Tara felt ashamed. Not for what she'd said, but because she'd hurt her mother. Amy never bore grudges, perhaps that's why she had forgiven Dad so many times?

'Are you still sad about Dad?' she asked in a small voice.

Amy gave a soft sigh and Tara turned in her seat and buried her face in her mother's chest.

'I didn't mean to hurt you,' she whispered. 'It's just that I can't see him the way you can.' She knew without looking up that Amy was crying again and all she could do was hold her mother tightly and hope that it would help.

'No one in this world is entirely wicked, not even your father,' Amy finally said.

'If I fall in love with a man and he puts one foot wrong, I'll leave him immediately,' Tara said firmly.

Time and again she had tried to work out why women liked men who were cruel to them, but, however she looked at it, there was no answer except weakness.

'I think you'll find it's not quite as simple as that.' Amy laughed through her tears. 'I hope the man you fall in love with will be worthy of you. But don't go through life expecting perfection, darling.'

Lesley Pearse spent most of the Sixties living in London's bed-sit land and experienced first hand what 'Swinging London' really meant to the mini-skirted dolly-birds. She now lives in Bristol with her three daughters.

Tara was shortlisted for the Romantic Novel Award in 1996.

LESLEY PEARSE

Tara

ARROW

Reprinted in Arrow Books, 1998

17 19 20 18

Copyright © Lesley Pearse, 1994

The right of Lesley Pearse to be identified as the author of this
work has been asserted by her in accordance with the
Copyright, Designs and Patents Act, 1988

First published in the United Kingdom in 1994
by William Heinemann

This edition first published in 1995 by Mandarin Paperbacks,
reissued in 1997 and reprinted 13 times

Arrow Books Limited
The Random House Group Limited
20 Vauxhall Bridge Road, London, SW1V 2SA

Random House Australia (Pty) Limited
20 Alfred Street, Milsons Point, Sydney,
New South Wales 2061, Australia

Random House New Zealand Limited
18 Poland Road, Glenfield, Auckland 10, New Zealand

Random House (Pty) Limited
Endulini, 5a Jubilee Road, Parktown 2193, South Africa

The Random House Group Limited Reg. No. 954009

A CIP catalogue record for this book
is available from the British Library

Papers used by The Random House Group Limited
are natural, recyclable products made from wood grown in
sustainable forests. The manufacturing processes conform to
the environmental regulations of the country of origin

Printed and bound in Germany by
Elsnerdruck, Berlin

ISBN 0 7493 1808 2

In memory of Ralph Pearse, my father-in-law,
one of nature's true gentlemen.
It was Ralph who inspired me to use
Chew Magna in Somerset, as a setting for
part of the story. He was born and grew up there,
and to all of us who loved him,
he will always be there.

Acknowledgements

To Louise Moore, my editor, for her unfailing enthusiasm, wisdom and encouragement.

To Darley Anderson, my agent, for believing in me.

To Richard and Vivienne Flowers in the hopes they don't mind me creating an entirely fictitious history at the farm. To Margaret and Mike Barber for their memories of growing up in Chew Magna.

Thank you to Dennis Spear for your invaluable reminiscences of village life. Tower Hamlets library for their help in my research, and Westminster Training and Development Association for letting me take a peek into their offices in Paradise Row.

Apologies to Port Lympne for wandering round your grounds when you lay empty and unloved. One day I'll go back to see the tigers and gorillas.

Last, but not least, thank you to James Kellow and Tony for teaching me to play poker.

Chapter 1

'Tell yer Dad I want the rent tonight. Or else!'

Anne stopped in her tracks, shame staining her pale face. Her mouth dropped open like the cod on the fish stall, arms weighed down by two string bags full of end-of-the-day cheap meat and vegetables.

'Dad must have forgotten,' she whispered.

Sid Bullock threw back his head and cackled mirthlessly. The golden light from the stall's hurricane lamps caught him under the chin, giving his long bony face a sinister look.

'Forgotten!' he roared, making people crane their necks to see what was going on. 'The only thing Bill MacDonald remembers these days is how to pour drink down his throat!'

Whitechapel Road was always busy, but at five o'clock on an icy January Saturday it developed a manic, desperate air. Stallholders anxious to rid themselves of perishable goods bawled out inducements to buy. Buses disgorged passengers to swell the already heaving throng of last-minute shoppers. Acrid, throat-burning traffic fumes mingled with smells of fruit, raw meat, hamburgers and onions. Yet even amid all this noise and confusion, Bullock's cruel jibe managed to make at least a dozen heads turn.

He might as well have announced it on the BBC. By the time the stalls were cleared and the rubbish swept

1

up, it would be common knowledge that the MacDonalds were in trouble again.

Once she'd called this tall, skinny man Uncle Sid. He doled out free chips from his shop and sixpences for sweets as if he was a real relation. Now he only spoke when he wanted to get back at her father.

'I'll remind him as soon as he gets in.' Anne wished she could melt into the rail of dresses behind her.

'C'mon, Sid! Ain't you ashamed of pickin' on a kid?' George's growling voice preceded his red face and plump body as he burst through a rail of jackets. 'If you've got a disagreement with MacDonald, pick it with 'im, not little Anne.'

She was twelve going on thirteen, a skinny kid in a long-outgrown, threadbare green coat. Her red-gold hair hung in pigtails, huge amber eyes welled up with tears and her wide mouth was sore in the biting wind, a red gash across a white, strained face.

Sid heard the veiled threat behind the jovial words and backed off.

'Tell him I want it, before he pisses it away tonight,' he tossed over his shoulder, and slipped away through the crowd.

'Bleedin' weasel!' George slid an arm round Anne's shoulder and drew her close to his thick sheepskin coat. 'Too scared to 'ave a go at yer dad, but don't mind ripping into a kid!'

Anne didn't see herself as a kid. Her childhood had gone down the pan as soon as she became aware that her father was a drunk, wife-beater, a thief and a blackguard. But she appreciated George sticking up for her.

'Got all yer shoppin'?' George bent down, enveloping her in his comforting smell of King George cigars, bacon sandwiches and a faint whiff of brandy. He took her cold hands in his and chafed them together. 'Anythin' you need 'elp wiv?'

2

Anne loved George, not only for his kindness and his generosity, but for his outrageous appearance. With his bald head, port-wine coloured bulbous nose and quivering belly he would have looked comic even in conventional clothes, but George never did anything in half-measures. A Russian fur hat, a glimpse of brocade waistcoat beneath his sheepskin and a red and yellow spotted bow-tie was his usual working attire.

George Collins was the top man in the market; a spieler who could sell anything to anyone and entertain them as they parted cheerfully with their cash. Master magician, juggler and clown, he could toss plates into the air and somehow land them neatly in straw-lined baskets without breaking one. He could find a half-crown behind a child's ear, sing a song, tap dance, insult his audience then two minutes later have them shrieking with laughter. But George wasn't just a sharp salesman. He sprinkled gold dust on people's lives, lifted their spirits and warmed their hearts, and Anne had wished more than once he was her father, not a mere pretend uncle.

'I've got everything now.' She wanted to remain in the circle of his arm, but she remembered her mother and Paul were waiting. 'I'd better be going, Uncle George, Mum's not too good.'

'That cough still?' There was no trace of teasing now, only concern in his watery blue eyes.

Anne nodded. 'It's not getting any better, and she's so thin, too.'

George patted Anne's shoulder and cleared his throat as if there were something he wanted to say but couldn't.

'Go on home, sweetheart, make her some honey and lemon and put a dash of yer dad's whisky in it.'

Anne looked over her shoulder as she reached the last stall, shifting her shopping to one hand. She raised

3

the other in a wave, then blew him a kiss before slipping away into the darkness.

It was the blown kiss that made George's eyes prickle. Somehow it summed up their relationship, the affection between them and the need to keep it hidden.

Anne wasn't pretty. The combination of red-gold hair, white skin and huge amber eyes was fascinating enough to attract stares, but her shabby clothes and obvious neglect were all most people saw – a navy school skirt dangling beneath the coat, grey socks bunched round stick-thin ankles and chilblains on exposed wrists and knees.

Yet George could see beyond the pre-adolescent gawkiness to what she could be. Those eyes like polished pebbles held a yearning for a better life. Right now her wide mouth was too big in her pale, pinched face, but in another two or three years it might tell a different story!

George turned back to his stall piled high with china and fancy goods, suddenly chilled by a glimpse into the future. He noticed the filth underfoot, the tawdry cheap clothes on sale and the stink of poverty in the air.

He should have been more forceful with Amy Mac-Donald all those years ago. Why hadn't he convinced her that a stepfather would be better for Anne and Paul than their natural one? Didn't it come down to cowardice at the end of the day, whatever excuses he offered himself at the time?

Bill MacDonald had crushed Amy underfoot just like these cabbage leaves lying in the muck. He'd turned Paul into a cringing shadow, and who could blame Anne if she grew into womanhood with the idea that all men were drunken bullies? Now a tragedy was brewing in the family and he could no longer get close enough to prevent it.

A couple of girls with headscarves over their curlers

were checking out his boxes of glasses, chattering and giggling about a party planned for later. Across the aisle three Teddy boys lounged at the record stall. They nodded their greasy heads in time to 'Jail House Rock', tapped the toes of their brothel creepers and dragged deeply on cigarettes as they eyed up his customers.

'Champagne glasses, is it, girls?' George recovered his composure. 'Invite me along and I'll make sure your party swings!'

'You're too old for us, Georgie Porgie.' The petite dark one chucked him under the chin. 'But you can send along your 'Arry!'

Anne noted the air of expectancy as she made her way home along Whitechapel Road. Saturday night was always special, there was a buzz in the air, a feeling that the grimmer side of life in the East End was held in suspension for a few hours.

Girls darted out of hairdressers', dress-shop bags in their hands, hair lacquered in place for the night's dancing. Young women with loaded prams, older women staggering under the weight of the family shopping, all looked less drawn than usual. Men were coming home from work, dirt-smeared faces cheerful at the prospect of Saturday night down the pub and a day off on Sunday. Young men ran after packed buses, daringly leaping on to the open back platform, cigarettes nonchalantly dangling form their lips as they contemplated whether tonight they might meet their dream girl.

Even the London Hospital across the road appeared to be waiting for the influx of casualties later tonight. Every one of its many windows sent a shaft of welcoming light out into the darkness. Soon the market would be packed up, hurricane lights taken down. A man would come and sweep away the squashed tomatoes,

5

cabbage leaves and sweet papers. Whitechapel was too soot-ingrained, too shabby ever to be considered beautiful, but lit up by car headlights and bright shop windows it had a raw excitement that Anne loved.

'Shakin' all over' by Johnny Kidd and the Pirates blasted from a café door as a girl breezed out, her full red skirt swirling over a froth of net can-can petticoats.

'See you up the Empire,' she shouted back then, pulling a scarf over her beehive, she tottered on four-inch heels to the bus-stop.

Anne paused for a moment, pretending to adjust the handles of her bags so she could peep in through the steamed-up window.

Teddy boys in drape jackets played the pinball machine, girls only a couple of years older than her drank coffee and flirted. She noted their pencil skirts, tight sweaters and carefully made-up faces and felt a stab of envy at their gaiety, freedom and their knowledge of who and what they were.

She wasn't a child. How could she be when she already knew that romance and happy-ever-after marriages existed only in films? Yet she couldn't think of herself as an adult, either, not when she couldn't find a way of protecting her mother and brother.

A sense of isolation grew with each passing week. Her mother and Paul's dependence on her increased each time her father laid into them. She had no friends, school only meant laying herself open to ridicule because of her shabby clothes. Now even shopping involved running the gauntlet of prejudice and hostility.

She hitched the two bags up into her arms for the last dash past Sid's fish and chip shop. Golden light spilled out on to the pavement, accompanied by tantalising smells that made her stomach contract with hunger. The black and white tiled floor, gleaming steel fryer, even the jars of pickled onions and bottles of pop arranged in neat rows were a sharp reminder of what her mother called 'Top Show'.

Once she opened that door next to the shop, the stench of frying food and mildew would engulf her, taking away her appetite. If Sid's customers smelled this, saw the filth in his kitchen or the maggot-ridden dustbins out in the yard, they wouldn't be quite so enthusiastic about his rock salmon.

Anne turned the key in the lock and slipped in hurriedly. She didn't put the light on as it was better not to see the bare wood stairs, wallpaper stained and rubbed away by her father's shoulders. The splatters of dried blood here and there testified to his explosive temperament, the neglect proved how little he valued his family.

The landing light came on as Anne reached the half-way point, and her mother looked anxiously down.

'Did you manage to get everything?'

Amy's voice was as small and gentle as herself. From a distance they could have been sisters just a year or two apart. They shared the same slender build, height and dainty features, though Amy's hair was pure blonde compared with Anne's red gold. But closer inspection revealed the ravages not only of time but of hardship and disappointment.

Anne's colouring grabbed the eye, there was a boldness in her stance and expression which couldn't have come from her mother. Amy's powder blue eyes seemed to reflect her feelings of hopelessness, her pinched face, stooped shoulders and lank hair spoke not only of poor health but a woman who had given up considering herself important.

Anne could barely feel her fingers or toes, her lips were chapped from the raw wind, but she managed a bright smile to reassure her mother she hadn't minded

7

being a scavenger at the close of the market.

'I got half a shoulder of lamb, some bacon, sausages and all the veg. Queenie gave us some bananas, too, she said to put them in some custard right away.'

Amy's hands reached to take the bags from her daughter, but she winced with the effort.

'It's all right, Mum.' Anne dismissed her help and bounded up the last few stairs. 'You sit down and rest. I'll make the tea.'

Anne had learned from her mother how to make the best of things. But, unlike her, she resented the necessity.

She felt no anger at being poor, or at living in three small rooms with no bathroom – she knew of plenty of other families far worse off. What really hurt was knowing her father was responsible for shaming them.

Drinking, gambling, even thieving could be over-looked if he was loving and amiable when he was at home. But Bill MacDonald was slowly killing her mother and her brother Paul and there was nothing she could do to prevent it.

'You are a little love.' Amy ran one hand caressingly over her daughter's cold cheek as Anne unpacked the shopping on the table. 'I wish I didn't have to rely on you so much.'

'She was sick again with her cough!'

Anne turned at her brother's shrill voice. He was poised on the edge of a chair, like a rabbit keeping watch for predators. Just eight years old, but so small and thin he looked nearer five, with big, despairing dark eyes that made Anne's stomach churn with anx-iety and love for him.

'You must go to the doctor again.' Anne ran a hand over her mother's straggly hair in comfort. 'Do you want some aspirin?'

'No, I've taken some more of that cough mixture.' Amy caught hold of her daughter's hand and pressed

8

it to her bony cheek. 'It's nothing, love, don't worry so much.'

Anne knew there was a great deal to worry about. Her mother was only thirty, but she looked closer to fifty. On the mantelpiece was a photograph taken on her wedding day, showing a curvy, plump-cheeked beauty with shining hair and sparkling eyes. Now she was so thin her ribs stuck out through her worn blue jumper. To hug her was to feel a bag of bones.

Countless beatings had left her skin yellow with bruising, two teeth knocked out, and a permanent scar above her right eye which opened up with each successive punch. The racking cough she had now was weakening her every day. Anne knew she got up in the night for fear of waking her husband. Sometimes she could eat no more than a couple of mouthfuls without vomiting. But worst of all was hearing her cry in despair.

'It's cold in here.' Anne shivered as she hastily peeled potatoes, one eye on the clock anticipating her father's return.

A polite visitor to the flat would describe the room as cosy, but a room which had to serve four people as kitchen, dining and living room could only be cramped. Amy tried to compensate for the lack of space by tidying, cleaning and polishing constantly, and camouflaged the shabby furniture with her exquisite needlework.

The ugly utility table was hidden under a cloth embroidered with poppies and cornflowers. A brown three-piece suite sported lace chairbacks and ruched satin cushions that wouldn't have been out of place in a Mayfair shop window. Even the hideous mock marble fireplace was softened by a scalloped-edged red cloth running along the mantelpiece.

During the long winter evenings Amy taught Anne these crafts, too. A pale lemon blouse lay on the back of the settee, waiting for the time when they could do the buttonholes together.

But however much Amy worked at making their home cosy she could do nothing about the noise. From the front came the constant roar of traffic, at the back a rumble of Tube trains behind the house. Windows became encrusted with soot and grime within hours of cleaning them, black grit found its way in like an insidious disease.

'The fire won't seem to draw today.' Amy reached down for the poker, giving it a feeble riddle. 'It might be choked up with ashes, I hadn't the strength to rake it properly this morning.'

'I'll just get these spuds on and then I'll see to it.' Anne glanced round at her mother and brother. Anxiety crackled between them; Amy worrying what sort of mood her husband would be in, Paul picking up the message like a radio receiver, turning it to terror.

Anne had realised some time ago it was this very atmosphere which drove Bill MacDonald to violence, a circle that none of them could break. Bill escaped to the pub because he felt their fear. Later, with the beer in him and half his wages gone, he would lash out, often hurting them so badly he felt compelled to run out again.

She had some good memories of her father. A day at Southend, a picnic in Epping Forest and walks down by the docks when he held her hand and tried to explain what had gone wrong. Few people remembered now that he had been a hero during the War. His medals were as tarnished as his reputation, the press cuttings as ageing and yellow as Amy's skin.

All that remained were hideous images. Police rushing up the stairs, turning her and Paul out of their beds as they searched for stolen goods. Bill lying downstairs in the hall in a pool of his own vomit and pee, too drunk to even move to the lavatory just feet away. Paul stripped naked, tied to the banisters and Bill beating him with his belt just for wetting the bed. So many times he'd knocked her mother out cold – broken ribs, black eyes, bruises, cuts and even burns.

'Shall I lay the table?' Paul's shrill voice cut through Anne's reverie.

Everything about Paul was sharp. His small features, ears that stood out like wing nuts, even his voice was squeaky and high-pitched. He had inherited his father's dark eyes and hair, but none of his sturdy build and height. Paul MacDonald was a human mouse, constantly on the alert for trouble.

Had he liked football, swimming, cars or even just raking the streets with other kids, Bill might have left him alone. But Paul clung close to his mother and sister, preferred books to people. Right now his soft, dark eyes were asking for reassurance that he wasn't going to be hurt tonight, but no-one could give him that.

'We'll lay it together,' Anne suggested, giving him a quick hug. 'Don't look like that, Paul, if Dad's in a mood we'll go into the bedroom till he's gone out.'

Of all the things Anne hated about her father, his attitude to Paul was the one thing she could find no excuses for. To pick on one child, continually to deride and find fault until he stuttered, wet the bed and had nightmares, then beat him for that too – that was barbaric.

Anne had her own way of escape. She would cut out models' and actresses' faces from magazines, then draw clothes for them. A coloured pencil in hand, she could immerse herself in luxurious dreams that hid the ugliness of her world. Poor Paul had no such hiding place.

It had just turned six-thirty when they heard Bill's feet on the stairs. Paul ran for his seat at the table, Amy moved quickly to the stove to pour the gravy into a jug.

Anne added another lump of coal to the fire and, leaving the poker as a lever to bring more air from underneath, she stood up, wiping her sooty hands on her skirt.

'Hullo, Dad.' She took a step towards him to take his donkey jacket, mustering a false smile of welcome. 'Tea's just ready, you must be frozen.'

Bill MacDonald was described by most people as 'a handsome devil', though drink and a loss of self-respect had spoiled the face that had once been likened to Clark Gable's.

When Amy met him in '45 he'd been in uniform, just back from the Far East. His black hair gleamed like a raven's wing, a wide smile revealed perfect teeth, his eyes were meltingly brown and his body iron-hard.

Now there were gaps in his teeth, his belly hung over his belt and a scowl was more common than a smile. But despite all this he still had a certain something which men envied and women desired.

Anne saw nothing in his face tonight to be alarmed by. He wasn't scowling, he didn't smell of drink, in fact he just looked cold and a little tired.

Hanging up his coat on the landing, she willed her mother not to mention the mud on his boots. Once he used to leave them down by the front door and walk up in his socks, but then he used to wash and change before eating in those days, too.

'What's going on?' he said, frowning as he looked across the small room to see Paul's head bowed over the table and his wife seemingly engrossed in filling the salt cellar. 'Someone died?'

That current of anxiety crackled and Anne's heart sank.

'Mum's been bad again today.' She laid one hand on his big forearm. 'I think Paul's going down with something, too.'

'Oh, shit,' he exclaimed, rubbing his filthy hand over several days' worth of stubble. 'There's always summat wrong with 'em. What's for tea?'

Amy turned round to face him, struggling to produce a weak smile.

'Sausages,' she wheezed, and promptly broke into a spasm of coughing.

Bill sat down at the table as his wife tried to control her cough. Drinking water seemed to aggravate it still more. Finally, with streaming eyes, she ran out of the room clutching a handkerchief to her mouth.

He showed no concern, just flicked his braces down from his shoulders and unbuttoned the top button of his checked wool shirt. A smell of stale sweat wafted out as he reached for a slice of bread with unwashed hands.

Anne wanted to use the opportunity to insist he got help for her mother, but the grim set of his mouth deterred her. Instead she poured him a cup of tea, dished up his dinner and attempted to amuse him.

'There was a right to-do in the market this afternoon,' she giggled nervously. 'Some boy threw a tomato at Mr Singh and he chased him down the road. While he was gone Queenie nicked his bag of money from under the counter for a joke. When he got back and found it gone he nearly had a heart attack.'

The market was at the heart of Whitechapel. Characters like George in his Russian hat, Mr Singh in his turban and the voluptuous blonde Queenie on the fruit and veg stall were as dear to the locals as the smoky pubs and the Pearly King and Queen.

Anne embellished the story with actions of Mr Singh clutching at his heart, mimicking his Indian accent.

'Oh, goodness me. What am I to do? These are very bad boys.'

Bill smiled but it froze on his face as he saw his son staring at him.

13

'What are you gawping at? 'Ave I got a bogey hanging out me nose?'

Paul blinked furiously and bent over his plate. From the lavatory below they could hear Amy hacking away and then a violent retch.

'Just what a man needs when he's been out freezing his balls off all day,' Bill exploded, pushing his dinner away. 'This place is like a bleedin' zoo. A witless zombie staring at me and the wife throwin' up.'

Paul began to quiver with fear, and as he stuck a fork in his sausage it flicked off the plate on to the tablecloth, splattering gravy.

Anne dropped her knife and fork as her father leaped up, hand raised, but before she could intervene he had struck Paul across the head, knocking him so hard he fell sideways to the floor.

'You bloody animal,' he yelled and, picking up Paul's plate, threw the dinner down on top of him. 'Behave like a fuckin' animal and you can eat like one.'

The plate slithered off Paul's shoulder and smashed in pieces on the floor.

'Don't, Dad.' Anne reached out and caught her father's arm. 'He couldn't help it!'

Bill MacDonald's moods were mercurial. Sometimes he could be defused with as little as a cup of tea or a joke. But this time his brown eyes were full of spite and his lip curled back, showing his missing teeth.

'He can't 'elp nothin', that's 'is trouble.' Bill slapped away her hand. 'The boy's soft in the 'ead.'

Paul aggravated the situation by not getting up. He curled up among the food, whimpering, and to Anne's dismay she saw a spreading wet stain on his trousers. Before she could move round to hide this from her father, Bill was on to him. He yanked Paul up by the neck of his jumper, only to kick him across the room, smashing him into the stove.

'You filthy little bastard,' he yelled. 'I've got the

perfect place for a fuckin' maggot like you!'

'No, Dad,' Anne screamed, shielding her brother with her body. Bill had often threatened to lock Paul in the coal shed out in the yard and tonight, somehow, she knew he meant to do it.

'Get out of my way.' He caught Anne by the shoulders and hurled her back against the couch.

'Don't you dare touch him!'

Both Anne and Bill turned at the small, firm voice. Amy stood in the doorway, white-faced and shaking.

'You lay one finger on him and that will be it!' Even in anger Amy didn't shriek or bellow, but her words were a clear enough warning.

'Whatcha goin' to do about it?' Bill's eyes narrowed.

The room was smoky from the sausages, thick with a smell of fried onions, but even so Anne could smell fear, from herself, Paul and her mother.

In that second, as Bill waited for his wife's answer, Anne noticed the glass lampshade quivering on its chains above her and she was reminded again just how fragile her mother was.

'I've taken as much as I'm prepared to. Hurt either of my children and I'll get the police.' Amy's maternal instinct was stronger than her own fear.

'*Your* children!' Bill moved nearer her. Anne could only stare in horror as she scrambled to her feet. 'I always knew that maggot wasn't mine, but are you trying to say Anne don't belong to me neither?'

'I wish I could say that.' Amy's chin stuck out defiantly. 'Because I'm ashamed of you.'

There'd been many times Anne had wished her mother would stand up to her father, but she knew with utter certainty this was the wrong one to pick.

Bill lowered his head and charged towards Amy like a bull, punching her first in the stomach with his right fist, the left thundering into her jaw. His assault was too fast to prevent one blow. Even before Anne could reach him he was laying into her mother in a frenzy.

'No, no!' Anne pulled at his braces from behind, but he was raining blows down on her mother as if she was a punchbag. For a moment Anne stood helplessly. Her father blocked the door, her fists alone would make no impact on his hard body. In desperation her eyes swept the room for a weapon. Her hand reached out for a brass candlestick on the mantelpiece, but as her fingers curled round it she saw the poker still stuck under the hot coals and heard her father punch her mother again.

'You slag!' he roared, hauling Amy up by one shoulder and driving his fist into her face. 'I've had it with your mealy-mouthed martyr bit. I know what you really are.'

Suddenly there was no alternative. Grasping the poker, Anne drew it out of the fire. The end glowed red, even the handle was so hot she could barely hold it.

'Leave her alone, you bully,' she screamed and lunged with the poker, thrusting it against her father's back.

His yelp made her jump back, but as he turned towards her she jabbed it forward again.

'I'll blind you,' she hissed.'Get out!'

Amy slumped to the floor as Bill let go of her. He hopped from one foot to the other, grimacing with pain, his hands vainly trying to reach his burned flesh.

'You know how it feels now,' she screamed. 'Go on, try and stop me! I'll stick this in your eyes without thinking twice.'

'Put that down,' he yelled, but there was indecision in his eyes.

The hot poker felt good in her hands. Bill might be six feet tall and fourteen stone, but three feet of hot iron made them equal.

'I want you to try and take it,' she said through

clenched teeth. 'I want to stick it in your face and mark you for life.'

It was quieter now, even Paul had stopped crying. Outside the traffic rumbled, car doors slammed, faint music drifted from the juke box in the café down the street, but in here there was nothing but her father's laboured breathing, and the dripping of the tap.

'Get out!' She jabbed at him again, just touching the front of his shirt, singeing a small hole. She hated his red, raw face, despised that sagging belly, and the smell of sweat made her want to retch. 'Get down the pub and drink yourself stupid. That's all you're good for.'

He backed away towards the door, past Amy lying like a rag doll. Anne knew she'd knocked the fight out of him, temporarily at least.

'Come on now, Anne, we've always been mates,' he said, his voice wheezy and uncertain. He had that imploring, cheeky look on his face that explained why women still found him attractive, his brown eyes soulful and questioning.

'Go.' She prodded with the poker again. 'Now.'

As he backed out on to the landing the sound of a train rattled the bedroom window. She kicked the door shut in his face and leaned her back against it.

'Go on, get going,' she shouted through it. 'Come back in here and I'll be ready for you.'

She waited, trembling so hard the poker twitched up and down like a water diviner's rod. Amy was motionless at her feet, her blood trickling on to the worn carpet. Anne knew her father was just standing there, perhaps trying to weigh up his chances of charging back in. Then, just as her arms were tiring from holding the poker, she heard him lift his donkey jacket down from the peg and move towards the stairs.

'Paul, watch the window!' she ordered. 'Tell me if he comes out!'

17

She counted each of the thirteen steps, heard the front door open, then slam behind him.

'Has he come out yet?'

'I can't see him,' Paul whimpered.

Bill was cunning enough to pretend he'd left and Anne was taking no chances. Bracing herself, she opened the door of the living room and peered out.

The naked lightbulb was swinging in the breeze above the stairs, but that meant nothing. He could be hiding in the lavatory by the front door, or even in the back yard.

'I can see him now,' Paul called out. 'He's going down towards the Black Bull.'

Still holding the poker she ran down the stairs and bolted both the front door and the one to the yard. When she returned to the living room her legs nearly gave way.

Amy's face was a mass of raw flesh surrounded by blood-soaked blonde hair. She was out cold, a lifeless broken doll. Paul had a split lip, a swollen eye and a lump of mashed potato stuck in his hair.

'What will we do when he comes back tonight?' Paul's voice was a squeak of terror.

Anne knelt by her mother, trembling all over, for a moment afraid she was dead. This was no ordinary beating; Amy's jaw was twisted to one side as if it were broken or dislocated. Her right arm lay at an unnatural angle, but as she put her head close to her mother's chest she could hear the faint sound of her heart still beating.

'I have to get an ambulance.' She turned to Paul, trying to control her own rising panic. 'Get some dry trousers on while I phone for one. I won't be a minute.'

It struck her on the way downstairs that an ambulance would only take her mother to the hospital across the street and that would be the first place her father would look. He would come for them, take them home and continue what he'd started.

George sprang to her mind. Time and time again he had offered help and a month ago, when Amy had a black eye, he had given Anne his telephone number. Did that mean he really wanted to help, or was it just politeness?

There was no time for hesitation. She ran back upstairs, found the number and four pennies, then belted out the back door and down the back alley to the phone box in the next street.

'I'll be there right away, sweetheart.'

That was all George said. No hesitation, no questions. All those other people Amy had implored for help in the past, doctors, social workers and even police, had shrugged their shoulders and looked the other way. Yet George, who wasn't even a relative, said he'd come.

She didn't immediately recognise the tall, dark man in a smart Italian pin-striped suit as George's son. It was three years since she'd last seen Harry and then he had been a gangly sixteen-year-old in an oversized red drape jacket, with a terrible crop of spots. This man barging up the stairs two at a time had brilliant blue eyes, sharp chiselled cheekbones and perfectly groomed black hair.

'Don't worry, sweetheart.' George hugged her briefly. 'Me and 'Arry'll soon have you all out of 'ere.'

There was no time to be embarrassed about anything, Harry simply strode in and took over.

'Jesus!' he exclaimed as he squeezed his way round the living-room door to see Amy crumpled behind it. 'What sort of animal does that to a woman?'

Anne found it odd later that she remembered so much detail about Harry that night, and virtually nothing about the role George played. Old Spice aftershave, cufflinks like small pistols and the side lacing on his winklepickers – how could she notice all this when her mother was so badly hurt?

Her father had conditioned her to think men were capable of no emotion other than rage, yet Harry, with his sleek college-boy haircut and his fashionable mohair suit, cradled Amy tenderly in his arms and his bright blue eyes were full of compassion.

'I'll make the bastard pay for this,' he vowed to her in a croaky voice as he looked down at Amy's battered face. 'So help me, Anne, I'll swing for him before I let him touch any one of you again!'

It occurred to Anne on the way to the Middlesex hospital that there was a triangular relationship between George, Harry and Amy that she knew nothing about. As Paul clung to her on the front seat, she glanced around at Harry supporting Amy in the back and wondered. She didn't understand it. Harry didn't even seem to notice the blood stains on his white shirt and expensive suit as he tried to protect her mother from further jolts.

There was plenty of time to study Harry further while they waited at the hospital, and a certain comfort to be derived from remembering that he had once been a skinny ragamuffin like herself. This was the dirty-faced boy who'd fired his catapult at fat old Mrs Maloney's backside and made her stumble and reveal her large pink bloomers. He had once entertained the kids in the road by doing handstands on his pushbike and he'd been known as the best runner in the East End.

He had grown into a handsome man without losing the qualities he'd had as a kid. His angular face, which could look fierce and uncompromising, broke into a warm smile effortlessly. He had developed muscle yet kept that nimble grace intact. But of all the things Anne found to like in Harry it was the sensitivity he showed to Paul that touched her most. Not only had he taken

Paul off to find a toilet, washed his hands and face and got the potato out of his hair, but now he sat with him close beside him, sharing a magazine in companionable silence.

Each hour seemed like a week as they waited in the small glassed-in cubicle that passed as a waiting room. The air was heavy with anxiety, not just theirs but that of the countless tense relatives who'd permanently imprinted their bottoms on the sagging plastic chairs, scuffed the carpet and left tea stains on the cream paint. No-one had to point out that Amy's condition was serious, the number of grave-faced doctors and nurses scuttling in and out of the side ward along the corridor made that quite clear.

'Don't you worry, my little flower,' George said after they heard one of the nurses mention pneumonia almost casually. 'She'll be fine, I know she will, and Uncle George will look after you until your mum's better.'

Anne knew George wouldn't willingly relinquish her and Paul, but she also knew that he might have no choice if the worst happened and her mother died. George was called out for questioning several times, both by nurses and police. Through the reeded glass she could see him gesticulating wildly, and on several occasions his voice rose in anger.

'I won't give any assistance to find that animal. Why d'you think I brought her here, rather than the 'ospital in Whitechapel?' she heard him shout. 'D'you really think she'd be comforted by seein' his face? I know he's their father, worse luck, but they've bin through enough!'

For years now Anne had daydreamed about escaping from their father. They were childish, silly dreams of finding a suitcase full of money, or wicked thoughts like hoping Bill would get run over and killed. But not once had she imagined life without her mother.

21

There was a horrible smell, George said it was disinfectant, but it seemed to get right down in her lungs so she could smell it with every breath. There were scary noises, too – clanging sounds, rubber wheels on the lino floors, sudden screams of pain and rushing feet.

Paul drooped against Harry and finally slid down until his head was on his knee, his small bruised body curled up on the seat. Anne noted the hole in the sole of his shoe, his bony legs covered in old scars and bruises and the way his eye was turning black where Bill had hit him. Down the passage she heard a man shouting.

'It's OK.' George held her tightly. 'It isn't Bill, just the usual Saturday night drunks. He won't show his face here, darlin', if he did he'd be arrested and you gotta believe you're safe with me and 'Arry.'

Finally Anne blurted it out. 'She's going to die, isn't she?'

George didn't answer immediately, just held her even more tightly.

'She's managed to hang on this long,' he said eventually. 'That's a good sign. And she won't willingly leave you two behind.'

The unasked question about her future hung in the waiting room along with cigarette smoke. Harry had been almost asleep but he opened his eyes and looked right at Anne.

'You'll come home wiv us whatever happens,' he said gently. 'It ain't much, Anne, but we'll look after you both.'

It was daylight when a nurse came in. Anne's stomach lurched with fright and instinctively she covered her ears so she couldn't hear what she feared was coming.

'It's all right, Anne.' The dark-haired nurse knelt down before her and removed her hands. 'Mummy's on the mend now. She's been very poorly but she's going to get better. You can have just one quick look at her and then I want you to go home and get some sleep.' She looked up at George and smiled. 'You too, Mr Collins, you can't look after two kids if you're exhausted.'

Anne was too sleepy to notice anything much when they arrived at George's house in Bethnal Green. She was aware she had arrived in Paradise Row, a terrace of tall thin houses standing back from Cambridge Heath Road, backing on to a high railway line, but took in no detail other than a sudden warmth and a great many stairs. One moment she was swaying on her feet looking at a rose coloured satin eiderdown, the next she was tucked in beside Paul.

It was George's bed, she could smell him on the sheets, and the last thing she remembered was hoping Paul didn't disgrace them by wetting.

'Well, sweetheart, how do you feel?'

Weak January sun flooded in through the lounge window and lit up the vivid orange carpet with its autumn leaf pattern. Anne could only stare at it, terribly afraid she was going to cry.

'Funny,' she whispered. She wanted to thank George for the new clothes that had miraculously appeared by the bed, for the feeling of safety when she woke. But she couldn't find adequate words.

When things had been bad back in Whitechapel, Anne had often resorted to daydreams as comfort. When she and Paul were woken by George around two, it was like stepping into one of them. The smell of roast lamb coming up the stairs, soft carpet under their bare feet, and that tension she'd lived with for so long fading.

How could she explain what it felt like to be in a blue

tiled bathroom with hot fluffy towels on a heated rail, when all she'd ever known was the public baths? To wash every inch of her skin knowing the hated smell of fish and chips or mildew was going for good. To lie under the water after she'd washed her hair listening to the echo of the dripping tap, knowing that today she wouldn't hear her father yelling at Paul, that her mother was safe in hospital.

Could George possibly know how it felt to pat 'Soir de Paris' silky talcum powder on her skin? How did a widower with only one son know to buy her white soft underwear with lace trimming?

As she put on the new Black Watch kilt with a matching green jumper she wanted to dance with joy. Yet at the same time she felt guilty. Surely it was bad to be revelling in such luxury when her mother was so ill? And shouldn't she have a bit more pride than to accept all these nice things so eagerly?

She managed a wobbly smile.

'Me and Paul haven't ever been anywhere as posh as this, Uncle George.'

'Posh!' Laughter made his belly quiver and he sat down sharply on the white fur-covered settee, waving his hand around. 'Posh, sweetheart? Look at the mess. It's like a bloomin' slum!'

Paradise Row was a Georgian terrace built originally for the middle classes. With four floors and a basement the houses may have degenerated between the Wars as the wealthy merchants moved further out of London, and each room became home to an entire family, yet they retained their old-world quaintness.

Overlooking a narrow strip of grass between its cobbled street and the busy main road, the old railings had been put back, the steps up to its front doors were scrubbed again and developers anxious to flatten it and raise council flats were being held back by conservationists.

Anne knew nothing of architecture, but she could sense the house's graceful proportions. Vast by her standards, its high ceilings, fancy roses round the lights and sense of elegance fired her imagination.

She could see by the new carpets, curtains and furniture what George was trying to achieve, but his home also had an air of neglect, revealing the absence of a woman's touch. Piles of clean washing were dumped on chairs. A car engine lay in the lounge, only a thin sheet of newspaper underneath it protecting the bright carpet. Pictures were propped up against walls, boxes of china for his stall, spilling straw, stood everywhere.

The kitchen was dull under a film of grease, burned saucepans had been left soaking and the floor couldn't have been washed for weeks. But it was lovely and warm. They had central heating, which only rich people had, and fabulous gadgets she'd never seen close up before – a toaster and refrigerator, even a Bendix washing machine like the ones they had down the launderette.

'I 'ad 'igh 'opes when I bought this place a couple of years ago.' George grinned cheerfully round at the mess. 'Me and 'Arry planned to make it a palace, maybe let out a few rooms. We got the heatin' and the bathroom done, we decorated it all, but we ran outta steam.'

Anne knew George's wife had died of tuberculosis when Harry was about two and he had brought up his son alone. She also knew what long hours he worked.

'I can clean up for you.' Anne felt bolder now and sat down next to him. Harry was out in the kitchen seeing to the dinner and he'd taken Paul with him. 'Would that pay for our food?'

George looked stunned for a moment, then spluttered with laughter.

'You're a little worry-guts. Money don't come into

the picture when it's old mates. This is your 'ome now, until your mum decides otherwise.'

'But school . . .' she protested. 'And Paul wets the bed sometimes, Uncle George.'

'Neither of you are fit to go back to school just yet.' George slid his arm round her shoulders. ' 'Arry used to wet the bed, too, after his mum died. I know all about sad little boys.'

Anne felt as if all her life until now she'd been crawling along a narrow, dark shelf. Isolated from others, yet able to sense they didn't share the same kind of miserable life she had. But now through the open kitchen door she could hear Harry talking to Paul about clearing out a spare bedroom for them both, and his words showed her a sun-filled world, where she and her brother had a chance.

'I know you're going to miss yer mum,' Harry said, 'but I'll take you both down to see her every day, Paul, and meanwhile you'll be like my little bruvver and sister and we'll share all the chores, like.'

She wanted to understand so much.

'Why was Harry so upset about Mum?' she asked.

'She was kind to him when he was a little 'un.' George smiled and patted her knee with his plump hand. 'I'll be straight wiv you, Anne. Both of us saw her as more than just a customer. Nuffin' improper, mind! Just maybe wishful thinkin'.'

Anne felt a bubble of pleasure rise inside her.

'Like I used to wish you was my Dad?'

'Just like that, Anne.' George beamed down at her, his bulbous red nose and fat jolly face suddenly handsome. 'And now we got a crack at it, ain't we! So we'd better be feedin' the pair of you up and gettin' this place ship-shape for Amy when she comes 'ome!'

Chapter 2

The ringing sound woke Anne. She leaned up on her elbows in the dark and listened.

She found it hard to distinguish between the telephone and the front-door bell, as both were luxuries she hadn't encountered till arriving at George's house, but the continual ringing suggested this was the phone.

'What time of night is this to bleedin' call?' George muttered as he padded barefoot down the stairs.

George and Harry joked a great deal about being foster-parents, but Anne knew their humour was intended to hide how nervous they were. They wouldn't leave her or Paul alone in the house, not even for a moment, and they checked out visitors before opening the door. George thought she didn't notice the rigorous locking-up before bed, or that he had blocked up the letterbox.

When Harry drove them to see their mother at the Middlesex hospital he was always on his guard. They were hurried into the car, after the road had been checked, shopping was done miles away and George kept telling them they weren't strong enough yet for school. But it was the absence of any mention of her father that convinced Anne they were hiding something. Bill MacDonald was a man everyone always

27

talked about, even if only how drunk he'd been or who he'd thumped. Harry and George knew something, and they weren't telling!

But despite this niggle of anxiety, the three weeks they'd been in Bethnal Green with George had been the happiest time Anne remembered in her short life.

Good food, warmth and the secure, calm atmosphere were a great part of it. Not a day passed without Anne noticing amazing improvements in Paul. He had put on weight, his bruises had faded, he was less nervous, sometimes he even managed to ask a question or comment on something of his own volition.

Pleasing though Paul's happiness was, Anne's great delight was in suddenly finding herself able to look ahead. She had always been good at household chores; cleaning the cooker, scrubbing the floor and polishing furniture were second nature to her. But the challenge of turning George's house into a home appealed to her creative side.

The stall's stock was now up in a spare room on the top floor, the car engine out in the back yard and the piles of shirts ironed and hung up in wardrobes. But while Harry and George were impressed by her housekeeping skills, they praised her talents at drawing and sewing still more.

Harry bought her a box of expensive paints and George brought home remnants of material and even a wonderful teenage doll with long blonde hair, so she could make it clothes. Sitting at the table in the lounge armed with scissors, reels of cotton and scraps of lace, she could immerse herself in a fantasy world of high fashion.

There was noise here like there was in Whitechapel, traffic at the front, trains at the back, but it was subdued, just a comfortable hum in the background. Beyond the net curtains she saw the trees, the strip of grass where old men sometimes sat in the sunshine to chat. Across the busy road was the park George called 'Barmy Park', named because the library had once been a lunatic asylum. St John's Church on the corner of Roman Road made her think of the palaces she used to build for Paul out of building bricks, a big, plain square church with only a small dome on top to give it a bit of dignity.

'You could be a designer,' Harry said one day as he picked up her doll, now dressed as a bride. 'All that smart gear up in Regent Street starts off like this.'

Her father had never shown any interest in her hobby. More than once he'd swept her bits and pieces off the table and told her to do something useful, like getting the coal in or making him a sandwich. Harry and George both loved clothes and they applauded Anne's talented attempts at dressing her doll.

'Your mum used to make fabulous frocks back before you was born,' George told her. 'I remember seein'' her standing in the window of Modern Modes up in Aldgate, just after the War ended. She was only about sixteen then, as pretty as a flower, dressing a dummy. It was a red evening dress, all beads and stuff; she told me that she was the one who did all the fancy work.'

'Yeah, she used to do it at home, too,' Harry chimed in. 'I went to see her one day when your Dad was in nick. She was sewing hundreds of sparkly things on to this frock. I never saw anything so lovely.'

Anne knew that her mother was a first-class needle-woman; Amy often told her stories about her days in the workshop. But until now Anne had never considered that she herself could actually make a career out of doing something she loved.

'How do you get to be a designer?' she asked Harry.

'Dunno' exactly.' He grinned, his blue eyes twinkling at her. 'I guess you go to art college, or maybe get an apprenticeship wiv one of the top shops. Just you keep on drawing and sewing, Anne, and remember to think big.'

George and Harry thought big about everything. They weren't scared to branch out with new lines on the market stall, they loved challenges, deals and living a bit close to the edge. Life to them was a series of poker games. Some they won, some they lost, but skill and keeping their cool kept the odds more often than not in their favour.

But now this mysterious phone call in the middle of the night reminded Anne her new-found happiness could only be precarious while her father was still out there.

'Was it about Mum?' Anne came out of her door and switched on the landing light as she heard George coming back up the stairs.

George looked at the Anne and a lump came to his throat. Mostly he saw her as a young woman because of her practical nature, her adult poise, but now with her face rosy from sleep, hair tousled, she was a small child.

'No, it ain't yer mum.' He tried to sound light-hearted and hide his rising panic. 'Just a problem down at the warehouse. I've got to go there now.'

'What's happened?' Anne could see tension in George's face and she knew he was hiding something. 'Who telephoned?'

'Now, now,' George turned her back towards her bedroom. 'It's nothin' serious, just a few louts making a bit of mischief, I expect.'

'Is it Dad?'

George's stomach heaved. Anne was perched on her bed now, eyes like two big toffees. Although he didn't like to lie to her, he knew this time he must.

' 'Course not.' He forced himself to laugh. 'Now back to sleep, 'Arry's here to look after you, and I'll be back in two shakes.'

Anne did as she was told but she still pricked up her

ears when George came out of his room again dressed. As she expected, he went straight to up to Harry's room on the next floor. Unable to hear anything more than a low rumble of voices, she got out of bed again. Sound carried easily in the tall, thin house and, with Harry's door open, George's voice drifted down the narrow stairs.

'Stay in the lounge,' she heard him say. 'It could be a trick to get us out of the house. Keep your eyes and ears open!'

Anne peeped round the door as the two men went downstairs. George led the way, rotund in his sheepskin coat and a woolly hat. Harry had pulled on jeans; his shirt was in his right hand. But as he reached the turn of the stairs she saw something was concealed beneath the shirt, something long and thin.

A shiver went down her spine. She knew that shape could only be a shotgun!

She wasn't exactly surprised to find George and Harry owning such a thing, they were ten-a-penny round the East End. But the fact Harry was arming himself with it meant he didn't anticipate her father turning up drunk and throwing stones at the windows.

Anne didn't dare go downstairs because she knew women didn't ask questions, they didn't poke their noses in; hadn't her own father made that clear often enough? Instead she climbed into bed with Paul, curved her body round his so they lay like two bananas and tried hard to shut out the images of George being hauled into a dark alley and clubbed to death, or Harry trying single-handedly to prevent a dozen of Bill's mates swarming in here to get his children back.

George parked his van at the end of Winthrop Street and looked towards the blaze in utter despair. There was over five thousand pounds' worth of stock in the little mission hall and it was obvious from the intensity of the flames that nothing could be salvaged.

Winthrop Street was narrow and badly lit, with mean little houses on one side overlooking rubbish-strewn bomb sites, wood yards and a totter's yard. At normal times it would be hard to distinguish anything at this time of night, but now fire lit the street up like arc lights.

Fingers of red flame flicked up from the narrow windows, licking the roof as if testing it. Popping sounds came from within as china cracked in the heat, then whooshing sounds as flames found an easier target in cellophane-wrapped towels and sheets.

But mingled in with the smell of smoke was the distinct whiff of petrol.

George could almost see the progress of the fire, he knew the layout of his warehouse so well. His paper-littered desk was already engulfed; soon the flames would reach the five gallons of paraffin kept for the stove and that would set alight the old wooden stair-case that led to the small storeroom above. China ornaments were stored there, the floor littered with pack-ing straw and that damned drum of meths he kept for the hurricane lamps.

Four fire engines were in full use, and dozens of firemen, muscles braced as they held high-powered hoses, yellow helmets standing out like Belisha beacons.

A crowd of residents from both Winthrop and Brady Street around the corner were huddled together, coats over their nightclothes, faces orange in the reflected light, some anxious about their own homes, others excited by the unexpected drama.

'I'm Collins, the owner.' George tapped one of the firemen on the arm. 'The police called me.'

He had never felt so impotent. If someone would

32

stick a bucket of water in his hand perhaps he could quell his fear and nausea. It wasn't just seeing a lifetime's work being destroyed in front of him, but the sickening knowledge that this was an act of revenge.

Three hours later the flames had been reduced to steam rising in the cold air and an acrid stink; the spectators had gone home to their beds. As the first rays of daylight appeared the firemen were reeling in their hoses, others stamped through the charred wreckage. Against the background of a pink grey sky the blackened walls and roof timbers of the old mission hall stood out in grim relief.

'To think it missed all the bombs in the War.' Old Mrs Graham shuffled out of number eight in an ancient dun-coloured dressing gown, and handed George a mug of tea. 'How could it have happened?'

'Arson.' Her husband behind her sniffed knowledgeably, clutching a blanket round his shoulders. 'I smelled petrol straight off, there was even pools of it in the yard 'cos the fire licked it all up, didn't it? You wasn't doing it for the insurance money, was you, George?'

The police and a couple of the firemen had made similar remarks and at any other time George might have seen the funny side of it. He'd lost his valuable warehouse, his stock and in effect his business would take a tumble. With full insurance he would have been laughing, probably got enough to retire if he wanted to.

But there was no insurance. It had lapsed just after Christmas and he'd put off renewing it because he had other things on his mind. This was something he should have anticipated and it was another reminder that MacDonald wasn't just a drunken bully, but a devious and dangerous man.

Right from the night he had taken Amy to the

Middlesex hospital and asked them to treat her under a false name, he'd been careful. And when Bill didn't come hammering on his door, he thought he had cracked it. His friend and fellow stallholder Queenie was the only person he had taken into his confidence and she was as trustworthy as the Pope. It was Queenie who had bought the children's clothes, the extra food, books and toys. She had kept her ear to the ground and alerted him to Bill's movements, the rumour and speculation.

But though he'd expected Bill to catch him one night in a dark alley, to have his stall smashed up, or his van trashed, tonight's events proved MacDonald had lost none of his cunning, the ability to plan; his hatred of George blazed as strongly as the warehouse fire he'd started.

George didn't drive straight home, he had too much thinking to do before he could face the children. As he passed Sid's fish and chip shop, and the MacDonalds' home above, he noticed the window upstairs was smashed and the front door boarded up.

It was no surprise. Two snooker halls, a drinking club and a pub had been on the receiving end of MacDonald's explosive temper already. No doubt the damage here was due to Sid giving him notice to quit.

'Amy won't be able to cope with this,' he muttered to himself as he motored on past Bethnal Green.

She had come within an inch of death. Progress was very slow, feeding her through a tube because of her broken jaw, pumping her full of iron, vitamins and antibiotics. If she were to read about the fire in the paper she'd be terrified that Bill might torch the house next.

'It's no good, mate.' He stopped cruising and turned the car around to go home. 'Either you get out there and finish MacDonald off or you find some safer place to send the kids.'

34

As he drove into Paradise Row he looked up at his house reflectively. He loved the fancy brickwork round the door and windows, the black railings and the wide steps. Once there had been many terraces like this in Bethnal Green, but between Hitler and half-witted do-gooders, most of them were gone now.

It was a whim that had made him buy it, prompted by the words of the song his wife used to sing.

'On Mother Kelly's doorstep, down Paradise Row.' He hummed the tune softly. He'd got it for a song, too, because it was almost derelict and he'd had more pleasure doing it up with Harry than from anything else he'd ever done. So maybe the neighbouring houses were neglected, but two had changed hands recently for a great deal more money than he'd paid for his. Other people would be charmed by the old gas lantern, the cobbled street and the graceful lines of a gentler period, just as he had been. One day it might prove to have been his best investment yet.

'That is if you can get MacDonald off your back,' he said softly to himself.

'Put that away.' George pointed to the gun lying across the settee the moment he got in. 'If the kids see that it'll spook them.'

Harry ran upstairs to hide it and came back seconds later pulling on a sweater over a checked wool shirt.

'How bad is it?' he asked as the pair of them went through to the kitchen and closed the door behind them.

'Wiped out,' George said curtly, putting on the kettle. 'Everything gone. It was MacDonald's doing, though whether there's enough evidence to put him away for it is debatable. But I don't want you running off half-cocked, 'Arry. We've gotta think things through.'

George eased himself down on to a chair. He was

35

exhausted, filthy and he stank of smoke. Harry glanced round at his father as he made the tea and he was shocked by the sudden change in him. He looked his fifty-five years now; his face had lost its ruddy glow, his shoulders were hunched in despair.

'It don't matter, Dad.' He laid his hands on his father's shoulders and massaged them comfortingly. He had a pang of guilt that he hadn't always worked as hard as he should, that he ought to remember that his father was no longer the stronger of the two. 'We can flog the land the warehouse was on, and we can get tick on new stock till we get ourselves together. Besides, I bet you've got a fair wedge tucked away somewhere.'

George had always been a constant in Harry's life, a boulder to lean on, a font of wisdom and understanding. Most of his mates had no respect for their fathers, but George wasn't just a father to Harry, he was his closest friend.

'It ain't money I'm worried about.' George's voice was shaky. He did have a few bob tucked away out of sight from the tax man and after a good night's sleep he'd be on top of it all again. 'It's Amy and the kids. MacDonald's a nutcase and he won't stop at torching the warehouse. This place could be next.'

'But why? He hates 'em anyway.'

George looked up at Harry and half smiled. He was such a handsome lad, that combination of black hair and blue eyes was enough to make any girl's heart flutter. But though half the girls in Whitechapel chased after him, George knew his son still hadn't found out what love could do to a man.

'You've got a lot of learning to do, son.' He shook his head and wiped his watering eyes. 'He don't hate Amy, she's probably the only thing he ever loved in his whole life. He might have taken out all his disappointments and failures on her, but he ain't stopped loving 'er.'

'He's a bleedin' shitbag!'

George sighed deeply. 'Now he is, but it weren't always like that, 'Arry. He should'a stayed in the Army, that's the place for men like him. But his weakness was Amy and that's why he come out.'

Harry raised an eyebrow.

'Bill MacDonald came back from the War a fuckin' hero.' George smirked. ' 'E even looked the part. The papers was full of what 'e'd done. Captured by the Japs, but escaped through the jungle taking 'is men with 'im. We all looked up to 'im, I guess that's why fifteen years on there's still blokes that want to drink wiv him and women still fancy 'im. Mad Mabel, Amy's mum, was the only one who reckoned there was summat dodgy about him.'

Harry grinned.

'The Witch of Durwood Street!'

He remembered the funny old girl chasing him down the road with a bread knife when he was a small boy. She'd had some sort of religious mania and used to stand in the market raving about hell and the end of the world. She always wore a long black coat and a shiny black hat and it had been a test of valour to play knock down ginger at her door.

Mabel had disappeared from Durwood Street some years ago and for all George knew she might now be dead.

'She wasn't ever as barmy as you kids liked to make out,' he said reprovingly. 'She had some sort of breakdown when her husband Arthur was killed at Dunkirk. Up till then she was a real beauty. Amy was their only child and when Mabel cracked, she took the brunt of it. Anyway, religion was what got Mabel back on her feet a couple of years later. She met some dodgy Holy Rollers and got sucked in.'

Harry's eyes widened at this glimpse into history.

'Then Amy fell for Bill?'

'Unfortunately. Amy was kept under. Never played in the street, made to go to church wiv her ma, wore dark clothes, just what you'd expect. When she was fourteen she went to work at Modern Modes, a right little drudge her ma made her. She must 'ave bin fifteen or sixteen when Bill came back from out East, God knows where she met 'im, she was kept under lock and key when she weren't working. But they fell in love and Mabel threw her out. She went down to Limehouse to stay wiv 'is folks. A right rough crew they was, an' all.'

'Go on. So they got married, did they? Was Amy up the spout?'

George shook his head.

'I suppose so, but it was real love all right. They was the best-looking couple for miles around. We was all glad for them.'

He shut his eyes for a moment, letting his mind wander back to that summer of '47. It had been around five or six in the evening and he was packing up his stall in pouring rain when he spotted Bill and Amy running hand in hand across Whitechapel Road, trying to shelter under an umbrella.

It was obvious they'd just left their own wedding. Bill's smart navy suit and trilby hat were peppered with confetti. Amy wore a white lacy costume, a dainty hat tipped over to one side and a spray of pink flowers on her breast.

Love shone out of them, and they were oblivious to anyone but each other. Bill's rugged face, his wide shoulders and lean body set off to perfection her utter femininity.

They were bound for the flat above Sid's fish and chip shop, everyone knew Bill had been painting and papering it for weeks. But as they reached the door, Bill scooped Amy up into his arms. It had brought tears to George's eyes to see them. Their faces were

38

pressed together and laughter wafted back to him as he stood there in the rain.

Amy had been trying to hold the umbrella aloft and her hat fell off. Bill kissed her then, and Amy dropped the umbrella. There in the rain, in all their wedding finery, a kiss had been more important than the umbrella bowling away, and the hat lying on the dirty pavement.

Cars honked their horns, people skirted round them with smiles on their faces, but Bill and Amy were in a world of their own.

'It should have lasted forever.' George sighed. 'They was so 'appy together. No man was ever prouder of 'is pregnant missus. When Anne was born Bill was like a dog with three tails. I seen 'im out pushing the pram, all on 'is own, and not many blokes are that way inclined, specially tough ones like 'im.'

'So what went wrong?'

' 'E got stitched up for a blag in Sussex.' George shrugged his shoulders. 'Charged wiv whacking some old geezer over the 'ead with an iron bar. I don't reckon 'e did it. But 'e'd bin in this village in Sussex before, in fact 'ed bought an Anderson shelter off the old man. Anyway, 'e got fingered and was sent down. Didn't 'ave an alibi! 'Is van was placed just along the lane from the robbery. It didn't make no difference that someone else 'ad borrowed it that night. 'E got sent down.'

'I suppose the bloke what borrowed the van never owned up?'

George shook his head. 'Bill got even from inside. The bloke was kneecapped and 'e's still limping around 'ere somewhere. But that didn't 'elp Bill. Meanwhile Amy was 'aving a tough time, alone wiv the baby. She 'ad to take in sewing to feed them.'

'But why did he turn on her?' Harry still couldn't quite grasp how a man could change so much.

George spread his hands wide. ' 'Is dreams was down the Swanny, his reputation ruined for summat he didn't do. 'Is baby was two now, walkin' and talkin'. He couldn't get work 'cept on the buildings, and 'e 'adn't got no money to find a better 'ome. Loss of pride does funny things to people. Drinkin', a bit of gambling and soon things were turning sour, so he slapped 'er once or twice.'

'Then back to nick?' Harry only knew this side of Bill – in and out of prison, fighting drunk in the Black Bull.

George half smiled. 'I 'oped she'd leave 'im. But there was nuffin' between us, son, only friendship. But then you'll remember 'ow good she was to you?'

Harry smiled at the warm memory of Amy's kindness to a motherless, lonely little boy.

'You spent quite a bit of time with her that winter.' George smiled tenderly. 'I tell you, son, I envied you! But when Bill got out of prison she couldn't look after you no more. Not with 'im being so prickly an' all. Then Paul was born and that's when everything went really bad.'

George didn't like to dwell on the night Bill had knocked him out and claimed he was Paul's father. He wasn't ashamed of being knocked out – after all Bill was younger and fitter. But to this day he regretted not going back to Bill and convincing him there had never been anything but friendship between him and Amy, and telling him straight she had no eyes for anyone but her husband.

It was half past eight in the morning now, but the railway wall so close to the back of the house, and the leaden sky above, made it dreary and dark in the kitchen, even with the yellow paintwork. George knew he should get down to the market and put his affairs in order. But for the first time he could remember, he wanted to stay at home.

'I want to kill him!'

Harry's words jolted George.

'No, son.' George's watery blue eyes flashed with fire. 'I know how you feel but violence ain't the answer.'

What Harry was suggesting was the way in their manor. They could round up a few men, lie in wait for Bill and take him off to one of the old warehouses down by the river. George had never taken part in such a thing, but he knew all about nailing a man's hands to the floorboards, burning him with a blow torch, breaking his bones one by one until the victim screamed for mercy.

But Bill wasn't an average man and, unless they actually killed him, he'd come back fighting and someone innocent was bound to get caught in the crossfire. 'It would start gang warfare,' he said firmly. 'Bill still has mates, remember, just a spark could trigger it off. We've got to think of Amy and the children.'

The door opened suddenly, startling both men.

'What happened, Uncle George?'

Anne was still wearing her long white wincyette nightdress, with her feet bare, hair tangled, and sleep in her eyes.

'It was a fire, darlin'.' George felt sickened by the anxiety in her eyes. 'I should 'ave got the place re-wired. One of the plugs was overloaded.'

She knew he was lying. She could sense the tense atmosphere, she saw a nerve twitching in George's cheek. Harry was looking the other way.

'How bad is it?' she asked. The smell of smoke on his clothes was overpowering and she could see the same kind of defeat in his eyes she'd seen a thousand times in her mother's.

'Gutted,' he laughed jovially. 'But every cloud 'as a silver linin', darlin'. I'll cop the insurance and sell the land, most of the stuff was dead stock anyways.'

She knew she wouldn't get the truth, but his lies were meant kindly.

'I'm so sorry, Uncle George.' She ran to him and put her arms around him. 'I'll go and run you a bath.'

'You ain't fooled her one little bit,' Harry said gloomily as she ran back upstairs. 'That kid can look right through you like an X-ray!'

'Hullo, darlin'! 'Ow you doin'?' George bent over Amy's bed and planted a kiss on her forehead. 'I was coming by to get some stock so I thought I'd just pop in to see you. 'Arry's coming later wiv the kids.'

He plonked down a huge bunch of flowers and a bag of fruit. He looked his old self again after a bath and shave. His bulbous nose glowed bright red, and he wore his favourite black and white checked suit.

Amy put her good arm up to hide her missing teeth as she smiled. George looked a real wide-boy today and she knew he'd dressed up because he thought it would fool her.

She was feeling so much better. With a plastered arm, stitches above her right eye, no upper front teeth and her skin yellow with fading bruises she wouldn't win any beauty contests. But her cracked jaw and broken ribs were mending, and the infection in her chest was almost gone. She had even begun to relish the thought of proper food instead of the soft minced-up things they brought her.

'Where are you going to put this new stock with no warehouse?' she chided him gently, taking his hand and squeezing it.

George gulped.

He glanced round the ward and waved to the other seven women while he gave himself time to think. He had intended to tell her the same story he'd told Anne, but clearly she'd seen a newspaper already.

'I'll bung it all in the 'ouse.' He flashed a brilliant smile. 'Like I said to Anne, it's a Godsend really. It was all dead stuff and I'll cop the insurance.'

The morning paper had bemoaned the loss of the old mission hall rather than his stock. He had checked it carefully and there had been no mention of arson.

'Don't even attempt to tell me any fibs.' Amy shook her head, a knowing look in her blue eyes. 'I know you want to spare my feelings and I'm sure you've told the children a good story. But I know it was Bill's doing.'

George shrugged non-committally and deftly changed the subject.

'Listen. A thought crossed my mind on the way here, about your mum. What happened to her?'

Once the stern-faced, black-coated figure handing out religious tracts by the Black Bull had been part of everyday life in the market. She'd moved into Durwood Street with her husband way back in 1929. As a young man George had often flirted with the curvaceous, beautiful redhead, before Arthur's death had changed her into a mean-faced old woman. Her disappearance had gone uncommented on for some time; but it must have been around six or seven years ago.

'I don't know where she went.' Amy sighed, a cloud passing over her face. 'You know she never spoke to me after I went off with Bill?'

George nodded.

'I used to walk up and down Durwood Street with Anne in the pram, hoping I'd run into her. I wrote to her so many times, but she never weakened. She must have heard how things were between Bill and me, I was surprised she never came round to gloat. I asked her neighbour where she'd gone when she disappeared but all she could tell me was that Mum went to work for a priest, as a housekeeper.'

'Suppose we could find her?' George asked,

squeezing Amy's hand. 'Would you be prepared to make the peace?'

Amy closed her eyes for a moment. If she projected herself back to the time before the news of her father's death had unhinged her mother she had golden memories, but the more recent ones were all tinged with bitterness.

'I don't know,' she said softly. 'I can't forget the hell she put me through during the Blitz, or the misery of later. I'd like to think I was big enough to put that aside, but I don't know that I am.'

George saw a need in her eyes, whatever she was saying with her lips, but he changed the subject and moved on to market gossip to make her smile.

'You and Queenie ought to get together,' Amy teased him as he told her a hilarious story about Queenie catching a woman with a stolen cabbage stuck up her jumper. 'She's been a widow for ten years now and you get on so well.'

Queenie had been in to see Amy the night before. She was as powerful a character as George with her blonde bouffant hair, red talons and sparkling jewellery. Although she was fifty and overweight, she was still an attractive lady and she was lonely, too.

'I'll think on that one,' George said as he got up to leave. 'Trouble is, love, me and 'er 'ave always bin mates. She'd think I'd gone daft if I tried to court 'er now.'

'Well, I might just stir things up.' Amy smiled, offering her cheek for a kiss. 'It's about the only useful thing I can do from this bed!'

'You can hurry up and get well.' George enveloped her in an awkward hug. 'And don't forget it was faulty wiring that started the fire! We stick to that story for the kids.'

Chapter 3

It was pure impulse that led George to the vicarage of the Church of St John's. He hadn't been near the place since his wife Irene died but he remembered the kindness and understanding Father Glynn had shown him then.

The old Gothic house hadn't changed much. It was as spooky as ever with its narrow windows, dark red brick and studded oak door set in an ornate porch. But council flats overshadowed it now, creating the impression it had only been left behind on sufferance.

Weeds grew up through the broken-tiled path, the benches in the porch where he'd sat as a small boy were broken, but the windows sparkled and he could see a bowl of bright pink hyacinths on the sill.

'Well, well, well.' Father Glynn beamed with pleasure and surprise as he opened the door. 'There's a surprise and no mistake. How is it with you?'

The wizened little Irishman had left his native Cork at eighteen and hadn't been back in fifty years, but his Irish brogue was as strong as if he'd just stepped off the boat at Holyhead. He had embraced the East End from the day he was sent there as a young curate. He kept his finger on the very pulse of life in Bethnal Green and made it his business to know everyone in his parish.

George dwarfed the little priest, the hand held out

was as small as Anne's, yet his firm grip and piercing blue eyes belied the bent body and wrinkled face.

'Not too bad.' George grinned. 'That is, if I don't think about the burned warehouse.'

'Sure and I read about it in the paper this morning.' Father Glynn beckoned George in. 'That's a fearful piece of bad luck, my friend.'

The house smelled of age and there was a dull film over the handsome black and white tiled hall floor. Father Glynn led George into his study and poured him a large Irish whiskey. This room too was shabbier than George remembered, but just as cosy, with two winged armchairs covered in rugs to conceal the splitting upholstery, walls full of leather-bound books and a threadbare rug in front of a coal fire.

George had sat in one of these chairs some twenty-three years earlier and Irene had sat on a small stool, a girl of twenty with long black hair and eyes as bright as Harry's, while Father Glynn talked to them about marriage vows. They had been so happy, unaware that, even then, tuberculosis was creeping into her lungs. Father Glynn had baptised Harry, too, and just a couple of years later conducted Irene's funeral.

They drank their whiskey and talked about mutual friends, Harry and boxing as if it was quite natural for George to pop in.

'I heard you bought a house in Paradise Row.' The old man gave him a sharp look as if to remind him his church was just across the road. 'I expect you know the Jewish boxer, Daniel Mendoza, used to live at number three?'

'Is that right?' George was impressed that a man of the cloth knew so much about the sport and its heroes.

'But you didn't come for a chat about boxing.' Father Glynn smiled, small dark eyes studying George closely. 'And I can see trouble sitting on your shoulder, so why don't you tell me about it?'

46

'You promise you won't tell anyone?'

The old man shot a reproachful look at George.

'Need you ask that?' he said gently.

Shamed, George quickly told him all about Amy and the children, and Bill.

'I see.' The priest nodded. 'And you think he may do something more to his family?'

'That's it.' George shrugged his shoulders. 'I've got to get Amy somewhere safe. You knew Mabel Randall; have you got any idea where she went when she left Durwood Street?'

'It was here she came!'

George blinked in surprise. Mabel's religion had been fired by some unorthodox church. The last thing he would have expected was to find her sheltering here.

'Here!'

'Well she's gone now.' Father Glynn smiled at George's surprise. 'She was a very troubled woman, she stayed for a while, but then she went off to Somerset.'

'How, why?' George stammered. He hardly knew what to say.

'She saw an advertisement in the personal column of the *Telegraph* from her mother, living in Somerset, asking her to get in touch. Apparently Mabel's father threw her out when she took up with Arthur Randall and Mabel had vowed never to return to the farm she'd grown up on as a child until he was dead.'

'So Mabel was booted out of home, too!' George chuckled at the irony. 'They say history repeats itself!'

'Mabel told me a great deal about her life while she was with me,' Father Glynn said pensively. 'Of course I can't repeat it, but let's just say that her experiences with Arthur taught her to be wary of handsome charmers like Bill MacDonald.'

'D'you think she might help her daughter now?' George asked.

Father Glynn didn't answer immediately; he was remembering the night Mabel had left him, some six years earlier.

Her suitcase was packed in the hall and, despite her usual abstinence from drink, she took a glass of whiskey with Father Glynn as they sat in his study.

He had known of Mabel when she first arrived in Whitechapel with Arthur, but then she had been the sort of woman no-one overlooked.

Back in 1929 Mabel was beautiful, her red-gold hair, tawny eyes and a body like a goddess had been enough to get her noticed. But people soon discovered she was gently bred and very talented both at music and painting. They didn't know much about Mabel, though her husband was a local lad. The couple had been on their uppers, Durwood Street then was only one step away from the workhouse. The street ran behind Whitechapel Road, one of many grim, narrow streets into which sunshine never found its way. Why such a handsome couple came there had remained a mystery, the fact they stayed was even more strange.

The Mabel sitting opposite him twenty-five years on showed no resemblance to that vivacious beauty. Her hair was iron grey, dragged back from a face that had forgotten how to smile; her body was concealed in a shapeless black dress.

'So how d' you feel about going home?' the priest had asked her. She was a stubborn, proud woman, but nonetheless he was sorry to lose such an efficient house- keeper.

'Frightened!'

'Not you, surely?' He laughed as he said it, knowing she induced terror in half his visitors. 'You're going home to see your mother who is anxious to see you!'

'Not of Mother.' She dropped her eyes to her lap. 'Of

the emotions I buried so long ago. Of my failure.'

'Failure?'

'Yes.' She lifted her eyes defiantly and he saw a flash of the younger Mabel. 'I had intended to go home in triumph one day, on the arm of my Arthur, with beautiful clothes.'

'Your mother will be happy just to see you,' he had assured her.

'But I've got nothing to take to her,' she had whispered in reply. 'I'm nothing but an empty shell.'

'I think she might be persuaded to help Amy,' Father Glynn said thoughtfully, coming back to the present. 'I heard from her when her mother died four years ago and the letter was that of a lonely, unhappy woman. I could try to mediate between them.'

George's sunny face clouded.

'I don't want 'er taking Amy and the kids on sufferance. Tell me what's worse, Father, a barmy, cold mother or a vicious husband?'

The priest reached out and put one small bony hand on George's great paw. 'You care for Amy and you feel powerless now to protect her and the children. But don't be tempted to condemn Mabel out of hand, and resist the temptation to strike back at MacDonald.' Father Glynn raised one eyebrow and smiled. 'Continue for now to look after the children and meanwhile I'll write to Mabel.'

It was only as George drove home that he realised Father Glynn hadn't suggested calling the police in or using the courts to keep Bill at bay.

' 'E knows 'is flock.' George smiled to himself, despite the heavy weight of responsibility on his shoulders.

Few men in the East End would be bound by a restraining order and the police were loath to intervene in family matters. They might try to pin the fire on MacDonald, they probably even despised him as much as George did. But at the end of the day they wouldn't put even one bobby outside his house to protect Amy and the kids.

Chapter 4

'Come on, girl, don't sit there gawping.' George opened the car door with a flourish.

'I didn't expect –' Amy broke off abruptly. Perhaps it was rude to say 'anything so nice'?

Her recollections of Paradise Row were coloured by the Bethnal Green disaster in 1943 when scores of people were crushed to death in the panic of an air raid. Someone in Paradise Row had set up an appeal for bereaved relatives and her mother had sent her there with two shillings. All she remembered clearly were masses of grieving people congregating on the cobbled street, wilting bunches of flowers laid on the grass, and going into a gloomy room in one of the houses that had stunk of unwashed bodies.

'What did you expect? A doss house?' George retorted as he helped her out. Her arm was still in plaster, but the sling had been abandoned.

Now she saw that Paradise Row was in fact a Georgian terrace built for the middle classes when Bethnal Green was on the outskirts of London. The big trees on the green outside were just coming into bud and it had an air of genteel tranquillity.

'Oh, George, you can't know how good it feels to be out of hospital at last.' She noticed the snowy white net curtains, sparkling windows and scrubbed front steps and guessed that spring cleaning had been done in her honour.

'And you can't know 'ow chuffed we are to get you 'ome,' he replied, taking out his key.

The door burst open before he could get the key anywhere near it and Anne leaped out to envelop her mother in a fierce hug.

Paul stood uncertainly on the doormat. A red crêpe paper hat rested on his sticking-out ears, one finger preventing it from falling over his eyes. He was self-conscious about his first pair of long trousers, even more so of the red and blue striped tie. Sheer delight at seeing his mother showed in his chocolate brown eyes.

'Paul!' Amy glanced past Anne's shoulder at her son, her eyes brimming with tears. 'Is that hat in honour of me?'

'He's had it on since first thing.' Anne disengaged herself to let Paul get closer.

'My big boy!' Amy exclaimed, taking her son's hand and looking him up and down. 'Don't you look splendid?'

Paul took a step closer, his arms slipping round his mother's waist, head buried in her chest.

'I'm so glad you're home,' he whispered.

'Wait till you see the other stuff we've done!' Anne said gleefully.

Amy understood now why the children had been so impressed by George's house; the hall alone looked sumptuous by her standards. But it was the heat she noticed most, and the delicious smell of roast beef.

'Isn't it wonderful?' Anne gabbled. 'I can't wait to show you the bathroom and your room. It's hot like this all the time. We've never been cold once.'

'One fing at a time,' George said from behind her. 'Remember Mum ain't quite the ticket yet.'

Seeing her children in an ordinary setting brought home to Amy just how much George had done for them. Anne was wearing yet another new outfit. Her hair was up in a pony tail, and her face was flushed pink with excitement. Paul's dark hair had been cut beautifully, not shaved remorselessly the way Bill used to insist on, and his little features looked less sharp.

Harry came up the hall as George finally managed to shut the front door behind them.

'Welcome home!' He couldn't quite meet her eyes and he blushed with unexpected shyness. 'How do you feel today?'

'Wonderful.' Amy beamed, but once again hid her mouth with her hand. 'I know I saw the children every day but it isn't the same as living with them, is it?'

'Certainly ain't.' Harry made a play of cuffing Paul's ear. 'Never stops talking, this one, wears you out!'

Paul giggled. He still rarely spoke unless asked a direct question, but he enjoyed Harry making these jokes.

'Come on in, Mum.' Anne drew Amy into the front room, putting one hand over her eyes. 'Now you can look!'

A 'welcome home' banner was strung across the chimney breast, huge bunches of balloons hung in each corner of the room and a bouquet of flowers lay on the coffee table.

'We went with Harry to choose those.' Anne's amber eyes sparkled and excitement fizzed out of her like a shaken-up bottle of lemonade. 'The flower shop was dead posh and the lady let us pick all our favourite ones. You've never had a bouquet before, have you, Mum?'

The beautiful flowers in their cellophane wrap with a huge pink bow weren't the only thing here she'd never had before, and for a second Amy was choked with emotion. There had never been a time when she was the object of everyone's attention. Never before

53

had her children looked so happy and healthy. Here she was in George's warm, comfortable home, and she knew for certain he would never withdraw his affection.

His character was stamped indelibly on the lounge, from the eye-popping autumn leaf carpet to the ostentatious simulated fur three-piece suite and electric imitation log fire. It was showy like him, perhaps a little vulgar, but it was a real home, furnished with love.

'I owe you so much, George,' she blurted out, afraid she might break down and spoil the children's pleasure. 'How can I ever thank you enough?'

'You just get better.' George looked at his feet and turned scarlet. 'Besides, Anne's our little housekeeper!'

'They've got all the gadgets, Mum.' Anne helped Amy over to the settee and made her sit down. 'A Hoover, a washing machine like down the launderette and a food mixer.'

'Which we ain't never used,' Harry joined in. He looked even more dashing than usual in light grey slacks and a pale blue shirt. 'Anne tried it out, though, to make a cake for you. She's good at cooking, ain't she?'

'Anne's good at everything, Mum,' Paul said in little more than a whisper. 'But I blew up most of the balloons for you!'

Amy slid her good arm round Paul and drew him close to her, aware he felt he hadn't done as much as everyone else.

'The balloons are the best part,' she said as she kissed his bony forehead. 'I couldn't blow up so many, I doubt even Uncle George could.'

'Everything's gonna be good for you now.' Harry grinned boyishly, his blue eyes sparkling. 'Anne's decided she's going to be a famous dress designer and

Paul's planning to be a doctor, so they'll keep you in your old age.'

'And I'm going to change my name to Tara Manning.'

Amy looked at her daughter in astonishment. In hospital they had discussed keeping the surname Manning which had been allocated to Amy as a safety precaution, but she hadn't expected Anne to take it so seriously.

'I mean it.' Anne's lower lip stuck out defiantly. 'I don't want to take anything of Dad's on with me.'

These two months at George's had made Anne aware of many things. One was that another move was inevitable and, although she was saddened by this, she realised it was an opportunity to wipe the slate clean. A new identity was the first step, the second was to look ahead and plan a career. She had no intention of ending up working in Woolworth's, or an East End sweat shop. She was going to be a success.

'OK, we'll stay "Manning",' Amy agreed, guessing what was behind the determination in Anne's eyes. 'I've got used to it all these weeks anyway. But why Tara?'

'Dress designers have names like that.' Anne lowered her eyes, sure everyone was going to laugh at her. 'Anne sounds like a schoolteacher or something stuffy.'

'It's a good name,' Paul piped up. 'She got it out of *Gone with the Wind*. She thought of Scarlett at first.'

Amy giggled. 'I suggested calling you that myself. I saw the film three times, but when your dad saw your red hair he said it was cruel. I never thought of Tara.'

'She wants to call me Ashley, too.' Paul glowered at his sister. 'But I'm not changing. I like Paul.'

'It's as good a time as ever to change,' George said cautiously, winking at Amy. 'Of course I can't promise I'll remember to call her Tara, even though she's been harping on about it for days. But it will help, Amy.'

He meant it would help to make her children more difficult to track down; maybe even give them new confidence to lose a name that had brought them so much shame.

Amy held out her arms to Anne.

'OK, Tara Manning,' she laughed. 'You'd better make sure we see your name on dress labels one day. And we'd better invent an interesting background for ourselves!'

Amy had been home a week when anxiety crept back in.

It was Sunday afternoon and she'd come up to her room for the afternoon rest George insisted on. Her room was the smallest and warmest, on the second floor overlooking the railway at the back. According to the children it had been a dumping ground for stock before Harry decorated it specially for her.

She wriggled down further under the satin eider-down. Weak sunshine was playing on a family of little china cats George had arranged on a what-not shelf and from below she could hear Harry, Tara and Paul washing up. George, she knew, would be dozing in front of the television.

It was so easy to live here. She woke to bacon frying and the next thing she knew George was staggering through the bedroom door with enough food for three people. Slowly she was regaining lost weight and her looks.

George's philosophy of life was very simple. He believed personal happiness was the cornerstone to success and so anything that gave one pleasure was good. Eating, drinking, chatting with friends, making money, spending it, laughing and loving, these were the ingredients he thought important. He had soon found three willing disciples as far as food was con-cerned, and never a day passed without him coming in with some delicacy for them.

Paul had all but dropped his stutter, and he rarely flinched any more when someone moved near him. Tara said he had only wet the bed a couple of times and he had gained almost a stone in weight. Tara's figure had begun to develop, tiny buds of breasts in a chest that at Christmas had been almost concave. Her hair shone, her skin had a bloom to it. She was growing very pretty.

All this luxury was dangerously seductive.

'If you were the only girl in the world' wafted up through the floorboards. Tara and Harry were singing it together, and judging by Paul's laughter they were doing a comic routine. Tara's sweet girlish voice mingled with Harry's gruff one, and the words brought back memories to Amy of Bill singing it to her.

She knew Tara was already getting a crush on Harry. It was entirely understandable, she was almost thirteen and he was as kind and attentive as he was handsome.

There was so much Amy liked about George's son – his quick mind, generosity of spirit, courage and ready laughter. But every time her daughter laughed at Harry, gazing at him adoringly with those big amber eyes, a cold chill ran down Amy's spine. Harry had the charisma, daring and charm of Bill. But he also had the same hunger for money and a place further up the social scale.

'I want to own a nightclub,' he had admitted dreamily to Amy one evening. 'I can't spend my life out in the cold like Dad, working for peanuts. I want to be someone.'

'Don't try any short-cuts,' she'd urged him. 'It would break your dad's heart if you ended up in trouble. Find another job if you like, break away from the market, but don't be tempted to rob to get what you want.'

It was Harry who constantly brought back reminders of the past. His conversations were peppered with phrases Bill used, he loved to talk about the gangsters and villains Bill had mixed with. Without realising it, he was influencing both Tara and Paul. Unless she could get her children away from the East End now, Amy feared they would grow up accepting its double standards. Tara would undoubtedly fall for Harry. Paul would grow up to hero-worship him.

Harry had fine principles now, just as Bill had had when they first got married, but instinct told Amy that corruption was just around the corner.

And then there was Bill.

He wouldn't give up, Amy knew that for certain. He was biding his time. George was brave and kind but he failed to take Bill's cunning into account. Amy knew she had to get away, but where could she go? How would she feed the children and pay rent? Maybe she could make enough at private dressmaking eventually, but how would she live until she got established?

'Look at Mum, Uncle George!' Paul was so excited he jumped up and down on the spot. 'She's got real teeth and she's had her hair done!'

Harry patted Paul's head and grinned.

'She looks like a film star now, don't she?'

At George's insistence Harry had been her chauffeur for the day, first for the last stage of her dental treatment, then to a hairdresser's up West.

Amy blushed but she couldn't prevent herself smiling in the hall mirror. She had believed false teeth would be the only answer, but George had found a dentist who did astounding bridge work and now she looked almost like she had on her wedding day.

Her blonde hair had been cut short, layered into an elfin style that accentuated her dainty features and big blue eyes. Good food, rest and loving care had brought back roses to her cheeks, flesh to her bones and a spring to her step.

'I'll pay you back when I get work,' she insisted. 'Goodness knows how I'll ever get out of hock to you, George, whatever would I have done without you?'

'It's payment enough seeing your pretty face.' George took her coat and hung it on the hall stand. 'By the way, a letter came for you while you were out.'

George was seriously worried. Four times in the last two weeks he had seen the same car parked up along Cambridge Heath Road, watching his house. Reynolds, the butcher at the market, had been quizzed by a man who claimed to be an old army buddy of George's, and down at the snooker club someone else had been making enquiries about why Harry and George never seemed to drink together these days. MacDonald was rumoured to be working away on a road building gang, but he had obviously enlisted some help.

Harry was spoiling for a fight. He wanted to go straight for the jugular, find MacDonald, give him a good kicking and send him packing, so they could get back the life they had before Amy came to stay, and right now George was beginning to think that this was the only avenue left open to them.

'A letter!' Amy's face fell. 'No-one knows I'm here!'

'Father Glynn from St John's does.' George's gravelly voice grew husky. 'Maybe this is his doing.'

Panic and hope jostled for position on Amy's face.

'A new home for us?' she asked.

'Open it and read it,' George suggested.

The letter lay on the coffee table. Tara and Paul were watching Rin Tin Tin on the television. Harry had gone out into the kitchen.

59

'It's from Mother,' Amy's voice was so faint George could barely hear it. She looked down at the white envelope in shock. 'I recognise the handwriting.'

'Well open it, then,' George urged her.

'I can't.' She shrank back, all colour fading from her face. 'I'm scared. You open it. If it's a horrible letter don't tell me.'

George ripped open the envelope and pulled out the single sheet of paper. He read it quickly and sighed deeply.

'It's bad, isn't it?' Amy whispered.

'No.' George shook his head. He cleared his throat and sat down on the settee to read it aloud.

'The address is Bridge Farm, Chew Magna, Somerset.' He glanced round at Amy who had moved to sit on the arm of the children's chair. ' "My dear Amy, I am distressed to hear from Father Glynn that you have been badly hurt. Although MacDonald has proved me to be right about him, I take no pleasure in that. Come here immediately, this is your home and where you belong, and we must save your children from the anguish we both experienced in London. I have no money to send you but I'm sure Father Glynn will help you with the train fare.

Mabel, your mother." '

Amy stared at George for a moment, a hundred different images of her mother flashing through her mind.

The beautiful red-haired Mabel of her early childhood, the woman who painted, played the piano, laughed and sang. Later, the unkempt, wild-eyed woman who wouldn't take Amy to the shelter during the air raids, who would have let herself starve to death and her child with her. But the image Amy recalled most clearly was the stern-faced, cold-hearted person who read aloud from the Bible, who saw even a new pink ribbon on a dress as one of the Devil's hoofs coming through the door. The woman who didn't even put aside her prejudice when her grandchildren were born.

'Well?' George raised a questioning eyebrow. 'Two fingers up, or do we give her a whirl?'

Amy took the letter and read it again, lingering over such words as 'distressed' and 'anguish'.

'She must be sixty now.' She was shaken by the rush of long-buried emotions. 'I don't understand why she's at a farm, though.'

George explained all he knew. 'Didn't she ever talk about it when you was a kid?' he asked.

'No.' Amy frowned as she tried to remember. 'Dad used to say things about his childhood and the boarding school he was sent to, but Mum never did. Why do you think that was?'

'Father Glynn reckons she vowed never to go back until her old man was brown bread.' He shook his head slowly. 'That letter's summat, Amy, but it ain't exactly what I had in mind.'

'You were hoping for the return of the prodigal daughter.'

'You don't have to go,' George assured her, his forehead furrowed with frown lines. 'I only thought it might make you feel easier, to know where she was.'

'Why don't she like us?' Tara asked as Amy tucked her and Paul into bed. 'What did we do to her?'

'The word is doesn't, not don't,' Amy reproved her.

They had talked of nothing but Mabel all evening. George had made them laugh with funny stories from before the War, and Harry had chimed in with his recollections. But Amy had kept quiet.

At this stage she didn't want to sway the children one way or another. She wanted them to want to see their grandmother, but at the same time not be too shocked if she turned out to be even stranger than

61

Amy remembered. Filling them in on the missing years would be like walking a tightrope, but she knew she must take the first tentative steps.

'Neither of you did anything, she never even saw you.' Amy sat down on the bed, tucking a teddy bear in beside her daughter. Paul bounded out and on to his mother's lap, his arms creeping round her neck.

'Tell us about her?'

'There's so much to tell.' Amy smiled down at her son and held him tightly. 'But I'm not sure it's right to tell tales on someone we might be going to see soon.'

'We won't tell her you told us.' Tara sat up in bed, pulling up her knees to her chest and hugging them. 'Tell us how she went barmy.'

Amy shook her head, not sure whether she should reprove Tara, yet at the same time knowing she couldn't avoid the subject for ever.

'Going barmy, as you call it,' she said gently, 'is often nature's way of blocking out pain. Not pain like with a broken leg or a bad cut, but a pain in the heart. Until the day Mother got that telegram about Dad, she was a happy, lively woman. She had the kind of personality that made everyone like her. She was an artist, she painted the most beautiful water-colours, she could play the piano very well, and she was very pretty.'

'Like you?' Paul asked.

'Not really, more like Tara. The same eyes and hair. Of course I was only nine when everything went wrong and I didn't know much about anything except what went on in our street, but I remember people looking up at her. One of our neighbours called her "the Duchess of Durwood Street". You see she spoke well, like a lady, she had good manners and made sure I did, too. As a child I never questioned why someone like her ended up in Whitechapel, after all I didn't know anything else.'

'It looks like she got thrown out for marrying Grandpa,' Tara said.

'Perhaps, but I know they were together for at least ten years before I was born, maybe even more than that. She told me once they had given up hope of having a child, she was thirty when I was born and your grandpa joined the Army because it was the Depression and there wasn't any work.'

Paul frowned. 'You mean he couldn't find any job except being a soldier?'

'That's right, and it must have been difficult being apart when they were so happy together. Funnily enough, though, I only remember clearly the times he was home. We used to go to Southend on the Tower Belle. Sometimes we went in a charabanc with other families and had picnics in the country. Other times it was just the three of us going to Victoria Park together, or the street parties. We had one for the Coronation of George VI in 1937 and it lasted two days! Dad took the piano out into the street and there was an old man who played the accordion. It was wonderful, coloured bunting, flags, paper hats. All the grown-ups danced and got tiddly, us kids played musical chairs and scoffed all the food.'

'Was Grandpa shot by a German?' Paul asked.

'I suppose he must have been, but up till then the War didn't seem real. We saw him off on a train, I remember, the station was packed with soldiers, kitbags, women and children. He picked me up to hug me and told me to look after Mother.'

Even now, Amy remembered it all so clearly. There must have been thousands of people crowded into Charing Cross station and from the viewpoint of her father's shoulders it was very exciting.

Her small hands caressed her father's blond hair absentmindedly as she surveyed the people all around her. There were splashes of bright colour – her mother's emerald green costume and her vivid gold hair curling on her shoulders; an old lady wearing a pink hat with an artificial rose on it. But mostly it was khaki uniforms, stretching as far as she could see. Steam belched from the waiting engines, the smells of oil, cigarettes and beer filled the air.

It was from her high perch that she noticed sadness wasn't peculiar to her own mother and father. Soldiers were hugging their wives, many women were dabbing hankies at streaming eyes.

'You are coming back, aren't you, Daddy?' Amy twisted her father's head upwards with her small hands so she could see him better, suddenly aware this was different from all the other times they'd seen him off back to the camp.

He reached up and caught her under her arms, lifting her right up above his head and down in front of him.

'You don't really think I'd leave my two best girls for long?' He looked down at her and smiled.

An icy chill ran down her spine, not because she didn't believe him, but because for the first time ever she saw fear in his face. She turned to her mother and caught her wiping away a tear.

Her parents were a handsome couple, Amy had heard that said since she was tiny. Arthur's blond hair, twinkling blue eyes and peachy skin suggested a boyish innocence, but the thin scar from his ear to his jaw, broad shoulders and rippling muscles spoke of an underlying toughness. Mabel, with her fiery colouring, hour-glass figure and beautiful face, demanded a second look. If there were ballots in Whitechapel for the most envied couple, the Randalls would have won.

Amy pressed her face into the rough serge of her father's uniform and drank in that smell of Blanko, cigarettes and Lifebuoy soap that was peculiar to him.

'Princess!' His hands gripped her sides, lifting her up into a fierce hug. 'You look after your mother for me and just be a good girl.'

She couldn't remember the train pulling out, just the image of her parents' last embrace.

'Mum! You were going to tell us about Grandma!'

Tara's voice brought Amy back to the present.

'Sorry, I was remembering seeing Dad off at the station. That was in '39 and it was only a few days after that I was evacuated to Kent with the rest of my school.'

Paul's eyes went very wide. 'Was that scary?'

'A bit.' Amy smiled at Tara's wide-eyed look of horror. 'But I wasn't there more than a month. No bombs dropped or anything so most of us went back home. Mother was worried because Dad was off in France somewhere, but she spent that winter painting greetings cards and talking about how when Dad came home we'd move out of London for good. In May, Holland and Belgium were invaded. I remember her sitting on the arm of an armchair in the parlour, her ear practically stuck to the radio listening for news, but she got a letter from Dad soon after.'

Paul yawned, snuggling down on Amy's lap, his eyes drooping.

'Into bed with you, my boy.' Amy stood up, lifting him in her arms, and tucked him in beside his sister.

'Don't stop, Mum,' Tara implored her. 'Tell me about when the telegram came.'

'It was a beautiful, hot summer's day in June,' Amy said thoughtfully, sitting back down on the bed. 'I was sitting on the floor in the parlour reading a Dorite Fairly Bruce school story. Mother was in the kitchen making a rhubarb pie.'

The little parlour was so clear in her mind she could even smell wax polish. The sun had rarely penetrated into Durwood Street – aside from it being very narrow, opposite was a big old warehouse – but that day the rays had caught the top of the window at an angle and filtered through the lace curtains, making a pattern on the round supper table. The front door was propped open with a flat iron to let in the breeze and Mother was singing 'Barbara Allen' as she rolled out the pastry.

They had been listening to the news of the evacuation of Dunkirk on the radio for what seemed like days and her mother had been on tenterhooks, waiting for news of Arthur. But only an hour or two earlier she had been her old optimistic self.

'He must be all right, I'd have heard if he was hurt by now,' Amy had heard her say to Mrs Penny over the yard wall. 'Bet you he walks in here the moment I put my hair in curlers!'

Amy could afford to be smug about her mother. Not for her the common headscarf or the crossover pinny. Mabel's lustrous hair tumbled on to her shoulders, her clothes, although just as cheap as anyone else's, had a certain flair. But it wasn't just that she was prettier and more lady-like than any other woman, more that she had the knack of getting what she wanted with seemingly no effort. While other mothers worked in munitions factories, Mabel painted greetings cards. Some women queued for hours to get meat; Mabel had only to smile and the butcher pressed a parcel into her hands.

There were often fights in the street between women, but Mabel learned to sidestep them. She had a smile for everyone, a cheery greeting, yet she kept her distance, never allowing people to become over familiar.

Amy never knew back in those days that they lived

in what was termed a slum dwelling. She'd never been to a house with an inside lavatory or a bathroom. In Whitechapel terms there were much worse places than where *they* lived. In Cable Street and Limehouse there were reports of babies being bitten by rats and two families living in one room.

'Time changes most things.' Amy patted Tara's cheek. 'You look back and find the details have gone fuzzy; you can't remember exactly who said what, or even in what order things happened. Yet I can see the moments just before the telegram boy arrived at our house as if it were just yesterday.'

Paul was fighting sleep and losing the battle. His eyelids drooped, then he would force them open, only for them to close again.

'I can pinpoint the very moment my cosy little world caved in,' Amy mused. 'I was sitting in our hall watching the dust flying around in a shaft of sunlight, because I liked to pretend it was fairies. Then suddenly there was this black shadow. It could have been a neighbour, the rent man or anyone, but I knew it was *something* nasty.'

'What did Granny Mabel do?' Tara asked.

'She stopped singing. She was out of the kitchen and up to the front door before I even got up off the floor. She just stood there with the telegram in her hand. I even remember her dress, it was green, with little pin-tucks down the bodice.'

Amy couldn't tell Tara the full story. Even twenty years later, after enduring countless other harrowing scenes, the way her mother had gone to pieces that day still frightened her. Mabel had stood in the hall, bent over slightly as if she had a stitch, one hand on her stomach, the other supporting herself against the wall. All colour had gone from her face, she bit her lower lip so hard Amy saw spots of blood.

Looking back, Amy knew her mother's spirit had left her body along with the last note of 'Barbara Allen'. Whatever was left behind didn't recognise her daughter, didn't seem either to hear or see.

She had shaken off Amy's hand, stumbled into the parlour and sunk to her knees by the couch. Her daughter could only stare in horror as Mabel began to beat the seat with her fists. Dust had flown round the room, mingling with the screams of anguish.

'I didn't know what to do.' Amy shrugged her shoulders as she told Tara the censored version of the story. 'I ran in to Mrs Penny next door and got her to help.'

In fact there has been no need to run for help. Half the street had seen the telegram boy and by the time Amy reached the door they were already converging on number ten, faces wreathed in sympathy and understanding. There must have been twenty women, crossover print pinnies over the shabby dresses they wore day in, day out; headscarves over their heads knotted at the front turban-style.

'Is it your dad?' Mrs Penny had shuffled towards Amy, leaning on her walking stick.

'Mummy's gone all funny,' was all she could get out, but the agonised screams from behind her made her clamp her hands over her ears. 'Make her stop, Mrs Penny, I can't bear it.'

'Did she go funny then, straight away?' Tara's eyes were shrewd and calculating; she guessed that her mother was leaving a great deal out.

'She was very, very upset,' Amy said gently. 'I stayed with neighbours because I was just a little girl, remember, I didn't really know what was happening to Mother. By the time I went back home again she was just sad, staying in bed all day, not wanting to eat or take care of herself. But you must go off to sleep now, this isn't a nice story for bed-time.'

Amy went straight to her room after tucking the children in. She sank on to the bed and struggled mentally to seal the old wound that she had unwittingly opened.

She was lost in a seething mass of women – one little girl in a blue smocked dress, unseen by those who elbowed their way in to offer sympathy. Tongue-clucking, tea-drinking, cigarette-smoking harpies who smelled of sweat and cheap scent. They spoke of distant relations who had died unexpectedly, women taken in childbirth and even people knocked down by trams, yet not one of them noticed that Mabel was withdrawing further and further into a corner, blank silence taking the place of her wild screaming.

Someone put the rhubarb pie Mother had been making into the oven, but it was forgotten in the confusion until a smell of burning filled the tiny house. They seemed to forget, too, that Amy was sitting on the stairs as they launched into graphic suggestions of how her father might have been killed at Dunkirk.

'A lot of them were blown up by mines,' one woman said, a cigarette dangling from the corner of her mouth. 'I 'opes it weren't that with Arthur, he was so 'andsome.'

'It said in the paper they was mown down as they raced for the boats,' another voice piped up. 'They said it was like 'ell, blokes wiv legs blown off and stuff floating in the sea.'

Amy didn't know then that her father was a hero, that he had manned a machine gun giving cover to the rest of his platoon while they escaped to the boats. It might have helped that day to know his death had saved hundreds of others, and that he had been killed by a single bullet, instantaneously. But all Amy knew that day was that her wonderful, warm daddy was never coming home again and in all probability parts of his body were scattered to the four winds.

Someone took her down to the Muckles at number twenty-four later that day. No-one asked if she wanted to go, or explained why they thought she should. In fact it brought it home to Amy just how bad things were, because her mother always sniffed at the Muckles. Amy assumed this was because the youngest children often had bare feet and lice; certainly their house was very dirty and overcrowded.

She was given some bread and dripping and put to bed between Doris and Sadie Muckle, two teenage girls who smelled fishy. Johnny, Alf and Colin were on a mattress on the floor and across the tiny landing were the rest of the eight children with their parents.

The next day Amy watched women trooping in and out of her house as she sat on the doorstep. The curtains were drawn and Amy thought her mother was dying, too, when she saw Doctor Graham arrive. Only by sitting quietly on the doorstep with her ears pricked for street gossip did she glean any information at all.

'She's gone right off 'er rocker, poor lamb, tore up a picture of 'im saying he shouldn't never have joined up.'

'She ripped her nightgown off and swore at the doctor when 'e tried to give 'er some medicine.'

'Disgraceful behaviour, if you ask me. She ain't the first woman to lose her 'ubby, and she won't be the last 'afore this lot's over. She should pull 'erself together and remember she's got a kid.'

The sound of pots and pans being thrown into the street alerted Amy a few days later. It was almost nine in the evening, as hot still as it had been at noon, the sun was like a huge orange, just about to slip down behind the clothing factory.

China followed the pots and, between loud bangs as plates, cups and saucers shattered on the cobbles, Amy heard her mother screaming abuse.

'Get out, you bitches,' she raved. 'Leave me alone, can't you? I want Arthur, not people who just want to nose through my things.'

Mr Muckle was drinking some beer, sitting on the back step with his shirt off. He was very fat and his stomach oozed over his trousers. Mrs Muckle was changing the baby on the kitchen table and the rest of the younger children were tumbling around on the dirty kitchen floor wearing nothing more than their worn underclothes.

' 'Ark at that!' Mr Muckle looked round at his wife and smirked. 'Some people got no gratitude!'

Amy darted out of the Muckles' front door just in time to see Mrs Hanley from number fourteen being forcibly ejected by her mother.

'How dare you ask me for Arthur's clothes? I wouldn't let a man like yours within a mile of them.'

Amy pushed through the crowd gathering to gawp and into her own house, seconds before the door slammed shut again.

'You don't want me to go away too, do you?'

Mabel turned and stared, almost as if she didn't know her, and in that second Amy understood why she'd been kept away.

Her mother looked like a witch; hair tangled and wild, skin mud-coloured, eyes bloodshot and her nightgown covered in stains. Even from a distance of three or four feet she smelled bad.

'You'd be better off without me,' was all Mabel said, and swept back up the stairs.

'The Duchess' was a title soon dropped by the neighbours. Once it had signified Mabel's artistic talents, her good manners and manner of speaking. She had been

71

the person they all asked for help with letters, on clothes, etiquette, education and even health. They had accepted her because she was married to Arthur and he had been one of their own.

Arthur Randall had been the kind of man who made women's hearts beat a little faster. Blue eyes with a hint of mischief, a man tough enough to lay another out with a single blow, yet generous and sympathetic to anyone less fortunate than himself. He had been born in Whitechapel and, when his father was killed in the docks, his mother had become housekeeper to a doctor. Arthur may have had a good education, travelled to India before he met Mabel, but he had been one of the lads. Bad luck had brought him back to the dark streets of his childhood with his new wife, but he brought sunshine with him. Now he was dead, Mabel's accusations and tantrums were befouling the air and making lies of everything Arthur had believed in.

'They called her "Mad Mabel" after that,' Amy whispered to herself.

She wished she could forget how the tiny house had turned into the worst kind of hovel, her mother lying upstairs in filthy sheets while Amy was forced to forage for food.

Those terrible nights of terror in the Blitz when she had huddled alone in the Morrison shelter watching the blackout curtains shredded by broken glass, as the warehouse across the street took a direct hit. She could still smell burning shrapnel in the back yard, see the night sky lit up like a horrific firework display and all the time the banging and thumping coming closer and closer.

Could she possibly seek refuge now with a woman who had so totally neglected her nine-year-old child?

It had been the evangelists who brought her mother

back to a kind of reality some eighteen months later. But even though Mabel cooked and cleaned again, she never recovered her old personality. From then on it was scripture meetings, prayers and Bible readings and the humiliation of knowing everyone in Whitechapel laughed at Mabel and pitied her daughter.

Yet sitting in her bedroom at George's now, reading the letter again, Amy found no mention of God's will, or even the Devil. Maybe going back to Somerset and seeing her own mother again had brought back the real Mabel Randall? Perhaps this was one last chance to reach out for one another?

'I'm stronger now,' Amy whispered to herself. 'I can stand up to her. I don't have to let her push me around.'

'Are you all right, Amy?' George's voice drifted up the staircase. 'Queenie's come round to see you.'

'You took a long time seeing them off to bed tonight,' Harry said as Amy came down the stairs a few moments later. 'Or have you been admiring the new gnashers?'

He was going out. He wore the pin-striped Italian suit he had worn the night he took her to hospital, and was drowning in Old Spice aftershave.

'I was talking to the kids,' she said, watching him as he flicked a comb through already perfect hair. 'Going courting?'

'No, boozing.' He grinned. 'My mate Needles got off in court today, we gotta celebrate.'

A shaft of light caught the side of his face, showing up his angular cheekbones and giving him a slightly furtive look. Suddenly Amy's mind was made up.

She halted in the doorway, looking at Queenie and George as they sat on the settee together looking at some old photographs. They looked like a couple – two outrageous characters, similar in age, size and mentality.

Queenie's hair was like yellow candy floss, back-combed into a halo round her plump pink face. Dressed to go down the pub in a black Lurex frock, she oozed sensuality, warmth and good humour.

'Hello, luv.' She looked up and smiled, blue eyes almost disappearing in a coating of vivid green eye-shadow. 'Blimey, you look the cat's whiskers!'

George struggled to get up to pour her a drink, but Amy pushed him back into the seat.

'Stay where you are,' she ordered. 'I'll get us all a drink, we've got something to celebrate.'

'You've decided to stay?' George's red face broke into a grin.

Amy poured three glasses of whisky.

'No, I'm going.' She smiled as she handed them the drinks. 'It's the best thing for everyone, George. I think you know that really.'

She saw conflicting emotions flicker across his face. Relief that she and the children would be safe, but sadness too.

'I'll miss you all,' he whispered.

'We'll miss you, too.' She sat down on a chair oppo-site him. She wanted to hold his hand, stroke that big, kind face and tell him he was a man in a million, but not with Queenie there. 'We'll keep in touch, and there'll be holidays.'

'You're doing the right thing, love,' Queenie said, her loud voice soft because she too had known Amy and the children their whole lives. 'It ain't as if it's forever, neither, get the kids through school in all that good clean air and maybe you can all come back one day.'

Amy could see George was struggling to find the right words.

'Don't be sad.' She smiled, hiding her own feelings. 'Just think of us all on a farm, George, and the satisfaction Mum will have at being proved right about Bill!'

'If it don't work out,' he said slowly, filling his chest up with air, 'if she treats you mean or anything, I'll come and get yer.'

'Well, 'ere's to a new beginning.' Queenie held up her glass. 'I reckon's you'll be all right down there meself.'

'You must look after George for me.' Amy raised her glass to theirs. 'Here's to a new future for all of us!'

Chapter 5

'Well, this is the right village.' Harry stopped his car at the crossroads. 'Now we've only got to find the farm!'

It was a straight choice: on up the main street, or turn left. Tara and Paul moved forward on the back seat, chins almost on Harry's and Amy's shoulders to see better.

Their journey down had taken them through dozens of sleepy villages, but their reaction to their first glimpse of Chew Magna was slight relief.

Not just because the interminable journey was over, but because there were shops. Not the big brash type they were used to, of course, but old-fashioned, genteel ones like those they'd seen in picture books. A saddler, an ironmonger, a chemist with four large bottles of coloured water in the window, bakers, butchers and greengrocers, even a Co-op.

'It's pretty,' Tara volunteered weakly. Her heart had been sinking further and further since they left London. She wanted to be with Uncle George and Harry, not going off to live in the wilds with a crazy grandmother. But even though she didn't want to be here, she had to admit this village was better than she expected.

To the right of the street the shops were raised up from the road, reached by a few steps. The walkway was railed off, as if people had once tied their horses up there. Although the shops were built in a terrace, there was no uniformity of either age or size which gave a delightfully quaint feel to the place. Late afternoon spring sunshine played on soft grey stone and twinkled on shop windows.

They had stopped by a little corner sweet shop. Jars of gobstoppers, aniseed balls, pear drops and Pontefract cakes were arranged in rows behind the bow windows, and from there they could see down the turning. Here again was a high pavement, with pretty cottages and a small fire station beyond; after that it seemed to be open countryside.

'Shall I ask in the bank?' Harry waved his hand towards an imposing Westminster Bank, set back on a wide pavement which led to an old church almost concealed by big trees. 'Or should I try the Pelican?'

'The pub and the bank are closed, silly,' Paul giggled.

'Just testing your powers of observation,' Harry said.

'The sweet shop's still open, Harry. Shall I ask in there?'

'I'll go.' Harry leaped out, then stuck his head back through the window. 'Don't go talking to any strangers!'

Amy laughed softly. Harry had been cracking jokes about country life all the way down. It was his way of preparing the children for what he regarded as being 'buried alive'. Amy had been suffering some pangs of anxiety herself, but now she saw the village she had a different view of things. There had to be a good few people coming in and out of here if there was a bank and so many shops. Besides, everything looked so pretty and clean.

Harry was worried. They had left London at ten. Paul had been sick four times on the way, and he guessed it was from nerves rather than travel sickness. He had to admit Somerset was beautiful, but it was such a long way from London and so very different.

'Would you know the way to Bridge Farm,' he asked the old lady tucked away behind the sweet jars. Although it was sunny outside, in here it was gloomy with a faint whiff of fish coming from somewhere.

'Bridge Farm?' The old girl put her hand behind her ear and leaned forward across the counter. 'Who you be looking for?'

'Mrs Mabel Randall.'

A light came into her eyes, like a cat who's spotted a bird close at hand.

'Bridge Farm, eh?' She peered at him over her glasses and chomped her false teeth up and down. 'I went to school with Mabel! Are you family?'

'Not me,' Harry said. 'I'd better take a box of chocolates, hadn't I? Which ones does she like?'

'It'll take more than chocolates to sweeten her up.' The woman reached up behind her and pulled down a big box with a couple of puppies on the front. 'But she does like these.'

Harry recognised salesmanship rather than real concern. He paid for the chocolates and waited for directions, sensing unasked questions hanging in the air.

'Turn down here.' She pointed to the turning between her shop and the pub. 'You go over the bridge then it's just a few yards further on the left. Stands back a bit from the road, there's a sign outside saying "Milk for Sale".'

'Thanks.' Harry smiled and moved towards the door quickly.

'Did they tell you how fierce she is?' The old woman's voice held a note of alarm and she leaned her plump arms on the counter. 'Are you expected?'

'Her daughter and grandchildren are.' Harry

paused with his hand on the latch. 'Why, is there something wrong?'

Her shocked expression chilled Harry to the bone. He could feel the old girl watching him through her sweet jars as he got back into the car. Why hadn't Mabel Randall announced her family were coming to stay? Any normal grandmother would have been in that shop, buying sweets and boasting about their intended visit.

'Only round the corner.' He grinned as he tossed the chocolates on to Amy's lap. 'Now don't get greedy, Amy, those are for your mum. I hope they ain't gone off, the stock in that shop looked like it 'ad bin there since rationing ended.'

As they turned off by the sweet shop Harry could see the bridge ahead, and felt heartened to discover at least the farm wasn't isolated.

'That must be it!' he said. Between the river and a dry-stone wall with a milk sign attached to it was a meadow, yellow with a million buttercups. Beyond the wall they could see a barn and the side view of a farmhouse.

No-one spoke as Harry drove closer and pulled up in front. Four pairs of eyes stared, as if unable to believe the messages their eyes were sending to their brains.

Even in bright sunshine it looked spooky, a long, low stone house with the upper windows tucked into the eaves. The walled front garden was so choked with weeds they almost obscured the downstairs windows, many of which were broken and filled with cardboard. Green paint was peeling off the front door and a wooden porch hung drunkenly to one side, so rotten it could be pulled down with one hand.

'It looks like a wicked witch's house,' Paul whispered. 'I'm scared!'

'Don't be daft,' Tara said brightly. 'She probably lives at the back. Let's drive up the lane.' She was appalled, yet pleased. This could be the reprieve she'd hoped for. Mum might insist that Harry took them back to London.

Harry said nothing, turning the car into the narrow muddy lane tucked between a wall and the house. All four of them stared wordlessly as he drove into the yard.

It was enclosed on three sides – by the house on the right, sheds and chicken coops straight ahead, a barn and stable on the left – and the filth and smell were unbelievable. They saw a sea of cows' mess. Here and there was a little dirty straw, a puddle of indeterminate depth, a mound of dryer cow pats, but there was no clear path to the back porch. An old tin bath was filled with dark green water. Rusting equipment lay around, an old tractor half inside the barn, a fearsome gadget with great spikes just behind the car. An old bicycle, bits of ploughs, rakes and shovels were strewn around, and a dozen or so plump hens picked their dainty way across the stinking morass.

'She's an old lady, maybe she can't manage to sweep it up,' Tara said in a small voice.

Paul had his hands over his nose and mouth to keep out the stench and Harry had a job even to breathe.

'The hens look healthy enough.' Amy managed to force a strained smile at her children. 'Like you say, maybe it's too much for her.' She wanted to turn tail and run. Filth in a house could be cured with soap and water, but it would take an army to sort this out.

'There's someone coming.' Paul's voice trembled and they all turned to look through the rear window.

At first glance it was a shabby old man, flat cap shadowing his face, coming up the lane from the fields, but as he came closer Amy recognised the face.

'It's Mother,' she whispered, flushing with shame that her children should meet their grandmother for the first time dressed in working men's boots, an ancient tweed jacket and trousers more suitable for a navvy.

'I remember'd her different.' Harry's voice reflected his shock.

'So did I,' Amy whispered.

The last time Amy had seen her mother was Christmas Eve at least seven years ago and she had been standing outside the Black Bull, dressed all in black, urging men to turn from the wickedness of drink and go home to their families. Her face had been alight with the fire of righteousness. Their eyes had locked, just as Amy reached the corner of Valance Road opposite where her mother stood. Mabel had turned her back and walked away.

Now her mother appeared to have shrunk. What little Amy could see of her hair was white and she'd become wrinkled, those plump cheeks she remembered now sunken in. Yet for all that, she looked as right in her surroundings as the chickens pecking in the straw.

Harry jumped out of the car, leaving Amy and the children staring in horrified fascination.

'Mrs Randall?' He smiled beguilingly. 'I'm Harry Collins, I was just wondering if I'd brought your Amy to the wrong farm, or if we should knock at the front door.'

'You'd be knocking there all night and I wouldn't hear it,' she replied sharply. 'Well, what are they waiting for? Get them out of the car and inside.'

Amy hadn't expected hugs or kisses, though she'd hoped for a welcome. But there was nothing. Not a hand held out, an inclined cheek or even a smile. For all the enthusiasm Mabel showed they could have

81

been a band of marauding gypsies. She pointed out they would need wellington boots, ordered them to scrape their shoes on a metal scraper by the back door, told Harry to bring in their cases immediately and swept in ahead of them.

After picking their way through the filth in the yard, the dirt in the kitchen came as no real surprise. A chicken was pecking around bold as brass on a cluttered table, the floor was covered in more droppings.

Amy's heart sank. Not only was the room dirty, but it was hot, smelly and gloomy. Little light came through the dirt-splattered window overlooking the side lane, and the dark beamed ceiling added to the feeling of oppression.

The sink, with its scummy water and mounds of unwashed dishes, took Amy back to the last days in Durwood Street. Spiders had festooned webs over each and every rusting, dusty pot hanging on the beams. A sticky fly paper turned slowly by the window, a graveyard for thousands, and a dresser was strewn with papers, jampots and what looked suspiciously like a pair of old knickers. Walls and ceiling were thick with grease, the stone floor sticky underfoot. There was a smell too, more than just manure. Rotting apples, mildew and a strong hint of cat's pee.

Did this mean her mother was mentally ill again? Had she brought her children all this way merely to be terrified half to death the way she had been before?

'Harry bought these for you.' Amy held out the box of chocolates. Her mother took them without thanks and put them on the table, shooing the hen away with her hand.

'Well, young man, you got them here.' Mabel looked scornfully at Harry and threw her cap on to the dresser. 'You might as well clear off before it gets dark.'

Amy sprang forward. 'Just a minute, Mother! Harry

is a dear friend, not a taxi driver. He's hungry and tired, as we all are.'

'It's OK.' Harry shook his head. 'I'll get a room down at that pub on the corner. I won't drive back tonight.'

The message in his eyes was clear. He couldn't bear to leave them here. They had until tomorrow morning to make a decision and he hoped they'd come back with him.

Silence fell. Mabel stood with her back to the window, hands on hips, looking at the children. Tara stared defiantly back, but Paul's eyes dropped to the floor.

Harry shifted his weight from one foot to another, uncertain whether to go immediately. Amy's eyes swept round the filthy room. She could see no sign of prepared food and doubtless the beds were unmade but her mother had invited them here.

'Mother and I have a lot of catching up to do.' She moved nearer Harry and touched his arm. 'Come back tomorrow morning before you leave.'

'If you're sure!' Harry's grin was watery. He ran his fingers through his dark hair as if wanting to say something more. 'Be good to your gran, kids, see you tomorrow!'

Amy's heart sank as Harry reversed out of the yard and she saw panic in the children's eyes.

'I don't like the look of him,' Mabel said as Amy turned back into the kitchen. 'A smart Alec if ever there was one.'

It was clear Mabel hadn't changed much in temperament since the day when she had refused to speak civilly to her son-in-law Bill. Her hair was white now, pulled back into a rough bun. Wrinkled skin ingrained with dirt, and the absence of a top set of teeth belied the beauty of her amber eyes, so much like Tara's. Her rudeness, however, acted as a spur. Amy knew she had to take a firm stand now or she would be trapped in humble servitude again, just the way she had been before she ran away with Bill.

'You don't like the look of Harry?' Amy used her anger to give her strength. 'Well I'll point out now, Mother, I don't like the look of you or this place! It's like a pigsty. I'll overlook that for now, but don't you ever say anything about Harry and George because they've been the best friends anyone could have. So just watch it!'

'Well, Hoity Toity,' Mabel snapped back. 'You've got a bit lippy for someone who's been knocked about. It's all your own fault, too. I warned you about MacDonald!'

'So you did, Mother.' Amy took a step towards Mabel and looked right into her amber eyes. 'OK, you were right, and I hope it made you very happy. But while we're getting things out in the open, how about considering what a mess you made of bringing me up after Dad died! Maybe if you'd done a better job as a mother I wouldn't have been attracted to Bill in the first place.'

'How dare you?' Mabel's lip quivered.

Amy went back to the children and put an arm round each of them. 'I didn't ask to come here, you invited us. I'm prepared to put aside the past and try to make a life with you. But only if you meet us half way.'

'You should consider yourself lucky I've offered you a home.' Mabel pursed her lips.

'Lucky! To live here?' Amy laughed mirthlessly. 'This place is disgusting. It's a far worse slum than Durwood Street!'

'It is a mess,' Mabel agreed, glancing round the room as if seeing it clearly for the first time. 'But I can't help it, there's too much to do for one person.' There was a forlorn, almost bewildered look on her face which suggested things really had got on top of her.

Amy felt a flicker of sympathy for her, despite her anger.

'All the more reason that you stop being so stupid then,' Amy snapped. 'I've got a deal to put to you.'

'What deal?' Suspicion wafted out of Mabel like body odour.

'If you treat us in a civilised manner, show your grandchildren some affection and share your home with us, then I'll work for you. I'll clean up this house, do the garden, sweep that yard.'

'Bill MacDonald *has* taught you a few things then?' Mabel almost smiled. 'Never used to be able to say boo to a goose!'

'I can when my children's happiness is at stake,' Amy said tartly.

The two women stared at one another, but it was Mabel who dropped her eyes first.

'A bargain,' she said, somewhat reluctantly. 'But don't you think I'll kowtow to you!'

'Nor me to you, Mother.' Amy smiled. 'Now, shall I introduce your grandchildren?'

'I'm Tara.' Tara moved forward just an inch or two. She had been concerned for the last hour or two about her crumpled kilt, the tomato sauce stain on her green jumper and her untidy hair, but compared with her grandmother she looked immaculate.

'I thought your name was Anne?' Mabel frowned.

'We changed it when we all changed our name to Manning,' Amy explained. 'She wants to be a fashion designer and we all thought Tara Manning sounded right.'

Mabel sniffed, but her mouth moved slightly in amusement.

'This is Paul.' Amy held on to his shoulder tightly, trying to give him confidence. 'Paul wants to be a doctor, but he's very shy, Mother, till he gets to know people.'

To Amy's surprise Mabel bent down towards Paul.

'Farms are good for shy people,' she said. 'Animals like gentle folk and you can practise talking to a horse until you're braver with people.'

'I like animals,' Paul volunteered hesitantly. 'Will I be able to help feed them?'

'Of course you will,' Mabel said. 'I'll take you over later to meet my old mare Betsy, she likes little boys.'

Those few words comforted Amy. She dimly remembered that tender voice from before her father died. It was odd that Paul had brought it back. Paul wasn't attractive like Tara, but if Mabel reacted like that to him, things were looking rosier.

'Right,' she said. 'Before we can even think of eating, I'll have to clean this kitchen. Is there hot water?'

'Of course,' Mabel snapped back. 'The Aga heats it.'

Amy looked blank.

'The stove, ninny!' Mabel turned to something behind her, lifted a large, heavy-looking hinged lid and heat wafted out. 'We cook on it, it keeps us warm and heats water. Look, it's got four ovens, all of them different heats. There's a rabbit stew in one of them.'

It was after midnight when Amy climbed into the big double bed with its feather mattress. It felt damp, it smelled musty but she was so tired she didn't care.

Despite the exhausting hours of work she'd put in already this evening, she'd barely scratched the surface. The whole house was totally neglected and all she had managed to do was roughly clean the kitchen, make up the beds and sweep a clean path through the yard. The floor alone had taken five or six buckets of water before the red quarry tiles appeared beneath the dirt.

But looking objectively, Amy could see that her mother had her priorities right. The animals were well looked after, there were crops in the fields, rows of vegetables in the garden. Her work in the dairy was almost a full-time job. Aside from Stan, a local man who came in to help with the milking, she had been struggling to hold it together alone.

This was never going to be a soft option like living with George. Her mother was prickly, self-opinion-ated and mean-spirited. She would harp on forever about Bill, and Amy would probably work her fingers to the bone without any thanks.

It was no good considering all the big jobs that needed doing – the holes in the barn roof, the broken windows, the front door that wouldn't open. Creating a clean, comfortable home was the first priority; turn-ing out all those fusty rooms, clearing the accumulated rubbish, washing windows and curtains.

The children's reactions were difficult to gauge. Mabel had taken them on a tour of the farm while Amy was washing the floor, and when they came back they were calling her Gran as naturally as if they had known her all their lives. They made no comment even when Amy tucked them into bed, and that seemed almost like approval.

As to her own feelings, Amy couldn't even begin to sort them out. But now, as her eyes drooped and she felt sleep overtaking her, she had a sense that fate had sent her here for a purpose.

'Are you sure, Amy?' Harry stood by his car, his bright blue eyes troubled. 'She's worse than Attila the Hun! And what about the kids? They'll hate it.'

'Do they look as if they're hating it?' Amy nodded towards Tara. She wore a pair of navy blue shorts, an old sweater and her bare legs were half hidden in a huge pair of wellingtons. She was hosing and sweep-ing down the yard, crowing with delight as smooth cobbles revealed themselves under the dirt.

Paul was hidden in the barn, but they could hear him

chattering away to two new calves as if they were old friends. Amy had never seen him eat such a big breakfast – porridge, bacon and eggs and at least three slices of bread and honey.

'Once the novelty wears off they'll wish they were back in London,' Harry argued. 'We could help you to find a flat there, and you could get a job easy.'

Amy shook her head. 'Look around you, Harry. Forget the dirt in the yard, the greasy windows and the hole in the barn roof. Look at what I'm being offered here and what it could mean long-term.'

The sun was shining on a clump of white dog daisies by the barn, the old mare Betsy was looking out over the stable door. The only sounds were Paul talking softly to the calves in the barn, Tara sweeping and the chickens clucking.

'There are meadows all around that belonged to my ancestors.' She gestured behind her. 'Mother tells me if we go down the lane it leads to the river. A couple of miles over there' – she pointed beyond the house – 'is a huge lake full of wild geese, swans and other birds. You tell me where I'll find that in London.'

Harry had never seen Amy like this. In a pair of jeans and a cotton blouse she looked more like twenty than over thirty. Her hair was tousled, her hands were already red from scrubbing, but she had a determined look in her soft blue eyes.

'Well, you know where we are,' Harry said as he opened the car door. 'If it don't work out, any trouble, anythin' at all, just phone and we'll be down to sort it out.'

'Are you going now, Harry?' Tara shouted, running across the yard as fast as she could in her huge boots.

'Paul!' Amy called out. 'Harry's leaving now.'

Somehow it showed the full measure of Harry when Paul came racing out of the barn, running full tilt to the older lad's arms, beating his sister. Harry swept

88

him up, pressing his face against the smaller one.

'You'll come and see us, won't you?' Paul asked, his small grubby hands cupping Harry's face. 'And teach me to box?'

Harry hugged Paul one last time before putting him down. 'And I hope I get such a good hug from you too, Tara?'

Tara looked bashful, but she put her arms round his waist and buried her head in his chest.

'I never had such a good friend as you,' she whispered. 'I won't ever forget you.'

'You won't get a chance.' Harry prised her off his chest and lifted her chin so he could see her face. 'I shall be checking up on you, so don't think you can marry some spotty-faced farm boy and forget about being a famous dress designer,' he said. He kissed her cheek, then reached out for Amy, a stricken look on his face.

Amy hugged him. 'Promise me you won't go astray, Harry?' She wiped away the dirt Paul had smeared on his face. There was strength and character in that angular face, his blue eyes were compassionate. If he didn't wander from the straight path it would be a lucky woman that had those sensual lips to kiss and that lean, strong body in her arms.

He shook his head, kissed her cheek and got into the car.

'You don't know how much Dad and me'll miss you. Keep in touch!'

'Can't you sit down for a minute?' Mabel said tetchily as Amy put back the last piece of washed china on to the dresser.

The children were in bed, exhausted from exploring and cleaning their bedroom. They hadn't even noticed the absence of a television in the excitement of so many new experiences.

'I'll stop now.' Amy hung the teatowel on the rail in front of the Aga to dry and leaned back against it, looking round at the clean room. 'It looks much better, Mother, but it needs painting.'

She had worked on the kitchen since Harry left that morning – walls and ceiling washed down, the pine table scrubbed with bleach, cupboards and drawers turned out, every last utensil and piece of china washed. Some of the old pots were copper and now they gleamed up on the beams, free of cobwebs and dust. The prettiest china was displayed on the dresser and faded checked curtains had been washed and replaced at sparkling windows.

It was far brighter now, already a pleasant family room, but Amy's head was buzzing with ideas, for new upholstery on her mother's rocking chair, maybe a rug beneath it, and bright cushions on the wooden settle.

'I can't afford painters.' Mabel's rocking chair scraped on the tiled floor.

'I can paint it.' Amy studied her work-reddened hands; they hadn't look like this since she left Bill. 'If I'm going to live here we have to make it nice.'

She'd barely had time to examine the other rooms but a quick glance had daunted her. Boxes of rotten, forgotten apples lay in the dining room, stuffing spilled out of the armchairs in the sitting room and an inch of dust covered everything. The bathroom upstairs smelled as if something had died in there, and she found mouse droppings in the airing cupboard. There were cupboards and trunks stuffed with ancient clothes, letters and photographs, strange old gadgets that ought to be in a museum, glimpses of a past Amy wanted to know about. Yet she sensed a deep reluctance on her mother's part to discuss it.

'There's paint out in the barn.' Mabel sniffed. 'I bought it all before Mother died. I was like you then, but losing her knocked the heart out of me.'

Amy pulled out one of the chairs from the table and sat down.

'Why didn't you ever tell me about this place when I was little?' she asked. The question had been in her mind all day and now it suddenly seemed very important. 'Did you fall out with your mother, too?'

Mabel didn't answer for a moment, she just sat and rocked, almost as if she was dozing off to sleep.

'Not Mother,' she said eventually. 'Just Papa.'

'Tell me about it now.' Amy moved her chair a little closer. 'There's so much time to make up for, Mother.'

Mabel chomped on her false teeth and looked hesitant.

Amy had been surprised this morning to find her mother had obviously bathed, washed her hair and put on clean clothes. Her white hair was fluffy now, trying to escape from its bun, and with her teeth back in she looked ten years younger. She still wore men's trousers and a sweater, but Amy had seen for herself that such an outfit was far more sensible than a dress.

She wasn't mad, not even depressed. Eccentric, certainly, but she had all her faculties. Loneliness and bitterness had put those permanent scowl lines on her face, but Amy had heard her laughing with the children several times today and that meant the Mabel Randall of pre-War years was still there somewhere.

'I never told you about this place because I once swore I'd never set foot in here again while your grandfather was alive.'

'Why?'

'Because James Brady was the cruellest man I ever met and I hated him so much I could have killed him. I only came back to nurse Mother.'

'He was dead?'

'Had been for a couple of years,' Mabel said.

'Thrown from his horse in a thunderstorm coming back from Wells. They reckon he lay there all night with a broken back before someone found him. I laughed when I heard, I hoped he died in agony.'

'Father Glynn told George Collins that your mother advertised to find you. What was it like when you got back here?'

Mabel closed her eyes and let herself go back six years.

Everything had seemed so bewildering, familiar yet totally different. The train was so much faster. Temple Meads station at Bristol didn't look so huge or so grand; then there was the bus ride out through Bristol, houses where once there had been only fields. She had got off the bus at Pensford Hill thinking that it was only a short walk down the lane from there, only to discover it was miles. Her case was heavy, her shoes were too tight and when she looked out over the fields towards the farm she was puzzled to see a lake where once there had been only farmland.

But once she got to the village her heart was pounding with excitement. The sweet shop on the corner was still there, though it looked as if it had changed hands. Pearse's the baker's was now called The Old Bakery and looked very much smarter. The High Street looked narrower than she remembered, but maybe that was just because of the parked cars. She could remember boys playing cricket there with only the occasional horse or pony trap disturbing them. But as she turned towards the farm she forgot her tight shoes and the heavy case, put aside the bitter memories and thought only of seeing her mother for the first time in thirty-four years.

She was sitting out in a wicker chair by the barn, almost asleep, as Mabel turned the corner to the yard, an old lady of eighty in a navy and white print dress

with a handmade lace collar, her white hair twisted up
into a bun. Smaller, thinner, her once delicate skin was
furrowed with deep lines, and brown from the sun.
Her eyes flew open as she heard her daughter's step
on the cobbles.

'Oh, Mabel.' She had struggled to get up, tottering
towards her daughter on bowed, arthritic legs, arms
wide open in welcome. 'You can't imagine how I've
longed for this moment.'

Tears pricked the back of Mabel's eyes unexpectedly
as she thought of that time now.

'It was good to see her again,' was all she managed
to say, but she was ashamed to compare the welcome
she'd offered Amy and the children with the joyous
one she had been given by Polly. 'She had all her
faculties, but she was too weak to cope with everything. You take after her, she couldn't bear mess
either.'

'Was it good to be together again?' Amy wanted to
know what had caused the rift in the first place, but
she knew better than to rush her mother.

Mabel's face softened. She leaned back in her chair
and rocked gently, her eyes closed.

'There was so much to say, so much that needed
explaining. But somehow we could never get it out.
Mother used to sit in this chair.' Mabel looked round
at her daughter and smiled. 'I used to sit where you
are and read her the paper. We gossiped about the
people in the village, but never about us.'

'But you hated your father, did you talk about
that?'

'I tried to once. Mother stopped me, she said she'd
married my father because she loved him. If he didn't
turn out to be kind of man she'd hoped for, then that
wasn't his fault, but hers for being a bad judge of
character.'

93

'She sounds like a saint,' Amy said with a wry smile. 'Do you go along with that?'

'I certainly don't. She should have stuck a knife in him.' Mabel was quite animated and flushed now, almost as if she'd spent some time considering killing her father.

'What was her answer to that?'

' "You must learn to be kinder, Mabel. To accept what is, and not to try to change people or events to suit yourself." '

'She sounds lovely, I wish I'd met her,' Amy said.

'You have a great deal of Polly in you.' Mabel saw sweet perfection in her daughter's face. The straight line of her small nose, the clarity of her complexion and yet sensuality in the lips inherited from herself. 'The funny thing is I could see it in you even when you were small. It irritated me sometimes because I knew you'd just accept things the way she did. But on balance I wish I'd inherited more of Polly and less of James.'

Amy realised that was meant to be a compliment, even if it hadn't come out like one.

'My grandfather?'

Mabel nodded and screwed up her lips in disapproval. 'He was like a mad bull. Red-haired, hot-tempered, arrogant and self-opinionated. He didn't have a friend in the world, you know. He had acquaintances, men who kowtowed to him because he was tougher and meaner, but not one real friend. I'm the same, who'll miss me when I'm gone?'

'We will,' Amy said stoutly. 'Besides, you had that breakdown, you weren't like that before Dad died.'

'I was.' Mabel shrugged her shoulders. 'I might have liked dancing and parties in those days, I might have laughed a great deal, seemed popular, but I didn't make close friends. I didn't need anyone other than Arthur. My breakdown didn't come from grief, you know.'

Amy's eyes widened. Surely she wasn't going to hear now that Mabel didn't ever love her husband?

'It was rage!'

'Rage?'

'Rage and fury,' Mabel said with satisfaction. 'Before you were born my life with him was like being on a switchback. Here and there we were up on top, but mostly plunging down to the bottom again. He was a gambler, you see.'

'A gambler? What sort – horses, cards?'

'Mostly cards, poker was his game. He was known in just about every casino, club and dive bar in England.'

Somehow that explained a great deal to Amy.

'That's why we were living in Whitechapel?'

So many times in her adult years Amy had pondered that question. So they had got trapped there as she and Bill had!

Mabel nodded grimly. 'We were only one step away from the workhouse in 1929. We had nothing left to sell, we were being chased for Arthur's gambling debts. It was January, thick snow on the ground, and I pawned my wedding ring to pay the rent on that house.'

Amy's mouth fell open. 'But Dad always seemed so . . .' She couldn't think of the right word; 'sensible' hardly seemed appropriate.

'Your father was feckless, a wonderful, stupid man. A bounder, a lazy good-for-nothing, but I loved him with every breath in my body. But the first day we spent in that filthy slum in Whitechapel I swore I'd leave him if he gambled one more penny.'

'Did he?' Amy hardly dared ask.

'No.' Mabel smiled. 'He didn't, at least not to my knowledge. He couldn't get any work, then I found I was expecting you and that's why he joined the Army. Sometimes I wish I'd turned a blind eye to his gambling, then he would have been called up for the War, but he wouldn't have been a sergeant and no-one would have expected him to be a hero. But instead he gets himself killed and leaves me.'

Amy shook her head in amazement at her mother's selfishness.

'I'm going to bed now,' she said, getting up and moving towards the door. She paused, her hand on the knob, suddenly wanting to wound her mother.

'Just tell me, Mother, did you ever wonder how Dad might have felt if he'd looked down during the Blitz and seen me on my own in the kitchen with the windows caved in, and lumps of burning shrapnel embedded in the floor?'

Mabel's eyes dropped to her lap and for a moment she was silent.

'I've had that coming to me for years,' she said in a small voice. 'I haven't forgotten any of it. Not the time I found you trying to sweep out the rats when the sewer broke open and they ran in the house. Or you scavenging for fuel for the fire with that old pram. Those memories are trapped in my head too, Amy. It was as if I was locked behind glass at that time, able to see you but unable to do anything for you.'

Amy closed her eyes. All these years she'd clung to the idea that her mother knew nothing of her suffering during the Blitz.

It was like holding a firework in her hand, ready to light it and throw it when the opportunity came to create mayhem. But Mabel had tortured herself already with those memories.

'I think we should both heed my grandmother's words,' Amy said.

'What words?'

'Accept what is, and don't try to change people or events,' Amy said haltingly.

'Apologies are useless now.' Mabel's voice shook,

and she got up from her chair and walked across the room to Amy. 'One day I'll find a way to redeem myself in your eyes.'

Amy knew she should hold out her arms to her mother, but she couldn't, not yet. Instead she backed out of the door, turning to flee up the stairs.

Time was on their side. One or two bricks had been knocked off the wall between them. That was a start.

Chapter 6

Mabel

Mabel stayed in the kitchen long after she'd heard the creak of bedsprings above her. She was exhausted, but she was loath to go upstairs because she guessed Amy was crying. Until two days ago Mabel had gone to bed soon after it was dark and slept soundly until first light, but now that kind of peace was shattered.

She should have known it was folly to contact Amy. The moment she stepped out of that car with her two children, the shell Mabel had carefully built round herself broke right open.

This shell had begun to grow around her heart when she met the evangelists back in '41. They promised salvation, a purpose to her life, and in her fragile and troubled state she believed that meant she must renounce everything that had gone before. She burned everything connected with Arthur and her former life and slowly, as she immersed herself in prayer and trying to convert others, the shell grew thicker and thicker, shutting out even her daughter.

The first cracks in her armour had appeared when she came back here. To feel the warmth of her mother's love, undiluted by all the years apart, made her question for the first time the rightness of expecting others to live by her rules.

Father Glynn's letter about Amy had further stirred up the muddy waters. Half of her wanted to remain in isolation, but the other half wanted a chance to redeem herself. But nothing could have prepared her for that moment when she first saw her daughter and grandchildren.

'All these years you've laid the blame for everything that has gone wrong in your life at others' feet,' she muttered to herself. 'Now Amy wants to know the whole story and you're scared of it.'

She knew it was right that Amy should know about her mother's past. But she couldn't know just how much it would hurt to dig up the family skeletons.

Sitting here in the kitchen with only the sound of hot coals shifting in the Aga, Mabel could sense the presence not only of Polly, her mother, but of Hannah, her grandmother. Hannah had taken her own life by drowning herself in the river after the death of three of her children from diphtheria. Who could blame her? Her husband Silas had been a cold, cruel man and James, her only surviving son, was just like him.

Mabel had felt this presence many times before, though she would never admit such a thing to anyone. They comforted her, gave her hope and now she was sure they were urging her to open up her heart to Amy.

There was so much here on the farm to evoke James Brady. Betsy's hooves on the cobbles reminded her of Papa galloping into the yard on Duke, his piebald stallion. Taking a sandwich down to Stan in the lower meadow took her back to carrying pasties and a stone bottle of cider to Papa during haymaking, and of course that bedroom upstairs!

James Brady might be six feet under in the church yard but, until she found the courage to tell Amy the whole story, his malevolence would remain, choking any hope of happiness.

But how could she explain something which had started from her own vanity, lies and deceit?

She was born wilful. Even with a father as frightening as hers, Mabel had a spirit that countless beatings couldn't subdue. That was why in August 1919 Mabel Brady, aged nineteen, the prettiest girl in the village, was embarking on her first visit to London.

'Be sure to write the moment you get there.' Polly Brady lightly touched her daughter's cheek with her own.

To a more seasoned traveller, Bristol's Temple Meads station on a hot summer morning would be a place to avoid. But to Mabel it had all the magic and excitement of a fun fair. Everything thrilled her – the huge engines shrouded in steam, people shouting above the riotous noise from pistons, guards' whistles, slamming doors. Porters laden down with luggage, and squeals of delight as people ending their journey met friends and relatives.

'Are you sure you have a handkerchief?' Polly's lips trembled, and she dabbed her own lavender-scented one to her eyes.

Polly maintained an air of genteel elegance despite a lifetime of hard work and the deaths of two sons in their infancy. In her only good dress, of blue artificial silk with pin tucks on the bodice and leg-of-mutton sleeves, she didn't look like a farmer's wife. Gloves hid her work-worn hands, a straw bonnet covered hair that was still a deep brown and her slender figure was still comely enough to attract admiring glances.

'Yes, Mother.' Mabel lowered her eyes and tried to conceal her impatience to get on the train. Already her new apple green dress was collecting smuts from the engine and she was beginning to wish she'd heeded her mother's advice and worn something old to travel in.

But the dress was a triumph! She loved its well-fitting bodice and long tight sleeves, with tiny pearl buttons from wrist to elbow. The skirt lay flat across her stomach, but was gathered at the back to create a small bustle. The length of material had been donated by a friend of her mother's, a pattern from one neighbour, the cream lace collar from another. With a ribbon of the same material on her jaunty straw hat, surely no-one would guess she was a country girl?

She wished too she didn't have to be chaperoned by Mrs Grey. The parson's wife was aptly named, everything about her was grey, from her clothes and skin to her conversation. She was already ensconced in the carriage with her picnic basket, smelling-salts and embroidery.

'You'd better be getting on now.' Polly reached into a little Dorothy bag and pulled out a couple of half-crowns. 'Buy yourself a little treat, but don't let on to your father. Now remember to act like a lady! Keep your gloves on and don't stare at people.'

For just a moment Mabel felt ashamed of herself. Her mother had to account to Papa for every farthing and she would have to sell a lot of extra butter and eggs to cover that amount. While Mabel was gone she would have all her daughter's tasks piled on to her already exhausting workload, yet still her smile was full of affection and pride.

'Thank you, Mother.' Mabel hugged her impulsively with real warmth. 'Don't try to do everything. I'll catch up when I get home.'

Polly was still standing on the platform when the trained chugged slowly out. As it snaked round a bend Mabel glimpsed her again, a small, slim figure in a faded blue dress, one hand still raised in farewell, the other holding a handkerchief to her eyes.

It was a blessing Mrs Grey nodded off to sleep soon after Bath because Mabel didn't want to talk about needlework, favourite hymns, or Reverend Grey's last sermon on avarice. What she really wanted was to fling the window down, throw off her hat, let her hair down and whoop with joy.

101

A whole week with her friend Lucy in London! Parties, dinners and a whole new circle of people to enchant. Suppose she was to fall in love with one of Ralph's doctor friends?

'Clever Lucy,' Mabel thought as she took out the letter from her friend and read it yet again.

'Dearest Mabel, Would it be a terrible imposition to ask if you could help us out? I've been so poorly since baby arrived, I just can't seem to get back on my feet. Ralph suggested asking you to stay with us for a week to give me a little rest. London is awful during the summer months and I know you'd make me feel so much better.'

Mabel folded up the letter and put it back in her purse, not bothering to read the more boring details about Edward's weight and his sunny disposition. Her father had pursed his lips when she showed it to him and said something churlish about 'surely a doctor could afford a nursemaid', but her mother had been completely taken in by the winsome note.

What a job it was to keep a straight face as her mother packed a bag full of homemade preserves, honey, bottled fruit, cheese and butter for her ailing friend. She seemed to have forgotten that she once considered Lucy Meredith 'a little fast'. But marrying a doctor, especially one as stuffy and dull as Ralph Soames, seemed to wipe out her memory of Lucy flirting outrageously with a travelling salesman in her parents' post office.

'If Mother only knew,' Mabel thought gleefully, stretching out her legs so she could see her elegant little buttoned boots peeping out from beneath her skirt. 'I just hope my white organza doesn't look too countrified up there among all that high fashion.'

The white dress in her bag had been made in secret, away from her father's sharp eyes. He didn't approve of dancing or parties and he certainly wouldn't approve of a dress that showed her shoulders!

Mabel Brady was ten when she discovered a world beyond Bridge Farm. Her mother had taken her to visit an old friend who worked at Chew Court, a mansion set behind huge iron gates. In that one afternoon she knew she was going to be a lady or die in the attempt.

Not for her rising at dawn to milk the cows, to see her hands red from scrubbing, or blistered from haymaking. Someone else could muck out the stables, feed the hens and hoe round the cabbages. Mabel Brady was meant to wear beautiful dresses, take tea on the lawn and drive around in her own carriage.

Seeing how the rich lived had given her a whole new sense of direction. She was fortunate her mother had encouraged both her and her younger sister Emily to paint, to play the piano and embroider, and she had been able to ride since she was old enough to sit on a horse. But things like dancing and playing tennis were frowned upon by Papa, so she had to learn those in secret, away from the farm, with Lucy as a tutor.

Lucy had always been fortunate. The only child of doting parents, she'd been taught to dance and to play tennis just because such things were fun. On days when Papa was off to Winford market, she and Lucy would spend hours in the shop's storeroom with the wind-up gramophone, practising their steps for the day the right partner came along. On sunny afternoons it was down to the cricket field for tennis, hoping that soon they'd get to play on a real court.

Mabel knew her looks set her apart. She had skimmed from childhood into womanhood knowing she was beautiful. Her father's fiery hair was tempered with her mother's brown, creating a golden red that was likened to new pennies. Creamy skin and eyes like polished amber pebbles were combined with an enviably full bosom and tiny waist.

But however beautiful she might be, Mabel knew she could never break into society in the village. She had to work so hard accounting for almost every minute in the day, and the only people she mixed with were at the same social level as herself, or lower.

At church on Sunday she would watch the gentry's carriages roll up and disgorge their passengers. There were the Plowrights, father in a silk top-hat, mother and daughters in the latest London fashions. Lady Constance Harringer, who was said to have millions but always wore rusty looking black crêpe. The Osbournes, who were 'in tea'. The Averys, just back from India.

But her main disadvantage was her father. James Brady might own much of the land in Chew Magna, he might terrify most of the locals into doing his bidding, but even at an early age Mabel knew her father's violent reputation would prevent any gentlemen pursuing her, even though she would one day inherit the farm.

Lucy had met Ralph Soames when he was studying medicine in Bristol, through a family friend. They had a whirlwind romance and married just before he went into a practice in King's Cross. All Mabel clearly remembered was a thin, pale man with spectacles, rather shy, with an earnest expression. But then all doctors were romantic.

Mabel was exhausted by the time they arrived in London late in the evening. Her dress was crumpled, her face freckled with soot, and Mrs Grey had spent the last couple of hours of the journey talking about children.

Ralph came striding down the platform. Although he had put on weight since his marriage, grown a droopy moustache and developed a more confident air, Mabel was shocked by his dishevelled appearance.

'So good of you to come, Mabel,' he said heartily, sweeping off his hat and dropping a kiss on her cheek.

His dark suit was shiny with age, his chin had a thick growth of stubble and behind his spectacles his eyes were bloodshot.

'Now, Mrs Grey.' He turned to the older woman, ignoring Mabel. 'How are the children and where are you meeting your relatives?'

Mabel smarted at his obvious concern for the older woman. He took Mrs Grey's bags and left Mabel to trail behind them carrying her own. It wasn't until he'd seen Mrs Grey off in a hansom cab with her brother that he turned to Mabel and took her case.

'I thought you were only coming for a week!' He grimaced at the weight. 'You won't need much more than an apron staying with us.'

Mabel's face fell. Surely this was a joke in poor taste? But Ralph didn't laugh; instead his pale face looked drawn and anxious.

'I'm so grateful you could spare a week with Lucy.' He sighed deeply. 'She hasn't been herself since Edward was born. I would have packed her off home to Somerset, but quite honestly I don't think she could cope with such a long journey.'

'She's really ill then?' Mabel gasped. 'I thought –' She broke off, unable to admit to Ralph that she'd believed the plaintive letter to be a carefully thought-out ruse to get her old friend to London for some fun and excitement.

As their cab made its way through London, Mabel's heart sank even further. It was too dark to see clearly, but the shops, public houses and hotels didn't look at all like the London of her dreams. Maybe the smart people were all in the other cabs that milled through the narrow, dimly lit streets, but the people she had glimpsed sitting out on front steps, standing at street corners and thronging along pavements were all shabbily dressed, worse than farm labourers back home.

The warm air was thick with acrid fumes and unpleasant smells. She held her lavender scented handkerchief to her nose delicately and listened to Ralph, but everything he said depressed her further. It seemed he had no motor car, or even his own carriage as she'd expected. He talked of trams, the poor people who were his patients, and worse still he seemed to live above his practice.

She had imagined Lucy in an area like Clifton in Bristol – elegant townhouses with shiny painted doors and maids to polish the brass knocker and white-stone the steps. But although the cab whisked them through such an area, which Ralph called Regent's Park, immediately afterwards they were plunged back into mean streets.

The horses' hooves went from a canter to a trot, then a slow walk and all at once they were surrounded by light and noise.

'What's going on?' Mabel popped her head out of the open window to see a place heaving with people.

'This is King's Cross.' Ralph smiled at her surprise. 'That's St Pancras station next to it. It looks like a palace, doesn't it?'

Mabel merely glanced at the huge building with its gothic windows, intricate carvings and spires, her attention diverted by the scene in front of it.

It was like a huge market, with a carnival atmosphere. Cabs, buses, trams and automobiles milled around the congested crossroads in what looked like utter confusion. Stalls selling everything from boots to toffee apples were stretched along the pavements, their hurricane lamps boosting the gas lighting. People were strolling leisurely as if it were afternoon instead of ten o'clock at night.

Excitement fizzed up inside her. The closest she'd ever got to such a scene was Winford market on Christmas Eve, but this wasn't a safe meeting of family and friends. This had a distinct air of danger.

Young children in ragged clothes mingled with old ladies all in black; girls younger than her with painted faces held the arms of soldiers in uniform. Men in top-hats and winged collars jostled with others in cloth caps and working clothes. Street vendors yelled out their wares, tram bells rang, horse's hooves, music and laughter rose together in a cacophony of joyous sound.

She could smell fruit, beer and fried onions, mingling with horse manure. The music came from several different directions, a hurdy gurdy, an accordian and someone playing a spirited polka on a piano.

A group of soldiers lounged on kitbags. There were sailors clearly the worse for drink, and a policeman was vainly trying to get the traffic moving.

Even the public house was like nothing she'd ever seen before. This was a vast gin palace, lit up like a Christmas tree, and each time the doors swung open more music and laughter wafted out to mingle with the activity on the street.

'I've never seen anything like it,' she said in wonder.

'There's so much sadness, though, in all this gaiety.' Ralph frowned, his pale face yellow in the gas light. He pointed out a man sitting in a wheeled box, his legs missing and a row of medals across his chest. There was another on crutches with one trouser leg pinned up. 'They fought so bravely for their country and now they have to beg for food.'

The War had barely touched Mabel back home in Somerset. Aside from reading the newspapers and knitting socks and scarves for soldiers, it was a distant problem that hadn't affected their farm. Mabel had attended the memorial service for the men from the village who were killed, shed a few tears as all the girls did and put flowers under the roll of honour for them.

But even when she went with her mother to take gifts of produce to the bereaved families, she had never considered the wider implications of war.

'So many women widowed, children forced out to work because their fathers are suffering from the effects of mustard gas and shell shock. We all thought it was the war to end all wars, but now, a year later, we're paying the real price.'

Mabel's smooth brow furrowed into a frown. 'I don't understand. What price?'

'The economy is at rock-bottom, homes gone in the Zeppelin raids.' Ralph shook his head sadly. 'On Armistice day we rejoiced, we looked ahead and believed in a bright new future. But here we are a year later still with overcrowded, insanitary housing, people dying for want of medical care. The class structure is as strong as ever. Factories are making enormous profits while they pay their workers a pittance. Is it any wonder people turn to the gin palaces or young girls sell themselves on the streets?'

Mabel's excitement at the display of London night life was dampened not only by Ralph's gloomy words but by the cab lurching round a corner into a narrow, dimly lit street overshadowed by a railway bridge. Garishly dressed women lurked beneath the arches, many displaying most of their breasts.

She was glad of the darkness now to hide her blushes; even in her innocence she guessed what they were. Here an overpowering smell of rotting refuse made her gag and a sense of menace in the soot-filled air made her flesh creep.

This wasn't the London she'd dreamed of, but a nightmare vision.

Her worst fears were realised when the cab stopped on the corner of a murky side street. She saw a dirty little shop, the windows painted dark green with 'Surgery' in white letters.

'Is this it?' she asked weakly. She could smell sewage, and a whiff of beer from an ale house on the opposite corner which provided the only light. As Ralph paid the driver, its doors burst open and two men came out fighting and yelling.

'Not quite what you expected?' Ralph took her bag and ushered her to the door. There was a slight hint of sarcasm, as if he were amused by her reaction. 'These people need my help far more than wealthy ones.'

One thought alone dominated as she followed Ralph up a rickety gas-lit staircase. She would never get a chance to wear her white organza here!

Lucy was propped up in bed by a mountain of white lace-trimmed pillows, but the vivacious friend Mabel had expected to see now looked nearer forty than twenty-one. Perspiration beaded her pale forehead, and her dark-circled eyes looked forlorn. She had lost weight, and when Mabel bent down to embrace her she smelled of sweat and stale milk.

'Thank you so much for coming,' she wheezed, clinging on to Mabel's hand. 'I didn't think you would, you never were one for visiting sick people.'

'How could I turn down a friend in need?' Mabel gulped hard to hide her disappointment. But before she could add anything more, a deafening wailing assaulted her ears.

'Could you get him for me?' Lucy raised herself weakly against the pillows. 'It's feed time.'

It was hard to say which was worse, picking up a howling, sodden baby, or seeing Lucy unbutton her white nightdress and produce an engorged breast.

'Could you manage to change him?' Lucy whimpered. 'The nappies are over there.'

Mabel didn't have a clue where to start; she just held the wet, noisy wretch in her arms, knowing her artificial silk dress would be ruined.

'More experience with calves than human babies?' Ralph laughed cheerfully at her stricken face, taking his son from her and stripping off his long gown with practised hands. 'There are times when I'd cheerfully swop him for an animal who can survive on its own.'

Even Mabel had to admit there was something quite soothing about seeing the clean baby plugged into its food source, and listening to the soft sucking sound. Ralph brought her tea and cake while she filled Lucy in with all the village gossip. She enjoyed feeling like Lady Bountiful, producing all the food from her bag, even if the butter had run out from the waxed paper.

'Your mother's so sweet.' Lucy dipped her finger in the honey. 'Does your father know she sent all this?'

'That was his contribution.' Mabel blushed a little, embarrassed that Lucy still remembered her father's meanness. 'Mother slipped all the rest in while he wasn't looking.'

'Is he still as stern?' Lucy leaned forward in her bed and reached for Mabel's hand. 'Does he let you walk out with anyone?'

Mabel tossed her hair back impatiently.

'There's no-one in the village I want to walk out with, but he's as suspicious and grumpy as ever. You can't imagine how pleased I was to get away for a while.'

She couldn't bring herself to admit that her father was set on her marrying Sydney Luckwell, a farmer in the neighbouring village of Stanton Drew. He was at least thirty-five, with rotten teeth and a fat stomach, and the mere thought of him turned hers.

'You look exhausted, Mabel.' Ralph's narrow face was concerned. 'Perhaps you'd like to go to bed now, the journey must have been tiring for you and I don't want yet another patient on my hands.'

'What would you like me to do tomorrow?' Mabel asked, unsure whether Lucy was just in bed early or actually bedridden.

'If you could just manage to take Edward out for a walk during the day,' Ralph said brightly, dashing her hopes of shopping in the West End. 'Perhaps a little mending and ironing and make some lunch for us? It will give Lucy time to get her strength back.'

'Don't you have a nursemaid?' Mabel asked before she went off to the little room next door. She had already adjusted to the small, cramped flat which was clean and cosy even if it was unbearably stuffy, and Ralph was a great deal nicer than she remembered.

'We can't afford one,' Lucy said without a trace of embarrassment. 'We have a woman to come in and do the rough work, but most of Ralph's patients are very poor. We usually have to wait for months to get paid, and sometimes we never get it. Everything will be all right when I'm strong again. We're very happy here.'

Mabel's opinion of Lucy's new life fluctuated over the next two days between horror and envy. She overheard the rough Cockney voices from the waiting room below, glimpsed the ragged wretches who waited patiently for their turn to see Dr Soames and recoiled in disgust at the smells which wafted up the stairs. Yet for all the squalor below, Lucy and Ralph had something special.

The cramped rooms upstairs were an oasis of tranquillity. Old furniture handed down from their families was shiny with polish; white lace curtains softened the misery beyond the windows. But it was love Mabel could sense – the caring way Ralph tucked Lucy's feet up on a stool; Lucy's dark eyes soft with pride as she spoke of Ralph's practice, and fat, happy Edward lying in his crib gurgling and smiling, adored by both his parents.

Mabel had never experienced such warmth. Mother scampered to attend to Papa's meals like a frightened mouse as soon as he strode into the kitchen. He criticised everything, or sank into his chair by the range in sullen silence. Both Mabel and Emily had learned to keep quiet until spoken to, learned to anticipate his every need and never once had they heard their father ask his wife's opinion on anything.

'It's nice here,' Mabel blurted out after returning with some vegetables for lunch. As a guest of Dr Soames she had been treated like a lady in the local shop, and she was beginning to see the worthwhile nature of Ralph's work.

'The people are kind and caring, even if they are poor,' Lucy said, putting Edward up on her shoulder and looking out of the window. 'I know it's not quite the racy life we planned when we were playing tennis on the cricket pitch, but I'm happy here.'

'I don't think I'm ever going to fall in love,' Mabel said wistfully.'How can I ever meet anyone when I'm at home all day?'

'Maybe you shouldn't think of a husband being the only way out,' Lucy said softly. 'If I could draw and paint like you I think I'd try to find a job using my talents.'

'Papa wouldn't hear of it.' Mabel sighed.

'He couldn't really stop you if your heart was set on it.' Lucy smiled. 'The War has changed things for women, you know, thousands have to get jobs now.'

'She's right,' Ralph said as he came in to have his lunch. 'Don't be intimidated by your father, Mabel, it's your life.'

That afternoon was hot and sunny and, armed with a bottle of sugar water and a clean nappy, Mabel walked Edward in his baby carriage towards Regent's Park. As the roads widened and the dark rows of squalid houses were left behind a joyful feeling of expectancy rose inside her. All at once she was in the London of her dreams – elegant crescents with carriages waiting outside, smartly dressed couples walking arm in arm, nursemaids wheeling their charges, small boys in sailor suits armed with hoops and toy sailing boats, little girls in white frilly dresses and sun-bonnets.

Mabel turned into the park, sat down on a bench under a tree and watched the fashion show pass by, gently rocking the pram with one hand. She was aware of a man coming towards her, just a glimpse of broad shoulders in an immaculately tailored grey suit, fancy waistcoat, winged collar and top-hat. At that very moment Edward began to scream.

Mabel had become quite enamoured with the fat, placid baby, who had Lucy's dark curls and cherubic features, but at that moment she loathed him for drawing attention to her. Rocking the pram made no difference and when the man stopped, raised his hat and smiled, she blushed and felt hopelessly inadequate.

She saw a flash of blond hair and white, even teeth. Even though she tried not to meet his stare she was aware of dark blue eyes studying her. He was what they called a dandy back home.

She hoped that if she ignored him he'd go away, but he stood and watched her feeble attempts to quieten the child. There was nothing for it but to lift Edward out, though by now she was flustered.

'Oh, do stop it,' she snapped.

'Fine nursemaid you are,' the man said. 'Do his parents know you speak to him like that?'

She should have walked the pram away, nose in the air, but instead she answered him.

'I'm not a nursemaid. He belongs to a friend who's ill. I was hoping he wouldn't wake up.' She hoisted

Edward up into her arms and sat down with him on the bench. Almost immediately he wet himself, soaking the front of her dress and shaming her further.

'Where are you from?' The man moved closer. 'I know the accent but I can't place it.'

'Somerset,' she said grudgingly. 'And I wish I was back there now.'

Edward stopped yelling and belched loudly, bringing up some milk, then smiled beatifically.

'Mucky things, babies,' the man said. 'May I sit down?'

Mabel knew exactly how to flirt – making bright frothy conversation was second nature to her – but not with a baby in her arms, and a wet dress.

'I'm surprised you want to,' she snapped.

'Well, it's a lovely day. You're the prettiest girl in the park and he's quite a bonny baby.'

Reason told her it was madness to encourage a total stranger, particularly one as young and handsome as this. But she couldn't help herself. There was a bright, boyish quality about him, though she guessed he was at least twenty-five. Without being impertinent he asked her questions and in no time she had told him her whole story, even admitting she'd thought she was coming to London for fun.

'So you're a bit disappointed?' His blue eyes glinted mischievously at her description of the patients in Ralph's surgery and her narrow view of London. 'Suppose I asked you out to dinner, somewhere you could wear the white organza. Would you accept?'

She felt a sudden tingle, a rush of blood to her head and goose-pimples popping up all over her. She lowered her eyelashes demurely and giggled.

'How could I?' she asked. 'I don't even know your name.'

'Arthur Randall.' He took her hand and lifted it to his lips. 'Miss Brady, would you take dinner with me?'

He was teasing her, she felt the laughter inside him even though his face was serious. She noticed his long lashes and slightly upturned nose, and the softness of his lips on her hand made her blush.

'I don't know.' She was torn now.

'You mean you don't know what to say to your friends, or you don't know if having dinner would be agreeable?' He raised one blond eyebrow.

Edward had fallen asleep in her arms, thumb firmly in his little mouth.

'I must go back.' Mabel's voice sounded shaky. 'It's a long walk.'

'I'll get a cab,' he said quickly. 'You could tell your friends I'm someone you met back home and you just bumped into me in the park. I could be a friend of the family, perhaps?'

'Charles Plowright,' Mabel said. 'He lives in a big house nearby. Lucy only knows him by name, he's something in shipping.'

She giggled with excitement. 'He's the kind of man who does have many friends, we could say we met at a tennis party.'

Lucy was completely bowled over by Arthur, as he picked up little Edward and commiserated with her about her illness. Lies tripped off his tongue so effortlessly, Mabel found herself almost believing the tale about the game of tennis the previous summer.

'I haven't seen Charles since,' he said convincingly. 'I was down in Bristol doing some business with his company, but unfortunately my work rarely takes me beyond Tilbury these days. What a surprise it was to see Mabel sitting in the park. We'd been talking for some time before I realised little Edward wasn't her baby.'

He hit just the right note. 'I'm having dinner tonight with some business associates and I was short of a partner. Could you spare Mabel for one evening?'

'Just as long as you bring her home at a reasonable hour,' Ralph said. 'Lucy is so much better since Mabel came, we owe her at least one night of dressing up and conversation that doesn't involve babies or sickness.'

'You look beautiful,' Arthur said once they were back in the cab, speeding away down Gray's Inn Road. 'I've booked us a table at the Café Royal.'

Mabel had fallen for Arthur even before the waiter tucked her chair into the table and placed the napkin on her lap. It wasn't the grandeur of the place, the soft lights, the quartet playing softly or the elegant people. It was just him. That tingle she'd felt in the park was becoming more intense; when his hand reached out across the table and covered hers a strange feeling came over her and she found herself looking at his mouth and wanting to kiss it. Such fleshy, succulent lips, curving in a way that gave the impression of a permanent smile.

Whatever Ralph had said about the sad state of the country, there was no evidence of it here tonight. Aside from the peals of gay laughter, sumptuous food and the conspicuous consumption of wine and Champagne, the clothes alone said Ralph was over-reacting. The women wore silk and velvet dresses, in styles too new for Mabel to recognise. Diamonds sparkled on throats and fingers, wafts of French perfume reached her nostrils.

Ralph had implied that half the men in London had been injured in the War, yet she saw no sign of that, either. The men in dinner jackets, silk cummerbunds and bow-ties who leaned so attentively towards their partners were all able bodied, fit and healthy.

Perhaps she ought to have felt an urge for caution when Arthur let slip snippets about his past that didn't

116

quite add up, but each time she looked into his bright eyes, or his hand brushed hers across the snowy table-cloth, she felt herself falling deeper and deeper.

'How did you get that?' she asked, lightly touching a thin scar that ran from his ear and disappeared under his collar.

'In India.' He grinned ruefully, a dimple in his chin growing deeper. 'A cavalry charge to quell the natives. I was lucky to get off so lightly, most of my regiment were killed.'

He spoke of tiger hunts, the heat of Calcutta, playing polo and his bungalow in the Himalayas, weaving an image for her of the gallant men who protected the British Empire.

'I've hardly ever left my village,' Mabel admitted. She couldn't bring herself to tell him she'd never eaten in a restaurant before, or that the only person she'd danced with was Lucy in the storeroom at the back of the post office. 'But now I've come to London I've got a terrible burning to see more of the world. Papa wants me to marry a farmer. I don't think I could bear that.'

'Mabel, you are much too beautiful to waste yourself in the country,' Arthur said, lifting her hand and kissing the tips of her fingers. 'People like you and me, with imagination and daring, should live in places like America or Africa. England's too small for us.'

No man she'd ever met talked like Arthur. He painted scenes so bright and vivid she could see them as clearly as if she were there. There were no awkward silences; he moved on effortlessly from India to his spell in the trenches in France, making light of the conditions and the carnage. He made her laugh about the characters he'd met. Her long-held dream of the big country house, vast lawns and servants faded. Instead he was building her a new one. Now she was in an elegant townhouse, throwing smart dinner parties and soirées. She would become a famous artist, travel extensively and together they would be the couple on everyone's lips.

What was there for her back in Somerset? Washing clothes, scouring milk churns, feeding the hens. Marriage there wouldn't release her from drudgery; a suitable husband in Papa's eyes would be a man as hard and penny-pinching as himself.

Later, they danced. With Arthur's arms around her she forgot Papa. Somehow she had to stay in London long enough for Arthur to fall in love with her. A man who had fought natives in India and been in the trenches of France wouldn't crumble when faced with James Brady.

She let him kiss her on the ride home without so much as a faint protest. If he had suggested taking her on somewhere else she would have agreed without a second thought. But he made no such suggestion, just delivered her home and promised to be in touch soon.

Late-night plans and schemes were one thing, but by daylight Mabel saw the problems she faced. Lucy was so much better that Ralph spoke of taking her and Edward to Brighton at the weekend. There was no alternative but to go home; but how could she when her heart was still in the keeping of a man whose address she didn't even know?

On Friday night, her bag already packed for home, Arthur finally called. This time Mabel didn't wait for him to win Ralph round and charm Lucy, instead she threw on a light shawl and went out with him for a walk.

Everything was against them. It began to rain soon after they left the house and Mabel knew Lucy was hurt that she didn't want to spend her last night with them. She felt shamed when Arthur suggested sheltering from the rain in a public house. Drinking in a restaurant or at a party was one thing; sitting in a smoky dive with rough men and dubious women was quite another.

'We can't stand out in this,' Arthur said, as they sheltered under a shop canopy. 'We've got to talk, Mabel, if you're going home. Come home to my lodgings.'

He took her there in a cab, rain belting down so hard they could barely hear the wheels or the clopping hooves of the horse.

She noticed little of the house, or where it was, other than an image of a tall, narrow building between two shops on a busy road. A woman popped her head round the door as Arthur led her up the stairs. She had a pinched, spiteful face with a tooth missing.

'No women in this house, Mr Randall,' she screeched. 'I told you that when you came here.'

'This is my cousin, Miss Brady,' Arthur said quickly. 'She's just on her way to the West Country and we wanted to talk out of the rain.'

'As long as she's out of here by ten,' the woman snapped. 'I've got my reputation to think of.'

'I'm sorry.' Arthur took Mabel's shawl from her shoulders and laid it over a chair back to dry. 'I should have planned something the other night, instead of leaving everything so late.'

'It doesn't matter,' she whispered, surprised by the shabbiness of his room, yet aware that this was her last chance to make a lasting impression on him.

'Oh, Mabel, it does.' He sighed deeply, leaning on the mantelpiece and looking at her long and hard. 'To be honest I didn't intend to get in touch again, but I couldn't let you go without telling the truth.'

Her heart sank – he was going to admit he was married. She could see her reflection in the smeared mirror behind him. Wisps of hair had come loose; the little green hat she had thought so smart showed her to be the little country girl she really was. Now she was going to make herself look even more pathetic by crying.

His grey suit was the same one he had worn the day they met. The stiff wing collar was wilting now with the damp, and his blue eyes looked sad.

'I've fallen in love, Mabel.'

She gasped, turning pink with embarrassment. Telling her he was married would have been bad enough, but to admit he'd met someone he liked better was an insult.

'I hope you'll be happy with her.' She bit back tears and stuck her chin out defiantly. 'Now you've made your confession I'd better go home. Kindly get me a cab.'

His face broke into a wide smile. 'Not with another girl, silly goose,' he laughed. 'It's you I've fallen for. I didn't think it could happen to me. I tried to fight it off and forget you.'

She couldn't speak, a lump was growing in her throat and all at once the damp clothes, Lucy and her parents' disapproval didn't matter. She flung herself at him, raining kisses on his mouth, his cheeks and chin.

'I love you, too, Arthur. I couldn't bear it when you didn't come round. I want to stay in London with you.'

She heard no warning bells in her head. She was alone in a man's bedroom, but all she could feel were the crazy beating of her heart, the warmth of his body and a delicious melting sensation.

One moment he was kissing her, standing in the middle of the drab little room, the next they were on the bed, straining to get closer.

She knew she shouldn't let him unbutton her bodice and touch her breasts, but somehow she couldn't prevent him. The wonderful sensations washing over her as his lips nuzzled and sucked at her dispelled her fears and swept her into a world where nothing mattered but the moment.

She had only the vaguest idea of the male anatomy and most of that was learned from the bullocks on the farm and by changing Edward's nappy, but when Arthur's hand crept up under her skirt and he somehow relieved himself of his trousers too, suddenly she understood this must be what married people did.

'Is that nice?' he whispered as his fingers explored her.

'Oh, yes,' she whispered back, knowing she should stop him but liking it so much she couldn't. 'You do really love me, don't you?'

'This is the way a man shows he loves a woman,' he said, parting her thighs wider and kneeling between them. 'I want you, Mabel, for ever.'

It hurt when he thrust himself into her, but his deep kisses and the way he wound her hair round his fingers reassured her. She moved with him, running her fingers over his silky back and buttocks, trying hard to block out the farmyard images that kept creeping into her head.

All at once Arthur was still, lying panting on top of her.

'Oh, Mabel,' he said softly. 'What a brute I am. You should have stopped me. I just wanted you so much I forgot everything.'

'It doesn't matter.' She wound her arms round him, not understanding what he meant. 'I love you.'

Bittersweet memories of that night both plagued and soothed her back at the farm. She was a woman now, a once mysterious part of adult life had been revealed to her and she loved and was loved. But there was fear, too, that perhaps Arthur's feelings weren't as deep as hers, and a sense of shame because she'd let hers get the upper hand. Yet each time she closed her eyes she could feel his body; smell him, taste him. How could something so powerful be wrong?

She wrote to him every day, tucking the letter into her drawers till she could get out to post it. Waiting for his infrequent replies was agony. She had to slip out to waylay the postman before he reached the farm, running the risk of being seen by her father. On the days when there was a letter for her, delight was tarnished by fear. She would hide it in her clothes, burning all day until an opportunity came to read it away from prying eyes. Sometimes it would be late at night before she got the chance, and she'd spend a whole day fearing that he was tired of waiting for her, that this latest letter would be the last.

'Whatever is the matter with you?' her mother asked on several occasions. 'Ever since you came back from London you've been a changed girl!'

She wanted to confide in her mother but how could she admit what had happened?

Arthur spoke loosely of coming down to Somerset, without any sense of urgency. When would this be? How was she supposed to pave the way for him? Did he have any idea what he was doing to her?

The farm had never seemed more tedious and mucky; she resented the days spent washing, ironing and mending when every hour away from Arthur hurt. Even the haymaking in September and the harvest home supper and dance which followed it brought home to her how little she had in common with the neighbours and even her family.

Until the trip to London she'd accepted her mother's peace-making docility and her father's sullen bad temper. Now she viewed her parents with scorn. Her father was a miserly bully; there was plenty of money yet he wouldn't spend a penny to make his family's life more pleasant. Never once did he praise any of his family, he only spoke to belittle them.

As for her mother, how could anyone be so weak? Each year she seemed to get smaller and thinner, lines deepening in a face which had once been beautiful. Why didn't she stand up to him? Why not take some of that money she made for him in the dairy and spend it on a new dress?

Mabel's unhappiness grew a couple of weeks after her return when Emily began walking out with Giles Henson, the only son on the neighbouring farm. Emily was only sixteen, yet she was being given freedom for courtship just because James Brady considered it a match made in heaven.

'Don't look at me like that, girl!' her father roared at her when once again Emily had skipped off and left the supper things for Mabel to wash up, as well as a mountain of mending. 'I've been too soft with you, it's time you buckled down and did some real work around here.'

She got up at five every morning and helped with the milking, then fed the chickens and pigs – all before breakfast. Mornings were spent either washing, weeding the vegetable garden or making bread. If she was lucky sometimes she could read or paint for a couple of hours in the afternoon before milking time came round again, then she had an hour or two in the dairy making butter and cheese until it was too dark to see. If that wasn't real work, what was?

'Let me go to Bristol or London to work?' Mabel asked her mother one evening when her father had gone down to the Pelican.

'Don't be silly, dear.' Her mother smiled faintly. 'What would you do there?'

'I want to be an artist.' Mabel stuck her lip out belligerently. 'When I was in London I saw advertisements for illustrators. I want to earn money for myself, be independent.'

'You are only equipped to be a wife and mother.'

Mabel wanted to scream at her mother; ask why, when her own husband treated her with less respect than he showed his pigs, she was anxious for her daughter to marry someone just like him?

She lost her appetite, even her interest in painting. And when her period didn't come, fear was added to frustrated love.

Mabel knew little about how babies were made but she had overheard a neighbour once telling her mother she was 'late' and remembered that a short time later the same woman's belly had begun to show. Having a baby in wedlock was a cause for celebration, but out of wedlock it was shameful. She remembered a girl had been drummed out of the village with her hair cut off for that crime. What would she do if that happened to her?

It was Lucy who unwittingly betrayed her. In a letter to her parents in the post office she mentioned the highlights of Mabel's visit and the gentleman who took her out to dinner. Before the day was out nosy Mrs Meredith had buttonholed Charles Plowright to ask about 'his friend' and before sunset the whole village knew Mabel Brady had not only spent time alone with an impostor but was in regular, secret correspondence with him.

Mabel was lighting the oil lamp in the kitchen when she heard Duke whinny as Papa reined him in too roughly. She heard the bang of the stable door and the metal tips of his boots sparking on the cobbles, and she knew by the speed he'd left his horse that he was in a bad mood.

Mother was still in the dairy, Emily upstairs changing her working dress for a better one to meet Giles. The kitchen table was laid for supper, a beef and vegetable soup simmering on the stove. She hastily replaced the chimney over the lamp and was about to go to the pantry to draw her father some cider when he appeared in the doorway.

One glance was enough to know this wasn't his usual grumpiness. He filled the doorway, puffed up by rage. His face glowed red to match his hair and beard, his pale blue eyes rolled like a madman's.

'Who is this man, you little slut?' he thundered.

Mabel had no idea then how or what he'd discovered, but his high colour and the wrath in his eyes warned her to tread carefully. All at once she understood why her mother never stood up to him.

'His name is Arthur and I love him,' she said, hoping by admitting everything she could defuse his anger. 'I'm sorry I didn't tell you before, Papa, but I was scared.'

She had no idea such a big man could move so fast. He brushed the chair aside, scooped her up under one arm and swept upstairs.

Mabel screamed at the top of her lungs. Her mother came running in from the yard, Emily met them halfway down the stairs but turned, lifted her skirts and ran back up. As Papa reached the top of the stairs, he turned and glared down at Polly.

'No daughter of mine will shame me in this way,' he bellowed. 'Fetch the strap!'

From her position under his arm, Mabel saw the colour drain from her mother's face, heard Emily cry out, but her father just turned around and marched into her bedroom, flinging her down on the bed.

'No, James,' her mother's voice came from the door. She had the big leather strap in her hand, because she hadn't dared refuse him, but she held it tightly to her breast. '*No*, James, you can't beat her for this.'

Mabel curled up tightly, too scared even to think, willing Papa to change his mind.

'Get out of here,' he shouted, grabbing the strap from Polly's hand and pushing her out of the door. 'If you hadn't been so weak this wouldn't have happened.'

He wound the leather round his big fist and lifted his arm.

'Turn over, girl!' he ordered.

Her dress was thin cotton with just one petticoat beneath, and as the strap cracked in the air she knew clothes would offer no protection.

It licked across her back with such force the pain took her breath away. Again the crack and this time she screamed out in agony. On and on he went, lash after lash, on her back, buttocks and thighs until finally she hadn't the strength to shout or even flinch.

It was then she realised he enjoyed inflicting pain. This wasn't really about what she'd done, but a sadistic act that gave him pleasure.

'You'll stay in here until I see repentance.' His voice trembled in the way another man's might after making love. She remembered then the farm boy he'd beaten nearly senseless several years earlier for some trivial misdemeanour. Mother had found him unconscious in the barn and dressed his wounds. The silence she had maintained about the whole incident, the way she got the boy home to his family, now took on a whole new meaning.

'If that man comes sniffing around here he'll get the same,' her father added. 'You are my property. Don't ever forget that!'

The door slammed, the key turned in the lock.

The pain she'd felt during the beating was nothing to the aftermath. It was as if a fiendish torturer prodded her slowly with a red-hot poker, paused to re-heat it, then drew it malevolently across her flesh. Hating was all she had left – imagining her father falling on to his plough, trampled by his bull or burning slowly in a fire.

'It's all your fault, woman,' she heard him snarl at her

mother in the kitchen below. 'You encouraged her high and mighty ideas. If I'd had my way she would have been married off a year ago. No man will want her now.'

She heard Emily shutting up the stable and her mother shooing the chickens into the hen house, but neither of them came to her. A rattling of plates, scraping chairs on the flagstone floor and a meal eaten in silence.

It was much later when she heard his feet on the stairs. His stumbling footsteps indicated he had been drinking and she braced herself for more abuse, but moments later the creak of bedsprings and his boots dropping to the floor told her that for tonight at least he had put her out of his mind. Snoring from across the landing soon confirmed it.

'Mabel!' Emily whispered through the keyhole. 'Are you all right?'

Mabel raised her head an inch. It was daring for her sister to take such a chance, for they both knew if Papa caught her at the door she would be punished too.

Emily was like her mother, timid, gentle and kind-hearted, with blonde shiny hair and soft brown eyes.

'I'm fine,' she forced herself to call back. 'Go to bed, Emily.'

There was no sound of movement and she guessed her sister was crouching there in the dark, aching with helplessness.

'I'm on your side,' Emily whispered back and Mabel could imagine her round, sweet face damp with tears. 'I hate Papa!'

Later still the key turned quietly in the lock. She heard a faint shuffle of slippers on the bare boards and the golden glow of a candle crept into the room.

Mabel was too weak and stiff even to turn her head. She was still in the same position her father had left her, lying sideways across the bed. She was so cold she felt she could die, her teeth chattered, yet her back was on fire and she had sweat on her brow.

'My darling. What am I to do?'

Mabel lifted her head enough to see her mother. She was in her long white nightgown, a cap over her hair. Her eyes were puffy with prolonged crying and she looked old and haggard in the candlelight.

'Was I really so bad I deserved this?'

'Nothing is bad enough to make you beat a child like that,' Polly whispered. 'Let me see to it!'

Her dress was split open with the force of the blows, the fabric congealed with blood from the wounds. Gently her mother softened the blood by bathing it, gradually peeling away the material to expose Mabel's entire back. Polly's sharp intake of breath proved the sight was shocking.

'Lift up just a bit,' she whispered. 'Let me get your petticoat, and drawers off. I've got some ointment to soothe it here.'

Mabel could see them both reflected now in the mirror. Her slim back and taut small buttocks were dark red, glistening where the skin was broken. Her mother bent over her, gently smearing on the ointment, hardly daring to touch. A soft nightdress was slid over her head. She was moved round so her head lay on the pillows, and covered with a warm quilt.

'I'm just going down to make you a drink,' Polly whispered.

Mabel recognised from her childhood the evil-tasting liquid as a herb tea to bring down fever and reduce pain. She drank it eagerly, wanting nothing more than oblivion.

'I'll come back tomorrow when he's out in the fields.' Polly bent over her to kiss her cheek. 'I'm so sorry.'

'It's done now.' Mabel's voice was just a weak croak. 'I'll be gone as soon as I can walk again.'

'Don't go.' The words came out with a sob.

128

'I have to, Mother. I think I'm having a baby.'

She waited for a gasp, and then the recriminations, but to her surprise there was nothing but a cool hand on her cheek, a caress of profound tenderness.

'Don't tell Papa, will you? He'd kill me.'

Polly didn't answer immediately and for a moment Mabel wondered if she'd been wrong to confide in her.

'Is this man kind?'

'Kinder than Papa,' was all she could manage, and she buried her face in the pillow.

It was three days before Mabel could get up without assistance and every pain-filled hour was filled with hate.

She would never forgive him. She would go to London. Even if Arthur didn't want her bruised and pregnant then she would find a job and a room somewhere. While James Brady was alive she would never enter the farm again.

By the end of a week she could dress herself and the door was left unlocked, which meant her father expected her to come out and beg his forgiveness. Her back still hurt, many of the lacerations were still weeping, but she knew she didn't dare stay any longer. Slowly she gathered together a few things in a carpet bag.

'You're going?' Her mother's eyes fell to the bag packed in readiness by the bed when she brought in some dinner.

'Tonight. I'll walk to Bristol.'

'You can't walk fifteen miles.' Polly's hand flew to her mouth in horror. 'Wait till tomorrow, I'll ask John Ames to take you on his cart.'

'No, Mother.' Mabel was resolute. 'John Ames would talk. All I ask is that you lend me some money for the train to London. I'll send it back as soon as I can.'

Polly could see cold determination on her daughter's beautiful face.

'How will I know you're safe?' She reached out for her hand, tears rolling down her cheeks.

'I'll send word to Reverend Grey,' Mabel whispered. 'I wish you could come with me, but I'll be back one day to dance on his grave, just you wait.'

'Don't tell Emily.' Polly stifled a sob. 'She's been breaking her heart over all this, but if she knows you're going she just might let it slip to her father.'

Mabel knew what her mother meant. Papa would be likely to punish Emily for aiding and abetting, and though she ached to say goodbye to her sister it was impossible.

Mabel heard the church clock strike one as she closed the bedroom door behind her. She had waited till Papa was snoring, her mother lying beside him awake and tense. She sneaked one last look at Emily asleep in bed, a plump arm curled round her sweet, innocent face.

Holding her breath she crept down the stairs and out into the night. The five pounds hoarded by her mother over the years, intended for her daughters' weddings, was tucked into her bodice. Her carpet bag held a change of clothing and Arthur's few letters; not a photograph, a book or any other reminder of her family. The stripes on her back were all she needed to remind her of her father. Mother and Emily would stay in her heart.

Her back stung intolerably. The weals opened up again as she walked and she could feel her chemise stuck with drying blood. It was icy cold, pitch dark and every mile past bare fields seemed like ten. Dawn's first light was penetrating the inky sky as she reached the outskirts of Bristol and down the hill she could see Temple Meads station in the distance.

It was ten at night before she sank on to a bed in a cheap hotel in Paddington, too exhausted even to undress.

A rap on the door woke Mabel and she was surprised to find it was dark again outside. That morning she had posted a letter to Arthur with her address, then gone back to bed again.

Every bone in her body ached as she got up, lit the gas light and made her way to the door. Her feet were blistered and swollen and her stomach was churning.

She expected the housekeeper, as she had only paid in advance for one night. But it was Arthur. He leaned nonchalantly against the wall, a bunch of wilted roses in his hand, hat tucked under his arm.

'Arthur!' Her head spun and she had to hold on to the door for support. 'You came!'

His smile vanished. He took a step nearer then stopped short.

'What is it, Mabel?' He seemed poised to move away. 'No letter for over a week from you, then that sharp little note. And you look so ill.'

'I couldn't write,' she blurted out, tears pricking her eyelids. She knew she looked frightful. Her face was white, hair lank and unwashed since the beating, and her old flannel nightdress was fit only for dusters.

All that week in her room she had kept herself sane by remembering him. Picturing him in the park in his grey suit and top-hat; in the restaurant in his dinner jacket; but mostly imagining the way he'd looked when he held her in his arms, loving and tender. Now he seemed taller somehow, shoulders broader and his face brown from the sun. His slightly upturned nose and wide, soft mouth made her heart leap, yet his blue eyes seemed cold now, and suspicious.

'I've got something to tell you,' she whispered. 'I

131

want you to hear me out. Then tell me how you feel.'

He came into the little room, shut the door behind him and sat down. The light caught the angles of his cheekbones; his lips curved into an amused smile.

'Aren't you going to kiss me first?' he asked.

She shook her head and even that gentle movement sent stabs of pain through her back.

'I'm going to have a baby, Arthur,' she said softly, searching his face for evidence of his real feelings. 'I've run away from home and I've got very little money.'

This wasn't how she'd envisaged their reunion. She'd expected a letter first, arranging a meeting. She would have bathed and washed her hair, dressed up and flirted with him until she felt certain of him. Now she had to tell him the truth straight out and take the risk that he would make his excuses and run away.

Arthur put one hand over his eyes and slumped back in the chair. Of all the girls he had known, Mabel was the only one he'd dreamed about continuously. He'd done his best to put her out of his mind, even toyed with not opening her letters and moving on from his lodgings. Yet he'd written back to her, and his heart had leaped when he found the note from her this evening. But now here she was, looking ill and neglected, saying she was expecting his child. Should he run for the door, get out now before he got trapped?

'You don't have to marry me,' she said in a low voice. 'I'll find a job and even a room of my own. All I want for now is some help until I can get on my feet.'

Even pale and worn she looked beautiful, the dark circles under her eyes emphasising their colour and size. But it was the sweet bravery in her direct approach that made him leap up and take her in his arms.

'Oh, darling,' he said. 'Don't make me out to be a cad.'

He felt her wince as his hands touched her back and instinct told him it was with pain, not revulsion. With-

132

out saying a word he turned her round and, taking the hem of her nightgown, lifted it up.

The weals began at mid calf, growing bigger as his eyes swept up over her buttocks and waist. But on her back they were some three inches across, in places still weeping. Her tiny shoulder blades stood out like small wings.

'Who did this?' he gasped.

'Papa,' she said simply. 'He didn't even know about the baby. He'd have killed me if he knew everything.'

He wanted to hold her more than anything in the world, but his arms would only cause her more pain.

'I love you, darling,' he whispered, taking her hands in his and kissing them. 'You brave, sweet girl. I could kill that brute!'

'Can I stay with you?' She looked up at him, her lips trembling, amber eyes full of doubt.

'Of course.' He sighed deeply, suddenly knowing he wanted her by his side forever, even with the burden of a child. 'The only trouble is I haven't much cash at the moment. I'm trying to arrange some business. I didn't expect this.'

'I won't cost you much.' She sat down on the bed looking up at him. 'I'll help you with things. I don't mind living in one little room for the time being. If you really do love me we'll find a way.'

It was only later, when he'd moved her to a better hotel further along Praed Street and tucked her back into bed, that Arthur knew he'd have to admit things about himself to Mabel that he normally concealed.

He had taken off his jacket, waistcoat and stiff collar, and in his white round-necked shirt he looked boyish and far less intimidating. He lay on the bed next to her, leaning up on his elbow.

'I'm not quite what I seem, Mabel,' he said softly,

bending to kiss her mouth. 'I know you think I'm a gentleman and perhaps I've led you to think I have business interests.'

'You haven't?'

He shook his head, dropping his eyes.

'In India the old colonels used to call me a bounder.' He half smiled at her look of surprise. 'Loosely, that means I live off my wits. To do that I've had to fool people.'

'You mean you tell lies?' Somehow she wasn't entirely surprised.

'Not exactly lies, just a bit of embroidery. I went to India as a young lad, just a clerk in a shipping company. I won't go into it all now, let's just say it gave me ideas and taught me things I'd never have learned here. I came back and joined the Army. I was in France, of course, but not as an officer.'

He told her how his widowed mother had become a housekeeper for a doctor in the East End of London when he was small. Later the old man, who had become fond of him, coached him and got him a scholarship to a boarding school in Essex.

'I mixed with boys from good homes.' He grinned. 'I was good at sport, a bright spark, and it didn't take much to get invited to their homes. It was the father of one of my friends who got me the post in Calcutta.'

Mabel listened with growing admiration. She could see nothing wrong with wanting a life better than the one you'd been born into, and even when he admitted the so-called sabre slash on his neck had actually been acquired in a fight over a game of cards she could only giggle.

'But how do you make money?' She thought how much that dinner at the Café Royal must have cost, his suits, cabs and even this hotel.

'I gamble.'

Mabel knew about old men playing dominos for ha'pennies, bets placed on horses and even bridge and whist where money changed hands, but she'd never heard of anyone making a living at it.

Later, as he got into bed and turned out the light, he told her more. He wanted to make love to her but, in the light of her injuries, talking was all they could do. He spoke of poker games, roulette, horse racing, even dog fights and boxing. He painted a world that seemed only to exist after sunset, full of gentlemen and racy women, fine clothes, grand hotels and Champagne.

Losing the baby at five months was the first of the bad times, an indication of what was to come.

They had married a few weeks after Mabel arrived in London, in a register office with a couple of Arthur's shady-looking friends as witnesses. It wasn't the wedding she'd dreamed of, but she adored Arthur, and when they moved on to a smart hotel on the sea-front in Brighton she couldn't have been happier. But it wasn't long before they had to do what Arthur called a 'flit' after he lost most of his money at the races, and they moved into a squalid room in Kentish Town.

'Only a temporary setback,' he'd said as he stamped on a cockroach. There were bugs in the bed and Arthur showed her how to whip back the covers and catch them on a piece of damp soap. The lavatory was out in the yard, serving at least a dozen other tenants, and they had to light a fire just to boil water to wash.

A week later she tripped on the rickety stairs and fell down a whole flight. She lost the baby later that night and the only person to help her was a woman from the room below who had lice in her hair.

Arthur promised, with tears in his eyes, that he would stop gambling and find a real job. But that day a doctor told her she was unlikely ever to have another child and Arthur not only got drunk but disappeared for four days, till she thought he'd left her for good.

But he came back, like the proverbial bad penny,

with pockets full of money and a taxi to take her away from that terrible house. Soon she was shopping for new clothes in Marshall & Snelgrove; they stayed in a hotel in Mayfair, and he seemed to have forgotten his promise.

Up or down, she loved him. He infuriated her with his fecklessness, saddened her with his disregard for her need for a proper home, astounded her with his resourceful nature and made her laugh more than was good for her.

But it was the loving that made her stay. Sometimes she felt like a slut, she wanted him so much, but he had only to kiss her, to press his body against hers, and she forgave him everything.

All through the Twenties Mabel saw both sides of the era. One week they were at clubs and parties with other bright young things, dancing the Charleston, listening to hot jazz and thinking tomorrow would never come. The next they were doing another flit, pawning her jewellery, even selling their clothes to pay the rent in some hovel.

He said they would go to America, or Canada, but each time the fare was gambled and lost. Once they had got together enough cash to buy a small boarding house, but three months after moving in she discovered he'd lost the deeds in a poker game.

Again and again it was her painting that saved them from starvation; a delicate water-colour here, a design for a greetings card there. Though she was offered several jobs that might have started her on the road to success as an artist, Arthur always had plans that involved moving on.

Finally they arrived in Durward Street.

They had only the clothes on their backs, that icy January day. Mabel in a brown second-hand coat, a battered felt hat hiding hair that was too bright for such a place; Arthur in cloth cap and a working man's jacket, with a muffler taking the place of a tie.

As they crossed the railway bridge and turned into Durward Street she knew they had reached the last step before the gutter. A huge square four-storey coffee mill and warehouses created permanent dusk in the narrow cobbled street. A terrace of tiny houses, uniformly soot-ingrained, seemed to cower under the shadow of their taller neighbours. Many windows were broken, stuffed with old rags and cardboard, and the gutters were blocked with debris.

Later she was to learn that this street had once been called Buck's Row, and Jack the Ripper had slaughtered one of his victims there thirty odd years before. It was provident she didn't know at the time, or that this would be her home for the next twenty-five years, or she might have turned tail and run.

She pawned her wedding ring to pay the shilling rent, and all they had were a few faded photographs to remind them of happier days. That first night they had to break up old chairs and orange boxes to make a fire and as they huddled together on a filthy mattress Mabel told Arthur she was expecting another baby. Eight months later, Amy was born.

Chapter 7

'Oy, bacon bonce!'

Paul stopped and looked around the narrow lane, but he couldn't see the owner of the voice.

Something wet hit his bare arm – a great glob of spit.

'You wanna keep your eyes open!'

He looked up and to his amazement a boy just a little older than himself was lying along the branch of a tree above him, virtually invisible.

Paul wiped his arm on the seat of his shorts, deciding discretion was the greater part of valour, and grinned nervously up at him.

'That's a good place to hide,' he said, wishing he had the nerve to climb any tree, let alone creep along a branch as thin as that one.

'You're the kid at Bridge Farm, aren't you?' The boy moved, held the branch in his two hands and lowered himself till he dangled three feet from the road, then dropped as silently as a cat. 'Can you do that?'

'I'm not much good at climbing,' Paul said apologetically. 'But I do live at the farm and you can come and see the calves if you want.'

For a second the boy just stared. He was dressed almost identically to Paul, in grey flannel shorts and shirt, but his pullover was bottle green instead of Paul's navy. He was sturdy yet quite small, with mousy hair in need of a cut and a sprinkling of freckles across his snub nose. But he had an open, guileless face, and his hazel eyes registered curiosity rather than malice.

'Is the old woman summat to do with you?' The boy looked just a little apprehensive.

'She's my gran.'

The boy made a sort of whistling noise between his teeth and the expression on his face showed that on a one-to-ten scale of shock, Paul had managed to hit him with a ten.

'Gran? Cor!'

They had been at the farm a week now, and this was the first child Paul had seen close up, let alone spoken to. Both he and Tara were due to start at their respective schools on Monday, something Paul was very nervous about.

'Why d'you say it like that?' Paul knew quite well, but he desperately wanted the boy to like him.

'She's nuts, everyone says so.'

To deny this may be to lose prestige.

'She's OK once you know her ways,' Paul said carefully. 'Come home with me now and see.'

For the first time in his life, Paul felt secure. Even at Uncle George's he had still jumped at shadows and imagined his father coming crashing through the door. His gran was a bit weird, but he liked her for all that, and what was even better, she liked him, even more than she liked Tara.

'She waves a stick at kids that go into her yard.' The boy looked doubtful. 'She threw a sugar beet at me once and it made a bump on my forehead.'

'You'll be all right with me,' Paul insisted. 'I expect she'll even give you some lemonade and gingerbread.'

Gran made the most wonderful lemonade. She said she hadn't made it since Amy was a little girl, but she certainly hadn't forgotten the recipe. She put it into some stone bottles in the pantry and said they could help themselves whenever they wanted.

'What's your name?'

'Paul Manning,' Paul said. 'I'm eight and a bit. My sister's called Tara.'

'I'm Colin Smart, I'm ten.' The boy grinned. 'I've seen your sister, she's getting tits.'

Paul wasn't sure how to take this. Not only had he not noticed this phenomenon, but he didn't think it was the sort of thing brothers were supposed to talk about. Instead he ignored the remark and walked down the lane with Colin, back towards the farm.

Tara didn't like it here. She turned her nose up at the little shops, she didn't like the farmyard smells, or the taste of the milk straight from the cows. But young as he was, Paul knew she was cross because she wasn't in charge any more.

Back in London she made decisions – what to have for tea, where to buy it, where to go to escape from their dad. Mum relied on her for almost everything back then, especially when Dad had given her a slapping. And Tara always took Paul to school to prevent anyone bullying him.

Everything was different here. Mum and Gran weren't always very friendly, and sometimes it seemed as if they were on the point of hitting one another, then Mum would go all quiet and broody. Tara hated it, she said they should stop harping on about the past and remember she was here too.

But Paul loved it. The old farmhouse with its beams and odd nooks and crannies, the ancient furniture that Mum had polished till it shone like conkers. He liked climbing on the bales of straw in the barn, petting the calves, feeding the piglets and collecting eggs. Everything here was magical, from looking for crayfish in the river to watching the water wheel at the old mill and seeing the men haul up huge sacks of grain on a hoist.

'Can you ride a bike?' Colin asked as they made their way down the hill.

Paul shook his head, deeply ashamed.

'Can you swim?'

Again a shake of the head.

Colin gave him a withering look.

'But I'll learn if you show me,' Paul volunteered.

'OK.' Colin grinned. 'I'll be your best friend if you want.'

An hour or two later Paul was deliriously happy. Gran had dug out an old bike from the shed. Stan the cowman had lowered the seat, oiled it and blown up the tyres and now Colin was teaching him how to ride.

'I've got hold of the saddle,' he shouted as they went careering down the narrow rutted lane at the side of the farmyard. 'Just steer and pedal. I won't let you go.'

He had claimed he wouldn't let go a dozen times already and Paul had fallen off into the stinging nettles twice and skinned his knee, but he was determined to master it.

'That's right, keep going,' Colin bellowed, too far behind to be holding the saddle now. 'You've done it, bacon bonce!'

Paul came to the end of the path, wobbled and fell off, but his grin spread from ear to ear.

'I can ride it,' he shrieked. 'Let's go and tell Gran!'

Riding into the yard was the proudest moment of his life. He wobbled a bit, he still couldn't use the brakes and had to use his feet instead, but already he could see new horizons opening up to him.

Colin ran up the lane, huffing and puffing. Gran sat on a small wooden bench in the sun, plucking a chicken between her knees, and his mother was hanging sheets on the line.

'I can do it,' Paul called out proudly. 'Look at me!'

Amy laughed, standing there with her hands on her hips, but Gran dropped the chicken on the floor and came over to him.

'You clever, brave boy,' she said, clapping his little face between her hands.

He wasn't wild about her kiss. She didn't have her top teeth in again and she had prickly hairs round her upper lip, but it was good to bask in her admiration.

Between them they'd cleared the yard and many of the rusting old farm implements had been dumped round the back of the barn by Stan. Paul liked Stan, too, he had an even redder face than Uncle George, which Gran said came from drinking cider, and he had bowed legs that looked too thin for his big body. Paul had thought he was even older than Gran because sometimes he talked about Great-grandfather Brady, who he'd come to work for when he was just a lad. But Gran said he wasn't more than fifty and she called him 'a gurt lazy dollop, with the brains of a mangel wurzel'.

'Can you ride a bike, Mum?' he called out, flushed with excitement, standing with the ancient bike between his legs.

Amy put on a rueful look and shook her head. The sun had caught her nose and cheeks and she looked so pretty he wanted to hug her.

'I never got the chance,' she said. 'Maybe you can teach me, too!'

'You'll have to teach Tara first,' Gran said quietly, turning towards her granddaughter who stood in the kitchen door looking white and spiteful. 'It's a long walk to her school, much better by bike.'

'I'll teach her now,' Colin offered, still out of breath from his run. 'I'll give Paul a "backy" round to my house to get my bike, then we can take it in turns.'

Tara didn't answer; she just folded her arms and looked away defiantly. She knew she should thank

142

Colin and praise Paul, she was glad really that he was so happy. But she felt so terribly alone.

She'd never had any real friends, but in London she hadn't been so aware of it. There were children she'd talked to at school and played with in the park but, because of her troubled home life, that's where they stayed. She would be thirteen soon, too big to play yet not old enough for adult company.

But most of her unhappiness was about this place. Would she ever grow to like it?

There was a certain satisfaction in cleaning really filthy things. She'd loved hosing down the yard and making it nice, but next morning when the cows came in for milking they made another mess just as bad! It was the same with the milking shed and the stables. Was she really going to have to clean them all, week in, week out, endlessly?

It was OK helping Mum clean out all the rooms, poking into boxes and cupboards and asking Gran about things. She was happy because Mum was going to do the smaller room upstairs for Paul, then tackle hers. She was thrilled that Gran had a sewing machine she could use and a whole drawer full of remnants of material, but sometimes she just wanted to lie in front of a television and be entertained, not to work all the time like her mother did. But Gran didn't have television, said she didn't approve of it, all she had was a funny old radio.

Above all else she missed George, Harry and London ways. George was big about everything, from the quantities of food he dished out to his extravagant praise. Gran cut bread so thin it was like net curtains. She kept going on about only using one electric light at a time, and her praise was so sparse it was almost non-existent. She missed George's roaring great laugh, the warmth of his hugs and the feeling that nothing bad could ever happen when he was around.

On Monday she had to go to Chew Valley secondary school. Gran had got her a uniform second-hand and the dark green blazer suited her, but that couldn't make up for not knowing anyone.

'Are you cross with me?' Paul's small voice close by surprised Tara.

'No. Why do you say that?' She spun round to find him standing almost at her elbow, a hang-dog look on his face.

'You don't seem pleased I learned to ride it,' he whispered, dark eyes worried.

Tara was immediately chastened. She glanced across at Colin waiting by the barn and sensed the boy was weighing them up, ready to report to others what the kids at Bridge Farm were like.

'You were brilliant.' She reached out and tweaked his cheek. 'Yeah, teach me too!' she yelled across to Colin, patting her brother's hand surreptitiously. 'I'm not as quick as Paul, though!'

Amy observed the interchange between her two children and, though she couldn't hear what was said, she gathered the gist of it. She was aware that her daughter was unhappy and understood the causes of it, but there was nothing she could do about it.

Mabel had taken Paul under her wing. When she was feeding chickens, collecting eggs or milking, Paul tagged along. She showed him how to groom Betsy, where the greenfinches were nesting in a hedge, and put her father's saddle over a box in the stable so Paul could pretend it was a horse. She didn't ignore Tara, but she kept her distance and Amy guessed why. Mabel was seeing herself mirrored in her granddaughter and it threw her.

Amy picked up the empty laundry basket and went back inside as the two boys and Tara went off with the bike.

'I hope she picks it up as quickly as Paul did,' Mabel

said. She was standing at the window and had presumably been watching as the children went by.

'She's finding it difficult to adjust.' Amy put the washing basket down and returned to the sink to wring out the clothes left rinsing. 'I suppose I'm trying to give her back the childhood she missed out on, and she's just too old now.'

'At thirteen she's still a child,' Mabel said quietly.

'And what would you know about that?' Amy spat out suddenly. 'I seem to remember when I was thirteen you made me wear black clothes, cut off my hair and broke all the mirrors so I wouldn't feel smug and think I was pretty. You forced me on to my knees on a stone floor to pray every bloody night and made me embroider altar cloths instead of making dolls' clothes.'

Mabel slumped down on to a chair at the table. 'Oh, Amy! Will we ever be able to overcome all this bitterness?'

As suddenly as Amy's anger had flared up it was gone, leaving just an ache in its place.

'I don't want Tara to be like us.' She took a step towards Mabel, yet couldn't quite bring herself to reach out for her. 'There's so much poison in both of us. For the children's sake we've got to try to break with the past.'

During the long evenings, Mabel had revealed their family history and it was clear that all the women in Bridge Farm had suffered tragedy. Emily, Mabel's sister had died in childbirth only two years after her wedding. Her mother Polly had lost two sons in infancy and her grandmother Hannah had drowned herself in the river at the back of the farm after losing two of hers in a diptheria epidemic. Amy had visited the graves in the churchyard, seen the old sepia photographs and from what her mother told her she had built up a family history of beautiful, sad women and callous and brutal men.

'The children are scarred already,' Amy said. 'But it's Tara I'm frightened for. She's on the threshold of womanhood, and she has never seen a normal, loving relationship between a man and a woman first-hand. How can she possibly distinguish between a good man, a strong one who'll protect, look after and love her, and a sweet-talking faker who'll end up hurting her? I tell you, Mother, she won't be able to. And once the pattern starts she'll accept it, the way I did, because history has a habit of repeating itself.'

Mabel got up and went over to the Aga, sliding the full kettle over on to the hotplate. Tiny pearls of spilled water ran across the hot surface, hissing before they disappeared.

'We'll find a way,' she said softly. 'We'll make those two children laugh, we'll show them love and kindness. We'll teach them to be two whole, perfect people. It won't happen to them.'

'How can you be certain, Mother?'

'I can't.' Mabel looked her daughter in the eye. 'But I'll do my damnedest to prevent it.'

Tara walked up the side lane, her shoulders weighed down with the heavy load of books in her satchel, her green blazer over her arm. Although she was hot and tired she wanted to dance with joy.

They had been at the farm for two months now, her thirteenth birthday had come and gone, but today was the first day that she'd actually felt she belonged.

'I timed that well.' Her grandmother looked round from the Aga as she stepped into the kitchen, a tray of scones in her hand. 'They're best eaten hot.'

Tara hung her blazer over the chair and sat down at the table. It was laid for tea, with slices of home-cooked ham, salad and a big plate of bread and butter.

Sometimes Tara thought she'd dreamed how awful the farm was when they arrived, because it was all so different now. Her mother was so good at making things look nice, like finding pretty china to put on the dresser and painting the kitchen all by herself. It never smelled nasty now, except when Gran cooked fish for the cats that lived in the barn. Mum had even persuaded Stan to dig up the weeds in the front garden, and planted petunias and marigolds.

'Where are Mum and Paul?'

'Amy's just seeing to something in the barn, Paul's gone up to the grocer's to get me some sugar. I can't believe how much we get through since you all came.'

There was no suggestion of complaint in this remark, in fact Gran looked very pleased about something.

'How was school today?' she enquired.

'Pretty good.' Tara beamed, unable to hold back her news a moment longer. 'You know the smocked baby's dress I was making in needlework?'

'Yes.' Gran sat down to listen. She was still wearing men's clothes, an old grey shirt and baggy twill trousers, but Amy had washed and set her white hair for her and it looked pretty.

'Well, Miss Ames put it out for display for the parents' meeting tomorrow night. She said it was the finest piece of needlework she's ever seen at the school.' There was no way she could explain adequately how it felt to be singled out for such praise.

'Quite right, too,' Gran said stoutly, taking in the suppressed glee in Tara's amber eyes. She was growing very pretty, her skin had a peachy glow, her plaited hair was like two thick hanks of shiny gold embroidery thread and the green and white checked school dress suited her admirably. 'You've inherited your mother's nimble fingers.'

Tara's face was split in two with a wide smile, her eyes dancing with happiness.

'I told her I wanted to be a dress designer and she said she couldn't think of a more suitable job for me, or anyone more likely to succeed.'

She couldn't possibly tell Gran how all the other girls had crowded round her in admiration, asking her if she'd give them a hand with their projects. How all at once the ice had been broken and she had become one of them. Beryl Jones had asked her over to tea and she was the most popular girl in her class, and a boy called Clive Spear said she had the loveliest hair he'd ever seen.

Coming home from school she'd walked with Beryl and Carol, and they said if the hot weather held they could all go swimming in the flash-hole in Dumpers Lane on Saturday. Beryl even offered to lend her a costume when she said she didn't have one.

'We've got lots to celebrate tonight.' Gran smiled with real warmth.

'Why! What else has happened?'

'Wait till your mother and Paul get back.' Mabel looked mysterious.

Paul came bounding in seconds later.

'Gran! Can I go out with Colin on the bike after tea?' he asked. He looked like a little ragamuffin, with his grey shirt hanging out of his school shorts, his tie somewhere round his ear, hands, knees and face filthy.

'How many times have you been told to change before you go out playing?' Mabel gave him an affectionate box on the ear, and pulled some straw out of his hair. 'Do it now, and wash while you're up there!'

'But Gran,' Paul's face screwed up into a plea, 'can I go out later?'

'We'll see.' Mabel pointed to the door. 'Change, and quick about it before your mother sees the state you're in.'

Tara sensed an undercurrent. Gran was really

happy, almost bursting with something. What on earth could it be?

Paul came clattering back down the stairs just as Amy came in. Tara noted the sly smiles passing between the two women and knew the pair of them had been up to something.

'What did you do?' Gran asked Paul. His face was smeary rather than clean. 'Just look at the flannel?'

'Come here.' Amy took him over to the sink, wet the corner of a towel and wiped his face. 'Don't you think a big boy like you could learn to wash his face properly?'

Paul wasn't listening, his eyes were on the tea table.

'Tara's got some good news,' Mabel said. 'But shall we just go and see the other first?'

Both Paul and Tara pricked up their ears.

'What?' Paul caught hold of his grandmother's arm. 'What other, Gran?'

'A surprise,' she said, ruffling his hair.

'Come on then,' Amy said. 'I think they're ready.'

As Gran led the way to the barn, Tara felt a surge of disappointment. It was just another new calf. She'd expected something more dramatic if it was more important than her good news.

'Flossie's had her baby?' Paul raced ahead, reaching up for the big swing bar to open the barn. The bar clonked down and the door swung open.

There on the clean straw were two gleaming new bicycles. Paul's eyes nearly disappeared into his hair line; Tara's mouth dropped open in shock.

'Oh, Gran,' she whispered in awe.

'Well, go on then!' Gran prodded the pair of them. 'Try them for size.'

Paul's bike was sky blue, an in-between size, neither a child's, nor a grown man's. But Tara's was the 'Pink Witch' she'd seen in magazines – shocking pink with white saddle and tyres, a basket on the front and even a place to put a lipstick. It was the dream bike for every girl of her age. It wasn't just something to ride around on, but a status symbol.

With a whoop of pure joy Paul ran in, moved his bike away from the bale of straw, swung his leg over the crossbar and rode out.

Tara approached hers with due reverence, stroked the gleaming handlebars and saddle, and rang the shiny bell.

'I can't believe it,' she said. 'All the girls at school want one. They'll be green with envy.'

'Well make sure you look after it.' Gran slipped back to her usual caustic manner. 'Otherwise I'll skin you alive.'

Tara looked back to her mother as she slipped hers off its stand and jumped on.

Amy stood back, watching. Her blonde hair shone in the afternoon sun. In her jeans and checked shirt she looked only a few years older than Tara, and her expression was every bit as joyful as those of her children.

'Go on then, a quick spin to test it, then we'll have tea,' Amy said, wiping a stray tear away with the back of her hand.

Her mother had pleaded poverty, she said she didn't even have the money to send fares, but that was just a smoke screen. In fact Mother had admitted at the time she suggested buying the bikes that she had several hundred tucked away in the bank.

There was no holding either child now as they rode round the yard, scattering the chickens, shrieking with laughter. Paul stood up on his pedals, holding the handlebars with only one hand to prove his expertise.

'I can't wait to show Colin,' he shouted. 'Thank you, thank you, thank you!'

*

Teatime was a party. Both children were bubbling with excitement, Amy was a little giggly and Gran presided over the teapot with a wide smile on her face.

'I don't ever remember so much noise here,' she said. 'James Brady will turn in his grave!'

To Tara much of the pleasure came from discovering her mum and Gran had hatched this surprise together over a week ago. She heard how Amy had cut out advertisements from magazines, then taken the bus into Bristol to track the bikes down.

'Your mother thought you should wait till Christmas.' Gran's expression was slightly superior, yet gleeful at the same time. 'But I said you needed them now, during the summer. That old bike isn't much good, and we can't have you fighting over it.'

'What was your good news?' Amy asked Tara, suddenly remembering there was something else.

'Compared to the bikes it was nothing.' Tara helped herself to another scone, spreading jam on it thickly. 'This has been a magic day.'

She would tell Mum everything at bedtime. She would hug her and tell her how happy she was they had moved here, and apologise for being a misery for so long. Tonight she didn't ever want to live anywhere else. London was smelly and dirty. Chew Magna was where she belonged.

Amy found out Tara's news from her mother once the children had rushed out after tea, leaving them to clear away.

'That's wonderful.' Amy beamed, guessing there was more to the story than just praise for a smocked dress. 'I've been so frightened she wouldn't ever accept life here.'

'She's so much like me.' Mabel shrugged her shoulders. 'A bit self-centred, stubborn and too proud to make the first move. I often felt alone, even when I was surrounded by people.'

'Well, it looks as if she's unbent a little,' Amy said as she caught a glimpse of Tara flying down the lane, her hair streaming behind her like a gold flag. 'I can't thank you enough for this, Mother!'

Mabel leaned over the draining board to watch the children through the window as they raced against each other back up the lane. Tara's gymslip had ridden up, exposing long slender legs. Paul looked as stocky as a pit pony, his face red with exertion.

'There's no need for thanks,' Mabel said gruffly. 'Just seeing their faces is enough.'

Chapter 8

May 1961

Amy was sitting on a bench in the yard shelling peas, enjoying the unexpectedly hot May sunshine, when Paul looked furtively round the edge of the dairy.

'What on earth have you been doing, Paul?'

She knew even without seeing him properly. She could hear the squelch of his shoes, smell the river water, and she remembered only too well what a magnet water was to children on a hot day. It was hard not to laugh as he crept out from his hiding place, head down. He looked like a half-drowned dog, dark hair plastered to a mud-streaked face, water dripping from the legs of his grey shorts.

'We were playing. I kind of slipped,' he said.

'You haven't been in the flash-hole?' she asked, raising an eyebrow. 'It's too deep, you can't swim properly and there's lots of weed and stuff to pull you under.'

'We weren't there, Mum.' His voice was plaintive. 'We were only down Dumpers making a dam.'

Dumpers Lane was a child's paradise. In winter it was often flooded, and it boasted a spooky old farm, an old stone bridge and thick woods. Any parent with a child missing had only to go down there to find them.

'So how did you get that wet?'

'I lost my footing.' His dark eyes implored her not to keep him in for the rest of the day, his sticking-out ears were almost transparent with the sun behind them.

'It seems to me you've got in too many scrapes since you made friends with Colin! Take your clothes off out here, then get washed and changed.'

Paul pulled off his clothes in record time, glancing round to check no-one was watching before removing his soggy pants and adding them to the pile on the ground.

Amy watched him with amusement. He had filled out so much in the last year he could be a different child. Satin-like olive-toned flesh so much like his father's now concealed his ribs and spine. His legs and arms were sturdy, even his bottom had what Gran laughingly called 'a bit of upholstery'. The malnourished mouse of a slum kid had been replaced by a country boy, and Amy had no doubt that Paul would eventually outstrip his father, not only in intelligence, but in height and strength.

'Don't be cross with me, Mum.' Paul came over to her, sliding one grubby hand across her shoulder. 'I'll wash my things.'

Tara still spoke with a faint Cockney accent, but Paul had adopted the Somerset burr as if born to it.

'I'm not a bit bothered about your clothes, they'll wash and dry,' Amy said evenly, catching hold of his naked little body and pulling him on to her lap. 'But I am concerned when you make a nuisance of yourself to our neighbours. Since you palled up with Colin you've been in trouble up at the Co-op for knocking over a display. You've been caught walking through crops, attempting to ride Mr Branston's goat and climbing on the church hall roof. To say nothing of plaguing the men at the mill by climbing on the sacks of grain.'

Paul's mouth drooped at the corners. 'I don't mean to be bad.'

'You aren't bad,' Amy reassured him. 'You're just a bit thoughtless, that's all. So when you go back down

154

Dumpers Lane, if you've dammed up that river so it floods someone's land, kindly un-dam it.'

'It's our land down there.' Paul's eyes sparkled as he realised she wasn't cross at all. 'D'you know, Mum, that's the best thing about living here – so much of it belongs to us. I can run through fields shouting that they're mine.' He paused for breath. 'Well, Gran's! But that's kind of the same, isn't it?'

'Yes, love.' Amy hugged him to her chest. Even through the winter, when the wind shook the windows and frost stayed on the bare branches all day, Paul had found new pleasures here. He didn't seem to feel the cold as he skipped out to collect eggs, or staggered over to the pigsty with a bucket of hot swill. 'It's ours. I hope one day your little boys will be paddling down the lane. Now off with you to wash and put some clothes on, and wear your wellingtons this time, that's what they're for!'

'That boy goes through trousers like a fox through hen houses.' Mabel picked up a pair of grey school shorts from the mending basket and examined the tear in the seat. 'Is this the new pair?'

Amy was sewing buttons on one of his shirts, wrenched off because he rarely stopped to unbutton them.

'I'm just glad he's behaving like a real boy at last,' she said. 'I didn't think he'd ever have the courage to go out and mix with other kids, let alone be naughty. I don't care if I mend a hundred pairs of shorts.'

Mabel snorted as if in disapproval, but Amy knew better. The relationship between Paul and his grandmother was based on mutual approval. Paul liked his gran being considered weird, he liked her old men's clothes, the fact she could shin up a ladder, drive a tractor and help deliver a calf or a litter of pigs. He sat enthralled while she drew him fantasy pictures of dragons and monsters, he helped her bake bread and he considered her the font of all wisdom.

In turn Mabel adored him. She loved his sensitivity, the way he turned his sad brown eyes on her like a dog. She saw how bright he was, his love of animals and his natural sympathy with all humanity. He looked very like Bill MacDonald, even she agreed to that, but maybe it was because Bill had never acknowledged Paul that she wanted him for her own.

Paul had something special about him. All those years of anticipating his father's moods had left him super-sensitive. He knew instinctively when someone was sad, ill, anxious or just in a bad mood, and he had the knack of deflecting it. He was such a serious little boy, and sometimes that alone made people laugh and feel better.

'Look at him now!' Mabel chuckled. 'To think a year ago he was even nervous of the chickens!'

They went over to the kitchen door to watch as Tara and Paul rode up the lane on Betsy.

Tara sat at her desk idly stroking her cheek with the end of one thick, golden plait. It was sixteen months since the day the family had left their father for good and the changes in Tara were dramatic.

She had grown two inches in height and her skinny gawkiness had gone. Small breasts pushed out the bodice of the checked school dress, the long slender legs wound round the chair were shapely and lightly tanned. Her plaits, dress and sturdy sandals signified she was still a child, but her face and body were those of a beautiful young woman.

Delicate fair eyebrows framed her wide amber eyes above a small straight nose. Her mouth, once too big for her face, was now perfection. Full, luscious lips with a well-defined bow shape gave more than a hint of her generous and loving nature.

She was supposed to be writing an essay on the birds

at Chew Valley lake, but instead she was dreaming about Harry.

Gran had been very prickly about George and Harry, in fact she still had reservations about them. Although they kept in touch by letter, so far Gran hadn't agreed to invite them down. But she was softening now, mainly because George had written telling them he had proposed to Queenie. Tara was delighted by this news. Although, unlike Gran, she had once hoped Uncle George would marry Amy, this suited her better.

They all liked Queenie, and they all knew she was the perfect partner for George, but just now Tara's pleasure was based on entirely selfish thoughts. Once he was married off, Uncle George's would make an ideal place to have holidays without her mother. Then she could be alone with Harry.

An interest in boys had come around the time her figure began to develop. Beryl had a boyfriend called Tom and she was always mooning over him and talking about kissing. Tara had looked around at the local boys and found herself comparing them all unfavourably with Harry. Even the sixth-formers seemed such country bumpkins next to his sophistication. They didn't have smart suits, they couldn't drive and she hadn't spotted anyone as handsome.

A year apart from him, with letters the only contact, had created a kind of golden aura around his memory, a collection of mental pictures she liked to dwell on.

The picture of him lifting her mother up from the floor that terrible day had stayed with Tara. His strong features had shown anger and disgust at the injuries her father had inflicted on Amy, yet such tenderness, too. Once she had taken him an early cup of tea and caught him asleep, dark hair falling over those bright blue eyes, prickly stubble on his chin. But best of all was the memory of the last hug out in the yard – the

157

strength of his arms around her, the smell of Old Spice wafting from his skin, his lips against her ear and the words he had said to make her strong. 'Don't think you can marry some spotty-faced farmboy, I'll be watching you.' In reality she knew he had been telling her not to give up on her dreams of being a designer, but now she preferred to interpret his words as an admission of dawning love.

Loving Harry was a secret she hadn't shared with anyone. It made her feel good inside, like knowing your school report was excellent or getting the most goals at netball.

She was happy to be living in the country now. She had friends at school, she knew most of the neighbours and shopkeepers. During the long winter nights her dressmaking skills had improved dramatically, with Mum teaching her the difficult bits of collars and sleeves. Gran had let her use the old treadle machine, and she quickly progressed from dolls' clothes to things for herself.

Gran encouraged big ideas. She didn't throw a wet blanket over ideas of art college, of painting in Paris, or opening her own boutique. She said anyone could do anything if they had a mind to stick at it. Well, she would make it to the top. One day she would be driving a Mercedes down Park Lane, there would be pictures of her and her designs in every fashion magazine and, best of all, Harry would be her man.

An outraged yell outside made her start. Pushing her chair back from the desk Tara stood up and went over to the window.

She saw Paul scrabbling over a pile of timber in the woodyard on the other side of the river. Colin was with him and, even at a distance of some five-hundred yards, Tara could sense their panic.

'Stop, you little toads!'

She laughed at the abusive order coming from an unseen man and wondered what Paul and Colin had done this time.

It was just after seven in the evening. The sun perched just above the square church tower and the shadows of the tall poplar trees were reaching out like fingers across the meadow. As Tara leaned out of her window to see better, she saw the owner of the loud voice come into view. He too was climbing up the wood pile, a big, dark-haired man wearing a singlet and waving a stick.

The two boys disappeared for a moment, then emerged seconds later to jump down into the river from a low wall, and wade across. They looked over their shoulders fearfully as they reached the bank of the meadow but, as the sound of the man's boots rang out from the stone bridge, they began to run to the farm.

Another shout of outrage made them halt for a second, but as they saw the man leap over the meadow fence they fled, arms and legs going like pistons.

'I'll get you, don't think you'll get away with it!' The man ran after them, brandishing the stick.

'What's happening?' Gran called out from the yard below. She stood with one hand on her hip, the other shielding her eyes from the sun. 'Who's that shouting?'

'There's a man chasing Paul and Colin,' Tara shouted down, realising her grandmother's line of vision was obscured by the dry-stone wall between her and the meadow. 'They must have upset him!'

Gran frowned in irritation. 'They'll get a hiding from me, too, if they've been up to no good.'

The man was gaining on the two boys with each long stride.

'Getting back to your gran won't save your skin!' he yelled. 'Stop now or it'll be the worse for you!'

The air was so still Tara could hear the boys' feet thudding on the uneven ground and the rasp of their breath. She was laughing, wishing she dared cheer her brother on, when out of nowhere came a premonition of disaster. Fear caught her stomach, freezing the smile on her lips, clutching at her heart and throat.

Paul was some three-hundred yards from her now, purple with exertion, cheeks puffed out, eyes bulging with effort as his thin legs sped over the rough ground. But it was mindless terror that drove him, the kind of wild-eyed panic she'd seen on heifers' faces as they were herded into the abattoir.

'Whatever is all the noise about?' Amy came out of the dairy drying her hands on her apron.

Tara froze at her window, unable to move a muscle. She saw Colin give up the race and sink panting to his knees in the long grass, but Paul raced on relentlessly towards the wall between him and the farmyard.

From her position Tara could see everything – her gran striding over to the wall, her back stiff with indignation; Amy standing still, blonde hair tucked under the white cap she always wore to work in the dairy, her hands flapping as if she sensed something was about to happen. Paul was steaming towards the wall at break-neck speed. As he lifted his arms in readiness to vault it, suddenly Tara screamed.

'Stop, Paul! The potato digger!'

The ancient rusting implement had two big spiked wheels on the back and it was hidden from his view, on her side of the wall. How many times had Gran warned them not to climb on it? How many times had their mother suggested it should be disposed of?

It seemed to Tara that everything went into slow motion. She saw the man bend over Colin and haul him up by the shoulder. She saw her gran put her hands on the wall and peer over. But in the same instant Paul's body hurtled up and over in a graceful, perfect arc, and she heard her mother scream.

*

She had no recollection of running from her room, down the stairs and out through the kitchen. It was only the screaming she remembered, but whether it was from Paul, her mother, grandmother or even herself she didn't know.

The only vivid picture was of Paul impaled on those spikes.

He could have been a guy ready for a bonfire, a doll-like figure tossed carelessly as washing over a thorn bush. But one hand was still twitching, stained bright red with the strawberries he'd been stealing. His dark eyes and mouth were wide open in shock.

It wasn't until her mother tried to lift him that Tara realised the full horror. One spike had entered his neck, the other penetrated his spine at waist level. As Amy tried to free him blood gushed out, splattering her clothes, and trickled down to the ground beneath.

'Don't try to move him.' Gran took command, pulling Amy back, shouting at Stan to phone for an ambulance.

The man from the field came over the wall and in that second Tara knew exactly why Paul had been so terrified. He bore a strong resemblance to Bill Mac-Donald, with the same purple-tinged face, dark hair and big, muscular frame.

'I would never have chased him if I'd known.' The man's face blanched as he saw Paul. 'I was mad because they trampled on my strawberries. God forgive me!'

The sequence of events following that was all mixed up. Was it then that her mother clawed at the man's face, or later? Did Gran really strike Amy to stop her screaming? Or was she silenced when the ambulance men pulled Paul from the spikes?

But Tara did remember Gran standing by Paul with her hand all bloody on his throat and saying he was dead. She recalled Amy showering his face with kisses and she wished she could touch him herself, only she seemed to be frozen to the spot.

It didn't seem real. Tara expected that any minute someone would shake her and point out Paul and Colin cruising down the road on their bikes.

But it was real. People were thronging into the yard. Some immediate neighbours, such as Mrs Hewitt and Mrs Parsons, sobbed openly. Others just stared at the potato digger as Tara did, watching the blood drip down its vicious spikes, forming a puddle on the cobbles beneath.

Colin vomited in a corner, tears making clean stripes on his grubby cheeks.

'We never meant no harm,' he bleated to one of the many policemen who arrived. 'We was only eating a few strawberries.'

'It's times like these when I wish I was anything but a doctor.'

Mabel Randall looked up at the rosy faced man with kind brown eyes and bit back her customary sarcasm.

'Will she be all right?' Her heart was beating too fast, she felt giddy and weak with the events of the evening and she didn't know how to comfort her daughter or Tara.

She was holding back her own anguish; trying hard not to think that she would never feel that little hand in hers again, or pat that firm little bottom. She had loved him so much. She had envisaged him taking over the farm one day. He was her future. Now he was gone.

'I'm certain it's just a temporary state brought on by shock.' Dr Masterton touched Mabel's shoulder reassuringly. 'It's just nature's way of protecting her.'

Among all the drama, noise and questions, no-one but Tara noticed that Amy had withdrawn into a silent world. Mabel had given the police all the information she could and Tara had been able to go up to her bedroom and point out what she'd seen. But even when everyone had gone and silence and darkness descended on the farmhouse again, Amy was still sitting dry-eyed on the old kitchen settle, staring into space, unaware of anything.

'It's not the silence, that's understandable.' Mabel lifted the boiling kettle from the Aga and filled the teapot. 'I feel it's something more dangerous, something that might hold her for ever unless we nip it in the bud quickly.'

The doctor glanced across at the open hall door. Tara had led her mother up the stairs after his examination and he could hear her murmuring something to Amy as she put her to bed.

He had witnessed the strong bond between Amy and her two children almost as soon as they arrived in the village. Their reluctance to speak of their past, a certain distrustful nervousness in all three, suggested to him they'd suffered prolonged hardship and violence.

'It may just be that she's holding on until she feels strong enough to let go,' he said carefully. 'Like you, I'd feel better if she was handling her shock and grief in a more demonstrative way, but all of us have different ways of coping with disaster.'

Gregory Masterton was in his late forties, the third generation of Mastertons to be doctor in the village. Except for his years at university, medical school and his national service he had always lived in Chew Magna. He knew everyone, every child, farm worker and landowner, and in his profession he often uncovered secrets he would rather not have been privy to.

He had been called to Bridge Farm perhaps only four or five times in twenty years, but each time he had left disturbed by its atmosphere.

163

Bridge Farm always had an air of tragic mystery. He felt in his heart that Paul's death was possibly just the start of more tragedy for the little family. What would happen to them now?

Mabel seemed so controlled, but only a short while ago the children in the village had dared one another to creep into the farmyard to spy on the woman who talked to herself. They had frightened each other by saying she cut children's throats and fed their bodies to her pigs. Would losing the grandson she'd come to love so dearly push her back that way?

What about Tara? She'd said something about Paul believing it was his father chasing him; that made the boy's death even more tragic. How could an adolescent girl come through such an experience and not be permanently scarred?

Then there was Amy. How could she stay here and keep her sanity? She must have brought her children here for some good reason, and now each time she looked across the yard or out of the window she'd see Paul on those spikes. What could anyone do or say to comfort her?

Amy Manning was one of the loveliest women he'd ever met. Now her big blue eyes were vacant, but only two days ago, when he'd passed the time of day with her in the High Street, they had sparkled at his clumsy attempts at flirtation.

She was the kind of woman any man would yearn for, not least a sometimes lonely bachelor like himself. He admired her quiet, gentle manner, her ability to listen and to draw people out. A mother, sister and friend to all, she was held in esteem by everyone in the village. Why should fate be so cruel to her?

'Tea seems inadequate, but it's all I've got.' Mabel shuffled over to the table and put down the teapot and two mugs.

'I'll just see if Amy needs anything first,' Gregory said.

Mabel merely nodded, sitting down heavily at the table.

It was happening again! What had she or her family done to deserve another kick in the stomach? If God had wanted a sacrifice why couldn't he have taken her?

Two years ago she had sat in this very kitchen contemplating killing herself. She could remember looking up at the beams and wondering if there was enough of a drop to hang herself, or whether to slash her wrists with her butcher's knife.

Mabel lifted her eyes up again to the beams. Not one spider's web hung there now, just polished copper pots and bunches of dried flowers. New red gingham curtains at hung the windows, and pots of geraniums stood on the sills.

All Amy's doing! Battered and abandoned as she was, she'd got down on her knees and polished the tiled floor, scrubbed everything clean and made it a real home. But instead of happiness and prosperity, life had slapped her in the face again, and taken her son.

The doctor paused on the landing, looking through the open door, not wishing to intrude.

Tara had her mother sitting on the edge of the double bed, wearing a pink cotton nightdress, and she was brushing her hair. Amy sat just as she had done earlier, eyes vacant, staring straight ahead, her lips slightly apart, her hands resting on her knees.

But it was Tara his eyes were drawn to. In the soft light from the bedside lamp her hair was pure gold. He had a vague memory of something someone had told him about Mabel when she was young – colouring that grabbed the eye and forced a man to turn his head and stare in wonder.

'Go to sleep now.' Tara gently pushed her mother down on to the pillow and tucked the covers around her. 'I'll stay with you.'

She lay down beside her mother now, stroking her forehead. Blonde and gold hair mingled on the pillow, as the doctor watched. He had no medicine as strong as a child's love. He was just an old quack with a bag full of pills and a few worn-out platitudes.

Chapter 9

Rain beat down like stair-rods as Paul's small oak coffin was lowered into the ground. Tara huddled closer to her mother, trying to hold the umbrella over Amy's head.

Tara had been crying incessantly since the first glimpse of the hearse. Just the thought of Paul lying in that flower-covered coffin made her stomach churn, and once again she blamed herself for his death. If only she'd run downstairs that evening and got up on the wall! She had always protected him before. Why hadn't she done something?

She wasn't listening to the vicar any longer. She didn't even feel the rain or see the crowd of mourners. Harry and George's presence didn't help either, all she could think of was that this was a place where Paul loved to play, even though Gran scolded him for being so irreverent.

'Time to go now.' Uncle George took her arm and led her away from the grave, towards the gate.

Her mother still stood at the graveside with Gran, their heads sunk on to their chests. Their two black-dressed figures looked shrunken against the flower-covered mound of earth and the huge yew tree. Behind them loomed St Andrew's church, with its square tower, and the strange broken-off monument with steps round it that people said was a market cross from medieval times. Gran was holding the umbrella over both of them, but it was shaking as she sobbed.

Amy had remained dry-eyed throughout the service, but the vacant look in her blue eyes was far more disturbing than tears. She wasn't aware of the vicar's comforting words, in fact she didn't seem to know why she was standing there in the rain.

Tara could smell the soil, not the flowers, and all she could hear were Gran's sobs and the sound of rain drumming on the coffin.

'Come on, into the car.' George's voice shook and when Tara looked at him she saw red-rimmed eyes and tears mingling with the rain on his face. 'I wish I could say summat to make it better, sweetheart, but I can't.'

The funeral car was waiting just outside the church gates by the old school house. Tara sat in it alone, shivering as Harry helped Amy and Mabel from the graveyard. With a protective and supporting arm round each of them, he looked almost indecently strong and healthy.

Amy was walking like a puppet, staring straight ahead through the black veil of her hat, unaware that every shop and cottage had blinds or curtains drawn across its windows as a mark of respect and sympathy.

Harry almost had to lift her into the car, then Gran followed. Tara shrank sideways against the door, frightened now by her mother's silence. Harry closed the door, said something to the driver which she couldn't hear through the glass partition, then ran ahead and jumped into his father's car. They drove off ahead and she guessed they were rushing to get to the farm before them to tell Mrs Hewish to make the tea and uncover the sandwiches.

'I wonder how many will come back?' Gran said. Tara knew this question didn't require an answer, it was the only thing she could think of to break the silence.

'The flowers were lovely,' Tara said, wondering if the gravedigger was already shovelling soil on to the coffin. She and Paul had spied on the funny little man once after a funeral; he had sat on a grave, poured himself tea from a flask and smoked a cigarette before he started.

'You must eat something.' George stood in front of Tara as she leaned against the kitchen wall. He held out a plate with a shrimp vol au vent, a sausage roll and a couple of sandwiches.

He didn't look right in a black suit. It made him seem thinner and older. The light shone down on his bald patch and his big bulbous nose made a strange shadow on his chin, almost like a beard.

'I can't,' she sighed. 'It just won't go down.'

Everyone was congregating in the kitchen, despite the food laid out in the dining room. Mr Atherton, the headmaster from Paul's school in the village, was there, his teacher Miss Candrew, along with Gregory Masterton, Mr Miles from the post office and old Mrs Smart from the sweet shop. There were others Tara didn't know, old people in the main, acquaintances of Gran's from her youth.

Colin and his parents had been at the service, all three of them crying openly. Tara had wanted to speak to Colin, to try to make him see it wasn't his fault. It made her feel even worse to see his little freckled face, usually wreathed in a grin, looking pale and drawn.

Mr Hodges was at the back of the church with his small blonde wife. As they walked out she saw his eyes were red-rimmed and he hung his head. He hadn't looked a bit like her father close to, but Tara still wanted to hate him because he was responsible.

Heavy rain battered the window, creating a murky

greyness that wasn't entirely dispersed even with the lights on. The heat from the Aga combined with the damp clothes made an atmosphere like a Turkish bath, with an overpowering smell of damp wool.

'For me,' George wheedled, holding out a teaspoon with a shrimp on it. 'I brought these specially for yer. They're kosher Whitechapel ones, none of yer Somerset muck.'

She wanted to laugh at his little joke and tell him how kind he was. George had come as soon as he heard about Paul's death and it was him who'd made all the funeral arrangements, leaving Gran free to look after Amy. Harry had come just this morning, bringing armfuls of food, including these shrimps.

'What's going to happen to Mum?' she asked. Amy was sitting on the settle, staring vacantly into space, the same way she'd been ever since the accident. Gran had removed her coat and hat and put dry shoes on her feet, but she acknowledged nothing.

'Give it time, luv.' George made her open her mouth and he popped in the shrimp. 'The Doc says it's 'er way of coping with it, and she will come round.'

'I could bear it if she cried,' Tara whispered. Everyone was talking so softly her voice seemed too loud. 'But this silence is scary.'

George had weighed up the situation when he arrived and he was far more worried than he let on. Amy was docile, picking at the food put in front of her, obediently doing as she was told, but she made no move to do anything of her own volition. Mabel escorted her to the toilet, ordered her to wash and dress, but they all sensed that if left alone, she would just stay where she was last put. Her speech was limited to yes and no. It was like looking after a brain-damaged child.

Doctor Masterton, a man George had come to respect for his care and concern, had said her behaviour was partly due to the tranquillisers he had given her. But even he could offer no reassurance that this wouldn't go on indefinitely.

'Your Gran understands what's going on in yer mum's mind.' George lowered his voice to a whisper. 'She went through something similar herself. The way she sees it is that your mum will snap back. If she doesn't then we'll get help.'

George had been surprised by Mabel. The patience and care she showed Amy came from the heart and when she broke down during the service he realised just how much she loved both her grandchildren.

'She will get better.' Harry joined them, and slipped his arm round Tara.

Tara was finding Harry disconcerting. She had expected his arrival this morning would ease the misery inside her. But instead it had added embarrassment to her burdens.

He looked like a spiv in his expensive suit and winklepickers, too noticeable among all the round, rosy country faces and shapeless suits of men who normally wore tweed. She was aware that his muscles were created in a gym rather than by manual labour, and his gold cufflinks and identity bracelet were too flashy. But worse still, his Cockney charm reminded her too much of her father.

She wriggled away from his arm and avoided looking into his eyes.

'We'll be all right once all this is over,' she said. 'Gran's been so good with Mum and Doctor Masterton comes two or three times a day.'

Harry didn't reply immediately, but lit a cigarette and puffed it thoughtfully.

'Don't try to shut us out,' he said 'We want to help.'

Tara felt a new batch of tears welling up inside her.

'I didn't mean to,' she whispered. 'It's just that . . .' She broke off, unable to explain.

'I'm a reminder of bad things?' he prompted, moving in front of her and tipping her face up to his.

When he drew her into his arms she could do nothing but lean against his damp jacket and cry. His head was bent to hers.

'I know I don't fit in down 'ere,' he whispered. 'I don't speak proper and me whistle is all wrong. But I've always bin like a big brother to you, I can't switch it off now.'

She heard George move away to speak to someone else; she could hear Gran slamming the kettle down again on to the Aga and Gregory Masterton talking to Paul's schoolteacher, and she wanted Harry to take her somewhere quiet to just hold her and convince her that she could be happy again.

'I hate Dad,' she murmured against his shoulder. 'I just wish I'd killed him that night. That's why Paul was so scared, he thought for a moment it was Dad chasing him. I don't ever want to go to London again.'

'Your Dad has gone away up North to work,' Harry whispered. 'I've got my ear to the ground and I know he won't be coming back. In a year or two you'll be leaving school and London's where it's all happening for anyone in fashion. Right now you want to hide away down here with your gran, and that's all right, but don't forget you're a Londoner, sweetheart. You'll want to come back some day.'

Harry had been staggered by the changes at the farm. His memories of the filth and neglect were almost wiped out when he saw the front garden bright with towering delphiniums and Canterbury bells. So the front porch still tottered to one side, the barn was still full of holes, but the farmhouse gleamed welcomingly inside and the yard was a pleasant place, even awash with rain.

'I won't ever leave Mum,' Tara sniffed. 'I'm all she's got now.'

Harry sighed. He guessed that Amy was responsible for all the changes here, that she worked like a slave to keep it up, and now Tara felt she had to take over her role. He wished he and George could take her away and let her grow up without responsibility.

'Promise me you'll come up to the Smoke for a holiday in the summer?' he said.

Amy had sent George some photographs of both children just a few weeks earlier and they'd both been stunned by how beautiful Tara had become. But today she looked like a waif again, wearing a black dress that was clearly borrowed, her hair scraped back in a bun. Queenie had warned him only last night that grieving was important and there were no short-cuts in the process. Yet even though he knew instinctively this was true, he had to make some attempt to try.

'You just wait till you're fifteen or sixteen.' He lifted her tear-stained face and wiped it with a handkerchief. 'I'll take you out dancing wiv all my mates and show off my beautiful girl. We'll go up West and look at all the clothes. I'll take you to Southend and we'll eat jellied eels and winkles till we're sick.'

A wan smile warmed her pale face.

'You'll be married by then,' she said.

'Who, me?' Harry laughed, with a flash of brilliant white teeth. 'I've got to wait for you to grow up first!'

'It's kind of you to offer us a bed.' George shot a sideways look at Mabel as he carefully wiped up plates and stacked them on the table. 'But I think we'd better 'ead on back to the Smoke.'

Everyone had left now, with the exception of old Mrs Hewitt, who was pushing the carpet sweeper round the sitting room. Amy, Harry and Tara were in there, too. Tara was showing Harry some old photographs; Amy sat silently in the armchair, staring blankly ahead.

It was still raining outside, and the lane up the side of the farm was a quagmire. Stan had enlisted the help of a young lad to help with the milking and it seemed to George that Mabel was putting her house in order.

'I misjudged you, George.' Mabel's drawn grey face broke into something resembling a smile. 'I don't know what I would have done without your help.'

'If there's anything I can do. A private doctor, a holiday, anything. You only have to pick up the phone and ask.'

'You've done more than enough already.' Mabel laid a hand on his arm. 'Thank Queenie for sending down the coat for Amy, and all that food.'

'We're getting married in August.' George's face broke into the first real smile of the day. 'I'm 'oping you'll all come! There's no fool like an old fool, they say, all these years we've bin friends but until Amy pointed out a few things I never saw her in that light.'

It was a great relief to Mabel that George was getting married, because she sensed the way he felt about Amy. She didn't mind a market-man as a friend, but she certainly didn't want her daughter marrying one.

'I'm sure you'll be very happy.' Mabel remembered Queenie. A mouthy baggage with a taste for flashy clothes, but even she had to agree the woman had a big heart and she was perfect for George. 'That only leaves Harry to marry off.'

Harry disturbed her. He had reminded her of Mac-Donald the first time she saw him and, even though she couldn't help but like him, he seemed too close to Tara for comfort.

'I wish I could get him married off and settled.' George sighed deeply and a cloud crossed his rosy face.

'Is he getting into mischief?' Like Amy, Mabel knew all the temptations in the East End. It had its own laws; thieving and fighting were just part of the rich tapestry.

174

'Hanging around with the wrong sort, more like.' George drew in a breath, then exhaled noisily.

'He's a good lad, he won't come to any harm,' Mabel reassured him. 'It's just his age.'

'Well, you know what it's like round our manor.' George bit his lip thoughtfully. 'I wish now I'd pushed 'im into an apprenticeship, buildin' or summat. Running the business wiv me don't exactly fill 'is time.'

'As I would have said in the old days, "The devil finds work for idle hands".' Mabel chuckled softly.

George smiled. It was good to see Mabel had dropped her obsession with religion, even better to hear her laugh at herself.

'Exactly.' He patted her shoulder. 'But lecturing 'im and playing the 'eavy father don't 'elp none, Mabel. I've offered up a few prayers meself in that quarter. But when I see 'Arry coming home wiv a flashy suit and diamond cufflinks and 'e tells me he won the dough down the dogs, what am I supposed to think?'

'He's a bit big to put over your knee and spank.' Mabel raised an eyebrow.

' 'E could lay me out wiv one punch.' George laughed. 'Solid muscle, 'e is, and 'e can run like Roger Bannister. But 'e's a truthful lad, Mabel, and 'e's got a good 'ead on 'is shoulders. So we just 'ave to 'ope it's just a phase 'e's going through.'

Amy sat motionless in the armchair.

Everything seemed remote, as if she were just an eyeball and an ear stuck in a block of concrete, observing, listening, but not feeling anything. Was it those pills Dr Masterton gave her? If she stopped taking them would the pain be so unbearable she'd want to scream?

They didn't stop Paul's face dancing in front of her, though. She could feel his hand creeping into hers and his lips kissing her cheek. She remembered how he'd squealed when she washed his neck and how it felt to wrap him in a towel and hug him dry.

She would never see him riding the horse her mother had promised, never be able to tease him when his voice broke or give him his first razor. It didn't matter how many pills they gave her, no matter how many kind words people said, she knew it was her fault he was dead, and nothing could change that.

Tara felt close to tears again as George and Harry prepared to leave.

George had been here for a week, filling the house with his presence, making her strong. Harry had made her feel marginally better since the funeral, but now he was going. Mabel was talking to George in low tones back in the sitting room. Her mother had been taken up to bed. Harry was perched on the edge of the kitchen table and he'd scooped up his jacket ready to put it back on.

'I'll come down in a few weeks to see what I can do.' Harry got off the table and put his arm round her shoulders. 'Your gran told Dad she intended to get another man in to do the dairy work, so she can look after the house and Amy. So don't go trying to do everything.'

The grief came over her in waves. 'I'll be all right.' She bit back the tears and gulped. 'I'm going back to school on Monday. Don't worry about us.'

'Come 'ere,' Harry said, taking her hands and pulling her closer. 'I gotta do one thing before I go.'

He put his hands behind her head and one by one pulled out all the hairpins that secured her bun.

'That's better.' He smiled at her as he ran his fingers through her long, silky hair. 'Paul loved your hair, 'e wouldn't want you to hide it. And 'e wouldn't like to see you looking sad forever.'

'Oh, Harry.' Tara flung herself at him, burying her face in his chest. 'Were you ever scared when you were my age?'

His body was like a warm rock, she could hear his heart beating and smell the Old Spice that evoked so many happy memories of staying with Uncle George.

'All the time.' He put one hand on her cheek and rubbed it gently. 'Can't you remember me down Mile End Road with Dad, the seat out of my trousers, skinny as a whippet? I was scared of bigger boys, scared 'cos I didn't think the girls would like me. I was even worried 'cos I couldn't dance.'

Tara almost laughed. She could only ever remember Harry being more handsome, more sophisticated and more daring than any other boy.

'Suppose Mum has to go off to the loony bin?' she whispered.

Harry held her arms firmly while he looked into her eyes.

'Your mum's just closed the shop for the time being,' he insisted. 'She ain't goin' barmy, just so terribly sad she can't cope for the moment. You wouldn't think nothing if she 'ad a bad cold or a bellyache, and that's all this is, only in her mind.'

Tara looked into those dark blue eyes and wanted to believe him.

'I hope you're right, Harry,' she said softly. 'Please be right!'

Chapter 10

August 1961

'Bloody 'ell!' George's rosy face drained of colour as he watched the six o'clock news.

'Harry!' He backed towards the door, his eyes glued to the television screen. 'Come 'ere. Quick!'

Harry raced down, three steps at a time, wearing only a pair of Y-fronts, his face covered in shaving foam.

It was Saturday evening. They had all just got back from the market and Queenie was out in the kitchen preparing a meal.

Harry was getting ready to go out for a few drinks down at the Blind Beggar with his mates, and maybe he'd go somewhere later and pull a bird.

'What is it?' Harry was irritated at being interrupted and he was afraid there was a lecture coming about getting into bad company. To his surprise his father was staring at the television, his face grey. He had taken off his waistcoat, his braces were loose around his hips and his stomach bulged over his loud checked trousers.

'Murder,' George said grimly.

'That's Sceptre Road!' Harry gasped as he recognised the street on the television.

Harry perched on the arm of the settee as the journalist at the scene of the crime spoke.

'At midday today the body of Father Glynn of St

John's Church, Bethnal Green, was found by a young couple who'd gone to the parsonage to discuss their forthcoming marriage.' He waved towards the old house behind him. 'When they got no reply, they walked in the unlocked front door and called out, thinking the priest might be in the garden. They discovered Father Glynn lying dead on his study floor, the victim of a brutal murder. The police haven't officially released the cause of death, but here in Bethnal Green it is widely believed that the old priest was knocked out, then strangled. Burglary seems to be the motive, though that has still to be confirmed.'

'No-one would turn over that place.' Harry looked at his father and frowned. Did George think this was the work of one of his mates? 'What would they expect to find in there?'

'Shush!' George silenced him as neighbours were interviewed. They were all in deep shock. One by one they spoke emotionally of the old man's kindness, the ever-open door, his total involvement in the community he'd adopted as his own, his sense of humour and understanding of his parishioners.

'There was no sense in killing him,' one woman sobbed. 'Father Glynn was a saint, he'd give his last crust to someone in need.'

'What sort of maggot would kill an old priest?' Harry sighed. Violence was an everyday occurrence around here, but it was always between men of equal age and size and almost always stopped short of death. He got up from his seat and made his way back towards the door.

'You don't understand.' George put out his hand to stop his son. 'That was the priest who told me where Mabel Randall was.'

'Yeah!' Harry stared at his father for a moment. Slowly, realisation dawned in his eyes. 'You don't think . . . ?'

George nodded. 'I'd like to be wrong, but I got this feeling in me gut the moment I 'eard the 'eadline. Maybe someone told MacDonald the old girl worked for the priest and 'e went round there to find out where she went.'

'Oh, shit.' Harry's face went as pale as the shaving soap. 'You don't think Father Glynn told him?'

'Don't be thick, 'Arry boy.' George winced. 'Why d' yer think Bill killed 'im? You can bet a week's wages that Father Glynn wouldn't put a woman and kids in danger. I expect 'e gave MacDonald a lecture an' all about laying into them, Bill got angry and hit 'im, then panicked and finished 'im off.'

'It might not 'ave bin him,' Harry said. 'Everyone says 'e's gone up North. Look, let me finish shaving and get dressed, then we can decide what to do.'

Harry, dressed ready to go out in a clean white shirt and grey trousers, sat at the kitchen table deep in thought while Queenie dished up pork chops and chips. George sipped a glass of beer, his pale blue eyes cloudy with anxiety. All three of them had discussed the murder, but they were still undecided about what ought to be done.

'I don't believe even Bill MacDonald would kill a priest,' Queenie said firmly.

She and George had been married just a fortnight before. They had a small reception in the room above the Blind Beggar and a brief four-day honeymoon in Ramsgate. All three were sad that Tara, Mabel and Amy hadn't been able to come, but there had been no real improvement in Amy and neither Mabel nor Tara felt they could leave her.

'MacDonald is capable of doing anything,' Harry said quietly. Only a few days before he'd heard a couple of old mates of Bill's talking about a job they'd done together a few years earlier. There had been an old lady in the house and she had caught them red-handed. Both the other men merely wanted to rip out the phone so she couldn't get help easily, but Bill had punched her in the jaw and tied her to a chair. Later they read in the press she'd been tied up for two days before she was discovered. He had heard other things, too, which turned his stomach, but he had no intention of putting anyone off their tea.

'The days when villains was like Robin 'ood is long gone.' George sighed.

Until tonight he hadn't had a care in the world. Marrying Queenie had felt like the best thing he'd ever done, and he couldn't be happier. But even a lovely new wife couldn't prevent him from having an acute attack of panic at something as close to home as this.

'We'd 'ave heard if MacDonald was around again,' Queenie argued. ' 'E ain't a man that can creep around unnoticed.'

'Unless 'e wants to,' George said darkly.

Silence fell again as each one remembered just how devious MacDonald could be. Both Queenie and George had known MacDonald all their lives. They had shared in the celebrations when he came back from the War and sadly watched his slide downhill. In their position in the market they were privy to tales that even Amy didn't know.

'On the other 'and 'e could have found their address after he killed the priest,' George said glumly. ' 'E could be on 'is way to Somerset now!'

It could be devastating for Amy. Aside from the trauma of having MacDonald turning up on the door-step in her present state, she could be in mortal danger. If he'd killed an old priest, he probably wouldn't think twice about hurting her or Tara.

'Harry should go down to Somerset now.' Queenie's double chin wobbled with fright. 'Just in case, George.'

'Me old darlin's right.' George looked hard at his

son. 'Take some tools and make out like you've come to mend the barn and stuff. We can't warn Mabel 'cos they ain't on the phone, but I don't think she'd turn you away. If MacDonald turns up, well, we'll know then he got it out of Father Glynn, won't we? You can get right round the nick and get 'im locked up. But if 'e don't show, then no 'arm's done. They ain't none the wiser.'

Harry nodded in agreement. Even as he finished shaving he had made up his mind he was going down there, and now his father had offered the perfect excuse.

'We should speak to the old Bill, though.' Harry frowned. 'I mean, Bill MacDonald ain't a man who'll slip naturally into the frame. Killing a priest for the church collection ain't 'is style. While they ponce around, MacDonald could be leaving the country.'

George didn't answer for a moment. Grassing was something totally alien to him. Even though he hated MacDonald for what he'd done to Amy and himself, his whole life had been ruled by a code of never squealing on anyone.

'Just think of little Tara.' Queenie patted his hand. 'It ain't wrong to tell tales when a kid's gonna get hurt.'

Harry flashed an appreciative smile at Queenie.

She was a big woman in every sense – voluptuous curves, larger-than-life personality, big-hearted, with a wonderful sense of humour. She could get up in a pub and belt out a song, drink anyone under the table and hump her boxes of fruit and veg down the market like one of the men. Yet she was entirely feminine. She could rock a baby in her arms as tenderly as its own mother, she was always the first to offer help to anyone in trouble and her affection, once given, was never withdrawn.

Now they were married Harry wondered why the pair of them hadn't realised what had been under their noses for the ten years since she was widowed. They were made for each other.

'I'll see to it,' George assured him. 'I know the right ear to whisper in without ever givin' away where Amy and Tara are. While you're down there, try and get Mabel to get the phone put in. I'll pay for it, but three women like that shouldn't be cut off with no way of getting 'elp.'

'Who on earth's that?' Mabel put down the coal scuttle as a car came up the side lane. It was after eleven and she was just topping up the Aga before going off to bed. Amy and Tara were already asleep and the only reason Mabel hadn't joined them was because she had been doing some accounts.

Peering out of the tiny diamond-shaped window in the back door she recognised the tall, slender youth as Harry by his silhouette against the car's interior light. Despite knowing who her visitor was, she still waited until he tapped on the back door before opening.

'What time of day is this to call?' she snapped.

He towered over her in the porch, his big shoulders filling the door frame, and even in the dim light she saw tension in his angular face.

'Dad sent me.' Harry blushed at her sharp tone. 'He thought you could use some help around the farm, mending the roof and stuff. We would have rung, but you aren't on the phone.'

Mabel pulled her dressing gown round her tightly and beckoned him in. She peered closely at him, and it occurred to her that he might be on the run from the police.

'I came as soon as we closed the stall.' Harry grinned. 'I would have been 'ere hours ago, but I took a wrong turning.'

She knew he was lying. A boy his age would have been out on the town on a Saturday night and, besides, smart lads like him didn't get lost.

'Just tell me the truth.' She closed and locked the back door, then shut the door through to the hall.

Harry wanted to lie as his father had told him to, but Mabel was too sharp. He stood there with his bag in his hand wishing he'd stopped at the pub until tomorrow morning.

'Well, boy, don't just stand there like some half-wit. Out with it! Are you in trouble?'

Harry hesitated. He had expected her to grumble about the late hour, but he hadn't considered she might think he was on the run.

'Dad didn't want me to tell you the real reason.' Harry lowered his voice to little more than a whisper. 'But it looks like I'll 'ave to now. Father Glynn was murdered in his parsonage. We think it could 'ave been MacDonald.'

The colour drained from her face, she swayed and Harry rushed forwards to catch her arm.

'I'm sorry.' He held her tightly and hoped she wasn't going to faint. 'We knew it would be a shock. But one of us 'ad to come, just in case 'e got your address.' He helped her to a chair, and gave her a glass of water. 'Dad will see they pick 'im up,' he assured her, sitting down beside her at the table. 'But we didn't want the police rampaging round 'ere unless it's absolutely necessary. Did we do wrong?'

She seemed to have lost some weight since Paul died and grief had made her facial lines deeper. For a moment she just sat there, digesting the shocking news.

'No, you did right.' She patted his hand in an uncharacteristically affectionate gesture. 'Father Glynn was a good man and a friend to me when I most needed it. Maybe it wasn't MacDonald who killed him, but we should be prepared just in case.'

Harry was always inclined to forget Mabel had lived in Whitechapel for years, but right now he was reminded. She hadn't lost that East End mentality when dealing with family matters, or her distrust of police and social workers.

'How are Amy and Tara?' he asked, as Mabel got up to make him tea and a sandwich.

Mabel looked round at Harry as she put the kettle on. She was surprised that a twenty-year-old lad could be so sensitive, and suddenly she was glad he was here. It seemed odd to see a man so smartly dressed in her kitchen. His grey suit, white shirt, polished shoes and striped tie were all symbols of the city. Yet his bony face, that resolute chin and the muscles rippling beneath the expensive clothes all suggested the kind of masculine strength this place was short of.

'Tara's terribly sad,' she replied. 'She tries too hard to please, trying to do the jobs Amy used to do and some of mine.'

'And Amy?'

Mabel sighed deeply. 'She's better in many ways. She answers when she's spoken to now. She washes, dresses and everything. But if Tara and I weren't here she'd just sit doing nothing all day.'

'Can't the doctor do anything?'

'She's still on tranquillisers.' Mabel frowned as if she didn't approve. 'I sometimes think they just keep the grief in. She still won't go out of that door.'

Harry looked at the back door and understood entirely. The spot where Paul died was so close.

'If I fixed the front door and porch Amy might be tempted to go out that way,' he suggested. 'It's worth a try, isn't it?'

Mabel spread mustard on some ham and added the top slice of bread, pressed it down and cut it in two.

'Anything's worth a try.' She pushed the sandwich towards him. 'But I don't know where to put you, Harry. Paul's room is just as he left it, but – ' She stopped, a tear rolling down her cheek.

It was almost three months since Paul's death. For George and Harry back in London, grief and horror had been overtaken by preparations for the wedding. Even on the drive down Harry's thoughts had been of MacDonald rather than Paul. Now Mabel's stricken face reminded him that time had stood still for these three women; that the wound was still raw.

'I'll just sleep in the dining room in my sleeping bag.' Harry touched her arm gently, understanding she couldn't bear to see him in there, not yet. 'It's better for me to be down here anyway.'

'Not a word to Tara or Amy about this.' Mabel sniffed and wiped a tear away with the back of her hand. 'I'll tell them I wrote and asked you to come and do a few odd jobs.'

'Harry!'

Tara's shriek of delight as she discovered him outside pulling down the old porch made his uncomfortable night worthwhile. It was just after seven, but Harry had risen when Mabel came down for the milking.

'Hello, princess,' Harry returned her warm hug. 'Dad thought I should combine a holiday with a spot of hard labour and get this place shipshape before winter.'

She wore a pair of faded cotton shorts and a pink scoop-necked blouse, and all at once Harry was struck by her new adult shape. Tara had become a woman while he wasn't looking; she had full breasts, a tiny waist and long shapely legs that went on forever. All at once he felt tongue-tied.

'Mum's not getting any better.' Tara's bright smile faded and her wide mouth slumped into dejection. 'I don't know what we're going to do.'

Tara couldn't adequately describe her real feelings. Sometimes it overwhelmed her so much she would go off somewhere alone and just cry and cry. Other times she wished everyone could forget as she did occasionally, and that made her feel guilty.

But worse still were the times she felt anger at her mother for sitting there so silently. She wanted to shake her and remind her she had a daughter, too.

'It's early days yet.' Harry guessed a little of what was going on in her mind. 'Now let me go and dump this rotten wood and sort out some bricks for the porch. We'll catch up later.'

Harry had dug foundations for the new porch and was just filling the trench with some cement when he became aware of Amy watching him.

She was standing at the bottom of the stairs, wearing a white blouse buttoned up all wrong and a full summer skirt with big pink roses printed on it.

'Hullo, Amy!' He made a point of not making too much of it, not even breaking off from working. She had lost weight, her skin looked so thin it was almost transparent and her eyelids had an odd purple tinge. 'Beautiful day, ain't it, shall I get a chair for you out here?'

The front garden looked beautiful, the grass a little long and daisy strewn, but the flowerbeds a mass of bright colours. Hollyhocks and foxgloves had replaced the earlier delphiniums and there were clumps of lupins, snapdragons and dog daisies.

She didn't reply, just stared at him, so Harry went by her into the sitting room and carried out a high-backed wicker armchair he'd noticed earlier.

'There we are.' He patted an extra couple of cushions into it, moving it back into the dappled shade of a cherry tree. A curved flowerbed bright with huge dahlias hid the chair from the road. 'We can chat while I work.'

In the old days she would've quizzed him about his work, his friends and would certainly have wanted to know every last detail about George and Queenie's wedding. Now he wasn't even sure she knew who he was.

'It's pretty, ain't it.' He turned round to face her and held out a hand. 'Come on, it's lovely, and no-one can see you if that's what you're scared of.'

She came forward hesitantly, looking around like a frightened deer.

'We'll have to stop gassin' if anyone comes along,' Harry joked as she gingerly sat down. 'Otherwise they might want to come in and join the party.'

Once she would have laughed, but now she just looked at him curiously, her head on one side.

'When Tara comes back I'll ask 'er to bring you some tea.' Harry moved back to his work, picking up the first brick and a trowel.

'Are you comfy?' he asked a few minutes later.

'I'm fine,' she replied in a low voice. 'Don't worry about me, it's nice watching you work.'

Something about her tone made Harry feel very odd. He had the distinct impression she thought she was with someone else.

As Amy dozed in the sunshine she *was* with someone else, and way back in time. The smell of flowers as she came down the stairs had brought a hidden memory sharply back. She let her head loll, closed her eyes and remembered.

She had a white rose pinned to her chest. It was an artificial silk one Mr Cohen had given her to finish off her blue dress and Flossie dabbed it with musk rose perfume that made it smell like the real thing.

The Empire, Leicester Square, on New Year's Eve 1945 was packed solid with revellers, and Amy Randall was overwhelmed by it all.

Everyone looked so sophisticated. So many of the men were in uniform – soldiers, sailors, airmen and

Royal Marines. Recently demobbed men in those all-too-obvious ill-fitting suits danced cheek to cheek with marcel-waved girls. A huge mirrored globe turned slowly on the ceiling, making snowflake patterns on bare arms and dark suits. Smells of scent, lavender hair oil, starched shirts and cigarettes mingled with the sounds of the big swing band, lifting her into a new world of intense excitement.

'Stop looking like a scared rabbit!' Flossie shook her arm. 'Let's have a drink and eye up the fellas.'

Amy was fifteen, a seamstress at Modern Modes in Aldgate, and two older workmates, Flossie and Irene, had insisted she came with them to see the New Year in.

They looked like film stars. Flossie, with her dyed-red hair curled and swept to one side like Ava Gardner, wore a tight green satin dress that showed off her voluptuous figure. Irene had a red crêpe dress with padded shoulders and flattering ruching across her curvaceous hips. Her black curls shone like tar under the spinning globe, and black pencilled eyebrows gave her a permanently surprised look.

Amy's mother would have had a fit if she could have seen her daughter in such company. Girls like Irene and Flossie who came from Cable Street were sluts or worse. But she believed Amy was babysitting for her employer in Stoke Newington, staying the night in his guest room, not sharing a bed with Flossie in a rooming house down by the docks.

'What do you want to drink, then, Amy?' Flossie leaned closer and shouted above the music. 'A drop of gin to liven you up?'

Amy had been staring at the band, watching the fifteen men in white tuxedos swaying with their instruments, but as Flossie spoke she saw him.

He was leaning on the bar, one foot up on the brass rail, talking to another soldier, and Amy's heart lurched dangerously. He could have been Clark Gable.

The same shiny black hair, dark brooding eyes, a small moustache over a wide smiling mouth and even the cleft chin.

'Steady on, girl.' Flossie's eyes travelled to where Amy was looking. 'Don't try to run before you can walk, he's a bit old for you!'

Amy was a small, slender girl in a childish blue dress with a sweetheart neck, blonde hair curled and loose on her shoulders, wearing her first-ever pair of nylons and a borrowed pair of shoes, in a place she wasn't even old enough to be. But as the man turned and smiled at her, she knew nothing would ever be the same again.

Her mother had told her a thousand times how dangerous men were. They told girls lies to get their way with them, then ditched them as soon as they'd got what they wanted. She'd pointed out girls with swollen bellies and frightened Amy half to death with terrible stories about what could happen to a girl who let herself get into that situation. But as he stood up straight, smiled and held out his hand, she forgot everything her mother had told her.

'I'm Bill MacDonald. Can I buy you a drink, have a dance, anything so you'll stay with me?'

Maybe if she'd had some experience of men she would've laughed at that line and doubted its sincerity. But instead his words went straight to her heart.

She didn't know how to dance, but somehow she managed it in his arms. His hand on her waist gave her the funniest feeling inside, and his deep voice gave her goose-bumps of pleasure.

He did most of the talking. He told her he'd just got back from the Far East and that he came from Grafton Buildings in Limehouse. Then she remembered why his face seemed so familiar. She'd read about him in the local paper, he was the sergeant who'd escaped with six of his men after being captured by the

Japanese. Without any weapons or provisions, his survival tactics had kept his men alive. For two months they'd trekked through dense jungle, bitten alive by mosquitoes, delirious with fever, wounds turning septic, but somehow Bill managed to lead them back to the coast where they were rescued by some Americans. He just laughed about that, made out it was like a Sunday-school picnic.

'Any man would have done the same.' He shrugged his wide shoulders and grinned. 'It's what I was trained for. Anyway, the newspaper exaggerated it.'

Flossie and Irene were with two of his friends, but Bill monopolised Amy. He asked her about her job, her home and sympathised because her father had died.

'One of my brothers copped it there, too. Ma's still cut up about it. Mind you, she thought I'd bought it, too. Got the letter to say I'd been captured, then the Red Cross couldn't trace me so everyone reckoned I'd died and been buried somewhere on the march. She got the shock of her life when she heard I was coming home!'

Bill had everything – looks, charm and yet a sensitivity which made her skin prickle.

She knew the part of Limehouse he came from only by reputation; knew it had slum dwellings that made Durward Street look almost desirable. When he spoke of wanting more than what he'd been brought up with, she guessed at the grimness and poverty of his childhood.

'I want a clean life now. Green fields, fresh air and space. I've seen enough crowded bars, fighting and drinking. I want a girl like you, Amy.'

He told her he'd once had a pet rabbit called Alice.

'You remind me of her.' He smiled, his perfect white teeth brilliant against skin still tanned from the Far East. 'She was so nervous when I first got her, she would buck and squeak to get away. But I kept stroking her, talking to her all soft and gentle, and eventually she'd come to me of her own accord, and lie in my arms like a cat.'

At midnight, the whole dance hall went crazy. A huge net of balloons was dropped from the ceiling, hooters went off, whistles blew and streamers flew through the air. Among all the popping balloons and people singing 'Auld Lang Syne', Bill kissed her for the first time.

He held her face in his hands and stooped to kiss her, his lips gentle, yet with an underlying strength that suggested he was biding his time.

'I knew as soon as I saw you,' he whispered. 'You're my girl, Amy. I just know it.'

Irene disappeared, and Bill's friend had to shoot off to pick up a lift to go home to Yorkshire, so Bill took her and Flossie home in a taxi. It was foggy as they got out in Cable Street. A lone lamp on the street corner sent out a murky yellow light, heightening the menace of the old railway arches and bombed houses like broken teeth.

'Don't you keep her out here long,' Flossie warned Bill, waving a reproving finger at him as she pointed out her room in the house. 'She's only a kid.'

Amy didn't feel like a kid when he kissed her again. He put his arms around her under her thin coat, and pulled her tightly against his hard body, his lips touching hers with such passion and sweetness that she never wanted the moment to end.

'This is no place to make love to a princess,' he said softly against her neck. 'You're so little and so beautiful, Amy. There's got to be a place for us somewhere.'

Amy stirred in her chair.

'Here's a cup of tea, Mum.' Tara was leaning over her. 'Were you asleep or just daydreaming?'

'I don't know,' Amy replied. She wasn't pleased to

be brought back to the present. She wanted to stay in Bill's arms, keep inside her the wonderful elation of being in love.

'Gran suggested I brought out your embroidery.' Tara opened the half-finished tablecloth to show her. 'You wanted to get it done in time for Christmas, but you never managed it.'

Amy obediently took the cloth on to her lap, but made no attempt to examine it. She had embroidered so many altar cloths, vestments, even church banners. Back in 1946, just days after she'd met Bill, that was what mother had her doing night after night until her fingers were sore.

Amy picked up her tea and sipped at it.

She was in the parlour at Durward Street. On her lap was a red altar cloth, and she was stitching gold crowns along the edge.

It was icy outside. When she came in she had to put her hands in warm water to thaw them out, and all there was for tea was Spam and bread and marg. There ought to have been enough money for good food now she was on higher wages, but Mother just gave the extra to the church.

The parlour was austere. She remembered it being bright with colour and cluttered with knick-knacks when her father was alive, but her mother had swept away all reminders of the frivolous past. No piano hid the damp patch now, all her mother's water-colours had been burned, with only dark patches of wallpaper to show where they'd been. The china shepherd and shepherdess on the mantelpiece that her mother once laughingly put together 'for a kiss' were long gone, replaced with a jam jar holding a few spills to light the fire. All the framed photographs of her parents had been burned. There had been one of her mother in a long fringed dress, a long cigarette holder in her hand;

another of her father in top-hat and tails, taken at a race meeting. Now there was only the one of Arthur Randall in uniform, taken just six months before he was killed. The frame was draped in black crêpe and her mother polished the glass every day.

The room badly needed redecorating. The wallpaper had once been a light beige with small roses, but now it was brown with vaguely pink blobs, and the coal fire had turned the ceiling dark brown. Everything else was scrupulously clean – the lace chair-backs were washed almost weekly, the hearth rug taken out and bashed with the bamboo beater daily. A dark green chenille cloth covered the round table in the window. On it stood an aspidistra in a glazed brown pot, and the Bible.

Mabel read her passages every night while she sewed, but tonight for some reason she hadn't picked it up and instead sat in her chair looking into the fire.

Amy was dreaming of Bill. Each time she closed her eyes and thought of his kisses a tremor of bliss ran through her.

'What on earth are you doing?'

Amy started as her mother's stern voice woke her from her reverie.

'Look at the mess you've made of that one.' Mabel reached forward and snatched the altar cloth from her hands. 'You'll have to unpick it, it's all crooked.'

Amy looked down. To her surprise it was a mess, with loops of embroidery silk sticking out all over the place.

'The light's so bad,' she said weakly, glancing up at the gas light above the parlour table. 'And I'm tired.'

She started work at Modern Modes at seven-thirty and tonight she hadn't arrived home till nearly seven. Of course she hadn't been working all that time, but she didn't dare tell her mother that Bill had met her outside work at five-thirty – just an hour to hold hands, kiss and talk, yet it seemed like five minutes. Tomorrow he was going back to camp as his leave was up and she didn't know how long it would be before she saw him again.

'If you're so tired you'd better get to bed,' Mabel snapped at her. 'It seems to me, though, that you're getting into bad company in that workshop. I've a good mind to come along and have a word with Mr Cohen.'

'I don't get into any company,' Amy said quickly. 'I'm the youngest, no-one talks to me much. I've told you that before.'

As soon as she was sixteen in April she'd own up about Bill, but until then she'd better keep her mother sweet.

Amy was never sure how she felt about her mother. Love and hate, fear and affection were all mixed together and at different times each one struggled for supremacy. She accepted having to hand over her entire wages each week, yet she resented never being allowed to have any fun. She still felt bitter about her terrifying experiences during the Blitz, although she understood her mother had been through some kind of breakdown.

The girls at work said she should pack her bags and leave. Neighbours said she should stand up for herself. But Amy's compliance was partly due to the belief that, now the War was over, Mother would put aside her religious fervour and regain her old personality.

She went off to bed then, glad to be alone so she could dream about Bill. She had fallen in love with him completely and he with her, and every moment away from him was torture. Just lying in bed thinking about him made her pulse race and a hot flush creep all over her body. He was twenty-five, and experienced with women, yet despite his background he was a gentleman. Not once had he tried on anything that frightened or embarrassed her. The truth was that if an opportunity arose where they could be alone, somewhere warm, then she knew that it would be she who would forget herself. Only tonight he had slid his hand inside her blouse while they were kissing. As his fingers squeezed her nipple she found herself pressing hard to him, understanding perfectly well what that hard lump in his trousers was, even though no-one had ever explained such things to her.

They had written to each other secretly for almost a year while Bill was in Germany. During that time Bill urged her continuously to tell her mother the truth and prepare her for when he was demobbed.

It was late November in 1946 when he finally came home and she remembered so well that reconciliation when he took her to see *Gone with the Wind*.

'I'm coming round tomorrow night, when you get back from church,' he insisted. 'I didn't come through fighting the Japs just to cower before your mother, Amy. I love you. I want to marry you. Where's the shame in that?'

But Bill didn't know what her mother was like. She saw all men as representatives of the devil, ready to draw girls into evil. She even seemed to have forgotten she ever loved her husband.

In church on Sunday evening Amy offered up frantic prayers for support when Bill arrived. They had only been indoors long enough for Amy to rake the fire into life again and put the kettle on when the knock came on the front door.

'Who on earth can that be?' her mother snapped, getting up from her armchair. Amy froze in the kitchen, praying silently. She heard the heavy wool curtain swish back, the bolts drawn and the door creak open.

'Good evening, Mrs Randall,' she heard Bill say. 'I'm

a friend of Amy's. Might I have a word with you?'

Amy took a peep round the door, her heart in her mouth and her legs turning to jelly. Bill was wearing his dark grey demob suit and a striped tie, his hair neatly slicked down.

'Amy?' Mabel turned towards her daughter with a look of consternation. 'Do you know this man?'

Amy patted her hair and took a deep breath.

'Yes, mother, this is Bill MacDonald, he called on Mr Cohen the other day.'

Bill's lips were set in a strained smile, and he held out a bunch of chrysanthemums.

'These are for you, Mrs Randall. I wanted your permission to ask your daughter out.'

If Amy hadn't been so frightened she might have laughed at Bill's demeanour. He was speaking correctly as if born to it, the polite, slightly servile smile more in keeping with a man in a hatter's than a tough docker's son from Limehouse just out of the Army. Mabel took the flowers and opened the door wider.

'You'd better come in.'

Amy quickly made the tea, adding another cup for Bill, but her hands shook so much the tray rattled as she carried it in.

Bill made the parlour seem tiny. He looked even bigger in a suit than in his uniform. The wide reveres made his shoulders huge, his white shirt accentuated his golden skin and his neat moustache added a note of distinction to his fine bone structure. He stood awkwardly, twisting the brim of his hat in his hands.

'Take Amy out?' Mabel sat down heavily by the fire. 'She's much too young for that.'

'She's sixteen.' Bill shrugged his shoulders and his easy smile showed perfect white teeth. 'My mother was married then.'

'Sit down,' Amy whispered to him, guessing her

197

mother would never suggest it. Bill sat on the edge of the couch.

'I've just been demobbed,' he said. 'I'm taking a job as a motor mechanic, starting tomorrow.'

'How old are you?' Mabel spun round in her seat, fixing her eyes on Bill.

'Twenty-five.' He smiled warmly, dark eyes fixed on her mother's face. 'I wouldn't keep her out late or give you anything to worry about.'

A chilling silence fell. Amy poured the tea and passed it round, guessing what her mother was thinking. Why hadn't Amy said something about this young man? Why the haste to call on her at home?

Bill's hands looked too big for the dainty cup. He held it awkwardly, but kept his eyes resolutely on her mother.

'Please, Mum,' Amy whispered.

Still no answer. Mabel's mouth was pursed and her back stiff with disapproval.

Bill was shocked. He had prepared himself for a frail old lady, imagined himself overcoming her resistance with charm and chatter. But Mrs Randall was an attractive woman who didn't look a day over forty, despite her black clothes and her hair scraped back off her face. Those strange amber eyes worried him, though, they were studying him minutely, and he felt she'd already decided he was lower than a cockroach. His eyes wandered to the black draped photograph of her husband in uniform.

'I'm so sorry about your husband. The War took a great many good men. My brother was killed at Dunkirk, too. I know how you must feel.'

For a moment Amy thought Bill had found the right opener, his remark was so kind and sincere it was bound to touch her mother's heart.

Mabel turned her head slowly towards him, studying his face intently.

'Get out, you snake in the grass,' she hissed suddenly. 'I don't need to be patronised. I know what you're after.'

Bill's face turned pale. 'I'm not after anything. I just want to take Amy out.'

'Don't use that tone with me,' Mabel screeched. 'My daughter will not be going out with anyone.'

'Mum, please.' Amy dropped on to the floor in front of her mother's chair and grasped her hands. 'I want to see Bill, but I want it with your blessing.'

'You hussy,' Mabel dragged her hand from under Amy's and slapped her hard across the face. 'How long has this been going on?'

'Don't hit her!' Bill was on his feet instantly, knocking his tea on to the floor in his haste. 'I only came back from Germany last week, we've done nothing to be ashamed of.'

Amy moved back from her mother in horror, holding a hand over her stinging face. Mabel's eyes blazed insanely, the corners of her mouth twitching as if she were possessed. Had Amy seen sadness or fear she might have felt sympathy, but instead all that sprang to her mind was how much misery this woman had put her through.

'I will go out with Bill,' she shouted. 'If I'm old enough to work, then I'm old enough to choose my friends. I'm not going to stay here alone with you and end up an old maid.'

Bill instinctively put his arm round Amy, drawing her away from Mabel as she rose from her chair in fury.

'A guttersnipe, that's what he is! To think the Lord spared him instead of my Arthur. Don't you know what this is, child? The devil come to tempt you! Get him out of this house now!'

'I was good enough to fight for my country, surely I'm good enough for your daughter.' Bill took a step towards the older woman, his voice cold. 'If you are refusing to let me court her, then I'll take her with me now.'

Mabel raised her hand as if to strike him.

'I'd kill her sooner than let her leave with you!'

'Go and get your things, Amy,' Bill said quietly. 'I'll take you to Ma, she'll welcome you.'

Amy hesitated. She knew if she backed down to her mother now she'd never win at anything, but in the same instant she was afraid.

Upstairs she threw everything she owned into a bag as fast as she could. Her mother's voice rose up the stairs, shrill and hate-laden. Grabbing the bag, she ran down the stairs, snatching her coat and hat from the peg in the hall.

'If you go now, you can never come back,' Mabel screamed like a harpy behind them as Bill hurried Amy down the dark street. 'You've made your bed, my girl, now lie in it.'

'Tell me, Mum?' Tara took her mother's hands in hers and squeezed them. 'Tell me what's making you cry?'

Amy looked like a child as she lay in the chair, sobbing. She was rubbing her eyes with her fists, angry rather than grief-stricken. Instinct told Tara that some memory from the distant past had caused this outbreak.

Harry had returned to his work behind her on the porch, laying bricks so fast it was obvious he felt awkward. She could hear Gran shouting some instructions to Stan out in the yard and willed her not to come round and interrupt.

'Tell me, Mum?' she whispered. 'Don't keep it in!'

'She was so mean to Bill,' Amy whispered. 'If it hadn't been for her forcing me to leave, things might have been different.'

'It's all so long ago.' Tara tried to jolly her along. 'Does it matter now?'

'No, nothing matters now,' Amy sobbed. 'I had happiness in the palm of my hand for such a short while, but it's gone now, and I'll never feel that way again.'

Chapter 11

Mabel and Tara were convinced that the morning's events were a major breakthrough. Although Amy had scuttled off into the house later and stayed in her room for several hours, at tea-time she had reappeared looking much more relaxed. After the evening meal she got up and cleared the table without any prompting, and she'd even asked questions about Betsy and a litter of pigs.

It seemed to Amy as if she was waking from a long, deep sleep. For weeks now she'd been aware of little more than heat and cold, but now pain hit her from every direction. It was like watching her life on Pathe News at the cinema. Every unpleasant incident, each mistake, misjudgment, wrong turning – they were all there, larger than life, faithfully recorded.

With hindsight she could see now that she alone was responsible for how things turned out. By allowing both her mother and Bill to manipulate her that night in '46, she had blindly stumbled into the world which Bill himself was so anxious to escape. She forced herself to relive every moment of that evening and the events which followed, knowing that until she did so she couldn't make sense of the present.

'I don't think I should trouble your parents,' she said weakly as she and Bill made their way down to Limehouse that Sunday night. The icy wind whipped through her thin coat and she had to hold on to her hat and trot to keep up with Bill. 'Couldn't I just get a room somewhere instead?'

She only had five shillings, but that was enough until she got paid on Friday.

'I'm not taking the risk of letting you stay in one of those places.' Bill glanced up at a sign saying 'Room to let' on a dismal house in Cable Street. He lifted her bag under one arm and put his free one round her shoulder. 'They're full of sailors, dockers and brass. A pretty little thing like you wouldn't last five minutes there. Our place is grim, but at least you won't come to no harm.'

She wanted to ask him to take her to Flossie's house but the grim set of his chin deterred her and instead she let him take her further and further into the area which she knew only by its grim reputation. Street lighting was almost non-existent and again and again she almost slipped on foul-smelling refuse and muck. Children were playing in the shells of bomb-damaged houses, despite the dark and cold. Skeletal dogs barked warnings, raucous laughter spilled from pubs, and the fog sirens from boats on the river added to the sense of danger.

Bill appeared not to notice any of this; he even waved cheerfully to a couple of blowsy-looking women huddled outside an eel and pie shop.

'Hitler had more respect for his bombs than to drop one here!' he joked as they approached his home.

It was like catching a glimpse of the end of the world. A wasteland lay before them – pits full of slimy water, uncleared rubble from bombed buildings and piles of stinking rubbish. Grafton Buildings lay just beyond this morass, one of four tenements left standing where once were twelve. A lone gaslight illuminated the central spiral staircase that led to a rabbit-warren of flats. Amy's heart was sinking even though Bill kept her hand in his.

'I know it's horrible,' he said. 'This is why I want to get out of London. But it's only for a couple of nights till I can find you something else.'

Amy barely breathed as he led her up the dark staircase. She could smell the shared lavatory on each landing as they approached, and that was enough. It was so noisy, too! Sunday night, but there were babies screaming, women shouting, a drunk yelling abuse and a group of small boys firing their catapults at milk-bottles down on the waste ground.

The front door was almost off its hinges, as if it had been kicked in, and it led straight into a living room which doubled as a kitchen. There was no rug on the floor, dirty brown paint peeled off walls and ceiling and the only furniture was a rickety table, two stools and two armchairs greasy with age. The cooker was an ancient, rusting range with socks and underpants hanging from string above it to dry. Amy took in the sink full of blackened pots, the table strewn with the remains of a meal and the cracked lino and almost ran straight out.

'I'm sorry, luv.' Bill took her in his arms and kissed her. 'I know it's not what you're used to.'

Amy knew that her own home was far superior to most in East London and she hadn't expected the same standard here. But this place was like a hovel.

'Where are your parents?' Amy looked around fearfully.

'Down the boozer.' He shrugged his shoulders. 'They'll be back soon. You can sleep in my bed, I'll kip down in here.'

Bill's bedroom was even tinier than her own at home, yet once four boys had lived in it. No curtain hung at the window, and the sagging, lumpy bed made her itch to look at it.

Bill did his best, he prodded the stove back to life, put a kettle on to boil and washed up the pile of pots and plates. Amy sat on the edge of one of the chairs and listened to his explanation.

'Mum had eight kids in ten years.' He smiled ruefully. 'Two died at birth, three more before they was five. I came along ten years after the last one, the same year Dad lost his arm in an accident down at the docks, so we was on welfare from then on. They ain't never seen the country or the sea, all they know is round here. I prayed this place would be bombed so they'd get a decent home, but they weren't even lucky enough for that.'

'But your brothers. Where are they?'

'Mick, the eldest, was the one killed at Dunkirk.' Bill sighed. 'Our Frank did a runner years ago when the bluebottles were after him. He ain't never showed 'is face again. Ernest, the next one up to me, joined the Navy as a lad and he lives in Portsmouth. He writes at Christmas, that's all, and I'll get away too as soon as I can.'

The arrival of his parents was heralded by dogs barking furiously and the sound of arguing.

'Don't mind Ma, she's all right really,' Bill said quickly. 'Just a bit sharp-tongued.'

Gertie MacDonald was fat, old and slatternly, with wispy white hair and pale brown eyes that swept over Amy in astonishment.

'Who the 'ell's this?' she asked, wheezing as she sank into the other chair and spread her fat thighs wide enough to show long pink bloomers.

Norman MacDonald lurched in unsteadily; a tall, thin man with a hangdog expression, his empty sleeve flapping.

Bill explained briefly what had happened and Amy turned pink as the old couple studied her. It seemed impossible to her that such a pair could have a fine-

205

looking son like Bill. Gertie was short, with a deeply lined face that held traces of grime, made worse by having only two or three blackened teeth left. She wore a crossover pinny ingrained with grease over a shapeless mauve print dress, and stockings that only reached her knees, held up with elastic garters, above which purple, veiny flesh bulged.

Norman needed a shave. His collarless shirt was black with dirt, his brown trousers several sizes too large. He looked as if he'd lost weight dramatically, leaving folds of skin just hanging.

'Clear off, you two.' Gertie pointed to the door and nodded her head. 'I want a word with 'er.'

Norman obediently staggered off, his eyes glazed with drink. Bill followed him, looking round once at Amy as if to reassure her.

'Well, out wiv it,' Gertie said immediately they had left. 'Are you up the spout?'

'Of course not!' Amy said indignantly.

'You mean you ain't bin 'aving it off with our Bill?'

Amy was shocked by the crude question, but she shook her head, tears filling her eyes.

'Don't cry,' Gertie's tone softened. 'Our Bill's a good-looking fella, I could 'ardly blame you if you 'ad. Sounds like yer ma's a bit cuckoo!'

'She's never been right since Dad was killed.' Amy explained about the religion and her mother's coldness. 'Bill only came round to make it right courting me.'

For a moment the only sounds were Gertie sucking her gums and a murmur of conversation from Bill and his father in the next room.

'I tell you now, I want somefin' better for my lad than what me and Norm got,' she said at length. 'You're a pretty little thing and you speak nice. If Bill can get on his feet and get a bit of cash behind him you'll do nicely for 'im. But use yer 'ead, girl, not the bit you sit on. I don't want no hanky-panky 'ere, and no babbies.'

Amy had a feeling this speech was meant as approval. Still stunned by her mother's reaction to Bill, she felt a wave of affection for the woman.

'I'll find somewhere else soon,' she said quickly. 'I've got a good job, Mrs MacDonald.'

'You'll need it, luv,' Gertie snorted. 'Just you save your pennies, keep yer drawers on and you and our Bill will do fine.'

But they didn't do fine. Weeks slid into months and still Amy was at Grafton Buildings, hating it more each day.

The winter of 1947 was the worst on record. Snow came at Christmas and it lasted until the end of March. An icy wind whistled through ill-fitting windows, buses were stopped and pipes froze up.

The lavatory was so disgusting Amy would leave home an hour early to walk to Aldgate to use the one in the workroom. They had to get water from a standpipe down in the street and lug it up the steep flights in buckets.

Bad weather meant Gertie and Norman couldn't even get out to the Two Brewers and they spent the evenings huddled in front of the stove, bickering. There was no opportunity to be alone with Bill unless they braved the cold outside. Just the brush of his body against hers, or the touch of his hand, was enough to inflame their senses, so they avoided close contact.

Bill came home from work frozen stiff and exhausted. His suit and best shirt hung on a nail in the bedroom as a reminder of better days. He wore old grease-smeared trousers, matted sweaters that stank of engine oil, and by the time he got home he had a dark shadow of bristles on his chin.

'We'll have to wait till spring,' he said wearily each time she asked if they could find a room somewhere. 'I ain't got the energy to do a place up now.'

There were many times when she wanted to go home. She dreamed of her clean, tidy bedroom, getting into the tin bath in front of the fire and a table laid properly with a white cloth. But to go home now would be to lose face. Even if her mother eventually accepted Bill, she would always believe he had failed to provide for her daughter.

Rats grew bolder. They lurked on the stairs, waiting for an opportunity to run into the flat to forage. Once she felt one run over her bed at night and she screamed so loudly the neighbours thought someone had hit her.

When the thaw came things were worse in many ways for at least the snow had hidden the ugliness. Rubbish, putrid and stinking, was revealed, heaving with maggots and rats. Bomb holes were full of black slime and the frozen earth turned into thick, glutinous mud. The warmer weather brought back noise, too. With windows open again and children playing outside, Amy's ears were bombarded with shouting and shrieking from first light until long after dark.

Durward Street was rarely quiet, especially on a Saturday night, but here it never let up for a minute. Babies screamed, couples fighting, women yelling down through open windows and kids running up and down the stairs. No colour or beauty ever showed in these dismal streets; even the weeds that sprouted up over the bomb sites had a grey, distorted look about them, just like the residents.

Amy learned to go to the public baths once a week, pushing an old pram with the bag wash. She black-leaded the stove, scraped at saucepans till they looked fit to use and cleaned the flat as best she could. Now she understood why so many women gave up. It was an effort to keep any standards of cleanliness when there was nowhere to put anything, no space or privacy.

And Ma was making a mint out of the pair of them. Bill worked twice as hard to try to save, but the more he worked, the more Ma wanted. For six months he was unaware that Amy was paying her, too. He was happily convinced Amy was stashing money away for a home of their own when in fact it was going into the till at the Two Brewers or down the dog track.

Amy heard from neighbours that Bill had been part of the Limehouse gang before he joined up. Although he claimed he had put that all behind him, men often called to see him and he would have muffled conversations out on the landing. Sometimes he would disappear with these men, never explaining later what it was about, but on several occasions he returned with skinned knuckles and dried blood on his clothes.

Everything was frustrating. The slow rate their savings built up, the long hours they both had to work, the lack of privacy, even the secrecy which Bill maintained about his friends, but most of all suppressing desire.

All around them was evidence of what happened when passion got out of control – girls with swollen bellies, screaming babies, and so many children. They weren't going to be trapped in Limehouse. They could wait.

On June 2nd 1947 Amy heard Bill calling to her from below. Opening the window she saw him standing by a gleaming black Austin Seven, its chrome glinting in the sunshine. It was just seven in the morning and, though he'd hinted the night before he was taking her out for her birthday, she hadn't expected anything more than a day in Victoria Park.

That morning she didn't notice the weeds sprouting up through broken concrete, the bomb holes, the rubbish or even the evil smells. All she saw was Bill.

He was wearing grey slacks and a fine white cotton shirt she'd made him during the winter. He had shaved off his moustache and he looked so boyish as he grinned up at her.

She put on her new pink sundress and sandals and ran down the stairs to join him.

'Happy birthday.' He ran to meet her as she reached the bottom stair and swung her round in his arms as if she were a child. 'The car's only borrowed, but we're gonna have a day in the country.'

He smelled of lavender hair oil and soap, and he kissed her there in the yard with no concern for the nosy neighbours peering out of their windows. His brown eyes sparkled the way she remembered from their first meeting and his lips were as warm and soft as the sunshine.

Amy hadn't been out of London since she was evacuated at the start of the War and the air was so clean and fresh she wanted to sing with delight. Green fields, woods and hills, then every now and then a little village basking in the warm sun.

'Are we going to the sea?' she asked, seeing a sign-post to Folkestone.

'Maybe. After you've seen my special place,' he said mysteriously.

'Is this it?' Amy stared in surprise at the little garage Bill pulled up by.

'No, that comes later.' He took her hand and squeezed it. 'But this is the kind of place I want to own.'

The garage was nothing more than a shed with a petrol pump, next to a row of cottages, a pub and a post office running along the main road into Folkestone, fifteen miles away. The garage was a messy place, straddling one corner of a crossroads, the ground covered in oil and bits of engines left to rust. But at the side of it was a small cottage and a young woman was pegging out a line of nappies in the garden.

Bill's face was a picture as he stared longingly at the place, lost in a silent dream of a sparkling forecourt, gleaming cars parked ready to be collected by their owners and his name above the garage door.

'It's in a good spot.' His smile was infectious. 'People on their way down to Folkestone, and the local folk wanting repairs done. I'd clean it up, paint the workshop, maybe even make a little shop. And look at that house, Amy! Wouldn't you like to live there?'

Amy's heart lurched at his question. Would she like to live there? She would almost kill to! No rats or smells, no fighting and screaming. She could make that place into a little palace.

'Oh, Bill.' She sighed, leaning her head against his shoulder. 'It would be heaven.'

'I want you so badly, Amy,' he whispered, holding her face in his hands with such tenderness she could scarcely bear it. 'This is how I want it to be forever, just you and me.'

They left the car there and hand in hand they walked up a country lane, as Bill told her of his vision of their future.

'Everyone will have a car soon,' he said, eyes shining with confidence. 'We get a little place like that to start, then another. We live right by the garage, so it's no trouble to keep it open all hours. You could build up the shop, look after the house and maybe even do some dressmaking. I'll grow vegetables in the garden.'

It was hard not to touch him in London, but here, with no-one to cast disapproving glances, it was impossible. So many times they stopped to kiss, so wrapped up in one another they barely noticed the odd passing tractor or a child on a bicycle.

Amy had visions of washing drying from the sun, a baby kicking its fat brown legs in a pram beneath an apple tree, and a kitchen with hot water and a gas stove.

Bill had mentioned a spot with a magnificent view on their journey down, and it was here they ate their lunch of pork pie, apples and two lumps of bread pudding, bought in the village shop.

The softly rolling fields ended sharply at an escarpment where they sat with pine trees behind them. Below them was marsh, stretching for perhaps fifteen miles to the distant sea. A few cottages and stunted trees were scattered here and there, and the whole area was criss-crossed by streams and small rivers. Amy preferred more picturesque scenes; old churches, half-timbered houses, rivers and ponds. Yet she understood why Bill liked it here so much. It was wild and natural, land snatched back from the sea as it had retreated over centuries, the home of birds and flowers.

'I get scared in London,' Bill admitted suddenly. 'Afraid I'll get drawn into something. Know what I mean?'

Amy knew all right. In Grafton Buildings few people were blameless. Stealing wasn't a crime in their book, just a way of life. She guessed his old childhood friends were trying to draw him back into the fold and that every day they lingered in Limehouse, so the pressure to conform grew greater.

She sensed he felt she was the bridge between his world and the one he'd glimpsed from afar. She loved this sensitive, gentle Bill far more than the strutting, aggressive man his mother was so attached to.

'Can't we find a place today?' she urged him. 'Chuck everything and move here?'

'What would we do for money?' He squeezed her tightly. 'Finding a job down here ain't going to be easy.'

'Couldn't you work on a farm?'

'I don't know nothing about that.' He grinned. 'Only motors and driving. What we need is a little nest-egg first.'

Later on, he led her through a broken fence, into a private estate.

212

'Don't worry.' He laughed at her anxious face. 'No-one lives here and we aren't doing any harm.'

The house was a palace to Amy, a great, grand place, the kind she'd only ever seen in films. She half expected a carriage to come rolling up the gravel drive, and a liveried footman to jump down and ring the bell on the huge front door.

'I found it when I was based at Shorncliffe, near Folkestone,' Bill explained. 'I don't think anyone's lived here for years, they just use it for meetings and stuff. Someone told me an oil company owns it.'

It was beautiful yet mysterious. A swimming pool lay empty, though old urns were filled with flowers. Hedges were shaped meticulously around a manicured rose garden, but the woods behind the house, shielding it from the road, seemed almost to pervade the lower rooms. Amy felt a stab of anger that someone owned this lovely place yet had abandoned it, while they couldn't even get a couple of rooms to live in.

'It doesn't seem right,' she said indignantly. 'You fought in the War, but I bet whoever owns this did nothing.'

'He was probably an officer tucked safely behind a desk.' Bill shrugged his shoulders. 'But no-one ever said life was fair, darlin'!'

There was a tall horse-shoe shaped hedge round the lawn. Twelve statues of naked ladies in different positions, bigger than Amy, stood around it, half hidden by foliage. Amy studied them wistfully.

'Fancy having enough money to spend just on things to look at in a garden,' she said.

Bill put his arms round her and held her tightly.

'I can't promise a place as grand as this,' he said. 'But our kids won't ever see a rat or a bomb-site, don't you worry.'

As he led her into a lawned area concealed by privet hedges, Amy knew that this was the testing time. The sun was hot, the grass strewn with buttercups. There wasn't a living soul for miles, just the cries of curlews from the marsh below.

'I love you, Amy.' His voice shook with emotion as he drew her down beside him on the grass. 'I want you so much I can hardly bear it.'

His body fitted against hers, hot and hard, making her arch against him. Her nipples seemed to be prickling through the thin cotton dress, her belly thrusting itself into his instinctively. His lips were on hers, tongue teasing and probing, making her shake with desire.

All those nights she'd lain awake at Grafton Buildings, thinking of his hands exploring her body, were nothing to the reality. Just one finger sliding down her neck produced a raging fire in her belly, every nerve-ending twitching as her tongue found its way into his mouth. He held her so tightly, rolling with her, consuming her. A hard lump in his trousers pressed against her groin and he groaned in ecstasy. He had touched her breasts before, but never like this. Now he caught hold of one tightly, squeezing the nipple and bending his head to bite it, making blood rush to her head and an involuntary moan of pleasure rush from her lips.

Buttons came undone without her even noticing and suddenly her naked chest was burning to meet his. Feverishly she pulled out his shirt, gasping at the touch of his flesh against her fingers.

'Oh, Amy,' he whispered. 'I want you!'

He moved down until his face rested between her small naked breasts, holding them against his face, moving from one to the other, squeezing, licking and sucking until she felt she would explode inside. His back under her fingers was smooth and silky and as she caressed him she felt tremors from within him matching her own. A hand slid under her dress but she was powerless to stop him, caught in a need so strong it drove all thought but him from her mind.

Feelings she never knew existed erupted as his fingers found their way inside her and she cried out in bliss.

'Tell me where it's best,' he whispered, as his mouth closed over hers.

How could she single out one particular sensation when her whole body was singing with strange thrills? The deep probing, the soft, delicate strokes to her vagina lips, all so delicious, made her pant and throw her legs wider apart, undulating under him.

Amy could hardly believe she was fumbling to undo the buttons on his trousers, it was unthinkable. Yet her fingers wanted to hold him, to make him feel the way she did. His penis was far longer and thicker than she'd imagined, but her hand closed round it, and she moved her belly closer. She opened her eyes for a moment to watch him as they lay on their sides, touching each other intimately. His eyes were shut, dark lashes like brushes on his tanned cheeks, his mouth curved into a tender smile.

He made no attempt to get inside her and, although she had always been nervous of just that, now she wanted it. His fingers weren't enough, she wanted all of him.

'No, darlin',' he whispered, moving away slightly as she guided him towards her. 'We mustn't.'

His reluctance surprised and yet stimulated her still further. She pressed his fingers into her, feeling the hot stickiness of herself and the burning need for more.

'Please,' she whispered. 'Please, Bill? I love you!'

Despite her ignorance of sex, she sensed when he moved against her he was holding back, not intending to go right in. But as his penis touched her hot flesh, she caught him tightly, thrusting herself upwards, giving him no time to withdraw.

It hurt momentarily, but the sensation of holding him completely overrode the pain. His face was buried in her neck, his breath hot on her skin. He called out wildly, then suddenly he was still, lying heavily on her, panting by her ear.

'Oh, baby, I didn't mean that to happen,' he whispered breathlessly. 'I meant to stop.'

Amy was still writhing beneath him, lips searching for his, wanting more. She was wet, sticky and a sad feeling washed over her, as if she'd been cheated, but she didn't know why.

'Was it OK?'

She opened her eyes and found he was leaning up on his elbows, still straddling her, a look of profound anxiety in his eyes.

'Yes,' she whispered, knowing that wasn't all he hoped to hear, but too ignorant to understand the real question.

He sat up and buttoned his trousers, then turned to her and pulled her dress down over her knees. He said nothing, just sat there, turned aside from her, rolling up the sleeves of his shirt.

In profile his face was exquisite perfection. She put her hand out tentatively to his strong chin, letting her index finger touch the small cleft.

'Bill!' she whispered. 'What's wrong?'

'Nothing,' he said, getting to his feet and holding out his hand to her. 'Come on.'

Her knickers lay on the grass. Somehow the act of putting them on in front of him seemed more vulgar than anything. She hastily picked them up and slipped them in her pocket, buttoning up the bodice of her dress.

Had she done something wrong? Why wasn't he speaking as he took her hand and led her down through the grounds and out through another bit of broken fence?

'Are you cross with me?' she asked fearfully as he pulled her along behind him on an overgrown path which appeared to be leading towards a river.

'Not you.' He stopped and pulled her to him, kissing her eyes gently. 'I'm angry with myself for not being prepared, for expecting you to fight me off, but not *with* you.'

He had never looked more handsome than he did at that moment. His eyes were soft, red lips still swollen from kissing, and his black hair gleamed in the sunlight. Yet Amy felt awkward. She was wet and sticky, she wanted to wash herself. She dropped her eyes to the tow path, trying hard to find the words to explain.

'Let's have a paddle,' he said unexpectedly as they reached the canal bank. 'Look, it's shallow here, almost like a bit of beach.'

There was shingle just under the water's edge for three or four feet, and an obliging overhanging branch acted as a support.

Bill had his socks and shoes off and his trousers rolled up within seconds, and he moved in to try the water.

'Cold.' He grimaced, holding out his hand for Amy. 'But it's nice.'

Amy entered cautiously, clutching on to him for support.

'You wouldn't be much good in the jungle.' Bill laughed as she winced at the pebbles under her bare feet. 'How would you cope with leeches and water snakes?'

'There aren't snakes here?' Amy's blue eyes flew open in alarm.

'You really are a city girl.' He shook his head, eyes twinkling. 'I'm the most dangerous creature around 'ere.'

The sun had caught Bill's nose and cheeks, giving

217

them the same golden blush she remembered from their first meeting eighteen months earlier. The cold water felt delightful and she leaned against his chest.

'Let me wash you.' His lips slid across her ear. 'You must be sore.'

She blushed, burying her face against him.

'It's OK, I understand,' he said, holding her tight with one arm and pulling up her skirt and tucking it into her belt with the other. Then leaning over he cupped his hand, filled it with water and brought it up to her.

She squealed, more from embarrassment than the cold. As she looked down she saw a smear of blood on her white thigh and she averted her face from his in shame.

'Don't be shy,' he said softly. 'You've got a beautiful body and I love you, there's no shame in it.'

He moved her over to the branch, pushed her gently back against it, then brought up more water in his cupped hands.

Tears filled her eyes for no reason she could explain. Perhaps it was his hand touching her again, the tenderness in his eyes, or the way he leaned to kiss her again and the afternoon sun glinting on his hair.

'Women can come, just like men,' he whispered, turning her face to kiss her. 'Let me make it happen for you.'

As his fingers stroked her the feeling so recently interrupted all came back, this time twice as strong. She leaned against him, unbuttoning her bodice so he could suck at her breasts. The sensations grew stronger and she held his head tightly to her breasts, aware she was calling out his name, yet not caring if anyone heard. It felt like being inside a corkscrew, going round and round, closer and closer to something she didn't understand. She opened her eyes and watched as he stroked her, his cheek against her breast, a look of supreme tenderness and pleasure on his face, and only for a second did she wonder how he had learned such things about women when she didn't even know about them herself.

Her feet were still in the cold river, the sun hot on her arms and head, and somewhere between the two sensations was this wild and beautiful emotion that lifted her into another sphere.

Chapter 12

Mabel stared out the kitchen window. Amy was in the sitting room sewing, Harry was out in the cowshed but she had no idea where Tara had gone to. That troubled her, for she knew her granddaughter had a crush on Harry and the sooner he left, the better. It wasn't that she didn't like him, she just wanted someone out of the top drawer for her granddaughter.

But even as she thought this, she felt guilty, after all he'd done so much for them. He'd mended just about everything on the farm. The new porch, every window had been repaired and painted, countless jobs that would have cost her a fortune to get done by a builder. But it wasn't just his help around the farm she had to thank him for, his male presence appeared to be the catalyst that brought Amy back to health and sanity. She and Tara had leaned on him too, his jokes and masculine strength had pulled them all through.

But it was time he left, and let them get back to normal. Amy was improving in leaps and bounds and MacDonald hadn't turned up.

A phone call with George revealed that the police were searching for Bill, as his fingerprints linked him decisively with Father Glynn's murder. His picture had been in the local papers, with a request for people who knew him to come forward. But he'd gone to ground, and after some discussion they'd decided it was safe for Harry to leave.

Harry was pressing some putty into the glass in the cowshed when Tara looked in. She didn't let him know she was there for a moment but just stood deep in thought, watching his nimble fingers and his look of concentration.

Setting aside Mabel's funny ways and the desire to see his mates and father again, he really liked the farm. It was good to work with his hands, to smell fresh air and see green fields rather than crowded markets and noisy pubs. There was no need here to keep up appearances, for acting tough. He had become really interested in farming, talking to all the old blokes down at the Pelican over a pint. He would miss that sweet exhaustion from a day well spent, the animals, but especially Tara.

Tara didn't let him know she was there for a moment. She watched his nimble fingers pressing in the putty, the look of concentration on his face. Seen sideways on his eyelashes looked like black brushes, his tongue peeping out between his lips.

She had watched him working many times over the past few weeks, noticed the silkiness of his skin when he took his shirt off, his slender hips, the tufts of black hair just above his navel and the width of his shoulders. Time and again she had wanted to run her fingers through his black hair, make him smile so she could see the curve of his lips and a hint of a dimple in his right cheek. She would sit in her room and draw his angular face, wishing she could capture that impish look and the depth of his dark blue eyes.

He was planing a piece of wood out in the barn one day and as his finger caressed the grain she felt a tug inside her, wishing it was her leg, arm or even breast he was touching so reverently. But how could she make him see her as a sweetheart rather than a little sister? For the last couple of weeks she'd been wearing her best clothes, brushing her hair till it shone, even putting on lipstick and mascara, but his attitude to her remained stubbornly brotherly.

'Gran says you're going home!'

Harry looked over his shoulder in surprise. He had been so engrossed he hadn't heard her come up behind him.

She looked so pretty in a new circular green skirt she'd made, with a tight knitted cotton top, but there was a frantic look in her eyes he couldn't quite identify.

'Yeah, tomorrow.'

'But why?' She was pouting, golden hair hanging down over those delicious pert breasts. She had mastered this sexy pout since she'd seen a picture of Bridget Bardot doing it and Harry had to admit it turned him on.

'Because you don't need me any more now.' He took a rag out of his overall pocket and wiped his hands on it. They smelled of linseed oil, and his fingernails needed cleaning.

Harry leaned back against the rails of the stall. Any minute now Stan would bring the cows in for milking and the hosed-down cobbles would once again be a sea of muck.

'I need you,' Tara blurted out. 'Please don't go, Harry. I can't bear it here without you.'

Harry recognised the pleading tone, he'd heard it from girls before. All at once he realised who the smart clothes and the make-up were for.

'You won't even miss me once you go back to school next week.' He felt awkward now, remembering how painful his own first crush had been. 'Anyway, what about my dad and Queenie? They've had to do all the work while I've bin down 'ere.'

'I don't care about anyone but you,' she insisted. 'I love you, Harry.'

At least thirty girls had told him they loved him since he was fourteen, but he hadn't expected this from Tara.

He took a deep breath. He wanted to laugh it off but a prickle touched his own heart.

'I love you, too.' He calmly went on rubbing his hands, eyes deliberately on the rag. 'You're like my sister.'

'I didn't mean it like that.' She moved so fast he didn't have a chance to avoid her and suddenly her arms were round his neck. 'I mean like this!'

It was an innocent's kiss, lips pressed hard against his because she hadn't yet learned the way adults did it, but somehow it was more moving than an experienced one.

'Oh, Tara.' He didn't know what to do – he couldn't hold her at arm's length because his hands were dirty and it would show on her white jumper. 'You're too young for me.'

'I'm not,' she insisted, pressing herself closer. 'I want you.'

Harry waved his dirty hands helplessly out to the sides. That young, sweet body against his was enough to make any man forget her age. Her hair smelled of lily of the valley and he wanted to hold her and kiss her more than he'd ever wanted any other girl.

'Stop it, Tara. It's not right.' If Stan or Mabel caught him like this he'd be picking shot out of his backside for weeks!

'You think I'm just a child, don't you?' she said scornfully. 'Well I'm not, I'm a woman, and I love you.'

He couldn't win. If he held her in his arms and kissed her he had no doubt as to what that would lead to. If he rejected her, the loss of face would hurt her, too.

'I've got a girl back home, sweetheart,' he lied. It was all he could think of. 'You and your mum are part of my family, I love you both, but not in that way.'

'You never said you had a girl.' Her look cut him to the quick.

There were lots of girls who would be pleased to have him at home, but not one he really cared about.

'I didn't think you were interested in things like that,' he said easily, stepping back from her.

Her eyes filled with tears and she turned away and ran out of the cowshed.

'Oh *shit*!,' Harry flung down his old rag. 'Women!'

'Autumn's sad, isn't it,' Amy said as she looked out of Mabel's bedroom window at the rain beating down. 'All the leaves have come down during the night.'

It was a Saturday in late October and Mabel was still in bed because she had a chesty cold which wouldn't go.

Amy had regained not only her health but her looks, too. Her hair had grown long enough to have it cut in a sleek bob on her shoulders and a feathery fringe drew attention to her big blue eyes. Jeans and a pink sweater showed off her slender yet curvaceous shape – she could easily pass for twenty-five.

She felt as if she was breaking out of a cocoon. Everything seemed sharper – sights, smells, sounds and feelings. Each day when she collected eggs, fed the chickens or cooked a meal there was a kind of joy, as if she'd been reborn.

Right now she could smell oranges and cloves from the homemade pomanders her mother hung in the wardrobe. When she looked around and saw Mabel sitting up in bed in her pink flannel nightdress she felt a surge of affection. The heavy old dressing table, the ancient carved bed that both James Brady and Mabel had been born in, were indescribably dear to her.

'The seasons all have their purpose,' Mabel said hoarsely, slicing the top off her boiled egg. 'Papa always relished autumn because it meant a lull in the farm work. We should see it like that, too, a chance to go shopping in Bristol. Go to the cinema with Tara, or to Bath to explore.'

Mabel was thrilled to see roses back in her daughter's cheeks. Slowly as the weeks passed Amy had grown stronger. She began to sew again for neighbours, she gossiped with other customers at the shops, laughed at the stories Greg Masterton told her about his practice. As summer finally drew to a close she had thrown herself into harvesting with joyous enthusiasm.

The growing friendship between the doctor and Amy pleased Mabel too. Greg Masterton was a gentleman, kind and understanding, and, although she felt a little nervous that it might lead to a romance and perhaps even marriage, for now it was a good thing.

'Tara seems happier now, doesn't she?' Mabel nibbled a slice of toast. 'She was a bit down after Harry left, but I suppose that's understandable.'

'I think she had a little crush on him.' Amy smiled. She had seen the torn-up sketches of Harry in the wastepaper bin and guessed her daughter had been rebuffed. 'I'm not surprised, of course, so had most of her friends from what I can make out. But I looked in on her just now and she was scribbling away on her sketch pad, that's a good sign.'

Mabel's eyes lit up. 'She really has talent. I mean, it's one thing to be able to draw an imaginary dress, quite another to actually make a pattern and turn it into a real dress.'

Amy smiled to herself. In many ways her mother was just as obstinate, prickly and awkward as she always had been, but where Tara was concerned she'd softened. Not outwardly – she still shouted at her for cutting out on the dining-room table and leaving a mess; she would snort and turn up her nose at some of Tara's wilder ideas. But privately she thought Tara was another Coco Chanel in the making.

It was true, Tara was clever. Her sewing skills left a great deal to be desired, she still rushed things, forgetting that patience was as important as flair. But she had an instinctive eye for colour and the use of textures, Amy could tell.

Amy stood up, taking her mother's breakfast tray from her.

'I'll light the fire in the sitting room,' she suggested. 'Then if you want to come down you can sit in there. I must go now, I've got some work to do in the dairy.'

She glanced out of the window as she crossed the end of the bed. The road was covered in fallen leaves and the red door of the fire station stood out clearly through the rain. Bare branches gave a clear view right across to the mill and she could see a bag of grain being hauled up on a hoist.

'Do you know anyone with a white Vauxhall?' She turned back to her mother. 'There are a couple of men in one out there looking at the house.'

'What sort of men?' Mabel asked.

'Just ordinary. Perhaps they've lost their way?' Amy replied. 'I'll go and see.'

She was just going down the stairs when she heard a knock on the front door. Balancing the tray against her hip she pulled back the curtain covering it and drew back the bolts.

'Sorry to take so long opening it.' She smiled as she opened the door. 'No-one ever comes in this way.'

'Mrs Manning?'

They were both tall, stocky men, one around fifty, dressed in a beige raincoat; the other younger, in a short navy car coat.

'Yes.'

'I'm Inspector Hawkins from the Metropolitan Police,' the older one said, pulling an identification card out of his pocket. 'This is Sergeant Harrison. Could we come in to speak to you?'

She led them into the kitchen and put the tray down on the draining board. She had an uneasy feeling in her stomach.

'Do sit down, I'll make a fresh pot of tea.' She whisked away a loaf and bread board and brushed the crumbs into her hand. The kitchen smelled of burned toast and she was embarrassed by the pile of breakfast dishes in the sink. 'What can I do for you?'

'Is your real name Amy MacDonald, wife of William Henry MacDonald?'

She could only nod. Blood rushed to her head and and she had to clutch the back of a chair for support.

'We're sorry to give you a shock,' she dimly heard one of them say as he guided her to a chair. 'We understand the reasons for your change of name and we don't want to upset you. I'm afraid MacDonald is dead.'

For a moment she was incapable of speech. She noted Inspector Hawkins had a beaky nose and his skin was so badly pitted he might have had smallpox. She noticed a button had come off his shirt and each time he moved she saw a flash of dark hair. She even wondered why men with so much hair on their bodies almost always lost it from their head, as he had. But she still couldn't put a sensible sentence together.

Harrison was a good ten years younger than Hawkins, fresh faced with blond hair cut so short he looked like a convict. He made the tea while Hawkins sat beside her and explained everything.

'Your husband's body was found in a burned-out car that crashed off the coast road near Berwick. The car was stolen, he had been drinking. A witness reported seeing him earlier trying to fill up the tank from a can of petrol outside some shops; he'd stumbled and spilled petrol on his clothes. It seemed he must have

227

forgotten this and just a few miles further up the coast road, lit up a cigarette. He must have gone up like a torch. The car went right over the cliff, landing on rocks beneath, and the whole thing caught fire. They found his bag in the boot untouched by the flames. In it the police who were called to the scene found his passport, driving licence and a few other things, and were able to identify him.'

Amy listened with growing horror as they described how money traced to a post-office robbery had also been found in the boot of the car.

'What's going on, who are these men?' Mabel appeared suddenly in the kitchen in her dressing gown, face alight with indignation.

Amy could only sit with her head in her hands as the police went through the grisly story again.

'Your friend Mr George Collins spoke to us late last night,' Inspector Hawkins explained. 'He was very concerned about not being able to break the news to you himself first but, as we pointed out, a phone call out of the blue is every bit as bad as us coming round.'

There were things Amy still didn't understand when they'd finished their tale, yet she realised her mother knew exactly what they were talking about when a murdered priest was mentioned.

'That's why Harry came down here,' Mabel explained. 'We didn't know for certain if Bill *had* killed Father Glynn, but he came to keep an eye on us.'

Amy heard them explaining how Ernest MacDonald, an older brother who lived in Portsmouth, had identified the body. Ernest couldn't be sure at first, but the small tattoo of a bluebird on the right shoulder had proved it to be him.

Amy covered her eyes with her hands.

The mention of the bluebird took her right back to Grafton Buildings. She could remember the first time she had ever seen Bill without a shirt, shaving at the sink, and how she had run her finger over it.

'I got it done in Singapore.' He grinned round at her, his face white with shaving soap. 'Pretty, ain't it?'

That day she'd been more impressed with the rippling muscles under his smooth olive skin, the width of his shoulders tapering down to slim hips.

'Did it hurt?' she asked.

'Not so much as my septic foot, or the dose of dysentery.' His brown eyes twinkled with laughter. 'I was so glad to be alive, I wanted a permanent reminder.'

'But you can't see it yourself!'

'I wanted it behind me,' he had said, suddenly serious. 'Now I've got you and a future, I won't always be looking over my shoulder.'

Inspector Hawkins knew almost everything there was to know about Bill MacDonald, yet he was surprised that this gentle, beautiful blonde was his wife.

Even though Hawkins had been transferred to Bow Street years ago, he'd heard the gossip about MacDonald knocking his wife and kids around, and their disappearance. He heard about the fire at Collins' warehouse and guessed old George had stuck his neck out to protect them.

Seeing Amy's tears shocked him. How did a man go wrong with a woman like her behind him?

'I'm so sorry.' He touched Amy's hand gently, wishing he could find something good to say about MacDonald.

'Is someone going to tell me what's happened?' A girl's voice made them all look up.

Inspector Hawkins stood up; the sergeant's mouth fell open. They knew there was a teenage daughter, but neither of them was prepared for her beauty. Her gold-red hair flowed over the shoulders of a green sweater; her amber eyes sparked with indignation.

'This is my daughter, Tara,' Amy said, a little nervously.

'It's your father,' Mabel said curtly. 'I'll explain later.'

'Is he dead, or has he been nicked?'

For a moment no-one replied or even moved. Her words sounded so blunt, cold and devoid of emotion.

'He's dead, Tara.' There was more than a trace of delight in Mabel Randall's voice and the inspector noticed that Amy winced. 'Go to your room, we'll explain everything later.'

'I want to hear everything now,' she said firmly and, sitting herself down at the table, folded her arms.

'I said go upstairs,' Mabel repeated.

'I won't.' Tara's voice was openly defiant now. 'I want to hear all the details. I'll enjoy it!'

Inspector Hawkins told her. He had a feeling this girl would like to know just how badly burned her father had been, that they couldn't even finger-print him because there was no flesh left on his hands. But he didn't tell her any of that, just the incidents that led to his death.

'What happens now?' Tara asked calmly. 'Does he get a funeral?'

'That's happened already,' Hawkins said. 'His brother took care of it. It took us some time to discover where you and your mother were.'

'So it's all over?'

Inspector Hawkins nodded.

'Is everyone here going to find out about us now?' The girl's amber eyes looked directly into his.

'No. Not even the local police know about it, and that's the way it will stay.'

'That's good.' She stood up and left the room abruptly, not even looking at her mother.

'I'm sorry.' Amy's voice quavered. 'Tara can be very headstrong.'

*

230

It was later that afternoon when Tara heard her mother crying in the stable.

'What is it, Mum?' she asked softly as she crept in to find her mother with her face nestled against Betsy's neck. She could see perfectly well that Amy had been crying for some time. It was dusk now, and gloomy in the stable, but she could still make out her swollen eyes.

'You're crying for Dad, aren't you?' she said in astonishment. 'What on earth for?'

'Because of what he used to be. Because no-one else cares enough.' Amy patted the white flash down Betsy's nose.

'Well, I'm glad he's dead,' Tara spat out. 'It's the best thing that's happened in my life so far.'

'You can't be, not really?'

'I can. He gave us such a horrible life.'

'Well, today I'm just remembering the man I fell in love with.'

'You're so weak,' Tara exploded. 'You'd find something good in a maggot. I can't stand it.'

She turned and ran back into the house, up the stairs into her bedroom. Only then, in the privacy of her room, could she let go. She didn't want her mother teasing those little memories out of her – of Sundays down Petticoat Lane riding on his shoulders; of riding the Wild Mouse at Southend or walking through the tunnel to Greenwich from the Isle of Dogs when he used to howl like a dog to make her laugh.

She wanted to keep her hate alive, she wanted to remember her mother with a black eye and Paul shaking with fear. Her father had been a bully and a thief, and today she'd discovered he was a murderer too.

'I'm glad he's dead!' she sobbed over and over again.

Tara stayed in her room all evening. Mabel called out

that tea was ready, but she didn't go down. She sat at her desk with her reading light on, drawing.

Her room was always warm because it was over the kitchen and pipes from the Aga ran through it. Gran had told her many stories about this room, that had been hers as a girl. How she and her sister Emily used to take the big drawers out of the chest and pretend they were boats. How they would hold on to the footboard of the bed to tie each other's stays. It was here that Gran had got the beating from her father.

The feather mattress was gone now, replaced by a new spring one, but aside from the drawing board Gran bought her last Christmas, and a green carpet, everything else was as it had been then. Her friends had modern bedrooms with Formica-topped dressing tables and sliding doors on their wardrobes, but Tara loved the big pine chest of drawers, the carving on the bedstead, the tile-topped washstand. The pictures on the walls of Adam Faith, Gene Vincent and Elvis Presley were a reminder that she was a modern teenager, but she loved Victoriana.

She and Paul had once dug out a lot of old dresses tucked away in a trunk, and spent a whole day up here trying them on. It made her smile even now to think of Paul in a girl's navy and white striped dress, he had looked so pretty in it once she'd found a sun-bonnet to hide his short hair. Gran had laughed, too, when she saw him, she said it had been her Sunday dress and described the lacy bloomers she used to wear underneath it.

It occurred to Tara that the memories of her brother were becoming less painful. She could think of him without crying, smile at the funny things he had done and said. She wished she could be that way about Harry, too; forget how she'd thrown herself at him out in the cowshed. Now she could never go and stay in London.

The wind got up and was chasing round the house

lifting the loose sheets of corrugated iron on the hen house, sending a milk pail rattling across the cobbles and banging the branches of the plum tree against the cowshed.

She was drawing her fantasy shop, its big windows displayed with her designs. First the shop front, dark green paint with 'Tara Manning' written in gold leaf; then the interior, with ladies posing before long mirrors, their husbands sitting waiting on a couch.

A knock on the door surprised her. She had expected to be ignored.

'I thought you might like a sandwich.' Amy peered round hesitantly. 'Can I come in?'

'Yes, of course.' Tara felt a little awkward now, wondering if she should apologise.

Amy came right in, pushing the door to behind her with one foot. She had milk, too, and a slice of walnut cake. She put the tray down on the bed and came to look over Tara's shoulder.

'Your shop?'

She could tell her mother had been stuffing the chicken for Sunday lunch, she smelled of sage and onions. Tara wondered if she was still sad.

'You're lucky you can draw, Tara. I see dresses in my head and I could make them the way I think them, but I couldn't put them on paper.'

Tara felt ashamed. Not for what she'd said, but because she'd hurt her mother. Amy never bore grudges, perhaps that's why she had forgiven Dad so many times?

'Are you still sad about Dad?' she asked in a small voice.

Amy gave a soft sigh and Tara turned in her seat and buried her face in her mother's chest.

'I didn't mean to hurt you,' she whispered. 'It's just that I can't see him the way you can.' She knew without looking up that Amy was crying again and all she could do was hold her mother tightly and hope that it would help.

'No-one in this world is entirely wicked, not even your father,' Amy finally said.

'If I fall in love with a man and he puts one foot wrong, I'll leave him immediately,' Tara said firmly.

Time and again she had tried to work out why women liked men who were cruel to them but, however she looked at it, there was no answer except weakness.

'I think you'll find it's not quite as simple as that.' Amy laughed through her tears. 'I hope the man you fall in love with will be worthy of you. But don't go through life expecting perfection, darling.'

Chapter 13

1963

'I hate school. I want to leave now!'

Tara faced her mother in the kitchen, eyes blazing. She was just sixteen, still in her school uniform, though she had done her best to disguise it by leaving off her tie and wearing a wide belt around her skirt.

'If I have to stay here another year I'll end up as loopy as you and Gran!'

Amy slapped Tara across the face.

'Don't be so cruel,' she shouted. 'I've been trying to explain to you that if you get "A" levels you can go to Goldsmith's College in London. Leave school now and you'll never get in there.'

'Who cares about college? I just want a job.'

Amy turned away, sickened not only by Tara's stubborn and short-sighted view, but also by herself resorting to violence.

'Go and get one, then,' she threw over her shoulder. 'Just don't blame me in a year or two when you regret it.'

Tara ran upstairs. Once in her room she wasn't sure whether to do a gleeful dance, or continue to sulk. She'd worn her mother down and got her own way at last, but somehow the triumph felt a little hollow. But then Mum was good at making her feel like that!

A job wasn't the real issue. What she really wanted was to move to London.

She stood in front of her mirror and looked critically at herself. A ravishing natural beauty, that was how Mr Haig the English teacher described her. He'd raved about her glorious hair and her wide sensual mouth. He had been teaching them how to write a poem, improvising on the spur of the moment, but she knew he felt what he was saying, even if he did laugh about it.

In the two years since Paul's death Tara had become a woman, and now the village didn't have enough to offer her. Aside from the odd dance at the village hall or the Young Farmers' Association, there was absolutely nothing to do – no youth club, no coffee bar. Even if she went into Bristol, the last bus back left soon after ten. She wasn't old enough to go in the pub and, anyway, even if she had been, she wanted a bit more excitement than sitting about with old men who talked about the days before the War and played shove ha'penny. Other girls from school were into riding in a serious way, taking part in gymkhanas, exercising their horses, but Tara wasn't that keen on riding and anyway, most of the girls were terrible snobs. Fashion magazines were her lifeline. She studied each designer's collections, she dreamed of clothes when everyone else mooned over actors and pop stars.

London had preoccupied her mind for over a year now, since she had got over the embarrassment of Harry. Once she had been convinced she could never look him in the face again, but now she merely laughed about it. George and Queenie had been to visit twice during this time, and little snippets of information about Harry disturbed her. He still worked with George, but now he had moved into a flat of his own near the Angel and George was clearly afraid he was getting into bad company. But Harry no longer figured in her scheme of things. All she wanted was to find a job in the fashion industry, and that meant London.

'They were all talking about this actor chap who's staying at Stanton Drew.' Mabel dumped the shopping on the kitchen table and sank down on to a chair as if she'd walked ten miles instead of just nipping up to the Co-op. 'Apparently he's been in a detective series on the television, but I've never heard of him.'

Amy looked up from her ironing. 'What's his name?'

'Wainwright.' Mabel took sugar and flour out of the bag and looked suspiciously at a bunch of bananas. 'Look at these, half of them are black. I should've been watching what Muriel was doing instead of listening to tittle-tattle.'

Amy smiled weakly. She was still brooding about Tara and wishing she hadn't smacked her face, but her mother could be very funny sometimes. She pretended to have no interest in gossip, yet she always knew everything.

Mabel looked round at her daughter.

'You've been crying!'

Amy shrugged her shoulders. 'Tara upset me. I told her she could get a job if that's what she wants.'

'She wants to leave home,' Mabel said brusquely. 'And you can't stop her, Amy.'

Amy was surprised by her mother's attitude; she had expected opposition.

'I can't bear it,' she said. 'Why has she turned against me, Mother? She can hardly be bothered to speak to me these days.'

'She hasn't turned against you. You didn't want to be with me, either, when you were her age,' Mabel said in a surprisingly gentle manner. 'I know I gave you good reason to want to be away from me, but I think you'll find that, even in the closest families, girls of her age want to get out.'

'I wouldn't mind her leaving home to go to college,'

Amy said. 'But she's being so foolhardy, refusing to take her "A" levels. At college they'll channel her into a proper career, but left to her own devices she'll just drift.'

Mabel got up and slid the kettle on to the Aga. Tara was the best in school at art and her needlework had improved vastly in the last two years, but she was as impatient and obstinate as herself. In just the way Mabel had imagined herself sweeping into a studio and becoming a successful illustrator overnight, Tara believed she had enough talent to take the fashion industry by storm.

'She doesn't understand that if she wants to become a dress designer she'll have to work up through the ranks,' Amy continued. 'She wouldn't last five minutes in a workshop. And don't tell me things have changed since I was a seamstress, Mother, because they haven't.'

Mabel smiled. Amy was right. Tara would be put to work picking up pins, machining seams and pressing. Even Amy, whose needlework was exquisite, had never got a chance to put forward her own ideas.

'The trouble with us,' Mabel said thoughtfully as she warmed the teapot, 'is we both want everything for Tara we never had. Perhaps we want her to achieve the things we never did.'

Amy's fame as a dressmaker had spread since she made a wedding dress for the local headmaster's daughter. With a sixteen-feet train, every inch of it embroidered with tiny seed pearls, it had been the talk of the village for months afterwards. Now she mainly made evening dresses and bridal gowns, all rich with embroidery or beading, but even so she knew she couldn't expect to walk into one of the leading fashion houses and call herself a designer.

'So what should we do?' Amy asked, knowing in her heart Mabel was right.

'Don't argue with her.' Mabel shrugged her shoulders. 'If she has set her eyes on London, I suppose we'll just have to accept it. Suppose we said she could take a summer job in London and asked George and Queenie to put her up?'

Amy's face brightened. A few weeks of having to kowtow to other women would probably bring Tara back to heel!

'That's a brilliant idea,' she agreed. 'I bet Queenie could find her a place with one of the dress manufacturers. If we said she could go after doing her "O" levels, that might appease her enough to swot for the exams!'

She put the ironing board away, piling the clothes on a chair ready to take upstairs, then sat down with her mother for a cup of tea. From upstairs the sound of Cilla Black's 'Anyone who had a heart' was booming out of Tara's record player – clearly she was wallowing in self-pity.

'It's the dance on Saturday.' Amy smiled. 'If only she'd meet some local boy and fall for him.'

'Pigs might fly,' Mabel said dourly. 'I never saw one lad around here when I was a girl that made my heart race. And look at you! A beautiful woman in your prime and your only admirer is a tubby doctor!'

'He's a kind, generous man,' Amy said indignantly. Greg had become far more than just Amy's doctor in the past two years. It was his friendship and interest that sustained her when her mother's stubborn and crusty nature irritated her. Sometimes she went for walks with him and his dog Winston, and he often called in at the farm for tea. 'I don't know why you go on laughing about him, anyway. You're quick enough to pick his brains when you need some advice!'

'He just hasn't got much…' Mabel broke off, unable to think of the right word.

'Sex appeal.' Tara's voice from the door made them both look round.

Both Mabel and Amy laughed. They hadn't known Tara was within earshot, but in fact her remark was true.

'What would you know about such things?' Amy giggled, glad that Tara had at least stopped sulking.

'Only what I've read in magazines,' Tara admitted. 'But I can't actually think of one person in the village with sex appeal!'

'That's a relief,' Mabel said drily. 'We don't have to lock her up!'

'What about this actor then?' Amy was anxious to smooth over any bad feeling to pave the way for a serious chat later. 'You'd better tell Tara about that.'

Tara sat down and poured herself some tea. Like her grandmother she rarely apologised; merely joining them was supposed to indicate a slight change of heart.

'Apparently he's a real dish,' Mabel said slyly. 'And drives a flashy car, but I don't want you riding your bike up to Stanton Drew to gawp at him.'

'How old is he?' Tara asked.

'About thirty-five, they said.'

'I wouldn't even cross the road to see someone that old.' Tara put her nose in the air. 'You can borrow my bike though, Mum, he's nearer your age!'

Amy was picking over some raspberries for jam on Saturday evening, when Tara stalked into the kitchen.

'Well, how do I look?' She struck a pose like a mannequin in one corner of the kitchen, then turned on her heel to show the back of her outfit.

'Very nice, dear,' Amy said.

Tara had designed and made the outfit herself, an emerald green shantung sheath dress with bootlace straps, topped by a little bolero jacket. Her hair had been in rollers all day and now it was backcombed into a bouffant style, flicking up on her shoulders. Her eyes were heavily outlined in black.

'Only nice?' she asked waspishly.

240

'You've got a lot of make-up on, you don't need so much.'

Tara had bought the material for her dress in a Bristol market and it was the sort that creased badly. The dress's seams were puckered, but Tara wouldn't listen to her mother's advice and put them right. Amy also privately thought the dress was too tight, but she wasn't going to raise objections at this late stage.

'All the girls wear heavy make-up, it's the fashion,' Tara retorted.

It was hard for Amy to see Tara looking so grown-up. In her heart she knew there was no real danger at the village dance, but she remembered only too well the feelings Bill had aroused in her at sixteen.

'Where's Gran? I wanted to see her before I left?'

'Out in the dairy. Someone came to buy eggs and cheese, she's still with them.'

'I'll say goodbye as I go past, then.' Tara bent to kiss her mother. 'Leave the back door unlocked. I might be late.'

'This is my granddaughter, Tara.' Mabel's lined face lit up with pride as Tara walked into the dairy. 'She's off to the village dance.'

Tara stopped dead in her tracks as the man turned to greet her. It had to be the actor everyone was talking about.

He wasn't just handsome. He was devastatingly beautiful – butter-coloured blond hair worn just slightly longer than the local men's, deep brown eyes and the kind of rugged perfection she associated only with Martini advertisements.

'This is Mr Wainwright.' Gran beamed at Tara, as she slapped some butter between two pats, then wrapped it in greaseproof paper. 'He's not only an actor, but an artist, too. He's staying at a cottage over in Stanton Drew.'

'Simon, please,' he said, shooting out a slender hand to shake Tara's. 'Mr Wainwright makes me sound middle-aged.'

Tara forgot she had thought thirty-five was old. In his light grey slacks and checked open-necked shirt, casual elegance oozed out of Simon Wainwright. Even his voice was delicious, deep and resonant, the sort she'd only heard on the wireless.

'It's nice to meet you,' Tara said awkwardly, desperately trying to think of something riveting to keep him here. He was at least six feet tall and his brown eyes held all the sex appeal she'd found lacking in the local men. 'Has Gran told you she paints, too?'

'She has indeed.' His mouth curved into a smile that sent shivers of delight down her spine. 'She also told me you were very talented!'

'I'm not really.' Tara blushed. She wasn't usually so modest, but then she'd never met someone famous before and she was wary of showing off till she knew him better.

'I left it too late for the shops. In London there's always a shop open somewhere. Thank heavens I saw your sign, otherwise I'd be one starving artist!'

Tara saw that her Gran had not only sold him eggs, cheese, butter and milk but had found him a loaf of her own homemade bread, a pot of marmalade and some bacon. She was always one for making the most of an opportunity.

'Are your family with you?' Tara asked.

His brown eyes had a wicked glint. 'I haven't one,' he said. 'Just down for a few days of rest before an audition. Where are you off to all dressed up?'

'A dance in the village hall,' she said, blushing because it sounded so rustic. 'It's about the only thing to do around here.'

'Perhaps I can drop you off?' He raised one perfect blond eyebrow questioningly. 'That is, of course, if you

242

haven't got a partner coming to collect you?'

'It's only a couple of hundred yards.' Gran stiffened as she saw the effect this handsome stranger was having on Tara.

'But I'm going that way.' He smiled charmingly at Mabel and pulled a leather wallet from his inside pocket. 'Now, Mrs Randall, how much do I owe you?'

His car was a silver 'E' type Jaguar and he barely had time to change gear before they arrived outside the village hall.

'That's it there.' Tara pointed out the Old School House next to the churchyard gates. 'Hardly worth a lift.' She giggled.

Simon smiled at her, pulled across the street and up the slope till they were right in front of the door.

'Be-bop a lula' blasted out with more volume than musical talent and Mr Jakes on the door, in a funereal black suit, was waving his hands in protest.

'Sounds promising.'

She knew he was being sarcastic.

'What are you doing tonight?' she asked.

He made her feel so strange, all sort of prickly inside. There was something exotic about him, not just his beautiful clothes, the car or even his perfect profile. It was a glimpse of something racy, something dangerous and thrilling. She was reluctant to get out of his car.

'Nothing,' he said. 'I might pop down to the local later. Sketch or read a book.'

'Why don't you come in with me?' she asked breathlessly.

He looked round at her, smiled and took one of her hands in his.

'I don't think it's quite my scene,' he said softly, lifting her hand to his lips and kissing it. 'Teddy boys in bootlace ties and bumper shoes, giggling virgins and a few farmers' wives to keep it all in line.'

243

Tara laughed. 'You've missed out the spotty country boys in cavalry twill trousers.'

'I bet you'll be the only beauty in there,' he said, fixing his brown eyes on her. 'All the boys will be queuing up to dance with you. An old man like me wouldn't get a look in.'

He was flirting with her, but whether that meant he was angling at something more she couldn't be sure.

'I've always preferred older men.' She fluttered her eyelashes. 'Go on, come!'

'Maybe later,' he said, and got out of the car.

For a moment she was baffled as to what he was doing, but to her amazement he opened the car door for her.

It couldn't have been timed better if she had planned it. Shirley and Judith, two girls from her class, came around the corner just as he took her hand to help her out.

'*Au revoir, ma cherie,*' he said, lifting her hand up to kiss it again.

Shirley and Judith stood there, gawping.

'Struth!' Shirley said as he roared off up the High Street. 'Who was that?'

Tara smiled. Shirley and Judith were exactly what Simon meant by giggling virgins. They both wore cotton dresses with can-can petticoats, even though that fashion had gone out two years earlier, big plastic earrings and bright red lipstick with their hair back-combed like birds' nests.

'Who was he?' Judith took a step towards Tara and the smell of L'Aimant was overpowering.

'My dream man.' Tara smiled.

Simon Wainwright smiled too as he drove off. Tara was just the kind of diversion he needed and he sensed she was a ripe plum, ready for picking.

It was good to be out of London for a bit, not least

because he could play the part of a celebrity and get the kind of adulation he rarely got in town. Aside from the one detective series his face wasn't known; most of his work had been for radio, where his talent for accents and different voices came into its own. But he was on his way up. Today he was driving a friend's car, but if he got a film offer soon he might be buying his own.

Born in 1930 in genteel Cheltenham, his mother widowed just a few years later, he had been brought up in a house of women. A grandmother and two older sisters had pampered him, a select private school had prepared him to be a gentleman. Acting came naturally to him, but the breaks hadn't come as he expected and until quite recently he'd had to take a job as a cocktail waiter to keep himself while auditioning. But down here no-one need know that . . .

The dance was just like all the others. The band was too loud, with ear-splitting feedback. It played Buddy Holly, Adam Faith and Billy Fury songs, all with more enthusiasm than talent.

Mrs Cuthbert and Mrs Jones, two formidable matrons from the choir, handled the refreshments and kept eagle eyes peeled for signs of illicit alcohol being added to the orange juice.

The Scouts had decorated the hall and it seemed not one of them had an eye for art, let alone symmetry. Crêpe-paper streamers had been tacked up and twisted round anything available. Chinese paper lanterns were pinned up at random, vast bunches of balloons hung in clusters. But the stage decoration made Tara smirk most of all. They had tried to create an image of a barn; with bales of straw, pitchforks and a couple of old stone cider flagons.

Apart from the couples who were 'going steady', only girls were dancing. The boys propped up the walls, smoking heavily, their feet tapping to the music as they weighed up the talent, or got up the nerve to ask someone to dance.

Tara was totally bored. She knew most of the boys would die to dance with her; she knew, too, that half the girls hated her because of it. But what fun was there in it when not one of the boys was even remotely interesting!

She might have flirted with Graham Sweeting if she hadn't met that man Simon. Graham always had a half-bottle of gin or vodka in his pocket, he could jive really well and he wasn't bad at kissing either. He was what Gran called a 'bad lot'. He rode a motorbike, wore a leather jacket and had greasy black hair styled in an exaggerated quiff. Back at Christmas they had got into some serious snogging in his dad's car, and it had been enough to give her an inkling of what sex was all about. But looking now at his lean hips in tight jeans, his sullen, sexy mouth as he dragged on his cigarette, she knew taking things any further with him would be a mistake.

Her heart sank as she saw Robert Caldwell coming towards her. He was the type of boy her mother wanted for her, earnest, reliable, clean-living. He went to Bible-study classes and collected for the missionaries. One look at his sandy hair, red-tinged skin and bitten finger-nails was enough to put her off.

'Would you dance with me, Tara?' he asked, blushing even redder.

She couldn't refuse him – he was a nice enough boy – but his breath smelled, his hands were always clammy and, anyway, she couldn't bear anyone who wore hairy tweed suits.

'You look stunning tonight,' he said shyly. 'Did you make that dress?'

One of the most infuriating things about Robert was the fact he was actually interested in her as a person –

what she did, what she wanted to do – not just her looks. He read a great deal, knew about things other boys didn't and possibly, if one had the patience to work on his clothes and image, he might be worthwhile in a year or two.

She was just stepping out on to the dance floor when she sensed Simon had come back for her. There was no draught from the door, not even a bang, but she knew the way the little hairs prickled on the backs of her arms and neck that he was standing behind her, looking at her.

To show she'd noticed him would be a mistake; instead she declined Robert's invitation to jive, and chose 'the Shake,' so her hapless partner couldn't show her up with his over-enthusiastic leg and arm movements. After a respectable period of letting Simon watch her wiggling bottom, she turned, feigned surprise at his presence, then leaned towards Robert.

'Sorry, Robert, I'll have to go, a friend of my family's just popped in. I must go and have a word with him.'

'You came back then?' She stood in front of Simon, her arms folded across her chest defiantly. 'Why's that?'

Even if her mother's reaction to her dress had been lukewarm, all the girls admired it. Here on home ground she felt confident enough to try her famous pout.

'As if you didn't know!' He smiled wickedly. 'I popped into the pub, two pubs in fact, but I was lonely.'

'Come and dance?' She held out her hands, knowing all the girls from school were watching open-mouthed. It pleased her to see that he looked slightly unsure of himself, it meant he'd been giving her some thought.

'I'd rather take you somewhere a bit more private,' he said. 'I feel as if the world and his wife are watching!'

'They are.' Tara giggled. 'That's half the fun!'

Simon looked at the band and winced.

'Not for me. Come home to my cottage and dance with me there?'

'I shouldn't,' she said weakly, looking into those wicked eyes and knowing she would anyway.

'Yes you should. We artists have to live dangerously.'

It was dusk as they left the village; as they approached the small round Toll House at the turn-off to Stanton Drew, Tara suddenly felt uneasy. By day the walk back to Chew Magna was pleasant, but the prospect of narrow lanes in the dark was scary. And suppose someone reported back to her mother that she had left the dance with Simon?

'Isn't this idyllic?' Simon waved his hand at the view.

It was a beautiful scene – a pinky sunset, the road winding round over a stone bridge, pretty cottages half hidden by trees up ahead.

'I could stay here forever,' he said. His resonant voice gave her goose-pimples. He glanced at Tara and noticed the tight set of her lips. 'Don't look so worried, I'll get you back at a respectable hour!'

They passed the few cottages and the Druid's Arms, then turned up a narrow track with high overhanging hedges.

'This is it.' He pulled up by a farm gate, pointing out a tiny grey stone cottage with lattice windows, set up on a bank.

She was really scared now, wishing she hadn't come, but Simon came round and opened her door, taking her hand.

'You're quite safe with me.' He stroked her cheek gently. 'If nothing else, I'm a gentleman!'

'Who does it belong to?' she asked as he opened the front door and led her into a large, book-lined room.

Although everything was gleaming, somehow it had a masculine feel to it. A big desk sat under the window, a log fire was laid in the inglenook fireplace. There were barometers, clocks, boats in glass cases and even stuffed birds on the walls.

Simon flicked on a lamp on the desk and another on a low coffee table by the settee.

'An actor friend who writes,' he answered. 'He divides his time between acting in London and writing books here. Do you like it?'

'Yes.' She was fascinated by the stuffed birds, wondering why anyone would want to sit and look at a dead pheasant. 'Don't you think these are a bit creepy?'

'A bit.' Simon chuckled. 'But all this stuff is antique, been in his family for generations. I bet you've got things like this in your house?'

'Not stuffed birds.' Tara grinned. 'My great-grandfather was an evil old sod, he'd shoot it to eat it and that would be it.'

'Let me get you a drink.' Simon brushed his hand against her cheek then turned away. 'I've got gin, whisky, vodka, wine or sherry. Which is it to be?'

'Vodka, please.' She didn't like spirits at all – apart from brandy for medicinal purposes her gran wouldn't have booze in the house. But vodka didn't smell, she remembered, and if she refused to have anything he would think she was a baby.

'Mum and Gran have suggested I go to London to work for the summer,' Tara said. This had a nice sophisticated ring to it and she thought it might impress Simon. 'It'll give me time to look around and make up my mind about college.'

'That would make me happy.' Simon smiled. 'I'd be able to take you out.'

Tara felt her heart leap. What a start in London that would be, to have an actor boyfriend!

'Would you like to choose a record?' he asked. He pointed to a shelf crammed with them. 'I don't suppose you'll find the Beatles, but have a look.'

The records were mostly classical and jazz, but Tara found one by Ketty Lester, who she remembered singing 'Love Letters.'

'I've put some lemonade in it,' Simon sat down on the settee, put their drinks down on a low coffee table. 'Come and sit with me?'

'Gran wants me to stay on at school, but I don't – I want to live, have fun. What do you think?'

'I wouldn't presume to have an opinion.' He laughed softly. 'Most of the people I know who've done well have no real qualifications. Besides, Tara, you're so pretty I can't see you being alone for long.'

She bristled. People were always saying that she would 'soon be snapped up', or what a pretty bride she'd make. It was as if they thought she was some empty-headed doll.

'I'm going to earn my own living,' she snapped. 'I don't intend to marry anyone until I'm successful.'

'Well, that's very laudable and liberated.' Simon slid his arm along the settee. 'But how about a kiss for an old-fashioned chap who likes his ladies soft and clingy?'

He drew her so slowly into his arms that her pulse rate seemed to double with excitement even before his lips touched hers.

She had been kissed dozens of times, but never the way Simon did it. His lips touched hers so lightly, teasing, tempting, then the tip of his tongue slid over her lip, sending shivers of pleasure right down to her stomach. Just when she felt she could bear the suspense no longer, his mouth came down hard on hers and he pulled her tightly against him.

'You were made for loving,' he said as he finally released her, his deep voice husky. 'Everything about you is totally desirable.'

It was the kind of statement she'd dreamed of a man making to her, but now she found herself blushing.

'You're a virgin, aren't you?' he said softly against her ear, his tongue circling it. 'So I have a duty to make this evening especially pleasurable.'

This was the moment she knew she ought to stop him and point out that she didn't want to lose her virginity to a total stranger. But she wanted more of his kisses, she didn't want him to think she was a silly country girl, and she had a feeling inside her she couldn't really control.

'I don't want to have a baby!' she blurted out, blushing furiously.

'Just let me take care of that,' he whispered. 'Trust me to make this the most memorable night of your life.'

He set the scene to perfection. He drew the curtains, lit the fire and candles, even tossed a few sprigs of lavender into the hearth so it smelled heavenly. The Ketty Lester record was on repeat as he kissed her into delirium.

Nothing had ever made her feel like this. Each deep, searching kiss made her tremble and hold him tighter, her tongue probing his mouth, pressing herself closer to him as his fingers ran through her hair.

Her dress somehow slid to the floor, followed by her strapless bra, her knickers, stockings and suspenders, and he was doing things to her she had never imagined, even in dreams. His mouth moved from one breast to the other, sucking, licking, biting, and all the time his fingers were moving in and out of her, making her wetter and wetter and wanting more and more.

She was embarrassed when he moved down to kneel on the floor between her legs and insisted on looking right into her.

'I want to see your little virgin fanny,' he said, moving her hands as she tried to cover it. 'I want to kiss it

251

and make you come before I fuck you.'

She had never heard of anyone doing such a thing, but the way his fingers stroked her felt so good she couldn't stop him.

The fire hissed and crackled, and as his tongue flickered over her fanny she felt herself floating away on a cloud of ecstasy.

'Don't.' She took his head in her hands, embarrassed by her feelings.

He moved back to kiss her lips, his fingers deep inside her, making her writhe sensuously beneath him.

'Oh, Tara,' he whispered. 'I can't hold back. I have to possess you, that hot little fanny is begging to be fucked.'

Tara watched nervously as he unpeeled a Durex from a packet.

'Help me put it on?' he asked.

His clothes had come off around the same time as her own, though she hadn't really been aware of it. Now, seeing an erect cock for the first time, she was scared. She had never imagined it to be so big, or so ugly, but after all he'd done to her she couldn't lose face now.

'What do I do?' she whispered.

'Just stroke it for a moment or two,' he said, holding her hand round its width. His eyes closed and he smiled with pleasure. 'That's it, can you feel how much it wants to be inside you?'

She could certainly feel the force in it, and knew she couldn't back down now. The sooner she got that Durex on it, the sooner it would be over.

He was gentle with her, though, putting cushions under her bottom, stroking her again before he slowly pushed his cock into her.

'There, that's not so bad, is it?' he whispered, and showered little kisses on her neck and shoulders. 'Soon you'll be wild for this, rushing in here with no knickers on begging me to fuck you.'

It only hurt for a moment and she quickly found herself moving with him, forgetting her apprehension.

'It's like I said, you were made for loving,' he murmured. 'Oh, my beautiful Tara, we're going to have so many wild nights like this.'

When he dropped her back at the farm it was almost two in the morning.

'I hope they aren't waiting up for me,' she said nervously as she got out. 'I can't imagine how I'll explain where I've been till this time.'

'Say you went back for a coffee with someone,' he suggested. 'Ring me tomorrow and let me know everything's all right.'

As she crept across the yard she could almost imagine her great-grandfather James striding out with a riding whip to beat her. The back door was still unlocked, the kitchen in darkness. Holding her breath she locked the door behind her, then stole across the room towards the hall and stairs.

Gran was snoring loudly, which was a relief. Of course her mother might be lying awake waiting, but she wasn't as ferocious as Gran. But no soft voice called out as she tip-toed across the landing and into her room. She didn't dare put the light on; instead she threw her dress on to a chair, hastily pulled on her nightdress and climbed into bed.

It was love! She knew it with utter certainty. Simon was the man she would spend the rest of her life with; even the career she dreamed of wasn't as important as him.

Her hands travelled down her body and she trembled as she remembered how he'd made her feel. They had made love a second time up in his bedroom and that time it had been even sweeter because she had lost her fear. She still didn't quite understand what he meant when he asked if she had come, but he said he'd make it happen next time.

At seven-thirty last night she had still been a virgin, her head full of childish ideas about men and sex. Now, just seven hours later, she was a woman, and she knew everything.

Tara couldn't do enough for her mother the next morning. She peeled the potatoes, mixed up Yorkshire pudding, even promised to hose down the yard and cowshed.

When Gran mentioned Simon, she went cold all over. 'Such a charming man.' Gran smiled as if she'd been thinking about him. 'I hope he drops by again.'

It was all Tara could do to stop herself blurting out what had happened, but it was no good. However much Gran liked him as a man, she'd soon be singing another tune if she guessed what was going on.

He was reading in the garden when she propped her bike against his front gate. The Sunday paper almost hid him as he lay back in a deckchair, his feet up on a stool.

'Boo!' she called out.

'Oh, sweetie, I was just dreaming about you,' he said, dropping the paper and holding out his arms in welcome. 'That's about the best surprise anyone could give me.'

He peeled her shorts and sun blouse off before she'd even got inside the house.

'This is how you should be always,' he said, untying her pony-tail and running his fingers through her hair till it cascaded over her shoulders. 'Your body's too beautiful for clothes.'

She couldn't describe how he made her feel. It was delicious and embarrassing all at once. She could hardly believe she was standing in broad daylight totally naked with a man she'd only met the day before. But the moment his lips touched her breasts and his fingers went inside her, all her inhibitions disappeared.

He took her up to the bedroom and there, on a big old bed in a patch of sunshine, he explored her body with his eyes, fingers and tongue and made her tremble with passion. The way he liked to talk about her body made her blush, and he asked questions she barely understood.

'Such big, beautiful breasts for someone so slender,' he said, sitting behind her and facing her so she could see herself in the mirror as he fondled them. 'Open your legs and show me how you masturbate.'

She didn't even know girls could do such a thing and her whispered admission made him laugh.

'Then I'll show you, my darling,' he said, kissing away her blushes. 'How can you hope to tell a man what pleases you if you haven't found out for yourself?'

Deep down she felt dirty lying back against his naked chest watching his fingers delving into her, yet it was so exciting, too. She looked so sexy with her hair all over her shoulders, one breast being squeezed and stroked and his slim fingers parting her pubic hair, revealing the red, shiny skin inside her. His face over her shoulder made her heart pound faster. His eyes were closed, the tip of his tongue sliding over his lips, hair flopping over his tanned face.

He made it happen with his tongue – such an incredible feeling that she felt she was going to explode. Afterwards he lay beside her stroking her breasts and made her cry with his tender words.

'You mustn't be embarrassed,' he whispered. 'I love you, and it's a natural expression of love. Some women go years without ever having an orgasm and once you know what makes it happen it's so easy.'

Being with Simon was to sail in uncharted waters;

the way he spoke, the books he read, his education and the people he mixed with were so alien to the way Tara had been brought up. But she wanted to be part of his world so badly she was prepared to do anything he asked.

He showed her how to kneel in front of him and take his penis in her mouth and, even though she felt disgust at the thought of it, she wanted to please him.

'That's wonderful.' He sighed, making her mouth move faster and faster until she was afraid she'd choke. 'Stroke my balls too, lick me, make me come in that sexy schoolgirl mouth.'

It was almost nine when she left him.

'I wish I was that saddle,' he said, kissing her one last time at the gate, holding on to her crotch and stroking it, even though she was astride her bike. 'Come tomorrow after school if you can. Wear your uniform!'

She was so sore she could scarcely bear to pedal the bike and she was sure what she'd been doing was written large across her forehead. Mum and Gran weren't likely to disbelieve she'd been over at Sandra's on the other side of the lake, she often went there last summer for tea, but Mum was very good at guessing when something unusual had happened.

'I've got to go back to London on Sunday,' Simon told her on Friday afternoon. 'I've got an acting job.'

He had already stretched his week to ten days, and Tara was sure she could persuade him to make it at least a fortnight.

She was wearing her school uniform. Simon liked to sit fully dressed with her on his lap and pretend to be a teacher while he groped her up her knicker leg. Tara couldn't see what he saw sexy in her hated uniform but, as it would have been hard for her to visit him in

256

her everyday clothes, his little predilection made things easier.

'You can't go back yet!' She clung to him, burying her head in his shoulder. 'What will I do without you?'

'You'll do what I showed you to do.' He rubbed her fanny sensuously and licked his lips. 'Come on, do it now so I know you can do it properly.'

But Tara didn't want to play that game again, no matter how pleasurable it had been yesterday. It wasn't sex she wanted, it was love. She wanted him to say he couldn't live without her, that he would marry her just as soon as her mother agreed, that she could come to London with him.

'You'll just forget me in London.' She began to cry, even though she tried hard not to.

'How can I forget you?' he said. 'I'll remember that hot, tight fanny, those big firm breasts forever. London's where I earn my living, darling. I've got bills to pay.'

'Can I come with you?'

He slid his hand inside her shirt and caught hold of her nipple.

'You must do your exams first,' he said softly. 'When you come to London to work we can see each other. I'm going to miss you far worse than you'll miss me, I promise you that!'

Instinct told her that she mustn't keep on at him, that pleasing him sexually would hold him longer than tears and demands.

'You will give me your address, though, so I can write to you?' she asked.

'Of course.' His hand slid back into her knickers. 'But if you want it you've got to show me what naughty girls do when they're all alone in their rooms at night!'

'What on earth's the matter with you?' Amy asked as Tara stood at the window on Sunday afternoon, staring

257

out at the rain. Tara had only picked at her lunch, she had a far-away look in her eyes and her shoulders were stooped.

'We don't mind you going to London for the summer.' Amy put her arm round her daughter's waist and leaned against her shoulder. 'We want you to be happy.'

Tara felt a stab of guilt. She wanted to tell her mother everything, but she knew she couldn't.

They had had one last bout of lovemaking early that morning. Tara had gone out on her bike on the pretence of looking for mushrooms. Simon had left the door open and she found him still asleep.

Looking down on him she thought he must be the most beautiful man in the world. His smooth bare chest was tanned a golden brown and, even though his muscles weren't as well developed as Harry's, his shoulders looked strong. But it was his face she lingered on. The rugged chin, with golden stubble growing through, those fleshy, sensual lips that had explored every part of her, the straight, slender nose, and his hair. No man should have hair like his, so glossy and silky, the colour of buttercups, especially when his eyelashes were brown and long.

Then he opened his eyes, blinked for a moment, and smiled. She knew then she would love him forever.

But for now she had to live without him. She would have to remember his kisses and his touch. He was lucky, he had all those photographs he had taken of her, he could bring them out and enjoy all over again those wonderful games they had played when he got her to pose. She had nothing of his but a handkerchief, his address and beautiful memories.

'I'm OK, Mum.' She smiled weakly. 'Just thinking about all the revision I've got to do.'

Chapter 14

'Who's the letter from?'

'Nobody,' Tara snapped without thinking.

'I didn't think nobodies bothered to write letters,' Amy said lightly.

Tara realised immediately she'd made a blunder. Although Amy carried on frying bacon, not even considering that there might be something sinister about a letter from London, Gran's head came round like an owl looking for prey and her eyes glinted.

'Just one of the girls that left last year, actually,' Tara lied frantically. 'Sally Webster. She's got a job in London. I'd better rush, I'm late.'

It was just six weeks since she had said goodbye to Simon, but it felt like months. The exams were over, school was about to break up for the summer holidays, and this was the letter she'd been waiting for.

She never knew first love could be so painful. Every romantic story she'd ever read, every poem, every sad song cut through to her heart. He was on her mind from the moment she woke up till she finally fell asleep. Every doodle she drew had his name in the centre of it. She wanted to confide in someone, but was afraid, and she tortured herself with the thought that he might have someone else in London.

He had written her just two short notes, the first saying he was rehearsing for a new play in the West

259

End, the second that the show had opened and it would be some time before he'd be free to come down.

Tara had made plans after his first note. She got a few dressmaking jobs, and some work washing-up glasses in the Pelican. The money was stashed away ready for the end of term.

There wasn't time to read the latest letter now, especially with Gran hovering, dying to know what was in it. Tara stuffed it in her school bag, planning to read it in the first free period.

It was almost ten before that chance came. There had been an extra-long assembly because of all the school-leavers, and every minute of it she'd been thinking about Simon.

She rushed up the stairs to her form room two at a time, practically threw herself at her desk and opened her bag. The envelope was pale blue and quite distinctive, but at the first flick through her bag she couldn't see it. She tipped the contents on to her desk, leafing through each book and file.

'Lost something?' the girl at the next desk asked.

'My letter,' was all Tara could wail. 'My letter!'

But it wasn't there.

She tried to think back. Could it have dropped from her bag in the house? Her blood ran cold at the thought. She knew her Gran, if she saw the letter lying on the floor, she'd definitely read it.

Suppose Simon had said something saucy, made some reference to his time at Stanton Drew. What if he mentioned the photographs? The prospect made her feel sick. They would never let her go to London if they knew about Simon! How could she have been so careless?

Other girls were discussing an end-of-term party as they got out of school, and they waved Tara over, but instead she ran to the bike-sheds.

She couldn't ride her bike, she had to search. Every hedge, every scrap of grass, every front garden, gutter, pavement and road was scanned for the blue envelope. But it wasn't there! All she could do was offer up a silent prayer that someone thoughtful had picked it up, seen the address and popped it back through their door.

'Please don't let Gran open it,' she pleaded with God as she pushed her bike into the farmyard. 'Please, please. I'll behave myself from now on.'

'Did you see that letter of mine?' she asked her mother, as casually as possible given her rising panic. 'I must have dropped it.'

'No.' Amy shook her head. 'No, I haven't, you'd better ask your gran.'

Tara went upstairs first, hoping it might be lying on the floor of her room. It wasn't, neither were the jumper or the jeans she'd dropped there. Someone had been cleaning up, or snooping.

'Was it you who cleaned my room, Mum?' she asked once she'd changed and gone back down to the kitchen.

'Yes, of course it was. And if you were to pick up your clothes it wouldn't take so long, either.'

Gran was out helping Stan with the milking. Tara couldn't bear the suspense any longer so she joined her there.

'Hullo, love, come to help?' Gran asked. She was squatting on a stool dressed in a pair of men's white overalls, her forehead stuck right up against the big Friesian.

Tara liked milking, but today she hated everything about the farm.

'I wondered if you picked my letter up?' she asked. 'I thought I'd put it in my school bag to read later, but when I got there I hadn't got it.'

'I haven't seen it.' Gran shrugged her shoulders.

'Mind you, I've barely been in the house today.'

Tears pricked at Tara's eyes. She needed words from Simon, she wanted reassurance he still cared. Why hadn't she read it before leaving this morning?

'What's up?'

Tara turned away from the older woman's gentle question; she couldn't face the third degree now.

Tara sat in silence all through dinner. She just didn't know what to do for the best now. He might have said he was coming down. He could even have suggested she came there. If only he'd given her a phone number.

She could try asking directory enquiries! Almost immediately she felt more cheerful, and as soon as the washing up was finished she ran along to the phone in the High Street.

'Can you give me the number of S Wainwright, 27 Godolphin Road, Shepherd's Bush, please?' she asked.

There was a silence while the woman looked.

'No-one of that name listed at that address,' she said in a bored voice.

'Well, can I have the number anyway?' Tara asked. 'Mr Wainwright might be sharing with someone.'

'The two listed numbers are both ex-directory,' the voice informed her. 'I can't give either to you.'

'But I've got to have it! It's an emergency!'

'I'm sorry. We aren't allowed to give these numbers under any circumstances.'

Tara slammed the receiver down in a temper, kicked the telephone box open and glowered at a man waiting outside.

She was still in a temper when she got home. She snapped at her mother, ignored Gran and went up to her room without even a goodnight.

'That letter wasn't from a girlfriend.' Mabel winced as she heard Tara kick the bedroom door shut. 'It's a man!'

Amy took Tara a cup of tea the next morning. She put it down by the bed and pulled back the curtains.

'Wake up, sweetheart,' she said. 'It's a beautiful morning!'

It had rained heavily for an hour or two during the night, but now the sun was up and everything gleamed.

'I think it's going to be hot again.' Amy opened the window and leaned out. 'Why don't you come to Wells with me today instead of going to school? There's that lovely fabric shop by the Cathedral, we could pick out something for a new dress each.'

There was a time when she couldn't bear to look out this window, because she relived what Tara had seen from it. But now she saw only the meadow and re-membered Paul alive, riding Betsy.

Tara sat up sleepily and reached for her tea. Her face was pink and sleepy, golden hair tousled, her wide mouth like a crushed strawberry.

'I ought to go to school,' she said wistfully. 'We're putting on that end-of-term concert today.'

'I'd forgotten that.' Amy perched on the edge of the bed. She'd been up since five, feeding the chickens and helping with the milking, and the whole time she'd been thinking about the best way to get Tara to open up. 'Well, maybe we could do something another day, just the two of us. We never seem to be on our own these days.'

Tara was tempted to blurt it out right then. Amy wasn't old and fusty like some of her friend's mothers. She would understand some of it!

But not all of it. Not the deceit, the lies. Or that he was nearer her mother's age!

'It's only a week to the holidays,' Tara said quickly, before she admitted things better kept to herself. 'We'll go to Wells then.'

Tara pushed her way through the gymnasium door, a

263

box of paper flowers she'd made in her arms.

It was a hive of activity, first-years putting out rows of chairs, while up on the stage some of the drama club were laying out artificial grass, others arranging the cardboard forest. Miss Parks was thumping out the musical score on the piano, her thin shoulders and head moving in time, glasses slipping down her nose.

Wendy Carter, the head girl, was rehearsing her part as Guinevere with Michael Trotter as King Arthur. They looked and sounded ridiculous. Wendy was big and horsy-looking, with a posh accent, while Michael was small and weedy with a Somerset dialect so thick it sounded put on. Every time they rehearsed someone got the giggles when they had to kiss. Michael was enthusiastic enough, but Wendy behaved as if she'd rather swallow poison.

'These flowers are beautiful.' Miss Kemp, the Bohemian drama teacher, lifted out one of the crêpe-paper roses. 'I take it you made these, Tara? They have that special Tara touch!'

'Mum and Gran helped.' Tara smiled. Miss Kemp was her favourite teacher and, even though Tara had no real interest in acting or singing, she helped out with costumes and props in the drama club just because of her.

'I don't know how we'd have managed without you.' Miss Kemp sighed. 'It was a bit foolhardy picking on something medieval. If you hadn't come up with the idea of painting sacking silver, our knights would have no chain-mail.'

'I'm sure you'd have managed very well.' Tara smiled shyly, pleased she was appreciated. 'I'd better go and get my costume on.'

'Where's your hat?' Miss Kemp looked askance at Tara's duffle bag. 'Surely you haven't squashed it in there?'

Tara clapped her hand over her mouth. She wore a

long pointed bonnet with trailing chiffon, and she'd left it adorning her dressing table.

'Hell! I left it in the bedroom!' she exclaimed.

'Then you must go home and get it at lunch-time. It will entirely spoil the effect if one of you is dressed differently.'

Tara rode into the yard, propped her bike by the back door and paused for a moment to catch her breath. The only sounds were the tractor way down in the lower meadow where Stan was cutting hay, and the scratch of the chickens' claws on the cobbles.

She gagged as she went into the kitchen. Gran was boiling up some fish for the cats and it smelled disgusting. Holding her nose she ran straight through, up the stairs and across the landing to her room.

She stopped short in the doorway. Gran was sitting on the bed, rifling through Tara's handbag.

'What are you doing?' Tara managed to get out. 'Why are you rummaging in my bag?' But even as she spoke, she knew! Simon's first two notes lay there in her lap.

'Is this Simon the actor I met?'

Tara looked at her grandmother and in that moment hated her – for her age, her wrinkles, her sarcasm and her prying.

'What's it got to do with you?' Tara rushed forwards snatching up her things and shoving them back into her bag. 'How could you go through my private things?'

'It's a good job I did, isn't it?' Gran pursed her lips the way she always did when she thought she was in the right. 'He's old enough to be your father! You'd better tell me what he means by "my sexy little school-girl"! Are you pregnant, Tara? Is that why you got so upset yesterday when you couldn't find that letter?'

'Leave me alone!' Tara screamed out. 'No wonder Mum ran away from you! You want to know

265

everything, to control everyone, and you don't care how you do it. I hate you!'

'Well, that's nice after all I've done for you!' Gran rose from the bed, hand raised as if she were going to strike Tara. She was formidable when she was angry, but Tara wasn't going to be brow-beaten.

'Don't you lay one finger on me,' Tara warned her, backing away. 'I'm not like Mum. I'll hit you back.'

The smell of fish wafting up the stairs now had a different tang. Gran momentarily paused, sniffed the air, then looked back at Tara, her face like stone.

'I'll deal with you in a moment,' she said. 'That fish is burning.'

Tara waited till she'd gone downstairs, then she quickly ran to her grandmother's room.

'She must have had that letter,' Tara muttered, scanning the dressing table with its silver-backed hair brushes, the big carved bed, the bedside cabinets and even the bookcase.

It was clear to Tara now. Gran found that letter and there was something in it which put the wind up her. Perhaps Mum was in on it, too. Was that why she suggested going to Wells today, to give Gran time to search for more evidence? Maybe Simon had said something about the photographs! What if he enclosed one?

She couldn't see it. In panic she fled back to her room, her heart thumping. She wasn't going to stay here to be punished; she would run away to London now.

A car came into the yard as she grabbed some clothes and stuffed them into a rucksack. She could hear Greg Masterton's voice through the open window.

'How are you, Mrs Randall? What's that awful smell?' He sounded as if he was holding his nose. 'Where's Amy today? Or is that her you're cooking?'

Any other time Tara would have laughed. Greg Masterton always made jokes about Mabel being a witch, but today it was too near the truth. Hastily she tore off her school uniform and pulled on jeans and a shirt.

Greg had obviously come to see Amy, but now he was politely setting off towards the lower meadow with Gran as if to see something. It was a golden opportunity. If she ran for it now she could be well away from the village before Gran even realised she'd gone.

The contents of her money box went into her purse, Simon's notes, her address book, make-up and hairbrush into her handbag, and she was ready. As she got down to the hall she heard her grandmother's voice back in the yard. She was offering Greg a drink and telling him Amy would be back on the five o'clock bus.

Tara looked round in alarm. It was no good trying the front door, it had too many bolts. But just as she heard her Gran's feet on the metal scraper by the back door, she noticed the sitting-room window was wide open! She was out of it faster than a hare with the hounds behind it, across the front lawn, down the little brick path and on to the road.

The school play, her mother, everything was forgotten as she tore up the road, her rucksack bumping up and down on her shoulder.

The High Street was deserted, the shops closed for lunch. Mr Hewish was just going in the Pelican but he didn't notice her as she scooted up the road and round the corner by the sweet shop, towards the Bristol Road. She had gone about two hundred yards when she heard a lorry coming up behind her, and it was pure impulse that made her put her thumb out.

The squeal of brakes surprised her, she hadn't actually expected it to stop. But she ran up to the lorry and looked up at the man in the cab. He was middle-aged, with a fat, jolly face, and he looked fatherly.

'Where to, love?' he asked in a Birmingham accent.

'Bristol?' she asked hopefully.

'Hop in.' He grinned cheerfully. 'I hope you know the way, because I'm lost.'

She didn't admit she was running away, pretending that she'd simply missed the bus. He'd just emptied his load of fertiliser out at a farm and the noise of the empty tipper truck drowned any real conversation. She wondered how long it would be before Gran realised she'd run away. Would Greg drive down to the station to try to head her off?

'Would it be easy to get a lift all the way to London?' she asked the man. 'I think I've missed the train, too.'

'Sure,' he said. 'I usually have a cuppa at a transport café. I'll get you a lift on from there.'

It was after seven when she finally found her way to Godolphin Road in Shepherd's Bush, and her heart sank into her plimsolls.

Her first real glimpse of London when she was dropped off at Hammersmith had excited her; the noise, traffic, shops and coffee bars had been so thrilling. But Shepherd's Bush was every bit as seedy as Whitechapel had been, and this particular road was awful. Tree-lined it might be, but the leaves were heavy with dust and overflowing dustbins stood outside almost every dilapidated house. A smell of drains and pungent curry filled her nostrils, a group of black children played in the gutter and further down an old wino was sitting on a wall drinking from a bottle.

Adam Faith's 'What do you want if you don't want money?' blasted out from a house with broken windows. Next door a couple of blowsy women sat on the steps gossiping. They broke off to stare as she walked past. She had expected grandeur; modern blocks of flats, or at least elegant townhouses. Not to be plunged back into her childhood.

Number twenty-seven was marginally better. The steps

up to the blue front door were clear of litter and the net curtains were clean, even if the stonework was crumbling.

There were three bells, but none for Wainwright. Tara stabbed at the bottom one, crossing her fingers. She heard the bell in the distance, but no-one answered it.

She tried the next one, marked 'Nichols'. A wave of panic washed over her. It hadn't occurred to her that he might be out, or even away for a while. What would she do if there was no reply? She couldn't get home even if she wanted to, and where would she sleep?

But she could hear footsteps now. Fierce hope ran through her, she patted her hair, ran a finger over her teeth and wished she'd thought to put on something prettier than jeans. The door was opened by a vaguely oriental-looking young man with slanting eyes and jet black hair. He was slimmer and shorter than her, and wore a pink shirt and white jeans.

'I'm sorry to trouble you,' she said. 'I'm looking for Simon Wainwright. His name isn't on any of the bells.'

'That's because he doesn't live here.' The man had an affected way of speaking, he flared his dainty nostrils and looked cross.

'But he gave me this address.' Tara's heart began to thud.

'Well, he stays here.' The man spoke very deliberately, as if he was thinking about each word. 'It just isn't his place. Anyway, he's out now.'

'Of course, the show!' It hadn't occurred to her before, but he must work every night. 'Oh dear, I forgot about his job.'

The man sighed deeply. He didn't speak for a moment or two, just looked at her as if he wished he could shut the door in her face.

'Can I wait for him here?' Tara asked weakly. 'I haven't anywhere else to go.'

He looked her up and down and his lip curled.

'You can come up to my place for a while. I'll try to

get hold of him, but if I can't you'll have to go. He doesn't always stay here, you see.'

Despite feeling faintly relieved when the man led her to his flat, Tara felt there was something odd going on here. Could this be another girlfriend's place? What if Simon was married?

The young man led her into a big room at the back of the house on the first floor. It was a bedsitter, the kitchen section was partially concealed by shelves housing a collection of old medicine bottles. The room had a gay, arty feel about it.

'I'll just go and use the phone,' he said, picking up a bunch of keys. 'Sit down.'

Tara watched him as he went out. He went up the stairs again and she could hear him unlocking a door. Moments later she heard a low murmur of conversation, then the sound of the phone being put down and the door relocked.

'I've left a message for him to ring,' the man said on his return, crossing the room to switch on the TV without looking at her. Tara sensed he didn't want to talk, in fact resented her presence.

'I'm sorry if I'm a nuisance,' she said softly. She wondered if she dared ask why he held the keys, why she couldn't go and wait in there and, indeed, who actually did own the flat.

He looked round from the television and gave her a cold, long stare, but said nothing.

It seemed that she waited hours, through *Take your Pick* then a documentary about seals. Tara sat stiffly on the only proper chair while the young man sat on his bed watching the screen intently. She was hungry and thirsty, but he didn't even offer a cup of tea.

Just after nine, the front door opening downstairs in the hall made the man leap up.

'I'll just see who that is!' He implied that she was to stay where she was.

The moment Tara heard Simon's deep voice she ran out on to the landing and looked down.

In the past few weeks she'd often wondered whether he really was as handsome as she remembered. But that first glimpse confirmed she hadn't exaggerated anything.

He looked up as the young man hastily explained something and, instead of the expected gasp of delight at seeing her, his expression made Tara's blood freeze in her veins. His lips were straight and disapproving, brown eyes cold.

'What on earth made you come?' he snapped at her. Worse still, he wasn't alone. By his side was a sleek black-haired woman in her forties, wearing a smart cream outfit.

'I'm sorry.' Tara could feel tears pricking her eyes. 'I lost your letter . . .' She tailed off, aware that both the young man and the woman were staring at her contemptuously. 'Can I speak to you on your own?'

There was a kind of conspiratorial nodding between the three of them, then Simon came up, took her arm and led her up a further flight of stairs.

'I'm sorry, Simon. I shouldn't have come,' she blurted out, following it with a garbled résumé of all the events since she lost his letter. 'I don't mean to be a nuisance. I was going to come to London anyway. I'll find a job and a flat.'

There was no attempt at a smile, no hasty reassurance.

'I explained myself when I wrote.' He drew her into a huge room covering the top floor of the house. 'I said I'd be glad to see you if you came to London, but this flat isn't mine and therefore I couldn't put you up here.'

The events of the long day, his lack of warmth and the presence of that woman were all too much, and the tears Tara had tried so hard to hold back finally flowed.

271

'I'll go,' she sniffed. 'Just give me a moment or two to think about it.'

She wanted to throw herself into his arms, tell him what agony the separation had been. But his eyes were showing irritation, not love.

'Don't be silly,' he said briskly, walking away from her and opening a window. 'You can stay here tonight, but we'll have to make some other arrangement tomorrow.'

He said something about going down to see the woman, who was a business associate, suggested she made herself some tea and he'd be back.

Tara wanted to lie down and sob. All these weeks she'd thought of nothing but seeing Simon again and now it seemed she'd mis-read everything. He'd made no attempt to kiss her, and he hadn't even tried to comfort her when she cried. Who was that woman? And why was the other man so hostile?

She looked around the room and her eyes were drawn to a photograph of a child lying loose on the desk, a seven-by-five black and white print on top of a file. It showed a naked boy of about ten caught squealing in the spray from a garden hose. He was blond, very pretty for a boy, and she wondered if he was Simon's son. Tara picked it up thoughtfully. Maybe that was why he was so odd – he was married with children and he didn't want anyone to find out he'd had an affair with a sixteen-year-old!

Opening the file wasn't even a real act of curiosity, it was just there, but as she opened the stiff blue cover she got a shock. It was full of pictures of naked boys, some, like the loose one, taken in a garden, some in the bath and shower, others on beds or couches. Sounds of feet on the stairs made her shut the file quickly and move away.

Simon disarmed her by coming through the door smiling, his arms held out for her.

'Come and give me a kiss! I'm sorry I wasn't more welcoming, but I had a lot on my mind.'

He looked like her Simon again, his eyes warm. But she was still smarting from the embarrassing rebuff.

'Where's that lady gone?' Tara asked cautiously.

'Home. That's Alice Kennedy, who runs my agency. I had a chat with her, explained the circumstances and she's gone now.'

'Agency?' She didn't remember him mentioning a business.

'Child actors.' He frowned, waving his hand as if that wasn't important. 'Quentin downstairs works for me, too. I hope he wasn't rude to you, he can be a bit hostile when he feels threatened.'

'Threatened?' She knew she sounded like a parrot, but she was so confused.

'He's nervous of girls, especially ones as pretty as you. He thinks he might lose his job.'

It only took a few kisses, a cup of tea and a beef sandwich for Tara to get over her qualms. Simon explained that he ran a theatrical agency, specialising in children. Alice Kennedy worked from here, and this flat was owned by another partner. He said he'd recently moved out of one flat, which was why he'd taken a break in Somerset. Since then, because he hadn't managed to find a permanent home, he was sleeping here.

'Does that explain why you can't stay with me?' he asked. 'You see, I'm responsible for many children. If the parents of one of them should see me with you, they just might think the worst. You do understand?'

He still wasn't quite as he had been in Somerset. Perhaps it was because she'd caught him unexpectedly. Or was it because she looked untidy and grubby? Too young, too country-girlish?

'But I'm not a child. I'm sixteen,' she said indignantly.

'That's a child to people with dirty minds,' he insisted. 'I have to be above reproach, you see.'

He suggested taking her tomorrow to a house he knew in Highgate, where there were lots of girls her age. He also suggested she slept in a spare room downstairs next to Quentin's.

'I want you in my bed really,' he said, stroking her breasts. 'But getting carried away now could wreck everything.'

As sad as she was, Tara saw the sense in everything he said. He talked about taking her away for a weekend somewhere, loving her where no-one knew them, and what fun it would be to keep it secret.

'I bet I can get you some modelling work,' he added. 'In no time you'll be able to afford to rent somewhere really smart, but just for tonight it's the room downstairs.'

It was a tiny room, nothing but a single bed, a chest of drawers and a wardrobe, but Tara was so exhausted by the day's events she dropped off to sleep immediately.

For a second when she woke she didn't know where she was, but then the sounds of London reassured her. It was all so familiar, the sounds she had heard every day until she was twelve – the distant hum of traffic, the rattle of the milk-float, faint BBC voices reading the news in one direction, music coming from another.

This was what she wanted! Not meadows, cows and old Betsy. She was sixteen, she wanted to have fun, be outrageous. She could stay in Somerset till she was ninety and never see half of what she'd see here in a week.

Her excitement grew as she considered the day ahead. She'd read about all the boutiques springing up; she would find them, see if any of them wanted an assistant who could sew and design as well as serve people. Simon would be impressed if she found work immediately.

She showered in a tiny bathroom she found opposite her bedroom and put on an apple green dress with a long droopy collar, the only thing in her bag suitable for job-hunting. She brushed her hair, put it up in a French pleat because it made her look older, then did her make-up.

Her dress needed ironing! However much she tried to smooth out the wrinkles, it looked bad. Her plan had been to slip out unseen leaving a note for Simon explaining what she was doing and that she'd be back by five in the afternoon. That way she hoped he'd be so touched by her adult independence he'd think twice about taking her over to Highgate. But she couldn't go out with such a screwed-up dress.

Hearing the radio coming from Simon's flat was a good sign, at least it meant he was awake. She knocked on the door. No voice came from within, no sound of feet, so she tried the door-handle and to her surprise it turned.

'Simon!' she called timidly, peeping round the door.

The bed under the window was empty, its crumpled covers thrown back, and she could hear the sound of the shower coming from her left along with the music. Tara giggled as she went in. Elvis Presley was belting out 'Teddy Bear' and she had a mental picture of Simon acting out the role in the shower.

She hesitated at the bathroom door. It was open slightly and steam belched out through the crack. Back in the cottage in Stanton Drew they had had some wonderful moments under the shower and she wondered if she could join him. Anticipating him pulling her into the shower with him, she slipped out of her dress and underwear and tip-toed to the bathroom.

The record changed to Cilla Black's 'Anyone who

had a heart'. Tara bit her lips so she wouldn't giggle. She pushed open the door, slid her hand round to reach the shower curtain, then with one swift movement pulled back the curtain.

But Simon wasn't alone under the jet of water. Quentin was with him.

Tara gasped in horror. Even though the two men jumped apart when they heard her, their erections made it obvious what they had been doing.

For a second Tara froze. She was aware of Quentin's long, thin, purple-tipped penis, a red handprint across his buttocks as he tried to shield himself from her stare. Simon's mouth hung open and clearly the shock was enough for him to lose his excitement as his cock shrivelled before her eyes.

The pictures of the naked boys, the meaning of what she had stumbled on and her own nakedness made her back away in horror, covering her body.

'How could you?' she said weakly, her voice cracking.

'It was all right when he was screwing you, then?' Quentin's shrill voice was loaded with spite.

There was a roaring sound in her ears, her eyes were blinded by tears, yet somehow she managed to grab her clothes and rucksack. She ran down the stairs, pulling them on as she went.

As she reached the hall, a young woman opened the front door with a key and it was clear she lived on the ground floor.

'Do you know what goes on up there?' Tara sobbed out, nodding back up the stairs as she struggled to zip up her dress. 'Do you know what perverts they are?'

The girl shrugged her shoulders, looking nervous, as if Tara was an escaped lunatic.

'They're queer! You should call the police, they need locking up!'

'Queer'! The word kept going round in her head like

276

some kind of crazy password as she ran full-tilt down Goldhawk Road towards the Tube.

People were milling down the road yet she barely noticed their curious glances.

How could Simon be that way? How could a man who seemed to worship the female body, who had loved to look at her nakedness, possibly make love to another man?

As she ran blindly up the steep steps to the Metropolitan line, Tara knew she needed help. She had felt this way before, when Paul was killed; the same terrible trembling, the need to be held and comforted by someone. Yet who was there?

When a child dies the whole world sympathises, but how could she expect anyone to understand what it felt like to discover not only that your lover was unfaithful, but that it was with a man.

Once on the platform, she realised she didn't even know where this line went, she hadn't even bought a ticket. She sank down on to a bench and sobbed, barely seeing the dozens of people around her.

A dirty feeling crept over her skin, nausea gripped her stomach. If she closed her eyes she saw the two men in the shower. But as disgusting as that image was, there was another far worse. Those boys in that album! Who were they? Why did Simon keep pictures like that? Every mother has pictures of her own naked children, but a businessman keeping them in a file?

She had to tell someone. But who?

She couldn't tell Gran or Mum. Not anyone back in Somerset. That left only Uncle George and Harry. Not George. Fresh tears broke out as she imagined the distress on his big florid face.

Harry!

It was the people going to work who brought her to her senses. Office girls in high heels and summer dresses looked at her curiously. Older women studied her as if any moment they might address her. She got up and walked further along the platform, wiping her eyes, and struggled to control herself.

The years fell away as she walked out of Whitechapel station into the sunshine. The noise was the same, the ceaseless hubbub of people shouting, buses and lorries whizzing past, children clamouring for attention as their mothers dragged them along to the market.

A group of boys stood on the corner, just as they always did. They had been Teddy boys then, with greasy quiffs, bumper-soled shoes and drape jackets. Today's boys were mods, sporting short college-boy haircuts and mohair suits. A couple of Lambrettas were parked close by.

George was on his stall. He was hidden by the crowd yet she could hear his voice. Queenie was with him; Tara caught a glimpse of platinum-blonde curls and that infectious laugh.

She crossed to the other side of the wide road, melting into the crowd. It wouldn't do for George to spot her now. Harry wasn't with them, so he was probably in Tod's Gym, just a few doors down from the flat where she used to live.

Things had changed. There were far more black people, and Indians, too. What had once been the eel and pie shop was now selling fabric for saris and the dilapidated Pavilion Theatre on the corner of Valance Road had finally been pulled down.

Sid's fish and chip shop was now called The Swinging Plaice. Inside it was tiled floor to ceiling, with new fryers right at the back and tables and chairs installed to seat perhaps forty customers.

The door which had once led to her home had been replaced. It was painted bright red, with half glass and even one of those posh entryphone grilles. Tara hesitated outside. Did it still stink? Had the new people installed a bathroom and put carpet on the stairs?

Tod's Gym had seen no such refurbishment; if any-thing it looked even more seedy. The door was propped open and the narrow, steep staircase straight in front of it obviously rarely saw a broom, much less a wash.

A man in a grey singlet and shorts was coming down the stairs. He looked like a boxer out for a run, muscu-lar, snub-nosed and vicious. But he smiled warmly at her, pale brown eyes flicking over her face and body.

'Looking for somebody?' he asked.

'Is Harry Collins in there?' She blushed under the man's scrutiny, terribly aware of her crushed dress.

'Yeah, he is. Go on up.'

She hesitated, frightened of entering such a male preserve.

'Go on, love,' He smiled, inclining his head towards the stairs. 'I could stand you interrupting my training.'

Tara took a deep breath and made her way up the wooden stairs. She could hear thumping sounds, grunting and a man shouting what sounded very much like abuse.

The gym was far larger than she'd expected, clearly it covered more than just the one shop. Strange-look-ing equipment covered the floor area to her right, on her left a group of men were lifting weights and in front of her was a raised boxing ring. A man lay on his back quite close to her, pushing his feet against a steel platform which rose and fell with his grunting efforts. He turned his head slightly, sweat streaming down his cheeks.

'What'cha want, darlin'?'

'I'm looking for Harry Collins,' she said.

'Over the back.' He thumbed towards the boxing ring.

She picked her way past men straining under weights, doing press-ups and sit-ups. The smell of sweat made her gag and she was aware that everyone was looking at her.

Harry was practising on a punchbag, head hunched forward, fists shooting out alternately, whacking the bag as if he hated it.

'Harry,' she said hesitantly.

He glanced round while still thumping away, but stopped the moment he saw her.

'Tara!'

He didn't look as handsome as she remembered, but twice as powerful. His bare chest glistened with sweat, his dark hair practically stuck to his head; even the grey shorts he wore had huge damp patches on them which made her feel faintly embarrassed.

'Sweetheart!' He came towards her, arms out-stretched, but stopped a foot from her, looking at his boxing gloves.

'I can't hug you,' he grinned. 'Not like this!'

Tara smiled weakly, clutching the strap of her ruck-sack, hopping from one foot to the other.

'Can I talk to you somewhere? Something awful's happened and I don't know what to do.'

Harry looked over his shoulder, whether it was to see a clock, check up on someone else, or just see who was watching she couldn't guess.

'Yeah, of course, sweetheart. Give me ten minutes to take a shower. Go along to the stall.'

'No.' She shook her head furiously. 'I don't want to see Uncle George. I'll wait in a café or somewhere.'

Harry frowned, his deep blue eyes almost black.

'OK.' He looked round again. 'The Black and White, it's about two hundred yards that way.' He pointed down towards Stepney.

'Black and White,' she repeated, backing away. 'Sorry to disturb you.'

'I'll be as quick as I can.' He made towards a chang-ing-room door. 'Ten minutes!'

280

When she was small the shops along Mile End Road had always seemed wonderful. But now she saw the unpainted fronts and dirty windows, and blushed at some of the goods on display. The lingerie shop with its collection of red and black scanties, the Durex sign in the barber's. Even the newspaper shop displayed far more pin-up magazines than ones with knitting patterns. Had the whole world gone crazy about sex or was it just that she hadn't noticed before?

Harry took her up to a booth right at the back of the café and sat down opposite her.

He smelled of soap and his hair was still wet, slicked back, black as a raven's wing. She was beyond admiring any man for now, but even so his sheer animal magnetism was hard to ignore.

'Come on, then. Out with it!' His voice was soft, yet there was an edge to it which demanded she tell the whole truth. His angular face had filled out and matured since she last saw him.

'Oh, Harry.' She hung her head. 'You see, I met this man and . . .'

Harry listened without interrupting. Somehow he ordered two teas, and sausage, eggs and chips, and put hers in front of her without disturbing the flow.

'He's queer,' she ended up saying. 'Queer!'

Harry took her hand across the table and squeezed it. He knew she hadn't told him the whole story. She spoke of 'having coffee' back at his cottage as if it had been an innocent romance with a boy her own age, but her comprehension of what the two men had been doing proved to Harry her relationship had been a sexual one.

'You've been a right silly mare.'

Tara's eyes shot wide open at his harsh tone.

'I thought I'd get some sympathy from you,' she stammered.

'Did you now?' Harry frowned, and held her hand

even tighter. 'Well, in my opinion you're lucky that you just *saw* something nasty. What were you thinking of having a scene with a man of his age? Can you imagine how your mum felt when she discovered you'd run off?'

'She's been in touch?'

Tara's heart sank. She hadn't given her mother any thought, but of course Amy would have phoned George immediately. And Harry had sat there just listening, without mentioning he already knew she'd run away.

'She was on the dog the moment she found you missing,' Harry said. 'Unfortunately Mabel couldn't remember the address on the bloke's letters, otherwise me and Dad would've been straight round there last night.'

'You don't understand.' Tears crept down her cheeks. 'I fell in love with him, Harry. I thought he was wonderful and I would have told Mum soon. But Gran spoiled everything, she had to go snooping and I panicked. None of it was planned or anything.'

Harry saw the desolation in her eyes, guessed at the pain inside her.

'Are you up the spout? When was your last period?'

Tara turned purple with embarrassment.

'It isn't any good shying away from it.' He shrugged his shoulders. 'If you think you're old enough to have sex, Tara, you're old enough to consider the consequences.'

For a moment she was tempted to deny things had gone that far, but she could see in his eyes that he knew.

'I'm not used to men asking such things.'

'It's a man who got you into this, remember? You chose to run to me instead of Queenie, your mum or even my dad. So I reckon that puts me in the position where I have to ask. Come on, stop hedging round the subject.'

'Two weeks ago, since I last slept with Simon, so I'm not pregnant,' she snapped, tossing her head.

'Well, that's a relief.' Harry smiled and patted her hand encouragingly. 'Now first we have to phone yer mum and stop her worrying, then we'll let George know you're safe too.'

'I'm not going home.' Tara reared up in fright.

'We'll talk about that later,' he said.

'My heart's broken,' she whispered. 'You make it sound as if you don't think anything happened to me. I'm hurting.'

Harry gulped. When he heard yesterday she'd run off with a bloke he'd felt murderous; the picture of Tara in his mind had been that of a sweet, innocent young girl. But when she'd walked in the gym, he'd been staggered by her adult beauty, despite the red eyes, mascara on her cheeks and a crumpled dress. He leaned across the table and put his big hands on her arms.

'I know, darlin'. First love is painful and there ain't anything gonna cure it but time. You mustn't dwell on what you saw. And you mustn't start thinking all men are the same. There's dozens of men waiting for you out there. You've got a whole lotta fun to go through before you need to get serious about anyone. One day you'll meet the right man and it'll be magic, you'll see. But until then you have a good time.'

'I want to stay in London, Harry.' She looked at his handsome face and remembered the crush she used to have on him. 'If we tell Mum everything she won't let me. Can't we kind of edit it?'

Harry smiled and shook his head slowly.

'She knows you've had sex with the bloke. That's a big shock for a mother.' He waved a finger reprovingly at her. 'But I don't reckon there's anything to be gained by telling her he liked boys too. You can just say he had another bird.'

'What about those children in his file?' Tara shuddered, hating Simon. 'Do we tell the police?'

'You leave that maggot to me. I'll get him sorted, don't you worry.'

'Will Queenie mind me staying?' Tara meant she was afraid Queenie and George wouldn't like her any more, but the words wouldn't come out.

'Course not, she was expecting you to stay soon anyway.'

He stood up, tucking his cigarette packet into the sleeve of his T-shirt, then winding it up to hold it in place.

'Time to see Dad.' He inclined his head towards the door. 'And phone yer mum!'

'I'm scared, Harry,' she whispered.

He put one arm round her shoulders and led her outside.

'Don't you think your mum and gran remember what it's like to fall in love?'

Tara just looked glum.

'As I recall they both were guilty of running off with the first charmer who crossed their path!' He pulled her to him for a hug, not caring that people were watching. 'You're luckier than them, babe. You've got people around you who care more that you're safe than what you've done. Now switch that lovely big smile on again and put all this down to a spot of experience.'

Chapter 15

Queenie waited until she heard Tara put the phone down before she came back into the sitting room. As she expected, Tara was crying, sitting straight backed, silent tears dripping down her cheeks. She looked the picture of misery.

'That bad?' Her heart went out to Tara, yet at this stage she didn't think it was appropriate to be too sympathetic. She put a cup of tea down on the smoked glass coffee table.

'It was OK.' Tara sniffed loudly and wiped her eyes on the back of her hand. 'But I know Mum. I bet she's crying now too.'

Queenie sat down heavily on the settee and waited a moment before speaking. She'd sent George down to the pub with Harry. They'd done their bit for the day.

It was seven in the evening. Queenie was still in her working clothes, a gaudy red and blue print dress, plump bare arms freckled with the sun, her bouffant hair-style held back with a red band.

'We've all done just what you did,' Queenie said gently. 'Me, your mum and gran, and probably just about every other red-blooded woman in the world. Some strike lucky with the right man, some of us make right Charlies of ourselves. But it ain't gonna do you one bit of good regretting it, it's done. What'cha gotta do now is make sure you're a bit more cautious the next time some Jack the Lad whispers a few sweet words in your lugholes.'

Tara smiled. Queenie tackled everything in the same straightforward, irreverent manner and after the strained voice of her mother and the brusque tones of Gran, it was very comforting.

'I'm so glad you married Uncle George,' Tara blurted out. 'You're so lovely!'

'And so are you, my little love,' Queenie's blue eyes swam with emotion, her double chin wobbling. She would have liked a daughter of her own, but fortune hadn't smiled on her in that direction. 'Now all we've got to do is find you a job, and make them stop worrying back 'ome. The first one's easy, the second may take a little longer.'

Tara felt as if she'd been put through an emotional mangle. It was only twelve hours since she caught Simon in that shower but it seemed more like days. Anger, shame, love and hate were mixed up with a sense of betrayal, but above all else she felt a fool.

'I feel so silly,' she whispered, moving on to the settee beside Queenie. Silly wasn't quite appropriate. A slut, a tart, dirty, were all far more apt, but she couldn't voice those words.

'I expect you do, love.' Queenie put her arm round her. 'I've had more than my share of that, but there ain't no-one in this house is going to throw stones, so drink up your tea, go and have a hot bath and off to bed. Tomorrow everything will look better.'

Tara didn't move from Queenie's arms. They were much too comforting.

Queenie had stamped the house in Paradise Row with her personality and taste since Tara had last been here. Like so many East End women brought up in poverty, Queenie was house-proud. The furry three-piece suite

286

had been replaced by a vivid green Dralon one and George had a reclining chair with a stool coming out from underneath to put his feet on. New Axminster carpet had been fitted, purple with green and white swirls. Heavy velvet curtains with fringed pelmets and a cord to shut them hung at the window, a showy teak wall-unit, fitted with strip lighting, housed her collection of crystal glass. But the thing that amused Tara the most was the bar. George had had one before, but it was small and unobtrusive. This one was stupendous. Kidney-shaped, with an imitation marble top, it took up the entire alcove by the window. The padded, studded white leatherette front had a narrow glass compartment, lit from within, displaying gilt-encrusted glasses never meant to be used. The top of the bar held a gilt Champagne bucket, an ice-bucket like a pineapple and a gilt cocktail shaker. Behind the bar was more of the same. Real optics like a pub, shelves holding rows of liqueurs and a collection of cocktail and Champagne glasses that wouldn't have shamed the Ritz. The whole thing sparkled as if it was polished daily. Tara could imagine that George and Queenie saw it as a toy, to play at having their own pub, something to impress their friends.

'I like the bar,' Tara said.

'Vulgar, ain't it.' Queenie's chest shook with laughter. 'We got to talking on our honeymoon and I confessed I'd always wanted one. George went right out and bought it, bless 'im. I kept tellin' 'im that toffs go in for a little drinks trolley, not bloomin' great things like that. Know what 'e said?'

'No, what?' Tara sat up, knowing whatever it was it would make her laugh.

' 'E said, "We ain't toffs, Queenie, it ain't no fun sticking yer loot in the bank. A bar in yer 'ouse is all about swankin'. Showing you've got plenty of dosh, but you ain't mean neither, 'cos you like folks to share it." '

Tara giggled. She could imagine just how many raucous parties this room had seen, with Queenie in her glittery frocks, festooned with jewellery, George in his embroidered waistcoat and bow-tie. Their way wouldn't be hers, but she loved them for their generosity and flamboyance.

'Off you go now.' Queenie elbowed Tara. 'You're dead on yer feet and the world will look a bit brighter tomorrow.'

It was only when she was alone in the little room that George had done up for her mother that her mind turned again to Simon. With it came tears. All day hatred had raged inside her, for the humiliation and the pain he'd caused her. But now, in the darkness, she felt empty. Love had made her a whole person for such a short while, and now it was gone.

Tara stood at the crossroads looking over to St John's Church, soaking up the sounds, sights and smells. Queenie was right, the world did look brighter!

She had woken to find Queenie and George long gone to the market and a note telling her to go out and buy herself something snazzy to wear. There was a ten-pound note and a front door key. A postscript said they'd be back around five-thirty.

Her green dress hung over the back of a chair in the kitchen miraculously washed and ironed by Queenie overnight. As she put it on it felt like turning the clock back and starting again.

It was Saturday morning and the whole of London was at her feet, waiting to be discovered.

Traffic roared through the busy crossroads. The streets were busy – women with prams loaded with washing and shopping, smaller children in tow; young girls with headscarves over their rollers; lads lounging outside the Salmon and Ball pub, eyeing up the girls.

There were the usual oddballs, a bearded man with a strange greasy quiff muttering to himself as he paced up and down, an old woman with her world in a wheeled basket and a much younger woman with wild eyes wearing a moth-eaten fur coat, despite the heat, chain-smoking by the public lavatories. Crowds milled up towards Roman Road for the market and old women were feeling the fruit laid out in inviting piles in front of the shops.

It was all so familiar, yet there was a different air to the place now. It was more prosperous, more cosmopolitan, with many black faces amongst the white. Tara had a feeling that this was a good place to be, or was that just because she had ten pounds to spend and six whole weeks stretching ahead of her without seeing one cow, pig or chicken?

Two hours later Tara's delight hadn't faded, but her feet were aching from wearing high heels. She'd inspected Roman Road market, been tempted to spend her money on everything from dress material to shoes and a black velvet jacket. But now she had come back to the crossroads of Cambridge Heath Road and Bethnal Green Road.

She was torn between going home and putting on flat shoes and then catching a Tube to the West End, or having a cup of coffee in the smart new place on the corner of Bethnal Green Road. But going into a coffee bar alone was scary. London girls were sharper, more formidable than the ones at home and she was afraid of being stared at by those Cilla Black look-a-likes with their pale faces and heavily outlined eyes.

'The hippy-hippy shake' was wafting out of the coffee bar's open door and it reminded her of the village dance back home. It was as she hesitated on the kerb, trying to pluck up courage to go in, that she saw the shop.

It stood slightly back from the rest of the rank in Bethnal Green Road, which was why she hadn't seen it before. It was double fronted, painted maroon, with two circles of glass left unpainted, and one outfit displayed in each of them. It had the kind of modern style she associated with *Honey* magazine. There were no old-fashioned dummies, but bentwood hat-stands. The two outfits were 'mod' styles, both in navy and white—calf-length skirts and striped tops, dressed up with berets, beads and wide leather belts. The shop was called 'Josh'.

Forgetting coffee, and even her aching feet, Tara darted across the road through the stream of traffic. The Beatles' 'Please, please me' reached her long before she got to the shop doorway and she paused on the pavement to look through the window.

She had never seen anything like it, not even in Bristol. The dress-shops she used to frequent catered for all ages, with dragon-like salesladies waiting to pounce. This one was exclusively for the under twenty-fives, with not a beady-eyed saleswoman in sight.

It was dark inside, painted the same dark red as outside, with spotlights here and there focused on garments hanging on the walls above the crowded rails. Dozens of girls were milling around, she could hear laughter and chatter above the music, as if they were at a party rather than shopping.

As Tara moved to go in, something caught her eye. There was a small notice stuck to the window – 'Junior salesgirl required, apply within'.

It was there for her. She knew it. Fate had drawn her to this shop because it was right. If she hesitated she might never pluck up courage.

Once inside the music was so loud she could scarcely think, but she took in everything at a single glance. In the centre was a raised counter; behind it stood a man with black curly hair operating the till and a busty blonde folding garments and putting them in bags.

Instinct told her he was the owner. His dark eyes watched everything at once and she knew he had noticed her the moment she stepped through the door. Taking a deep breath, she walked up to the counter and smiled.

'Hullo. I'm Tara Manning. I've come for the job!'

He didn't reply immediately, just looked her up and down. She guessed he was Jewish by his olive skin and prominent nose, he looked no more than thirty.

'How old are you?' He carried on ringing up a garment.

'Sixteen.'

'Where are you working now?'

'I'm not. I've just left school.'

He was almost handsome, with soulful dark eyes. It was a good-natured face, she decided, and he was dressed impeccably in light grey slacks and a pale blue buttoned-down shirt, with a heavy gold identity bracelet on one wrist and a sovereign ring on the other hand.

'Take over, Angie,' he said to the blonde girl, stepping down from his platform to come round to her.

He was only a fraction taller than her, carrying a little too much weight, but when she glanced down at his feet she saw his shoes were crocodile.

'That's not a London accent!' he said, and as he smiled his teeth flashed brilliant white. 'The West Country?'

'Somerset,' she said. 'But I'm staying up here with my aunt and uncle.'

'It's too noisy to talk here.' He took her arm and led her towards the door. 'I'd take you out the back but Saturdays are always busy and I have to keep my eyes open. I hope you don't mind talking outside?'

It wasn't that much quieter. A long traffic queue had formed, and the pavement was full of jostling shoppers. The air was thick with petrol fumes, a smell of fried onions wafted from a hamburger stall and it was very hot.

'Tara's a pretty name. What makes you want to work for me?' His voice was attractive. It had just enough of a London accent, but with the edges rubbed off.

'Because I love fashion.' She gave him her most winning smile, tossing back her hair from her shoulders the way she imagined models did. 'And because your shop looks exciting.'

'What's exciting about it?' He put his head on one side and she had a feeling he was trying not to laugh.

'The bustle, the music, the darkness and the clothes. As soon as I saw it I knew it was for me.'

'Did you now?' His eyes travelled down her body. 'Where did you buy that dress?'

She knew he liked it by the inquisitive look in his eyes, and she was flattered that it passed as a professionally made one.

'I didn't buy it. I made it. I make all my clothes.'

He raised one bushy dark eyebrow.

'What patterns do you use? Style? Simplicity?'

'I make my own,' she said. 'I just draw it first, then I make it up.'

'Can I look?' He moved nearer, bending down and lifting the hem just an inch or two to look at the seam. 'Very good!' He smiled up at her. 'You could make more as a machinist in a factory than I could pay you.'

She felt drawn to him, though she didn't know why. His black curly hair looked almost wet it was so shiny and those dark, treacly eyes were very appealing. It was a shame about his big nose and the fleshy lips, they detracted from his good points.

'I don't see myself as a machinist. More a designer.'

It came out without thinking and she blushed at her own arrogance.

He grinned, showing in that one facial movement that he appreciated ambition.

'Well, as a designer, what do you think of my clothes?' Tara knew he was trying to put her down, but as she'd started blowing her own trumpet, she felt she might as well continue.

'The cut and styles are super,' she said, glancing back through the door at two girls holding up skirts. Even at a distance she could see prominent faults, such as an uneven hem and patch-pockets sewn on askew. 'The finish could be better, though.'

She waited, half expecting him to tell her to push off, but instead he laughed.

'Well, Tara, for your honesty I'm going to give you the job. But I'd be grateful if you wouldn't pass on your observations to my customers. In time you'll realise that to produce high fashion at low prices we have to compromise. How does four pounds a week sound?'

Her face lit up, eyes flashing with delight. She had no idea if that was good or bad, but it sounded like a fortune.

'Thank you, that's wonderful.' She beamed. 'I'm sorry, I don't know your name.'

'Joshua Bergman,' he said. 'But everyone calls me Josh. Now, if you come here at nine o'clock sharp on Monday morning, I'll sort you out something to wear. What size are you?'

'Ten.' She was bubbling with excitement now. 'You won't be sorry you took me on.'

Josh let his eyes slide down her. He took in the glorious red-gold hair, the pale gold eyes, the dress and the long, slender legs.

'No, I don't think I will be!'

'Josh Bergman!' Queenie screwed up her face in disapproval.

Forgetting her aching feet, Tara had run almost the whole way to Whitechapel market to tell George and Queenie her news.

'Oh, don't be like that!' Tara pleaded. 'I love his shop. Do you know him, then?'

'Well, only by reputation.' Queenie shrugged her shoulders. 'Now if it was 'is dad you was getting a job with I'd be delighted. He owns Bergman's, a big company that makes quality coats and suits. But Josh is a bit of a wide-boy.'

'He didn't seem like that to me.' Tara pouted. 'Anyway, I thought you'd be thrilled.'

'Well, it's a job.' Queenie's tone changed and she put her hand on Tara's shoulder. 'Come and 'ave a cuppa and tell me all about it.' She looked over her shoulder and beckoned to a thin elderly man sitting on some boxes. 'Hey, Frank, do us a favour and mind the stall for a while?'

They sat on a wooden bench by the tea stall soaking up the hot sunshine.

Aside from George and Queenie, Tara didn't recognise any of the stallholders now. Instead of Mr Reynolds' meat van with its drop-down counter and striped awning, there were a couple of young men selling huge joints from a much bigger truck. She could see many Indians in turbans, but not one of them was Mr Singh, and the old lady selling sweets in paper cones had been replaced by a stall with giant-sized plastic bags already filled and priced.

'Everyone's different,' she said.

Queenie glanced around her, wrinkling her nose disdainfully.

'Mr Reynolds retired,' she said sadly. 'I wouldn't get my meat from those two crooks if they was giving it away.' She nodded towards the two men in the truck who were attracting a large crowd. 'Lots of the others

294

moved down to Roman Road. Old Betty with the sweets died last year. It ain't the same any more luv, too many thugs and nig-nogs.'

It was every bit as colourful as Tara remembered, but with a different, foreign flavour. 'My Boy Lollipop' was belting out from a record stall and a couple of black girls were jigging about in time to it. Indians manned all the fabric stalls, and roll after roll of vivid satins and rayons were piled up with embroidered sari material. A vegetable stall held strange-looking produce she'd never seen before and a black man sat in front of dozens of sacks filled with rice, herbs and pungent-smelling spices.

But there were just as many people as before. Children still clung to overloaded pushchairs and their mothers' legs, and the crowd in front of George's stall was bigger than ever.

He was standing on a box, with Harry passing things up to him. Sun gleamed on his bald patch, the remaining hair snow white and curling up around his ears. In a bright red waistcoat and bow-tie that matched his face, he was in fine voice.

'Look at the quality of these saucepans. You wouldn't get anything finer in the kitchens of the Savoy. Up West you'd pay thirty quid for this set, but I'm not asking even twenty for them. Not eighteen, not fifteen, not even twelve. First four people to put their hands up get them for ten!'

Tara laughed as the notes fluttered in hands.

'Do they really come planning to buy a set of saucepans?' she asked Queenie.

'Doubt it, darlin'.' Queenie's plump face broke into laughter. 'I 'spect they get 'ome and think "What the 'ell did I buy those for?". 'E's a genius at winkling money out of pockets. The Jamaican women love 'im, they buys 'is china like they're planning a street party. Last week 'e 'ad a load of lace tablecloths.

Flogged the lot, 'e did, in about twenty minutes and to fink I said 'e'd never sell one 'cos they was too fancy.'

Tara sipped her tea and looked at Queenie. Her round face didn't show the rigours of time and hard work. Maybe the pink and white skin was only make-up and the blonde hair out of a bottle, but she hardly looked fifty. In a blue and white striped summer dress, with her dark green apron and money bag round her waist, she looked as plump and juicy as the fruit on her stall.

'Come on, then.' Queenie lit a cigarette. 'Tell me about this job.'

Tara poured it all out, pleased to see the older woman seemed to be warming to the idea.

'What's 'e like?' Queenie asked. 'I've met Solly, 'is dad, a couple of times, but I've never set eyes on Josh.'

'A bit flashy,' Tara admitted. 'Gold bracelet and stuff. Black curly hair, a big nose and sort of squishy lips. I'm not sure how old he is, though.'

'Same as our 'Arry.' Queenie puffed thoughtfully. 'They used to play together when they was little. 'Course, the Bergmans went up in the world, moved away to Golders Green when they made their pile. But they did live in Cable Street.'

'Really?' Tara was surprised. Cable Street had been notorious when she was little, for its slums, gambling dens and prostitution. 'How old was he then? I can't imagine him anywhere that wasn't posh!'

'He was about seven when they moved out,' Queenie said. 'I 'eard he went to a private school soon after. 'Is dad's still got 'is factory down there. Bought the place cheap, but now he goes there in a flash motor. I was surprised when I 'eard Josh opened up a place round 'ere. I would've expected 'im to go for Chelsea or Kensington.'

'What do you think about the job, then?' Tara held

her breath, knowing that if Queenie wasn't behind her, her mother and Gran wouldn't approve. 'It's perfect for me, it's a shop for young girls. Josh might let me design once I've been there a while. And it's close to home.'

Queenie sighed.

She'd had a hard life. She was married at seventeen, to a man who saw her as nothing more than a warm body in his bed and a willing pack-horse to do all the work for him. Dick came from a long line of coster-mongers, but he had been a lazy boozer with a vile temper. She had never wanted to work on a stall, but the alternative had been starvation. Out in all winds and weathers, the only thing Dick did was buy the produce in the morning, then go off down the pub while she sold it. Time and again she'd been tempted to leave him, but she'd made her vows in church and she couldn't go back on them. Friendships with people like George had sustained her all those years, and she let people think she was happy with Dick because that was the way then.

Dick had died when she was forty, and she had the money then, without Dick drinking it away, to indulge herself with nice clothes, and move into a better flat. Then finally George had turned from a lifelong friend into a sweetheart. Now she had everything any woman could want.

Like George, Amy and Mabel, she wanted more for Tara than they'd all had. A summer job to her meant a West End shop, mixing with girls from good homes, not coming back to a place that held only bitter memories and people who would drag her down. But when she looked at Tara's eyes dancing with excite-ment, she hadn't the heart to pour cold water on her dreams.

'Let's just see this as a temporary thing,' she said cautiously. 'I think you ought to go back to school in

September. And if you must work local you've got to stick to the story.'

George had pointed out the dangers of anyone recognising her as Bill MacDonald's daughter. Although they all agreed Tara had changed so much from the skinny, carrot-haired child she had once been, there was always a danger of slipping up and revealing she'd lived here before.

'I only told Josh I was staying with my aunt and uncle,' Tara whispered, looking round to make sure no-one was listening. 'I won't ever let on about him.'

'Well, leave it to me to talk George round.' Queenie smiled. 'Now off you go and let me get back to the stall.'

'Cor, you don't 'alf look nice,' said Angie, Josh's other assistant, as Tara came out of the changing room on Monday morning. 'I wish I was as tall as you!'

'You're more feminine than me.' Tara smoothed the calf-length skirt down over her hips, turning round to see herself in the mirror. She didn't really like these long tight skirts the mods wore, and she certainly didn't want to turn into a replica of all the other girls in Bethnal Green. They all seemed to be small, with identical backcombed bobbed hair plastered forward on their pale cheeks. But this dark green skirt and the striped green and white top weren't too bad, in fact she thought she looked quite elegant.

Since she'd arrived at nine and been introduced to Angie by Josh, no customers had come in. Josh had instructed them to find a suitable outfit for Tara, then went upstairs to his office.

With a Wilson Pickett record on full blast, both girls were enjoying themselves, pulling out clothes willy-nilly and getting to know each other.

Angie was from South London and she'd come to work for Josh when he first opened the shop because at the time she'd had a boyfriend close by. Since then she'd finished with the boyfriend, but moved into a bedsitter in Stepney. It was clear she had an almighty crush on Josh. She reminded Tara of the girls in the *Carry On* films, wide-eyed and busty. Each time she giggled, her blonde curls shook. Although she was eighteen she looked younger than Tara, though from things she said she was no little Miss Innocent.

Already she'd talked endlessly about 'pulling blokes', her hangover from Saturday night and her anxiety last week because she hadn't come on. Yet when Josh came back to the shop for a few minutes, she was all batting eyelashes, provocative pouts and pretend dumbness.

Tara liked her, though. It was good to have another girl to work with, especially one who made her laugh.

'This is the sort of dress I want to wear,' Angie said, pulling out a slinky black crêpe number. 'But I always meet fellas whose idea of a good time is to drag me down the dog track, or they've got motorbikes. I have to wear jeans all the time, and me bum's too big.'

The shop only got busy at twelve, as girls started to come in during their lunch hour. Tara was amazed at the amount of money girls only a little older than herself had to spend, and at their slavish following of fashion. When she saw short, dumpy girls putting on long pleated skirts, she wanted to lead them to slimmer shapes and encourage them to wear softer colours than the grey, bottle green and black they seemed so struck on, but she hadn't the confidence yet.

Again and again she saw girls turning away because there were no real summer dresses. The sun was blazing outside, they were going away for a holiday at the weekend, but they could find nothing revealing to wear.

'Daft, innit.' Angie giggled as yet another disappointed girl walked out. 'Here we are in a heatwave with only things with long sleeves to sell. I'm going down to Southend on Sunday if it's still nice and I ain't got nothing new to wear either.'

The afternoon was very quiet and, although Josh brought in some new stock for them to price up, there was nothing much to do. Tara sat behind the counter and idly drew a summer dress on a scrap of paper.

'That's nice.' Angie rested her breasts and elbows on the counter to look at what Tara was doing. 'I wish I could draw.'

'Would you wear that on Sunday?' Tara showed her the sketch of a scoop-necked print shift dress, the back cut very low.

'Yeah, I would,' Angie said enthusiastically. 'You can never get dresses like that when you want them, though.'

Tara tucked the sketch away under the counter, her head spinning with an idea.

Josh sat back in his chair and smiled to himself.

He called the room above the shop his office, though in reality it was more of a stockroom. But at his big desk under the window, swivelling in his leatherette chair, with dress-rails behind him, he could imagine he was a tycoon surveying his empire.

His good mood was entirely the result of hiring Tara and, although it was only four in the afternoon of her first day, he knew he'd picked a cracker. He would've taken her on just for the way she said 'I've come for the job'. Josh liked positive people who weren't afraid to be pushy. He was that way himself, and he understood it.

Joshua Bergman hadn't been born with a silver spoon in his mouth, though people tended to forget this. He had been almost eight when they moved to Golders Green and early memories of poverty and hunger were etched on his brain. He could barely recall the expensive private school he went to later, other than having elocution lessons to rid him of his Cockney accent. Yet he could still remember waking in Cable Street to find a rat sitting by his bed, and his mother cooking chicken soup over an open fire.

His father, Solly Bergman, had come to England from Germany in the 1920s with nothing but his tailoring skills and a smattering of English. Until 1939, when he met and married Rachael Steinway, he had resigned himself to poverty, accepting a home in Cable Street as his lot. Rachael, however, was ambitious, and soon after Josh was born in 1942, she persuaded her husband to use his tailoring skills on women's clothes.

Josh had been brought up on the story of the elegant royal blue costume Solly made for Rachael and how she toured the West End shops in it until someone gave her an order. That first small order was the start of Bergman's. By the time the War ended Solly had a small workroom with two machinists, but his home was still the single squalid room Josh was born in.

'Build up the business before you spend any money' was his father's motto, and he stuck to it in those post-war years as his business flourished. Josh had patches in the seats of his pants, his mother cooked on an open fire, and every penny went into bigger and bigger workshops.

The end of 1949 was when everything changed. Rachael put her foot down and insisted on a decent home, and Solly reluctantly bought a small house. The first one was in Stoke Newington, but later they moved on to Golders Green.

Josh had a great deal of respect for Solly's business acumen, but his father's way was too slow for him. He intended to be a millionaire by the time he was thirty and have a good time while he was getting there. Art college, then an extensive business course gave him all the knowledge he needed. A little wheeling and dealing in bankrupt stock gave him enough capital to start and, when the shop in Bethnal Green came on the market at a low rent, he took the plunge.

He didn't need to know every step that went into the making of a garment, the East End was full of little sweat-shops. All it took was a few sketches of clothes he'd seen in magazines, and picking up fabric at the right price. His father's name, and his degree in art, persuaded people the clothes he produced were his own designs, and he kept the truth under his hat. Josh was nobody's fool. He knew he couldn't steal other people's ideas forever. If someone tumbled he'd lose all credibility. But good designers cost money, they wanted their name on the labels; furthermore they balked at making cheap clothes.

He wasn't going to bank on anything with Tara. She might turn out to be as full of bullshit as himself. But, all the same, he had a good feeling about her. She had a discerning eye. He noticed the way she skimmed through the rails, really looking at the clothes. She'd winced at several garments, and he was tempted right then to ask what was wrong with them.

A consumer boom had started. All the post-war babies brought up on free orange juice and the welfare state wanted to live now. There was work for everyone, fat pay packets waiting to be spent, and Joshua Bergman was determined that he was going to get a big slice of the pie.

'Did I do all right?' Tara lingered by the counter as Josh cashed up the till. Angie had already shot off home and the shop door was closed.

Josh looked at the takings and smiled. Considering the heatwave he hadn't expected as much and he had a feeling that Tara dancing attendance on the few customers had helped.

'You did well,' he said, shoving the notes into a bag. 'I think you were born to it.'

Tara fidgeted nervously. Josh seemed easy to work for, and he clearly liked people who used their initiative, but he was still the boss. He was hard to read. Although his dark brown eyes seemed soft and gentle, his manner suggested he could be ruthless.

'We lost a lot of sales because we haven't got any summery dresses,' she said tentatively. 'People kept asking for sleeveless things and there's only those left.' She pointed to a rail of ugly eau de nil frocks with full skirts.

'That's always a problem at this time of year.' Josh sighed. 'If only we could predict the weather! It's too late now to get some new designs and patterns made.'

Tara took a deep breath and pulled her sketch out of her pocket.

'I could make a pattern for this.' She put it on the counter cautiously. 'There are three bolts of lovely print out the back. I could even make up a sample for you tonight, if you liked it.'

Josh looked at the sketch and his pulse quickened. The dress was simple, but it was classy. He hadn't even considered that fabric out the back and she was quite right, it would be perfect. Under the pretence of considering it, he studied Tara. She had moved away from the counter and was straightening a rack of skirts, obviously afraid she had overstepped the mark. A spotlight caught her gold hair and profile. The curve of her cheeks, her long neck and determined chin were achingly beautiful. She looked so vulnerable.

'I'll give it a try.' He shrugged his shoulders in an effort to look unconvinced. 'Take a length of fabric home and if it works you can keep the sample.'

'You mean you'll get my pattern made up and sell

them?' Tara spun round to face him, eyes flashing with pleasure.

'Only if it's right.' Josh had to bite his lower lip to keep from laughing. 'A sketch doesn't always work out. Let's just say we'll see!'

Tara wolfed down her tea and between mouthfuls told George and Queenie all about her day.

'I didn't expect him to agree,' she said rapturously. 'Just think, if he likes it I could be in business.'

'You'd better use the dining-room table.' George smiled at her excitement. 'But don't get carried away, love, be prepared for disappointment.'

At nine o'clock Tara heard Harry at the front door. He went into the lounge with Queenie and George and a rumble of laughter and chinking of glasses suggested they were all having a drink. She was too engrossed in her work to go and say hello.

Queenie's sewing machine was a hand one, but far more modern than her Gran's treadle. It sat on a small table under the long narrow window that looked out on to the side of the kitchen and the back yard. The high wall up to the railway blocked out a great deal of light, but Queenie had made George paint the walls white and she'd planted a creeper up the railway wall, so it wasn't half as gloomy as it used to be.

The dress was cut in six panels, but it had no collar or sleeves and already she was at the pressing stage, with only the edges of the facing and the hem to finish off. Her face was flushed with the heat but she glowed with pleasure.

'What's this, a sweat-shop?' Harry came in just as she took it off the ironing board. He had clearly dropped in on his way to a club and he wore a sharp navy suit with a red handkerchief peeping out of the breast pocket. She wasn't sure she liked him looking like a spiv, with every hair in place and reeking of expensive aftershave – the Harry in jeans down at the farm had been much more approachable.

He sat astride one of the dining chairs, leaning his arms on its back, taking in the brown paper pattern and the floor covered with off-cuts of bright fabric.

'I'm making a sample for Josh,' she said. 'What do you think?' She held the dress up against her.

George had already told him the story, but Harry smiled at her expression. Ecstatic was the only word that sprang to mind. She had bits of cotton all over her jeans and T-shirt, her hair shoved back behind her ears, and she looked adorable.

'It's brilliant.' He grinned. 'At least, as far as I can tell with you just holding it. I dare say it fits as well as everything you make.'

'I love it at the shop.' She sat down at the sewing machine again, but turned her head towards him. 'It's just perfect.'

'What are you going to get out of making this sample?' Harry asked.

'I'll keep it.' She bent her head over the machine and turned the handle.

Harry looked at Tara's back and frowned. Her hair had parted to reveal her neck, her small shoulder blades stood out through her thin T-shirt, and all at once he felt fiercely protective.

Something had happened to his feelings about Tara since she had arrived last Friday. It wasn't a purely brotherly thing any more; he kept looking at her shape, her face and wanting to stroke her hair.

The feeling was so strong he hadn't even trusted himself to do Wainwright over personally, he'd sent some of the lads instead. If he'd been there it might not have stopped at a good kicking. Thank heavens he had a pad of his own now. If he kept bumping into Tara in her nightie there was no telling what would happen!

'If 'e gets it made up and starts selling them you must keep a tally of them,' he said brusquely.

Tara stopped machining and turned round in her seat. She didn't like his tone, it sounded disapproving, and he was scowling.

'Don't be a wet blanket. It's a start for me. I might get to be his designer.'

Harry checked himself. He could drop in on Josh and make sure he didn't take advantage. He didn't want to dampen her enthusiasm.

'Yeah, of course you might. I only meant that if it takes off you need some figures and stuff to bargain with. That's a lot of work for someone who's been in a shop all day.'

'I don't mind.' She bent back over her work. 'Anyway, it doesn't seem like a real job. I love it, and the other girl Angie is nice.'

'You 'aven't told them you used to live round 'ere?'

Tara shook her head.

'Keep it that way, darlin',' he said softly. 'And don't go mentioning me to Josh Bergman neither, not yet.'

Once again Tara broke off and turned, puzzled by that last sentence.

'Why? I thought you were old friends?'

Harry shrugged his shoulders. 'It might prejudice 'im. I mean, I ain't no angel, darlin'. People with shops get a bit edgy when one of their girls knows "a face".'

Tara felt uneasy. She knew he meant that if the shop got broken into he might be suspected. But only a guilty person would think that way!

'OK.' She didn't feel she could question him. 'Just until I've settled down. But I can't keep it a secret forever, Harry. I'm too proud of you for that. Besides, Angie would go weak at the knees if she saw you.'

Chapter 16

Harry climbed over the high wire fence like a monkey, dropped silently to the concrete below, and ran to the shelter of the warehouse.

It was a wild night. Not just rain but a deluge, driven sideways by strong wind. But the unexpected foul weather pleased Harry. It meant less chance of nosy-parkers showing up, and footprints and tyre marks would be eliminated. He pulled the hood of his black oilskin coat over his head, wiped the worst of the rain off his face with one gloved hand and looked around.

The warehouse had been built as a store during the War, a single-storey brick building with a corrugated iron roof. Further down the road leading to Tilbury a new industrial estate was being built, but this place was surrounded by scrubby Essex marshland.

In the far distance he could see a row of lights leading towards the docks, but here there was only inky darkness. The rain obscured everything, even the black dress van they'd stolen earlier this evening in Gray's Thurrock. Harry smiled to himself, imagining Needles peering anxiously out into the darkness, waiting for the signal.

The big double gates were only more wire mesh over an iron frame, the gate-man's tiny hut next to them was in darkness. It looked like a prison camp, but without the arc-lights and sentries, and the only sound was the

307

rain beating down on the iron roof and gushing from an overloaded gutter.

Harry made a reconnoitre. Stealthily, he climbed up on to a raised wooden loading bay and peered into two dirty barred windows. There were no lights here either, and he smiled with satisfaction. Jumping down from the platform he skirted right round the building. At the back a small brick office had been added in recent times. By standing on tip-toe he could just make out a typewriter on a desk, a couple of filing cabinets and a Xerox copying machine. Further round the building the concrete gave way to rough grass and mud. Another window here was barred, but then as he came back on to concrete he saw a narrow door.

Harry took out his torch, shielding the glow with his hand as he examined the lock. Just an ordinary Yale type, and even if it was bolted on the other side, the door was little more than strengthened hardboard. No dogs, no nightwatchman! This would be a cinch.

Making his way back to his point of entry, Harry flashed his torch twice as a signal, then moved back under the shelter of the warehouse wall.

'What sort of mug leaves a load of leather coats in the middle of nowhere, with no security?' he whispered to himself.

It was a bird called Janet who had inadvertently put him on to it. Just a girl he met from South Ockenden who he'd taken out a few times. One Sunday she had to work overtime and she asked him to pick her up here in the evening instead of at her office in Tilbury. After a few drinks she'd revealed it was a holding place for goods about to be shipped overseas. She'd been doing the paperwork for engine parts, but all kinds of different goods got stored here.

It didn't take Harry long to discover what went in and out. A couple of days of watching revealed goods as diverse as food stuff and refrigerators, and at six every night the staff locked the doors and went home. There wasn't even an alarm system.

He hadn't seen Janet for months now and, though he'd been thinking about robbing the place for some time, he might never have done it. But early this morning he'd been in Tilbury picking up a shipment of china and drove out here again on impulse. His eyes nearly popped out of his head when he saw rail after rail of leather coats being unloaded. Food and household goods were notoriously hard to get shot off, but leather coats were a different ball-game – high value, easy to lift and store, and he had contacts up and down the country who would pay cash on the nail for them.

Needles, Tony and Eric, his old childhood mates, were the obvious men to come in on it with him. Every one of them could be trusted implicitly, none of them had a criminal record. But, though Needles and Tony were only too anxious to join him, Eric, who was the demon driver and brilliant at nicking cars, couldn't make it. It was Eric who'd suggested Ginger.

Harry could see Needles and Tony running towards the gate, Needles' huge gorilla shape a few paces behind the smaller, more athletic Tony. Both wore the same oilskin coats as himself, and Needles carried a pair of bolt-cutters. He ran to the gate to meet them.

'It's a doddle,' he said through the mesh. 'Come on, Needles, do yer stuff.'

His real name was Albert, but they'd christened him Needles when they were seven, after he picked up a hedgehog to stroke it in Epping Forest. Now they told other people it was because he was sharp, but sometimes when they were alone they still teased him. His huge lumbering body, great physical strength and adenoidal voice suggested an empty-headed, hard man, while his black curly hair, bright shoe-button eyes, florid complexion and penchant for flashy clothes were hallmarks of a bully boy. In reality he was a warm-hearted family man with two small children and a dainty wife who adored him. Harry had never heard him raise his voice, let alone his fists, in anger. Although he worked the West End clubs as a bouncer, he used his gentle charm, not his size or strength.

'Just 'old the chain tight, Tone,' Needles said, brandishing the bolt-cutters. 'Wot a poxy little chain. I could bite that off wiv me teeth.'

'Save them for a steak tomorrow.' Tony grinned as the chain snapped like a piece of plastic. 'Which way in, 'Arry?'

'Round the back.' Harry opened the gates wide and signalled with his torch for Ginger to drive in. 'Ow's Ginge doing? It seemed like 'is bottle was going!'

Ginger was the only fly in the ointment. Harry was prejudiced against men with red hair for a start, especially when they had white eyelashes. Not that there was really anything to dislike about Ginge, he always stood his round down the Blind Beggar. But he did tend to brag – whatever you'd done, he could top it.

He'd spotted the right kind of van straight off, was into it like a ferret and had it hot wired before they could even draw breath. But Harry didn't like the way he chain-smoked, or the shaking of his hands.

' 'Ard to say if he's losing it.' Tony glanced round at the van moving towards them. ' 'E don't say much. But this is a straightforward blag, 'e should be OK.'

Tony's mother was Italian and he had inherited her velvet dark eyes and olive skin, with his father's thin foxy face and wiry body. Boxing was his sport, so far only amateur, but he hoped to turn professional soon.

Needles stayed to close the gates after Ginger drove in while Harry led the way round to the back of the warehouse.

'Know what this reminds me of?' Tony said as they stopped at the door.

'Canvey Island?' Harry smiled.

'Yeah, right.' Tony chuckled. 'We was right little sods, getting in all them caravans. Remember that night we stayed down there and that bloke caught us?'

Tony pulled a jemmy out of his pocket and with one quick flick he had the door open.

'I wet me pants,' Needles said behind them.

These childhood memories had forged links of steel between them. Girls came and went, even Needles getting married hadn't loosened the bond. They understood one another. They were brothers.

'Don't wet them tonight, or else you can walk 'ome,' Harry said over his shoulder as they walked in.

'Leave it out!' Needles gave a low rumbling laugh. 'I'm more likely to shit meself these days.'

The rich, warm smell of leather almost knocked them back.

' 'Struth!' Tony exclaimed as he flashed his torch around. 'There's bloody millions in 'ere!'

Inside, the warehouse looked as big as an aircraft hangar, the torch revealing only small sections at a time. Rail after rail was crammed with coats. They couldn't see well enough to make out the styles or colours, but the feel of them was to know they were quality.

'Fuckin' 'ell,' Ginger gasped behind them. 'We'll never get this lot in the van.'

'Wheel 'em down to the door,' Harry instructed. 'Ginge, you get in the van and we can toss 'em up to you. Hurry now, just 'cos there ain't no guard don't mean the police won't come and check the place over. If it comes on top of us, leg it over the fence and we'll all meet up back at my van.'

Needles and Tony stood by the door tossing the heavy piles effortlessly into the van, as Ginger stacked them. Harry went back and forward, returning rails and bringing new ones. They were silent now, each working flat out, the only sounds the slap of leather on leather, grunts of exertion and the constant drumming of rain on the roof.

'That's enough,' Harry said when he saw the van was piled high with just a small space at the back. 'Needles, Tony, get in there. It's less 'suss at this time of night with only two up front.'

'This beats chucking out drunks,' Needles chuckled as he clambered in.

'I ain't even 'ad the collywobbles.' Tony got in beside Needles. 'Remember not to drive like a loony, Ginge, I don't wanna be the first man to drown in leather.'

It was only then that Harry took a look at Ginger. He was shivering violently, though it wasn't cold. Even in the dark, Harry could see he was white as a sheet.

'I'd better drive,' Harry said as he locked the back doors and pulled the warehouse door closed behind them.

Harry knew Needles and Tony inside out, and he could predict their reactions to almost anything. Ginger, however, was an unknown quantity. Nervous men were dangerous.

'No, that's my job,' Ginger said quickly. 'I'm all right, 'Arry. Just a bit cold.'

'OK then.' Harry didn't want to shame the man. 'But drive carefully. We don't want to draw attention to ourselves.'

As they steamed up along the side of the warehouse and turned the corner, to Harry's horror he saw a man bent over by the gates, looking at the broken lock.

'Shit,' he muttered.

'What do I do?' Ginger bleated, the van swerving to one side.

Harry took it all in at a glance. A Ford Popular was parked up beyond the gates. This man was clearly a nightwatchman, but he'd gone home instead of staying here as he was supposed to. By his stooped shoulders he looked elderly and maybe they could come to an amicable agreement with him.

'Keep driving,' Harry said. 'I'll jump out, push the bloke away and open the gates. Drive straight through. I'll leg it after you.'

It was an old man; Harry could tell by his slow reactions. He stood up slowly, holding his back, and stared at the van, his face white and featureless in the headlights.

Harry leaped out of the side door and ran towards the gate. Close up he saw the man was in his sixties, tubby and paralysed with fright. His hands were clinging to the mesh of the gate, his mouth open in horror.

'It's OK, we ain't gonna hurt you,' Harry shouted. 'I'm just going to open the gates and let the van out.'

'The police are on their way.' The old man's voice was croaky. 'Don't do this, son!'

In that moment Harry guessed he was ex-service, had probably been tough in his time given the bluff about the police coming. If he had phoned from that box he would be on their side of the fence now.

Harry wrenched the gates back from him and they swung easily in the wind, but still the man stood in the path of the van.

'Look, I'll lock you in that hut,' Harry said frantically, not wanting to manhandle him. 'You can make out we shoved you in there when we arrived.'

The van revved up behind him and startled him for a second. He jumped back, pushing the old man slightly to one side, and turned angrily towards Ginger, intending to warn him not to run the old chap down. In that split-second the van lurched forward between them. Harry was blinded by the headlights, then a shot rang out.

The van was between him and the man, and the speed at which Ginger drove didn't give Harry time to think. He sprinted along beside it and leaped in the open door.

' 'Struth, the old bugger was armed. Put your foot down before he fires again.'

As the doors slammed shut, the engine revved and Needles and Tony yelled from the back wanting to know what had happened, Harry could hear and see nothing outside. They were six or seven hundred yards down the road before he realised the smell of cordite was inside the van. His head jerked round towards Ginger and he saw an old service revolver still in his hand while he struggled to steer.

'You shot him?' Harry gasped, so thunderstruck he could hardly get the words out.

Everything seemed out of control – the wipers weren't clearing the rain properly, the van was lurching on and off the grass. Even Harry's brain seemed to have seized up.

'What's goin' on?' Needles bellowed from the back. 'Are you hurt, 'Arry?'

It was like a nightmare, one of those when he found himself walking down the High Street with no trousers on. Only it was real. Ginger's thin white face was smirking and there actually was a gun in his hand.

'You slag! You shot that old geezer! What on earth for, you shit-bag? He wouldn't hurt a fly!'

'He was going to stop us.' Ginger's mouth was quivering, the van was veering all over the road.

'All you had to do was push 'im away. What 'ave you got a gun for, anyway?'

They were coming into the industrial estate and, although it was after one in the morning, one factory was ablaze with lights and men were loading a lorry.

Harry tried to think. 'Did you hit 'im?' he asked.

'I might 'ave winged 'im.' Ginger was shaking now, and the van was going right up on the kerb.

'Pull up,' Harry ordered. 'I'll drive while I think about this.'

He was out of the van before it had even stopped

314

completely and round to Ginger's side, dragging him out by the lapels of his raincoat.

'You bastard.' He wanted to pummel that white face into a pulp. 'D'you know what they give yer for armed robbery? He was a brave old man. He probably only went home for a cup of tea and some sandwiches. Now you've hurt 'im and 'e might lose 'is job. Suppose he ain't got a phone in that little hut of 'is?'

Harry threw Ginger against the side of the van and punched him in the stomach. Ginger doubled up and vomited in the road. Harry's blood was up now. He caught hold of Ginger's shoulder with his left hand, about to drive his right into the shivering man's face.

'Harry!' Needles' voice came from the back of the van. 'Will you tell us what's going on or 'ave I gotta break out of 'ere to find out?'

It was the voice of reason. He let go of Ginger, looked down at the vomit, already dispersing in the rain, and glanced up the road at the lit-up warehouse they'd just passed. Aside from that one warehouse, all the others were in darkness, but this sort of place had high security. Even now someone could be watching them.

'Get in, you maggot,' he hissed. 'And don't say a fuckin' word until I ask you to.'

Harry climbed into the driving seat, then turned towards the back. The smell of leather was almost suffocating in the enclosed space.

'Needles, Tony,' he called softly. 'Did you see anything out the back window?'

'No, just 'eard the shot.' Tony's voice was muffled. 'Then Ginge drove off. Who was it? Watchmen don't 'ave guns normally.'

'We can't talk 'ere.' Harry fumbled under the dashboard for the wires to start the van. 'I'll drive to our van, then I'll fill you in. I'm for dumping this lot.'

It took no more than twenty minutes to reach the van. Harry let Needles and Tony out of the confined space and into the back of his van, leaving Ginger to stew in the stolen one while he spelled out what had happened.

'I want to go back,' Harry said, sitting on his haunches. 'That old geezer might have had a heart attack, anything. He might be lying out in the rain.'

'We can't go back,' Tony said quickly, running a hand through his dark hair. 'If he has called the police they'll be there now.'

'We could phone an ambulance,' Needles said. His small eyes glinted in the darkness and he kept cracking the bones in his fingers.

'OK, we'll do that.' Harry felt marginally better. 'I don't want no part in those coats. Let's just lock the van and leave it 'ere.'

It showed the measure of his two friends that there was no argument. Harry had always been their leader and they trusted his judgment.

There was a single light in the car-park and it shone on to Needles' and Tony's faces. Needles' small eyes had all but disappeared in a deep frown, and his usually jovial mouth drooped at the corners. Tony seemed to have shrunk.

'What about that slag?' Tony thumbed towards the stolen van. 'It's all 'is fault. Shall we dump 'im 'ere?'

All three were thinking the same thing. Ginger was boastful, there was a strong chance that by tonight the whole of the East End would be sniggering about this robbery. Ginger might well make out he was the only one who didn't lose his bottle and he'd shot the man so they could get away. Such talk was dangerous; it could get all four of them nicked.

'No.' Harry shook his head. 'We give him a good verbal bashing, promise we'll kick 'is 'ead in if he squeaks. But right now we've gotta get 'elp for the old chap. Please God don't let him be badly hurt!'

Harry was gone less than ten minutes but, when he

316

walked back into the car-park, the stolen van had gone with Ginger in it.

'What 'appened?' He ran over to his van, where Tony and Needles were sitting.

'When we got out the van he must've thought we was goin' to do him over,' Needles said glumly. 'He drove off like the 'ounds of 'ell were after 'im.'

'Fuckin' 'ell,' Harry exploded. 'A bloody loose canon careering around town!'

Harry got in the driving seat and started it up. There weren't many times he wanted to cry, but this was one of them.

' 'E shot the geezer,' Tony said softly. ' 'E's got the coats and the van. It's 'is funeral now, 'Arry. Let's just get 'ome.'

Harry didn't go to bed when he got in. It was almost five in the morning and in an hour he'd be picking George up. The three of them had gone straight to the Regency Club in Dalston in an attempt to create an alibi. To ask anyone to lie for them would be an admission they'd been up to something, but they knew the owner well enough to know that he'd cover for them if necessary.

Harry sat in an armchair, watching the dawn come up. His flat was a small serviced apartment on the third floor, a tiny, functional and austere place which he'd never felt enthusiastic enough about to turn into a home.

He wasn't thinking about himself now, but of the effect this would have on his father. He recalled all the times he'd been warned not to look for easy money, to keep out of fights and not to mix with villains. How could he possibly tell George about this?

With luck he could keep Tony and Needles out of it. Needles had small kids, Tony's dad was out of work and he had to help support the family. The old man had only seen two men; if he could just find Ginge before the police did, then he could mark his card.

Later he scrubbed the bottom of his boots until there was no trace of mud on them, and rolled up the oilskin coat and his gloves to dump them later. But all the time his heart was sinking further. Why on earth had he taken Ginger along? He never played poker with people he didn't know, all his life he'd gone by the code of never taking anyone on trust. Yet now, as the sky gradually lightened, he saw he was to blame entirely.

George once told him that, if a man assumed the role of leader, it was his duty not only to look out for his men, but also to set the ground rules at the outset. Harry had failed on both counts.

The rain had blown itself out as he drove towards Bethnal Green to pick up George. The sun was peeping through the clouds and, when he stopped to buy the morning paper and found nothing in it about the robbery, he thought perhaps the gods had decided to smile on him just this once.

Tara was in the kitchen as he walked in, wearing a frilly pink gingham housecoat. She turned and smiled at him.

'Want a bacon sandwich?' she asked. 'I'm just making one for Uncle George.' She looked as fresh and pretty as the morning.

'Just a cup of tea will do.' He sat down at the table and, without thinking, put his head in his hands.

'What's up?' she asked softly, putting one hand on his shoulder.

'Just tired.' He forced himself to smile. 'Bin up all night playing cards, so don't waste your sympathy on me. Tell me 'ow you're doin'. I don't see enough of you these days.'

It was getting on for two years now that she'd been in London working for Josh. She'd never gone back to school. Although in the first few months he had taken

318

her out dancing and introduced her to his friends, since then he had distanced himself from her.

Both George and Queenie were very protective. They wanted her to make friends of her own, and certainly didn't want her running around with shady characters. Besides, she was immersed in her work.

'Everything's wonderful.' Her mouth curved into a wide smile.

Tara was eighteen now. At the end of the summer holidays a year and a half ago she had persuaded her mother and gran, with Josh's help, to let her stay and work permanently. That first dress she designed was one of many that Josh had subsequently made up and sold. He gave her a small percentage on each of her designs, she had a wardrobe full of samples to wear herself and she had money in the bank. But although she was happy with her job, she could see her limitations.

She knew next to nothing about the costing and manufacturing side of the business. Josh gave her very little credit for all the hours she put in and she was still a long way from being given a free hand. But, as her mother had pointed out, if she left now and went somewhere else she would have to start at the bottom again.

'You've done brilliant.' Harry gave a weak but encouraging smile. 'But a pretty girl like you should be thinking about 'aving fun, not workin' all the bleedin' time.'

'I don't work all the time.' Tara tossed her hair back from her shoulders. 'I go out with Angie and her friends. I go down the Rising Sun with George and Queenie.'

'What, no boyfriend?' Harry raised one eyebrow questioningly. He kept his ear to the ground where Tara was concerned and he knew she had enough admirers to go out every night of the week if she wanted to.

'No-one special.' She giggled. Twice she had briefly thought she was in love, but both times it had fizzled out after a couple of weeks. 'Boys don't like ambitious girls.'

Harry grinned. He'd heard her put blokes off countless times because she was engrossed in her work, and it made him happy.

Tara poured the tea and stirred some sugar into Harry's.

'What about you?' she asked. 'What's happened to that girl Janet?'

She had been so jealous when he brought the small blonde girl round once for Sunday dinner that she'd found it impossible to stay in the room with them. She knew this was entirely unreasonable, but Harry was very special to her.

'History.' He smiled wickedly. 'She was boring!'

'I've got to go and get dressed.' Tara sensed he had something on his mind and she wished she had the time to dig deeper. 'Why don't you come home to the farm with me one weekend? Mum and Gran would love to see you.'

A lump came into Harry's throat. Right now he could think of nothing better than being alone with Tara in Somerset. But he couldn't make any plans until he knew whether that nightwatchman was all right.

'Maybe in a few weeks,' he said. 'Give us a hug, babe?'

He didn't get up and Tara moved over to him and put her arms round him.

'Have you done something wrong?' she whispered, as his head nestled against her.

Harry gulped. She smelled beautiful, of soap and talcum powder. He could feel the warmth of her skin through the thin housecoat and her hands caressing his head were so soothing.

'Just bin a bit of a prat,' he murmured, wishing he could stay in her arms all day and forget what had happened. 'Nothing for you to worry about, babe.'

She wanted to question him further but she could hear George's feet on the stairs. She bent and kissed his forehead.

'Come for that weekend,' she whispered. 'Soon!'

'That nightwatchman's died!' Mabel was sitting in her rocking chair reading the newspaper.

The kitchen smelled of onions and herbs and although it was only two in the afternoon it was gloomy because of the rain belting down outside. Amy was mincing leftover cooked meat for a cottage pie. She broke off from turning the handle and looked at her mother questioningly.

Mabel had begun to take a great deal more interest in the outside world since Tara left home. She not only read the newspapers, but studied farming magazines. At long last they had a milking machine, electricity in the out-buildings, a washing machine, refrigerator and vacuum cleaner to make life easier. Even the changes in her appearance, which started when Amy had the breakdown, had been maintained. Her white hair was always cut and permed, she no longer slopped around in men's trousers and boots. In a tweed skirt and navy blue sweater she looked just like every other middle-aged woman in the village.

'What nightwatchman?'

'The one that was shot last week out at Tilbury,' Mabel took off her glasses and looked at her daughter. 'Didn't you read about it? Two men robbed a warehouse and the old man tried to stop them getting away. They shot him and left him lying in the rain. He died last night in hospital. Poor old chap!'

Amy sighed. 'What's the world coming to? Once it would've been just a cosh over the head or tying him up. Why did they shoot him?'

'Greed, what else.' Mabel folded the paper and rose from her chair. 'I hope they hang him when they catch him.' .

Amy put the last piece of meat through the mincer, and glanced out of the window.

'It's still raining,' she said in irritation, unscrewing the mincer from the table and shaking the last few bits into the dish of meat. 'I wanted to go for a walk this afternoon.' She had felt on edge all morning, though she couldn't exactly say why, other than that she'd been cooped up in the farmhouse for days.

'You aren't made of sugar.' Mabel looked round at her daughter and noticed she looked pale. 'Put a rain-coat and boots on and go anyway.'

'You don't mind?' Amy knew there was work to be done in the dairy and the stable needed mucking out.

'Why should I?' Mabel said. 'I'll see to the butter and grade the eggs. You work too hard as it is.'

Amy stood on the wooden bridge at the end of Dumpers Lane and gazed reflectively at the river beneath her. This place made her think of Paul because it had always been his favourite.

Trees crowded around her, the drumming of rain softened by the canopy of leaves. The river was high today, cascading over stones, brown with churned-up mud. She could smell wild garlic and damp earth and the undergrowth was shiny with rain. To her left was the spooky old mill, the river gushing through the tunnel beneath the house. To her right a narrow footpath led through the trees to the village.

She wondered what Paul would have been like now. Sometimes she stopped to speak to his friend Colin and found it hard to come to terms with a burly teenager in jeans and a leather jacket, instead of the little freckled-faced boy in shorts he had once been. It didn't hurt to think about Paul now. She could see him here so clearly, with his fishing net and a jam jar with string tied round the top, wading in with his tongue darting in and out between his lips as he tried to catch sticklebacks.

Her thoughts turned to Tara. She had all the chic of a city girl now, hair regularly trimmed, false eyelashes and impeccable make-up. They didn't see her often, just for a few days at Christmas, a week in the summer and odd weekends. There was nothing for her here now. Her mind was always on fashion, her conversation all about Josh, Angie, George and Queenie.

At least that affair with Simon Wainwright hadn't affected her too deeply. She'd had other boyfriends, by all accounts, and often made Mabel and Amy laugh with stories about the lengths she went to to avoid them once they were cast off.

Amy had been so anxious in the first few months after Tara left. London, and particularly the East End, was a dangerous place for a young girl, though George and Queenie assured her that Tara's life revolved around her work and, even when she did go out, she never gave them cause for anxiety.

But it was hard to find herself no longer a mother. All those years of looking after children, and now she was obsolete. Of course there was the work at the farm, more than enough for anyone, but it wasn't the same as running after children. Sometimes, like today, she felt terribly alone.

She walked on back through the woods towards the village. The rain was getting heavier and she could feel it creeping right down to her underwear. She knew she ought to go home, but she was loath to spend another afternoon cloistered with her mother.

The High Street looked desolate in the rain. Aside from the brightly lit Co-op, the shops had a bleak,

323

closed-up look about them. Rain gushed down the gutters, spilling out like a river across the road at one point. Even the windowboxes of the cottages up on the raised walkway had a bedraggled air.

'Amy!' The shouted greeting made her look round. Gregory Masterton was coming round the corner, almost dragged along by Winston, his golden labrador. Greg was as wet as the dog, in a yellow oilskin, thinning hair plastered to his face. 'Fancy a cup of tea?' he called, his jolly red face breaking into a wide smile.

Amy didn't think twice. 'I'd love one,' she called back, and ran across to meet him.

They had become close friends since Paul's death. Greg was the one she poured things out to, with whom she shared her anxiety about Tara and even her irritation at her mother. Sometimes she felt that without him, she might have slid back into depression.

'Hello, Winston.' Amy patted the wet dog, smiling at his exuberant expression. 'Did you drag your dad out in this?'

'What's your excuse for wandering in the rain?' he asked as they walked up the High Street towards his house. 'Escaping the troll?'

They always shared the joke about Mabel being a troll who lurked under the bridge waiting for unwary travellers. Mabel hadn't entirely lost her caustic tongue and sometimes she treated Greg like a young farmhand.

'I suppose so.' Amy smiled. 'It's this rain. I want to do the garden, anything rather than be stuck in the house. Do you think it's ever going to stop?'

'The weather forecast doesn't offer much hope.' Greg paused momentarily at his grey stone garden wall. Clumps of purple aubretia were showering over it, behind a lilac tree in full blossom. 'Look at that, Amy! Now you don't notice how beautiful purple, green and grey are together until it rains.'

Amy looked a bit down in the dumps to him. He knew Mabel shoved a great deal of work on to her, but this seemed to be more than tiredness.

'You're a very calming person.' Amy smiled properly for the first time that day. 'Maybe I need rain to see the best things about you, too.'

Amy had loved Acacia House from the first time she took the children to see Greg. His home and practice were in a fine Georgian grey stone detached house that reminded her a little of both that old house Bill had shown her in Kent, and Paradise Row. A little neglected, perhaps, with its big wrought-iron gate practically rusting away and the old sash windows in need of a lick of paint, but it was so gracious.

In the days before she knew Greg well, she used to try to guess what the rest of the house was like. She imagined a grand piano in the drawing room, velvet armchairs – everything precisely in its place like a showroom. But when she finally went in there, she found it was nothing like that. Not only was it very untidy, without a piano, but the furniture was all unmatching, bits and pieces passed down through several generations, and she found herself loving it even more for its warmth and lack of ostentation.

'You'll have to ignore the mess, I wasn't expecting visitors.' Greg grinned as he opened the door.

'You always say that.' Amy laughed. 'I know for a fact that your cleaning lady bends your ears about her troubles rather than doing any work. I suspect you like living in a muddle!'

Black and white tiles covered the hall floor, as usual covered in Winston's muddy pawprints. To her right a door led through to a tiny study, the surgery and waiting room. To the left was a formal dining room he used more for meetings; at the back a big bright sitting room. The kitchen was tucked away behind the wide staircase.

Winston jumped up at her the moment he was let off his lead, covering her raincoat with muddy smears.

'Down, Winston,' Greg bellowed. 'Into the kitchen!'

Amy followed him as he shooed the dog into the back and took down an old towel to dry him. Usually when she went into his kitchen she cast her eyes enviously over the modern units, the many cupboards, the view from the sink over the garden, but today she found herself watching Greg.

He had taken off his oilskin as they came in. Now, dressed in a brown cardigan and tweed trousers, he bent down to rub the dog's coat. Winston allowed himself to be subjected to this for a couple of moments, then turned over on his back to have his belly tickled. The tender way Greg obliged brought on the oddest feeling inside her; it was almost jealousy! She turned away, taking her boots off in the hall, and wandered into his sitting room.

It was the most cluttered room she'd ever seen. The walls were lined with books, a big desk under the window strewn with papers. More books were heaped on the floor; a big sagging Chesterfield was covered in a crotcheted blanket, because of its bald patches and Winston's habit of sleeping there. There were so many things to look at. Old clocks, a couple of model sailing ships, Toby jugs, a collection of pipes, pictures embroidered by his grandmother. It was like being in a museum of the Masterton family, things hoarded not because of their value but for sentimental reasons.

She felt that Greg knew more about her than anyone else in the world. He had a knack of drawing out her innermost thoughts and often told her things about himself which led her to believe they were strangely similar.

Professionally he was a very successful doctor, held

in great respect by everyone. But on a personal level he had an innate shyness, and she suspected he was often very lonely.

'Let me take your coat.' She was startled by his hand on her arm. She hadn't noticed him come out of the kitchen she was so deep in thought.

'Amy!' he said reprovingly. 'You're soaked right through. How long have you been wandering about?'

'An hour or two,' she said absent-mindedly, letting the coat slip off her shoulders.

She felt his fingers touch her hair and run down her neck to her shoulders, and an unexpected tremor ran down her spine.

'You're wetter than Winston,' he said, turning her towards him.

Amy glanced at the hand on her shoulder and slowly raised her face to his. There was naked tenderness in those gentle brown eyes. His lips were slightly apart, his round ruddy face suddenly inexplicably dear.

'Hold me,' she whispered.

Silently he pulled her into his arms and drew her head down to his shoulder, one hand caressing her back. She could smell the wet dog, a faint whiff of antiseptic and damp wool, and could hear his heart hammering beneath his sweater.

It was she who instigated the kiss. Lifting her head, she put one damp hand on his cheek and brought his head down to meet hers. She could hear the rain swishing down the gutter outside the window, and the ticking of the grandfather clock in the hall. But his lips on hers were full of such sweetness and passion she felt herself moving into a void where nothing mattered but him.

'Oh, Amy.' Greg sighed as they broke apart, their faces still close together, bodies pressed up against one another. 'If you only knew how many times I've longed to do this.'

She wished she could admit something similar, but the truth was she'd never felt any pang of sexual desire for him until now. Yet, like a person dying of thirst given the first sip of water, she wanted more.

Her whole body seemed to erupt into flames as he kissed her again. This time his tongue moved into her mouth, his breathing was heavier. She undulated her hips against him, unable to control the sensations rushing through her. The same pent-up longing was in him, too; she felt it in his quivering body, the touch of his hands and the heat of his lips.

'You're so wet,' he whispered in her ear. 'Shall I get you a dry sweater?'

Amy guessed he was scared by this sudden turn of events, however much he might have longed for it.

'I want you, Greg,' she whispered against his neck. 'Take all my clothes off.'

His lips came back on to hers and she felt a bolder surge running through him as his fingers found the zip of her skirt. It dropped to the floor at her feet, and his hands moved under her sweater, pulling the damp wool up and away over her head. He paused to look at her for a moment, as she stood in a white cotton petticoat, then his arms reached out for her, enveloping her in a fierce hug.

They moved on to the settee. It was cramped but Amy was past caring. His hand slid up her leg and as his fingers touched the bare skin beyond her stocking top, she cried out and held him tighter still.

Everything was frenzied – their kisses and the way they caressed each other. Too much haste to possess, too much hunger. As his fingers found their way into her Amy called out, arching her back and opening her legs wantonly.

He couldn't get his trousers off; instead he just unzipped them then, pulling her round on the seat, he knelt on the floor before her and pushed himself inside her.

328

It was short-lived, a few hard strokes as he held her buttocks tightly and called out her name, then suddenly he was withdrawing, leaving a sticky mess on her thigh. They were still locked in each other's arms, panting, when they heard a woman's voice calling out.

'Cooeee, Dr Masterton, are you there?'

Amy's eyes flew open in horror. The woman was clearly in the back garden, having wandered around the side of the house after getting no reply at the surgery door.

'Damn.' Greg jumped up, tucking himself away. 'I forgot, I've got an appointment with Mrs Spear!'

Amy jumped up too, aware that any minute the woman was likely to look through the window. Greg pulled down her petticoat, grabbed her damp sweater and skirt from the floor and ran with her into the hall. His eyes looked stricken.

'Get dressed, I'll head her off round the front.'

He ran back to the kitchen and she heard him open the window.

'Just catching up on some paperwork,' he called out. 'I must have dozed off and didn't hear the bell. Come back round the front and I'll open the surgery door for you.' He was smoothing down his hair as he came back. 'I'm sorry about this.' He looked flustered. 'Would you mind slipping out the back way once she's in? You know what a gossip she is.'

Winston thumped his tail against the kitchen cupboard as she put her raincoat and boots back on.

'No, you've got to stay here,' she whispered, opening the back door just wide enough to slip through.

She felt humiliated as she stole down the garden path. It was still pouring, more water splashed on to her from overhanging bushes and her sweater felt like a wet flannel beneath her coat. Her face was burning, her eyes swimming with tears. Sliding sideways through a hole in the fence, she reached the river and took the footpath back to the farm.

What had she done? A long, warm friendship broken because of some crazed animal lust. How could she ever face him again?

'What on earth's the matter with you tonight?' Mabel snapped at her. It was almost nine and they were watching television in the sitting room. Amy had got out a dress she was making for a neighbour, but it lay untouched on her lap. 'You've hardly said a word since you came in. Are you sickening for something?'

'I think I've got a cold coming.' Amy got up and folded her work, leaving it on the chair. She was unbearably ashamed of herself, and afraid that if she stayed down with her mother she might just end up confessing. 'I think I'll have an early night.'

As she walked out into the hall she saw that an envelope had been pushed through the door. She closed her eyes for a moment, wanting to pick it up, yet afraid. She could tell by the handwriting it was from Greg. His big, bold hand was unmistakable.

Once in the bedroom, with the door firmly closed, she opened it.

'My darling,' he wrote.

'Whatever must you think of me? I loved you from the first day you came into my surgery with the children. For four years my love has grown stronger and stronger and then, just when it seemed you finally felt something too, I spoiled everything.

I pictured seducing you in some romantic spot, loving you so tenderly you'd never leave me. But instead I acted like an animal. I can't believe I bundled you out of the back door. My only excuse was that I was afraid of you being caught in a

330

compromising position. I wanted to hold you, tell you I loved you. To make love to you again with only your pleasure in mind. Instead I haven't even the nerve to face you and this letter will have to suffice until I know whether you are disgusted by me.

If there is any hope please let me try again? Can I cook you a special meal, with wine and music? Tomorrow night at seven?

You are everything in the world to me, Amy.

Deeply ashamed, Greg'

Amy felt a bubble of joy running through her veins as she read and re-read the letter.

It was his sensitivity that affected her most. Not just his guilt about bundling her out, but his fears that he hadn't pleased her sexually.

All at once she knew what had been niggling away at the back of her mind for weeks now. She wanted and needed love. Now she was being offered a second chance, a fulfilling, adult relationship built on under-standing and deep friendship.

'Oh, Greg.' She sighed, wishing she dared run up to Acacia House immediately. 'Of course I'll come.'

Chapter 17

July 1965

'What's age got to do with it? She's got imagination and flair.' Josh sat back in his swivel chair and lit a King Edward cigar with a flourish.

It was just after one on another hot summer day in early July. The windows were closed to keep out the noise and dust from the busy street outside. Only a small fan fluttering the papers on Josh's desk made the office bearable.

'Don't be a fool, my boy! You can't upset manufacturers for a mere slip of a girl.' Solomon Bergman shook his head, his German accent more pronounced as it always was when his son's behaviour troubled him.

They were total opposites. Solly was white-haired, small and stooped. After a lifetime of tailoring, nothing more than an expensive suit, a gold watch and a Daimler separated him from the hundreds of wizened Jewish men who had grown old long before prosperity reached them.

Josh wasn't a giant at five feet ten, but he exuded power from every pore. Since his boutique had taken off he seemed to grow in stature and confidence daily. His suits were made to measure, his hair impeccably styled.

They were in the office above the shop in Bethnal Green. In the two years since Tara had come to work for Josh, things had changed. Prosperity showed. It really was an office now, with a huge black ash desk and a real leather chair, carpet on the floor and dress rails relegated to a fully equipped stockroom downstairs. Swatches of fabric were piled in a filing tray, sketches of designs pinned to a board and samples of buttons and trimmings were mounted on cards.

'There are plenty more manufacturers crying out for work.' Josh shrugged his shoulders, but beads of perspiration on his forehead showed he wasn't quite as calm as he tried to pretend.

'But she doesn't cut the patterns professionally, does she?' Solly snorted. His eyes had been as big and mournful as his son's once, but now they were almost concealed by folds of wrinkled skin. 'Look at it from their point of view.' He waved his hands expansively. 'You take them brown paper stuck together with Sellotape and call it a pattern. Then when they make a mistake, you blame them. Of course they don't like it! I can't understand why you're so struck on her. She's not that special.'

Word had reached Solly some time ago that Josh had been upsetting old friends in the rag trade. Now he wanted to borrow an enormous sum of money to open three new branches, and this girl seemed to be at the bottom of it.

'If you think Tara isn't special then you're the fool.' Josh smirked at his father. 'She's got ideas like no-one else. Every one of her drawings I've had made up has been a winner. She started drawing short skirts just after she came here. Now that bird Mary Quant's in all the papers with them. If I'd been brave enough to back her, maybe *my* name would be in the newspapers. Then there's the colours she puts together, the cut and the sheer sexiness of her ideas. She's exciting, Dad, and she's right for me.'

'Listen, son.' Solly leaned forward across the desk.

333

'Calm down, sit back and work things out before you even think about expansion. You've had this shop less than three years. You've done good, trebling the turnover this year, but don't assume it will continue. Opening shops all over London won't necessarily make you a millionaire. It could go the other way. This shop was right for Bethnal Green, you struck lucky, that's all. Try the same formula in Kensington and you'll probably fall flat on your face because the rent will be ten times as high as here.'

'Dad, Dad, Dad.' Josh shook his head wearily. 'You haven't noticed anything, have you? There's a revolution going on out there. This is 1965, young people want to live, not save their money. Girls want a different outfit every week, they want to show off, be outrageous, and according to Tara, who seems to have a nose for this, it's going to get a great deal wilder.'

'She must be a great lay.' Solly sniffed.

'I wouldn't know. She doesn't put it about,' Josh retorted. 'I wish you'd just give the kid credit. She's worked like a slave for me, always on time, reliable, trustworthy and creative. I know she's only eighteen with no qualifications, but that cuts both ways. She doesn't make any demands, she doesn't throw her weight around. Tara just gets an idea and goes for it. Her designs are what's selling.'

Solly lapsed into silence, irritated by his son's cockiness. The reason he had money now was by sheer hard work and attention to detail. Every suit and coat that went out of his factory was checked by him. If they were short-staffed there wasn't one job he couldn't do himself. He was aware that times had changed, that the youngsters had money and didn't give a damn about quality, but Josh was building his business on shifting sand.

He delegated everything. For all those years at art school Josh didn't know how to cut a suit, or even press a seam. He got that slip of a girl to patch together designs and two-bit sweat-shops to make them up, then crammed the dress racks with them and raked in the money. But at the end of the day he was leaving himself wide open. The day Josh got tired of sitting at the top telling others what to do, the whole thing would crumble. He should be investing the profits, be here overseeing everything, not swanning around town in a flashy car with an empty-headed dolly-bird on his arm.

'I'm sorry, son.' Solly shook his head. 'I can't put money into such a risky venture. Wait until you've raised the capital yourself; plough back the profits instead of spending them.'

'You'll be sorry, Dad.' Josh forced himself to smile even though he felt as if someone had stuck a pin in his balloon. 'I wanted you to be a shareholder, do the whole thing properly. You'll be the loser.'

'I hope I am.' Solly took his walking stick in his hand and got up. His arthritis was playing him up. 'If you do well no-one will be more pleased than me and your mother, but it was a long hard road making our money, and we can't risk losing it now.'

Josh merely smiled.

'Give Mum my love,' he said dismissively, and watched as his father made his way cautiously down the stairs.

Solly took his time going out through the shop, stopping to look at the clothes, but watching Tara out the corner of his eye. She was helping a customer choose between two dresses.

'I thought the black one looked a bit ordinary,' he heard her say. Tara was standing by the changing rooms, talking to an unseen woman. She was wearing a black and white skirt that was at least two inches above her knees and a tight white top, her hair loose over her shoulders. He had to admit she was very pretty.

'The red one is sensational,' Tara went on. 'If you're going to a party you want to stand out.'

'You don't think it makes me look fat?' a voice called out.

'How can anyone size ten look fat?' Tara laughed. 'Honestly, it looked super.'

'OK, I'll have the red one,' he heard as both dresses appeared across the door of the cubicle. 'No, on second thoughts I'll have both. The black one will be good for work.'

He saw the pleasure on Tara's face as she came back to the counter with both dresses over her arm.

'Hullo, Mr Bergman.' She looked a bit startled. 'How are you?'

'Fine,' he said, wishing he could have concealed himself to make sure she rang up both dresses. 'I must be off now. Goodbye!'

He wondered about Tara. Why did a girl as pretty and talented as her want to work in Bethnal Green? Why hadn't she gone to art school, or into one of the big fashion houses? She must be after Josh, worming her way in because she knew his family had money.

She said her family had a farm in Somerset. Well, how come she was so street-wise? OK, she spoke nice, didn't have a Cockney accent, yet he could swear she'd been born and bred in these streets. She had the soul of an East-Ender.

'Time will tell,' he muttered as he made his way out to his car. 'Rachael ought to find him a nice Jewish girl, maybe he'd lose a few of his wild ideas then.'

It was quiet in the shop after Mr Bergman left. Angie was out in the stockroom pressing a few dresses and Tara busied herself sewing on a button that had come off a jacket.

She was disturbed by Mr Bergman. She sensed he didn't like her and she didn't understand why. In two years she'd been late perhaps three times, and never been off sick. She looked after the shop as carefully as if it was her own and she'd made a great deal of money for Josh. Why didn't he pick on Angie? She was the one who was always taking liberties, borrowing clothes from the shop, taking time off, not to mention sleeping with Josh.

The two years had flown by and she was a great deal wiser now. So maybe with hindsight she should have gone to art school, but then she wouldn't have got the experience she had now.

Living with George and Queenie was comfortable. She enjoyed the good food, the warmth and the convenience, but also their uncritical attitude. She didn't have to guard her words, or hide emotion. There was no suspicion, no frosty silences. If Queenie and George had something to say, they said it, cleared the air and moved on.

Tara had lots of friends now, mainly through Angie, and all the things she'd expected of London were there for the taking. Dancing at the Empire on Saturday nights, Sunday lunch-times down at the Blind Beggar, then often in the week she went to the Rising Sun in Bethnal Green with Queenie and George to see the music-hall acts they put on there.

Since making that first summer dress for Josh she'd put her heart and soul into fashion. Some of her wilder ideas didn't work, but she was learning every day, by listening to the customers and watching what the West End shops were doing. Soon she intended to make a stand with Josh and insist she got some of the credit for all her work.

'You're looking a bit glum!' Angie said as she came out from the back with an armful of dresses. 'What's up?'

In two years Angie had matured from a naive, giggly girl to a confident and glamorous woman. Her blonde hair cascaded over her shoulders in pre-Raphaelite curls, false eyelashes accentuated her green eyes and she made up for a her lack of height with four-inch heels. Although she had many boyfriends, it was Josh she'd set her heart on, even though he treated her badly.

'Nothing much. Old Solly was in here giving me the evil eye.' Tara grinned, getting up off her stool to help. 'He doesn't like me.'

'Can't figure you out, that's all.' Angie smiled. 'Neither can I, sometimes. But I like you anyway.'

They had become close friends, but they had entirely different outlooks. Angie lived for the minute, lurching from one emotional crisis to the next, her only ambition to find a wealthy husband who would whisk her away from work. Tara's reticence to get involved with any man puzzled Angie, nor did she understand the fierce ambition that kept her friend home at night slaving over a sewing machine.

'I ought to go home this weekend.' Tara sighed. 'Mum was on the phone last night and she had that tone in her voice.'

'The "you've forgotten all about me" tone?' Angie winced in sympathy.

Tara nodded.

'I get that all the time, and I've got a darned sight less excuse not going to visit than you. Somerset's such a long way.' Angie held on to the heap of dresses while Tara put them on the rail.

'I love it when I get there,' Tara said thoughtfully. 'Mum always gives me such good ideas, Gran feeds me up and makes a fuss of me. But I always feel I've disappointed them somehow.'

'Because you're still in Bethnal Green?'

'Yeah. They worry I'm going to get corrupted.'

338

Tara hadn't revealed her past even to Angie. Mostly she'd put it so far behind her she believed Anne Mac-Donald and all that went with her was just a dream. But sometimes, when she let slip about some of Harry's friends, she saw her mother's lips tighten and her eyes cloud with anxiety. Gran was even worse; not only was she convinced Harry was becoming a gangster, but she implied Josh was some kind of Jewish white slaver.

'How's your mum's romance with the doctor going?' Angie asked.

'Hotting up, I think.' Tara's eyes danced. She liked Greg, he was kind, funny and so good for her mother. In every phone-call home she asked her mother about him, hoping there'd be news of an engagement. 'She told me he took her to the theatre last Saturday, and supper in a posh restaurant in Bath. I suspect they're having it off now, though how they get around to it with Gran watching like a hawk I'll never know.'

'Maybe they'll get married soon. That'll take the heat off you.' Angie put the last few dresses on the rail and stretched her arms. 'My God, it's hot in here. No wonder it's so quiet.'

'How's things?' Josh's voice behind made them both turn.

'Not too bad,' Tara said. 'But like last year and the one before we're running out of summer clothes.'

'Any bright ideas?' Josh asked, ringing up a reading on the till. He smiled when he saw they'd taken two hundred pounds. One would have pleased him.

'What about that white broderie anglaise you've got upstairs? A sweetheart neckline, thin straps, maybe button-through?' Tara suggested.

She had made a sketch, but she didn't bother to show it to him as he took her description on trust now.

'Make one up.' He nodded. 'Can you do it tonight?

I've got a new manufacturer lined up. I'm going there tomorrow morning.'

'Well, I was going out.' She frowned, wondering whether she really liked David Gates enough to bother. He was another Cockney spiv who tried hard to be like Harry, but somehow missed out on the warmth and entertainment factor. 'But I could put it off.'

'I'd appreciate it,' Josh said. 'Go at five today. Angie can handle the last-minute stragglers.'

Josh went back to his office and sat down. He was no longer surprised by Tara's drive. He expected the sample the next morning because she never let him down. She seemed to have her finger right on the pulse of what the under twenty-fives would buy.

She was a dream employee, and hardly a day passed without him being afraid someone would poach her. To think he'd almost fired her when he found out her connection with Harry Collins!

She'd been with him for four months and in that time she'd designed six or seven garments that were all sell-outs, including a classic velvet jacket which he still kept in stock. She was happy with her tiny percentage and samples, his customers were delighted and Josh was rubbing his hands in glee at the effortless profit he was making.

Tara said little about her home life. Occasionally she'd mention the farm, her gran and widowed mother. When she confided in him that they wanted her back at school in September he wrote them a letter to confirm that he wanted to keep her on permanently, and praised her to the skies.

Her aunt and uncle she spoke of more often, but the names Queenie and George didn't ring any warning bells. If she had ever spoken of Harry, he didn't remember.

One evening in early December it was belting down with rain and Harry Collins ran into the shop with a

340

coat over his head, just on closing time. Tara was out in the stockroom and he was alone in the shop, so there was nothing to warn him of their connection.

'Long time no see, Josh.' Harry grinned, slung the coat over a stool and held out his hand.

They were the same age, born within streets of one another, and until the Bergmans moved up in the world they had been playmates. Harry had once broken another boy's nose for calling Josh a dustbin, the Cockney rhyming slang for yid, and forcing him to pull down his trousers to show his lack of foreskin. They were six years old, and Josh idolised Harry from then on, not just for being tough but for his compassion for a weak Jewish kid.

'Harry Collins!' Josh came round the counter and gave him a slap on the shoulder. 'How the hell are you?'

Even though Josh moved in a different circle now, he kept his finger in local affairs. Everyone had a great deal of respect for Harry, he was tough, shrewd and fair, but he could be a nasty bastard when someone upset him. Josh had seen him fighting often enough to know few men would get up and walk away after Harry had set about them. Then there were the girls! Harry had to be doing something right, because girls hung around him like wasps in a pub garden.

'Nice to see you doing well, Josh.' Harry's smile was sweet sincerity.

They made a few jokes about the past, about girls they both knew, then Josh made his boastful blunder.

'You should see the little darling I've got tucked away, Harry. A dream walking, and she's making me a mint.'

'I didn't know you went in for pimping.' Harry grinned.

'No, nothing like that.' Josh swaggered a little because he saw he had the man's full attention. 'She designs clothes for me and I hardly pay a penny for it.

Since she joined me I reckon I've made hundreds in clear profit from her.'

The next moment Harry had him pinned against the wall, holding him by his throat.

'That little darling is our Tara,' he spat into Josh's face, blue eyes turning almost black. 'You thieving bastard!'

'Your Tara?' Josh croaked. He knew Harry was an only child like himself, and he didn't remember a cousin or other close relative.

'You got it.' Harry's mouth was a thin angry line and Josh thought he was going to kill him. 'It's bad enough gettin' a kid to spend all her spare time making frocks for you, but when you don't bleedin' pay 'er properly and boast about it behind 'er back, that's fuckin' disgustin'.'

'I'm sorry, mate,' Josh stammered out as best he could with a hand at his throat. 'If I'd known who she was . . .'

'You shouldn't treat any girl like that,' Harry thundered. 'You bloody yids are all the same, sell yer own grandmother for tuppence. But I'm marking your card now, Josh. Pay her what she's due, or else.'

He let go of Josh suddenly as Tara came bounding into the shop from the stockroom with an armful of dresses.

'Hullo, Harry. What brought – ' She stopped in mid-sentence, suddenly aware she had interrupted something. She looked from one to the other, her eyes narrowing as Josh rubbed his throat.

'What's going on?'

'Nothing, sweetheart.' Harry smirked. 'Just been havin' a chat about how late at night you work. Josh was saying he was goin' to give you a bonus, weren't you, Josh?'

'Er, yes.' Josh gulped hard. 'We'll have to work out some commission or something.'

'That will be nice.' Tara still looked anxious.

'It certainly will.' Harry picked up his coat from the stool and waved his car keys. 'Come on, now, it's tippin' down outside. I'll be in touch, Josh. Good to see you again.'

That night he'd made up his mind to sack her. He didn't want Harry on his back or poking around in his affairs. But reason got the better of him in the small hours. He weighed up the money Tara had made him, and the money she'd continue to make him, and decided that a slightly higher commission on every garment she designed and a rise in salary wouldn't break him.

But it rankled. It cramped his style knowing Harry was watching him. At Christmas he might have been able to seduce her when she'd had too much to drink. He was frightened to ask her out, even to kiss her under the mistletoe in case it got reported back. He made up his mind he would get his own back one day.

The trouble was everything about Tara was desirable. He could sense she shared the same hunger as himself for money and position, a sure sign of a childhood pitted with deprivation. But her cool front excited him more than anything. She didn't giggle with the other girls about men, he'd never seen her flirting. Yet this wasn't the timidity of a virgin; rather a girl that knew about men and was biding her time until she met someone special.

One day all the care and attention he'd paid her would pay off. He intended to have her.

'You look pleased with yourself,' Angie said as Josh came into the shop a few days later. He practically bounced through the door, flashing a brilliant smile at the customers.

'I am,' he said, and swept through the shop up to his office.

'I wonder what's got into him?' Angie asked Tara.

'He had his dark suit on,' Tara mused. 'And his briefcase. Maybe he's done some deal?'

The phone in the shop pinged a few minutes later, which always meant he wanted someone to go up.

'I'll go,' Tara said. 'I expect it's about a design, anyway.'

Josh was sitting in his chair when she reached the office, his feet up on the desk, looking smug.

'I've got a new shop,' he said. 'I want to discuss it with you, but not here and now. How about coming out with me for a drink after work?'

Tara's heart leaped. This could be the opportunity to get what she wanted.

'OK.' She looked down at her dress, considering the image she needed to portray. 'I'll have to nip home first to change and leave a message.'

'Don't mention this to Angie.' Josh's brown eyes flashed a warning. 'You can leave half an hour early. I'll use that time to tell her everything.'

Tara wasn't sure if it was the drink part he didn't want getting out, or all of it. Something told her not to ask.

'All right,' she said. 'What shall I say you wanted me for?'

'To look at some trimmings.' He put his feet back on the floor. 'Off you go. I've got a lot of phone calls to make. I'll pick you up outside the library at six.'

Josh smirked with delight. Everything was coming together. Two days ago he'd seen the perfect shop in Kensington Church Street; today he'd got the finance from a merchant bank. But best of all was the whisper he'd heard last night.

Harry Collins was in trouble. He didn't know the details yet, but his source had said it was serious stuff, some blag that had gone wrong. When whispers like that were going around it meant the police wouldn't be far behind. Soon he'd be able to make a move on Tara.

Planning seduction was so pleasurable, like a snake luring a rat into its mouth. Tonight he'd just leave the bait and, if he was right about that ambitious little girl, she'd snatch it right up.

Josh waited until Tara had left the shop, then went downstairs, closed and locked the door.

'It's only five,' Angie reminded him.

She was wearing a short, tight red skirt, a clingy black blouse and very high heels. As always her make-up was a touch overdone, especially the false eyelashes, but her blonde curly hair gleamed as a spotlight caught it.

Josh smiled seductively. Tara was caviar and Champagne but it would be sometime before he managed to charm her out of her knickers. Angie was fish and chips, and available at any time.

'Come on upstairs.' He nodded towards the back of the shop. He was always ridiculing Angie for her South London voice and loud taste in clothes, but he had to admit she was a little sex-pot.

'Is that why you said Tara could go early?' She had been hurt about that, assuming it was favouritism, but now he had that lustful look in his dark eyes she felt warmer towards him.

'Yes, and because I had something to tell you.' He grinned.

He wasted no time in the office, remembering he had to meet Tara at six, and pulled Angie on to his lap.

'What's the secret?' she asked, smiling as his fingers moved to undo her blouse.

'Promotion for you,' he said, sliding his hand over her bra and tweaking her nipple. 'I've got another shop and I want you to be manageress here.'

'But I already am, aren't I?' She couldn't think straight when he was touching her.

'Not really, because I'm always in and out and Tara's

345

here. I want you to take sole charge and take on another two girls under you.'

'You mean Tara's going to the new shop?' It sounded as if Tara was getting the breaks, not her.

'Yes. I'd have sent you both, but I can't leave this one without someone reliable running it.'

'Where is the other shop?' For once she didn't respond quite so readily to his hands; she smelled something fishy.

'Kensington.'

Angie wanted to cry. She knew exactly why Tara had been chosen instead of her – because of her looks and the way she spoke. Her lip quivered and she bit back the tears.

'It isn't like that.' Josh guessed what she was thinking and the last thing he wanted was for her to leave him in the lurch with no-one running the shop. 'I want you here because I trust you, you know the people round here, and so I can see more of you.'

'Do you really love me, Josh?' She wanted to believe him, but he'd promised her so much in the past and never come through with it.

'Would I be here with you now if I didn't?' he asked. He had her blouse undone and was unfastening her bra. 'Give me a kiss, Angie. I've been thinking about you all day.'

He had been thinking about sex all day, because deals always made him randy. Any willing girl would do, but Angie was available.

She slid her arms round his neck. Josh was the best kisser she'd ever met, she had only to touch her lips on his and she got excited. His tongue slithered into her mouth as he played with her breasts.

One of the reasons she never quite gave him up was because he was such a good lover. Most men she's been with just jumped on, fucked her, then rolled over, but Josh turned it into an art form.

346

'What would you like me to do to you?' he whispered, his hand creeping up her skirt, lingering on the smooth skin above her stocking-tops.

Her lips went back to his, but she took his hand and pushed it up against her fanny.

'It's hot and wet already,' he murmured, fingers finding their way around her tight panties. 'You're a rude little girl, Angie, you've been thinking about me, too.'

She writhed as he pushed hard into her, his lips on her neck, moving down towards her breasts to bite them.

He could make her do anything he liked once his fingers started to move in and out of her. Somehow sitting half undressed on her boss's lap just feet from a window overlooking a busy street heightened it still more. If a bus passed she could be seen, but Josh knew that.

'I wonder what men out there would think if they saw you,' he whispered, pulling her skirt up and panties right off with one hand and turning her round on his lap so she faced the window. He kept pushing into her with two fingers and with the other hand he stroked her clitoris. 'Play with your tits, Angie, turn all those men on.'

In reality she knew the window acted as a mirror and the only person who could see her clearly was Josh, but it was all part of the fantasy. Her head began to swim, her eyes closed and she undulated her hips as his fingers moved faster.

'Harder,' she croaked, pressing her bottom back against him, feeling his hard cock straining to be loosened from his trousers. She opened her eyes and saw herself mirrored in the window, long hair falling over her naked breasts, her body so white against Josh's hairy arms and her black suspender belt. 'Fuck me, Josh.'

Josh smiled to himself. He loved to have women in his power this way. They would do or say anything under the influence of sex.

'No fucking tonight,' he whispered. 'I just want to make you come.'

She was bucking against him, making so much noise he was sure the people out there in the street could hear, and then suddenly she was still, lying back on his shoulder.

'That was wonderful,' she said a faint voice. 'I love you so much.'

He turned her round to kiss her. He was so hard it hurt, but if he stayed to fuck her now he'd be late to meet Tara, and he didn't want to go smelling of sex.

'What about you?' she said softly as he fastened her bra and buttoned up her blouse.

'I'll come round later tonight,' he said. 'I wanted to take you out tonight but I've got to meet someone.'

'Shall I cook you something?'

Josh smiled. She was very pretty, sexy enough to meet any man's approval and a first-class worker, but her cooking was awful and the bedsitter was so dingy he didn't like to linger in it.

'No, don't bother,' he said. 'I'll be late, I expect. Just keep yourself warm for me.'

She stood up, pulled her panties back on and smoothed her skirt down. She was aware of a part of him she never quite reached and it saddened her. Other men would go home with her right away, be glad to spend the whole evening with her, and she suddenly remembered Josh never did that.

'I won't ever go cold on you,' she said, bending to kiss him. 'I love you, Josh.'

Tara was outside the library ten minutes early. She'd had a quick shower and changed into a cream short-sleeved dress that Josh had turned down because he said it was too expensive. It was one of the things they argued about, he always wanted things to be cheap and insisted girls wouldn't pay for quality.

It felt as if she was betraying Angie by having a drink with Josh. Although common sense told her she had to look out for herself as far as her career went, Angie might suspect her of trying to lure Josh away from her. But whatever Josh's motive was for asking her out tonight, Tara's was straightforward ambition. If she could hang on in while he fought his way to the top, seize every chance to get known in the trade while she honed up her skill, then one day she'd stop holding the ladder for him and start her own company.

'This is lovely.' She smiled across the table at Josh. 'I never knew there were such pretty places in London.'

She had never been to Highgate village before, and it felt more like being back in Somerset than in a city. They had plumped for sitting in the pub garden as the sun was still hot, and the scent of honeysuckle and roses was wonderful.

'It'll be packed out later.' Josh looked round at people parking their cars in the already crowded road. 'But maybe we'll go somewhere else then. I wanted to talk to you away from the shop, because it's vital I know how committed you are to working for me.'

'Very.' Tara shrugged her shoulders. 'I mean, I don't see myself leaving.'

Josh looked pensive for a moment, his eyes half-closed and his thick lips set in a straight line.

'You see this new shop is in Kensington, and I'll want you to be manageress.'

'Kensington!' Tara's heart began to pound. She was always going there on her days off, wandering around the streets, looking in shop windows, dreaming of the day when her clothes would be in those boutiques.

'Bethnal Green was just putting my toe in the water.' He smiled smugly. 'One day I'll have shops in every major town.'

Tara listened to his plans carefully. Kensington was just the start, he wanted to open branches in Chelsea and Oxford Street soon after. Just the thought of what this could mean brought her out in goose-pimples – it was as if he was laying out her own private dream.

'What about Angie?' she asked. 'Is she in on this too?'

'Angie isn't right for Kensington,' he said carefully, knowing how loyal the two girls were to one another. 'She'll run everything at Bethnal Green. Don't worry, she's quite happy about it.'

Tara knew now that at least part of Josh's plans rested on her. But he was as cunning as a snake, he never came right out with anything, he had to sidle up, even attack from behind.

'I couldn't be your manageress and your designer.' She sipped her drink and looked innocent. She saw the startled look, guessed he'd thought he could go on putting on her for ever. 'I can't do both jobs efficiently, Josh. It's got to be one or the other. With two shops and more planned I'd be run ragged.'

'I was only thinking of you carrying on like we've always done.' He slapped on his most beguiling smile. 'I'd do the bulk of the designs.'

That meant he was going to steal ideas from others, just the way he had before she came. She had never dared allude to that for fear of making him angry, but now she knew it was time to put her cards on the table.

'You can't design,' she blurted out. 'You haven't made one sketch in two years that was workable. You can't go on copying other people's clothes either, Josh, not if you want to stay in business.'

She saw anger rise in his face and she wondered if she'd blown it.

'I'm sorry to be so blunt,' she added quickly. 'I'm only saying this now because you wanted to know how committed I am. I'll be your designer, Josh. I'll work some of the time in the new shop, but I'm not prepared to go on as we have been any longer.'

Josh was stunned, he'd underestimated the girl. He had thought offering her a carrot would turn this drink into a date. He hadn't expected an ultimatum.

'So what else would you like?' His lip curled petulantly.

'More money,' she said quickly, before she lost her nerve. 'And a proper workroom. I'm not working at night for nothing any longer.'

'You seem to be running away with yourself.' He wanted to wipe away all that confidence. 'I've got other designers lined up.'

Tara's heart sank. She was fairly certain he was bluffing, but she couldn't be entirely sure.

'If you get other designers in, then I'll be off.' She spoke gently but with a hint of steel in her voice. 'I haven't worked hard for you for two years just to be pushed back behind the till.'

He was stuck. He had approached other designers, but every one of them who was any good had merely laughed at the deal he put to them. Something told him Tara didn't know how to play poker; what she said was what she meant. He couldn't take the risk of her stalking off now.

'OK.' He sighed. 'But until the new shop gets on its feet I'd expect you to be there.'

'When are you opening it?' she asked, inwardly reminding herself how slippery he was.

'The middle of September.'

'How much room has the shop got above it?' she asked.

'Two floors. I suppose we could put a workshop there.' Josh had stopped trying to be cunning.

'Let me have a flat there and we're in business,' she said. 'Kensington's a long way from Bethnal Green, Josh.'

Josh's mouth dropped open. The quickness of her mind amazed him.

'I was thinking of letting it,' he shot back. But even

as the words came out he could see this was to his advantage. In one fell swoop he could remove her from Harry's influence and Angie's, she would be available whenever he dropped round and doubtless she'd work doubly hard without distractions.

'But what will Harry think about you leaving home?'

'It's nothing to do with Harry.' She looked at him with scorn. 'I love living with Queenie and George, they're the kindest people in the world. But I'm not crazy about the East End, Josh. I want a bit of style.'

For months now she'd been aware she was on the outside looking in. Kensington and Chelsea were where it was happening for young people. She wanted to mix with people who were free spirits, be a part of the swinging scene she read about in the newspapers.

'You'll get it, babe.' Josh felt a smile stealing over him. 'You and me, Tara, we're going places.'

'I get to be your designer, with a workshop, a flat and more money?' She went over it to make sure he'd fully understood her. 'And I only work full-time in the shop until it's up and running?'

He hesitated for only a second. Excitement had turned her cheeks pink, her golden hair shone in the evening sun and those strange, beautiful eyes were making his heart turn somersaults.

'It's a deal.' He grinned. 'Now let's have another drink to celebrate.'

Chapter 18

September 1965

'Are you sure about this, Tara?' Queenie looked up anxiously from packing a box with china. 'You're so young to be living alone!'

'I'll be OK, Queenie. It's a big adventure moving into your first flat, isn't it?' Tara replied, her voice quivering.

'Of course it's an adventure.' Queenie's usual smile switched back on. 'Anyone would think you was being shipped off to the salt mines of Siberia. You'll only be a bus-ride away and, anyway, you'll have more fun round there.'

'Will you come and see it once I've got it all straight?' Tara threw her arms round Queenie's plump neck and held her tightly. 'I've got this one big room and Josh got a man to paint it all white for me. I'm going to have big posters, huge plants and floor cushions.'

'I'd better bring my own chair, then,' Queenie joked, returning the hug. 'I'm too fat and stiff to sit on the floor. Just mind you don't invite any of those Bohemians round who take that pot stuff.'

'What do you know about pot, Queenie?' Tara giggled.

'Nuffin', worse luck.' Queenie chuckled and her chins quivered. 'I do know about fellas, though. So don't invite anyone in for coffee unless you intend to go to bed with them. In my experience men assume

353

sex is on the menu at just the mention of coffee. They can't help it, love. Their brains and their John Thomases are very closely connected.'

'Uncle George was lucky finding you.' Tara moved away to pack the rest of the cutlery and glasses Queenie had insisted on giving her. 'It was just a shame you didn't get together years ago while there was still time to have a family.'

'We've got Harry.' Queenie smiled and reached for the clothes she'd just finished ironing for Tara. 'And you. Who knows, in a few years we might get grandchildren.'

'I won't get married for years.'

'I hope not, love,' said Queenie. 'I was your age when I got hitched the first time, and it ain't all it's cracked up to be, I can tell you. Mind you, years ago we got married so we could sleep with our chaps, if the truth was known. Now you can get that pill and get stuck in without any of the boring bit.'

Tara bit back laughter. She knew Queenie was trying to instruct her on birth control, not enthusing about free love.

'I do know about it.' She dropped her eyes, slightly embarrassed. 'Don't worry, I won't get into trouble.'

Queenie understood Tara. Not because they were alike, but just the opposite. Tara kept her distance from people and things which might bring her down. She'd heard so many horror stories from both her mother and grandmother that she was determined not to go the same way. But Queenie sensed Tara's way was more dangerous. Avoidance didn't give you experience, in fact it just held closed floodgates which could be opened by a person with the right key. In Kensington she was likely to meet plenty of handsome charmers. Would Tara be able to see beyond a fat wallet and an expensive suit?

'That man hurt you, didn't he?' Queenie sat down on the settee, the ironing still in her arms.

'It could have been worse.' Tara shrugged her shoulders. 'At least it was a clean break.'

'You must try and trust men again, sweetheart.' Queenie's blue eyes looked misty. Unlike Harry and George she had never seen Tara's cool approach to men as mere ambition. 'Don't lock your heart away. God put us on this earth to love and be loved. It's more important than money.'

It was late when Tara got to bed on her last night in George's house. Mentally she ticked off all the things she would miss about Paradise Row, and the list seemed endless. The small but cosy bedroom, Harry's room which she had used as a workroom soon after she arrived. Clothes miraculously washed and ironed, the wonderful meals. Yet somehow she knew it would be the small touches she'd miss most. Queenie coming in to tuck her in. George bringing her a cup of tea in the morning and the way he always cleaned her shoes. The gleaming brass on the front door and welcoming smells of dinner cooking.

Lying in the darkness thinking about all the happy times here made her question her own family. Amy's sweet gentleness could be every bit as aggravating as Gran's stubborn and prickly nature. They didn't laugh much. Life for them revolved round work and keeping things going, enjoying life wasn't a priority.

There were a great many things still left unsaid about her running away to London, even two years on. She sensed her mother felt abandoned somehow. Gran sniped all the time, about Josh being Jewish, how he came from Cable Street. Then she'd have a go at Harry – he was a thug, a waster, a drinker and a gambler. With her mother it was more subtle; a frown, a sigh and always the same remark about how little they saw of her.

Up till now Gran's barbed comments about Josh

355

hadn't mattered, he was just her boss after all. But a change had come about in their relationship since that night in Highgate. There'd been no touching, no suggestive words or even looks to show her how he felt; just a glint in his eye and a certain softness in his voice.

Deep down inside she knew she was aching for a love affair. Not a grope in a car with someone she had nothing in common with, but a deep, meaningful relationship. Her dreams were becoming more and more erotic, visions of the things Simon did to her came crowding back, making her hot and damp. Josh figured in these dreams and she had an instinct that he felt the same way.

Harry pulled up outside the shop in Kensington Church Street and turned to smile at Tara.

'Pretty posh,' he said. 'A different league from Bethnal Green.'

It was seven in the evening, but although the shoppers and office workers had gone home the street was still busy. Restaurants, wine bars and pubs were crowded, people strolled up and down on the warm summer evening, the traffic was still heavy.

'Doesn't it look wonderful?' Tara waved her hand towards the new shop front. It was the same maroon as the one in Bethnal Green, but instead of circles painted on the glass this double-fronted shop had round windows and wide double doors with brass fittings. Inside it was still chaos; clothes-rails erected but as yet unfilled, boxes of stock strewn all over the newly fitted carpet.

'It's a nice place to live.' Harry looked across to Barker's, the big department store down opposite the crossroads. This part of Kensington had all the big stores and countless elegant small shops. 'I'm glad for you, sweetheart, but Paradise Row won't be the same without you.'

356

Harry had told George the truth about what had happened that night of the robbery, but they had kept it from Tara. At George's suggestion he'd kept away from both the house and the market and taken a job on a building site out at Ealing.

Ginger had disappeared. If anyone knew where he was, they weren't talking, but leather coats were appearing all over the place, and just about everyone had been taken in for questioning.

Harry had been pulled, as had both Needles and Tony soon after the old man died. They had all stuck to the same story about drinking in the Regency, and been released. But he knew the case was far from closed.

Time and again Harry had been on the point of going into the nick and admitting to his part in the robbery. Each time he thought of that old man, he felt lower than a slug. But he shouldn't feel guilty, he hadn't used the gun. Until he could find Ginger and force him to own up, he wasn't going to put his head on the block.

Tonight was his last night in London. First he wanted to see Tara settled in her new home, then he was going to find that slag once and for all. The police were closing in now the coats were being pushed out, and it was only a matter of time before Harry's face was in the frame.

'Come on, then!' Tara slapped at his arm. 'Heaven only knows where your mind is tonight, but I want my stuff moved in.'

'Slave driver.' Harry pulled himself together. It had been hard enough driving here with Tara firing questions about where he'd been, why he wasn't helping George any more, whether he had a new girl. He didn't want her prising a confession out of him.

She unlocked the shop door and together they unloaded everything from the van. She had a great deal more than the small rucksack she'd arrived with two years ago – a record player, her own electric sewing machine, a dressmaker's dummy and four huge cardboard boxes of clothes. On top of this was all the stuff Queenie had given her – lamps, bedding, china and saucepans.

'It's up two flights of stairs,' she warned him as she re-locked the shop door behind them. 'Wait till you see it, Harry! It's so big!'

Harry smiled. She was like a puppy, gambolling around full of excitement. In jeans and an old T-shirt, with her hair tied up in a pony-tail and no make-up, she looked just the way she had at fourteen.

They took a box each and Tara led the way out through the back of the shop.

'That's the stockroom.' She waved one foot towards an empty room, behind a curtained doorway. 'That's the staff room.'

This part of the building was neglected compared with the shop, with dirty cream walls and bare wood stairs leading up to a square landing with three rooms off it.

'That's going to be my workroom.' She nodded towards the first empty room right across the front of the shop. 'The other two I don't know about. But upstairs is my place.'

The stairs from then on were carpeted and the walls marginally cleaner, and sunshine flooded in through the front windows.

'This is my room!' She ran forward into the front room, dropped her box and flung her arms wide. 'Isn't it wonderful?'

Harry put his box down and as he stood up arranged his face into the sort of gleeful expression she expected.

'Yeah, it's wonderful,' he agreed.

It was a big room, just like the one beneath it, but the ceiling was lower and the two sash windows smaller. It looked very bare to Harry, who was used to cluttered places. It contained just a single divan, a fitted grey carpet, a small table and two upright chairs, but it was newly painted white.

'You just wait till I've got pictures up, lamps and stuff.' Tara leaped over to the windows and opened them wide to let out the smell of the new carpet and paint. 'I'll invite you round for supper, Harry, that's if you can tear yourself away from your villainy.'

'Who's been filling your ears with stories?' Harry caught hold of her arm and pulled her round.

'No-one.' Tara was surprised by his harsh tone. 'Why? Is there something to tell?'

Harry let go of her arm. He felt daft now, he knew if Tara had heard any whispers she would've told him.

'No, of course not.' He forced himself to smile. 'Over-reacting, that's all. People are always spreading rumours about me.'

'I was only teasing, Harry. I don't really see you as a gangster. Now let's get the rest of the stuff up.'

She found Harry hard to fathom sometimes. There were great areas in his life he never opened up about. He liked people to think he was shallow, that the side he showed the world was all there was. But Tara knew better. He was a deep pool and it would take a very deep plunge to reach the bottom of him.

'Come and look at the kitchen and bathroom,' she said, wanting him to show a little more enthusiasm. 'Look, isn't it great? A brand new suite all for me.'

Harry did smile right from the heart at the bathroom. Not so much at the pink suite, but because he knew that she had a quirk about bathrooms, stemming from the days when she didn't have one.

'It's fantastic.' He slung an arm round her shoulder.

'It was disgusting the first time I came here.' She wrinkled her pretty nose in disgust. 'It was all cracked and stained and it smelled awful. I don't think Josh really wanted to go to all that expense, but he had to.'

'He isn't thinking of moving in downstairs, is he?' Harry asked guardedly.

'No.' Tara gave him a sideways look. 'He took on the lease of a really smart place in Brompton Road just a short while ago. He wouldn't want me cramping his style. Come and see the kitchen!'

Like the bathroom this was at the back, overlooking the gardens of the big houses in Palace Green. It had new lino on the floor, a sink unit and cooker, and again the walls were painted white.

'I'm going to put shelves up there.' She pointed to the wall next to the cooker. 'And I'll have to get some cupboards and things. But look at the view!'

Harry looked out of the long narrow window. Trees obscured the backs of the houses straight ahead. Kensington Palace Hotel stood out to his right, and up here on the second floor he couldn't even hear the traffic above the sound of bird song. All he could think was 'If only'. Tara was setting out on a bright new road, while he was stuck in a hole of his own digging.

He was silent as he carried up the last few boxes.

'I'll have that one in here.' Tara came out from the kitchen as he came in with some groceries. 'I've put the kettle on for some tea, or shall we go along to the pub?'

'Tea, please,' he said, putting down the box. 'You shouldn't be drinking so much, either. You aren't old enough.'

Tara frowned, turning to look at him.

'You can talk,' she retorted. 'You were getting leg-less when you were sixteen. Besides, I'm eighteen and quite old enough.'

'And I'm a good example of what happens to people that get into 'eavy stuff too young,' he snapped. 'You can get sucked in, you know. Sometimes you get known by the company you keep.'

He was worried about her living alone. He imagined the other girls in the shop encouraging her to have wild parties up here, and men taking advantage. Back home with Queenie and George she toed the line and came home at a respectable hour, but here it could all change.

'Are you trying to tell me something?' Tara went over to where he stood at the top of the stairs.

He was wearing ancient jeans, almost threadbare in parts, and a tight black T-shirt. She could see an inch or two of hard smooth flesh between them and she had an almost irresistible urge to touch it.

'I suppose so.' He turned his head away from hers defiantly and in profile his face was beautiful. 'You've changed since you went to work for Josh, you've got very ambitious and kind of hard. I remember the sweet, gentle kid you used to be and it makes me sad.'

Tara felt a little uncomfortable. She wasn't sure if he'd heard something about her, if he was anxious about her moving in here, or if she really had changed.

'I'm the same inside. Look at all the things that have happened to me. I had to grow up fast, remember?'

'Yeah, I know.' Harry put one hand on her shoulder and squeezed it. 'I suppose I haven't any right to criticise, especially when all you're doing is bettering yourself. I'm just sliding downhill so fast I'm burning a hole in the seat of my pants.'

'What have you done?' she whispered, aware that the sadness in him wasn't caused by her at all. She had an urge to put her arms round him and hold him tightly, the way he used to do to her.

'I can't tell you,' he said softly, his blue eyes burning right into hers. 'I'll tell you when it's all straightened.'

She could see a nerve twitching in his cheek, a look of guilt and sorrow in his eyes.

'But wouldn't sharing it with me make you feel better? You're like a big brother. I want to help.' She reached out and put her hand on his cheek.

He sighed deeply, his eyes dropping from hers.

361

'I don't feel like big brother any more.' He caught hold of her hand on his cheek and pressed it with his. 'I haven't for some time, Tara, that's partly why I don't come home much.'

A quiver ran down her spine, she felt the warmth of his hand on hers coursing through her body.

'You didn't come home because I was there?'

He nodded, as if the admission were difficult.

'I wanted you from that day you walked in the gym. I thought if I waited it would pass, but it never did. I watched you going out with other blokes and I hated them. But worst of all was listening to you talking about Josh. Once he used to envy me because I was bigger and stronger, but now it's the other way round.'

Tara was shocked. Harry had never ceased to be important to her, especially after the way he handled her affair with Simon. He'd soothed that ache inside her, washed away the dirty feeling with his understanding. Then there were all the people he'd introduced her to, taking her dancing with his friends and showing her around. It had never occurred to her that his visits home had become less frequent because of her.

'Oh, Harry!' Flashes of that passion she'd had for him when she was fourteen were shooting through her brain. 'Why are you telling me this now?'

'I don't know.' His voice dropped and his arms moved, his hand going round her waist. 'Maybe just because I'm afraid I won't get another chance.'

His lips were moving towards hers, those lips she'd once drawn from memory and dreamed of kissing. A light touch, then they moved away, only to come back again, burning against hers with a fierce hunger. One hand lay against the small of her back, holding her tightly against him, the other was on her head, as if he were afraid she would back away.

There had been many other kisses since Simon,

362

many memorable ones that with the right opportunity might have led to lovemaking. But no man had ever created the all-consuming heat she felt now. Her nipples tingled, her belly contracted and her tongue moved against his.

It was Harry who drew back first, leaning back against the banisters at the top of the staircase, his hands still on her arms. His blue eyes seemed more brilliant than ever before, his lashes longer, his lips more desirable.

'You are the most beautiful girl I ever saw,' he said softly. 'I'll be back for you.'

She reached out and held his face between her hands, a feeling of exquisite tenderness welling up inside her.

'Are you trying to tell me you're going away?'

Harry felt the softness of her hands on his cheeks, he could still taste her mouth on his and smell her fresh talcum powder smell. He wanted to imprint every last detail of her on to his mind, so he could recall it if things got bad.

'I've got to.' There was deep sorrow in his eyes. 'I can't promise anything. I can't even tell you what's happening. Just promise me you won't run off and marry Josh or anyone else?'

She knew then that he was in serious trouble. Something about him, this conversation, tweaked cobwebs of old memories. Family history was repeating itself and she knew to her cost what came of giving your heart to a man who was in trouble.

'Promise me, Tara?' he repeated.

She wanted to, but she knew what it would mean. Putting her life on hold until he reappeared, worrying, wondering.

'I can't.' She looked him straight in the eye. 'There isn't anyone else, but I'm not making promises I don't know I can keep.'

He kissed her once more. His hard, lean body seemed to merge into her own, his breath become hers and she knew then he would be hard to put aside.

'Does that look the business or what?' Josh sat up on the counter, a smug smile on his lips.

It was all ready for opening the next morning. Pressed garments hung on the rails, the windows held wonderful displays of mini skirts and velvet jackets in jewel colours. There wasn't so much as a stray tag on the deep carpet; even the till was ready with a float.

Otis Redding was singing 'My Girl' on a tape of soul music Josh had prepared, coloured lights flashed on and off round the outside of the windows, creating an almost Christmassy feel, and inside spotlights played on garments displayed on the walls.

'It's brilliant,' Tara chuckled. 'But I've told you that a hundred times already.'

Josh had seemed very different in the last few days as they worked together here alone; warmer, and more fun. They had eaten supper together at the pizza place around the corner, laughing about so many things.

'I hope you're right about girls wearing skirts that short round here,' Josh said.

'The mini is going to be a sensation.' Tara put her hands on her hips defiantly. 'OK, so most people are only daring to show two inches above the knee so far. But this is Kensington, a place full of show-offs. I don't look ridiculous in mine, do I?'

Josh grinned. Tara looked wonderful in the short black and white skirt, but then she had perfect legs, and those boots she wore with it gave him a hard-on. But not all girls shared her perfection. She had overcome his qualms by insisting he stocked some of the new tights, in case girls fought shy of revealing so much leg. But he couldn't quite believe mini skirts were going to fly out.

'You look great,' he said. 'At least they don't take much fabric.'

'Well, if you've finished admiring everything – ' Tara tossed over her shoulder as she made for the door through the back – 'I've got some designs to show you. They're in my room. Come on up and I'll make some tea.'

Josh halted in surprise as he stepped into the room. Two days ago it had been bare, but already she'd made it homely. A Spanish rug in shades of blue and green covered the bed and she'd draped two lengths of green and gold fabric around the window rather than putting up curtains. Somehow she'd managed to persuade the carpenter who'd fitted out the shop to put up some shelves in here without charging anything extra, and a collection of odd little knick-knacks, from old inkwells to perfume bottles and fans, was arranged on one. The table was covered in more turquoise material, but he could barely see it, or the floor, for several different dresses in various stages of being made up.

'I didn't expect you to start this soon!' Josh shouted out to her.

'I had to,' she shouted back above the noise of running water. 'I kept having ideas as I saw people walking past the shop.'

Josh picked up the sketches from the floor and smiled. The top one was of a trouser suit, the jacket like a Regency frock-coat, trousers flared out at the bottom. Then there was a mini dress, a diamond shape cut out at the navel, a party dress trimmed with a feather boa, and several different short tops, all trimmed with beading, clearly meant to be diaphanous. Tara appeared with two mugs of tea.

'Well! What do you think?'

Josh had already noticed the climate here was very

different from Bethnal Green. The girls were tall and leggy, not a bit like the small mods he'd started his career catering for.

'I like them all,' he said cautiously. 'But aren't they a bit — ' He paused, not knowing the right way to describe them. 'Well, girls can't wear things like this to work!' He sat down on the bed.

'I don't think girls who shop in Kensington are looking for work clothes.' Tara put the tea down on the floor. 'I've been watching people and they all seem to go for way-out stuff. We won't last long unless we attract the outrageous girls.'

Josh picked up a gold chiffon bodice and held it up, frowning.

'Where did you get this material from?'

'Barker's.' She grinned. 'That's the beaded top in the sketch. I knew you wouldn't go for anything so expensive, but I thought I might twist your arm if I made it up for myself.'

She took it from his hands and held the unfinished top to her chest.

'Look, it's going to have long, floaty sleeves, and beading to hide all the rude bits. Can't you just imagine it?'

Josh shook his head.

'Not for us, too much work,' he said. 'Besides, it would be spoilt with a bra showing through it.'

'I don't think girls round here worry about bras.' Tara giggled. 'Besides, they sell tops a bit like this one in that shop called Top Drawer, the man in there told me they can't get enough of them, and they're nearly twenty quid.'

Josh whistled.

'Anyway, the beading comes in strips,' she carried on. 'It doesn't have to be sewn on by hand. We could try just a few!'

'I'll reserve my judgment till I've seen it finished.'

366

Josh frowned. 'Don't get carried away, Tara. We need bread and butter lines.'

To his surprise she didn't argue, just sat down on the floor, picked up the blouse and began pinning the sleeves in.

'How's Angie?' she asked.

'OK.' Josh shrugged his shoulders. 'She's taken on a new girl called Rose, they seem to be hitting it off.'

'I'm going to miss her,' Tara said thoughtfully. Hester and Miranda, the new girls here, were leggy blondes with rather superior attitudes and posh voices. She couldn't see herself becoming close to either of them.

'You'll soon make new friends.' Josh noticed she looked a bit sad and wondered if she'd found out anything about Harry yet. He had been hugging himself with delight since he discovered what that was all about. If the whispers were correct, Harry could be going down for a long stretch.

'Do you ever feel lonely?' Tara asked suddenly. 'I mean kind of surrounded by people, yet still feel alone?'

'Yes, sometimes.' The question caught him off his guard, in fact he felt like that a great deal of the time. 'Why, do you?'

'Yes.' She put her work down and smiled. 'I used to think it was because I was artistic, it set me apart somehow.'

'Maybe that's it.' He wanted to move over to her, but it would be too obvious to move from the bed to the floor. 'I hope we can become close friends now, Tara, we've got a lot in common.'

He hoped she was going to ask more leading questions, but instead she looked at her watch.

'I hope so too, Josh,' she said. 'But it's getting very late and it's going to be a big day tomorrow.'

Josh popped a pill in his mouth as he drove towards

his flat in Brompton Road. Tara might be going to bed early, but he was going home to get washed and changed, then out to a club. One purple heart should be enough for tonight; two of them and he'd never get it up.

He had a lot to celebrate tonight. The shop was ready, the press would be sniffing around tomorrow and, with luck, Tara would fall into his lap pretty soon.

Chapter 19

'Someone to see you, Tara!'

'Send them up,' Tara yelled back, leaning over the table as she marked out a pattern on brown paper. She didn't want any interruptions; she had four patterns to make today for Christmas party dresses. But then Miranda had enough sense not to send anyone up unless it was important.

The new shop had succeeded way beyond their expectations. The opening day's takings were higher than the best day ever in Bethnal Green and since then they'd gone well above the target figures daily.

The biggest problem now was getting stock made up fast enough. Josh would come staggering in with what looked like a mountain of it, but by Saturday evening most of it would be gone. She'd been right about the mini skirts. Everyone loved them and they were selling tights like hot cakes. Josh had had a few of the beaded tops made up, too, but his manufacturer balked at the work in them and he still hadn't found someone else to take over.

It was mid November now. Kensington High Street was crammed with Christmas shoppers and it seemed that everyone wanted a new dress to wear, the more seductive and outrageous the better.

Her head bobbed up from the work the moment she heard laboured breathing out on the stairs.

'Uncle George,' she shrieked with delight and ran out on to the landing to see him puffing up the stairs. 'What a lovely surprise!'

He paused at the top, holding on to the banister. Not only was he extra red in the face, his bald patch glistening with perspiration, but he looked suddenly old and tired. Even his clothes were different, a dark grey suit with a matching waistcoat. The only time she'd seen him so soberly dressed was at Paul's funeral.

'What is it?' She still went to hug him, but somehow his appearance didn't warrant her usual exuberance.

'Bad news, I'm afraid.' He responded warmly to her hug, but he couldn't even raise a ghost of a smile. 'I came to tell you myself, before someone else does.'

'Come in here.' She took his hand and led him into the workroom, aware that the girls downstairs might be listening. 'Is it Harry?'

Since the night she'd moved into the flat he had sent her one postcard with a gorilla on it and the cryptic message 'Don't forget me!' When George and Queenie didn't mention him in their numerous phone calls, Tara decided they were as much in the dark as her and avoided the subject.

'Yes, it's 'Arry.'

In the clear light of the workroom she could see his eyes were red-rimmed and his collar was grubby, as if he'd been up half the night.

'He's bin nicked!'

'Oh, no!' Tara's stomach churned. 'What's he done?'

'A warehouse blag back last June.' George groped his way through the boxes and packages on the floor and sat down on a stool like an old man, resting the palms of his hands on his thighs. 'A nightwatchman was killed. Do you remember it?'

Tara's blood ran cold. She remembered it only too well. Everyone had talked about it for days and the papers had said they should bring back hanging for such a brutal crime.

All she could do was nod.

'Harry didn't shoot the old man, you must believe that.' George's voice sounded strangled.

'But he was part of the gang?' she whispered, tears welling up in her eyes. She had imagined everything from protection rackets to bank robbery, but never something like this.

George's head sank down on to his chest.

' 'Ow can I explain.' His voice was low. 'See, I know my son, Tara, and 'e ain't a wicked lad. 'E planned this job all right, and I can't even claim someone talked 'im into it. But 'e never intended any violence, 'e weren't tooled up, that ain't 'is style.'

'But what happened? Who shot the man?'

'I can't tell you that because I don't know.' George reached out for her hand, a pleading look in his eyes. 'All I know is what he told me back then. 'Arry got out of the van to open the gates as they was leaving. 'E says the driver drove the van right at 'im and the old man and he pushed the old geezer away for safety. 'E 'eard a gun shot, thought it was the old bloke firing and jumped back in the van. Only then 'e discovers it was the driver what 'ad the gun.'

'But who was the driver?'

' 'Arry won't name 'im.' George shrugged his shoulders. 'All this time 'e's bin trying to track 'im down. But now someone's grassed 'Arry up. The police think 'Arry done the shooting. They've charged him with murder!'

Tara slumped down on to a bolt of fabric, covering her face with her hands.

'He was on the job, fair do's, he deserves punishing for that,' George said. 'But he ain't a murderer, Tara. He ain't.'

'But surely all he's got to do is tell the police who did do it?' Tara looked up at George.

'You know the unwritten laws round our way!' George pursed his lips. 'Thou shalt not grass even if the plod are kicking yer 'ead in and the person who did the crime is a shit of the first water.'

'What are we going to do?' Tears began to trickle down her face.

'You, sweetheart, are going to do nothin',' George said firmly. 'You've got a good job and having your name linked with a murder suspect won't 'elp it. I'm getting 'Arry a good lawyer and we'll just have to pray the police don't fabricate any evidence. 'E's going to get sent down, love, whatever 'appens. But 'ow long for depends on whether our brief can prove 'Arry didn't own, or fire the gun.'

'I must do something, Uncle George.' Tara went over to him and perched on his lap, laying her head on his shoulder.

' 'E don't want you nowhere near 'im.' George patted her back as if she were a small child. 'I saw him in the cells just now, and 'e said to tell you you're not to write or attempt to visit him. I'll be seeing 'im so you can send messages through me if you like.'

'He hinted something was wrong when he moved me in here.' Tara struggled to compose herself. 'But I never expected it to be anything as bad as this. It's like Dad all over again.'

This was part of the reason George hadn't let on before. He could see similarities himself, and Tara had been through enough. He and Queenie had hoped, perhaps foolishly, that the right man would give himself up, or be found by the police. But they'd seen no sense in casting shadows over Tara's happiness.

'I'll tell you something now, sweetheart.' George blew his nose vigorously. 'I always hoped you and 'Arry might end up together. I know 'e cares a lot for you and I see a spark of something in you, too. But even though 'e's my son and I love him, I'd disown him rather than see 'im screw up your life.'

'He said he was going to prove himself to me.' She bit her lip. 'I think he knew that he'd gone wrong, but he meant to sort it out.'

'I just hope 'e can, then.' George shook his head sorrowfully. 'You see, your dad weren't such a bad lad, either. He got in with the wrong crowd, was tempted by easy money. I just 'ope our 'Arry don't go the same way.'

'He couldn't, Uncle George!' She looked up at him with frightened eyes. 'Could he?'

'A long stretch does strange things to men.' George reached out for her hand and rubbed it between his own. 'Some 'ate it that much they never steal as much as a pin when they come out, but most of 'em are corrupted beyond 'elp. It's a sewer, is prison.' George paused, as if wondering whether he should be saying all this.

'Harry won't get corrupted,' Tara said confidently.

'I hope not, darlin'.' He got up from his chair. 'I gotta go now. I left Queenie on the stall and it'll be busy today, so I'd better hurry back.'

She couldn't bear to see him so sad. Her own feelings about Harry were swinging wildly between disgust that he'd been stealing, anger that he was foolish enough to shield the real villain and love because of all he meant to her. But Harry was George's whole life. He didn't deserve this kind of anguish.

'Give Queenie my love.' Tara held out her arms for one more hug. 'And Harry, too. Could I write just one letter to him?'

'OK, just one. But send it to me, not Brixton. I'll just slip it in a book or something. I expect 'e'll send something to you the same way, but 'e won't want anyone making a connection between you two.'

After George left, Tara tried to return to her work, but

373

all she could see was Harry's face the night he'd moved her here.

'You can't get involved with a jail-bird,' she whispered to herself. 'You know how it will end!'

It all came back, things she thought she'd wiped from her brain when they ran away from her father. The heavy feet of the police on the stairs, the shouting and the scuffling until he was subdued and handcuffed. Those interminable train rides to visit him in prison, Mum trying to hide her tears as they came home.

She could never allow her children to witness seeing their home torn apart in a search, or the humiliation of being pointed out at school because their father's name had been in the paper again.

Josh came into the workroom just as the shop was closing, with a bouquet of flowers in one hand, a bottle of vodka in the other.

Tara looked up questioningly. He usually burst in like a whirlwind, shouting instructions, rummaging through boxes, demanding everything from coffee to the figures for the week. But now he was just looking at her, as if preparing for something.

'I've got those four designs finished,' she volunteered. 'I did a little jacket, too, I thought it might go well with those plain black cocktail dresses we bought from GlamourWear.'

'I'm sure they'll all be fabulous,' he said. 'But that isn't why I came. I'm here to offer a bit of sympathy, to cheer you up and tell you not to worry!'

'You know already?'

'It's in all the papers,' Josh said gently, weaving his way through the many boxes and putting the flowers on her drawing board. 'He didn't shoot that old man, Tara, he couldn't do something like that.'

She knew that, of course, but Josh's opinion was confirmation she was right. Harry and Josh had known each other since childhood, who better to assess Harry's character?

'George came over this morning,' she explained. 'He's devastated.'

Josh put a hand on her shoulder.

'Come on,' he said. 'Put these flowers in water, then let's go and have a few drinks. You can't help Harry by sitting there moping about it, and he wouldn't want you to.'

'This room reflects your personality,' Josh mused as he downed yet another glass of vodka and lemonade.

He had been through the whole commiserating bit. He had told her all his stock of anecdotes and now he hoped the subject was laid to rest.

'What do you mean?' She was slurring her words, even Josh looked a little blurry.

'Well, we've got all the arty bit . . .' Josh waved his hand at a series of brilliantly coloured modern-art posters tacked to the wall. 'We've got the superb needlewoman bit in those amazing cushions and curtains.' The huge floor cushions all featured appliquéd animals – a lion complete with loopy wool mane, a tiger in fur fabric, panda, giraffe and zebra all amongst appropriate foliage.

'But the bit I find the most illuminating is the collecting and hoarding.'

The room was like a treasure trove. Old theatre posters, illustrated musical scores, even advertisements covered the wall round her rug-draped bed. Strange lamps, candlesticks and pieces of sculpture vied for space on the many shelves with tiny animals, boxes, even jewelled hatpins.

'I don't know what you mean.' Tara poured herself another drink.

'All those art books.' He gestured towards a shelf crammed with books in glossy jackets. 'Your collection of jewellery, I bet you've never worn half of it. All those old bits and pieces. I reckon it's some kind of security blanket.'

Tara giggled. She loved collecting unnecessary things, anything from old fans to paperweights, inkwells, and eggcups. At night when she was alone she liked to arrange them all, days off were spent scouring Chelsea antique market and the junk shops further afield in Fulham, Shepherd's Bush and Acton.

'I think it stems from when I was little,' she said dreamily. 'We never had anything much in our flat, no books, no pictures, just a few cheap china animals Dad won on a rifle range at a fair. Sometimes the man at the paper shop gave Mum a pile of old glossy magazines. I used to soak up the pictures of posh houses. I think I wanted them more than smart clothes.'

'I thought you lived on a farm?' Josh had not only picked up on the word 'flat' but also on the picture of extreme poverty.

Tara gulped. All this time she'd been so careful, now with too much drink inside her she'd let it slip.

'I'm talking about when I was very small,' she said hastily. 'We moved to my grandmother's place in Somerset when Dad died.'

'I'm sorry.' Josh looked sheepish. 'I never liked to ask before. What did he die of?'

'A heart attack. But I don't like talking about it.'

'So where was the flat? In London?' Josh was suddenly very attentive, sitting up on the floor and leaning towards her where she lounged back on the cushions.

'Acton. I can hardly remember any of it now,' Tara snapped, suddenly sober.

'OK, so you don't want to discuss it.' Josh wriggled round so he was nearer her. 'I don't like to think about the place we had down by Cable Street, waking up to see a rat by my bed, or hearing other kids calling me a dirty Jew. There's no shame in being born poor, only in not improving your own lot. Dad and Mum think they've arrived now they've got the house in Golders Green and a Daimler. I want more than that!'

'Like what?' Although plenty of other people had talked about his origins, it was the first time Josh had spoken of it, and the admission seemed to make them equal.

'It's not just money. I want fame.' Josh turned on his side, supporting his head on his hand, looking right into her eyes.

She looked exhausted, and very drunk, with a violet tinge beneath her lovely eyes. Even in jeans and an old shirt, with no make-up and her hair all tousled, she still looked more desirable than any other girl he knew.

So much of Tara was hidden. Through her designs he sensed a sensual woman, the way she kept her flat showed she was a home-loving person, yet he had never been able to fathom exactly what it was she wanted. He hoped by opening up to her, she might reciprocate.

'I want to be a celebrity, Tara. I want people to nudge each other when I walk by and say,"Hey look, there's Josh Bergman, he's only thirty and he's a multi-millionaire already".'

'You haven't given yourself long.' Tara giggled.

Josh had made her feel so much better. Maybe it was just the remnants of her childish crush that had made her think for a moment that Harry was for her. She was grown up now, she had a right to reach out for what she wanted, without feeling indebted to people from the past.

'I'm well on the way.' His eyes were full of fire now, face flushed with more than just the vodka. 'I want a plane of my own, holiday homes in exotic places and beautiful women on my arm.'

'Do I come anywhere in this dream?' she asked. 'Is your designer important or will you replace me?'

'You are part of the dream.' He lowered his voice and his hand moved to stroke her cheek. 'Together there's nothing we can't do, we'll rise up like shooting stars to conquer the fashion industry.'

Tara was very aware of his hand on her face, but his words thrilled her even more.

'That would be so wonderful,' she breathed. 'It's not money, is it? It's people looking up to you.'

His lips were moving slowly down towards hers, fleshy, pink and succulent, his dark eyes soft with tenderness. 'I'm hungry for you, Tara!'

His lips were so warm and soft against hers, his fingers in her hair soothing away any last doubts. There was no threat in his touch, just sweet warmth, lulling her into relaxation.

His kisses were thrilling, slow and teasing. At some point, though she never noticed when, he moved her slightly, placing another cushion under her head, and his fingers were slowly unfastening the buttons on her shirt. Flashes of lovemaking with Simon came back to her, memories of how she'd responded and the realisation she wanted that again.

'Tara, you're so beautiful,' he breathed softly against her neck as he opened her shirt and slid his hands round her back to unfasten her bra. 'I've dreamed of seeing your breasts since the first day I met you.'

A flush of desire washed over her as Josh's lips came down towards her nipple. She saw his face soften, his eyes half close and his lips move into a kiss. She watched as his lips took her pink nipple, his tongue snaking out to lick it, and her body arched involuntarily towards him.

She pulled out his shirt, running her fingers up and down his spine, pressing herself hard against the lump in his trousers she so much wanted to touch. But instead he moved back to her lips, kissing her again as he covered her breasts with her shirt. 'I must go home,' he whispered, tracing round the outline of her lips with his tongue. 'I won't be responsible for my actions if I stay.'

It pleased her that he didn't consider her a pushover, that he was too gentlemanly to pull off her clothes and his own on their first evening together, but all the same she wanted him. Wanting didn't quite cover it, she was burning for him, desperate, but how could she say so without appearing promiscuous?

'I don't want you to go,' was the best she could offer, kissing him with fevered lips.

'I must, babe.' He wriggled away from her slightly. 'We've got plenty of other nights, haven't we?'

It was next morning, when she woke up with a raging thirst and a headache, that she had misgivings.

'Thank heavens he didn't take advantage,' she thought to herself as she lay holding her head. Sober, she could see things that hadn't even crossed her mind last night. Angie's hurt, maybe even putting her job in jeopardy, not to mention the callousness of taking a lover the very first night Harry was in jail.

She couldn't concentrate on her work that day. She was making up some samples, but she kept making mistakes and having to unpick things. Each time she heard one of the girls go into the shop kitchen, she started, expecting Josh to come up the stairs.

Yet as hard as she tried to forget, images kept coming into her mind and she could feel his lips on her breasts, taste his kisses, and she knew she wanted him.

He rang late in the afternoon, hurriedly from a phone box.

'Are you all right today?' he asked. 'You put a lot of drink away.'

'Just a bit of a headache,' she said, wondering if she should try to cool things down, or encourage him.

'I don't know when I'll be able to get round again,'

he said. 'I've had a bit of a problem getting more material for the velvet jackets. I might have to go up to the Midlands.'

He left it at that. No date, no promise to come round, leaving her without the opportunity to turn him down.

That evening Amy phoned and the moment Tara heard her voice she knew she'd been crying.

'I don't know what to say,' she said in a weak plaintive voice. 'I can't believe Harry would hurt an old man.'

'I'm sure he didn't, Mum.' Tara felt sick now, she'd forgotten all those people back home reading about it and recognising it as the Harry Collins they all liked so much. 'George say's he's shielding someone.'

'But he was at the robbery,' Amy said. 'No-one can alter that.'

Tara tried to get her off the subject, asking about Greg and Gran, but still her mother kept coming back to it.

'We just have to believe in him, Mum,' Tara said. 'And hope the man that did it comes forward.'

After she'd put the phone down Tara put her head on her arms and cried. She was so confused. Harry's face danced before her, bringing back all the good memories. But even if he wasn't a murderer, he was a thief, and he was going to prison. She couldn't even think about loving a man like that.

As the run-up to Christmas grew more frantic, Tara had little opportunity to dwell on either Harry or Josh. There was no time for designing now, just helping in the shop, filling up the rails from the stockroom, supervising, displaying, rushing to the bank for change.

Josh baffled her. He only breezed in and out to collect the takings, or bring more stock. Sometimes he could spare five minutes for a coffee upstairs in her flat, but even though he always pulled her into his arms and gave her one of his thrilling kisses, she could feel the tension pent up inside him.

'I'll make it up to you soon,' he said one afternoon, sliding his hand up under her sweater and tweaking her nipple. 'What are you doing for Christmas?'

'I have to go home,' she said, wishing it wasn't necessary as she was beginning to feel she had no place there any longer.

'Could I come with you?'

Tara was stunned. 'You don't really want to?' she said disbelievingly.

'I do. I'd like to meet your family and see your home. Christmas isn't different to any other day at my parents, but if I'm in London they'll expect me to turn up. I could drive us down on Christmas Eve after we've closed.'

'I'd have to speak to Gran.' Tara immediately got a mental picture of her Gran sounding off about Jews and wondered if it was such a good idea. But on the other hand it would prevent Mum and Gran from going on about Harry all the time.

'Gran's a bit batty.' She slid into Josh's arms. 'Don't blame me if you have a terrible time.'

'I've got a way with ladies,' he whispered, pressing himself hard against her. 'Or so I'm told.'

To Tara's surprise both Gran and her mother seemed to welcome the idea of Josh when she telephoned them. They both agreed to stick to the same story about the flat in Acton and Mr Manning's heart attack. Even when Tara warned Gran not to make her usual disparaging remarks about Jews, she only chuckled.

'I know when to keep my lip buttoned,' she said.

Gran didn't mention Harry, but then she'd already made her feelings known in a letter. To her there were no grey areas, Harry was guilty of robbing the warehouse, so it followed he'd killed the watchman too.

When Angie phoned one evening and said she'd jacked in her job, Tara was shocked.

'But why?' she asked. 'I thought you loved it.'

'It was crappy money, and I'm fed up with Josh,' Angie said light-heartedly. 'He hasn't been near me since he opened the Church Street shop. I'm not wasting any more time on him. I'm going to work for a new boutique in Carnaby Street. I might even get a flat over your way, too.'

She spoke of people's faith in Harry in Bethnal Green.

'Everyone knows he didn't do it,' she said. 'His mates'll put the frighteners on the bloke what shot him, don't worry.'

It was one less thing to worry about. At least she didn't have to concern herself about hurting Angie. But as Christmas came closer and closer, there was no time to dwell on anything other than work.

The shop was packed with noisy, over-excited young people. Soul music played at full volume, coloured lights flashed over the central display of one green and one red velvet mini dress. It was the last Saturday before Christmas and it seemed as if the whole of London's youth had descended on Kensington to buy something to wear.

Tara stood by the side of the cashier, folding and packing the garments, keeping one eye open for shop lifters.

'That's the last of those!' Susie, one of the temporary staff, put down the white crêpe mini dress trimmed with fluffy feathers at the neck and wrists on the counter. 'We must have sold hundreds!'

'They've been going well in Bethnal Green, too,' Tara replied, mentally making a note to ask Josh to get some more.

'That was mean of Josh sacking the manageress there,' Susie said. 'She's been working for him since he started.'

'She left to work in Carnaby Street.' Tara looked sharply at the girl. Her eyes showed no sign of malice.

'Where did you hear that?'

'My cousin Rose works there,' Susie said. 'She told me. Josh accused her of wearing clothes from the shop and sacked her instantly. Rose reckons that wasn't the real reason, though. She thinks he's got another bird, and doesn't want the new one to find out he's been sleeping with Angie.'

Tara ruminated on this news for the rest of the afternoon. It was quite in character for Angie not to admit the truth; she didn't like to lose face, not even with an old friend. But Josh's behaviour was far more puzzling. He had known Angie borrowed clothes right from the outset. Why get funny about it now? Unless of course Rose was right and he wanted to remove the last obstacle in his way to getting her.

It was the deviousness of it that bothered her. What sort of game was Josh playing, and why?

Tara got into bed early on Sunday night. Saturday night had been a real laugh. Miranda had stayed behind after work and they'd had a couple of bottles of wine, while they chatted. She had been wrong about Miranda. She wasn't snooty, not once you got closer, it was just the way she'd been brought up – private school, rich parents with a big house in Barnes.

Later, when they were very drunk, they staggered off to the Zambesi club in Earl's Court wearing tinsel and mistletoe in their hair. There weren't anywhere near enough girls to go round, and the Australians and South Africans who had made the club their own were practically fighting each other to dance or buy them drinks. She had vague memories of snogging with some huge Australian and telling him she'd fallen in love with him, then running off to catch a taxi with Miranda while he was in the toilets.

But on Sunday when she woke around twelve she felt like a balloon with a slow puncture, all the joy disappearing leaving her flat as a pancake. She half-heartedly did the button holes on a sample jacket, took her washing to the launderette and cleaned her flat, then crawled into bed to cry.

'Let Josh come for Christmas,' she said to herself joylessly as she lay in bed, staring at the ceiling. 'But keep him at a distance. Don't trust him!'

'Try and find out who grassed me up,' Harry whispered to George through the grille in the visiting room. 'I've heard the name Joe Spikes mentioned a few times in here, too, try and get a starting price on him, where he's come from, his form, the works.'

'Where's he supposed to hang out?' George asked.

'I dunno, one bloke said he's come from over the river, Catford, Deptford. Thinks he might be part of the Richardson crew. I got this whisper that he's got some grudge against me. He could have leaned on one of the lads.'

George looked nervously round him. He hated coming to Brixton. Seeing his son through this grille was torture, the haunted look in his eyes, the way he kept biting his lip. There was nothing he could do either, not even squeeze his boy's hand.

In the waiting room the heat was stifling. Flustered mothers struggled with small babies, toddlers grizzled because they were tired of waiting. You could tell the women who'd been through this countless times, bold-faced and loud-voiced, ten minutes with them and they'd tell you every last thing about their old man. It was a sordid, dirty place, like lifting a manhole cover and finding a whole underworld you never knew existed.

'How's Tara?' Harry put his hands on the grille, as if trying to sap something of his father through the wire. 'I've put up that picture of her in my cell. It helps.'

'The shop's packed out all day every day, but she seems 'appy enough.'

384

'Has Josh moved on her yet?'

'Don't ask me questions like that, son.' George frowned. 'I don't know the answer, anyway it ain't any good brooding on such things.'

'She's such a kid still,' Harry looked gloomy. 'I don't trust Josh, he's such a fuckin' smoothie. I just can't bear to think he might be screwing her.'

'Well, use your loaf then.' George moved closer to the grille. 'Give your brief enough to clear you of the shootin', at least. You'll still get a year or so for the robbery, but you could use the time inside studyin' summat useful. I'll stick by you this time because you're my boy. But get in the shit a second time and that's it as far as I'm concerned.'

Harry looked at his father and felt a lump in his throat. George was a diamond. He never pulled a fast one on anyone, never lied or cheated.

'Did I ever tell you 'ow much I value you?' Harry said softly, wishing there was no grille and he could hug his father. 'I'll make you a promise here and now, I'll never let you down again. I'm through with thieving.'

George's eyes misted over. 'Glad to hear it, son.' His voice was gruff with emotion. 'Now tell me what else you've 'eard about this Joe Spikes. And while you're at it, what about birds you've dropped. One of them could be at the bottom of it.'

Chapter 20

'Push the other one away, idiot!' Tara sat back on a bale of straw laughing hysterically at Josh's attempt to feed the calf from a bucket.

'Don't just sit there laughing,' he shouted over his shoulder. 'Help me!'

It was Boxing Day morning and Tara was attempting to un-citify Josh. With her hair tied up in bunches, wearing old jodhpurs, boots and a donkey jacket, she looked as if she'd never lived in a town.

He had already failed miserably on feeding the pigs, by turning to run when the big sow Mildred put her front trotters up on the sty wall to roar out an ecstatic greeting. He could do no more than pat Betsy gingerly on the nose as Tara took in her oats. Now even feeding a couple of pretty black and white calves seemed beyond him.

The calves were penned with willow screens in the back corner of the barn, the floor ankle-deep in dirty straw. In an ancient jacket and trousers of Gran's, wellingtons borrowed from Stan, with his curly black hair and olive skin, Josh looked more like some poor tinker than a businessman.

The calves had moved in on him the moment he appeared with the bucket of skimmed milk, elbowing aside the screens and both trying to get their heads in the bucket at the same time.

'Be firm with them,' Tara called out as he nervously edged further and further back. 'Slap the little one on the nose and hold your ground.'

But Josh couldn't co-ordinate holding the heavy pail and he seemed reticent even to touch the animals. Tara got up to intervene, but before she reached him his boot landed on some manure, he skidded and toppled back. The milk flew up into the air as he fell backwards, the pail clonking down on to his chest.

Tara shrieked with laughter. Josh was spreadeagled on the straw, soaked in milk, and the two calves were advancing on him, limpid dark eyes glistening at their spilled breakfast.

'Get them off me,' he yelled, covering his face with his hands as two long tongues flicked out to lick him. 'They'll trample me to death!'

Tara shooed the calves back into their pen with one expert tap each on each rump, and put the willow screen back.

'They're six-week-old babies, not charging rhinos.' She was convulsed with laughter, but held out her hand to haul him up. 'Somehow I don't think you're ever going to get the hang of this.'

Josh wiped the milk off his face once he was vertical again, but he hadn't noticed where his hand had been and now he had a smear of manure right down one cheek.

'It's horrible in here,' he said petulantly, his face a picture of misery. 'It stinks, it's dirty, but I wouldn't mind it so much if you weren't enjoying my discomfort.'

'Oh, don't be daft. Can't you take a joke?' Tara took a step forward and wiped his face with a handkerchief. 'Go and change. I'll feed the calves.'

'He's no country boy,' Mabel said with a smirk as Josh disappeared up the stairs, wearing only his shirt and socks, leaving the mucky trousers, boots and coat in the porch.

'You and Tara have a cruel streak,' Amy said reprovingly, having seen the whole thing from her bedroom window. 'If Tara had just helped him with the calves he'd probably have enjoyed feeding them.'

'To each his own.' Mabel looked round from the vegetables she was preparing in the sink. 'I'll say that for Harry, he could handle everything here.'

Amy put the kettle on the Aga then turned to her mother, hands on hips. Mabel had been very jolly and amenable for the last few days, but her tone suggested she might be lapsing back into her usual prickly ways.

'Well, that is a turn-up,' Amy said sarcastically, knowing the only way to deal with her mother was outright confrontation. 'We've finally found something we like about Harry!'

'I only speak as I find.' Mabel pursed her lips and looked at her daughter defiantly. 'You know I don't really believe Harry killed that man. But he was thieving and he deserves to be punished.'

Amy shook her head in amazement.

'Mother, you're the most aggravating woman I've ever met,' she said. 'You've refused to allow me even to mention his name. You were rude to George when he telephoned. Now you say you don't believe he shot the watchman. Couldn't you have come down off your high horse for long enough to write Harry a Christmas card?'

'If I've been hard, it's only for Tara's sake,' Mabel said waspishly. 'If I showed the slightest softness towards him, Tara might take that as approval. Besides, Harry knows me better than anyone and for your information, Miss Perfect, I did write to him, soon after he was nicked.'

'You did?' Amy's jaw fell open.

Mabel leaned back against the sink, a smug smile on her lips.

'I told him what a disappointment he was to me. But I did say, too, that I knew he wouldn't take a gun to anyone. I also offered to help him get back on his feet when he gets released.'

For a moment Amy just stared in surprise, but slowly something dawned on her.

'You mean working for you, here?' She threw back her blonde hair from her face.

'Well, if Greg Masterton sweeps you off, I'll need help,' Mabel retorted. 'And the way things are going with Josh and Tara, she won't be coming back here either.'

'Mother, Mother.' Amy burst into laughter. 'I think you are the most contrary, cunning, obstinate woman I've ever met, but I love you anyway.'

Amy was still smiling as she went into the sitting room to tidy up and put more coal on the fire. All this time she and Greg had wondered how they could ever broach the subject of them marrying without Mabel flying off the handle. But in fact her mother was already making plans, albeit cock-eyed ones. She probably knew, too, that whenever Amy was missing in the afternoon or evening she was with Greg in his house, making love.

Since that first clumsy attempt back in the summer, their love affair had become so beautiful and fulfilling. Only yesterday Greg had suggested they become engaged and put a stop to the gossip about them. But Amy wanted to wait until after Harry's trial. It didn't seem right to be planning a joyful occasion when someone you cared for deeply was in so much trouble.

'I doubt if he'll take you up on the offer, Mother,' Amy said to herself as she swept up the pine needles. 'But he'll appreciate the thought behind it.'

*

Josh looked at himself in the bathroom mirror thoughtfully as he waited for the bath to fill. The milk had penetrated right down to his pants, he had straw and muck in his hair, and he doubted he could wash the farmyard smell off.

He was angry, not so much with Tara for showing him up, but at himself.

'You shouldn't have come here,' he whispered to his reflection as he drew a comb through his curls to remove the straw. 'You've blown it.'

Back in London he called the shots, he knew who he was and where he was going. He should have taken her out, shown her a bit of the high life until she was as besotted with him as other girls were. But coming here had weakened his power. These three strong women had showed him a way of life that made him question his own.

It had begun as soon as he walked into the kitchen on Christmas Eve. It was the atmosphere that knocked him sideways. Twists of red crêpe paper and holly adorned the old black beams among the copper pots. The big scrubbed table was laid invitingly for a late supper and every surface seemed to be groaning with more food. A huge iced Christmas cake sat on a dresser next to an equally large home-cooked ham, golden with breadcrumbs. There were mince pies on a cooling tray, a wooden trug full of vegetables waiting to be prepared, and dishes of sweets.

'This is wonderful,' Josh managed to get out. 'It looks and smells so festive. I didn't expect to find two more beauties in the same family, either!'

He had expected Tara's mother to be middle-aged and drab, not a stunningly pretty woman with a figure like an eighteen year old. Even the grandmother was majestic in a plum-coloured two-piece, white hair sparkling like frosting under the light.

Both women had laughed. Amy said he was 'gallant'

and fussed over him as she poured him hot beef and vegetable soup with delicious homemade bread.

'We practically sold out of all my designs,' Tara bubbled as she related tales of the last few frantic trading days. 'The new shop's a stupendous success. Josh is going to be a millionaire before long!'

'Is that so, Josh?' Amy smiled, 'or is this just Tara's excitable nature?'

'The shop has exceeded my wildest dreams.' He grinned, looking from Amy sitting at the table, her face rosy with pleasure at having her daughter home, to Mabel standing at the cooker basting the turkey. 'But it takes more than one good season to build a fortune.'

'Are you going to open other branches?' Mabel slid the turkey back into the oven and closed the door.

In a Jewish family this question would imply a collecting of information as to his suitability as a prospective husband. But Mabel sounded as if she already believed he was well on his way to building an empire.

'I'd like to,' he said cautiously, not wanting to brag. 'For the time being I want to build up both shops until I'm certain which way the wind's blowing. But that's enough business talk. Tell me about you, Mrs Randall. Tara tells me you paint!'

Josh could barely keep his eyes open as Mrs Randall showed him a couple of beautiful water-colours she was giving to people as Christmas presents. For weeks he'd barely slept, keeping himself going with purple hearts and blues. On Christmas Eve he'd limited himself to just two, relying on pure adrenaline to pull him through. But now, with the long journey behind him and the comforting knowledge that there was a huge wedge of money in the night-safe, exhaustion had taken over.

It was after ten. He heard Amy saying she and her mother were going to the midnight service soon and,

391

although he had hoped for such an opportunity to be alone with Tara tonight, he knew he was incapable of using it.

'Poor Josh, you look all in,' Amy said gently, ruffling his hair in a way that made him feel like a small boy. 'Let me show you your bedroom.'

'Go on.' Tara grinned at him. 'Mum's right, you're dead on your feet. I'll go to church with them if you don't mind being alone.'

She looked so pretty in a cream mini skirt and jumper, a bow of tinsel still in her hair from earlier in the day. Her cheeks were flushed and her amber eyes sparkled in a way they never did in London.

'If you won't think I'm a misery,' he said weakly.

'Of course not.' She patted his arm. 'I'll see you tomorrow and show you around. Off you go!'

He was awake enough to notice model planes hanging from the ceiling in the bedroom, to see a row of Dinky toys and a couple of teddy bears on a shelf, but too sleepy to consider who this room belonged to.

'I've put a bottle in,' Amy said, turning down a beautiful red and blue patchwork quilt which he guessed was her work. She plumped up the pillows on the old-fashioned wooden bed, and switched on a lamp. 'Sleep tight, Josh.'

Josh couldn't remember a time when he'd felt so cosy. The bed was so warm and soft and the linen smelled of lavender. He could hear plates rattling down in the kitchen and Tara giggling.

Christmas until now had been nothing more than a Gentile festival which gave him an opportunity to make money. His parents celebrated it half-heartedly, by putting up an artificial tree, loading up the cocktail bar and raiding Fortnum & Mason for the kind of delicacies they saw in glossy magazines. Now he could see that his desire to come here for Christmas had been based on the same reason his parents put up that tree each year.

He wanted acceptance.

Ever since he was a small boy Josh had been aware that his home life didn't conform with other children's. He knew his parents loved him, but they never had time for him. Even when they moved away from Cable Street, there was never much of a home-life. His father only came home to sleep, and as their wealth increased his mother involved herself in charity work rather than staying at home. Had they been orthodox Jews he might have had the stability of the synagogue and all its teachings. But as it was he straddled the two worlds of Jews and Gentiles uneasily, never quite fitting into either.

Until tonight none of this had concerned him, he believed making money was the answer to everything. But suddenly he wasn't so sure.

He woke on Christmas morning to the smell of roast turkey and the sound of laughter drifting up the stairs. He was horrified to discover it was after eleven, and he washed, shaved and dressed in record time.

Later he was to discover the women had been up since six, milking the cows and feeding the animals. But his first view of them preparing vegetables and sharing a joke with Dr Masterton, who lounged in the rocking chair drinking a pint of cider, didn't tell him that.

'We thought you were Rip Van Winkle.' Mabel smiled. 'You're a bit late for breakfast, and I doubt if you fancy cider when you've just woken. But how about a cup of tea and some toast?'

He liked the look of Greg immediately, and envied the way he looked so right in his tweed jacket and grey flannels. His own navy blazer had seemed perfect in Simpson's of Piccadilly, but now he felt overdressed.

'They've all been dying to open the presents.' Greg's plump, rosy face broke into a warm grin of comradeship. 'But we couldn't start without the guest of honour.'

Josh knew all about presents, he'd had plenty of practice with his avaricious mother, but the moment they began to open the parcels he knew his style only belonged in Golders Green. The pale blue cashmere sweater for Amy should have been bought by Greg. Mabel's eyes sparkled like his mother's when she saw the wooden box of paints, but the moment she saw the Harrod's label she looked embarrassed.

'It's lovely,' she said, lowering her eyes. 'But you shouldn't have given me such an expensive gift.'

She meant that she felt awkward because she'd only given him a pair of grey woolly gloves, and Amy a desk diary. Yet somehow he sensed she felt he was trying to buy them. Worst of all he knew this *had* been his ploy and he dreaded the moment when Tara would open her box and find the boots.

'It's a way of thanking you for inviting me,' he said quickly. 'And Tara, yours is because I could never have got this far without you.'

Her squeals of delight at the tight white leather boots almost washed away his guilty feelings, but not quite.

The whole day was wonderful – wearing his first paper hat for lunch, lingering over mince pies and brandy as they read each other the jokes from the crackers.

Later they played Scrabble in the sitting room. The fire crackled, the tree lights twinkled and the paper chains rustled in the heat. The scent of pine needles and oranges mingled with cigar smoke as they chatted and laughed.

Tara sat on the floor, her tongue peeping out of her lips as she concentrated on finding words. Amy curled her legs up beneath her on the settee, giggling girlishly each time Greg came up with a far-fetched word he claimed was a medical term.

Mabel dozed in an armchair, waking from time to time to top up their glasses with cherry wine. But Josh's eyes kept returning to Tara.

There was nothing artificial about her. She stuffed sweets and fruit, rubbed her mascara on to cheeks rosy from the fire and flicked her hair back behind her ears without any pretence. He wanted to kiss that long neck, lick away the stains of the cherry wine from her mouth and hold her in his arms forever.

Back in London he would have dismissed a country doctor with thinning hair and a pot belly as a boring companion. But the man sparkled with wit and incisive comments on human frailties. Josh saw the way his hands reached out to touch Amy now and then, the way their eyes met. He wanted it to be like that between him and Tara, to feel so safe and secure that he didn't have to guard his words, or cover things up.

In the course of conversation he discovered the tragedy that had killed Paul. He was touched to find he was the first person to sleep in his room, yet sad that Tara had never told him about her brother.

'The right moment never came.' She shrugged her shoulders in a way that suggested he'd never shown the slightest interest in her family. 'Besides, Paul belonged here, not London. It didn't seem appropriate to talk about it there.'

Was he shallow? Why hadn't he realised that deep sadness was part of her reason for remaining a semi-recluse when other girls were out dancing and partying? How many other secrets was she hiding while he used her talent?

He was a bit tipsy when he went to bed on Christmas night. He'd been far drunker, but had never laid his heart on the line before.

Tara followed him up the stairs. Amy and Greg were in the sitting room, Mabel in the kitchen. He turned to Tara on the landing and held out his arms.

'I love you,' he whispered, wanting more than a girl in his bed or even a fashion designer to help him fake it. 'You are everything in the world to me.'

She put her arms round him, drawing his head down on to her shoulder, and rocked him in her arms.

It was only the next morning that he realised she hadn't responded either way, and that worried him more than a rebuff.

He climbed into the big old-fashioned bath and lay under the hot water.

That was why he'd tried so hard to help this morning, dressing up in those awful old clothes in an effort to learn about the farm. Maybe seeing him away from London had made her uncertain that he could fit in with this part of her life, and he had to try. But now he'd made a fool of himself!

They were due to drive back tonight, but he had to try to make things right before they left.

He finished washing, shaved and put on a pair of slacks and a sweater, then went back downstairs.

'Lunch will be ready soon.' Amy smiled as he came into the kitchen. 'I hope you didn't hurt yourself. I've just been telling off Tara for being so cruel. The calves did that to me the first time. It's the same for everyone.'

'Sorry, Josh.' Tara grinned impishly. 'It was mean, but it was so funny.'

'I've a good mind to take you down to Bergman's one day and throw you in the deep end.' Josh ran a hand down her hair as she sat on a chair. 'Anyway, I've forgiven you. After all these years I've finally discovered why Jews steer clear of pigs. They're scared of them!'

'I'm glad you take it all in good part.' Mabel turned round from the stove. 'It's been good having you here, Josh. I hope you'll come again in the spring or summer and see the farm at its best.'

A feeling of joy rushed through him. He wanted to go over and hug the old lady, swing pretty Amy around the room and tell them both how much he liked them. Tara must have implied to them she really cared, otherwise they would've kept quiet.

'After lunch let's go down to the lake,' Tara suggested. 'I must see it before I go.'

'You stay on here till after the weekend.' Josh smiled generously. He didn't want to go back without her, but he had to cast bread on the water. 'We can manage quite well without you, and I think your mum and gran would like a bit more time with you.'

He hoped she'd refuse, but instead her eyes lit up.

'Oh, Josh, that's wonderful,' she said. 'Thank you so much. Are you sure you can find your way back alone?'

'I've got a map and a pair of eyes,' he said. 'Now, Amy, can I do something? Set the table, wring a few chickens' necks?'

They leaned against the rail and stared at the lake, their sides just touching.

Tara was childishly wearing all her Christmas presents at once; the white boots from Josh, a tartan fur-lined jacket from her mother, and the green hat, scarf and gloves from Greg. Her golden hair hung in great hanks on her shoulders, her lips red as cherries in the wind.

The sky was growing very dark, the sun was big and orange as a pumpkin. The lake seemed to stretch to infinity, almost black now, with silver flashes on the choppy surface. There had been dinghies earlier, but now they were all scudding off towards the yacht club on the far side and the water was left to the swans, geese and ducks.

'This is so beautiful,' Josh said softly. 'Imagine living in a house overlooking it. I'd never want to work again.'

'Paul and I used to come here nearly every day on our bikes,' she said, tucking her hand under his arm and huddling against his sheepskin coat. 'The first time we saw it he was scared by the bigness and wildness of it, but he grew to love it, learned all the birds' names and where they came from. Those big ones, the Canada geese, were his favourites. He used to bring cakes of fat with bits of meal in it specially for them.'

Josh knew there would never be a better moment, but he was scared by the bigness of what he felt.

'I meant what I said last night,' he said softly, turning to take her in his arms. 'I do love you, Tara.'

Her eyes were wide, glowing in the fast fading light, and the green bobble hat against the gold of her hair was painfully lovely. Her mouth quivered momentarily as if she was struggling to find the right words.

'I don't know how I feel,' she said finally, her eyes burning into his. 'Sometimes I think you're the one for me, but other times I know it isn't right.'

She was speaking the truth. Her emotions had swung in both directions so many times in the last few days. Here on home territory faults showed up that she hadn't noticed before – bragging, a kind of fawning manner and even insecurity. But the harshness she hated in London was gone, this new tenderness touched a place within her.

'Are you saying you don't want me as a lover?' He tried to keep his voice even and resist the urge to grab her fiercely.

'If you became a lover I might lose the friend.' She put her gloved hand on his cheek and stroked it. 'We've got a long way to go, Josh, and right now we need one another. Let's just be friends for now and see how it is in a few months.'

'Is it Harry?' He took her hand, peeled off her glove and held her fingers to his lips.

She gave him one of her strange looks that reminded him of the unblinking stare of a cat.

'Harry's like a brother,' she said.'Yes, I'm worried about him, he's very special to me. If he was to go down for a murder I know he didn't do I couldn't bear it. But he hasn't got anything to do with us.'

'One kiss for friendship?' Josh tilted her face up to his own.

She smiled, showing her even white teeth, and her eyes sparked with fire.

'For friendship,' she said. 'And maybe a tomorrow.'

Josh's flat was icy. It stank of stale cigarette smoke and whisky. He switched on the light, took one look at the mess left from before Christmas and shuddered.

It was a small apartment in a block above shops in Brompton Road, a stone's throw from Harrod's. He hadn't had the time or enthusiasm to make it his own yet, and the furniture and decor spoke of faded grandeur.

He drew the heavy plum-coloured curtains, switched on the electric fire and sat hunched in front of it. Empty bags from his pre-Christmas shopping expedition were strewn everywhere. Dirty shirts and pairs of shoes littered the floor, and the remains of a Chinese meal still sat on the marble coffee table. But he wasn't really seeing his customary bachelor squalor; he was thinking of Tara and the future.

On the long drive back guilt had overcome him and he knew in his heart what he had to do. 'If he goes down for murder,' he whispered to himself, rubbing his hand round his chin and feeling the stubble coming through, 'you'll never be able to look any of them in the eye.'

He reached into a cabinet inlaid with mother of pearl and pulled out a bottle of whisky and a glass. He half filled it and gulped it down in one, wincing as it burned his throat.

'Do it now, ' he said.

Picking up the phone he dialled a number in South London, glancing at his watch. It was just after one, a good time to catch him in.

'Joe?' he said as the deep voice answered. 'It's Josh. Good Christmas?'

'I'm calling it off,' he said after pleasantries had been exchanged. 'Make some excuse to bugger off after you've cleared the place of anything of yours. Is he asleep?' He listened patiently for a moment as the gruff voice erupted into argument and abuse.

'I know all that,' he said. 'But there's more than one way to skin a cat. I can't let Collins go down for murder, he'll get a fair stretch for the robbery anyway. Besides, it's been costing me a fortune keeping that little gutless wonder safe all these weeks. He isn't worth it.'

He could tell by Joe's voice that he'd had enough of playing nursemaid, however much he hated the idea of Harry getting off lighter.

'We'll meet tomorrow and I'll settle up with you,' he said firmly. 'Now get the fuck out of there and make sure the gun's somewhere the plod will find it.'

Josh put his hands over his face and sighed deeply. Joe could be relied on to do his part, in half an hour he'd be gone leaving no trace of himself.

The room was getting warmer now. Josh had another slug of whisky and rolled a joint to fortify himself for the walk down to a phone box to make the final call.

It was freezing out on Brompton Road. He turned up the collar of his sheepskin coat and walked past Harrod's, not even glancing at the illuminated windows. The streets were deserted, only the odd taxi passed now and then.

He was almost at Hyde Park before he stopped and pulled open the heavy door of the phone box. Inside it reeked of piss and vomit, but he still closed the door behind him.

He took out the card with the name and phone number on, took a deep breath and dialled.

'It's me again,' he said softly. 'I've got an address for you, and a name. Clive Dunning, known as Ginger, 134 Baytree Road, Brixton. Basement flat. He's the man who shot the nightwatchman, not Harry Collins. If you go there now you'll find him in bed. Some of the leathers are there, too. Watch the back way. He might try to leg it out that way.'

The air smelled sweet as he walked back home. Next week he'd look into finding a shop in the King's Road, and maybe Oxford Street too. He felt lucky.

Chapter 21

January 1967

'They've dropped the murder charge?' Tara was so astounded she almost dropped the receiver. 'Are you sure?'

She glanced round to see both her mother and gran standing stock-still, clutching each other's hands.

Bacon was sizzling in the pan. Pails of pig swill were steaming on the floor, ready to be taken out. Gran was back in men's trousers, boots and a sweater; Amy still had on a duffle coat and gloves.

'Well, I got it from 'Arry's brief,' George said, his voice rumbling as if he was trying to suppress a wild whoop of joy. 'Seems the plod picked up the other geezer in the early hours of yesterday morning.'

'They've picked up the man who really did it,' Tara quickly relayed back to Mabel and Amy.

'Oh, Uncle George, I'm so thrilled!' She giggled. Amy was gesticulating wildly, presumably sending love and kisses, while Mabel had sunk down on to a chair, her smile like a slice of watermelon. 'You should see Gran's and Mum's faces. They're both grinning like a pair of Cheshire cats.'

'Bless 'em.' George's voice broke. 'I tell you, sweetheart, there's going to be a lot of celebrating round our manor tonight. S'pose I'll 'ave to go and set up me stall in a minute, but I can't see me selling nothin', I'll want to give it away.'

'What happens now?' Tara asked, wiping a tear from her cheek. 'Will he get bail?'

'Doubt it, love. 'E's due back in court next Monday, but as this is a lesser charge, and he'll be pleadin' guilty now, I expect they'll fix a new date.'

'How long will he get?'

'The brief's hoping he might get probation, but I don't fink that's on. Maybe six months or a year. Anyway, I'm going over to Brixton this afternoon to see 'im.'

'Give him our love.' Tara let out a deep sigh. 'Can I go and see him when I get back?'

She sensed a change in atmosphere in the room and glancing round she saw Gran's smile had gone, replaced by a look of horror.

'No, love, you keep away. That ain't no place for you. 'E won't want you going to court, neither. There's bound to be a lot of press there and we don't want your boat race in the papers.'

She gave a reluctant sigh to indicate she would do as he said.

'Well, give him a hug from all of us. Of course we always knew he didn't do it.'

'You gotta remember he's still going down for thieving,' George reminded her in a gruff voice. 'A girl going up in the world like you must keep that in mind. Know what I mean?'

'Yes, Uncle George, I know. Well, bye, and thank you for the wonderful news.'

An hour later they were still sitting round the breakfast table when Greg came in.

'What's this?' He looked cold and tired, but he picked up the party atmosphere immediately. 'Didn't anyone tell you Christmas is over?'

Amy blurted out the news, her eyes shining. Greg took off his tweed jacket and sat down heavily.

'Well, that's certainly something to brighten my

day.' His round face broke into a wide smile. 'I've been out on calls all night. Mrs Purvis had a stroke just after midnight and I'd no sooner got her to hospital than I got a call to say Mrs Thrush's baby was on its way in a hurry.'

'You poor thing.' Amy ruffled his thinning sandy hair affectionately. 'I'll make you some breakfast. Was it a girl or a boy?'

'A great big boy.' Greg smiled. 'A ten pounder, no less. But never mind my patients. I want to know everything about Harry.'

Amy made Greg a bacon sandwich and a fresh pot of tea and Tara related what George had told her.

'Let's just hope this sets him straight.' Greg ran his hand round his stubbly chin reflectively. 'I like Harry, he's a man with tremendous abilities, but prison can change men drastically and not always for the good.'

'I think he'll pull himself round,' Amy said stoutly.

'Huh!' snorted Mabel. 'You're the worst judge of character I ever met.'

Tara looked at her grandmother and smiled.

'Oh, Gran!' She shook her head. 'You believe in Harry, I know you do. Why don't you just admit it?'

'I want to see proof before I go trusting him again.' Mabel tossed her head and flounced over to the sink. 'Now are you going to sit there all day, or can I have my kitchen back?'

'Eighteen months.' Tara put her head in her hands and sobbed.

She had come over to Paradise Row during the afternoon to wait with Queenie till George got back from the court.

'It ain't so long.' George slid his arm across her bent shoulders. ' 'E's already been on remand for three months, with time off for good behaviour he could be out before Christmas.'

It was a bleak, cold day in late January and for the last few days Tara had bolstered herself up with the possibility that Harry might just get probation and actually be here with them now.

'Ain't no sense in dwelling on summat that can't be altered,' Queenie said sensibly. 'Now I'm going to make the tea and you, my girl, are going to tell us all about Christmas, the shop and how quick we're gonna see your name in lights.'

George switched on the television to watch the news. He was a little puzzled by Tara's reaction to Harry's sentence; after all she was stepping out with Josh now.

He'd had to admit to Harry she'd taken Josh to the farm for Christmas and he knew his son was gutted. But judging by her tears, he suspected his son wasn't entirely out of the running.

' 'Ow's it going with Josh, then,' he asked a little later, when she had composed herself again. He thought she looked very pale, but maybe it was just the black sweater.

'He's not my boyfriend,' she said softly. 'We're just friends, that's all.'

'I didn't mean that.' He grinned, cheered by her reply. 'I meant the shop an' all.'

'Fabulous,' she said, but her smile was so weak it diluted her description. 'I'm busy getting a spring range together, but it's hard to think of spring when it's so cold.'

She lapsed into silence after that remark. George glanced across at her every now and then and wondered what was on her mind. He was certain it wasn't only Harry's sentence.

Tara paused in the shop after George had driven off, trying to see it as the customers did.

Considering the stock was old it all looked remarkably

fresh. Earlier today Miranda had changed the window displays to feature pin-striped trouser suits which had been sticking. She'd jazzed them up, one with a triby hat and a frilly white shirt, the other with a red scarf and beret, and the central display model wore a black and white checked suit.

Tara was speaking the truth when she said everything was fabulous. Two of her designs were to be in *Honey* magazine next month. The shop was becoming the in place for the young and trendy, and Josh was finding some wild fabrics that lent themselves to designs she'd had in her head for some time.

It was Josh who was the problem. Since she got back at New Year he'd been a bit strange. Before Christmas he had been like a mad dog most of the time, demanding this, shouting about that, but she could understand that kind of behaviour. What she'd expected when she got back, and perhaps dreaded, was the smarmy, creepy attitude of someone who wants to please. But it wasn't that either.

This was something else entirely. He was getting extravagant ideas, about two new shops, a townhouse in Chelsea, even a villa in Spain. He'd barely looked at her latest designs, just accepted them, even some that a year ago he would have thrown out as impractical. He was more talkative, too, sometimes so much she couldn't get a word in edgeways, and full of nervous tension.

He had a bee in his bonnet about publicity. Yesterday he rang the *Evening News* and told them his girls wore the shortest mini skirts in London, and Tara had to shorten three skirts to a mere fourteen inches before the photographer came to take pictures. Last week he was contemplating getting a girl to model topless in his window, but fortunately he was advised against that by his solicitor.

Tara sighed as she walked through to the back of the

shop. If Josh was doing all this to try to impress her, it was having the opposite effect!

The whole of 1967 was a confusing, yet thrilling year. She saw Ginger sent down for life in April and read the judge's chilling words which might have been said to Harry. 'You took a man's life coldly and deliberately and it is my duty to put you away to protect society.'

But while judges were taking a high moral tone, London was the Swinging City. Young people from all over the world were flocking to be part of it. Clubs and boutiques opened up like mushrooms overnight. Skirts got shorter, jeans got tighter. Messages were coming over from the States about Flower Children and the first 'love-in' was held in Alexandra Palace.

For a designer like Tara it was a heaven-sent opportunity. Anything went, from long velvet tubes to cheesecloth smocks and tapestry jackets. While every other person under the age of twenty-five was rushing off to the UFO club in Tottenham Court Road to listen to Pink Floyd, Procol Harum and the Soft Machine, she was hastily turning out the clothes to make it happen for them.

Gone were the days when one pattern would be made into fifty identical dresses. Now she had to produce dozens of different designs in one week. They had to be quick before other shops copied them, always one step ahead, keeping the stock changing.

Josh began to buy Nehru shirts from India and bales of flimsy cotton so cheap it was laughable. He opened the shop in Oxford Street in May and installed a book-keeper and secretary in a suite of offices above it. Next came the fourth shop in King's Road, opened in a blaze of publicity on the first of June with four bunny girls giving out free Champagne. The empty room next to her workroom became a stockroom, then the next one, too. Bales of cloth eight-feet high filled the landing and soon Josh had to employ a driver to handle getting it to all the shops.

Tara began to understand why Josh took drugs. His life was one of relentless pressure. He had to be first, he had to be best. He was on a treadmill going faster and faster, and if he broke his pace for a moment everything might collapse.

She often saw him swallow a couple of pills with a hasty cup of coffee before rushing off to the factory or a mill. Meals were eaten on the run, even a night out was always to do a deal or to impress someone. His hair was right down to his shoulders now, he had got so thin she could see his ribs through his cheesecloth shirts and she doubted he got more than a couple of hours' sleep a night.

The pressure was getting to her, too. Sometimes she started work at seven in the morning and at eight or nine at night she was still sewing on buttons. Occasionally she went out with Miranda to the UFO just to keep abreast of the rapidly changing scene, and often she was so tired she was tempted to buy some speed to keep her awake enough to enjoy herself.

But of all the things that affected her in this frantic time, sex was the dominant force. All around her girls were sleeping with anyone they fancied. In the parks, on the Tube, even on street corners couples were kissing and cuddling. The Pill was available to all, every poster, record and magazine promoted free love. There was no escaping it.

She had two brief experiences, she couldn't call them romances exactly as they engaged nothing but her body. The first was with an American who was trying to dodge his draft papers, the second with an Australian who was doing the customary tour of the Continent. But these two men left her nothing, not even laughter.

She was still confused about Josh and Harry. She

knew from George that Harry waited eagerly for news of her, yet she had to keep in her mind that he was a blueprint of her father. At night, alone in her bed, she would think of that kiss out on the landing and tell herself it was only the remnant of a schoolgirl crush.

Her feelings about Josh were no clearer. When he was close to her he made her flesh tingle. She knew she could start an affair with him at any time, but reason told her it was dangerous. Josh believed he was hipper, sexier and cleverer than anyone else. And his womanising was no longer a secret. All the girls he employed were the same type – long blonde hair, legs that went on forever and bodies like goddesses. Rumours reached her that he made love to girls in stockrooms, time and again he was in the papers with another glamorous girl on his arm.

He bought his townhouse in Chelsea in November. When she went to his housewarming party the only furniture was a huge double bed, and during the evening she saw him take two different girls into it.

Yet for all that they were friends. They could laugh about things together, both shared the same love of fashion. She had to remind herself that, if she let it become more than friendship, she would have to take her turn with all his other women.

It was just two days before Christmas when she heard Harry's release date was set for January 2nd. On the same day Greg bought her mother an engagement ring.

Although it was customary to throw a release party, George refused point-blank on the grounds that it might encourage Harry to think he was a hero. Instead Tara met Harry, Queenie and George for dinner in a Greek restaurant in Islington.

It was bitterly cold that night. She wore a white rabbit coat, a plain black mini dress with a scoop neck and her hair was loose.

They were already seated at the table when she arrived and Harry's pallor made her falter. His skin had always glowed from exposure to the sun and wind, but now it was grey, his cheeks sunken, emphasising his angular bones. She had seen his navy blue suit hundreds of times, but now it merely hung on a far leaner frame. Even his eyes looked dull. But he leaped out of his seat when she walked in, with all his old animal grace.

'You look even more beautiful than I remembered,' he said as he kissed her lightly on the lips.

She knew with just that brief touch that she hadn't imagined anything. All those feelings she'd tried so hard to banish were there, waiting for him to light the fuse.

Sitting opposite him was the sweetest agony, laughing and chatting, all the time wishing she could hold him. She wanted to run a finger down those sharp cheek-bones, kiss the hollows beneath them.

'He looks so thin, don't he?' Queenie said, patting his stomach as if he was a little boy. 'I can see I'll 'ave to do a bit of baking.'

'The food was so awful I couldn't eat it.' Harry grinned as if it hadn't mattered, but Tara could see pain in his eyes. 'It was the stink of the place, the sad, sick people who've never had a chance in life. I used to lie on my bunk and focus on your picture, Tara. It cut everything else out.'

'Well, it's over now, son,' George lifted his glass for a toast. 'And here's to the future!'

George wore a new waistcoat, scarlet with gold embroidery, and a red bow-tie. His plump face shone with happiness. Queenie lived up to her name in brilliant blue satin, a mink stole and diamond earrings, her blonde hair arranged in fat curls, each one studded with a tiny blue flower.

Tara told them about the engagement party on

Christmas Day at the farm, and how Gran got drunk but insisted she was sober even when she had to be carried upstairs.

'When are they going to set the day?' Queenie asked. 'Will it be this summer?'

'I don't know.' Tara shook her head. 'You know how awkward Gran can be. Greg made some sort of suggestion about building a practice in the meadow by the side of the farm and she went crackers.'

All through the meal Tara was painfully aware of Harry watching her. She saw his eyes travel down her neck to her breasts and felt her nipples harden under his gaze.

'Tell me what it's like to be famous?' he asked teasingly. 'How does Josh feel now his rival is out?'

She had avoided the subject of Josh and the shops. She didn't want Harry to feel put down by hearing such a success story when he was at such a low ebb.

'I'm not famous.' She blushed. 'There's only been one article about me. Josh is the one who's becoming a celebrity. Speaking of him, he wished you well.'

In fact Josh had turned red with anger yesterday afternoon when she mentioned Harry's release and this celebration.

'Don't go tangling with him,' he warned her. 'The media will be on to it in a minute. He's bad news.'

She had called him a turncoat, suggested he was getting too big for his boots, forgetting old friends.

Josh tried to get round her later, said he was frightened of losing her and how much he cared. He held out a hundred pounds and asked her to give it to Harry to help him out till he found a job.

'I bet he wished me a thousand miles away,' Harry smiled, looking into her eyes as if trying to gauge whether he had been told the truth. 'It must scare the hell out of him imagining me snatching you away. His business would crumble over night.'

'For the record, Harry,' she said softly, 'Josh tried to give me a hundred pounds to tide you over. I refused it, because I knew you would. And his business wouldn't crumble without me, he'd have dozens of designers jumping to take my place.'

She ought to have said he couldn't snatch her away anyway, but at that moment she knew he was maybe the one man who could!

'I don't believe that.' Harry's lips were twisted into a wry smile. 'The money was a bribe!'

'Come on now,' George interrupted. 'It's 1968 now, a new year, a new start. I'm going to order a bottle of Champagne and we'll leave the past behind us.'

It was after midnight when they left the restaurant. Harry slipped his arm round Tara as they stood together looking for a taxi to hail. Queenie and George were still in the restaurant doorway, chatting to the owner.

'Tara!' A male voice came from nearby but it wasn't one she recognised. She looked up at Harry in astonishment and a camera flash went off. It was a second or two before they got over the surprise and by then the photographer was jumping into a car and heading off down Essex Road.

'Who on earth was that?' Tara was so shocked her mouth fell open. 'How did he know I'd be here, anyway?'

Queenie toddled over to them, a little unsteady on her high heels.

' 'E must have followed you 'ere,' she said indignantly. 'What a slag. I wonder 'ow 'e connected you to our 'Arry?'

'Josh,' Harry said, his face turning hard and cold. 'That creep would sell his own mother for a spot of free publicity!'

'Don't be ridiculous,' Tara snapped at him. 'What good could it do him?'

'Wait till tomorrow and you'll find out,' Harry sniffed. 'I can see the headlines. "Top designer celebrates with East End villain on his release." Quite by chance there'll be a picture of the shop, too!'

It was as if someone had thrown a bucket of cold water over them. All the rosy dreams Tara had planned of perhaps going on somewhere so they could be alone to talk vanished. She didn't like Harry's accusation and she was even more perturbed at the prospect of her face being splashed across the papers. Jumping into a taxi alone was instinctive, but once she'd got into bed she regretted it.

She thought of Harry's slim, hard body, sensual lips and those brilliant blue eyes. She recalled the way he'd tried to grab her back from the taxi, his face aghast because it wasn't what he'd planned either. He would see this as loyalty to Josh. All that passion pent up from a year inside might be unleashed elsewhere. Why hadn't she just thought of his feelings instead of her own stupid pride?

All at once she knew where she belonged. It didn't matter what other people thought or said. She had to be with him. She got out of bed and, going down to the phone in her workroom, she dialled Paradise Row, pulling her silky negligée tighter round her body.

But Queenie answered.

'Could I speak to Harry?' she asked. 'I was a bit hasty running off.'

' 'E's gone out, darlin',' Queenie's voice sounded tense, as if something else had happened. 'Only a saint would spend his first night of freedom at 'ome!'

'Do you know where he's gone?' She was quite prepared to get in a taxi and go to look for him.

'No, love. He didn't say.'

'Was he angry with me?'

'Sad more than angry.' Queenie sighed deeply. 'I won't take sides. I understand how it is for you, and

413

him. But he's thought of nothing but you all this time. Whoever tipped off that reporter knew they would mess things up between you. You can't blame 'Arry for thinking it was Josh!'

'I know, that's why I rang.' Tara felt tears pricking her eyelids.

'Let's just pray he gets quietly drunk somewhere and lurches home without getting up to any mischief.' Queenie chuckled. 'I'll leave 'im a note that you phoned.'

Chapter 22

'Yeah, of course I've heard of Harry Collins. But I don't like the idea of some ex-con steaming into our game.' Duke Denning spoke in a low voice, glancing back over his shoulder to make sure there weren't any eavesdroppers.

He needn't have worried. At eleven in the morning in the shabby Town of Ramsgate in Wapping High Street, the only customers apart from himself and Joe were two comatose old men staring at their pints.

The pub was one of the oldest on the river, overshadowed by soot-blackened warehouses. When the docks were in their heyday it had been a cheery little place, but now it looked as sad and abandoned as the rest of Wapping.

'Well, he ain't a cheat if that's what you're thinking. I might not like the bloke, but he's straight. His track record will tell you that,' Joe insisted.

Duke had been a gambler all his life, but he'd learned over the years to shorten the odds in his favour. He was tall and powerfully built, with the kind of blond good looks that usually opened doors for him automatically. But he had to remind himself he wasn't in Manchester or Birmingham now. East End villains and gamblers were different.

When Joe Spikes rang him late last night and asked for a meet, he was surprised. Joe rarely came north of the river, and he wasn't one to ask favours of mere acquaintances. Perhaps this was why Joe insisted on this pub. It was close to the Rotherhithe tunnel, frequented only by warehousemen and a few hardened drunks. Anyone observing them together would assume their relationship was employer and employee, because of the gulf between their appearances.

Duke's height, blond hair and rugged face made women turn their heads and flutter their eyelashes. Joe's appearance did the opposite. A hideous scar covered the right side of his face, puckering his upper lip and pulling his nose to one side. To make matters worse his head was as bald and shiny as a billiard ball. At six feet tall, with shoulders like a barn door and a hard, lean body, nobody would want to run into him in a dark alley.

Duke wore a light grey Savile Row suit, but Joe was in rough corduroys and a donkey jacket.

'Why are you so anxious to get him in on the game?' Duke had already picked up the vibes that Joe had a grudge against Collins, but setting someone up at a game of cards was a strange way to get even.

They'd first met a couple of years ago, in Manchester. Duke had an interest in an illegal gaming house, and Joe was brought in as a debt collector. No-one they'd ever employed was so successful; one look at that face was enough to frighten even the most persistent 'welsher'. But Duke liked Joe, even if he knew little about the man's past. He was tough, entirely fearless and far brighter than people gave him credit for.

'I want him to lose, of course.' Joe grinned, but it did nothing to enhance his fearsome appearance.

'Fair enough.' Duke smiled back. 'So he's loaded. Right?'

'Dunno about that.' Joe shook his head. 'But I want him cleaned out of what he's got.'

'Come on! Why?' Duke asked, his piercing blue eyes homing in on the other man like lasers.

'That's between him and me,' Joe dropped his eyes from Duke's. 'It's quite simple, ain't it? You get the others to let him in, you take his wedge off him. What you got to lose?'

'Well, if he's a demon poker player, everything,' Duke smirked.

He couldn't make out why Joe didn't just give the guy a good thrashing, but then Joe was a devious bastard and maybe this way the hurt would last far longer than a few broken ribs.

'Harry ain't a gambler. Sure, he's had a game or two, but not in your league. I know why he's bin trying to get into a big game, because I was enough of a mug to do it once or twice myself. He thinks it's easy money. I want to teach him a lesson.'

'OK.' Duke finished his pint and stood up. 'We can all do with a couple of pigeons in a game, I'll send word he's in.'

Joe gave that evil grin again.

'Thanks, Duke. I owe you one! But do me a favour and don't let my name slip. This is just between us. You know where you can reach me to let me know the result!'

Harry nervously patted his breast pocket as he got out of the van by Swan Wharf in Wapping.

It was four weeks since his release and tonight was the first stage of the plans he'd made in prison. He'd drawn his entire savings, three hundred quid, out of the post office, and if his father knew he'd kill him. But what could he do with three hundred? Buy a second-hand motor, take a holiday or get a new suit. What he needed was enough dosh to buy a couple of derelict houses, a bit of spare to do them up and he'd be on his way.

It was all very well his dad saying they were partners and making out like he really needed his son around, but, aside from humping heavy boxes, Harry was just a spare part. Employers didn't want someone with a record, unless it was navvying. Harry wanted to work with his hands and marry Tara.

There was money to be made as a builder and he had a nose for places that were right for speculation. Hadn't it been his idea to buy the house in Paradise Row? So maybe he'd lose this wedge, but so what? He'd played poker inside enough, listened to all the tales of fortunes won and lost. As long as he didn't go beyond what was on the table and kept his cool, he'd be no worse off.

The tall warehouses looked spooky in the darkness. As a boy he had loved this place with its narrow cobbled streets and names like Cinnamon Street and Tobacco Wharf. Sailors and dockers crammed into the little pubs, a rich soup of every nationality. There were strange exotic smells of spices, coffee and tea, and noise and confusion everywhere. But now there was only the sound of his feet on the cobbles, the occasional fog-horn on the river, and wind whistling through dilapidated buildings.

He had taken it as a good omen that the game was to be played in Baxter's warehouse, as he remembered it from his childhood, when he and Needles used to go down the narrow alley at the side to watch the ships unloading their cargoes. But Baxter's looked sad now. Most of the windows on the front were boarded up, a bush grew out of the roof, and the old hoists creaked ominously in the wind. The old man who owned it, Stan Baxter, died a few years ago. Harry had done his homework about all the players tonight and one of them was Chas Baxter, the owner's son.

Harry flicked down the cuffs of his white shirt. He'd got to start bluffing right now and make them all believe he was a pigeon. The gun cufflinks were part of the image he wanted to portray. Only a naive eighteen-year-old or a mug would wear such things, but he'd known they'd come in handy one day.

He knocked loudly on the narrow door next to the loading bay, polished up his old winklepickers on the backs of his strides while he waited, and set his face to look like an arrogant twerp.

It was eleven o'clock and he wondered if it would still be dark when he came out.

He could hear footsteps coming down a metal staircase, the echo proving the place was no longer used for storing goods. Metal bolts were pulled back, a key turned in the lock and the door creaked open.

'Harry Collins.' He shot out his hand and gripped the other man's. He knew this was Duke Denning by the descriptions he'd been given, but he hadn't expected him to be quite so good-looking.

'Come in, Harry. The others arrived a few minutes ago. Ready for a good night?'

Aside from a description and the knowledge that this man was reputed to be one of the best players in England, Harry hadn't found out much else. He didn't seem to have any form. Rumour had it he was just a professional gambler.

The wind was howling through broken windows on the river side of the building, bringing with it that peculiar, tangy river smell Harry loved. Although there was only one dim light on the metal spiral staircase, he could see enough to know the place was in ruins.

'It's gonna be a bit chilly, ain't it?' he said as he followed Duke up the stairs.

'The old office is OK.' Duke turned to speak. He wore an impeccably tailored navy suit, a military tie and hand-stitched shoes. Even the man's voice was quality, deep, clear and accentless.

Harry had dug out an old suit tonight, dark green

419

mohair, with a flashy gold lining. But, like the cufflinks and winklepickers, it was just a prop.

Duke flung open a door and warmth, light and cigarette smoke came billowing out.

'Here we are, lads,' Duke said in an overloud voice. 'Harry Collins!'

Three men, all far older than him, sat round a table strewn with pub ashtrays, lighters and glasses. An almost full bottle of Scotch stood at the centre. Harry grinned as he waited to be introduced.

The office was oak panelled and still very gracious, despite the ruin elsewhere in the building. An electric fire was on in the old fireplace, and an oil painting of a stern-faced Victorian gentleman hung above it. Nothing else of the past remained. The floorboards were bare, the curved-topped windows taped up with cardboard. A single dim light above covered in a red fringed shade suggested someone's attempt at creating atmosphere.

'Chas Baxter.' Duke waved a hand towards a man in his fifties with a florid complexion and a huge beer gut. 'Alf Reed, Jack Somers.'

Harry shook their hands and sat down.

Alf owned two West End night-clubs; a flashy bastard of forty-something whose Rolls-Royce he'd seen parked along the road. Harry knew he lived in Millionaires' Row in Hampstead and, although he might not have quite reached that status yet, he was loaded. His light brown hair looked as if it had been blow-dried by some poof; his pale brown eyes were shrewd.

Jack Somers was a building contractor from South London who once had the reputation of being a hard man. Now he was close on sixty, as rich as Alf, with a permanent suntan, lean body and barely any hair.

Harry knew these men wouldn't be a pushover. Anyone who resorted to playing cards in such dingy surroundings had to be serious about the game.

They exchanged pleasantries and he was handed a glass of whisky. Jack commiserated with him about his prison sentence and asked what plans he had now.

Harry was certain they knew everything about him, including his inside leg measurement, but he couldn't show that.

'I gotta few deals lined up,' he said, grinning foolishly as if surprised to find the other players were men of stature. 'Nuffin' certain yet, but I might open a club.'

'Not on my patch, I hope.' Alf's thick eyebrows lifted, and fleshy lips curved into a wry smile.

'Where's that?' Harry asked innocently.

'Alf owns the Ace of Hearts in Wardour Street and the Purple Pussy Cat,' Duke said with a smirk.

'No!' Harry laughed, quickly pulling out his cigarette case and flashing it round. 'I got me heart set on King's Road, a place for dolly birds. Know what I mean?'

'Takes a lot of dough,' Alf said. 'You need experience in the club world, too.'

'I got both.' Harry looked smug. 'Well, the experience of clubs is only drinking in them, but it can't be that 'ard.'

He saw them exchanging glances and decided he'd said enough.

Duke was to deal the first game and, as Harry was already sitting to his right, he would have to make the opener. The atmosphere changed immediately Duke picked up the sealed pack of cards. The sit-down money, two hundred pounds, was slapped down beside them, cigarettes, lighters, drinks and ashtrays placed strategically, and Duke dealt.

Harry had a pair of sixes, but nothing else. He changed two and came up with another six. It was a fair hand, but he had to act cautious. He noted that neither Alf nor Jack asked for new cards, which could mean they had good hands, too. He picked up a ten-pound note and flicked it down. Alf raised him twenty. Chas raised twenty; already there was fifty pounds in the pot. Jack hesitated just a second but raised forty. Duke folded.

Harry smiled weakly and raised twenty, sliding a hundred pounds on to the pot. Alf folded.

He was sure that earlier hesitation on Jack's part meant he had a poor hand. Chas looked supremely comfortable, but Harry had no way of knowing whether that was his usual look. It was Jack's turn and he raised twenty. Harry glanced at Chas, but his face was impassive and he pushed his money on to the pile, raising thirty.

Harry didn't dare look at his money on the table. He just picked it up and threw it down in an expansive gesture. 'Raise you fifty.'

Jack folded and Chas smiled benignly as he threw a hundred on. 'I'll see you,' he said.

It was the moment of truth. He laid his three sixes down and waited.

Chas had only a pair.

A ripple of laughter went round the table, even from Chas. He pushed the money towards Harry and lit up a cigar. Harry didn't know what to think. Was this some sort of wild strategy on Chas's part, or everyone's?

He folded on the next game and lost his stake. But in the third he won six hundred.

The air was thick with smoke; it hung around the light above them like a blanket. The cardboard on the windows wobbled in the draught and Harry could feel another one from the door nearly cutting his ankles in half while his head was roasting. He was no nearer sussing anyone out, they were all steady players who gave nothing away, and seemed to have endless amounts of notes in their pockets.

'Bloody George Raft from the door,' he said casually

as he looked at his cards. He'd got nine hundred on the table now; maybe it was time to up the ante. He had a straight, and he knew the time was right.

Jack was dealing and Chas made the opener with two hundred pounds. Duke raised him a hundred and now it was Harry's turn. He dropped in the three-hundred stake and raised another two hundred.

Alf folded, quickly followed by Jack. Chas, still as cool as a cucumber although he hadn't had a win, tossed on his three-hundred stake and raised two hundred. Duke raised another hundred and Harry matched it, shoving his whole pile in. Chas folded.

It was between him and Duke now and he would have to fold if Duke didn't, or call him. But to his surprise Duke called. Harry put his cards down gingerly, sure Duke could beat them.

'It's yours, Harry,' Duke said. 'Only three of a kind.'

The feeling as he drew the money towards him was almost as good as Christmas morning. He had almost four thousand, and he still had his other hundred in his breast pocket.

They stopped for a beer, moving back from the table while they chatted. Harry sat back grinning while he studied them. The grin was meant to disarm them. They'd taken him for a sucker and he guessed each one thought his luck would soon break and they'd get the money back.

The night wore on. In the good games time flew, in the bad it stood still. At one point he'd had six thousand; then it went down to three. The temperature was rising in all ways. Chas stripped off his jacket. Duke dabbed delicately at his forehead with a maroon handkerchief. Only Jack and Alf looked cool, but perhaps that was because their sort of losses meant nothing to them.

Harry kept up the bluff – opening his jacket to show the gold lining, flicking his lighter, going down frequently to the filthy toilet below, drumming his nails on the table.

Pure adrenaline was keeping him going now as his pile reached ten thousand, only to be cut in half in the next game, but when he looked at the other men they showed no emotion.

Duke had the most wins; Harry came next, beating Chas by one game. He wondered how they could pull out that kind of dough without wincing, and how often they did this.

It was after four when finally Duke suggested the next game should be the last.

Harry was dealt three kings, but two low cards. When he changed the two and got the king of hearts he could barely believe his luck. He tried to remember what the old guy in prison had told him about the odds on someone having a better hand than that, but it escaped him. All he could think was that this was shit or bust time.

The raising was slow, Harry had to keep himself in check, wanting to raise wildly and get it over with, but knowing he mustn't. Jack folded first, putting his jacket on and smiling broadly as if nothing mattered but going home to bed. On and on it went after Jack's car had roared away into the night. It was nearly five, there had to be twelve thousand on the table, a great tottering pile of notes, and Alf folded.

'I'm off, lads,' he said cheerily, tapping Harry on the shoulder. 'You're a gutsy player. Hope the club goes well.'

Harry felt a little ashamed he'd taken so much money from a good sport. He just hoped Duke and Chas would be the same.

Duke folded and it was just like that first game all over again. Now it was between Chas and him.

Chas put the last of his money on the pot, but Harry had no way of knowing if he had more. He raised him

424

again, but his own pile was getting dangerously low. Should he call, or play one more?

He raised just a little, all he had left now was seven hundred on the table and the one still in his pocket. When he saw Chas reach into his pocket he groaned inwardly, but to his surprise Chas brought out a folded document.

'I'll be honest,' he said, still not moving a muscle or showing any emotion. 'I'm broke. But I'll put these in and see you.'

'What is it?' Harry's eyes were blurry now, his head aching and heart racing.

'The deeds of this place.' Chas shrugged. 'Put the rest of your dough on the pot and I'll see you.'

The cold impassive face chilled Harry to the bone. He looked first at his small pile, then at the mountain of notes on the table. Reason told him the bloke must have an excellent hand to risk everything, but then again so had he.

'OK!'

They laid out their cards simultaneously. Chas had a full house, but Harry's four of a kind beat them by a whisker.

A wild glee rose up in Harry. He wanted to shout, scream with joy, but he didn't dare. He hadn't got out yet!

Duke whistled through his teeth, but Harry was only looking at Chas. For the first time in the night muscles were moving in his face, as if he was struggling to control himself.

Harry had to steel himself. He didn't owe these men anything, they would cheerfully have taken the shirt off his back. But all the same, could he really take it all? There had to be twenty thousand there, more money than he'd ever dreamed of.

'Are you really broke?' he asked.

Chas shrugged his shoulders, his large stomach quivering.

Harry stood up. He was at his most vulnerable now. Duke looked capable of knocking him out with one blow; Chas was desperate enough to go along with it, and the river was far too close. In the back of his mind he remembered something Mabel had once said to him. 'Kindness is your biggest asset, Harry, don't ever lose sight of it.' He scraped the money together on the table and put the deeds in his pocket.

'Write me a note to say the building's mine,' he said quietly. 'Duke, witness it.'

The thick smoke was burning his eyes, sweat was breaking out all over him and he could sense Duke was like a coiled spring.

'How much did you sit down with?' he asked.

'Three thousand.' Chas tried to smile but his mouth was set. A nerve quivered in his cheek.

Harry took some notes from the top of the pile and slid them over to Chas, he guessed it was around a thousand.

'A stake for another game.' He felt deflated now and knew he would never play again. He couldn't risk ending up like this fat man. 'Just sign the paper.'

'You didn't have to do that,' Chas said in a curiously small voice, pulling a fountain pen from his pocket. 'You won it fair and square.'

Harry saw the oil painting out of the corner of his eye. 'Call it for that picture,' he said.

Chas smiled then, with real warmth. He took the sheet of notepaper Duke silently offered him and began to write.

'That was my great-grandfather,' he said as he finished. 'He was an honourable man, too.'

Duke's head was whirling. Harry was no real poker player, he was too wild, and he'd just drawn good cards. Duke had come out even himself, perhaps a little down, so he had nothing to reproach the man for. But this last act of chivalry touched him and he knew that Harry Collins was a force to be reckoned with.

Joe had been so sure Harry would lose that he'd offered no alternative plan and Duke wasn't thrilled to be the man to relay the outcome to him. But what could he do at this late stage anyway? Joe would have mugged him, that was a certainty, but Duke Denning wasn't going to lose his reputation that way. He witnessed the note without a word and handed it back to Harry.

Chas slid a set of keys across the table.

'It's all yours now.'

'I underestimated you,' Duke said as he watched Harry slapping the notes into bundles and putting them in his pockets.

Harry looked up. 'Most people do,' he said softly. Picking up his cigarettes from the table, he opened the door and left.

George was in the kitchen when Harry let himself in. He shivered in the narrow hall, pockets bulging, fingers stained with nicotine, his angular face pale with exhaustion. But the house was warm. He could smell coffee from the kitchen and Queenie's lilac soap wafting down the stairs on a cloud of steam from the bathroom.

'What time's this to come in?' George grumbled. 'It's bleedin' Saturday, son, the busiest day. You won't make a market trader if you stay up all night.'

He was wearing red pyjamas and checked slippers, the little hair left around his head standing out like a bottle brush.

'I ain't gonna be a market trader for much longer.' Harry grinned. 'You'd better sit down, Dad. I don't know if your old ticker can stand this.'

George just stared at the money on the table. He had the deeds of the warehouse in one hand, the note in the other.

'You crazy boy,' he said, and a tear rolled down his cheek.

'I ain't ever going to do it again,' Harry knelt beside his father's chair and leant his face against George's chest the way he did when he was small. 'I ain't got the stomach for it, really. I was just lucky tonight. But I'm going to use it now I've got it. Just think of it like me winning the pools.'

George held his son's head tightly. He didn't approve of gamblers, he'd seen too many end up in the gutter.

'Tell me what you want from life, 'Arry,' he whispered.

Harry knew what his father was afraid of.

'I want to build up a business,' he said, his voice muffled by his father's chest. 'I want to make something of myself. I'll make you proud of me.'

He couldn't tell him yet that he intended to have Tara beside him, that would be tempting fate.

George lifted Harry's face up in his big hands.

'I've always been proud of you,' he said fiercely. 'And I know if yer mum's looking down on you, she is too. But build an honest business, son, no more duckin' and divin'.'

Chapter 23

'You aren't serious, Harry?' Tara looked up at the dilapidated warehouse in horror. 'A night-club! Here in Wapping?'

Tara had gone over to Paradise Row for tea and Harry had whisked her round in the van to see this place he'd won. He looked like a navvy, in old trousers daubed with muck, a grey roll-necked sweater, big dirty boots and a donkey jacket. Even his black hair was dull with dust.

The news had reached her about the poker game long before George or Queenie got around to telling her. Angie heard it in a pub in Bethnal Green the evening after the game and telephoned straight away. The winnings had risen to forty thousand by that time and the building was made to sound like something grand.

Harry might be a hero to the whole of Bethnal Green, but not to Tara. It was an unwanted reminder of her father and a timely warning not to embark on a love affair with him.

'I'm completely serious,' he said. 'I've already had some rough plans drawn up and got someone to act for me with the council. Unless they turn it down, I'm on my way.'

In another hour it would be pitch dark, but even in daylight it looked forbidding.

'Who's going to come to a club here?' She wrinkled her nose in disgust. An icy wind was blowing rubbish down the narrow street, bringing with it the stink of the river, and she felt dwarfed by the menacing, soot-stained buildings pressing in all around her. Further along the street an uncleared bomb-site had become a tip, strewn with old mattresses and abandoned cars. The only homes she'd seen were tenements, many of which were boarded up. At night it would be terrifying. There was virtually no street lighting and she could imagine rats scrabbling out of the sewers to look for food.

'Toffs,' he said airily. 'They used to come in Victorian days for illegal gambling and it was a darned sight more dangerous then. Look on the positive side, Tara. We can make as much noise as we like, drunks wouldn't bother anyone. It just needs a good publicity campaign.'

'Show me inside,' she said in a weak voice, wrapping her rabbit coat round her. He'd obviously made his mind up and the sooner she got it over with the better.

He opened the narrow door beside the loading bay and led the way in.

'Careful now,' he warned her. 'I've pulled up a few floorboards to look underneath, so it's a bit dodgy.'

A smell of mildew and rotting timbers made her pull up her collar and bury her nose in the fur. She wanted to be enthusiastic, for his sake, but it was like the set for a horror film.

'The windows are a pretty shape,' she ventured, noting their curved tops. They were boarded up at the front, but enough light spilled through from the river side to see by.

'They remind me of prison,' he chuckled, taking her hand to lead her past a gaping hole where he'd pulled up some floorboards. 'They were the same in the

Scrubs, I used to lie awake and count the fifteen little panes.'

To her right a metal spiral staircase led up to the next floor and ahead, through a partially broken partition, was the main part of the warehouse. She saw a vast area, with girders across the ceiling and iron pillars holding it up. It was open to the full force of the wind on the river side, the loading door having long since rotted and fallen into the mud below. A few tea chests were piled in one corner and evidence of Harry's exploratory probing showed in more ripped-up boards, hammers, levers and a pickaxe.

'Look at that!' he led her over to the river, throwing his arms wide, as if showing her the Himalayas at sunset. 'What a view! Imagine yourself with a drink in your hand, soft carpet beneath your feet, the band playing and all this!'

Tara could only see a wide expanse of dirty river and a few barges. Below, the low tide revealed an expanse of stinking, oily mud, strewn with refuse.

'Harry, you can't possibly do it up,' she gasped. 'It's too far gone.'

She had to admit it was big enough. If it had been in Chelsea she might have been cautiously enthusiastic. But Wapping!

'This is the worst bit.' He grinned cheerfully, expanding his chest and breathing in the river air. 'But I've had a survey done and it's structurally sound. Once I've got the windows in and a new floor laid, it'll soon take shape.' He waved one hand towards the wall on the left. 'I'll have a long, curved bar there. Those bench seats that make alcoves, with a table, all along under the window. Then over there at the back, a small stage and a specially sprung floor for dancing.'

It grew more and more ridiculous as he showed her round the rest of the place. The spiral stair would be replaced by a wide grand one, a chandelier would hang above it. He even talked about removing part of the first floor to create a kind of gallery. There were to be gaming rooms on the next floor, and he even talked about making a flat for himself up in the top-floor rooms. His thin face glowed with a missionary zeal. He didn't seem to notice the cold and dirt, or be daunted by the sheer size of what he was proposing.

Until news of the poker game broke, Tara had fondly imagined he was staying away from her until he found a good job. Now she felt he was betraying her trust in him.

'So it's going to be a gambling club?' she said, tight-lipped. Her hands and feet were like ice, it was dusk now and every dark corner was scary.

'Of course. I won't lure rich people here otherwise.'

'Take me home, Harry.' She sighed. 'I'd like it to be a success, but I can't see it happening.'

He caught hold of her arm and spun her round to face him. His eyes burned brightly, his chin had a determined thrust to it.

'It will be a success, Tara, because I'll make it happen. I don't want you to come here again until opening night, then maybe you'll believe in me.'

Not a kiss, not even a few words to say that she was important to him. As the last rays of daylight left the sky she wondered why she'd ever thought he cared.

Hot June sun seared through the workroom window, even with the Venetian blinds closed. Tara sat on a chair by the sewing machine, her hair and flimsy cheesecloth dress damp with perspiration. She was hand-stitching the hem of a green crushed velvet dress, but she had to keep stopping and wiping her hands because the needle was sticking.

Below in the shop she could hear the pounding beat of Sergeant Pepper's Lonely Hearts Club Band; out in the street the ceaseless roar of traffic.

A fan beside her machine merely churned up the hot, stale air. Chemical smells from bales of fabric and damp cloth on the pressing machine mingled with joss sticks from the shop and gave her a headache.

She wanted to be at the farm, to sit under a tree and read a book, or bury her nose in her mother's roses. She wanted her own bedroom, the feeling of starched cool sheets against her skin, with a soft breeze ruffling the curtains. She wanted a man to love her, not to be torn between two crackpots who had put her life on hold while they played out their fantasies.

Harry was actually camping out in that awful building. She hadn't seen him since that day in February. He'd phoned a couple of times but all he talked about was steel beams, timber and the price of lighting.

Josh, meanwhile, was getting wilder and wilder. He'd bought a new silver Mercedes with the number plate JB 12. He continued to stage publicity stunts, including having a couple of models fighting over him at Annabel's nightclub, buying a picnic at Fortnum & Mason with a famous actress on his arm and getting Tara to make clothes for an entire rock group, for which he took the credit. He was making a fortune, there was no doubt about that, and if it wasn't for his wild social life he'd probably have opened more branches still.

Every time Tara complained about the work foisted on to her, he gave her a rise. But money wasn't really what she wanted, she never had the time or inclination to spend it anyway. Sometimes she barely went out of the building in a whole week and, aside from a night out now and again with Angie or Miranda, she had no fun.

She couldn't remember the last time she'd had a lie in, or a walk in the park. Just this eternal pressure to get things done, to solve problems, to fit in with what everyone else wanted.

The phone rang and she picked it up wearily, fully expecting it to be Josh asking when the sample dresses she was making would be ready.

'Hello, princess. Fancy a day at the seaside tomorrow?'

The shock of hearing Harry's voice and such an unexpected invitation threw her.

'I can't,' she replied, looking around her workroom at the piles of unfinished samples.

'Why not?'

She hesitated. It didn't matter how long she spent in this room, the piles of work never got smaller because someone always brought more.

'You can't think of a good reason,' he said teasingly.

'Oh, Harry, I can't take a day off . . . ' But even as she said it she glanced out of the window. Through the blinds she could see girls in sun-dresses eating ice cream and a couple of workmen with bare chests, and suddenly the room seemed even more airless.

'You can,' he insisted. 'Look, the club's nearly ready. I don't know when I'll find a spare minute again. Just imagine a day at Southend, paddling, eating ice cream and shrimps. I'll win you a teddy bear on the rifle range and we'll ride the Wild Mouse!'

His words pulled a cord somewhere inside her, making her feel light-headed and giggly.

'OK,' she said, biting her lip because she'd committed herself now without even thinking about it properly.

'Get the Tube to Bethnal Green,' he said quickly, as if afraid she'd change her mind. 'If I come to collect you it'll take forever getting out through town. Eight o'clock all right?'

'Fine,' she said. 'I'll see you then.'

She hadn't even had time to think up a plausible story when Josh came crashing up the stairs with some dresses in his arms.

He wore white jeans and a red shirt, black curls cascading over his shoulders. At least he'd had some time in the sun, his face was tanned and his big nose was even a bit red.

'Look at these,' he said gleefully. 'What do you think?'

He was buying a great deal of stock from India now, and one of his plans was to go over there later in the year.

Tara gave them a cursory glance. They were made from flimsy cotton, with bright embroidery down the bodice; pretty but very badly made, something he always seemed to overlook these days.

'Great,' she said without much enthusiasm. He didn't listen anyway and today she couldn't be bothered to warn him about continually lowering his standards for the sake of price.

'God, it's hot in here!' He wiped the back of his hand across his forehead. 'Why don't you open the window?'

'Because it's so noisy and dusty,' she said wearily.

Josh was usually too hyped-up to notice anything unusual about his staff, but her tone of voice made him look properly at her. She was very pale, with mauve shadows beneath her eyes, and her hair was decidedly limp.

'What's up?' He moved over to where she sat and put his hand on her shoulder. Through the thin fabric he could feel how hot she was, and she seemed bony. 'Let me take you out to supper tonight?'

'I can't, I've got all this to do.' She waved a hand towards the mountain on the cutting table.

'That can wait till tomorrow.' He barely glanced at them.

'I want to go home tomorrow,' she said.

Even as she said it she knew it was a bad idea to lie. He owed her umpteen days off anyway. But once it was out she made it worse by saying her gran was ill.

'Oh, dear.' His big dark eyes softened with concern because he liked Mabel. 'Nothing serious, I hope?'

435

'It's hard to say with Gran.' Tara was deliberately vague. 'Sometimes she makes a big fuss about nothing, other times she says nothing. But Mum thinks I ought to go.'

'Well, one day won't be much good,' he frowned, for once thinking only of the distance and how tired Tara looked. 'Take a couple and don't worry about work, there's no rush for anything here.'

He suggested she went that night, and once again she had to lie and claim Greg couldn't pick her up at Bristol and there would be no buses.

Josh fanned himself with his hand. 'Well, let's just go over the road now and have a couple of drinks, they've got air-conditioning and you could do with a break. Besides, there's something I want to discuss with you.'

She could see his pupils were tiny; there was no doubt his intake of speed was getting bigger every day.

'Just a couple then.' She smiled wearily at him. 'I'll just go and wash my hands. Won't be a minute.'

The pizza place he took her to hadn't been open long and, aside from being deliciously cool, it was quiet and pretty. They sat at a table by the window looking on to Kensington High Street and Josh ordered a bottle of sparkling white wine and two pizzas.

She felt better already, with her hair brushed and the damp cheesecloth replaced by a green and white spotted mini dress. The prospect of a day at the seaside was exciting, and maybe she could even catch the last train home to Bristol afterwards to make up for telling Josh lies. Throngs of people were out in the street, most of them tourists. Tara noticed Josh's eyes were glued to Biba, as if begrudging each customer who went through the door.

'You don't have to worry about them,' she said gently. 'There's room for all of us.'

'I heard they're buying Derry & Tom's.' He frowned.

Tara had heard the rumour that they were planning to take over the huge department store, too.

'If they do it'll be their funeral. It's too big, they'll never make a go of it. Don't worry so much about competition, Josh, we can learn by their mistakes. Anyway, what did you want to talk about?'

Josh launched into his idea of producing a range of clothes with his label to be sold in department stores, as Mary Quant had done. Unlike most of his ideas to expand, this one sounded sensible because it involved no real outlay. He told her he'd recently bought the freehold of a warehouse in Fulham and explained that not only could he move all the stock stored at Church Street there, but run the wholesale business from it.

'But would I be designing for this?' She was excited by the idea, as department stores would want better quality clothes than they churned out for the shops.

'Of course. Who else? But I thought I'd get another machinist in to help you.' He flicked his long hair back from his face, and smiled warmly. 'I know you're doing too much, sometimes I worry that you'll leave me.'

She saw a softness in his soft eyes that she hadn't seen since Christmas.

'I'm not going anywhere,' she reassured him, filling up their glasses. 'But I do need help, Josh. I can't go on much longer the way I have been doing. I never get any time to myself, any fun.'

'If I get someone experienced who could take over, does that mean you'd spend some time with me?' His voice was soft and sweet, but she heard the blackmail behind it and a dormant feeling of resentment was prodded into flames.

'Do you ever think of anyone but yourself?' she snapped. 'I'm run ragged, at the beck and call of everyone. What on earth do you want to spend time with me for anyway, haven't you got enough girlfriends?'

'Shush.' He grinned as two women turned round

to look. 'You know I've only ever wanted you.'

'You want me in your pocket more like,' she hissed, pushing her half-eaten pizza away in disgust. 'You think buying me this and a bottle of wine should be enough to keep me sweet for another few weeks while you pile work on to me.'

'That's not it at all.' He caught hold of her hand and squeezed it. 'I want to share everything with you. I want you to be the one beside me.'

Anger subsided, all she felt now was weariness.

'Josh, it wouldn't work.' She sighed. 'Apart from fashion we've got nothing in common. You live in a glitzy world of parties, drug-taking and fast cars. That isn't my way.'

'And you think you're great because you live like a nun,' he said sarcastically. 'Does it make you feel superior, sitting up all alone in your room while the rest of the world is having a good time?'

She knew then he'd been keeping tabs on her. Once he would've suspected another man, but he knew her private life was barren because he'd been prying.

'Stick your sodding pizza!' She stood up quickly. 'I'll put up with overwork, but I won't stand for anyone poking their nose into my private life.'

As she ran to the door, Josh followed her, throwing a note down on to the table as he went. He caught her at the traffic lights outside Barker's department store, and grabbed her arm.

'Calm down,' he said. 'I only know you're alone all the time because the girls in the shop tell me. I know you like me deep down, and I don't understand why you fight it.'

Jimi Hendrix's 'Hey Joe' was blasting out from Kensington market just along the road. A gang of young lads all with shoulder-length hair, wearing nothing but love beads and ragged jeans, were lounging on the pavement listening to the music. Three girls in tie-dyed T-shirts and minuscule denim skirts on the other side of the street were about to dart through the traffic to meet them. Their long sun-tanned legs and obvious freedom snapped something inside her.

'Has it ever occurred to you that trust might come into it?' She wanted to slap his smug face. 'Yes, I fancied you, but then I found out you sacked Angie because of me. I didn't like that, Josh, and it made me cautious. Since then you've done nothing to prove you can be trusted about anything. You get that photographer to follow me. You fuck girls in changing rooms, you take drugs until your eyes are like bloody great marbles, and yet you still think I should be there for you.'

'Well, I'm sorry. I didn't know I was supposed to go into sackcloth and ashes when you turned me down at Christmas. But then you are secretive about everything.'

'I'm not!' she retorted.

'Oh, yes you are. Half your life is covered in dust-sheets. You didn't tell me what happened to your brother. Or what made you come to London in the first place. All the time on the farm I kept picking up hints of other things you hadn't told me. If you were to open up to me we might find we had a lot more in common than just fashion.'

Tara dropped her eyes. 'Like I said, it's all about trust,' she whispered. 'Aside from Uncle George I've never met one man I could trust. You can't give that to people, Josh, they have to earn it.'

'Can't we start again?' He took her hand and lifted her fingers to his lips. 'You're so beautiful, Tara, and I love you.'

His lips felt beautiful against her fingers, his eyes deep pools of tenderness. She wanted to believe in him, to share her secrets and learn his, but first she needed evidence that he was sincere.

'Find me some help,' she said softly. 'Stop taking drugs and slow down. Then maybe.'

Chapter 24

Tara saw Harry through the railings as she came up the steps from Bethnal Green Tube. He was leaning against the bonnet of a grey Consul at the end of Paradise Row. Even across the street, a distance of perhaps forty yards, he looked different. Not just his hair, though it was a surprise to see it touching his collar, but something else she couldn't quite put her finger on.

He straightened up as he saw her and ran to meet her, jumping effortlessly over a small hedge on the strip of green between Paradise Row and Cambridge Heath Road.

The sun was already hot and temperatures were forecast to sweep up into the high eighties by midday.

'Morning, sweetheart.' Harry flung his arms round her and spun her round as she reached the pavement. 'You're looking gorgeous!'

'More accident than intent this early in the morning,' she said breathlessly. His short-sleeved white shirt smelled of Persil and his freshly shaven face faintly of Old Spice, just as it had when she was a child.

In fact she had been up since before five, worrying because she'd lied to Josh about going home, because she was excited at seeing Harry and because she didn't know what to wear. It was going to be hot, so she wanted something cool. On the other hand he might want to take her somewhere in the evening and she couldn't change. She wanted to look casual, yet sexy at the same time.

Finally she settled for a simple little turquoise mini dress with shoestring straps. It didn't crush easily, it had a little jacket she could roll up and stuff into her bag with her bikini and towel, and the colour looked wonderful against her hair!

Despite the early start Bethnal Green was busy, traffic swarming every which way across the crossroads.

'What do you think of my new motor?' Harry opened the door of the Consul. He had bought many cars over the years, but this one seemed a bit staid for him.

'Thinking of taking up mini-cabbing?' she teased.

'It goes.' He grinned. 'Besides, it was cheap!'

'I thought you said only poofters wore their hair long?' She reached over to ruffle it as he started up the engine. It wasn't long by Chelsea standards, merely touching his shoulders, and it had been styled properly, not just left to grow anyhow. But East End men had remained rigidly smart, suited and booted regardless of what was happening elsewhere.

'Short hair reminds me of prison.' He smiled round at her as he pulled out of Paradise Row. 'Just call it an upgrade of image!'

'There's something different about you,' she said reflectively. 'Have you put on weight or something?'

'A bit, what I lost while I was inside,' he said. 'I think what you mean is what Queenie calls my "working lad" face. I eat the right food. I work hard and I'm too tired to go out boozing. What you see is Mr Health and Vitality!'

'It looks good.' Just looking at his hard thighs encased in blue denim made her feel strangely aroused. 'What about ladies?'

He didn't reply immediately, just looked sideways

441

at her with that delicious smirk which made his lips curl.

'I've been saving myself,' he said eventually, reaching over and taking her hand. 'Saving my money, my body, my brain. I've worked a sixteen-hour day ever since I got the warehouse.'

'And it's finished now?'

'All but odds and ends. The carpets were fitted last week, but the tables and chairs haven't all come yet. You are going to come to opening night?'

'Of course I am.' She liked his hand in hers. It was rough from all his hard work, but it felt good all the same. 'Are you having any celebrities?'

'Dunno now Ronnie and Reggie are banged up.'

'You weren't going to invite them?'

'I'd have had to if they was at liberty,' he squeezed her hand. 'But don't look so horror-struck, Tara. The Krays policed our manor, they didn't do nothing to innocent people, remember, and they never did me no harm. In a way, they've done me a favour, people will be swarming to the East End now to get a whiff of the flavour.'

Tara gulped. It was totally in character for Harry to stick up for old pals, but it was another reminder he couldn't break free of his roots.

'Barbara Windsor's coming.' Harry smirked wickedly. 'David Bailey the photographer, Terence Stamp and Steve Marriott from the Small Faces.'

'They aren't! Really?' Tara's eyes widened.

'It's handy sometimes to have connections.' He smiled at her excitement. 'I'm sending Josh an invitation, too. I hope he might bring half of Annabel's. We've got more than enough local colour, but we are short of a few nobs.'

'I'll make sure he comes,' Tara said. 'Miranda knows umpteen debutante-type girls, do you want some of those, too?'

'The more the merrier.' Harry put his hand back on the wheel as the traffic increased. 'But let's forget about work for today, and just enjoy ourselves.'

Tara hadn't been to Southend since she was four or five, but the moment they got out of the car and walked across to the promenade, memories came flooding back.

At half past nine in the morning most of the holiday-makers were still tucking into big greasy breakfasts in the hundreds of little bed and breakfasts along the front. But the man selling beach-balls and buckets and spades was festooning them round his stall. A smell of frying bacon and sausages came from another and the cockles and whelk man was ladling them out on to little glass dishes in readiness.

'I remember it being so packed I couldn't see anything but legs,' Tara giggled. 'I remember Dad putting me up on his shoulders and telling me not to drop my cornet on his hair!'

'Looks like that family are expecting the same.' Harry pointed out a couple of big women staking out a huge patch of beach with towels and deckchairs, while their children ran straight down to the water's edge. 'But it don't get too busy in June, not mid-week.'

The tide was in, and a couple of men were already swimming.

'I wouldn't go that far.' Harry slid his arm round her as they leaned against the promenade rail to watch. 'I bet it's icy, with huge great turds in it!'

'That's horrible.' She pushed him away playfully. 'I won't even have a paddle now.'

The sea was calm, lapping softly on the shingle and patches of sand. A dozen seagulls scavenged over a dumped takeaway meal, a couple of dogs frolicked in and out of the water chasing balls. More and more families were arriving, arms weighed down with

443

towels and picnics. Men carried prams over the beach, women screamed at children not to go in the sea until they'd taken off their shoes.

'I learned to swim here,' Harry admitted. 'It was just after the War and there was still barbed wire everywhere and warnings about landmines. Dad held me under the belly and suddenly I realised he'd let go and I was swimming alone.'

'Dad swam the day we came here.' Tara had a mental picture of her father dripping wet, in woolly trunks. Paul was just a baby in a pram and they had to put it in the guard's van on the train. 'I can remember him kissing Mum while they were lying on the beach. I had one of those elasticated swimming costumes, when you came out the water you had to pull out the legs to let the water out!'

Tara's memories of Southend were all golden ones. Maybe it was smaller and shabbier, but it was every bit as colourful, noisy and exciting. Dozens of candy-striped stalls clustered together. She could see the fair in the distance, the skeleton-like track of the Wild Mouse rising above the brightly coloured awnings of the other rides. The big wheel was still just now, but tonight it would be a blaze of bright lights and music.

'Mum and Dad were happy the last time we came here,' she said. 'That fortune-teller over there told Mum she was going to move to the country. I can remember them talking about it. Dad even pushed Paul in the pram and we stayed until it was dark to go to the fair.'

'Well, she did end up in the country.' Harry smiled, touching her cheek gently. 'D'you want to go in there and find out what's in store for us?'

'She won't have got her crystal ball warmed up yet.' Tara laughed, aware he was making her heart race and tingles run down her spine. 'But I'll settle for an ice cream!'

'I don't like these as much as wafers,' Harry licked his cornet reflectively as they sat on a bench. 'I like to squeeze them and lick all the way round, then carry on squeezing and licking till there's nothing left inside.'

Tara giggled. It sounded very sensual and each time she looked at him, with his eyes half closed, dark eyelashes fanning his cheeks and that red pointed tongue slipping in and out, she had a strong feeling he wasn't only thinking of ice cream.

Even the people looked the same as she remembered, as if time had stood still. The promenade was filling up now and there was no-one in sight even vaguely in touch with 1968. Enormously fat women in flowery, full-skirted dresses waddled along, with their big handbags hanging from plump white arms that would be fiery red by the time they went home. Younger women pushed prams, many in tight skirts, their hair backcombed and sprayed stiff. Many of the men were wearing three-piece suits, despite the heat. There were old men in Panama hats and beige summer jackets and children in those same elasticated swimsuits she remembered, wearing plimsolls with the toes cut out to go in the sea.

A child's roundabout was playing 'The teddy bears' picnic'. From a café across the road Elvis was belting out 'Return to Sender' and from somewhere behind them a piano was tinkling out 'If you were the only girl in the world'.

So many smells! Hot dogs and onions, candyfloss and peppermint rock, seaweed, fish and chips, vinegar and coffee. She heard bangs from the rifle range, barkers shouting out from the hoopla stalls, waving goldfish in little plastic bags. Every seat was taken on the bingo stall, by fat ladies whose bottoms squelched over the small stools, blue-rinsed heads bent over their cards as they listened to the caller, pencils poised.

They walked to the end of the promenade. Harry

445

had won a hideous black gorilla on the rifle range. They'd eaten candyfloss and shrimps, then lay on the beach dozing in the sun.

Harry stripped down to black swimming trunks; she wore a pink and white spotted bikini she'd only ever had the courage to wear sunbathing at the farm.

The shop seemed just a distant memory. No sewing machine thundering, no thumping music from the shop below. Just hot sun searing into her skin, the sound of waves on pebbles, children's laughter, and the fairground music in the distance.

Tara was half asleep, lying on her side, when she felt his fingers lightly caressing her back. She opened her eyes and found Harry leaning on one elbow looking down at her.

'Bored already?' she asked.

'It's nearly one.' He smiled, moving closer to her, maintaining the stroking on her back. 'I've just woken up and I'm starving. Shall we find a pub and get some grub?'

He made no attempt to move and his fingers were sending ripples of pleasure up and down her spine. Lying here next to him wearing only a bikini made her feel very vulnerable, but also very aware of his masculinity.

There was no other man on the beach with a body so perfect. His shoulders rippled with muscle, his smooth, hairless chest was already tanned from his work outside. Mentally her fingers were reaching out to stroke him, yet if she moved the blissful spell would be broken.

His face was coming down to hers, she saw his lips part and eyes soften with desire. The kiss found her ear, nuzzling at her lobes, tongue running lightly round the rim, then moved across her cheek to find her lips.

She had received many different kinds of kisses

from him, but this kiss now was in a different league. It spoke of knowledge that she wouldn't rebuff him, that their friendship had only one way to go. But at the same time he was reassuring her she could call a halt if she wished to.

She found herself moving slowly on to her back, her arms coming up to hold him, and as his chest touched her breasts it was as if a touch paper had been lit. Salt on his lips, the sensual slide of his tongue on hers, even the smell of his skin and hair told her that this was meant to be. The tender way he held her face, his fingers running through her hair, the cry of seagulls high above and the waves breaking further down the beach, all made it a moment so perfect she wanted it to last forever.

'It's beautiful, isn't it?' he said softly, his nose rubbing against hers, blue eyes smiling. 'Let's go and eat. It won't go away now.'

She thought of that last sentence as she watched him at the bar. His shirt was open, showing a smooth, dark brown chest and rock-hard stomach. A little dark hair sprouted just above the zip on his jeans. She imagined slowly lowering that zip and sliding her hand inside.

'It won't go away.' He had said words she didn't know she wanted to hear. Not the standard cliché of 'I love you' or 'I want you', which could mean today, but not tomorrow. He knew whatever it was between them would be with them next week, next year, forever.

It was almost three when they came blinking out into the sunshine. They had talked constantly yet about nothing, laughing and sitting close, their fingers twining round one another's in a silent message of trust.

The beach was crowded now, children running shrieking in and out of the sea, teenage boys playing football, groups of girls strolling along arm in arm looking for boys to flirt with.

They found a few square feet of space, close to the promenade wall, spread out their towels, and Harry stripped off to his swimming trunks he'd kept on under his clothes.

Tara had the pants of her bikini on, but the top caused her problems as she tried to fasten it under her dress.

'Let me do it.' Harry shuffled up close behind her, reaching up under her dress for the bikini top.

His hands were warm, lingering on her side as if unable to prevent himself fondling her, and he moved closer still to kiss the back of her neck.

'You're giving me goose-pimples,' she whispered, not wanting him to stop.

'Just the sight of your body is giving me an erection,' he whispered in her ear. 'And that's a darned sight more awkward than goose-pimples on a beach!'

'Well close your eyes and go to sleep,' she suggested, wanting to kiss and hold him so much she couldn't even look at him directly.

He lay down on his side, propping himself up on one elbow. Tara finally got her dress off, folded it up neatly, then adjusted the top of her bikini before she lay down on her back.

'What are we going to do?' He undulated his pelvis against hers and she felt for herself that he really did have an erection. His fingers dug into her side and his tongue flickered round her lips.

'Lie here and sunbathe,' she whispered back.

'I didn't mean right now.' His lips were playing with hers even as he spoke. 'I meant about wanting one another, needing to make love. What are we going to do about that?'

'In the car?' she whispered back, blushing at her eagerness. 'A field?'

'I want to make love to you! To have a feast, not a snack,' he whispered back, his hand touching her

448

cheek, as light as a butterfly's wing. 'To fall asleep with you in my arms and to wake with the birds singing. Not ten minutes and being nervous that someone will see us.'

'We could go to my flat?'

'No, you wouldn't be mine back there,' he said, tracing round her nipple with one finger. 'Suppose we found a boarding house and stayed here?'

'I'd be embarrassed.' She blushed. 'We haven't any luggage or anything. They'd know we weren't married!'

'Who cares?' He smiled encouragingly. 'We just front it out, say we like it too much to go home. They don't care who we are or what we do.'

She was still hesitant. 'What happens when we get home?' she asked.

He leaned up on one elbow and looked down at her. His eyes said he understood.

'I've known you since you were a little girl, Tara,' he said softly. 'Do you really think I only want you for a one-night stand?'

'I can't be sure.' Her eyes filled with tears. 'My experiences of men haven't been too good.'

'Then it's time I taught you to trust again!'

'It's the only room we have left. I'm afraid it might be a bit noisy till after eleven because it's over the garden.'

'You don't expect Southend to be quiet,' Harry said, winking at Tara and making her giggle. 'I expect we'll be down there boozing with them anyway.'

The landlady had flame red hair, thinning and dull as if she permed it to death. Her eyebrows were pencilled on and she wore a gold Lurex blouse. She spoke very carefully, as if trying to pretend she wasn't a Cockney, but her blouse and her huge gold earrings gave her away.

'Now just come on down to the bar if you need anything.' She looked round at them as she opened the door and smiled broadly. 'By the look of you two you won't be needing much help from anyone, but just in case!'

'Oh, it's lovely!' Tara exclaimed when she saw the room. 'Look, Harry, it's so pretty!' The room had a ruffled pink bedspread, flouncy white curtains and a pink and white carpet. A pink velvet-studded headboard incorporated bedside lamps fringed with gold. Clearly the woman had the same over-feminine taste as Queenie.

'Well, thank you dear.' The woman gave a tinkly little laugh that set her many chins wobbling. 'It was my room, but my legs get bad in the winter so I moved downstairs. The bathroom's just along the passage and you can have a meal in the bar tonight if you want. Breakfast any time from seven till nine. I'll leave you to settle in.'

'The bed's OK.' Harry sat down the moment the door was shut, then made a trial bounce. 'Very soft and springy,' he added, smiling.

'It's not too crappy, is it?' He came up behind Tara as she kneeled on the floor, looking out of the low window. He slid his hands under her arms, cupping her breasts in his hands. 'I wanted to make love to you somewhere beautiful!'

'It's lovely, like being at your house,' she whispered.

It had been so easy to talk all day, but now Tara was lost for words, and embarrassed. Had Harry thought of buying some Durex while she got the toothbrushes and paste? If she asked him would he be offended? Should she go off and wash first? What did people do at times like this?

'What's wrong? Not second thoughts?' Harry's soft voice cut a swathe through her anxiety.

'No,' she whispered.

'Then kiss me!'

She knew it was right the moment his lips touched

450

hers. She felt herself lifted up, his arms around her tightly, lips still on hers as he moved with her to the bed.

'You are the most beautiful girl in the world,' he said huskily as he undid her zip and used his lips to remove her shoulders straps. 'I've imagined this moment for so long that now it's here I'm afraid.'

She lay back on the bed, her dress loosely covering her breasts, and held up her arms to him. His eyes held a message of love, his lips trembled, and as he moved down to her she caught his face in her hands, running her thumbs across his high cheek-bones. 'You're the beautiful one, Harry!'

Simon and the other odd men who had flitted through her life were all she had to compare with Harry, but now she was mature enough to feel the difference when a man's heart and soul were engaged in lovemaking. His gasp as his hands touched her naked breasts for the first time wasn't lust, but the wonder of skin against soft skin, dreamed of for so long.

It was the same for her, too, as she ran her hands down his back, fingers pressing into his spine. She loved his shudder of bliss, wanted to find a million ways of pleasing him.

As his fingers found their way inside her she cried out involuntarily, arching her back away from the mattress, wanting him inside her now. She was burning up, shuddering with need. Her lips searched frantically for his, wanting to be possessed.

'Please!' she heard her own hoarse whisper.

'Please do what?' he whispered back, moving his lips down her breasts and on to her belly.

'Please fuck me now.' She dug her fingers in his back, pulling him back to her.

She didn't understand why he was rustling something. Even when she saw it was a Durex, she didn't feel relief, only irritation that something was slowing him down.

'Oh, Tara!' he whispered, opening her legs and kneeling between them. 'Do you really want me that much?'

His fingers went back inside her as she opened her eyes to look at him.

'Yes,' she groaned.

Hands lifted her buttocks, drawing her right up to him, and at last she felt him sliding into her.

It was like riding on the Wild Mouse, climbing slowly higher and higher, then whooshing down with the wind catching her hair, only to spin round, then climb again. She was on fire, lips searching for his, every nerve ending tingling. An orgasm came like a rocket, she heard herself cry out, and while her body was still shuddering, sparks running through her veins, Harry thrust himself into her one last time.

Voices outside the window brought them back to reality.

'Get me a Snowball and a bag of cheese and onion crisps,' a female voice bellowed. 'And tell those little buggers to get off that garden or I'll do 'em a mischief.'

'There should be someone playing a harp.' Harry nuzzled his lips in her hair, wrapped his arms round her and rolled her over so she was on top of him. 'Doesn't that peasant out there know she's close to heaven?'

'It was heaven, wasn't it?' She sighed, rubbing her finger over sweat collected in the hollow of his chest.

'We'll have to get up if we want food,' Harry said reluctantly. 'But at least that will give us the strength to carry on.'

His stoical remark made her laugh, infecting him too. They rolled together, laughing until they were almost crying, and at that moment Tara knew for certain that she loved him.

Everything made them laugh that night. The sixteen-stone woman with a voice like a fog-horn who spent the evening flitting between drinking large gins and going out to slap her children in the garden. There was the pretty but tarty blonde in a pair of skin-tight shorts who eyed up every man who walked in the bar. Then there was the prim twin-setted woman who held her man's hand across the table, but had eyes like a dead fish.

'These people are supposed to be normal,' Harry sniggered as a perfectly ordinary-looking man suddenly burst into an Elvis Presley impersonation with a child's toy guitar. 'If they are, can you imagine what the ones locked up are like?'

'You wait till you open the club,' Tara warned him. 'When I help out in the shop I'm staggered by the nutcases that come in. I bet they're queuing up already to visit you.'

'What are we going to do when I open?' Harry was suddenly serious. 'You work all day, I'll be at it half the night. When will we see one another?'

'There's early evenings.' Tara didn't even want to think about that yet. 'You'll be able to get off one night a week, won't you?'

'I can't be sure of anything.' He sighed deeply. 'It's going to be an even bigger gamble than the game I won the place in. My customers will be villains and wide-boys in the main. I'll have to watch the staff like a hawk. I can't see me getting much time off. Not at first!'

He told her a little of how he'd taken Duke Denning in as a shareholder in return for some capital. About the many merchant banks he'd talked to before he found someone prepared to make him a further loan. He told her for the first time that he'd studied book-keeping in prison. That he'd spent a whole two weeks gaining experience at nights in a West End gambling club belonging to another poker player called Alf Reed.

'I didn't gamble.' He smiled at her worried look. 'Just served drinks and watched. Alf's been a great help, he even found me two straight blokes to work the tables.'

She felt a little ashamed now that she'd doubted his ability to pull it off, especially as he'd never for one moment considered she couldn't become a designer.

'Well, if you aren't going to get much time off, we'd better make the most of it now.' Tara moved nearer to kiss his cheek. 'Like now we could be tucked up in bed, not down here watching this circus.'

The first bout of lovemaking had been frantic and fast, but now the pace was slower, each caress savoured, whispered endearments heightening the ecstasy.

His tongue explored every part of her body, lapping at her till she was writhing under him, almost delirious with desire. The sheet beneath them was damp with sweat, pillows knocked to the floor as they rolled together as one.

Sounds of children crying, a jukebox blaring out 'Hey Jude', and a buzz of conversation from the bar below wafted through the open window, but they barely heard it. The sun sank down into the sea, the lights went on in the funfair and along the promenade, but they could have been alone on a desert island, drowning in a sea of tenderness.

When she came, she cried, holding his damp body to hers, his fingers still locked in her hair, and she knew he was her whole world.

They drank a bottle of Tizer between them in great greedy gulps, till it spilled down their naked bodies and they licked it off each other. Then, propped up on the pillows, lying in each other's arms, they talked.

Tara told him how she'd always felt like an outcast at school, how instead of trying to make friends she pretended she didn't want them.

'When people started to say I was beautiful, I thought it was some kind of cruel game, really they were still laughing at me.'

Harry looked at her face on his shoulder. The bedside lamp intensified the gold of her hair and the honey colour of her skin. He marvelled at the beauty of her amber eyes, the wide mouth, the small delicate nose and her perfect body. Yet he understood. He'd known her when all she saw was ugliness, remembered the little girl who took a poker to her father to protect Amy and Paul. The little girl who dressed painted pictures of brides, but never had a man standing beside them.

'I always thought I was weird because I didn't have a mother.' He stroked her face gently. 'Like I wasn't good enough to have one, know what I mean?'

Tara nodded.

'I suppose that's why I was always the dare-devil, the kid that went too far. Robbing that warehouse was part of that.'

'Mum and Gran will be wary about you because of it,' Tara reminded him. Her fingers crept up to touch his cheek-bones, tracing round the lines she'd drawn so often when she was a girl. 'They both like you, well, love you even. But they've both got this thing about dangerous men!'

Harry smirked. 'Me, dangerous?'

'They're both convinced our family is stuck in some kind of tragic circle we can't break out of,' Tara said softly.

'I'll win them over eventually.' Harry looked right into her eyes and she saw nothing but absolute sincerity.

'Did you ever love anyone else?' she asked. She didn't want to know, yet she had to.

'There's been loads of girls,' he said. 'But you know that, Tara. Sometimes I thought I was in love, especially when I was young. But I knew when I started to

455

fall for you that none of that was for real.'

'So when did you fall for me?' She giggled, snuggling closer into his arms with a delicious feeling of absolute safety.

'I think it got going that day in the cowshed when you kissed me.' He smiled as he pictured her.

'But you were horrible, you told me you had another girl?' She remembered how she'd cried up in her room.

'You were too young.' He kissed her forehead and smiled. 'But if you'd known what I was dreaming after that, you'd 'ave bin scarlet with embarrassment.'

'Tell me now,' she said, doing the old pout.

He bent his head to kiss her breasts. 'These figured in it a great deal,' he whispered. 'I used to imagine stripping off your school uniform and seeing your lovely little bum in tight white knickers.'

She giggled. 'Well, I used to wonder how big your willie was.'

'Is it as expected?'

She looked down at it curled up amongst his dark pubic hair.

'Not at this moment.' She bent to kiss it. 'But if I'd seen it like it was a little while ago it might have frightened me half to death.'

It was dawn before sleep overtook them.

'I love you,' Harry said just as her eyes finally closed, and it sounded to Tara as if he'd never said those words to anyone before. 'I always knew we were meant for one another.'

Chapter 25

'You look brown!' Miranda shouted above the sounds of 'Mony, Mony' as Tara walked into the shop just after ten in the morning. She was arranging some Indian cotton blouses on the central display, but she broke off and came closer. 'I hope you had a good time wherever you were, 'cos Josh is on the warpath!'

Tara gulped. 'You did give him the message that I'd be another day, didn't you?' she asked.

It was too early for customers; the other two shop girls were cleaning and straightening the rails.

'Of course I did.' Miranda put a hand on Tara's arm, green eyes grinning wickedly. 'I don't think it was the days he was upset about, more the nights!'

'Oh, shit!' Tara exclaimed, turning pale. 'Did he phone the farm?'

' 'Fraid so,' Miranda winced. 'He used the shop phone. When he put it down he said, "Fuckin lying bitch"! After that he was like a madman, none of us could do anything right. Where were you, anyway?'

'Between you and me, off with Harry by the seaside.' Tara laughed nervously. 'Looks like I'll have to make a confession!'

Miranda's eyes opened wide in alarm. 'You haven't got long to think up a good one.' She picked up the phone and shrugged her shoulders. 'He told me to ring him the second you walked through the door.'

'Act dumb,' Tara said quickly. 'I'll think of something before he gets here.'

She felt faintly sick as she walked upstairs. Reason told her she could spend her time with whoever she chose, but given Josh's sympathetic manner at hearing her gran was ill, she had every reason to feel guilty.

Mum and Gran wouldn't like it either. When they discovered she'd been with Harry, they'd probably freak out!

They had stayed a second night at Southend because they couldn't bear to part, and left early this morning to get her back to work. Her face was sore from Harry's stubble, she was tired from so little sleep, weepy because she wanted to be with Harry, and now this.

As she got up to her flat it began to rain, huge drops that sent the people out on the street scurrying for shelter. She put the kettle on the gas, lit the grill for some toast, then went into her room to change. She was buttering her toast when she heard Josh's feet on the stairs and, for the first time since she moved in here, she wished she had a place of her own with a proper front door.

'Want some tea and toast?' she called out, trying to behave normally.

He didn't answer but stood outside the kitchen door glowering at her.

'Well?' Tara put her hands on her hips questioningly. 'Do you want tea or not?'

The kitchen was long and narrow, with no room to sit. She felt cornered with him in the doorway and nothing but a window behind her.

'You managed to get back then? Gran wasn't at death's door after all?'

'OK, I give in,' she said lightly. 'I didn't go home, only said that because I didn't want the third degree about where I was going.'

When Josh smiled he could pass as handsome. Scowling did him no favours at all.

'And where was that?'

'None of your business.' She tossed her hair back and took a bite of her toast.

'None of my business?' he roared. 'You take two days off just when I wanted you to work on these wholesale designs, and then you say it's not my business!'

His face was red with anger. Josh wasn't an entirely reasonable man. She'd seen him sack girls for taking five minutes extra on their lunch hour. She was sure he wouldn't actually sack her, but bearing in mind his tender words to her just three days earlier, he was bound to flare up if she told him she'd been with Harry.

'Josh, you owe me so many days off I'll never catch up with them.' Her tone was crisp. 'Most nights I'm still working gone ten. There's never been a time I didn't have samples ready for a deadline, even if I've had to stay up all night to hand-stitch the hems. If I can't have a couple of days off when the sun's shining, I think it's time I found myself a new job.'

'Who were you with?' he shouted, taking a threatening step towards her.

'What's it got to do with you?' She turned her back on him and put another slice of bread under the grill.

'Off modelling for another porn magazine, were you?'

She had the boiling kettle in her hand, ready to pour it into the teapot, but her hand stopped in mid-air.

'You what?'

He didn't look normal at all. His pupils were so tiny she could hardly see them, his thick lips had flecks of foam at the corners. Could he have had an overdose?

'I said, were you off modelling somewhere for a porn magazine?'

'Don't be ridiculous,' she snapped, slamming down the kettle. 'If you've been taking drugs, go somewhere else and wait for it to wear off.'

'I'm as straight as an arrow,' he said haughtily. 'Which is obviously more than I can say for you. Don't I pay you enough? Aren't you getting enough glory? And to think all this time I've fallen for the timid little virgin bit.'

She realised then something else had happened. His anger went far beyond catching her out in one little lie.

'Look, Josh, I don't know what this is about. Come on down to the workroom. Sit down, have a cup of tea and tell me what I'm supposed to have done.'

She could hear the girls from the shop going in and out of the stockroom on the ground floor, and doubtless their ears were pinned back.

'I could put the modelling down to a lark,' he shouted. 'But blackmailing me! That's just the end.'

Tears glittered in his dark eyes, and suddenly she realised he was really wounded.

'Josh, I don't know what you think I've done.' She put her hands on his shoulders and propelled him towards her room. 'But we're going to talk about this properly, sitting down.'

He seemed shell-shocked, and he let her push him into a chair.

'I don't know how you could do this.' He sat on the very edge, rigid with anger.

The smell of burning toast made her run back to the kitchen. She turned off the grill and opened the window, then went back to him.

'OK, I lied about where I was going, but that's all.' Tara knelt down beside him. 'Now explain yourself!'

For a moment he just sat, staring at the floor. He was wearing a light blue suit, and a cream shirt which looked none too clean. He hadn't even shaved, he smelled sweaty and his clothes reeked of tobacco. His hand disappeared into an inside breast pocket and pulled out a foolscap-sized brown envelope.

'You explain those!' he snarled and threw the envelope at her.

Tara pulled out the contents – photographs with a
letter folded round them. As she removed the pictures
she gasped.

'Come on, now,' Josh needled her. 'Don't tell me
you've got a twin and that's her!'

One glance at the picture of the schoolgirl sitting
astride a chair masturbating was enough. She knew
exactly who had taken it, and where. She sat back on
her heels and covered her face in her hands.

Back in that little cottage it had seemed a bit naughty
to let Simon catch her in that pose, something to giggle
about. But now it sickened her.

'Oh, Josh,' she whispered. 'No wonder you're upset.'

'When were they taken?' he asked in a shaky voice.

'Not recently, if that's what you thought,' she said
weakly. 'And not to be sold. I was just sixteen. It was
down in Somerset, he talked me into it. I thought it was
just for him.'

'Who is this he?'

'A man called Simon Wainwright, he's an actor.'

'Was this before I met you?'

'Yes, of course. He was the man I ran to London to
be with, but everything went wrong.' She stopped
suddenly as the full horror of what this meant washed
over her. 'Is he blackmailing me?'

'You?' Josh gave a hollow laugh. 'No, me! Read the
letter, why don't you. Either I pay him a thousand
pounds or he sends these prints to *The News of the
Screws*. He reckons it will ruin me!'

Tara read through the letter. It was typed, with no
address at the top, but its style and content suggested
an articulate, well-educated writer.

'Dear Mr Bergman,
I enclose some photographs of your designer

461

Tara Manning. Recently in the press there was an article about this young lady's talent and how her designs have brought you fame and fortune. A quote I found particularly entertaining was 'Tara brings her own innocence and romanticism to her clothes'. These prints do not show either romance or innocence, surely?

I am fairly certain a man like yourself would not knowingly employ a girl who modelled for shots like these and I'm sure you would be frightfully embarrassed if such news should get out to the press or these prints sold on to them. We all know that the parents of your many young girl customers would be nervous about allowing their children into your premises once this got out.

Fortunately I am in a position to help you. I can locate the negatives these prints were taken from, round up the spare prints and return them to yourself and give an undertaking that the matter of your designer's modelling career in pornography is over. If you would be so good as to put a thousand pounds in ten-pound notes in a box and bring it to the Leprechaun on the Uxbridge Road at Shepherd's Bush, it will be exchanged for your photographs. Please do this within the next seven days, otherwise I will have no alternative but take them to *The News of the World* who will pay more than I am asking you for. As you approach the bar with the box, just say to the barman "Would you please exchange this for the envelope you have addressed to Patrick Mulligan".

I do hope you will take up this limited offer, needless to say should you try alternative methods to recover the negatives I will be forced to teach you and your company a lesson in obedience!

Yours

Patrick Mulligan'

'Oh, Josh!' She felt sick, but despite the embarrassment to herself, her first thoughts were for Josh and his business. 'It's just a try-on. This man Mulligan must have got them off Simon. Tell him to stuff himself. Why should you pay him?'

'Don't be naive!' he exploded. 'It's a well-documented fact that you've worked for me for almost four years. No-one will believe I'm nothing to do with this. He's quite right about the young girls. Do you think parents will want their daughters coming in here once these have been bandied around?'

'What do you suggest we do?' Tara asked later.

She had made him a cup of coffee, drunk two herself to try to calm her nerves, and told him the whole story. She had tried to make Josh see that the man was an actor and he could hardly try to get these published without smearing his own name. But Josh didn't see it that way.

He pointed out that Simon Wainwright wasn't a name anyone had ever heard of. Anyway he might not even be involved but merely passed on the pictures to this man Mulligan. If Josh was to march into this pub demanding the negatives it would probably only be minutes before either his head was kicked in, or the newspapers had the story. Then of course there were Tara's mother and grandmother. What would this do to them?

The police were suggested and then rejected. As Josh pointed out, this bit of smut would get round faster with them on the case.

'What hurts me most is that you never told me about this guy,' Josh said finally. 'It's just another of those secrets you keep hidden. How many more will come out before I get to the bottom of you?'

She had to tell him about Harry then. Not to hurt him further, but because she knew Harry was perhaps the only person who could sort it out.

'I see.' His face set like concrete, a chilly look in his eyes. 'I might have known.'

'I'm going to phone him now. He'll know what to do.'

'What can he do that I can't?' he jeered. 'Send round a couple of heavies?'

That was meant to insult Harry but Tara wasn't going to be rattled.

'Maybe that's just what this needs. Anyway, I think he'll feel it's his place to stop this man,' Tara said quietly. 'Remember, Josh, I've known him all my life.'

Strains of 'Bridge over Troubled Waters' drifted up the stairs, along with the perfume of joss-sticks. Tara made more coffee and insisted Josh ate a sandwich.

'I'll just pay the money.' He sighed deeply as he finished the sandwich. 'There's nothing else for it.'

'That won't work and you know it,' she said sadly. 'He'll be back for a second lot, then a third, and the more successful my designs are for you the more he'll want each time.'

But as Josh slowly calmed down, Tara's fears for herself grew. Not just over her smeared name, or her family's shame, but Harry, too. It was one thing having admitted to a relationship with Simon, another having to show Harry graphic pictures of the event. Would it taint everything?

Miranda's voice called up the stairs. 'Tara, here a minute!'

Tara wiped away tears from her cheeks and brushed past Josh. At the bottom of the stairs Miranda waited, an anxious expression on her face.

'It's Harry,' she whispered. 'In the shop. I told him Josh was up there with you and tried to make him go away, but he seems to think you wanted him here.'

'I did, Miranda.' Tara tried to smile. 'Sorry, I should have told you.'

'Is everything all right?' Miranda wiped a stray tear from Tara's cheek, her eyes full of concern. 'He hasn't sacked you or anything?'

Tara shook her head. 'Just a bit of a show-down. Tell Harry to come up.'

Harry seemed to tower over Josh as the pair coldly shook hands. Ironically it was Harry who looked the real businessman today, as he'd changed into a navy suit and striped shirt ready to see his bank manager.

'Let me see the letter,' Harry said quietly.

Josh passed it to him with the pictures. Harry held the prints with one hand and read the letter.

Tara felt so faint she had to sit down. Any minute now he would look at the pictures and the loving kiss he gave her at the bottom of the stairs just now might well turn out to be the last.

He folded the letter and put it in his inside pocket then, without even looking at them, he tore the batch of prints in half.

'You haven't seen them,' Josh's voice rasped.

Harry took out his lighter and held it to one of the prints, setting it alight and dropping it into the waste-paper bin. As they watched he did the same with all ten.

'There was no point in doing that,' Josh spoke up. 'He'll have copies.'

'I don't want to see them, nor do I want anyone else looking at them.' Harry looked at Josh as if he was a maggot. 'I'll go and sort that pervert out now.'

The flames in the bin died down and the room was filled with an acrid smell.

'You'll do more harm than good.' Josh's eyes went black with anger, irritated by Harry's quiet control. 'This is something that needs negotiation.'

'Fuck off, Josh.' Harry stood up, poised to leave. 'That louse wants stamping on and I'm surprised you're even considering anything else.'

465

'He might retaliate out of spite if you hit him,' Josh argued.

'He might end up dead if he tries.'

Tara looked from one to the other. Harry was far bigger than Josh, leaner and healthy, and she loved him. Next to him Josh looked insignificant, effeminate with his long curls and jewellery, but she valued his friendship. An electric current of jealousy sparked between the men and she knew for certain that, whatever came of this business, there wasn't room for both of them in her life.

'I'll come with you,' Josh said as Harry made for the door.

'No.' Harry shook his head. 'Tara's my girl. I do it alone!'

He was off down the stairs so quickly Tara was shocked.

'Harry, wait,' she called, running after him. She caught him at the door through to the shop. 'Be careful.' She reached up and kissed him.

'I'll ring or call round after I've seen him.' Harry held her briefly. His eyes were colder than a January morning. 'We'll have to find you a new place to live, too.'

Harry sat in his car, reproaching himself for not beating the shit out of Simon Wainwright personally four years ago. He had got a couple of lads round to give him a good kicking, whispered in the right ears that this bloke needed castrating. But clearly he hadn't frightened the man enough.

Reaching into his jacket Harry dug out the old envelope he'd just collected from his flat. He slid his thumb under the flap and pulled out the contents. Just a photograph of the man and the pitifully small list of productions he'd been in. Harry had got this from Wainwright's agent's office just a couple of days after Tara was tucked up safe with George and Queenie.

It had taken a few drinks to persuade the secretary to open up, but she'd been bruised by the man too and Harry convinced her it would be therapeutic to talk. He'd learned how the man used his charm on both sexes, but mostly on the rich and middle-aged who showed their gratitude with things like his Jaguar, holidays, expensive clothes and jewellery. The child modelling agency was owned by one of his lovers, as was the house in Shepherd's Bush. The woman went on to say she was sure Wainwright was involved with blue film-making.

Harry studied the black and white picture. It was out of date now, possibly taken ten years earlier. The man could have lost that blond hair, put on several stones and lines could cover that matinée-idol face. Maybe that's why he'd turned to blackmail now!

He looked at his watch thoughtfully. It was almost twelve, the Leprechaun would be open now and, if the clientele was as he expected, buying a few rounds of Guinness should encourage someone to give him a bit of information.

'What'll it be, sir.' The red-faced Irishman behind the bar with a nose like a diseased sausage polished glasses, pulled pints and carried on a conversation all at once. The pub was precisely how he expected it, a Victorian watering hole that had been left intact except for electric light, a juke box and a small stage in one corner.

'A pint of Bass, please.' Harry took out a handkerchief and mopped the rain from his face. 'I only parked a few yards away, it's piddling down out there.'

'Ah, we need the rain.' The barman smiled. 'That hot weather isn't good for trade!'

'I didn't think anything kept an Irishman from his drink,' Harry joked. 'By the way, is this the only Irish pub round Shepherd's Bush?'

'Well, it's the best-known one.' The barman seemed willing to chat.

'Do you know a guy named Tom Clancy?' Harry used the name of an Irishman who lived near his father. 'That's why I came in, I've got a message for him.'

'Tom Clancy?' The barman rubbed his chin thoughtfully. 'I know a Sean Clancy, but he's gone back to Dublin now and I don't think he had a brother. Tell me what the man looks like?'

'Good-looking bugger.' Harry leaned one elbow on the bar while he made up this fictitious character. 'Black hair, blue eyes, big shoulders, did a bit of acting at one time.'

The barman shook his head. 'I'd remember him for sure if he'd been in. Don't get many good-looking people in here.' He laughed at his own joke. ' 'Cept you of course, sir!'

'I'm sure this was the pub they said.' Harry frowned. 'He used to hang around with another actor called Simon, big blond-haired bloke.'

'I know a Simon,' the barman said. 'Yeah, he's an actor all right. He's not Irish though.'

'He wouldn't be a bit suspect, would he?' Harry grinned wickedly. 'Likes blokes as well as birds?'

The barman grinned and Harry knew he'd struck gold.

'Don't you go saying that to the boss.' The Irishman's eyes twinkled and his voice was lowered as if he didn't want to be overheard. 'She's kind of sweet on him, and she hasn't noticed anything odd yet.'

'Is it true, then?' Harry leaned forward conspiratorially.

'All I'm saying is, there are rumours.' The barman looked over his shoulder to check no-one was listening. 'Do you know where he lives?'

The barman shook his head. 'Must be somewhere close, he's in most nights.'

Harry changed the subject. He didn't want Wainwright warned someone had been asking about him.

468

The rain had stopped when he came out of the pub and the sun was shining again, making the pavements steam. He quickly checked his map, then drove round to Godolphin Road, where Simon had lived four years ago.

A girl was sitting on the wall outside the house. From a distance she looked pretty, but as Harry pulled up she looked at him with dead eyes and he realised she was on drugs.

'Do you live here?' he asked.

'Why?' She looked up at him but there was no real curiosity in her eyes. 'What's it to you? Charging rent for the wall?'

'No, love.' He noticed her neck was filthy and a sour smell was wafting from her. 'Just wondered, because I wanted to ask who lives on the top floor.'

'Noel,' she muttered.

'Noel who?'

'I don't know his fuckin' other name,' she said, giving him a baleful stare. 'He's just a bloke.'

Harry pulled a pound note from his pocket and waved it at her.

'Did you know a couple of blokes who lived there, one was called Simon, a big blond guy, the other was Quentin?'

She looked at the note and then at him. 'You queer?'

Harry shook his head and smiled.

'I knew Quentin, he was a dancer,' she volunteered. 'He left about a year ago. I didn't know the other one, except by sight.'

Harry gave her the pound. 'Thanks, love.'

So Wainwright had moved on. Harry wasn't surprised, but it had been worth a try.

As he drove back to the club Harry banged on the steering wheel in frustration. In the old days he would've turned up at that pub tonight mob-handed and torn it apart till he found Wainwright. But turning straight meant he couldn't do that. He hated the idea that Josh was now privy to a bit of Tara's past. Even more than that, he hated to see the fear and shame in her eyes which just a few hours earlier had been lit up with happiness.

At quarter to ten Harry walked back into the Leprechaun. It was so packed now he could barely see across the bar and at the far end four ageing Teddy boys were playing Fifties' rock and roll.

The barman with the diseased nose wasn't working, instead there was a woman in her forties who he suspected was the landlady, and two young barmaids. The barmaids were both very ordinary, with droopy long hair, short skirts and footballer's legs, but the landlady was a bit of a sensation – shoulder-length red hair, a figure like Diana Dors and vivid blue eyes that sparkled as if she enjoyed every moment of her life.

Harry made no effort to be noticed at the bar because he wanted to study her. Instinct told him she wasn't a tart, just a naturally sexy lady, but he could understand it if her customers were confused. Big bouncing breasts almost popped out of her low-cut black lace dress, and her small waist was clinched with a wide belt studded with imitation rubies and emeralds.

'What would you like?' She swept down the bar to serve him, bringing with her a cloud of the heady Madame Rochas perfume Queenie always wore.

'You,' he said, giving her one of his special grins. 'But until you're free, a pint of Bass.'

She laughed and those big soft breasts quivered.

'I haven't seen you in before,' she said, looking straight into his eyes without any pretence as she pulled his pint. 'I'd remember someone as tasty as you!'

'I bet you say that to all the blokes.' Harry laughed.

'Only the pretty ones.' She smiled, showing perfect white teeth. 'I'm Myra, the landlady.'

470

A sudden influx of customers prevented Harry from talking to her and he got shoved further and further away from the bar. Then the band paused for a drink and the whole bar seemed to have the same idea. He was trapped between a group of girls on a hen night and three very drunk Irishmen when he saw Simon Wainwright come in.

Age hadn't hurt him. If anything he was better looking now than in his picture. In fact Harry would have to agree that Wainwright could have been a film star. It was no wonder Tara fell for him.

Harry pushed his way through the crowd up to the far end of the bar, so he could watch Wainwright, and see how close he and Myra were. It was quite incredible to watch how she lit up when she spotted him – it was as if the Blackpool illuminations had been switched on.

Harry was too far away to hear the conversation, but he saw Wainwright take her hand and lift it to his lips, lightly kissing each finger-tip. She gave him a double gin and tonic but no money changed hands and even when she went to serve other customers her eyes constantly strayed back to him.

It was nearly eleven when Harry beckoned to her to give him another drink. Although the bar was even more crowded, fewer drinks were being served now as it approached the end of the evening.

'Another Bass?' she asked.

'Yes, please.' Harry took a chance and leaned over the bar. 'I was going to ask you out for a late drink somewhere, but I see you're already spoken for!'

She coloured, and for a moment looked flustered.

'It's an on-off thing,' she said, glancing over her shoulder. 'I'm not sure how things stand tonight.'

Harry knew exactly what that meant; after all he'd played that game with women hundreds of times. But he could also see she was tempted just this once to stand the man up.

'I could pop back at twelve to see if you're free,' he suggested.

'OK.' She pointed over to the small door by the side of the bar. 'I'll leave that one open if I'm alone.'

She waved away the money for his drink and moved to ring the bell for last orders.

Myra was talking to Wainwright again; she gave him another drink and he downed it in one. He took her hand again, but this time he pressed the palm to his lips and appeared to be trying to appease her about something.

The group played their last number, 'Summertime Blues', and people started to leave, first in ones and twos, but faster as the barmaids came round collecting glasses.

Myra looked a little cross now, while Wainwright leaned on the bar talking earnestly, still holding her hand in his. Suddenly he straightened up, leaned across and kissed her on the lips, then left without a backward glance.

Harry had to follow him quickly, but he blew a kiss to Myra, tapped his watch to say he'd be back and left by another door.

It was raining again, a light drizzle which made visibility more difficult. Harry turned up the collar of his suit jacket and wished he'd had the sense to wear a mac.

When Wainwright crossed the Uxbridge Road, walking towards Shepherd's Bush, Harry didn't follow him immediately. But as he turned off into Loftus Road there was no alternative. Keeping well back he watched every move the man made, relieved that he seemed to be going home rather than off to a club or restaurant.

Finally he stopped, opened the gate of a terraced house which was in darkness, and then the front door. Harry waited a few houses down. He saw the light go on in the hall, another further back in the house, then one on the stairs. He moved closer. The curtains in the front room were open, and though the room was in darkness there was enough light from the hall to make out a very average sitting room with a three-piece suite and television. He heard the lavatory flush upstairs and saw Wainwright come back down the stairs and go to the room at the back.

It was all Harry needed. The man was alone in the house, he was sure of that. The lock on the front door would be easy to pick later on, but for now he was going back to Myra.

The door was open as she'd promised, and Harry slipped through without making a sound. She was standing behind the bar wiping down the optics with her back to him.

'Boo!'

'Oh, my goodness!' she exclaimed, jumping a couple of inches. 'I nearly had heart failure.'

Harry sat down on a stool. There was no doubt she was pleased to see him.

'I only came back to say hello, really,' he said. 'I don't like to move in on a hot romance.'

She had put more lipstick on while he was gone and combed the lacquer out of her flaming red hair.

'It was hot, but it's cooled.' She sighed deeply. 'I suppose if I had any sense I'd tell him to sod off, he just uses me now. But you don't want to hear this, do you? Let me get you a drink? Is that jacket wet? You didn't tell me your name!'

'Mike. I'll have a scotch, please, and my jacket's only damp.' Harry smiled at her warmly. 'He's a good-looking chap. He looked pretty keen on you from where I was standing.'

Myra pushed the glass up on to the optic and made it a double. She put it down on the bar and got herself one, too.

'I thought I understood most men,' she said, coming round the bar and getting up on the stool beside him. 'But he has me puzzled. He seems to be keen, but there's a coldness in him. He wants me to do something for him at the moment and I've got a feeling the moment it's over I won't see him again.'

'What is it? Putting a bomb in the Midland Bank, topping his wife?'

'No, nothing like that, nothing dangerous or even illegal. I've only got to give someone an envelope, that's all.'

'What's in it? Why doesn't he post it?' Harry slapped on the innocent, interested face he'd perfected in school.

'He said it was some papers. Something to do with his father's estate. He'll only hand them over when he gets back the money he's owed.'

'Funny way to go about it.' Harry raised one eyebrow.

'That's what I said.' Myra smiled. 'I thought perhaps he was blackmailing someone at first, but he just laughed. He said they really ought to do this through a lawyer, but that's so expensive, and anyway if the taxman finds out about this money he'll have to hand half of it over.'

'I'd look at the papers if it was me,' Harry said, putting one hand over hers. 'I'd steam open the envelope and look inside just in case.'

'I couldn't, it would be a betrayal of trust,' she said, but she looked over by the till as she spoke.

'He might be betraying your trust.' Harry squeezed her hand. 'Let me look? I'll tell you if they're kosher or not!'

She shook her head. 'No, Mike. I've always tried to be straight with people. I tell them what I really think, I don't lie. That's why I've told you the truth about Simon. I like you, too, but I want you to get it straight in your head about how things are for me.'

'You love him?'

She took a deep breath. 'Yes, I do. I never wanted any man so much, if you want to know the truth. In my heart I know it's not right, but I can't help myself.' She blushed and giggled.

Harry really did like Myra, even if she was a good fifteen years older than him. He felt more than a little guilty he was fooling her, but somehow he had to get behind that bar to hunt for the envelope.

They had another drink and Myra told him several funny stories about her customers, about her ex-husband who was a boxer, and about her annual holiday in Spain with her sister.

'Come on up to my flat?' she suggested. 'I don't know why we're sitting here, it's not a bit comfy.'

She was already getting up, smoothing her dress down over her hips, and she had lust in her eyes. Harry took a chance, following her to the door that led to her flat, then suddenly he stopped.

'That door I came in by,' he said. 'Hadn't I better lock it?'

'Oh, dear.' She stopped in the doorway. 'I'd forgotten!'

'Don't worry,' Harry said. 'Go on in, I'll do it and visit the gents at the same time.'

He could hear her feet climbing the stairs and he felt a stab of pity. She was lonely, wanted loving. and she deserved more.

Slipping behind the bar, he saw a brown envelope sticking out next to the till and pulled it out. 'Patrick Mulligan' was written on it and he could feel something narrow, like a strip of negatives between sheets of paper. Sliding it into his inside pocket he nipped back round the bar and over towards the door, but as he put his hand on it, guilt overcame him.

'I can't stay, Myra,' he said as he found her in her sitting room. 'I want to, but I can't.'

She looked much younger up here, in the feminine pink room with its soft table lamps.

'Why, Mike? Are you married and just remembered?'

'That's about it.' He smiled. 'The trouble with you is you're too nice, Myra. It started out me just wanting a bit of excitement. But I can't do it now.'

'You mean you can't fuck me cheerfully then bugger off?' She had a half smile on her lips but sadness in her eyes.

'I could fuck you cheerfully. I just don't know if I could bugger off afterwards,' Harry said. 'I think I should just go now.'

'At least you make a girl feel good about herself,' she said softly, coming over and reaching up to kiss his cheek.

He held her face in his hands for a moment. 'You're a queen, Myra.' He kissed her lips very gently. 'Don't think too harshly of me.'

The rain was coming down heavily as he ran to his car. He jumped in and headed towards Loftus Road. He drove right past number 43. It was in darkness now, the curtains in the front bedroom pulled across.

It was half past one. The street was deserted, with only the odd light here and there to show some people were still awake. By the light of the dashboard he opened the envelope. There were what looked like two sets of prints and the negatives, wrapped in plain paper. He pushed them back in hastily, resisting the temptation to look at them, and shoved them into the glove compartment. It was awkward changing in the car and he had to keep looking round to make sure no-one was coming. Off with the suit, shirt and tie, on with a pair of jeans, dark T-shirt and plimsolls.

The thin surgical gloves were next, a length of rope round his shoulders, knife tucked into his sock and

476

the strip of plastic in his hands. One more look round to make sure he wasn't observed then out, leaving the keys in the ignition in case he needed to get away fast.

The front door opened effortlessly. Harry slid in, closing it silently behind him, then crept towards the stairs in the darkness.

He could sense the character of the house, even though he couldn't see it. Thin, cheap carpet on the stairs, textured wallpaper painted over. It smelt musty, of stale cooking and infrequent cleaning.

At the top of the stairs was a post, ahead a landing and to his right another few steps going up again. He took the steps. Ahead the bedroom door was open and he could see the glow of a street light shining through the curtain and hear a gentle snore. He knew exactly what he was going to do. The only problem would be not killing him once he got his hands round the pervert's neck.

He paused by the side of the bed, looking down at Wainwright and assessing the best way to grab him. His chest was bare, covered only by a sheet and blanket up to his waist. He lay on his back, head turned slightly to one side.

Silently he took up his position at the side of the bed, drew out his knife, and held it at Wainwright's throat. His other hand went down to the pillow where golden hair spread out. He gathered it up gently in his fist, then, as he felt himself in control, yanked it tightly.

'Wake up, you bastard,' he said softly. 'Wake up!'

Chapter 26

Wainwright opened his eyes and his body bucked violently.

'Don't fuckin' move,' Harry hissed, 'or shout, because this is a knife I've got at your throat.'

'What is this?' Wainwright's voice was just a squeak of terror. 'I haven't got any money.'

'It isn't money I'm after,' Harry snarled. 'It's revenge. Turn over, gently now in case this knife slips.'

'I don't understand,' he whined, but did as directed. 'Who are you?'

'Someone who doesn't like nonces.' Harry put one knee on the edge of the bed and got a better grip on the man's hair before putting his knife down. 'It's what you've attempted to do to my friends I'm concerned about. Now put your hands behind your back and clasp them together!'

Five minutes later Harry had Wainwright bound hand and foot.

'That's better.' He rolled Wainwright on to his side and turned on the bedside light.

It was the sort of room Harry had seen dozens of times before, cheaply furnished and battered by previous tenants. A scuffed and dusty dressing table stood in front of the windows, curtains barely covered the window. Brown patterned lino lay on the floor and yellow rose wallpaper was peeling off in one corner.

Harry sat down on the bed. 'This room ain't much to boast about.' He picked up his knife again and flicked it against his finger. Wainwright's brown eyes bulged with terror and he tried to wriggle back from him. 'Now you can list all your victims to me!'

'What victims? I don't know what you mean!'

'Oh, but you do.' Harry put the tip of the blade in Wainwright's nostril. 'Have you ever seen anyone with their nose cut open? It's not a pretty sight,' he said casually. 'Just be sensible now. I've got all night, you see, and I want to know about everyone you've blackmailed.'

Wainwright acted innocent, insisting he'd never blackmailed anyone. Harry waited patiently while the man spouted off about mistaken identity and if he didn't untie him now he had friends in high places who would see him locked up for years.

'You must think I'm as stupid as you.' Harry smirked. 'I've given you a chance to tell me without any rough stuff, but it seems to me that's the only thing you'll understand.'

He put the edge of the blade back in Wainwright's nostril and with a quick flick of his wrist he cut it. Not far, half an inch at most, but enough blood gushed on to the pillow to convince Wainwright his whole nose had been cut off. He cried then, great blubbering tears and Harry looked down on him with contempt as blood, tears and mucus mingled and ran over his lips.

'Tell me,' Harry ordered. 'Come on, the works, or I do the other one, too.'

It all came out then, a torrent of almost incoherent babble. But Harry understood enough to know there was a politician guilty of procuring a young boy, the wife of a rich man who'd had an affair with him. A policeman who was homosexual and a judge who'd had sex with two under-age girls, but still Wainwright didn't mention Tara.

'You don't expect me to believe that's all?' Harry threatened him with the knife again.

'It is,' Wainwright sobbed. 'I've told you everything.'

'Come on, I know there's more.' Harry put the blade against his other nostril. 'What about taking porno pictures of young girls? How many of those have you done?'

'I can't remember,' he sobbed, and to Harry's disgust he wet himself.

'You perverted, evil wanker,' Harry said as the stream of urine soaked Wainwright's dark blue pyjama trousers and ran across the sheet. 'Where's your bottle now, queer boy? Tell me where you keep all the stuff about your victims. Now – before I cut your cock off, too!'

'It's in a box under the stairs,' he sobbed. 'Look, I'm sorry, I'll give you anything, just let me go!'

'I haven't anywhere near finished with you.' Harry laughed, opening the dressing table drawer and pulling out a sock. 'Let's just shove this in your mouth for now, to shut you up. I hope you'll still be able to breathe, can't always with a split nostril!'

It took only seconds to check the dressing-table drawers. Underwear, a couple of sweaters, a bundle of notes which he threw across to Wainwright in disgust, and a packet of Durex.

'You ain't got much gear,' Harry said derisively, slashing his knife down the jacket of the expensive navy blue suit hanging up. 'Still, I expect you can still sell yer arse to make a few bob when I've finished with you. I ain't got any plans for that.'

He checked through the house quickly. There was no food, just a few teabags, coffee and sugar. No books, no letters, as if he'd come here in a hurry and abandoned all that went before. The bathroom revealed his true narcissistic nature, with shelves holding fake tan, face creams, expensive cologne and a galaxy of shampoos and bath oils.

In the cupboard under the stairs was a Johnny Walker whisky box. Harry dragged it towards him, then lifted it up and took it over to the kitchen table. Just a quick flick through revealed details of Wainwright's victims, filed in alphabetical order of their christian names, each in a cardboard wallet. There were at least twenty-five wallets.

Tara's file was plump, and as he opened it excitement at actually finding hard evidence instantly turned to nausea. First there were more prints, blown-up ones he couldn't avoid looking at, plus some slightly blurred black and white photographs taken without her knowledge. In some of these she was with Josh, getting into his car, going to a restaurant. One was of her standing in the window of her workroom looking down to the street, in another she was in her room wearing only bra and pants and it could only have been taken from the church across the road.

'You bastard, you've been spying on her,' he muttered, making a mental note to frighten him still more before he left.

Leaving the box in the hall, Harry went back upstairs. Wainwright had worked himself up into a lather, dripping with sweat, tossing and bucking around so much it was surprising he hadn't come off the bed.

'You're pathetic.' Harry looked down in contempt at the man and wished Myra could see him like this so she'd never look at him again. 'You're like a bloody great slug, leaving a trail of slime behind you.'

Wainwright's brown eyes pleaded with him.

'I want to know more,' he said, advancing towards the bed with the knife back in his hand. 'I want to know where you come from, your real home. If you don't want to tell me I'll slit the other nostril.' He pulled the sock out of Wainwright's mouth. 'Come on then, you've got two minutes. Real name, real address.'

'Wainwright is my real name.' His voice shook with fear. 'This is my real address.'

'Bullshit, there's no personal belongings here.'

'I was married.' Tears filled the man's eyes. 'She chucked me out.'

'Address,' Harry commanded.

'131 Gorse Road, Bushey in Hertfordshire,' Wainwright whimpered. 'But don't go there – my children.'

'You've got children?' Harry's lips curled in disgust. 'God help them, having a father like you. Why did your wife throw you out?'

Wainwright just shivered and whimpered.

'She found out you were a faggot, I suppose?'

The lack of reply seemed to confirm this.

'Well, I'll be going in a moment or two. I've had as much of your stench as I can take.' Harry reached out, took the sock off the bed and shoved it back into Wainwright's mouth. 'I'm taking the files, I'll drop by the police station to hand them over. I'll explain you would have brought them in yourself but you're tied up at the moment.' Harry sniggered at his joke. 'Don't panic, big boy, you'll be released by morning!'

He was just about to turn off the bedroom light when Myra sprang into his mind.

'By the way.' Harry bent over the bed and stuck his knife right up against Wainwright's cheek. 'Myra in the pub! She didn't tell me anything about you. Nothing whatsoever. I followed you here and I swiped that envelope from behind the till. If I discover anything has happened to her, or that you've been near her, I swear I'll come back for you and cut off your cock.'

He paused, sticking the top of the knife into his cheek far enough for the man to make a muffled squeal which had to be agreement. Harry drew his knife down Wainwright's cheek, just deep enough to draw blood and terrify the man.

'A scar on a man's face is a dead give-away, I always think.' Harry smirked. 'It warns people not to trust you, like a leper carrying a bell.'

He turned off the bedside light then, smiling as he heard more muffled sounds of distress.

'Calm down, Simple Simon,' he called back. 'The police will get here eventually, no point in struggling now.'

Harry sat at his desk, head in his hands. It was light outside now and he'd been through each of the files carefully. Reason told him it would be best to dump the whole lot on the police anonymously and let them deal with it, but his upbringing had conditioned him to distrust them.

It was a hot potato all right. Blackmail was a despicable crime, but some of the people in these wallets were beyond sympathy and Harry was tempted to just pass on the information to one of the sleazier Sunday papers. The politician who took two under-age boys to a hotel in Brighton posing as their uncle, yet only days later spoke out about cleaning up vice in inner cities. The abortionist who'd plied his trade round the bedsits of Paddington leaving carnage in his wake. But there were others, mere unfortunates – a transvestite, adulterers and homosexuals, and women like Tara, silly enough to let him photograph them in compromising positions. They shouldn't be punished with further humiliation.

But if he didn't give this stuff to the police, what should he do with it? Burn it, return it to the owners or merely sit on it? He moved from his desk over to the leather Chesterfield and lay down.

This was the one room in the building he'd made no structural alterations to, and he loved it. It would always remind him how fickle Lady Luck could be, and Great-grandpa Baxter on the wall with his disdainful look would make sure he took good care of business.

The windows were re-glazed, fifteen panes to remind him of prison, but the view was over the Thames. Once the Baxters must have stood at that window watching ships unloading below. He wouldn't be able to oversee that way, but he had a spy hole in the panelling to watch the croupier in the gaming room next door.

The oak panelling was re-varnished, a plain grey carpet on the floor. An old roll-top desk was a find from a junk shop in Shoreditch. It was a truly masculine room. Harry liked to lie down on the sofa and imagine himself in three or four years as a tycoon, sitting behind his desk barking out instructions to his minions.

He felt his eyelids drooping and told himself he would just have forty winks, then phone Tara, and the police to tell them Wainwright was tied up.

Banging woke him. Someone was trying to get in downstairs.

He raced out on to the landing, then down the big wide staircase towards the foyer and the front door.

'I'm coming,' he yelled as they banged again. 'Give us a chance!'

It was the delivery of furniture – twenty-four small round tables, sixty chairs and twelve button-backed settees in dark red velvet.

'We came earlier.' One of the men looked angry. 'There weren't no-one here. You're lucky we didn't take this lot back.'

It took some time to get it all unloaded and Harry felt obliged to give them both a drink in the bar when they'd finished. As he saw the men out, he happened to glance at his watch.

'Bloody hell!' he exclaimed. It was just after six, Wainwright had been tied up for some fifteen hours.

He dialled 999 nervously, asked for the police and left the message about a man tied up in Loftus Road, hastily putting the receiver down before they could trace the call. Then he rang Tara.

'I've been nearly out of my mind with worry.' Her voice sounded shaky and scared. 'What's been happening?'

'I got held up,' Harry said. 'But don't worry, I've got the negatives, he won't bother you or Josh again.'

He heard her exhale, it sounded as if she was crying.

'It's over, babe,' he reassured her. 'Now can I come over and see you? I want to kiss all those worries away.'

'So it's to be Harry, then?' Gran sat in her rocking chair and looked as if she was sucking lemons. 'After all the warnings you still want a jailbird and a gambler?'

Tara was ready to leave, in jeans and a T-shirt, her holdall on the kitchen floor beside her. It was three weeks since Southend and this three-day break at home had been intended as a peace-making mission, a chance to sort out her feelings and to find out if Harry would ever be accepted.

'Come on, Gran.' Tara folded her arms insolently and looked away in disgust. 'This is Harry we're talking about, not someone I picked up down the Salvation Army hostel.'

She was leaving now, a day early, because she couldn't stand any more argument. Instead of going back revitalised, she felt worse than she had when she arrived.

'I wrote and told you all about it,' Tara went on. 'You refused to acknowledge the letter, wouldn't even talk to me on the phone. Well, I've done everything I can, and if you won't accept Harry, then I'm going back to

London and I'll stay there.' She turned away angrily, opened the kitchen door and went out to say goodbye to her mother.

The yard was bathed in sunshine, a couple of chickens pecking at some straw over by their coop. The barn door was open wide, revealing a gap left by the new tractor which Stan was using down in the lower meadow. There was evidence everywhere of new prosperity, not just the tractor. There was a sturdier door on the barn, the room next to the dairy had a bright sign announcing 'Farm shop', with dozens of pots of jam and marmalade arranged in the window, and a recently painted bench stood outside so customers could sit down and have an ice cream or drink. Big tubs of petunias and a hanging basket on the dairy wall added to the idyllic scene.

Amy was washing the churns in the dairy. She looked up as Tara came in and smiled weakly. She had her big white apron on, her blonde hair tied back with a scarf, but there was defeat in her eyes.

'She hasn't come round?'

'No, Mum, and I don't think she will.' Tara put her bag down on the stone floor. She didn't want to leave like this, but Gran hadn't given her any choice.

Amy sighed and wiped her forehead with the back of her hand. She was piggy-in-the-middle again and she didn't know what to think, much less do.

'Mum, what do I do?' Tara began to cry and immediately Amy went to comfort her. 'I'm so happy with Harry, he's everything in the world.' She sobbed on her mother's shoulder. 'He isn't like Dad or Grandpa, he isn't.'

'There, there.' Amy held Tara tightly. 'I know he isn't like them. It's just this club that bothers us. All those shady characters. We can't help worrying, not just about what might happen to him, but you, too. You've moved out of the flat above the shop. What's going to happen when you're up half the night with Harry? Are you going to be able to work?'

'Harry's not living with me,' Tara said, lifting a tear-stained face to her mother's. 'He's got a place of his own again back in the Angel. I won't be going to the club every night!'

It wasn't strictly true that Harry wasn't living with her, because he had been with her every night since she moved in. But he had got a flat of his own, for when the club opened.

'Only time can resolve this one.' Amy dabbed at Tara's face with the corner of her apron. 'I'm not against you. I love you too much for that, and I do know how it feels to want to be with the man you love.'

'Oh, Mum.' Fresh tears started to flow. 'She's been nasty to you and Greg too, hasn't she?'

'She can be the most aggravating woman in the world,' Amy said bitterly. 'We wanted to get married this summer, but she's managed to scupper that plan by playing on my conscience.'

'How?' Tara asked.

'Well, we had a row when Greg suggested building a surgery here. I lost my temper with her and flounced out, saying I'd give her a taste of what life would be like without me on call.'

'That was when she twisted her ankle?' Tara asked. She had sensed there was something more to the tale of Gran slipping in the cowshed a month or two back, but she hadn't known Amy wasn't actually there at the time.

'Yes.' Amy blushed, the memory still making her feel guilty. 'It happened the day after I stormed out. She didn't call me or anything. Just strapped it up and hobbled about on a stick. Stan came round to Greg's in the end and said the farmhouse was in a terrible mess.'

'She couldn't manage without you, then?' Tara took just a little pleasure in this.

Amy half smiled. 'She looked after the animals, but that was all. The dishes were piled up in the sink, the floor was covered in pig swill because she couldn't carry the pails. You can guess the rest.'

'But unless you stand firm, she'll always expect you to do things.' Tara caught hold of her mother's arms and squeezed them. 'Can't you marry Greg and live with him, but come round here each day?'

'She'd be so lonely,' Amy's eyes welled up and this time it was Tara who comforted her.

'But if she was lonely she'd soon let Greg build the surgery,' Tara said. 'You mustn't let her blackmail you.'

'Easier said than done.' Amy broke away and dried her eyes. 'For now we're just waiting, chipping away at her.'

'I suppose that's what I'll have to do, too.' Tara smiled bleakly.

Amy looked up at the clock on the dairy wall. 'If you're going to catch the twelve o'clock bus you'd better go,' she said sadly. 'Give things time. Not just with your Gran, but with Harry, too. Keep your options open.'

There was nothing more to be said. Tara put her arms round her mother one more time and hugged her tightly.

'Bye, Mum,' she whispered. 'Keep in touch!'

'You're the most precious thing in my life,' Amy whispered back. 'I want you to be happy above all else. If Harry's the one that makes you happy, I won't fight it.'

Tara had to run to catch the bus and they were almost at the turn-off to Stanton Drew before she got her breath back.

The little round toll house with its thatched roof standing in the middle of the junction evoked memories of Simon. When Harry had finally phoned to say he'd dealt with Wainwright all she felt was relief. But the next day, when she read the story in the papers of the man tied up and tortured in Shepherd's Bush, she felt sick. It had to be Simon and, even though Harry was merely protecting her, it didn't feel good to know he could do such things.

Harry wouldn't confirm or deny what he'd done. All he was concerned about was getting her away from above the shop into her own flat. But Josh's words on the subject had chilled her.

'If that's his way of sorting out a problem, I hope you two don't ever fall out.'

Josh had been moody and sullen for a few days after the event; he said little when she got the flat vacated by one of Miranda's friends in Pembridge Road in Notting Hill Gate. But since then he'd grown warmer again. He'd found a girl to help her in the workroom, and even bought her a television as a flat-warming present.

Reason told her she should be entirely happy. The flat was just one big, sunny room with a tiny kitchen and bathroom, but it had its own front door, huge windows overlooking a much quieter road than Church Street, and it felt like a real home. Harry had got a friend in to paint it. She'd splashed out and bought a settee that opened into a double bed, and full-length curtains in a wild jungle print.

But even though when they were together passion wiped out all anxiety, a little voice kept telling her to be careful.

Chapter 27

'Please try and look as if you want to go to the party,' Tara begged Josh as he drove her through the City. 'You've known Harry since you were small, there'll be lots of people there who knew you then. It'll be fun!'

Josh looked his best tonight in a dinner jacket and bow-tie. His dark curls shone, his face was tanned. He looked like a man on the way to his first million.

'About as much fun as it was hearing them call me dirty Yid,' he said drily. 'I can't actually remember one nice person from that era.'

'You said Harry was kind then!'

'Well, yes, I suppose he was.'

'If nothing else you can flaunt yourself.' Tara giggled. 'What better than to come back stinking rich and rub people's noses in it?'

Tara didn't really know why she'd talked Josh into coming tonight. He was no fun when he was in this dour introspective mood and Harry didn't really care whether he came or not. But she knew the press would be there and Harry needed all the celebrities he could get on his side.

At least she knew that she was looking good. She'd made the outfit – a cream plunge-necked slinky cat-suit that fitted like a second skin, with flared trousers and a beaded wide belt slung around her hips. The matching jacket draped over her shoulders was studded with more bead work across the yoke and lapels. She had spent two hours at the hairdresser's having her hair curled into ringlets and for once even she knew she looked gorgeous!

As Josh turned off the main road just past Tower Bridge, Tara was reminded again what a gamble Harry's club was.

The Top Cat Club's green neon sign glimmered through the gloom ahead. The logo of a cat wearing a top hat seemed to defy the smoke-blackened brick-work surrounding it, the bricked-up windows, the rat-ridden air of the place.

She was surprised to see that Harry had kept all the pulleys and hoists and repainted them in the original red to match the huge loading-bay door. Aside from glass in the windows, paint and restored doors, it was just as she'd last seen it back in February.

'Doesn't look too promising!' Josh's jubilation was barely controlled. 'I'll give him till Christmas.'

'Don't be such a downer,' Tara snapped at him. 'He's never been like that about you. If I hear you say one more negative word tonight I'll be handing in my notice.'

'I don't mean to be nasty.' Josh turned his soulful eyes to her. 'Yeah, I'm jealous 'cos he's got you and I think he's wrong for you. But I do really wish him success, I promise you.' He pulled a magnum of Champagne over from the back seat. 'See, I even got him a present!'

Tara walked in the small door beside the loading bay with Josh close behind her, up three or four steps, and stopped dead.

It wasn't the shock of seeing Harry looking inde-cently handsome in dinner jacket and bow-tie, but the surprise of coming out of that dark, unpleasant street into somewhere so splendid. She clapped her hand over her mouth and stared in amazement.

The spiral staircase was gone. No more plaster partitions. Instead she was standing in a spacious, deeply carpeted foyer. To her left a wide oak staircase led up to a gallery, and suspended in the space was a huge chandelier. She barely had time to take in the splendour, or to notice the interested faces turning to look at her from beyond an archway into the bar, before Harry had his arm round her and she was being drawn further in.

'This is my girl!' he said, grinning like a Cheshire cat. 'Did I lie when I said she was the most beautiful girl in the world?'

'Harry!' Tara buried her face in his jacket in embarrassment, aware of all the men watching her.

'Well, it's true.' Harry prised her off him and kissed her lightly, looking across at Josh. 'Glad you could make it, Josh, it's good to see you again. Now let me introduce you both to the lads!'

Tara was torn between looking at the club itself and the four elegantly dressed men, Harry's sidekicks, waiting to be introduced. She wondered how Harry could have found a chandelier, brought it and hung it up without mentioning it once. Where did he learn to put in a staircase as huge as that? The striped wallpaper, the wood panelling, mirrors and carpets, how did he ever get all that together and make it look so perfect?

'You've met Needles before.' She was jolted back to the man in front of her. She'd met him when she first came to London, though he hadn't looked so formidable then. His shoulders were like a barn door, hands like hams, and he towered over her.

'You look very dashing tonight.' She returned his dazzling smile. He still wore his curly black hair cut very short, small dark eyes twinkling with merriment. His hand almost crushed hers and she wondered in passing whether anyone would ever dare throw a punch at him.

'Not as gorgeous as you,' he said gallantly, his voice as adenoidal as she remembered. 'You look a treat!'

'Well, thank you.' Tara smiled up at him. She could see instantly why Harry had clung on to this particular friend. Loyalty, trustworthiness and humour were all written on his big face.

Harry went on to introduce Tony, another childhood friend who would be bar manager. His father was Italian and he had inherited olive skin, flashing white teeth and dark, soft eyes.

Dennis and Alec would be running the gaming rooms upstairs. Dennis's voice had the plummy tones of public school, he was tall, thin and aristocratic-looking. But Tara felt a little uneasy looking into his cold duck egg blue eyes. His mouth smiled but somehow the rest of his face didn't join in. Alex was easier to like, a Cockney kid with a splash of freckles across his pug nose. Harry often talked about this one-time professional boxer, who'd let his passion for women get in the way of training. He wasn't handsome, too stocky, too pale-skinned, but his grin was warm and engaging; when he shook her hand he held it just a second too long.

'Well, let's get you both a drink.' Harry patted Josh on the shoulder, edging them through to the bar.

'Oh, Harry.' Tara's eyes shone as she looked around. 'I can't believe you've done all this!'

Three large windows stood in front of them, red velvet curtains open to show the view of the river. In front were bench seats and tables, each with a small shaded light. She understood Harry's fascination with the river now. The sun was sinking down over towards Tower Bridge, turning the sky purple and pink. The water was silver and, as a ferry passed on its way to Greenwich, she had a childish desire to wave to the passengers.

To her left was a long curved bar of gleaming mahogany, with a brass foot-rail, and a mirrored wall behind the optics. On the right in the corner furthest away from the windows was a small stage where a quartet of musicians in dinner suits played soft dance music, a minute dance floor in front of it. The walls elsewhere had a shelf at elbow height for standing-up drinkers, and a huge buffet was laid out on a long table in the centre of the room.

'Don't look too bad, does it?' Harry grinned.

'It's marvellous.' Tara slid her arm round him and kissed his cheek. 'I'm so proud of you.'

'I had a bit of help.' He looked vaguely bashful now. 'All the lads chipped in.'

He passed them glasses of wine from the bar.

'These are freebies.' He grinned. 'If you want anything else you have to buy it, I'm afraid. If I'd said free drinks all round I'd have been killed in the stampede!'

They'd come early, and as yet there were only a few people here. Josh sipped his drink and looked round.

'How many people are you expecting?' he asked.

'Five hundred or so,' Harry replied, his eyes straying back towards the foyer. 'Can I trust you to look after Tara? I've got to greet my guests. Have a wander round. There's another smaller bar up in the gaming rooms. I'll be back soon.'

'Isn't it wonderful.' Tara sipped her wine and waited for Josh to make a comment. She knew he was thunderstruck but she was silently laying bets that he would come back with something sarcastic.

'It's incredible,' he said eventually, making her eyes open wide with surprise. 'I came in here once a few years ago when Chas Baxter wanted to sell it. I didn't think anyone could do anything with it. But it would've been better for him if he'd made it a freaks' place, strobe lighting and stuff. This is a bit dated.'

In view of his praise Tara didn't shout him down about the other comment. People were arriving thick and fast and her gut reaction was that Harry was on the right track.

'Tara, sweetheart.' Queenie bore down on them, her mink stole flapping over one pink shoulder, blonde hair swept up into a mass of carefully constructed curls. 'Well, let me get a good look at you!' She twirled Tara around, her face rosy with excitement.

'You look the business,' she said, patting Tara's small round buttocks in the tight suit. 'Just don't get carried away wiv the dancing and split those trousers. I bet you've got nothing on underneath.'

'You're looking gorgeous, too.' Tara laughed. Queenie's dress was long, pink and sparkling, slashed to the knee. 'I bet you've got something on under there?' She patted her large rump and it was as hard as a wall.

'Eighteen-hour girdle with magic fingers to hold me gut in,' Queenie giggled, whispering behind her hand. 'I doubt I can sit down, though. Sometimes I fink I should slip into middle age gracefully and get meself a few crimplene tents!'

'Don't you dare.' Josh smiled warmly at her. He could identify with Queenie, she had the same style as many of his mother's Jewish friends. 'I like to see glamorous ladies.'

'Where's Uncle George,' Tara asked, handing Queenie a glass of wine which she gulped down in one.

'Out there with 'Arry.' She inclined one ring-covered hand towards the foyer. 'He's like a dog with two sets of balls tonight. Don't you just love it? Ain't our 'Arry a clever boy?'

Queenie's joyful admiration of her stepson was like warm balm on a sore place, so different to the cautious lukewarm praise her gran and mother gave her. But Queenie had come for a party and she had no intention of leaving tonight until she'd met every single guest.

Taking Tara by the hand she dragged her to a group of people coming through the door, and waded in.

Harry had the mix of personalities and backgrounds just right. Old friends of Queenie and George's generation gave colour and warmth. Older villains, with their scarred faces and four-hundred pound suits, added the danger, while a dozen pretty girls Miranda had rounded up from her haunts supplied the glamour.

The Cockney hard men were obvious by their short hair, brilliant white shirts, discreet ties and expensive three-piece suits. Their women, many with beehive hair-styles, glittering cocktail dresses and stilettos, bubbled and fizzed as their tables filled up with glasses of gin and orange. Barbara Windsor arrived, greeting old friends with squeals of joy. Terence Stamp stood by the door, smiling sardonically as if wishing he could let his hair down and forget he was a star. His girlfriend was as thin as a greyhound, with long blonde hair and eyes like giant cornflowers.

Steve Marriott from the Small Faces was chatting to George, who he'd known since he was a kid. Tara watched Queenie eyeing him up and wondered when she would ask him round for a meal to fatten him up. He'd brought a few friends with him, the men uniformly small, skinny and long-haired, looking like peacocks in jazzy shirts and velvet trousers. Their girls were model types with perfect features and skirts like wide belts.

By midnight the main bar was so packed that Harry had to get behind the bar at one point and serve drinks himself. The small dance floor was packed with couples smooching as a singer with a voice like Matt Monroe sang 'Moon River'.

'He's a clever boy,' Queenie said, beaming with pride. 'Good touch that, giving them wine when they first come in. Look at them now, buying drinks like they'll never get another.'

'I didn't think this would work, not until tonight,' George admitted, tweaking his bow-tie with one hand while puffing on a cigar. 'But he's got it just right. As long as the nobs turn up to play now and then, he'll make it.'

The party was swinging. The tables were covered in drinks, every chair was taken and the rest of the floor space taken up with people standing elbow to elbow. Laughter and chatter mingled with the dance music. A haze of smoke drifted up towards the lights, the air was filled with the smell of perfume and cigars. Behind the bar three barmaids were run off their feet as men stood three deep waving ten-pound notes.

Tara was having a wonderful time. Josh had finally gone home and she was the centre of attention, both from the press and Harry's friends. She could see for herself that the club really was going to work.

She was a bit drunk now, leaning on the bar watching. The band had gone, and Harry had put a tape on. Wilson Pickett's 'Wait till the Midnight Hour' was playing, the lights above the stage casting red, green and blue smoky beams of light on to the dancers.

A group of beehived girls, joined by Miranda and some of her stylish friends, danced. They'd kicked off their shoes, forgotten about their handbags and their partners.

Queenie was there too. She was a graceful dancer despite her weight, though clearly her girdle was cramping her style. George was sitting on the edge of the stage, his bow-tie dangling loose round his unbuttoned collar, and his braces on view. His eyes were on Queenie, too, a smile playing at his lips. Would she and Harry be like that when they got to their age?

'Penny for them?' She jumped as Harry spoke softly in her ear, she hadn't heard him creep up on her.

'I was wondering if we'll be like Queenie and George when we're as old as them?'

'No.' He shook his head. 'We'll be thinner, sexier and a great deal richer. Come and dance with me. I want an excuse to hold you.'

'Why do you need an excuse?' She leaned her head on his shoulder as they danced. She often wondered if she was the only woman in the world that got a buzz out of her man's body. Not just during sex, but any time. The sensation of hard flesh against her soft body, running her fingers down the muscles in his legs and arms, the flatness of his stomach. Even his hands made her feel weak, so strong, yet when he chose to be gentle his fingers were more sensitive than a child's.

'Because if I stood around cuddling you people would think I'd gone soft,' he whispered in her ear, running his tongue round the edge. 'It's all a matter of face, Tara. I've got a beautiful girlfriend, they know I'd kill anyone who tried to hurt you, but I can't act like I'm going over the top.'

'Are you going over the top?'

'Oh, yes.' He moved one hand against her cheek, the other holding her waist, blue eyes looking right into hers. 'You mean more to me than anything else in the world. This club is only a stepping stone to a better kind of life for us.'

Her heart thumped and she wished she could describe to him just how much she loved him. 'Would you really kill for me?' She put her lips to his cheek, ran one finger round his ear.

'I hope no-one ever puts me to the test.'

It was after three when the last guests left. Tara sat on the stairs, watching as Needles called cabs and helped women into coats. She was deliciously drunk, she didn't know where her shoes were and her jacket kept falling off her shoulders.

'All right, babe?' Needles called out. 'Anything I can get you?'

'Has Harry taken loads of money tonight?' she asked, slurring her words.

'Looks that way, darlin',' Needles hitched up his trouser legs and sat down beside her. 'He's up there in his office stuffing it in the safe right now. It's gonna be all right.'

'Where's your wife, Needles?' she asked. 'I didn't get introduced to her.'

'She's at 'ome, sweetheart, tucked up in bed waiting for me.'

'Wasn't she here?'

He laughed, a deep growl of a laugh from his belly.

'This is my job,' he said. 'She won't be coming 'ere. 'Er place is at 'ome wiv the kids.'

Tara was too drunk to digest that just now, but it seemed to her Needles' wife got a raw deal.

'I can't see you waiting till the end of the night with me very often.' Harry opened the door of the flat with Tara over his shoulder. She had fallen asleep in the cab and he'd carried her in.

'I'll learn to drive then I can come home alone,' she replied as he sat her down on the settee.

'I wouldn't trust you to drive safely,' he tossed over his shoulder as he drew the curtains. 'I'll put you in a taxi.'

'Afraid of me becoming independent?' She stood up a little unsteadily, threw the cushions off the settee and unfolded the bed. It was already made inside and she got the pillows out of the cupboard.

She could smell smoke everywhere, on her clothes, hair and skin. She wanted to have a shower, but she knew she was too drunk.

'I suppose so.' Harry looked faintly ashamed. 'That and the fact I don't approve of lady drivers!'

It was almost four in the morning. She had the day off this time, but it crossed her mind she wouldn't be able to stand this sort of pace for long.

'Will it always be this late?' She sat down on the bed and slipped off her shoes.

'Later sometimes.' Harry took off his jacket and the bow-tie he'd loosened in the car. 'Once we get big card games going it could be all night.' He sat down next to her and pulled her into his arms. 'We have to remember it's not forever,' he said softly against her hair, unzipping her suit. 'Once everything's running smoothly I'll be able to take time off. But it's going to be hard for the next three or four months. I bet Josh has predicted I'll be bust by then?'

'No, he's given you till Christmas.' Tara giggled. 'By the way, you never told me what Josh said about you sorting out Simon.' She had seen them talking, just before Josh left, and she knew it was about that.

'Not a lot. What was there to say? Just thanks.'

His chauvinistic attitude suddenly irritated her – first the suggestion she couldn't be trusted to drive and now this put-down. Didn't he realise her brain was as sharp as his?

'What exactly did you do to Simon?'

'Nothing. Just marked his card.'

Tara moved round to face Harry, her suit falling down over her shoulders to reveal her breasts. He looked unconcerned, as calm as if she'd been referring to someone back home in the village.

'Don't try to fool me, Harry Collins,' she said firmly. 'I know perfectly well the man who was found tied up and tortured was Simon, even though they didn't print his name.'

'Don't ask me about it.' His eyes suddenly grew dark with anger. 'I got the negatives, and the spare prints. So I used a little force to get him to open up. What did you expect me to do, charm him? Screw him?'

Tara drew back from him, suddenly nervous. She'd seen this attitude before – in her father!

'I only asked,' she whispered, pulling her suit back up over her body.

'Forget that man,' Harry almost snarled. 'Put him out of your mind. He got far less than he had coming to him, that's all you need to know.'

Tara got up and held out his jacket. 'You'd better go home,' she said in a small voice. 'Don't ever, ever speak to me like that!'

Harry looked up at her and instantly felt ashamed of himself for being so harsh. She looked so forlorn now, one hand clutching her suit over her breasts, her ringlets loose and bedraggled, mascara smeared under her eyes and that soft, sexy mouth quivering as she held back tears.

He'd been speaking the truth earlier when he said she was the most beautiful girl he'd ever seen. When she walked into the club he almost burst with pride. Until tonight he'd had a rosy idea that Tara would be at the club with him most of the time. He'd imagined her at his side, having a drink and chatting to the customers. But tonight, even though it was a happy, fun-filled evening, he'd sensed the club's real style.

It would become a villains' watering hole; he couldn't prevent it even if he wanted to. They would bring women, stylish, glamorous women, but they wouldn't be their wives. When the pubs turned out all around the East End they'd descend on him in their droves. It would be a place to take the tart you want to impress, and if you haven't got a girl, there's always the lads to chat to, or a game of poker.

But Tara didn't belong in that scene.

'I'm sorry, babe.' He got to his feet and reached out for her. 'It came out all wrong. I only want to protect you.'

Tara stepped back from him, her amber eyes filling up with tears she could no longer hold back.

'But I have a right to know what happened. It was my pictures you had to get back, remember!'

'There's ugliness all around us, darling.' He caught hold of her hands. 'You've got so much talent, you're so beautiful – I don't want you to be contaminated by people with ugly minds and dirty thoughts.'

She let him hold her again, she couldn't resist him when he spoke like that, with that tender expression in his eyes.

'Roses are beautiful, too,' she said, looking up into his face. 'They grow best in shit, Harry, and they have thorns. I might just be a little tougher than you think.'

Chapter 28

Christmas 1969

'Her place is with her family at Christmas,' Mabel snapped, 'not gallivanting round a gambling club. You should have put your foot down!'

'When are you going to realise you can't dominate everyone?' Amy tried to keep calm. It was eight o'clock on Christmas Eve, Greg would be arriving within the hour, and the last thing she wanted was another row.

Mabel was stuffing the turkey, rosy in the heat, wrapped in a big white apron. Bunches of holly tied with red ribbon turned slowly in the heat above their heads, the tree was lit up in the sitting room, gaily wrapped presents beneath it, and the whole house smelled of mulled wine, mince pies and pine needles. Everything was the same as it was every Christmas, but this year Tara wouldn't be there.

Amy lifted the tray of mince pies out of the oven, kicked the door shut with her knee and took them over to the table.

'Is it so extraordinary she wants to be with the man she loves?' She flicked back her hair from her hot face. 'I wouldn't call it gallivanting, either. From what I understand they're both exhausted!'

Amy was as disappointed as her mother, but she understood the pressure on both Tara and Harry. For weeks now they'd both been frantically busy and hardly seen one another. Besides, Queenie and George would give them a far more rapturous welcome than Mabel would!

'It's all right for you!' Mabel broke off from her task, put her sausage meat covered hands on her hips and glared indignantly at her daughter. 'You'll be spooning with Greg and I'll be left alone.'

'Don't be so ridiculous.' Amy banged the mince pies down on to the cooling tray in anger. 'We've got Ena and Herbert coming for lunch tomorrow and, as you well, know Greg is on call so he might not get here at all.'

'It won't be the same without Tara,' Mabel said stubbornly. 'Besides, both she and Harry could rest just as well here as in London.'

'It's a long drive,' Amy reminded her. 'Anyway, the club will probably be open till three or four.'

'Gambling on Christmas Eve!' Mabel snorted with disapproval. 'Taking food from children's mouths, encouraging men to drink when they should be home with their wives!'

'You are the most cantankerous, selfish old woman I've ever met!' Amy shouted. 'Has it occurred to you the real reason she's not coming home might be because she can't bear your nasty digs all the time?'

'The girl's a fool if she can't stand the truth.' Mabel's eyes flashed. 'She should marry Josh, he's rich, well educated, and Jewish men don't cheat on their wives. They've got so much in common, far more than she has with that piece of riff-raff!'

'In my eyes Harry has proved himself,' Amy said defiantly. 'How dare you call him riff-raff!'

'He'll let her down, I tell you,' Mabel insisted. 'He's a gambler, they always do.'

'Why do you always bring up that ridiculous argument?' Amy snapped back at her. 'Harry might own a gambling club, but it doesn't mean he gambles his own money away. Anyway, Greg will be here soon. Go and change ready for church.'

504

'I'm not coming.' Mabel's voice took on a plaintive note. 'I know what Gregory Masterton wants, you think it's you don't you?'

Amy gritted her teeth and left the room.

'It's not you he wants,' Mabel shrieked after her. 'It's this farm.'

Upstairs Amy slapped cold water on her face and resisted the temptation to scream aloud. 'Sometimes I hate you, Mother,' she whispered, taking deep breaths to calm herself. 'You'd try the patience of a saint!'

She peeled off her everyday clothes down to her white petticoat, looking at herself in the mirror. Next year she would be forty. She might still be as slim as the day she married Bill, but she could see tiny lines round her eyes and a slackness on her jawline. Tonight's anger wasn't only about Tara and Harry, it was about her mother controlling her. She had to make a stand soon, otherwise she'd end up like Mabel, a frustrated and bitter woman.

Looking down at her sapphire and diamond ring, she sighed. Surely no couple of their ages had ever had such a long engagement?

Mabel used Greg when it suited her. She saw him as another unpaid worker, a source of advice, an ear to bend when she chose. But the moment Greg mentioned setting the day, she bristled and made things impossible.

They were trapped. If they went to live in his house, Mabel would let things slide again. If Greg moved in here he would be insulted, treated with suspicion and derided if he made any suggestions. But they couldn't go on snatching odd moments together like a couple of teenagers.

All day Amy had had a feeling of foreboding. Was it because she felt herself being pushed to the edge by her mother? Or was it anxiety about Tara? There was nothing concrete to be worried about. Despite

Mother's fierce words about Harry before he opened the club, she had mellowed enough to invite him down with Tara on several occasions in the last eighteen months. Happiness and love shone out of them and there wasn't one person who wasn't charmed by both Harry and the aura that surrounded them.

But recently Tara's letters and many phone calls had had a wistful air to them. She seemed to be alone a great deal, yet reticent to talk about that, or Harry's business.

The Top Cat Club, and Harry, had become well-known. Personalities from the stage, screen and sporting world were always being photographed at the club and he had been on television several times himself.

But was Harry being sucked into the seamier side of clubland, as they'd feared? Was he really earning enough legitimately to pay for that brand new Mercedes? His hand-stitched jackets, shoes specially made in Curzon Street, monogrammed silk shirts and gold Rolex watch – were they all from the profits of drinks and gambling or was he involved in something more?

Protection rackets, drugs, prostitution, even gun-running passed through her mind. Could a man who'd tasted the high life ever settle down to a normal family life?

'Come with us, Mother?' Amy pleaded one last time as she stood in the kitchen ready to leave for church with Greg. They had smoothed over the early fight, but Mabel was still being awkward.

'No.' Mabel pursed her lips, looking at Greg's new camel overcoat disapprovingly. 'I've got things to do. Besides, he looks like a used-car salesman.'

'Mother!' Amy admonished her. 'It's a lovely coat, and anyway, what's that got to do with the midnight service?'

'Peace and goodwill to all men!' Greg said, laughter

in his voice. 'Come on, Amy, or we'll be late. I'll see you tomorrow, Mabel. I won't wear the coat!'

Mother was forgotten in the beauty of the service.

Candles beneath each of the windows cast a flickering yellow light on to the congregation; the air was rich with the perfume of pine and flowers. Amy knew every single one of the people there. Farmers, shopkeepers, girls from the bank and hairdresser's. Old people clutching their walking sticks, too bent to kneel; young couples who rarely came to church.

Her hand found Greg's during 'Oh, Come all ye Faithful', and a tear of happiness trickled down her cheek as his fingers entwined hers. She turned her head slightly so she could look at him, and another tear slipped out.

His pale brown eyes saw all the injustice, the hurt and pain in people's lives, and in his own way he did his best to alleviate it. Those square, practical hands could bring a baby into the world, stitch up a wound, calm a fractious child. He cared for every one of his patients, not just their health but their dreams and aspirations, too.

'Time to go!' Greg's voice startled her; she'd been so wrapped up in her thoughts she hadn't noticed people were leaving. 'You look miles away.'

'I was thinking about you.'

They shook hands with the vicar, wished a merry Christmas to dozens of people and made their way down towards the gate.

Greg stopped her, turning her towards him. The night sky was studded with stars, a frost in the air turning their breath to smoke. Old graves shone white against the dark grass, the huge yew tree was lit up by the light from the church porch, and all around them people called out to one another as they made their way home.

'Promise me you'll marry me soon?' he said, as if sensing she wouldn't go back on a promise made here by the church. 'I can't wait any longer.'

Amy tried to speak, the same tired old excuses surging around in her head.

He put his finger to her lips and stopped them. 'I need you, Amy,' he said softly. 'I want you in my bed, night after night. I want to start the day with you beside me, to share everything I have. We can't go on snatching odd moments, it cheapens what we feel for one another.'

'I know.' Amy sighed. 'I come home from your house glowing because it's been so wonderful, then Mother makes one of her sharp comments and I could kill her.'

'Well, it's crossed my mind to hire an assassin more than once.' Greg chuckled.

His humour decided her. He never complained about Mabel, he always saw things from others' view. It was time.

'Well?' He raised one eyebrow, his hand coming up to stroke her cold cheek.

'Yes, Greg. As soon as you can get the banns read.'

He kissed her.

She heard people chuckling, she felt the wind in the trees, the frost creeping across the grass, and knew that by lunch-time tomorrow this would be discussed in every house in the village. But all that mattered was his warm lips on hers, and the joy in both their hearts.

'Oh, Greg, I can't.' She pulled at his hand as he led her up the High Street towards his house, rather than left to the farm. 'Mother will be waiting!'

'You've got to stay with me tonight.' His eyes implored her. 'Mabel's gone to bed, the turkey's in the slow oven. She won't even know you haven't been there if you get back before she gets up.'

'But what if – '

Greg cut her short. 'She's not ninety, she can look after herself. You know as well as I do she sleeps like a log.'

Amy grinned impishly. 'You've succeeded in tempting me. You'd better make it worth my while staying.'

Acacia House looked festive. Greg had left the lantern on above the front door and it shone down on a red-ribboned holly wreath. Their feet scrunched on the gravel drive and Winston barked out a welcome from inside.

'I'm going to make love to you till you scream for mercy,' he whispered, bending his head to nuzzle at her neck. 'The neighbours will hear you shouting and think I'm treating a cow in labour in my surgery.'

'Is that what I sound like?' she asked as they went in. Winston came bounding up, all drooling tongue and wagging tail, demanding to be petted.

'No, you make beautiful sexy moans that make me feel like a god,' Greg pushed the dog away with one leg. 'Back to your basket Winston!'

Greg unfastened Amy's coat and slid his hands in to cup her small breasts. 'Oh, Amy, this is all I could think of while we were in church, imagining your nipples beneath my fingers and sliding my hands up your thighs.'

'Fancy thinking such things in God's house,' she reproved him, moving away towards the sitting room. 'You ought to be drummed out of the parish!'

'I think it's a shame women stopped wearing stockings.' Greg hung up their coats on the hall stand, then followed her. 'Nothing could beat that feeling of sliding your hand up sheer nylon, then suddenly finding soft flesh.'

Amy picked up the poker and prodded the fire back to life.

'You're a very surprising man,' she said, glancing back over her shoulder at him. He was getting some glasses out of the cabinet for drinks. 'I wouldn't have put you down as a sensual type.'

'I think most people are, with the right partner.' He added tonic to the gin, then went towards the kitchen to get ice. 'I didn't get so many erotic thoughts till you came along. You set me off,' he called back.

Amy smiled and sat down, holding out her hands to the blaze. Winston was creeping into the room, head down because he sensed he wasn't welcome. Amy smiled, she knew that if she caught his eye he'd bound across. She could hear Greg banging an ice tray on the table in the kitchen and knew he would come back with a plate of something nice to nibble on, too. This domesticity in a man was something she still found strange, in fact she found it hard not to wait hand and foot on everyone, she'd done it for so long.

'I wonder if Harry makes snacks for Tara?' she called out.

Greg came in with a tray of sandwiches and mince pies. 'Sorry, Winston.' He ordered him out and kicked the door shut behind him. 'There's a time for dogs, but this isn't one of them.'

He put the tray down on a coffee table, added some ice to her drink, put on a Frank Sinatra record, then sat down beside her.

'Still dwelling on them?' he asked. Amy had told him something of the row before they left for church.

She nodded and smiled, faintly embarrassed that she wasn't only thinking of him.

'Want my real opinion?' he asked.

'Yes, please.'

'You can't let Tara go. It isn't about whether Harry is right or wrong, it's about you being unable to set her free. You've never stopped blaming yourself for the unhappiness your children had in London. Somehow you think if you can keep Tara close to your side she'll never be unhappy again.'

Amy stared in surprise. It was rare for Greg to voice an opinion about Tara or Mabel, though when he did he was usually right.

'You can't make people happy by locking them away from harm.' Greg smiled, taking her hand in his. 'They have to experience grief to appreciate joy. The two things go hand in hand, I'm afraid. Do you think we could be so happy together if we hadn't both had bad experiences in the past?'

There had been many people to tell her about Greg's past. He hadn't had much luck with women. He'd been left virtually at the altar by one, another girl he was sweet on had been killed in a road accident. There had been girls at university and medical school, but each one of them had left him for tougher, more assertive men.

'You are a nice man.' She turned round to him and stroked his face. 'You understand so much.'

'We must get married.' His pale brown eyes held hers. 'We belong together, Amy. Maybe we can even have a baby, before it's too late.'

Joy welled up inside her. 'You really want a child?' she whispered.

It was all so perfect. He was offering her the one thing she wanted above all else, a chance to be a mother again.

'I never wanted anything more,' he said, his lips trembling, coming closer to meet hers.

'I love you, Greg,' she murmured as his lips covered hers. 'This time I'll be strong with Mother.'

Slowly he undressed her, kissing her neck, her shoulders, her breasts as her clothes fell to the floor. 'You're such a beautiful woman,' he said as he moved cushions on to the rug for her to lie on. 'I hope our baby looks like you.'

Greg's lovemaking evoked all those emotions she'd had at seventeen, but now it was sweeter still because

511

there was no anxiety or shame. His fingers were gentle. Love and tenderness guided him, rather than experience, and his sensual delight at stroking and licking at her turned sex to a feast of erotic pleasure. His half-closed eyes were dreamy as his tongue slid up and down on her fanny, he murmured sweet words, pushing his fingers hard into her till she was writhing in ecstasy.

The music, the fire and the soft lights all added to the moment. She was on fire, every nerve-ending jangling and demanding that he bring her to a climax, yet holding back because she wanted this bliss to last forever. He rolled her on to her side and entered her from behind, one hand holding her breast, the other stroking her fanny, whispering words that heightened the sensations still further.

'I'm coming,' she cried out, holding his hand against her. 'Oh, Greg, I love you!'

Mabel heard a car pass the farm then pull up further down the road, but it meant nothing more than a couple of youngsters stopping for a spot of petting before going home. She peered through the darkness to her clock on her bedside table. It was nearly two.

'I can't think what Amy wants to go home with him for,' she grumbled to herself. 'Shouldn't think he knows what it's for.'

In fact she was lying awake because she was ashamed of herself. She wished she hadn't said those sharp things to Amy, and in her heart she welcomed Greg as a son-in-law. If only she could admit to Amy that her bad moods and barbed remarks were brought on by fear – fear of being left alone again.

A sharp sound made her prick up her ears. A heavy boot against a stone?

Her bedroom overlooked the road and that sound had come from someone stepping into the little lane up the side of the house.

It was too late for Amy to come home now, and besides, Greg was far too much of a gentleman not to escort her. Had it been an odd drunk lurching home she would have heard the feet going on past. But there was nothing!

She could hear wind in the elms, the faint tapping sound of a loose piece of corrugated iron on the barn roof, and an owl down by the river. But whoever kicked that stone was now standing still outside. She got out of bed and looked out of the window. The fire station light was on as it always was, casting a beam as far as the bridge, but there was no-one there.

There was enough light through the window to see herself in the dressing-table mirror. 'You look like Mother,' she said to herself indignantly. She didn't like old age. To see herself in the ruffle-necked nightdress, hair thin and white, her face lined, made her smart with anger. It seemed such a short while ago that her skin was smooth and glowing, that her hair tumbled over her shoulders and her body made men turn their heads.

She heard another sound. This time it came from the yard, a scuffle of boot on cobble. Silently she padded across the room, out on to the landing and into Paul's old room next door.

She came in here a great deal when Amy was out, to touch his model planes, to look at his pictures and arrange his soldiers. Harry always slept in here when he came with Tara, but she'd never told him how right it felt to see him in there.

She saw a shadow in the yard. Just a momentary darkening on the barn door, but she knew it was someone creeping along by the back of the house. Standing very still, she listened. He was fumbling with the doorknob. She was scared now, suddenly all too aware of being alone.

'I must phone the police,' she whispered. 'Creep

513

down so he doesn't see me and phone before he gets in.'

How many times had Greg told them they shouldn't leave the door unlocked? She'd tried to explain that that was the way she'd always known, because she'd never considered she had anything worth stealing.

There was no time. Any minute he would be in; she must rush to the phone. But as she reached the top of the stairs she heard the back door creak open, then close a second later.

Indignation was greater than fear. How dare someone creep into her house at Christmas, uninvited? She continued down the stairs, peering over the banisters and considering her next move. A faint gleam of light suggested a torch. She couldn't hear the sounds of drawers or cupboards opening. He must be just looking around. All she could hear was the ticking of the grandfather clock.

Slowly she crept down the stairs, avoiding the one that creaked, proud of herself for not making a sound. The sitting-room door was open slightly, the smell of pine strong and warm. As she got to the bottom stair she darted in there to pick up the heavy candlestick. Her heart was thumping so loud it was surprising he didn't come to find the source. She wished she'd stopped to put her dressing gown on over her nightdress.

Taking a deep breath Mabel moved out of the sitting room back into the hall and towards the kitchen. She had it all quite clear in her head. Switch on the light and order him out. If he didn't go she'd hit him, then call the police. Her hand stole round to the light switch, she counted silently to three, then flashed it on.

'What the hell are you doing in my house?' she screamed. 'Get out!'

But even as her brave words came out, fear struck

her. Not so much because of his build, though he towered above her and seemed to fill the kitchen, but because he wore a black balaclava which covered his entire face except for his eyes, nose and top lip. The eyes were dark brown and they looked startled. He moved towards her threateningly.

She brandished the candlestick. 'Get out or I'll call the police,' she shouted, moving sideways towards the phone on the dresser.

He moved swiftly, his hand reaching the phone at the same moment hers did.

Mabel lashed out with the candlestick, but it merely glanced off his upper arm. He knocked it out of her hand on to the floor and pushed her back against the wall.

She knew then that he was more than a burglar. He wore camouflage trousers, a khaki pullover and heavy working men's boots.

'Who are you?' She looked hard into his brown eyes, trying to imagine the rest of his face. 'What do you want from me?'

His upper lip moved slightly, as if he saw something funny in her question. She could hear her heart thumping, blood almost bubbling in her veins.

'Speak, for God's sake!' she screamed at him.

His eyes reminded her of the heifers when she tried to get them into a truck to go to the abattoir.

'Look, you're scared. So am I, neither of us expected to run into one another,' she said quickly. 'Go now and I won't call the police. I'll even give you some money if that's what you want. Don't get yourself in deeper trouble by hurting me.'

She wanted him to speak so badly – anything to break that terrible silence, the feel of that hand pushing her shoulder back to the wall and and his dark eyes burning into her face. But still he said nothing.

'Are you mute?' she snapped.

He pulled a length of rope out of his pocket and at the same time grabbed her, pulling her towards a chair.

'There's no need to tie me,' she protested. 'Don't be ridiculous.' But she submitted, letting him tie the rope round her wrists behind the chair. It meant he was going to search the house; the worst that could happen was she might be in the chair till Amy got home.

Screaming wasn't an option. For one thing it was unlikely anyone would hear and, anyway, it would only make him angry. Better to just sit there quietly.

He had gone straight upstairs. She listened as he went into each of the bedrooms then came running back down the stairs, only pausing for a second to look in the sitting room.

'I could have saved you the trouble,' she said drily as he came back into the kitchen empty-handed. 'There's nothing worth stealing here. I never keep more than a couple of pounds and that's up there above the Aga, if you're desperate.'

It was something in the way his head jerked round at her words. 'I've got it,' she crowed triumphantly. 'I know who you are!' But as her words came out and he moved towards her she realised she'd made a fatal mistake.

His eyes turned black, she could see beads of sweat forming on his nose, and she knew he would have to kill her. She was blabbering now, saying whatever came into her head.

'Amy will be back soon with the doctor. You'd better get going because they'll call the police. Please don't hurt me!' She despised herself for speaking like that but she couldn't stop.

His hands were reaching out for her. He wore thin surgical gloves and they reminded her oddly of the waxworks in Madame Tussaud's. She bucked in the chair, hearing it scrape on the quarry tiles Amy had polished that afternoon, but those rubber-clad fingers caught her neck, thumbs pressing in on her windpipe.

So often in the days before Amy turned up with the children she'd wanted to die, but not now, not before she'd put everything right. The smell of turkey in the oven, the aromas of cooked ham, mince pies and pine needles, they all seemed overpoweringly pungent and so terribly dear to her. She could feel her eyes bulging as he pressed harder and harder and already the room was slowly spinning as she lost consciousness.

'I didn't come here to kill you,' she heard him say, as if from a very long way off. 'But I've got to now you know who I am.'

'It's still dark,' Greg complained as Amy got out of bed.

'It's after six. Stan will be doing the milking and he might wake Mother. Besides, I'll have to creep upstairs and change.' She wasn't going to tell him she had woken with that awful foreboding feeling, he'd think she'd gone cold on the wedding plans.

'I'll walk round with you.' Greg swung his legs out of bed as Amy disappeared into the bathroom.

'You stay here,' she called back. 'There's no point in you coming too!'

'I'm not having you going home in the dark,' he said, rummaging around for his underpants on the floor. 'Besides, Winston would love a walk.'

'What are we going to say to Mother about where we'll live?' Amy shouted out. 'We haven't talked about that.'

'Where do you want to live?'

'Here. But I doubt she'll like that.'

'Let's just tell her we're getting married,' Greg said evenly. 'Maybe she won't be as difficult as we imagine.'

'Pigs might fly,' Amy said darkly, coming back into the bedroom zipping up her skirt.

Daylight was just trying to break through as they walked down the High Street. Winston ran back and forth, sniffing everything with enthusiasm, his breath like smoke in the cold air.

As they approached the farm Amy began to walk on tip-toe so her mother wouldn't hear her high heels on the path. As she turned into the lane that led round to the farmyard, she moved to kiss Greg.

'I'll come right round, just in case she's locked you out.' He kissed her nose and grinned like a cherubic schoolboy. 'If that's the case I'll take you back home!'

As they walked across the yard Amy paused, looking up at the house.

'What's wrong?' Greg touched her arm. A shadow seemed to pass over her upturned face, something sinister that made him feel cold.

'I don't know, just a funny feeling.' She frowned, then shook her head. 'Weird! Probably what Mother calls James Brady's ghost!'

They were at the back door. Greg moved forward and turned the knob. 'Not locked.' He smiled and pushed the door open. The first thing he saw was Mabel's silver candlestick lying on the floor.

'Oh, shit,' he exclaimed. 'I think you've been burgled!'

Amy switched on the light and moved with him into the kitchen, Winston close behind. The kitchen drawers had been turned out on to the floor. The larder door stood open. Through the door to the hall they could see more papers strewn.

'Mother!' Amy ran to the door, Greg close behind.

'Let me look!' he shouted, but it was too late. Amy had already reached the top of the stairs and Winston bounded after them, barking, thinking this was some kind of game.

Amy paused momentarily as she reached the landing. She could feel Greg behind her, hear Winston

518

panting, and she was afraid of what she might see. Taking a deep breath she took another step, closed her hand round the brass knob and opened the door.

'Mother!' Relief washed over her as she saw Mabel tucked up fast asleep in the darkened room.

'She's OK, she can't have heard anything.' Amy turned to Greg and smiled in relief. 'Look, she's still asleep!'

But Greg brushed past her, pulled back the curtains and bent over Mabel. All colour left his face. There was no need to ask him what it was, his face said it all. But as Amy moved towards the bed Greg turned and tried to prevent her.

'No, don't look.' His voice was strangely shrill.

But she was already looking. Her mother's eyes seemed to bulge out of her face like two huge amber pebbles, and her mouth was open as if in a silent scream.

Amy felt Greg's arms go round her, then there was nothing more, just black mist swirling round her and a strange buzzing noise in her ears.

'So where was Mrs Manning?'

Amy heard the question as if the voice spoke down a cardboard tube.

'She was with me, at my house. I walked back here with her.'

Amy stirred on the sofa, felt her mother's crocheted shawl tickling her face and remembered.

'Stay calm,' she said to herself. 'Breathe deeply, think it through.'

The Christmas tree was still lit, the curtains drawn behind it, presents piled up beneath. The fire had long since gone out, leaving a greying pile of warm embers.

'Greg!' she called out hesitantly. 'Greg!'

'It's OK, darling, the police are here now.' Greg was at her side in a second, kneeling next to her, his plump face pale and anxious. 'You just stay there, I'll talk to them.'

'No, Greg.' She struggled to sit up. 'I'll speak to them myself. I have to!'

'I'm so sorry, Mrs Manning.' The uniformed policeman came into the sitting room. His bright blue eyes were soft with sympathy and she thought she recognised him.

'Have we met before?' Amy frowned, trying hard to think why his face seemed familiar.

'I'm Sergeant Rudges.' His weatherbeaten face seemed to turn a little red. 'I was one of the officers who came –' He stopped sharply, clearly embarrassed.

She nodded, remembering now. The young constable who turned white and shook like a leaf as they lifted Paul's little body from the spike. He was a man now, broader, stronger featured, but he still recalled the horror of that day as she did. Somehow it helped to soothe the rising panic inside her.

'You'll remember how strong my mother was?' she said softly.

He nodded.

'Why didn't she put up a fight, then?'

Sergeant Rudges looked at the woman sitting in front of him. Could anyone stand another such terrible blow?

He wanted to get out. Go home to his wife and children, see them open their presents, hear their laughter. He didn't want that picture staying in his mind after he closed his eyes. Eyeballs like brown boiled sweets bulging from a grey face, a slack old mouth gaping open, and those vivid red thumbprints on her windpipe.

It took years to put aside the memory of the poor kid impaled on that machine. Now there would be yet another horror story to add to the fund of legends about this farm. The whole place chilled him to the bone.

'It looks like he strangled her before he began the robbery.' He had already considered how odd it was that she'd been killed while still in bed. But the forensic boys would soon sort that out. 'Have you any idea what's been taken?'

Amy was glad of the diversion. She got up, clinging to Greg's arm for a moment.

'You don't have to do anything now,' he said softly. 'I'll make us some tea.'

'It's better for me to do something.' She opened the desk first and discovered that the money her mother kept hidden at least was there. 'The sooner they know what's gone, the clearer the picture will be.'

Once in the kitchen she looked around. As well as the strewn drawer contents, other things had been moved.

'Did you touch anything here?' she asked Sergeant Rudges.

'No.' He shook his head. 'We don't touch anything till forensic gets here.'

'The chairs have all been moved.' She looked round slowly and pointed to the abandoned cigar box on the floor. 'The egg and cheese money's gone. There was around ten pounds in there. Can I touch that?' She gestured to an imitation cottage above the Aga. 'That's where we kept the housekeeping money.'

It was gone, as was the five-pound note tucked behind the clock that was Amy's payment for making a dress for a neighbour.

'I'll have to check upstairs for jewellery,' she said.

'Don't worry.' Sergeant Rudges put one hand on her shoulder. 'I can hear a car, that'll be the Bristol police. I expect they'll want to take over now.'

It was such a long, long day. So many men coming in and out, so many questions.

The experts decided her mother had been strangled

521

in the kitchen, tied to a chair. The assailant must have carried her upstairs, tucked her into bed, then carried on ransacking the house. Why would anyone go to the trouble of putting her into bed? Understandable if he didn't want his crime discovered immediately, but why, then, did he tip out drawers on to the floor?

The police pored over everything, asking questions about who came to the farm regularly and what strangers had been there in the past few months. They dusted for fingerprints, picked up samples of fibres and even mud from the floor, took photographs before they removed Mabel's body. Through it all Amy wanted to scream that it was her fault.

If she hadn't gone home with Greg, the door would have been securely locked. If only she could take back those angry words she'd flung at Mother before Greg called, and replace them with words of love. She should have told her how much she admired her strength, that caustic wit and indomitable spirit. Thanked her for opening up her heart to her grandchildren, for being a rock when Amy most needed her, and giving Amy a place in society, pride and dignity again.

But time had run out. Now she would never discover the secrets her mother had locked away in her heart. She couldn't tell her that the past was wiped out. everything forgiven and forgotten.

Of all the hard tasks life had thrown at her, picking up the telephone and telling Tara was the hardest.

'Mum, I can't take it in,' was all Tara could say. 'Can you get Greg to explain it all to Harry? Then I'll phone you back.'

'My darling.' Greg held her in his arms on the settee in the sitting room, stroking her back and hair, crooning words of love to her. 'I wish I could find the right words to say to you.'

'I should have come home,' she sobbed. 'Why did you make me stay with you?'

'It was fate, Amy,' Greg whispered. 'The man might have killed you, too, and think what that would have done to Tara and me.'

'But we were making jokes about her.' Amy lifted swollen eyes to Greg. 'Now I'm always going to think of that.'

'My mother and I made jokes about my dad just before he died,' Greg said gently. 'He was a mean old devil and I said we'd shock him at his funeral by laying on a lavish party. It didn't mean we didn't love him, just that we weren't blind to his faults.'

Nothing seemed quite real. Not Greg cutting off slices of turkey and ham and wrapping them in foil to take home to his house. Not the calm way he went round the farm checking on the animals, or him going upstairs and packing a few clothes for her in a bag.

'You're coming home with me,' he said gently, pulling her to her feet and slipping her coat on. 'Tara and Harry can stay there, too. I've phoned Stan to tell him what's happened. Now we just lock the doors and walk away.'

If only it was as simple as that. Lock the door and walk away. Forget the place where Paul had died. Forget the police coming to say that her husband had murdered a priest then died himself in an accident. Forget the day she discovered Tara had run away. And now this, an old woman strangled in her own kitchen for less than twenty pounds.

Chapter 29

'Oh, Mum, it's so awful.' Tara ran into Amy's arms the second Greg opened the door. 'Who could do such a thing?'

'I don't know, darling.' Amy rocked her, tears streaming down her face. 'I keep asking myself that.'

'What can I say, Amy?' Harry stepped forward, putting his hand on Amy's shoulder. His blue eyes were dark with sorrow, his lips tight. 'I'm so sorry sounds a bit weak, but I'm sure you know how gutted I am. I've got a letter from Dad and Queenie for you. I'll give it to you later.'

He could hardly bear to look at Amy's eyes welling up with tears. He felt as helpless as he had at Paul's death, but this time there was rage, too.

Greg looked at Amy and Tara rocking together in each other's arms, and his eyes misted over. 'Come into my study, Harry?' He inclined his head towards a door in the hall. 'Let them talk it out between themselves. I'm sure you could use a drink.'

Harry hesitated. Amy lifted her head from Tara's and nodded at him, and reluctantly he followed Greg.

Harry had been to Greg's house several times, but he'd never been in here before. It was smaller than the other rooms, tucked between the surgery and hall, with a long, slender window overlooking the gravel drive. It was a masculine retreat, smelling of cigars and old books. A desk with a typewriter was slotted in under the window, sagging leather armchairs flanked an old gas fire.

'This was my surgery when I first joined my father.' Greg smiled weakly, bending to light the fire. 'He was a crusty old devil, I was glad to get in here and escape from him.'

Harry nodded appreciatively, feeling soothed by the room's calm atmosphere.

'I didn't mean to drag you away from her. It's just I think they've got a lot of talking to do that they can't do in front of us.'

'Of course.' Harry nodded, running his hand through his hair. He looked as if he'd dressed in a hurry, a Fred Perry shirt buttoned up wrong, a scratch on his cheek from shaving. 'Thank God Amy had you! I fully expected to find her like a zombie again.'

'She's bearing up well so far,' Greg said softly. 'How has Tara been?'

'Very quiet.' Harry sighed. 'I don't think she dropped off last night for a minute. But it's as if she's holding it all in. Maybe now she's with Amy she can let go.'

'Whisky all right?' Greg took a bottle and two glasses down from a shelf.

Harry nodded and sat down by the fire.

As a doctor Greg tended to view everyone from a health point of view, and he was surprised to see Harry looking so drawn. Although this was obviously due in part to the shock of Mabel's death and a couple of sleepless nights, instinct told him this really was the result of months of overwork. His eyes seemed dull, his black hair less glossy, and the vitality which was so much part of his nature seemed lacking.

'Have there been any further developments?' asked Harry.

'Not really. Mabel's fingerprints were on the

candlestick, which makes it look as though she picked that up as a weapon against him. They found a woollen mask up the road, seems he threw it out of a car window. It's been suggested he only killed her because she recognised him.'

'What makes them think that?'

Greg shrugged his shoulders. 'Well, he tied her to a chair first, they found rope fibres on it. That would be enough for most burglars, but he went on to kill her.'

'What was he after?'

'Money, I suppose.' Greg poured them both another drink. 'There were always rumours about Mabel having a fortune stashed away. People assumed she inherited it from her mother.'

'Did she?'

Greg liked Harry's direct questions. He would've made a good policeman, straight to the point.

'Well, some, but I doubt it was anything like as much as people like to think.' Greg pursed his lips. 'She always pleaded poverty, but she always managed to find a few quid when necessary. Recently they've been making more money, what with extra pigs and chickens. She bought a new tractor, and the farm shop was doing all right.'

In his brown cardigan and tweed trousers Greg looked the part of the calm country doctor, but Harry could see he wasn't as composed as he tried to pretend. His hands were shaking, his rosy face was pale and there were dark circles beneath his eyes.

'Any suspects?' Harry asked, getting out his cigarettes with trembling hands and offering them to Greg.

'I hope you've got a good alibi, Harry.' Greg took one and raised a sandy eyebrow. 'Don't take that as an accusation, but the police asked me about you immediately.'

'Mabel would've seen the irony in that.' Harry's eyes twinkled, relieved that Greg could be open with him.

'I was in the club from nine in the evening until three. We had dozens of well-known people in who can verify it. Don't worry, Greg, I've got nothing to hide. They can interview me any time they like.'

Greg nodded but he still looked anxious. 'They asked me for a list of anyone who'd ever worked for her, visitors, people who called at the farm. Anyone who might have had a grudge against her.'

'Was there anyone?' Harry leaned forward in his chair.

'Mabel didn't endear herself to many people.' Greg's mouth moved into a smirk. 'She was sharp with almost everyone. But I can't think of anyone who felt so strongly about her that they'd kill her.'

Harry felt sick. The moment Amy phoned yesterday, Wainwright had sprung into his mind. Harry felt like kicking himself for underestimating the man. He had seen him as a maggot, someone who once crushed would be too scared to even consider retaliation. Yet Wainwright could have murdered Mabel. He knew her, the farm and possibly the rumours about her wealth. He was certainly cold-blooded enough.

Perhaps he'd hoped Harry would be blamed, that during an enquiry other things might come to light. Maybe he'd even expected Tara and Harry to be asleep in the farmhouse and he actually came looking to kill them!

But whatever happened, Harry felt partially responsible for failing to hand over that box of files to the police. Why hadn't he? An ingrained reluctance to grass anyone up? The feeling that it was better for all concerned to just let it drop?

One thing was crystal clear. He couldn't let all that out now, not without making things a hundred times worse for Tara.

The oddest thing was that he felt as if Mabel's death was connected to all the other unexplained and strange things that had happened in the last few months. That sewage coming up in the basement! Even the plumber reckoned it was sabotage. The delivery of sand right in front of the club door late on a Friday afternoon. The visit from the health inspector, supposedly due to a complaint from one of his members. There had been so many incidents, ranging from the bust by the drug squad, rushing in like madmen and not finding so much as a cardboard roach, to the spirits room being broken into and stripped.

Yet was Wainwright powerful enough to mastermind all these incidents? Or did he have another enemy?

'Look, we ought to talk about practical things,' said Harry. 'I mean the farm, obviously Amy can't go back there, well, not to live. Could we get another man in to work there? I could pay his wages.'

'That's very generous.' Greg gave a wry smile. 'I wish it was that simple. Unfortunately Amy did far more than anyone realised, she was also very good at keeping Stan working properly. Once she's not in there, he'll start slacking.'

'I wish I could come down for a while.' Harry sat back in his chair, thoughtfully watching the smoke rise from his cigarette. 'But things aren't too good for me right at this moment.'

Greg raised a sandy eyebrow. 'I thought you were on your way to making the first million?'

'So I am.' Harry smirked. 'The club's making money hand over fist, but there's things going on that need watching. Sometimes I feel like a man making his way through a jungle. Behind every tree and plant there's an unseen enemy – success makes a lot of those. Just between you and me, Greg, I'm thinking of selling it.'

'But from the papers it sounds like you're flavour of the month?'

'I am at the moment. The press love the "Cockney

lad makes good" routine, but they'd like it better if I went in for a bit of excess. You know, bought a flash penthouse, a jet or a Roller. They watch all the time, Greg! Waiting for me to slip up, anything would do – drug bust, knocking off a fourteen-year-old,' Harry paused. Greg was looking a little worried, as if he didn't really believe this.

'This murder should show you what I mean,' Harry insisted. 'Right now the press only know an old lady's been murdered. But then they'll find out that Tara Manning, designer for Josh Bergman, is the old girl's granddaughter! That connection should keep the story hot a day more. Throw in Harry Collins, ex-con, night-club owner as boyfriend and we can keep it going still longer. Suppose, though, that they discover the very beautiful Mrs Manning is in fact Mrs MacDonald, the widow of a priest murderer? How do you think that will go down around here?'

'Oh, shit, I hadn't thought of that.' Greg's colour faded. 'Will they dig that out?'

'I hope not.' Harry shook his head. 'Amy's been through too much already, and the local police are bound to feel for her. But it is a possibility. My advice would be to refuse to talk to any press, it's usually a chance remark that leads them on to another angle.'

'Do you know what my biggest problem was on Christmas Eve?' Greg's face was a study of dejection.

'What to buy Amy for Christmas?'

'No, where Amy and I were going to live.' Greg shook his head. 'Amy wanted to be here, but I couldn't see how we could leave Mabel to fend alone.'

'Even after her death the problem is still there,' Harry said ruefully. He liked Greg, felt he and Amy were perfect for one another, and it made him angry to think anything could get in the way of their happiness.

'Mabel's will might settle that for us.' Greg got up,

rubbing his back. 'To be perfectly frank, I hope she's left the place to a sodding dogs' home or the church.'

'Come on.' Harry sensed Greg was close to the end of his tether. He stood up too and put his hand on the older man's shoulder. 'Things will work out, you'll see. Once the funeral is over, you and Amy must get married. If the farm's left to her she could sell it. You two don't need to be burdened with all this.'

'Thanks for coming Harry.' Greg looked up at him. 'You brought a breath of fresh air with you.'

'I can't leave you, Mum,' Tara insisted. 'Don't ask me to go back to London and leave you here.'

'Oh, Tara.' Amy put her arms round her daughter and hugged her tightly. 'You haven't changed a bit since Whitechapel. Still trying to protect me. I'll be fine, I'm stopping here with Greg.'

They were in Greg's sitting room, waiting for him to drive Tara to the station. It was the end of January now, Mabel had been put to rest alongside Paul in the churchyard and slowly the village was getting back to normal.

Harry had stayed until after the funeral but he'd had to get back to the club. He had been invaluable while he was here, going to the farm daily, sorting out Stan and finding a lad to help him permanently.

But the reorganisation of their lives was nothing compared with the terrible strain of having a spotlight trained upon them. Journalists telephoning, banging on the door and waylaying them as they walked down the street, and so many questions from police and neighbours.

Tara was surprised by the strength her mother showed, almost as if she'd taken some of Mabel's spirit on board. She refused to be swamped by the deluge of nosy neighbours, she slammed doors in journalists' faces and kept her head high even when she knew everyone was gossiping about her and Greg living together.

The police were no closer to finding the murderer. Amy, at Harry's suggestion, had put forward Wainwright's name as someone who had called at the farm, and through his friend who owned the cottage in Stanton Drew they had found him and interviewed him. But he had an alibi, as did all the people they questioned.

It was a mystery. A house-to-house enquiry had revealed nothing. No-one had seen a car late that night, spotted anything unusual either before or after. Although the police continued to search for clues, as the days slipped past it was apparent they'd run out of steam.

Amy and Tara both cried as Edward Grimes, the solicitor in the village, read them Mabel's will. In her words, 'My estate goes to my granddaughter Tara, because she has the good sense to use it wisely and hold it in trust for her children. Because of her youth and the possibility she could be swayed by others, I ask that my daughter Amy holds the farm until Tara's thirtieth birthday, without any structural changes or alterations to use, and that Tara gives her mother a home there as long as she needs it.'

Alone with Greg Amy had cried bitter tears. Like Greg she cared little about the farm, she would have been happy to see it auctioned off. But she saw her mother's devious mind behind this will, updated just a couple of months before her death. Even after all Amy had done for her and the farm, Mabel couldn't bear to think Greg might profit from it. She didn't want him to move in, to build a surgery, or even to make life more comfortable for Amy. She saw her mother's will serving a dual purpose. The hard work and responsibility might put a strain on Amy and Greg's life together and, if Tara came to the rescue, Mabel hoped that would finish off for good her relationship with Harry.

'We've talked it over,' Amy reassured her daughter. 'Greg and I will work out a plan for the farm to just tick over, keeping its value with the minimum of effort and work. You must get back to your life, darling, don't worry about all this.'

Amy was wearing black, her face still had a drawn, haunted look. Whatever brave words she came out with, Tara knew it would be some time before she recovered.

'Did I ever tell you how precious you are to me?' Tara flung her arms round her mother and buried her face in her neck.

'And you to me, darling,' Amy whispered back, kissing Tara's hair. 'Now off back to London, pick up the threads again. We'll always hold Mother in our hearts, but that doesn't mean we have to spend the rest of our lives being afraid to be happy.'

'Is there anything I can do to help?' Josh asked on her first day back at work.

Everything had been put on hold while she was down in Somerset. Old designs were just trotted out in new fabrics, and sales held in all four shops. Her assistant Margot must have had a very easy time of it; the workroom had never looked so clean and tidy.

It was good to smell the bales of cloth again, to hear the traffic rumbling by and Marc Bolan's 'Ride a White Swan' blasting out from the shop below. She would go over to Kensington Market at lunch-time and buy herself something extravagant from the antique clothes stall.

'That's sweet of you, Josh,' Tara was touched by his concern. He had come down for the funeral and asked Greg if he could help with the funeral expenses, but perhaps his real contribution had been giving her so much time off without hassling her.

532

As much as she'd hated to leave her mother, she was actually relieved to be back at work. All that emotion had drained her, and drawing had always been the perfect way to recharge her batteries.

Josh was straight today, his eyes soft and gentle again, his big lips curved in a genuine smile of welcome. There had been a bouquet of flowers for her and cards of sympathy from all the girls in his shops.

'You know how much I liked your grandmother,' he said, perching on a desk by her drawing board. 'She was like the Jewish matriarchs, formidable but a great character. Amy must be finding it tough without her.'

'She found it tough with her,' Tara blurted out and within minutes she found herself telling Josh far more than she meant to.

'You'll feel better now,' Josh predicted as he gave her a brotherly hug and dried her eyes with his handkerchief. 'Maybe she had her reasons for giving you the farm. Maybe she had a reason to distrust Greg.'

'Don't be ridiculous,' Tara snapped. 'Greg's a wonderful man!'

'Well, I suppose your gran's instincts could be off-beam sometimes. She liked me, didn't she!'

Tara laughed and suddenly she felt better. 'You are a ray of sunshine,' she said. 'It's time I put it all behind me.'

Gran's death and the end of a decade made Tara more aware that she could no longer just drift on as she had before.

Somehow 1970 seemed different. Flower Power was dying, revolution no longer seemed imminent. The innocence was dead, a new generation of teenagers was springing up who were more materialistic and showy. Platform shoes and maxi skirts were coming in and, instead of living by the maxim 'Turn on and drop out', people were cutting their long hair and working their way back in.

Ideas were running around in her head, clamouring to be put down on paper. Not just for actual garments, but fabric designs with bold, swirling colours. She began to be irritated by the limitations of Josh's empire, casting a jaundiced eye not only on the designs she did for him, but on his policies.

Everything had to be cheap. Fabric, trimmings, even the cut of the garment was influenced by the need for economy. She longed to produce sumptuous evening dresses in chiffon and silk, use lavish embroidery, appliqué, sequins and beads. She would look at Ossie Clark's designs with all their rich crêpe, covered buttons and swirling skirts, and feel green with envy.

One afternoon, when Josh had wandered into the workroom to show her his new platform boots, she decided it was time she showed him her ideas. He stood in the doorway, wearing green trousers so tight he had an indecent bulge in the front. They flared out at the knee to twenty-six-inch bottoms, and then the boots!

'What do you think of them?' He grinned like a schoolboy. 'I always wanted to be six foot!'

They looked ridiculous, but then so did mini skirts at first, and at least these were plain black, not the multicoloured ones she'd seen on some people.

'Ask me in a couple of weeks when I've got used to you towering over me!' she laughed. 'How long did it take to practise walking in them?'

'I nearly broke my ankle when I came out the shop in them,' he admitted. 'But you do like them, don't you?'

She saw no good reason for being brutally honest and she nodded. 'They're groovy,' she said, turning her head away so he wouldn't see her laughing. 'Now come and look at these!'

He rolled a joint, as he always did these days, and just sat and smoked while she turned the sketches over for him to see.

'They're all breathtaking,' he agreed. 'But not for us.'

He had noticed a new maturity in Tara even before the old girl's death. But since she'd come back to London it was stronger. She invariably wore long skirts now, with her lovely gold hair pinned up. He liked this new Tara. She had poise and elegance, without losing any of her warmth. He sensed, too, that she was disenchanted with Harry's club and her lack of social life and this was making her ambitious again. Maybe it was time he made a bit more fuss of her?

'Can't we produce a range of special clothes?' she begged him. 'Just a few trial ones to put in the windows and make people stop in their tracks?'

Josh had his own worries right now, although he was concealing them well. Bailiffs had called at the Oxford Street shop only a few days earlier for unpaid rent; he owed the Inland Revenue several thousand, too. Although he knew Tara's ideas were good, he hadn't got any spare money to waste on frivolous schemes right now.

'It wouldn't work.' He shook his head and laughed. He had no intention of telling her the truth. 'We have to stick at what we do best. I know my market and if I move away from it I'll lose it.'

'But, Josh, the shops are looking grotty,' she said. 'You've flooded them with all that Indian stuff.'

'That's what's selling.' He drew on his joint and switched the radio on. 'Listen to that,' he said as David Bowie's 'Space Oddity' came on.

Tara watched him patiently.

'Ground control to Major Tom,' he sang, playing an air guitar like a teenager, tossing his black curls. 'Take your protein pills and put your helmet on.'

She had to laugh, he was totally immersed in the song. Once it had finished she switched the radio off.

'Will you listen to me?'

'Come on then, what is it? More money?'

535

'The sales are down, Josh,' she said quietly. 'We're selling more Indian junk because that's just about all we've got.'

'The sales aren't down! Whoever told you that?' He opened his eyes wide and once again she saw only pupils and little of the iris.

'Because I stand in the shop from time to time and watch, like you should do,' she said. She was sick of the smell of joss-sticks, of hearing 'All You Need is Love' on tapes. 'The only time you spend in there is when you're trying to get a girl in the stockroom.'

'Well, I've got other business interests, too,' he said airily.

She didn't know if this was true, but it didn't concern her anyway.

'Real customers are getting more discriminating. I don't mean the hippy-trippy ones who wander in for a new cheesecloth smock, but the people with money,' she said. 'I see them every day examining hems and linings. Over in Kensington Market girls much like me are opening up stalls selling wonderful clothes and we're losing trade to them. If you don't pull the business back together pretty sharply, you won't have one much longer.'

'You sound just like my dad.' He laughed, but he was touched that she cared so much. 'Stop worrying, Tara. Be cool.'

Despite her anxiety that Josh was losing his grip, she found him easier to work for than ever before. He wouldn't go along with her ideas about revamping the shops and their image, but he did let her have her own way about designs as long as they could be produced cheaply. He often came to the workroom late in the afternoon to discuss something with her, and if she wasn't rushing home to see Harry it sometimes went on over a drink or a pizza.

The first time he asked her to go with him to a trade fair in Birmingham, she was hesitant. Not because she didn't want to go, but because Harry might misconstrue the relationship.

She adored Harry, but in his world she was just a pretty decoration, his 'bird' as one of his henchmen once called her. No-one at the Top Cat Club cared about what she did. The trade fair gave her wider vision, she met people who were passionately interested in the same things as her, and the ambitions she'd had before she started her affair with Harry came back more strongly than before.

The novelty of going to the club had long since worn off. Harry was always too busy to sit with her for long, and she had little in common with his cronies. It was better to see him away from the club, two or three hours before it opened, on his night off and Sundays. Their romance was one of snatched moments, full of high passion but with never enough time to share one another's interests, friends or even to really talk.

She needed a life of her own. When Josh asked her to go with him to mills and factories instead of staying in the workroom all day, she went, seeing it purely as a way of furthering her knowledge about the industry.

It was a night away in Paris that sparked the row, and all at once her grandmother's observations about Harry seemed a great deal less ridiculous.

Josh always went to see the Paris collections. He claimed he learned nothing from them, that it was all hype and the glorification of a few designers who made clothes only for the super-rich. But he thought it was time Tara experienced it, too.

Everything was totally above board. They left Heathrow at the crack of dawn on a Thursday morning and were back on Friday night. They had separate rooms in the hotel and there was no time for romantic boat rides along the Seine or whatever else Harry thought they might have been up to. But she was stimulated by what she'd seen. It was as if a curtain was pulled back to reveal a world of beautiful people, with exotic lifestyles. She wanted to design for them, not for little office girls with ten pounds to spend.

Best of all though, Josh seemed to be coming round to her way of thinking. On the plane home he said he was going to look into his finances with a view to a complete update.

Josh dropped her off in his taxi just after ten. Tara limped up the steps of the house; her feet hurt, she was exhausted, hot and sticky.

To her surprise Harry was sitting in her flat. He had his own key so he could come in late at night without disturbing anyone, but he rarely came round without phoning.

'Hello.' She grinned weakly as she flung her overnight case down. 'I didn't expect to see you!'

He didn't jump up from the settee to kiss her, there was no bright smile which said he'd missed her, no concern at her looking tired. Instead he stared at her slinky velvet maxi dress with a split up to her thigh, and it was obvious he disapproved.

'How come Josh didn't come in for a nightcap? Did he spot my car?'

Tara flopped down in an armchair, took off her shoes and massaged her toes. She didn't like Harry's tone.

'Neither of us were looking for your car,' she said, still rubbing her feet. 'We were both too tired to think about anything other than going to bed.'

Harry looked closely at Tara. It was some time since he'd seen her dressed up and she looked like a new girl. She wore her hair up, loose tendrils escaping at the neck. It made her seem older, more sophisticated. The combination of those alluring amber eyes and her wide pouting mouth was enough to make any man catch his breath. In the last couple of years she'd gained a little weight, just enough to make her more curvy. Her brown velvet dress wasn't tight but it clung to her body; he could see her hipbones slightly protruding, the cleft in her buttocks and her breasts jiggled as she moved. In that second he would gladly have locked her up so no man could look at her.

'You've been hitting the high spots, then?'

Tara looked up. Harry was in his dinner jacket and bow-tie ready for the club, his hair tied back in a pony-tail, and for a second she had a flash of one of his haughtier customers, the Hon Nigel Fitz-Makepeace, a man Harry called 'A prat of the first water'.

'You sound like Nigel the Prat,' she giggled. 'Hitting the high spots indeed!'

'Don't you take the piss out of me!' Harry jumped up and reached her in two big strides.

She thought he was going to hit her and involuntarily drew back, protecting her head with her arm.

'You must have done something to make you look so guilty.' He caught hold of her arm and twisted it slightly away from her face. 'I wasn't going to hit you.'

'I was neither taking the piss nor looking guilty,' she snapped back at him. 'And wouldn't anyone flinch when a man of your size and strength charges at them like a wild boar?'

'You've been up to something,' he insisted. 'That dress is hardly the thing to wear on a plane!'

As she moved to protect herself, she had revealed a flash of thigh. She looked down and swiftly covered it.

'I'm a fashion designer,' she said through clenched teeth. 'Maxi dresses are high fashion everywhere other than the Top Cat Club and, if you must know, we spent most of the time rushing about, talking to people about really thrilling things like buttons, accessories and industrial machines.'

'Did you sleep with Josh?' he asked, his voice as cold as his eyes.

'If you have to ask me that I suggest you fuck off now.' She tilted up her chin, refusing to be browbeaten by him. 'Would I tell you I was going to Paris with him, share a cab back here and not invite him in, if I had slept with him?'

'I don't know you any more,' he said, eyes narrowed. 'You've changed. Once you lived for me popping in to see you, now I've got to make an appointment because you're always gadding about with Josh!'

'I've got a job I care about.' She wriggled to the edge of the settee because she felt intimidated by him standing over her. 'All I'm doing with Josh is learning more about the fashion industry. I'm sorry I wasn't waiting stark naked in the bed for when you wanted to come and give me one. How terrible of me!'

She made to get up, but he pushed her back down. His face was mean-looking and there was a dangerous glint in his eyes.

'I didn't come round here for a screw. I could get that from one of my barmaids if that's all I wanted. I had something to talk to you about, but I'll find someone else to share that with, too.'

'You make me sick,' she shouted, eyes flashing with anger. 'I've had to make a life of my own because you're always stuck in that bloody club with your gamblers and villains. You could have asked me what Paris was like, about the designers I've met, show an interest in me for once. But no, all you think about is you.'

He turned on his heel and made for the door. Not another word, or even a look back. She heard the door slam, his feet on the stairs, then the outer door close behind him. A few seconds later his car engine roared into life.

Tears didn't come, she was too angry for that. She

didn't even go to the window. Instead she shook out her hair and stormed off to have a shower.

Later, in bed, her mind turned to the many warnings her mother and gran had given her. Harry had come close to hitting her, even though he would probably deny it. Was this what life would be like with him?

'Our life together just revolves round sex,' she whispered sadly, reaching out to turn off the lamp. 'There's no time for anything else, not talking, seeing friends or having fun together. You don't want a woman with a career and a mind of her own, Harry, you want an empty-headed doll who adores you.'

The tears came then, because she sensed this was the end of the line for them, and at its best it had been so beautiful.

Chapter 30

Harry wiped a tear from his cheek as he drove away down Pembridge Road towards Notting Hill Gate. It was a warm night and people were everywhere coming out of pubs and restaurants, looking in shop windows and just wandering about. A gang of freaks with long hair, bright coloured loons and flowing shirts stood at the corner by the Tube, chatting. He stopped at a zebra crossing for three girls in long dresses to cross. One waved at him and blew him a kiss. Any other time Harry would've blown one back, but he was too miserable for that.

He was angry with Tara, and even more angry that he'd got himself into this jam.

The goals he had two years ago no longer applied. He didn't want a club, he didn't even want to be in London. Tara was the only thing in his life he really cared deeply about and now it looked as if she was growing tired of him.

He put his Abbey Road tape on. 'Here Comes the Sun' usually made him feel better, but as the music filled his car it just made him feel more depressed. Summer was on its way, he and Tara should be visiting her mother, walking in the parks or going to the seaside, not going off in two different directions.

Everyone assumed it was so exciting having a club like his. Drinking with friends every night, making a heap of money at the same time, being in control dressed up like a damned penguin. They never saw behind the scenes, the workload of ordering, doing the books, taking on staff and training them, watching for dishonesty, discovering his toilets trashed by filthy mindless animals, and even having to clean them himself because his staff turned tail and ran.

What was he going to do? There was someone out there really trying to screw him up, and the worst of it was they were succeeding!

It had been stupid, with hindsight, to burn the files. But after Mabel was killed he panicked. The police kept turning up at the club with questions and more questions and he was afraid they might come one day with a warrant and find the lot. Now if he wanted to go and spill the beans about that Wainwright he had nothing to back it up with. Besides, how could he tell them everything without naming Tara?

Then there was this undercurrent at the club, something heavy that he couldn't quite put his finger on. As if some of them knew something was about to happen and were afraid to admit it in case they got it too.

Sometimes he wished he had taken Josh's advice and made it a club for youngsters. He felt old and in a time warp. The Top Cat Club was stuck back in the Fifties. The men were all booted and suited with short Brylcreamed hair; even a coloured shirt made you look suspect. Men with scarred faces drank intently at the bar, concerned only with creating a hard image. Their birds were usually dim-witted, dancing together round their handbags till they were so pissed they had to be shoved in a taxi. He'd tried to update the music, but all they wanted was Matt Monroe and Frank Sinatra. When did he last have an intelligent conversation with anyone?

Keeping Tara away from the club was a precaution he felt he had to take – he didn't want her involved

543

with whatever was happening there. But it was miserable. He loved to have her beside him, to show her off. He couldn't blame her for thinking he only went round to her flat for a quickie, it often happened after a couple of kisses and then he felt ashamed when he left.

That's probably why he'd been so stupid and tactless tonight. Why hadn't he just cuddled her, made her a cup of tea, asked her about Paris then told her that he was selling the club? Was he trying to send her off into Josh's bloody arms?

Still, it looked as if the sale would go through, even if he didn't really like the man. Funny how things turned out. Duke had been there when he won the club. He'd put up money to get it off the ground, and in the two years he'd not only got his stake back, but made a bob or two at the tables. Now he wanted to buy the place and, as far as Harry was concerned, he was welcome to it. He was hard-nosed enough to make a fortune out of the punters, and good luck to him!

After all this time Harry still knew little more about him than he had on the night of the poker game. He only turned up when there were big stakes; win or lose he kept his cool. But he was doing everything right, coming in night after night, helping out, meeting the members, and the solicitors said he had the finance organised.

Another two or three weeks and contracts would be exchanged. Harry would have enough cash to buy Tara her own shop and bid for that row of derelict houses in Islington. Building work was what he really liked – he'd never been happier than when he was gutting and rebuilding the club. It was clean money, too, restoring houses for people to live in, not watching mugs lose their shirt at cards.

Brooding about Tara had distracted him from the journey, and it was only when he turned into the dimly lit dockland streets that he realised he'd been driving on automatic pilot. Ahead he saw a flashing red light and two policemen standing in the road. He slowed down, opened his window and then stopped. The policemen were bending towards something by their car and one beckoned to him. Harry got out.

'Got a problem?' he called out.

He didn't see the person who jumped him, just heard a soft, light step behind him and then felt the crack on the back of his neck. The last thing he saw before hitting the ground was that they weren't police, just men in dark overalls.

Harry was aware of being in a van, of a thin blanket beneath him and a smell of petrol, even before he felt the rope and the blindfold. The pain in his neck reminded him what had happened and suggested he shouldn't let on to his captors that he'd come round.

He was on his side, wedged in by something behind his back. Although his hands were tied, he could reach it with his fingers and it appeared to be a rough wooden crate. His ankles were tied together, too, and he had pins and needles in his arms from lying in one position.

He could remember playing a game on the bombsites when he was a kid; they'd take it in turn to blindfold each other, then make noises and the captive had to guess where and who each one was. It was time to play it again.

There were three, possibly four men in the van. He could tell by the stuffy atmosphere, the number of times a lighter flicked on and several different body smells. One was sitting next to where he lay, it was his trousers that smelled of petrol and he could feel the heat from him. The others were in the front seat. Only two of the men were talking, but somehow he sensed a silent third. He was certain he'd never heard either of them before. Their voices were London but not

Cockney, more towards Essex. They weren't talking about him, just about drag-racing.

'No more talking,' a third voice spoke. 'He'll be awake any minute if he isn't already. Check him.'

He was right, there were three in the front, and he'd heard that voice somewhere before. It was Cockney, but ironed out somehow, as if the man had lived somewhere else for some years.

Rough hands were checking him over, a light shone on his face and the man's breath smelled of onions.

'Still out, guv!'

He didn't know that voice either, though it sounded more local than the other two. Only the deeper, older one rang a faint bell. But there was no further talking after that, just taps, a slight rush of air as Harry imagined one waving his hands as a signal, an occasional whispered word.

'Clever fuckers,' he thought, smiling behind his blindfold. 'Go on, try and frighten me to death. I'll just play doggo and wait for you to give the game away.'

It was painful lying on his side, every bump in the road jarred his hip and a cramp in the arm beneath him made him want to groan.

What had they done with his car? What message had they got at the club? How long would it be before anyone would realise he was missing? Needles would worry immediately unless he was told something plausible. Tony would worry less, but both would take charge and carry on as normal if the story told to them was convincing enough.

Harry thought hard. His father wasn't likely to raise the alarm, they sometimes didn't speak to one another for a week at a time. That left Tara! Once, two or three days' absence would have been enough for her to panic, but recently they hadn't seen each other more than once a week. And after the way he'd stomped off tonight, well, she'd be expecting him to apologise. When he didn't, she'd assume he just didn't care.

Someone at the club had to be in on this. Dennis was the most likely candidate, as gaming-room manager he knew everything that went on and he was intelligent enough to take command. Recently his attitude had changed slightly, too, a trace of sullenness, rarely chatting or wanting to stay behind for a drink. What could they want from him? Kidnapping was a possibility, but unlikely. Some new firm starting up who wanted to frighten the pants off him so the word would get out about them? Did someone believe he'd grassed? Or was it straight revenge?

Harry tried to concentrate on overhearing something from outside which would give him a clue where they were. He could hear heavy traffic. There was light getting through the blindfold frequently, but that meant little. It could be any busy road from the M1 to the Holloway Road. He was dropping off to sleep when someone spoke.

'Where to, Joe?'

He sensed anger between them that one of them had let slip a name.

'Joe'. Harry hugged the name to himself, sure it belonged to the man with the deep familiar voice. How many Joes had he known in his life? Joe Shepherd who went off to Canada, Joe Cohen whose father was a Rabbi and insisted his name was Joseph anyway. There was Joe Small, the ex-boxer who trained at the gym, but his voice was distinctive, like a fog-horn.

Joe Spikes. That was the name his father had mentioned when he was inside. It had never cropped up again and he'd forgotten about it until now. George had suggested he was something to do with a South London gang. To his knowledge he'd never met the man, but then he could have been to the club one night. Perhaps that was why the voice jangled bells. Maybe he'd been barking up the wrong tree about Wainwright being connected with the incidents at the club. Maybe it went back further?

The van was full of cigarette smoke, making him feel sick. His neck hurt, he had an itch on his foot he could do nothing about and his arms ached like crazy, but still he said nothing.

The journey seemed to be going on forever, and now there was seldom a flash of light from outside and no noise from other traffic. They had turned on to a smaller road, he could tell by the number of twists and turns and an occasional branch brushing the van. The man in the back with him was getting restless, stretching his legs out, flexing his arms and yawning. All at once they stopped, pulling over on to uneven ground.

'Get the gate!' The order came from one of the men up front and the van door slid back, a blast of cool clean air clearing the smoke.

The van moved forward and stopped again while the gate was shut, then the man jumped in, panting slightly.

It was rough ground, the van lurching and wallowing, going downhill quite steeply, winding, and he could hear branches slapping on the van. The wheels reached gravel and flat ground. More wind came in as the van came to a halt, which suggested they were now on open ground.

The men in front got out and the back door was opened. Harry's feet were tugged sharply and he was pulled out like a side of meat.

'Where are you taking me?' The words came out despite his determination to remain silent. They didn't reply, but the rope holding his feet together was untied.

Two of them frog-marched him forward, holding him by the elbows. One man was just in front of him; he couldn't make out where the fourth one was. They stopped, and to his right he heard something. Footsteps! They were muffled, but on a wooden floor. They were waiting for a door to be opened. There was a scrape of old bolts, the turning of a lock. An old house or church somewhere deep in the country? The door creaked.

'A Hammer Horror setting!' Harry remarked, and one of the men punched him in the small of his back. Fear clutched at his innards, and he struggled to get a grip on himself.

Their feet echoed as they walked along a passage with a wooden floor and he could smell cedar clearly. Another door opened.

'Down steps now. Take it easy or you'll fall!'

It was terrifying to walk in total darkness down stairs he knew were narrow and old. He could feel cobwebs. The smell of musty earth grew stronger with each step and it was cold, very cold.

Once they hit the bottom he felt uneven flagstones underfoot. Could it be the crypt of a church? The coldness, the ancient mustiness suggested it could be. Another door and this time they pushed him forward alone.

For a second panic rose up inside him, a conviction that he was being pushed to the edge of an abyss and they were waiting for him to fall in. He teetered, gained his balance and shouted. 'Take the fucking blindfold off!'

One of the men walked towards him. Harry had never felt so terrified.

'For God's sake, if you're going to kill me get it over with quickly!'

He regretted his outburst immediately. Before his words had even finished echoing round the walls, he sensed their amusement.

'I'm going to untie you, Harry, but before you get any ideas, we're tooled up. Any aggro and we just tie

549

you up again. Am I making myself clear?' The voice was matter-of-fact.

'Yes,' Harry replied. Why didn't the one called Joe speak, when he was obviously in charge?

'What's this about?' He tried to keep his voice calm and even. 'Am I supposed to have done something to one of you?' It was like playing Blind Man's Buff. His head kept moving around as he tried to work out exactly where the men were. He had a feeling they were very close, smiling at his discomfort.

'This is my club.' The man called Joe spoke at last. 'Here you'll do exactly what I say. I'll tell you only what I want you to know. Whether or not I choose to kill you in the end will depend entirely upon you!'

A cold chill went down Harry's spine. The voice was icy. No anger, or outrage. If this man could kidnap someone without either of those two emotions, he was capable of anything.

He heard the man's feet move away and at the same time another man came close and unfastened his hands. For a second Harry just stood there, rubbing his wrists, but as he heard the men move away he wrenched the blindfold off. Only three of them were still in the cellar. Their faces were covered in black stockinette masks with only their eyes showing. Two wore denim jackets, jeans and black T-shirts, the third was in a brown leather jacket, trousers of a similar colour and a white Fred Perry shirt.

'Go to sleep.' The one in the Fred Perry was the one who'd given the orders before. 'There's a bucket over there if you need it, a bottle of water and some biscuits. Don't bother to look for an escape route, there isn't one.'

They were gone before Harry could even work out how old they were. The heavy door closed and Harry noted it was made of steel with a small hatch, just like in prison.

He stood for some time, rubbing his wrists and just looking around. It could be a crypt, the flagstone floor and the uneven low ceiling would bear that out. But crypts were usually just rough stone, this looked like brick and it had all been whitewashed at some time. The worst thing of all was that it had no window. The ceiling curved down to four feet at the far end as if the room had literally been carved out of the earth. It measured around sixteen feet by twelve, with nothing in it but an iron bed, a rough wooden table holding the water and biscuits, and one chair.

He looked at his watch. It was almost one. Some men would be able to work out where they were from the time. But not him, he didn't drive out of London often enough.

He was locked in a place he didn't know, for a reason they wouldn't tell him, dressed in a dinner jacket and bow-tie. It was tempting to break down, to create a scene so the men came back, anything rather than be left alone in here. But reason told him that would be futile. They had planned this meticulously. They probably knew more about Harry Collins than he did himself!

Chapter 31

'What's up, love?' Josh was looking through some papers in the workroom when he heard Tara sigh deeply. 'Are you feeling ill?'

'No!' Tara put down her pencil and turned towards Josh, her face long with misery. 'Just wretched!'

'Tell me about it?' He came over to her and pulled up a stool. 'Harry?'

She had come in this morning wearing jeans, with her hair pulled back in a pony-tail. He'd noticed her puffy eyelids straight away, but he'd hesitated before making any comment.

Tara never discussed Harry with anyone, least of all Josh. She didn't want to now because she was sure he'd gloat, but it was hard to bear the pain alone.

Josh was wearing Brut aftershave today, one that Tara liked best of all on Harry. Each time she got a whiff of it she wanted to cry. A tear trickled down her cheek. Josh reached out and wiped it away with one finger, then cupped his hand round her face.

'You don't have to tell me the details.' His voice was gentle. 'I'm just your friend, ready with a hug, flapping ears, whatever you need.'

'I think it's over,' she whispered, trying hard to hold back the tears. 'We had a row the night we got back from Paris. He hasn't been in touch since.'

Josh slid his arms round her, the gentle, unthreatening

552

hug of an older brother. He wanted to laugh, sing and shout. But right now he'd got to keep it cool.

'Come on! I expect he's just giving you both time to simmer down. Was he jealous because you were with me?'

'I don't know if he was,' Tara sobbed. 'He was kind of sarcastic about you, but mainly it was directed at me being too engrossed in my work. He scared me, Josh, he was really heavy.'

'Sounds to me like he's got something on his mind. Can't be the club, that's doing brilliantly. He couldn't have got himself into something dodgy, could he?'

'What makes you say that?' Tara looked up at Josh curiously. She had expected him to suggest another woman or money problems, both of which she would have rejected out of hand.

Josh shrugged. 'I just heard a rumour the other day. Harry wasn't mentioned, incidentally, I'm just putting two and two together and probably getting five. There was some recruiting going on and a couple of the faces mentioned were mates of his.'

'He wouldn't go back to crime.' Tara's eyes grew wide with fright.

'No, of course not,' Josh reassured her. 'Like I said, Harry was never mentioned. Why would he need that kind of scene when he's doing so well?'

'Do you think I should phone him?' Tara asked. 'I don't want to be pushy. But on the other hand he might think I don't give a shit if I don't.'

'Of course you should phone him, ninny.' Josh grinned broadly. 'The man's probably too scared to contact you in case you bite his head off. Now look, I've got to go over to the Oxford Street branch, I'll pop in later on just before closing. If you haven't arranged anything with Harry for tonight, let's have dinner together and discuss some new plans of mine?'

'OK.' Tara still looked a bit glum, but Josh had made her feel quite a lot better. 'Thanks for the shoulder!'

He put a finger under her chin and lifted it. 'You can come to me any time, Tara, about anything.'

'You're a real sweetie.' She reached up and impulsively kissed him.

'Well, that's it.' He staggered back, touching his lips. 'I'll never wash again!'

Tara giggled. 'Off with you!' She pointed to the door. 'I'll see you later.'

She rang Harry's flat at the Angel first, but there was no reply. The phone in the club rang for around five minutes and was finally answered by a breathless Needles just as she was about to hang up.

'Hello, Needles.' She apologised for dragging him away from his work. 'Is Harry there?'

'No, sweetheart, didn't 'e tell you 'e were shooting over to Germany?'

'Germany!'

'Well, it was all a bit sudden, like,' he said tentatively. 'He belled me and said he was off on an impulse.'

'But why Germany? It's not the sort of place he'd go to for a holiday?'

'Would he go on holiday without you, sweetheart?' He gave a rich belly laugh that soothed her. 'No, it's just a club or summat he's going to look at.'

'So you're in charge, then?'

'In charge of letting in and throwing out.' He chuckled. 'Tony's minding the bars and Duke does the rest.'

'Duke?' She'd met Duke a few times at the club, and remembered him for his rugged good looks and piercing ice-blue eyes.

'Duke's the bloke what's going to buy the club.'

Tara was so shocked she was temporarily lost for words.

554

'I didn't know that either,' she said finally.

Needles felt uneasy. He liked Tara, she was a real doll, and anyway he didn't like to hurt ladies, but all the same! What if he was dropping Harry in it?

' 'Spect 'Arry wanted it to be a surprise. You'd better not let on I told you.' He sounded anxious now. 'Anyways, Duke's bin coming in for weeks now. 'Arry said this was a good chance for him to hold the reins.'

'So how long will he be gone?'

'Oh, luv, I've upset yer.' Needles' voice dropped to a sympathetic purr. 'He might be two or three weeks, but that's nuthin', is it? 'E'll be in touch with you before long. But don't let on I told you, will you?'

'I won't say anything,' she promised, and rang off.

Tara didn't know how to react to the news. She was surprised Harry was selling the club, hurt he'd gone away without phoning her, yet at the same time she wondered if that's what he'd come to tell her the night she got back from Paris. Had he taken the fact she rarely went to the club now as lack of interest? Was he as hurt by her attitude to his business as she was by his lack of enthusiasm for hers?

She spread out some fabric on the cutting table and began to arrange a pattern on it. She knew where he was now, and why he'd been a bit odd. Maybe he thought a bit of space would do them both good, and perhaps he was right.

'Well, are you ready for the new plan?' Josh asked after they'd ordered dinner.

They were in the Bistingo in Queensway, Tara's favourite restaurant, specialising in French farmhouse cookery. She loved not only the food – pigeon, duck and rich stews – but the atmosphere of the place, with its rustic pine furniture and clumps of dried flowers hanging from the ceiling along with copper pots and pans. Rich smells of herbs and garlic wafted out from the kitchen and soft guitar music was playing in the background.

Josh was glad to see she'd perked up. She'd washed her hair and put it up again, with little curls round her neck and she was wearing a midnight blue maxi dress that made her look like a princess.

'I'm dying to hear it.' She'd already explained about Harry and now she felt faintly silly that she'd let Josh see her so upset.

'I'm going to let you have your way.' Josh smiled, his teeth brilliant white against his olive skin. 'Not all at once, I can't do all four shops right now. But we'll start with Church Street.'

Josh was excited. He'd been through a difficult patch, but he was on top of it now and his new plans were giving him the kind of rush he usually only got from drugs.

'Sweep everything out and start again?' she said breathlessly.

Josh nodded. 'Not just new stock, an entire new image.' He grinned.

Tara's mouth dropped open as Josh pulled out a file of architect's drawings, showing a double-fronted shop with huge windows that curved into a central door.

The internal plans kept the same theme, an almost Edwardian image with lots of big green plants, raised areas with banisters round and huge pine dressracks which looked more like old-fashioned wardrobes. Old swivel mirrors, the odd dressing table or two and dressmaker's dummies completed the picture.

'It looks expensive,' Tara commented, putting the plans aside as their meal arrived.

'It will be, that's the whole point,' Josh explained. 'Expensive fittings, expensive clothes. We're aiming at under-thirties with money. As you so rightly said, there are enough shops catering for the hippy-dippy types. We're looking for the *nouveau riche*, people who want beautiful, outrageous clothes and don't mind paying for them.'

Tara picked up her knife and fork, closing her eyes and savouring for a moment the wonderful aroma of garlic, herbs and beef.

'And I can design for this shop?' she asked.

'All the evening wear will be exclusively yours.' Josh's eyes twinkled at her rapturous expression. 'I'm going to buy in knitwear, jackets, trousers and such like. But I want you to go to town on all those sequinned, beaded silk and velvet dreams you've been on about.'

She wanted to shriek with delight, order a bottle of Champagne and throw her arms round Josh.

'But I won't have time to do the everyday shops' clothes.' Tara was sure there had to be a catch.

'We can use all the old patterns.' Josh reached for her hand across the table. 'You'll spend all your time on this. As these clothes won't be mass-produced I'm thinking of starting a small workshop with around four girls to work exclusively on them.'

Tara beamed. With her own workroom she could dictate how things were done, get the sort of finish she wanted. It was a dream come true.

'So what's this shop going to be called?' Her eyes sparkled like newly polished amber and her cheeks were flushed pink.

'I'm not sure. Maybe Joshua Bergman written in posh gold script, but we'll see.'

Tara sat back in her chair, too stunned to think of any more questions.

'Finish your dinner.' Josh rapped her knuckle with one finger. 'And afterwards I'll order some Champagne to celebrate.'

It was almost a week later when Tara began to climb

down from the cloud Josh had thrown her up to.

She woke up on Sunday morning and suddenly realised that it was now ten days since she came back from Paris. Even accounting for the fact Harry was cross with her, he could at least have sent a postcard.

Phoning the club wasn't an option now. If Harry was simply tired of her she didn't want a barmaid or cellarman telling her so. Going to see George and Queenie was the answer. She could pretend she'd gone to tell them Josh's plans and see if they'd heard anything.

It was really hot, and Tara could imagine Queenie planning lunch outside. Every year she added something more to her tiny Mediterranean garden. The railway wall was completely covered in ivy now. Clematis, climbing roses and honeysuckle blocked out the neighbours' messy tips, a tiny pool sat in one corner with a fountain playing, and at night they had a couple of floodlights hidden under bushes.

'Well, this is the life, isn't it?' George held up his pint of beer for a toast. Petunias cascaded over the edge of pots. Exotic lilies, nurtured over winter in the house, were a blaze of red, blue and yellow.

'It certainly is.' Tara grinned, chinking her glass of wine with his beer. She had arrived in a long cheesecloth dress but she'd stripped off now to a turquoise swimsuit. 'Here's to more of it!'

'You'll be sunning yourself in foreign parts soon,' Queenie said, rubbing a little sun-tan oil on her plump arms. 'When Josh opens that shop it'll be all actresses and pop stars coming in. You won't want to slum it round 'ere no more.'

Tara laughed. 'When I'm rich enough to swan off to foreign parts I'll take you, too,' she insisted. 'I hope Harry's speaking to me again by then, otherwise it might prove embarrassing.'

She saw the looks exchanged by them, sensed their surprise.

'We had a fight,' she said, shocked he'd said nothing to them. 'He didn't tell me he was going to Germany and I haven't heard from him since.'

'We thought you'd come over because he was away.' Queenie looked concerned. 'I was just going to ask you how he's getting on there.'

'You haven't heard either?'

'No.' George sat up straight in his chair, tipping back his old straw hat and revealing his bald patch. 'To tell the truth, love, we was a bit narked he didn't tell us he was going. First we knew of it was when I rang Needles.'

A cold chill ran down Tara's spine. It was unthinkable Harry would go away without telling George.

'I don't like this.' She felt her stomach turn over the way it always did when something was wrong. 'It's understandable that he hasn't phoned me, because we parted on bad terms. But he wouldn't neglect you, especially if he forgot to say goodbye.'

'I'll ask Needles to pop over.' George got up quickly. 'He only lives around the corner, he said 'Arry's phoned the club several times. We'll ask 'im what he makes of it.'

'So you only spoke to 'im once?' George repeated himself, making quite sure he'd got it right.

'Yeah.' Needles looked too big for the dainty white garden chair he'd perched on. 'Most of the lads 'ave spoken to 'im at different times. I just ain't picked the phone up.'

'When did 'Arry leave?' George asked.

'Must have bin Friday, not last week, but the one before. He was in on the Wednesday and 'e didn't say nuffin' about going nowhere.'

'Thursday was the night I got back from Paris. He was at my flat when I got home.' Tara frowned. 'He said he was going to the club, he drove off there.'

559

' 'E never came. 'E belled me Friday morning.' Needles leaned forward, resting his elbows on his knees. 'Said 'e was at the airport, in a phone box, that's why 'e couldn't speak for long.'

'So where did he go Thursday night?' George pondered, looking a little pale. 'What was he wearing, Tara?'

'His dinner jacket, bow-tie, the usual.' Tara was worried. 'Needles, are you sure it was Harry that phoned you?'

'Don't be daft, gel.' Needles' face broke into a broad grin. 'I've known 'Arry since 'e were a nipper. Fink I don't know 'is voice?'

'Was it clear, Needles?' George asked. 'I mean the line, his voice. I can't see 'Arry bombing off on the town in a penguin suit meself. Neither can I understand why 'e didn't bell me before getting on a plane.'

'You'd have bin at work,' Needles retorted. 'But now you come to mention it, the line weren't that good. He kept banging the receiver and there was this 'issing noise.'

'Do you think it was someone pretending to be Harry, Uncle George,' Tara said in a small voice. 'Do you think something's happened to him?'

' 'Ang on a minute!' Queenie interrupted, leaning forward to pat both George's and Tara's knees. 'You're getting Tara all steamed up just because 'Arry's been a bit thoughtless. 'E'll turn up in a day or two, just you see.'

'Queenie.' George put one hand over his wife's. 'In Harry's whole life I don't think 'e's ever gone away for more than one night without telling me. 'E ain't bin abroad much. Not more than three times, I don't think. If he was going to Germany 'e would 'ave bin spouting on about it. But we can settle this right now by going to 'is flat and looking around. If 'is passport's gone, I'll believe 'e 'as!'

Tara got dressed again and went with George and Needles, while Queenie stayed home to cook the dinner.

Harry's flat was neat and tidy, a bit like a hotel room, his shoes in the wardrobe in a straight line, the bottles in his bathroom lined up like soldiers. Even the bed was made to military standards by his cleaning lady.

'Neat, ain't 'e?' Needles said as he rifled through the drawer by the bed containing letters bound up with rubber bands, receipts in a bull-dog clip and a box of loose change.

'Never was till 'e got banged up,' George offered. 'But some of this is that cleaning lady, anyhow.'

'It's not here.' Tara looked round from searching his desk under the window. 'This is where I last saw it.'

She wanted to cry. It was all these things of his, the box of cufflinks on the dressing table, his hairbrush, the smell of his suits in the wardrobe, everything she touched reminded her powerfully of Harry.

'His razor's gone, too,' she said sadly. It was a brass-handled one that usually sat in a pot on the bathroom windowsill. 'So's his toothbrush.' She rushed over to the wardrobe and found the light grey leather jacket he wore all the time. 'But look, George, when have you ever known him go anywhere without that!'

George shrugged his shoulders, as if he didn't know what to think. Needles went back into the wardrobe.

' 'Is brown jacket's gone,' he said. 'So's his best navy whistle.'

'Someone just packed those things,' Tara insisted. 'You know as well as I do he always takes that grey jacket. Is his dinner jacket there?'

Needles looked again. 'No, it ain't.'

'That settles it. He wouldn't take that with him. He's been kidnapped!'

'It don't mean nuffin', him taking the penguin suit,'

Needles said comfortingly. 'Only that 'e's expecting to go to a few posh places.'

'His car!' George was pale, suddenly older looking. 'Where's that?'

'It could be parked up at the airport,' Needles suggested. 'I'll take a run out there and look.'

'Come back to the house first.' George didn't look well at all, he was shaking so much that he couldn't lock the door and Needles had to take the key from his hand.

Back at Paradise Row Tara was all for going straight to the police to report Harry missing, but George stopped her.

'Look at it the way they will,' he said haltingly. ' 'E's phoned his club, stuff's gone from his flat, they ain't gonna believe anyone's snatched 'im.'

'But you don't think everything's OK, I know you don't,' Tara insisted.

George covered his face with his hands for a moment, leaning forward on to his knees.

'I'm more worried 'e's got 'imself in a tight spot. You gotta understand that 'Arry's always been in a difficult position, he grew up with some nasty people, even did time wiv 'em. Our 'Arry's loyal, I know 'e don't want to get stuck into villainy no more, but sometimes it ain't so simple.'

Needles appeared to understand perfectly, he nodded glumly.

'You really think he's in on something?' Tara was appalled. 'He told me he'd never go back to prison. I don't care how good a deal it seemed, he wouldn't take the risk.'

'Wait a bit longer, Tara?' George warned her. 'Needles and me will sniff around like, ask the lads what's going on. 'Arry might not be in Germany, that could be just a smoke-screen, but if we call the plod in and 'Arry suddenly turns up we'll all look bloody daft. Know what I mean?'

*

Tara sat in the window of her flat watching as twilight turned to dark. She ought to have felt reassured that Needles had found Harry's car parked at the airport. But then again, he hadn't managed to find his name on a passenger list. Was that just because Needles didn't have enough clout? Or because he wasn't on one?

Reason told her men like Harry were more than capable of looking after themselves, but still her stomach churned alarmingly. One thing came out of all this loud and clear. Harry's life was conducted on more than one level, and she would probably never discover all of them.

George and Needles had opened her eyes to things she hadn't even considered – gang warfare, policemen on the take, drugs. Now George said she mustn't confide in anyone, particularly Josh, as he and Harry had many mutual friends and one careless word could make things much worse. But even if Harry had done something really wicked, she had to help him, she owed him that much.

And she'd do it alone if necessary.

It was after three when she finally got into bed. She had made up her mind about Harry.

However much she loved and wanted him, reason told her there was no future in it. He came from a world she didn't want to move back into. However much he claimed otherwise he would always see women as second-class citizens. Fighting, gambling, drinking, wheeling and dealing, they were all so deeply ingrained in his character he could no more cut them out than you could try to stop a cat from stalking birds.

Her mother and grandmother were right, Josh was the right man to marry, to have children with. He might not make her feel weak at the knees, but did she want that anyway? She could put all her passion into her designs. She and Josh were real friends, they cared about the same things, had identical goals. With them there would never be a conflict of interests. People talked too much about love. You could love people in so many different ways, anyway. Who could say that the affection she felt for Josh was less valid than that painful, gut-wrenching feeling she had for Harry?

Chapter 32

'I've got to get in the club and search it,' Tara muttered to herself. She had been awake for more than an hour already and it was still only seven, far too early to get up on a Sunday morning.

Tara was convinced that the key to Harry's disappearance lay in the club, and she felt sure that if she could get into his office she'd find some clue as to what had happened. There was no way she could go there openly – Duke Denning knew her and would wonder what she was up to. If she asked for Needles' help he'd be so worried about her he'd probably give the game away. As for breaking in, that was impossible. Men who had all done time for breaking and entering weren't going to leave a club vulnerable to burglars.

There had been some developments during the week. One was that George rang her to say Harry had rung him twice. On the second occasion Harry had told him he'd flown back to England to pick up some more clothes, but he couldn't pop in as he didn't have time.

George checked the flat the next day and found that Harry had swapped the brown leather jacket for his grey one, hung up his dinner suit and taken clean underwear and socks.

Around a day later Tony took another call from Harry, asking him to collect his car from the airport and take it into his usual garage to get it serviced.

'I asked him why he hadn't contacted you, sweetheart,' George said in a forlorn voice. 'All 'e said was "Leave it out, Dad, I've got enough on my plate right now." '

That ought to have put Tara off, but in fact it made her more determined. It was beginning to feel like a conspiracy with even Uncle George joining in, but she was going to get to the bottom of it.

All she had to do was work out some way to sneak into the club and have a snoop around.

She got up soon after nine, unable to settle for her usual Sunday lie-in, pulled on a pair of jeans and went out to buy a newspaper. By eleven o'clock she had run out of ideas. She'd cleaned her flat, put clean sheets on her bed and read the newspaper, and the day loomed ahead of her endlessly.

Sundays had always been spent with Harry. He usually arrived at around four in the morning, letting himself in with his own key and snuggling down beside her. Usually she would get up around ten, creeping out to buy newspapers, then come back to make him breakfast in bed. Sundays were about being close; making love, chatting, cuddling and dozing. On a nice day they might stir themselves to go for a walk, sometimes they went out to a pub or restaurant, but mostly they just enjoyed being alone together.

Tara couldn't keep still. She moved the bed settee to a new position then moved it back because she didn't like it. She rearranged her collection of inkwells and paperweights, swapped prints round on the wall, then sat down at her drawing board in the window and tried to work on a new design.

But it was hopeless, she couldn't settle. She jumped up to make coffee, ate half a packet of biscuits out of sheer boredom, then rang her mother.

She hadn't mentioned Harry's disappearance, Amy

had enough worrying to do with the farm without that.

'What a lovely surprise.' Amy sounded as if she was smiling. 'You were lucky to catch us, we're just about to take Winston for a walk.'

Amy seemed to have taken on a new lease of life. She barely mentioned the farm but spoke instead of Greg, his practice, their busy social life and wedding plans.

'August 22nd,' she said. 'Just a small wedding – you, Harry, George and Queenie, then Greg's two old aunts and a handful of friends from down here. We've arranged to have a reception and buffet in the Crown. The bar there goes out on to a nice garden, so if it's good weather we can use that, too.'

'What about the farm?' Tara felt slightly irritated by her mother's bouncy attitude while she was feeling at a loose end.

'Greg found this super young lad, just out of college.' Amy was practically gushing now. 'He needs the experience of running a place on his own, and Stan likes him, too, so there's no conflict. I've let him have Paul's old room, so it means the house isn't standing empty.'

Tara bristled; not only at the idea of a stranger in Paul's room, but at someone taking over her farm without any consultation.

'You'd like Tim,' Amy carried on, unaware that her daughter's silence stemmed from anger. 'He paints, too. Sometimes in the afternoons when he's got nothing to do he takes his easel down by the river or the church.'

'Sounds like everything's just about perfect there?'

'Yes, it is.' Amy didn't appear to note the sarcasm. 'But you should come down soon for a long weekend and see for yourself. Make it before the wedding.'

Tara put her head in her hands after she'd put down the telephone. She was ashamed of being so ratty, cross with her mother for showing more interest in Greg and Tim than in her. And she was desperately in need of someone.

'Bloody Harry!' she exploded. 'Other girls fall out with men and it's over once and for all. Not you, you bastard. You have to go missing to prolong everything.'

The telephone rang, a shrill noise in the quiet room. She reached for it eagerly, willing it to be Harry. But it was Josh.

'I don't want you to think I'm crowding you,' he said gently, perhaps guessing her disappointment. 'It's just such a lovely day. I thought we could take a spin out to Windsor or somewhere. Have lunch and lie about in the sunshine.'

A glance out into the sun-filled road decided her.

'That would be wonderful. Come as soon as you like. I'll be ready.'

Was it coincidence that the first dress she came to in her wardrobe was a revealing one with a laced-up low-cut bodice? She tied her hair up in a high pony-tail, teasing one or two strands loose round her face and quickly curling them with her tongs. The flimsy cheesecloth dress was white, with a tiny green pattern, and she wore nothing beneath it but a pair of white lace panties.

A few squirts of perfume, a little make-up and a pair of sandals, and she was ready.

Josh watched as she ran down the steps from her house and felt an ache of desire. She looked so beautiful, her golden hair gleaming in the sun. Her dress accentuated her small waist, and pushed up her breasts so they almost spilled over the top of the bodice like two ripe peaches.

'I was so glad to hear your voice.' She slid into his open-topped Mercedes and reached across to kiss his smooth cheek. He looked quite different in an open-necked shirt and jeans, somehow less intimidating. 'I was feeling lonely.'

'Sundays can be like that,' Josh said as he pulled away. 'All those people out there in twos, everyone having fun but you.'

'I'm sure you never feel like that,' Tara retorted. 'You've got a book stuffed with girls' names!'

'Spending time with someone you don't care for much is worse than being alone,' he said with a smile. 'I often spend Sundays working.'

Tara's spirits rose as they sped out of London. The sun was hot on her arms and shoulders, she was in a smart car with one of the most eligible bachelors in London.

The pub he took her to had a garden sloping down to the river. All the tables and chairs were full, but Josh bought a bottle of wine and two glasses and they sat on the small landing stage, their feet dangling over the edge.

'I can't believe an hour ago I was getting so uptight,' Tara said. 'I wanted to shout at Mum for being happy. I didn't even want some poor farm lad sleeping in Paul's bed.'

Josh listened while she explained all that had been said.

'I'm horrible, aren't I?' Tara pulled a face and laughed at herself. 'What would you prescribe?'

'A holiday.' Josh smiled lazily. 'Somewhere hot, with white sand and brilliant blue sky and sea. Lots of good food and booze to make you relax, then a lot of good loving.'

'That sounds blissful.' Tara took a deep breath of the delicious fresh air. 'Umm, it's nice here in the sun, too!'

She wasn't sure she wanted Josh to talk about loving, but then she wasn't sure that she didn't.

They ate baked potatoes stuffed with salmon and mayonnaise, finished the bottle of wine, and Josh bought another one to take away with them.

'We need refreshments,' he said, his eyes twinkling as he stuffed two glasses in her bag.

Tara felt a bit tiddly once they left the pub.

'We'll find a place to lie in the sun, drink our wine and I'll roll us a joint,' Josh said.

She had long since given up being concerned about Josh smoking pot. Everyone in London was at it and, anyway, it was supposed to be far less damaging than the speed he used to take. Harry had tried it, too, lots of times. It was yet another reminder of his double standards. He would go crackers if he thought she'd tried it, but it was all right for him.

'Is it scary?' she asked innocently as Josh took a blanket from the boot of his car.

'What, sharing a blanket with me?'

Tara giggled. 'No, smoking dope. Harry wouldn't hear of me trying it.'

Josh tucked the blanket under his arm, handed her the bottle of wine, then took her hand and led her towards a footpath along the river bank.

'Men like Harry like their women barefoot and pregnant, in the kitchen.' He smirked. 'Letting them do mind-bending things like having a good job, smoking dope or even taking driving lessons is bad news.'

His gentle, almost affectionate way of putting Harry down didn't make her bristle; in fact it reminded her that Harry didn't approve of lady drivers. His memory somehow seemed blurred, and she was very aware of Josh's hand in hers. He could never compete with Harry, but today he looked almost handsome. Even the gold medallion nestling amongst the dark curly hair on his chest didn't make her want to laugh as it usually did. He was just Josh, an honest, ostentatious guy who knew how to be a real friend.

'Let's go in there.' Josh stopped by a hole in a hedge that led to a field. 'There don't seem to be any cowpats.'

It reminded Tara of the lower meadow at home – grass strewn with buttercups, unseen grasshoppers chirruping, rooks cawing in a tree. The sun was hot on her arms, the grass smelled fresh and clean and the only clouds in the sky were mere wisps of cotton wool.

Josh laid down the blanket, opened the wine and poured it, then sat rolling up a joint. She watched as he burned the lump of cannabis, then crumbled it on to tobacco. He rolled it expertly, licked the paper, stuck it down and twisted one end like a firework. Then he tore a strip of cardboard from a cigarette packet, rolled it tightly and slid it into the other end of the joint.

'What's that for?'

'A filter.' Josh grinned. He put it between his thick lips then lit the end. 'You're very curious today!'

'Sometimes I feel as if life's passing me by,' she said thoughtfully. 'I mean, I've been living in London now for years but I don't know much about what goes on.'

'Maybe I'm partly responsible for that.' He took a deep drag on the joint and slowly exhaled. 'I let you work all hours for me. I've taken too much from you and not given enough back.'

'I don't feel hard done by.' Tara giggled, taking the joint he offered her and dragging deeply on it. She coughed violently and took a mouthful of wine to stop it. Another drag and she'd got the hang of it. 'But I've decided it's time I lived a little. I'm going to learn to drive, and buy a car. And I'll smoke dope if I want to.'

'I don't feel any different,' Tara insisted half an hour later.

'Boring people say that!' Josh teased. He was lying on his back. Tara was sitting, her legs tucked away under her dress, looking down at him. 'If we were at my place now and I put some sounds on, you'd notice it immediately. If I was to kiss you, you might find you liked it more.'

He was very relaxing to be with. They had flitted from subject to subject like butterflies, laughed about things that happened in the shop, people they'd met in Paris.

'So we've either got to go home to your place, or start kissing for me to find out?' she grinned.

'It's too nice here to go home.' Josh closed his eyes. 'Why don't you just come and lie down, snooze a bit. You know, Tara, you're hyper-active, always wanting to be doing something. Did someone tell you that it's sinful to be idle?'

'Mum and Gran bred it into me.' She stretched out her legs and slowly moved round to lie beside him.

'My folks are like that, too.' He looked at her sideways. 'Every moment of the day has to be filled. Mum makes bread and cakes that no-one will eat rather than be idle.'

Tara knew she was just the same. How many Saturday nights had she spent on the drawing board instead of going out dancing with one of the girls from the shop? How many evenings had she spent cleaning her flat when she could have been laughing at a funny film, chatting to someone, or just been happy doing nothing?

'My parents seem to think anything pleasurable is sinful.' Josh grinned. 'They would be appalled if I married someone just because she made me feel happy. They'd expect me to choose her like you would a horse. Good breeding stock, strong enough to work hard and as frugal as they are!'

'Gran was always giving me dire warnings about being led astray by love.' Tara smiled. 'I daresay she'd approve of your parents' ideas.'

'So what would you marry for? Just love, however poor and unsuitable? For money? Or even friendship?' Josh leaned on one elbow and looked down intently at her.

'Once I would have said just love,' Tara replied. 'But I'm beginning to think my gran and your parents have a point. In the long term it might be better to marry someone who's a good friend, has the same interests and goals.'

'Like me?'

Tara looked into his eyes and she knew it wasn't a hypothetical question.

'In many ways you'd be perfect.' She couldn't stand the intensity of his gaze and looked away.

'But Harry's in the way?'

There was so much understanding and tenderness in his voice she felt drawn to him. She nodded. 'I always thought he and I were meant to be,' she whispered. 'I believed he wanted the same things as me. But I don't think he does any more.'

'You have to decide what you want out of life, Tara,' Josh reached out and stroked her face. 'Harry would be a fish out of water anywhere but London. But when we open this new shop and the new labels have "designed by Tara Manning" on them, the whole world will be your oyster.'

Tara gulped. She'd suggested having her name on labels before but he'd always shied away from it.

'Milan, Paris, New York...' The place names sounded like a prayer. 'There's no end to where it will lead, Tara. But it won't do if every time we need to hold a fashion show or go to one of the collections, Harry gets heavy.'

'Are you serious about the labels?' she asked disbelievingly. It meant so much to her.

'Totally.' His eyes were so soft she could feel herself sinking into them. 'I was very arrogant when you first joined me. I took and took. Now I see I couldn't have done it without you and I want to share from here on in.'

'What are you saying?' She could feel a bubbling of excitement inside her. 'A partnership?'

'I'm saying I love you, Tara,' he said, stroking back her hair from her face. 'I know it's too soon to ask you to marry me, I'd be afraid to ask in case you turned me down. But whether it's a partnership in marriage or just business, I want you.'

He moved nearer, leaning his head on her shoulder, his lips just touching her neck.

A tremor of wanting started in her belly. She was aware only of him, no longer feeling the hot sun, the grass tickling her toes where the blanket ended, or even hearing the boats on the river and people walking on the towpath.

His lips were soft and full, they nibbled their way up her neck, across her cheek and found their way to hers. She wanted him from the moment his tongue flickered against hers. It was like taking just a sip of water and finding it inflame the thirst still further. She let him push her down on to the blanket, her mouth reaching for his with hunger, her body arching up towards his.

A warning bell told her she was reacting like this because of the dope and the wine, that she must calm down, stop things now before they got out of hand. But it was too exciting, the burning inside her too strong. As he unlaced the bodice of her dress and moved down to kiss her breasts she panted with longing.

'Your breasts are lovely.' He ran his tongue over her erect nipple till she cried out with pleasure. 'I've done this in my dreams so often, but reality's even better.'

His breath was hot on her flesh, his fingers evoking a wild and savage response as they squeezed and stroked her breasts.

A dog barked close by. Tara opened her eyes and saw a golden labrador coming through the hole in the hedge. It was a reminder of home, of Winston and the farm.

'Sally!' A man's voice shouted from further along the towpath.

'A dog!' Tara said, rolling over and pulling her dress back over her breasts. 'His master's coming, too.'

'Lucky him!' Josh sniggered just as the dog gambolled over to them, tongue lolling and tail wagging. 'Hello, girl. Of course I'm not a bit bloody pleased to see you, but I'll pretend to be polite.'

'Sally!' The shout made them turn. A middle-aged man in khaki shorts and matching long socks was coming towards them. 'I'm dreadfully sorry,' he said, looking flustered. 'I hope she hasn't disturbed you, she's so friendly, she wants everyone to play with her.'

The moment had passed. Tara reached for the wine bottle and emptied the last inch or two into their glasses.

'It's just as well.' She smiled at Josh, amused by his grumpy expression. 'Suppose we'd gone a bit further and that man caught us at it? I'd have died of embarrassment.'

'We seem to be jinxed.' Josh's lower lip protruded petulantly.

'I don't think I would have gone that far without the joint.' Tara reached over and took his hand. 'I'm not really ready for that yet, Josh. I'm still too mixed up.'

'Let's walk, then.' He stood up, tucking his shirt into his trousers, then held out his hand to pull her up. 'Next time, Tara, next time!'

Tara walked past the front of the club briskly. Mrs Knight, one of the cleaners, was Hoovering just inside the open door, a cigarette hanging from her lips, hair bound up in a scarf. She was the mother of one of Harry's friends, a tall skinny woman who knew Tara well. Fortunately she was too engrossed in her work to look up, and Tara darted round the corner into the narrow alley beside the club.

575

It was two o'clock. Unless something unusual had happened this morning, Needles, Tony and possibly Alec would come out any minute now and walk further down the road to get some dinner at the café while the cleaners finished up.

Josh had given her a wonderful day out, even after the incident in the field he was still charming. They walked and talked, and later they went for a meal in Windsor.

It was after eleven when he dropped her home. He didn't ask to come in, or suggest another date. There was a quiet understanding between them that nothing needed to be pushed.

Josh had talked about taking a holiday together in Italy, taking in the art treasures, the fashion, the sun and sea. But first she had to find out about Harry.

Monday and Tuesday and Wednesday were the longest days she'd ever known. Anxiety, guilt, fear and even anger fermented inside her; she couldn't concentrate on her work, neither could she sleep. One moment she was mooning over Josh, remembering in detail how it felt when he kissed her breasts, the next she was angrily reprimanding herself for being so unfaithful.

It was her day off today, and the idea had come to her in the small hours. Now she was actually waiting to carry it out, she wasn't nearly so certain about it.

If someone caught her she would just act thick and make out she was looking for evidence that Harry was two-timing her. But she didn't intend to get caught.

Footsteps made her duck down behind a dustbin. 'I don't fuckin' like it,' Needles' voice rang out. 'Marcia's been with us since we opened and until Harry signs over the club to Duke, she should stay.'

'Don't make waves, Needles.'

Tara crept back down the alley and peered nervously out into the road. Needles was wearing the overalls they always put on for beer deliveries. Tony was almost running beside him to keep up, his short legs going like pistons.

'I can't take much more of this,' Needles snarled. 'If I didn't owe 'Arry I'd be out of 'ere now.'

They were out of hearing range now and Tara came out of her hiding place.

It was odd that Alec wasn't with them, she knew the three usually had their meals at the same time. But maybe now Harry wasn't around things had changed.

As she got back to the front door she could hear the sound of the Hoover coming from the bar and Mrs Knight shouting above it to her helper. Taking a deep breath Tara darted in, paused for a moment to get her bearings, then made a dash past the bar door to the stairs.

Everywhere looked so odd without lights. Sunshine came in the open door, a little more from the curved window over the stairs, but it was gloomy, a bit like being in a church.

Her feet were silent on the thick stair carpet, but as she reached the gallery she heard two men's voices coming from the direction of Harry's office. There was no time to consider who they were. She had to hide.

Running along the corridor to her left she darted into a windowless storeroom and hid behind the door. Her plan had been to reach the empty rooms, above this floor. She intended to settle down and wait until everyone left and the club was locked up, then she would have several hours to search without fear of interruption.

She could hear the men coming closer, talking softly. Suppose they came in here and caught her?

'The signal should come on Friday,' one of the men said. She didn't recognise this voice at all.

'I just hope they handle it properly.' She was sure

577

this was Duke's voice, and she held her breath as they went on past the storeroom.

'They've been training for long enough,' Duke said, but his voice tailed away as if they'd gone into one of the gaming rooms.

'Joe's a good man, he won't let us down.' The stranger's voice drifted to her, suggesting they were coming out of the room again. 'We ought to send some replacements down for the others, though. They aren't used to being cooped up.'

'There's no-one else to replace them.' Duke sounded angry at the suggestion. 'They knew there would be a lot of waiting, it's part of the deal.'

Tara held her breath, terrified they might just pull the storeroom door shut and lock it. There were spirits in here, boxes and boxes of them, and it shouldn't have been open. But they were going down the stairs now, their voices retreating. After a quick peep to make certain, she dashed for the small wooden staircase at the end, holding her bag firmly under her arm.

At the far end of the narrow, dusty passage upstairs was the room she was making for. Harry had brought her up here once when he had the idea of making it into a flat.

This was the room he'd thought of using as a bedroom. Because it was on the end of the building it had funny little arched windows on two sides. If she peered down from the front one she could just see the paper shop across the narrow street. The side one looked on to an alley, on her right a tiny glimpse of river. The room hadn't been cleared. Still the old armchair with one castor missing, a tea chest and a cardboard box of old printed price lists.

Tara turned the tea chest on its side as a precautionary hiding place, opened her bag and sorted through the equipment she'd brought. A torch, a flask of coffee, a pack of sandwiches, assorted fruit, sweets, cake and a book. She didn't anticipate staying beyond nine or ten, but it was as well to be prepared.

Getting in here had been a piece of cake, getting out would be far more hazardous. She would have to go downstairs in the early evening and hide in the cloakroom until someone came to open up for the evening, then, when an opportunity arose, nip out the door. But if she was caught! But she wasn't going to dwell on that! For now all she had to do was listen.

One of the advantages of this hiding place was the fact it was over the foyer. If Harry hadn't had delusions of grandeur, insisting on that oak staircase and a chandelier, there would be another room beneath this one. As it was, sound carried clearly up here. Harry once told her he came up here for a cigarette sometimes when they had a stand-in doorman, just so he could discover how many entrance fees went in his pocket.

An hour passed. The men came back. She could hear Mrs Knight clearly, grumbling about the mess in the ladies lavatories. She heard her bang her equipment into her cupboard, then shout goodbye to Needles. Then one by one Alec, Tony and Duke left.

Finally the front door was banged shut, Needles' voice drifting up from the street below as he shouted something to the shop owner opposite.

There was no sound other than the buzzing of the chiller unit down in the bar. She started to walk down, but the sudden, unexpected sound of the telephone made her stop in her tracks. The click of someone picking up the receiver reverberated through the silent building and she heard a man's voice speak. Hastily she turned and went back to her hideout.

Voices woke her. Startled, Tara sat up and checked her watch. It was almost nine in the evening.

She had waited and waited for the person on the

telephone to leave. But he hadn't, and she'd reconciled herself to searching at night instead, then waiting till morning to get out. Finally she had lain down on the dusty floor and fallen asleep.

Needles was in, she could hear him quite distinctly, Tony, too, and maybe Dennis and Alec, though she couldn't be sure. A girl with a harsh Cockney voice shouted out that they needed more mixers, then there was a peal of dirty laughter from her and one of the men.

Did she dare use the toilet along the passage? Maybe she should wait till the music was turned on and people arrived.

Tara sat shivering. It wasn't very cold but it was creepy. She could hear scratching under the floor-boards, creaking from the old hoists outside. It was one in the morning now, but still people arrived to gamble and drink. She could no longer hear the music, it was buried beneath the noise of people enjoying them-selves.

She shone her torch on her watch. Three o'clock! It was quiet now, the music turned down to a mere hum, but there was a big card game going on and so the bar was open in the main gaming room. Every now and then a drunken girl's laughter spilled out. Tara could see the scene as if she was in the room, she'd so often been part of it. The laughing girl would be sitting on a bar stool, possibly in a long evening dress. Her man is in the next room, deaf and blind to anything beyond the cards in his hands. She's getting drunk because she's anxious. She'll talk and laugh too loudly, trying hard to justify why she's there, and all the time he's losing more.

Harry had come to hate gambling and gamblers. He said he'd heard all the stories about fortunes won and lost. That he was sickened by men who dragged their families down, of women who came crying to him asking for help. She felt Harry's presence tonight and it made her feel brave.

At last she heard the door of the card room opening, and feet shuffling out. Someone down there had won, but there was no joy or laughter. The silly girl was crying now, saying stupid things she'd regret tomorrow. Needles' voice came from the foyer, she could hear him clearly as he comforted the girl and jollied her out into a taxi. Harry said they always paid for taxis for people who'd lost a great deal; he'd laughed and said he had to, in case they were still on the doorstep the next morning.

Cars were driving away now. If only she could see which was which and mentally check off each man.

'Come on, man.' Needles sounded irritated, he wanted to go home. 'It's late and I've had it with being polite.'

She had never heard Needles be anything but polite. His size was enough to deter most troublemakers. Tony said goodbye, quickly followed by the barmaids, Dennis and Alec. More voices she didn't recognise, discussing something about a car, then they left too.

'Good night tonight!' Duke's voice wafted up to her. 'That prat lost over two thousand to Reg. Both bars exceeded their targets, the door money was up, too. I hope you'll stay on with me once the sale's finalised, Needles.'

'I need to speak to 'Arry before I make any promises,' Needles said staunchly, and his cold tone revealed his loathing of the man.

'Your loyalty's touching.' Duke's sarcasm chilled Tara. 'But I'm going to be the boss here permanently. It might be a good plan to think on what that means!'

Tara heard the door open and a man's feet stepping down on to the pavement. She heard a click which could be Needles setting the alarm, then the front door slammed and keys were turned.

One set of feet went off to the left, stopped, then she heard a car door open. The others crossed the road and within seconds two cars pulled away. Tara watched the red tail lights till they were out of sight, then she made her move. She was stiff through sitting still for so long and her heart fluttered with fright. The narrow passage to the wooden stairs was pitch dark. Remembered tales of how Harry had found a rat playing in the men's urinal one morning made her flesh creep. She didn't dare switch on her torch, not until she was safely in the office.

She hoped that no alterations had been made to the alarm system since it was installed. Harry had been like a child back then, making her walk about in the bar till she stepped on the pressure pads. She remembered too that all windows and exterior doors were alarmed, so she must stay away from those.

She noticed the smells that Harry used to speak of, now the extractors were turned off. Not just stale beer, cigarette smoke and perfume, but old musty smells from the time this was a warehouse.

The office door was locked. For a moment she panicked. She had to lean on the door and take a few deep breaths before she remembered how the spare key system worked. The office key was in the main gaming room, the key for that was kept on a ledge up above the office door. She reached up and groped for it, smiling as her fingers touched the cool metal. Harry liked these rather childish puzzles and playing his game brought him nearer.

A sudden buzzing noise startled her. Goose-pimples came up all over her, but then she remembered it was only the chiller in the bar below. She took a deep breath to calm herself, then carried on.

Across in the gaming room, she found the key on a hook underneath the bar. Her teeth were chattering with fright so she helped herself to a measure of brandy from one of the optics to steady her nerves.

As she opened the door of the office all fear faded away. This was Harry's domain. The leather Chesterfield was where he slept when he worked late or drank too much to drive home, the brass desk lamp with a green shade was the one she'd bought him. Even the signed framed photographs on the wall reassured her – famous old boxers Harry admired, one of him and David Bailey when he took the pictures for an article in a Sunday supplement, and a score of actresses and actors who'd been to the club.

The steel shutter over the window was locked. She pulled the curtains over and switched on the desk lamp. Systematically she went through each of the small cubby holes in the desk, reading everything. Receipts for petrol, reminders of an unpaid water bill, letters from the electricity board, some of them so old she wondered why they were still there. A brochure of villas in Spain, even a seed catalogue!

It was in the middle section she found something unusual. She was quite sure it wasn't important, just a small dog-eared car-park ticket, but it was for Lympne airport. It was because she had no idea where this was that she tucked it into her jeans pocket. It was dated just two weeks ago and was tucked into an electricity bill, paid on the same day. There were more bills in this section, all receipted as paid in cash by Duke. This seemed to bear out the fact that he really was taking over the running of the club.

When Tara looked at her watch again it was almost five. She'd been through the desk, a filing cabinet and a chest of drawers. But all she had found that was out of the ordinary was a list of telephone numbers.

At first glance there was nothing odd about these either. They were all in major cities – Manchester, Birmingham, Cardiff, Plymouth, Glasgow and Leeds. But by each of them, instead of a name, was a type of bird. Sparrow, Falcon, Thrush. Were they some sort of code?

She was feeling very odd now. Not so much tired as strung out, every sound making her jump nervously. Jotting the numbers and names down carefully, she tucked her copy into her pocket and put the original back where she found it. The poker room was the only other room used for secret meetings, she didn't feel searching the whole building was justified. The poker room was another with steel shutters, so she could safely turn on the green-shaded light, which cast a murky beam over the baize.

It was disappointingly bare. No boxes to delve into, no briefcases, just an unemptied ashtray, a couple of dirty glasses and a Capstan full-strength cigarette packet with two left in it. A small cupboard stood in the corner with a locked drawer above it. The cupboard held nothing but new sealed packets of cards and a set of dominoes in a wooden box. Behind the bar was just as disappointing, nothing out of place but a bottle of red nail varnish and a baby's squeaky toy. The knife for slicing lemons caught her eye. She picked it up and looked thoughtfully at the locked drawer.

'There has to be something in it,' she reasoned. 'Why lock it otherwise?'

Harry was a dab hand at opening locks, she'd seen him do it to the door of her flat when she forgot her key. He made it look simple, but it didn't work for her. She twisted and poked, pummelled and scraped, but it didn't make any difference. Just as she was about to give up she remembered the keys still in the door. It was obvious none of them would fit, they were all too big, but one seemed to turn the lock partially. She pushed it in with one hand and turned it, driving the blade of the knife in next to it, and to her amazement the lock turned.

A gun lay in the drawer.

Tara recoiled in horror, her hand over her mouth. It was a fancy little pearl-handled pistol and she knew instinctively it belonged to Duke. It somehow went with his name, his looks, the way he spoke to Needles as they closed up. A ruthless man, who would push anyone out of his way with whatever means were to hand.

It was another reminder of the danger of being caught here. Beads of sweat jumped up all over her and she could hear her heart hammering.

There was a fair-sized brown envelope underneath it. Inside was a smaller padded envelope with something bulky in it and a single sheet of paper on which were written those same telephone numbers she'd found in the office.

The smaller padded envelope was sealed, but Tara knew she had to open it.

Sliding the lemon knife under the edge she tried to open it without tearing; with luck there might be enough sticky to close it again. She slid her hand in and knew immediately what it was.

Harry's passport and wallet! She'd bought the wallet herself for his last birthday, soft brown pigskin with his initials engraved on the stud fastener.

Tears came to her eyes, a feeling of abject misery washing over her as she pulled it out.

'I'll keep it next to my heart,' he'd joked as he transferred money from his back pocket into it. 'You'll be wanting me to carry a furled umbrella next.' There was nine pounds inside it and a receipt for petrol. There was space for a photograph, but he'd laughed when she'd suggested he put one of her in there.

'Pillocks carry their girl's pictures,' he joked. 'Hard men have one of their dog.' But even though he'd laughed about it, claimed his pocket was all the wallet he needed, she'd never known him go out without it.

His passport had no stamp for Germany, nothing but two old ones for Spain, several years before.

He had to be dead, she knew that with certainty. Someone had gone back to his flat to collect the passport and other clothes, they'd moved his car somewhere. But his wallet would have been in his pocket wherever he was!

Blinded by tears she shoved everything back, not caring now if they did discover the drawer had been opened. She had to get out of the club. But how? The downstairs windows were all barred. If she attempted to tamper with the door the alarm would go off.

She tried to calm down, going through the procedure of locking the door and replacing the keys where she'd found them, but even as she tried to think logically, the feeling of claustrophobia grew.

Standing on the gallery, with the first murky ray of daylight lighting up the sky beyond, she remembered something Harry had told her a year ago.

'Needles locked me in. He thought I intended to stay the night, but I'd promised George I'd go round there. I had to climb out of a window on the top floor and shin down the roof.' She ran there now, into each of the top-floor rooms. Two had barred windows, the third's were too small. As she peered out of the last window her stomach churned again. It was a drop of at least ten feet to the slanted roof of the poker room below, beyond that was a sheer drop to the Thames.

But what if it was alarmed? Harry had never mentioned this! Her heart thumping with fright, she reached up for the latch and turned it. Nothing! The window creaked as it opened, flakes of ancient paint falling off like dandruff, and the wind straight from the river came howling in.

It took only a minute to collect up her belongings, but far longer to brace herself for the climb out. The window was just the width of her shoulders, the drop seemed to grow longer as she looked at it.

Her bag went first, clonking down on to the roof below. Dragging a box over she rested her hands on it and put one foot out the window, then heaved the other leg up to join it. Pushing up with her hands she wriggled her body backwards until finally she was in a position to drop her body over the edge and hang by her fingertips.

She hung there, paralysed by fear. Looking down, the sloping roof seemed miles away from her feet, and slippery too. What if she fell? She might slide right off the roof into the river.

Her arms were almost pulled out of their sockets with her weight, she had to let go now as she couldn't get back. As she hit the roof a loose slate was dislodged and went hurtling over the edge. Miraculously her feet gripped the tiles, and crouching down she inched towards the edge.

'Shit!' she exclaimed. It was a sheer drop to the river, perhaps fifty feet or more, and the tide was out, leaving thick greeny-grey mud.

She sat down and shuffled back across the roof on her bottom. The wind was nearly cutting her in half now and she was so scared her legs felt like rubber.

Peering down into a dank gully between the club and the old warehouse next door, she knew this was the way Harry had got out, but her heart sank even further as she looked at it. Iron struts zig-zagged down to the bottom. The shaft was less than four feet wide, the struts perhaps four or five feet apart, but only a strong, agile man like Harry could swing like an ape from strut to strut.

The wind whipped her hair as she looked back longingly at the small window, but there was no way she could get back to it. She couldn't stay here either, unless she wanted to involve the police before she'd even had time to think about anything. She had to climb down!

She dropped her bag down into the gully, gulping as she saw how long it took to hit the mud at the bottom. Sitting on the roof with her feet dangling over the guttering she reached out for the first strut and gripped it.

Fear clutched at her, but taking a deep breath, she pushed herself forward and swung forward into space.

To her surprise her feet touched the next strut and by letting go of the bar with one hand she managed to find a sticking-out brick on the wall to steady herself. Slowly she lowered herself to a sitting position and shuffled sideways down the diagonal rail, clinging on for grim death. Now she had a different perspective she saw she was over the worst part. It was just like a child's climbing frame, all she had to do was cling on to the poles and zig-zag down with them.

She was down to the last one, the black slimy gully less than twelve feet beneath her. The smell was so disgusting she tried not to breathe. She lowered herself on to her stomach on the last horizontal bar and braced herself to swing. But this time the strut was wide, she couldn't get a proper grip and, as she let her arms take her weight, her fingers slipped away.

Her feet hit the slime and skidded out behind her. She landed face down, her arms shooting out in an attempt to save herself. The smell was worse than the shock – stagnant rainwater, seagull droppings and the accumulated filth of years. The horror of falling into such foulness made her scrabble to her feet, scarcely noticing the pain in her leg.

She was soaked to the skin, covered in black stinking slime. Hobbling over to the edge of the gully, she saw she still had to negotiate a nine-inch ledge just above the water line to reach the side alley.

It was broad daylight now. A river-police launch was coming in to dock as she scrabbled the last thirty feet. Crouching in the alley, trembling with the cold and stinking so much it made her gag, she knew no taxi driver would dream of letting her get in his cab.

'Josh!' She said his name aloud. 'He'll know what to do.'

Chapter 33

Harry forced himself to get up out of the bed.

'Exercise, you lazy bastard,' he muttered. 'If a chance comes and you aren't fit you'll blow it!'

He felt terrible. He hadn't shaved or had a bath since he got here, toothache nagged at him and his head hurt constantly from lack of fresh air. Down on to the floor, then press-ups – one, two, three.

'Keep going. Four, five, six.' He counted, trying to wipe everything from his mind, concentrating only on pushing himself further and further.

Harry looked rough, his hair falling over his face in greasy black rat's tails as he bobbed up and down. In only a pair of black underpants it was apparent his body hadn't suffered; the muscles in his arms, chest and legs still stood out under lightly tanned skin. But the yellow bruise on the back of his neck, thick black stubble and a drawn white face proved the strain of being held captive.

A stink of sweat, urine and stale cigarettes hung thickly in the air. A pile of newspapers and a couple of paperbacks with lurid covers lay on the table. Grey army blankets were tossed back on the narrow iron bed, a grubby nylon shirt hung over brown corduroy trousers on the back of the only chair. The bucket sat in the furthermost corner, covered in a newspaper.

'Keep going,' he urged. 'Thirty, thirty-one, thirty-two.'

This was the worst kind of prison. He didn't know why he was being kept here, or for how long, where he was, or who was behind it.

It had been three days before the men let him see them without masks, but that only made him more terrified. Keeping their identity secret meant they intended to let him go eventually. Taking off the masks meant the only way he'd get out was dead.

Micky was the only one of his captors who had a human side. The other three were animals, and Joe Spikes was the worst.

They didn't know he'd discovered Joe's other name. Micky had lost his temper one day and referred to him as 'Spikes'. No doubt Joe would slice his goolies off if he knew that. But then Harry wasn't going to give the game away, or admit he'd heard of the guy before, not yet. He might be able to get Micky on his side.

Several things had become clear since he was captured. Joe Spikes was a psychopath, totally immersed in whatever this project was. He didn't allow himself to get anywhere near Harry, almost as if he was afraid just talking to him might somehow weaken him, yet he kept tabs. Micky was given a slapping for getting too friendly, Frank, one of the others, got in serious trouble for not locking the far door while Harry was in the lavatory. Yet for all this, Joe Spikes wasn't the boss. Micky described him as the Sergeant, intimating there were officers above him.

The days were endless. Every morning he had to force himself out of bed like this, just so he had a chance of sleeping at night. At eight they would unlock the cell door, allow him to empty his bucket in the toilet out in the passage and wash in the sink there. Another door was beyond it, always locked except for that one time, and on that occasion he hadn't realised it.

Around nine he was brought breakfast, always

fried, invariably swimming in grease. Most days they brought him a paper to read, occasionally another cup of tea later in the morning, but usually he was alone until at least two when he got a sandwich and some fruit. The main meal was often as late as seven and it varied from fried, often burnt food, to meat pies and instant mashed potato.

He knew now it wasn't a church. He'd scraped into the walls and discovered brick, not stone. It had to be a big country house, empty because the men never worried about noise. He'd worked out for himself it was near the coast because he heard Frank mention tides once, and he remembered a kind of tang to the air as he was hauled out of the van. The advertisements in the newspapers seemed to be mainly for places in the South-east, so he could be anywhere from Margate to Brighton.

Setting Joe Spikes aside, Harry had tried to find out about each of the other men. Micky was the youngest, no more than twenty-three, with curly brown hair and a round, almost cherubic face. He was a good-looking, well brought-up lad who had fallen in with the wrong crowd and didn't have the brains to realise where he was heading. Harry never got enough time alone with him to find out the whole story, but he got the impression of a lad not unlike himself.

Frank, Micky's mate, was born nasty. Twenty-eightish, been in trouble since he got out of nappies. Dirty, straw-coloured hair, pale blue eyes and a mean, bony face. He was pretty certain Frank had only latched on to Micky because he felt he had a touch of class, and would sell him down the river if push came to shove.

Carl, the third man, had to be ex-Army. Harry felt he saw himself like some SAS man, taking his orders, doing the job, all without considering why. He was older than Micky and Frank, mid-thirties, with a square, raw-looking face. The sort of man Harry would pick himself to take on a job that required split-second timing, courage and dependability.

But Joe was the one Harry dwelt on, trying hard to place where he'd heard that gravelly voice before. Joe rarely came down here. When he did he said little, but it was the way the others revered him and his ugliness that scared the shit out of Harry.

Joe was the oldest of the group, around fifty. Bald as a boiled egg, he had a ferocious scar on his right cheek which pulled his lips into a terrifying grimace, and most of his teeth were rotten. Yet he looked like a man of iron. The most disconcerting thing about him was his dark eyes. They seemed to glow with an extraordinary hatred which turned Harry's legs to jelly.

Harry stopped the press-ups at fifty and began running on the spot. He closed his eyes as he always did and tried to imagine he was actually running through fields. He had to try to get Tara out of his mind, she was preventing him from looking at all the clues objectively and working out what was going to happen.

At first he'd thought this was purely kidnapping and that the aggravation at the club was merely a scam to make people like Needles, Tony and his father jumpy. He'd believed Wainwright was behind it; as an actor he could have come into the club disguised, maybe greased a few palms. But did a man who just wanted revenge take on a payroll of at least four men to assist him? And keep his victim in relative comfort, when he could just kill him and dump the body somewhere?

But anyway Harry hadn't seen anything about his disappearance in the paper. George couldn't lay his hands on enough bread to make a kidnapping worthwhile, anyway. The only money lay in the club. All the first week Harry had waited for them to come in and demand his signature on some papers. When that didn't happen he knew then he wasn't being held for a ransom.

He had to use some lateral thinking to work out what was going on. If someone hated him enough to lock him up, then they'd torture him too. That meant his being here must serve a purpose and the answer had to lie in his club. They wanted him out of the way to do something there!

Drug- or gun-running! Everything dropped into place once he'd faced that. Either one meant big money, enough to buy people's loyalty, to slip their own men in as staff. A well-planned scam that had probably started months ago.

Duke Denning!

Now he understood why he'd never been able to get close to the man. He was a plant. Harry Collins had been taken for a mug. He couldn't have made it easier for him, either. He'd been so thrilled someone wanted to take the place off his hands he'd bent over backwards to make the bloke feel comfortable. He'd even instructed his staff to do all they could to assist him in learning the ropes!

During the first week Harry had pictured Tara, George and Needles going spare because he was missing. But around the time he realised this wasn't a straightforward kidnapping, it dawned on him someone must be impersonating him.

Over the years, in prison and in the club, he'd heard the outlines of hundreds of plots and blags. In one particular case he remembered a couple of guys telling him how they held a businessman prisoner, tortured the man to give them personal details of his wife and office staff then, posing as him, rang his secretary and told her he'd gone to America on business. Their idea was to empty his bank accounts and they'd come close to doing so before they got caught. At the time Harry had been impressed with their cunning. The only reason their plan backfired was because the victim failed to tell them he had a pet name for his wife and she got suspicious.

Once again Wainwright was in the picture. He was an actor, noted for his mimicry, he could easily be calling George, Tara and the boys at the club, telling them some pack of lies to stop them from calling in the law.

Harry had inadvertently landed himself right into this. Most of his staff knew Duke was taking over, with the right kind of phone call they'd just carry on as if Harry was there. As long as Duke let Tony bank the money, the staff got paid and everything ran smoothly, why should they think anything was wrong?

But the worst thing of all was facing how this would end. When the job was done, Harry's body would doubtless be found and with it enough evidence to convince the police he was the Mr Big behind it all. And who would believe that his loyal and trusted mates, Needles and Tony, weren't in on it too?

The key turning in the lock made him stop running and look round.

'OK, Harry.' Micky smiled at him as he sat hunched on the bed. 'Slop out time!'

This had become the high spot of the day. Not only because it freed his cell from the stink of the bucket, but there was a small shaft above the the toilet down which fresh air blew. There was no hot water, but it was good to splash cold on his face.

Harry picked up the bucket and carried it out, his eyes immediately going to the door beyond to check if it was locked.

'I wouldn't dare forget,' Micky said behind him. 'Joe'd chop off my dick!'

Harry tipped the contents down the pan, filled up the bucket with water and swilled it around.

'You must realise they're going to kill me.' He spoke softly, not knowing if there was anyone outside.

Micky stood just outside the lavatory. The fact he didn't even glance towards the door suggested there was no-one there.

'Chances are they'll kill you too!' Harry said blithely. 'Even if they make out it was me that did the drug-running, I couldn't have done it alone, could I? I reckon you three guys are for the chop.'

He slammed the door shut between them, leaving Micky to think that one through.

The lavatory gave him an indication of the nature of his prison. Like his windowless dungeon, both were built from brick, whitewashed over. The tiny window, which was actually more like a ventilator, showed that the walls were over a foot thick and they were way down below ground level. By standing on the toilet and pressing his face up against the two slats of wood, Harry could see a tiny patch of sky and leaves at the end of the shaft. He could hear nothing, not the faintest sound of traffic or voices. There could be no escape this way. The shaft was less than nine inches across and possibly six feet long, but it was heaven to see a speck of blue sky, to breathe in fresh, earth-smelling air even for just a few moments.

He took his time washing. It was a matter of pride. Even if he would be locked up alone for most of the next twenty-four hours, he wasn't prepared to turn into an animal. He wished they'd give him a razor and some shampoo. There was no mirror to see what he looked like, but the beard itched like crazy and his hair was stuck to his head with grease.

Cleaning his teeth set off the toothache again. He wondered if it would get to the stage when he could pull it out himself like they did on survival films.

Micky was sitting on a box outside when Harry opened the door, staring blankly at the wall.

The space between the inner and outer door was around eight feet square, whitewashed, with one dim light stuck on the wall. Even in the murky light Micky looked fresh and healthy, big tanned biceps straining the sleeves of his white T-shirt, his jeans straight off the ironing board.

'Been home to Mum for the night?' Harry asked. 'You couldn't get her to dig something out for me, could you?'

'Yeah, I did go home,' Micky admitted, getting up from his box and moving towards the doorway of the cell. 'Mind you, getting a good feed and your things washed ain't worth the earache she gives me.'

Harry followed Micky in. He put his bucket down, then picked up the sweaty nylon shirt and slipped it on, anxious to do nothing that would make Micky clam up.

'She's sussed you're up to no good, then?'

'Mums do, don't they?' He looked up at Harry plaintively. His gentle brown eyes were anxious. 'I wish I could do something that would make her proud.'

Harry half smiled. 'I can think of something,' he said softly.

'What's that?' Micky didn't even have much curiosity in his voice. He smoothed back his dark brown hair from his face, his eyes meeting Harry's.

'You could help me get away. Blow the thing wide open. I'll tell the police and your mum it was your doing, then you can come and work for me.'

'I'd be dead meat.' Micky sniffed. 'Besides, from what Joe says about you, you ain't that much better than him.'

'Don't tell me you can't judge character better than that.' Harry grinned. 'You must know that man's a nutter. Something's wound him up like a spring and once that goes, God help us all. Look, I'm not suggesting you go to the old Bill, just ring up a friend of mine

597

and say where I am. I'll never let on it was you.'

He didn't for one moment think Micky would agree, how could he without being strung up himself by these goons? But he might just get something out of him.

'Fuck off, Harry. I can't do that and you know it.' Micky looked nervously over his shoulder. 'There's big money riding on this horse. It ain't just us here minding you. Know what I mean?'

'OK, Micky.' Harry put one hand on his shoulder and squeezed it. 'I ain't going to fall out with you over this. But just think about your own position. Remember what I said about Joe. He's a grenade, and one day someone's gonna pull the pin!'

Harry lay on his bed after Micky had brought him his lunch. Corned beef and pickle sandwiches today, the sliced bread going a bit stale. That was it now until about seven. He'd read yesterday's paper but he was saving the crossword till later.

He studied the ceiling. It wasn't so much a ceiling really, more like a cave, solid brick cemented together, no sharp edges where walls meet ceiling, just graceful curves. He tried to recall every escape story he'd ever read, in the hope he might get a bright idea.

He couldn't tunnel, he had no tools. There was no window, no suitable tool to bang his guard on the head. He could use his fists, but what was the point? A second man always locked the outside door and didn't open it again till he was locked in.

Of course he'd thought of taking the guard hostage, holding him in a throat lock and ordering the next man to open up. But he got the feeling none of the men cared about each other enough for that to work. They'd probably just shrug their shoulders and tell him to keep the body in with him!

He'd already tried to pretend he was having an acute asthma attack, he did the laboured breath and

598

rattling noises very well, but Carl didn't go for it. He just said it must be the feathers in the pillow, removed it and went out, locking the door behind him.

Swinging his legs down on to the stone floor he went back to running on the spot.

What could that phoney Harry have said to George and Tara to stop them worrying? Or had he told them something which made them so sick with fright they didn't dare do anything? That was the worst thing of all, the possibility they both believed he'd let them down again!

Day after day in here he had nothing to do but list the mistakes he'd made in life, and the one he regretted most was hiding things from Tara. If he'd been upfront about everything, she wouldn't believe he was doing something bad now. He shouldn't have underestimated her intelligence.

He had been running for fifteen minutes when he heard noise – a clanking sound of metal on the stone floor, then feet going away again. It was only four o'clock, an unusual time for anyone to come.

He carried on running on the spot, maybe they were just storing something outside the outer door, but a few seconds later he heard the feet coming slowly down the stairs again. It took longer than usual for the second door to open, and he could hear the same clanking noise.

He stopped running, wiped the sweat off his forehead with the back of his hand and peered through the small hatch. Micky was just by the lavatory door, bending over something.

'What'cha got there, Micky?' Harry asked. 'My coffin?'

'It's Christmas time,' Micky replied, opening the door. 'Look what I've got for you.'

As the door swung in, Harry saw two large pails of steaming water and a tin bath on the floor. Micky had a towel draped over his shoulder.

The man showed no sign of agitation; he was unhurried, as if this was the only task of the day. Could that mean the others had gone out and left him alone? He couldn't remember hearing another man come down the stairs with him.

'Brace yourself!' Micky grinned childishly as he lifted the bucket out of the sink. 'You'd better kneel down in the bath, or I can't reach your head.'

The water was freezing, but it felt good. Harry wiped it out of his eyes and reached out for the towel.

'This feels like the Last Rites!' he said as he dried himself. 'You sure you ain't got a shroud in that bag?'

He saw an odd expression pass over Micky's face, tightening his features.

'I asked Joe if he was going to kill you.' His voice lowered, more from shame than the need for secrecy. 'He said he wasn't.'

Harry decided Micky was naive rather than lying through his teeth. He reached for the carrier bag.

'These are my clothes!' He turned to Micky in astonishment. Pants, socks, jeans – they were all his! A Fred Perry cream shirt, a pair of shoes and his favourite grey leather jacket. 'How did they get these?'

'I dunno.' Micky looked down at his feet. 'Joe come back with them last week. I didn't know they was yours. I thought he was being, well, nice.'

'Nice! That guy couldn't be nice if he was on his deathbed!' Harry exploded. He put on the clean underpants and reached for the shirt. 'You do know what this means, don't you?'

'I don't follow you.' Micky sounded like a small boy.

Harry grabbed his jeans. He could smell Persil on them and it made him think of Queenie. Even if they were going to kill him later, at least for now he felt comforted by his own things.

'Well, it wouldn't do to leave me dead here with you lot in someone else's clothes, would it? Or with four weeks' growth of beard. My father would soon point out that proved I'd been a prisoner. I suppose they went and packed a bag in my flat to make out I'd left the country?'

'I dunno anything.' Micky's voice shook but his eyes widened as if truth was finally dawning.

'No wonder my dad hasn't kicked up a stink,' Harry said. 'Who's posing as me on the phone, then?'

Micky turned away, his silence proving he knew the answer to that but had no intention of naming names.

Harry zipped up his jeans, and sat on the bed to put on his socks and shoes. 'Just tell me one thing,' he pleaded with Micky, casting his eyes down the man's jeans to see if there was a bulge somewhere which would be the other key. 'Is Duke the top man?' His hips were as slender as Harry's own, jeans well fitting, and there seemed to be nothing to mar the smooth line.

Micky shook his head. 'Joe calls him Lieutenant. That means there's someone above him, doesn't it?'

'Do you know who it is?'

'No.' Micky gave a glum sort of smile. 'They don't trust me with anything much.'

Harry felt too sick now to even try to grill Micky any longer. He wanted to lie down on his bed and just think about Tara, not anticipate his own death knowing he'd broken his number one rule, never trust anyone, when he let Duke learn so much about him.

'I'd better tip that water down the drain.' Micky went out to the bath, bending over to push it towards the toilet. 'I'll go and make you a cup of tea if you like, you look as if you need one.'

Harry watched idly as Micky bent to lift the bath enough for the water to flow out. His mind was blank until that moment, sapped by a feeling of utter dejection. But as his eyes fell to Micky's groin, he saw something long and thin jutting out, revealed by the angle his legs

602

were bent. His mind shot back into action.

'Let me help with that,' he said casually, getting up slowly so as not to alarm him. 'You ain't a bleedin valet!'

One glance confirmed that the keys for the inner door were still in the lock. He moved into the confined space behind Micky, then grabbed him by the throat. The bath clattered down, slopping water over their feet. His life depended on using his strength and there was no time to consider not hurting the man. He squeezed his windpipe almost to the point of strangulation, then pushed Micky back into the cell.

Micky put up a fight, he wriggled and flailed his arms, but he was too intent on getting Harry's fingers from his neck. Holding him with just one hand, Harry quickly slid his hand into his pocket, pulled out the key then pushed the other man to the floor.

Micky leaped up just as Harry got the door shut.

'Don't,' he shouted. 'They'll get you!'

Harry locked it, but looked back through the grille. Micky was rubbing his neck, his face bright red, and he was clearly stunned.

'I'm sorry, Micky,' he called softly. 'I feel a bastard doing this, but it's the quick or the dead I'm afraid!'

'You won't get away,' Micky called out. 'Joe's got a gun. He was cleaning it as I came down.'

Harry sensed in that second that Micky wanted to help him.

'Which is the best way out?' he asked.

'Turn right at the top of the stairs. Climb out the back window and go through the woods.'

'I'll stick up for you if you get nicked,' Harry called back. 'Give me a few minutes before you start hollering!'

There was a fraught moment as he opened the second door, and he half-expected to see Joe lying in wait, gun in hand. But there was no-one in the gloomy passage. He locked the door behind him. The passage

603

was longer than he expected, with several more doors. The smell of musty dampness was even stronger, and there was no light here, just a small beam from the hatch in the cell door and daylight coming down the stone stairs.

The air grew sweeter and fresher as he crept silently up the stairs, listening carefully for the other men. He felt drunk with it, wanting to fill his lungs to bursting point. He could hear a radio playing in the distance, but the only other sound was from birds outside.

The stairs led to a small passageway. It was panelled and he recognised the cedar smell he'd noticed the night he came here, but now it was mingled with a smell of fried food and gun oil.

He turned right. The passageway ended with a locked door, but just before that on the left was a big kitchen with long sash windows looking on to dense foliage.

At a glance he took in the order. A box of groceries on a work surface, five plates, five mugs, cutlery and pans all stacked up together by the deep white sink. The room had a dated 1920s look about it.

He could hear voices in the distance. One of the windows was open just a crack at the bottom. He closed the door behind him and gingerly drew up the sash. Wriggling out on to the sill was no problem. He gently pulled the window down behind him, hoping to fool them, then leaped eight or ten feet into shrubbery.

After the cold of the cellar it felt like jumping into the tropics. He was almost blinded by the bright light and the spot he'd landed in was thick with nettles. Fighting his way through bushes, he felt the ground sloping steeply upwards and it was only when he felt completely hidden in the shrubbery that he paused to look round behind him.

It wasn't an ancient house as he'd imagined, but a

country mansion built perhaps at the turn of the century in Georgian style. The most remarkable thing about it was that the house was virtually built into the hillside, the shrubbery wrapped round it as if in another couple of years it would completely engulf it.

Harry pressed on. The air felt like Champagne, his wet hair was drying fast in the warmth, shoes squelching from the soaking. The thick shrubs and brambles gave way to woods, the ground still sloping steeply upwards. He dodged behind the biggest tree and checked to see if anyone was following.

All he could see of the house now was a slice of dark green roof. The key to the cellar was still in his pocket, so even if they went down to check why Micky was taking so long they wouldn't get in immediately to free him.

'I hope they don't hurt him,' he whispered, then turned to fight his way on through undergrowth.

He knew exactly what he was going to do. The very first house he came to he would rush in and ask them to call the police. Then he'd ask the people if he could make a reverse charge call to Tara.

When he turned now he couldn't see the house at all, just trees and dense shrubbery. It was getting thicker now, and he had to go sideways and sometimes back to gain just a few yards. His delight at being free was marred now by fear. He had no idea how deep this wood was. He could be heading in entirely the wrong direction!

His breath was laboured, he seemed to be making more noise than a herd of elephants. Brambles caught at his jeans and slashed across his face, and again and again he tripped on fallen branches. But at last the trees were thinning and he heard the sound of a car ahead.

His excitement was so intense it was painful as he crashed forward. Finally he saw a glimpse of road. A wire fence topped with barbed wire was all that stood between him and freedom.

Crouching down by the fence he peered out both ways. It was a country lane, opposite an open field. To his left the road was straight, no houses, no shelter. To his right the road looked equally exposed, but there was a bend around fifty yards down and at that point a hedge started. Holding a trunk of a tree he jumped on to the barbed wire and leaped into the road.

It was pure joy to run, to feel wind on his face and freedom in his heart. Wind caught his hair, drying the last moisture from it, his legs were going like pistons, lungs filling to the point of bursting. As he approached the bend he could see tall chimneys in the distance. A lorry was coming up the slight hill, the slow speed and the noise of its engine made him dive into the ditch just below the hedge and he waited, trembling, as it passed.

The lorry chundered slowly towards him, scrunching its gears as it reached the brow of the hill, then moved on past him sending out a blast of exhaust fumes. Harry jumped up, but to his horror saw the green transit van. He froze.

Joe stood beside it with a sawn-off shotgun in his hands, a brown woolly hat over his bald head. Frank was between him and the house. A glance over his shoulder showed Carl with a small hand-gun.

The van must have come up behind him as he was running, it engine masked by the noise of the lorry. Harry swallowed hard. He had no chance; run anywhere and Joe would shoot.

'Come on, Harry,' Joe called out. 'You've had your outing, time to go home.'

Harry saw in his mind that dimly lit cellar, smelt the bucket and remembered just how long it took from the evening meal until breakfast.

He sprang away from the ditch, running towards

Frank at full tilt, hoping his unexpected movement would confuse the bloke.

'Stop!' he heard Joe yell. Frank was poised ahead to catch him, but Harry ran on. Behind him Carl was coming up. He must reach that house! He crashed past Frank, pushing him aside with every ounce of force left in him, on to freedom.

A shot cracked out, but he was concentrating on the house ahead, coming nearer by the second. He saw his feet flashing along, his hands clenched, arms moving like pistons. Then he felt the stab of pain.

Blood spurted out from somewhere, he saw it fly past him a split-second before the road came up to meet him.

Chapter 34

'Josh, please help me.' Tara clung to the telephone receiver, shaking with fright and cold. 'I'm in such a mess.'

'Mess?' he repeated sleepily. 'Tara! Is that you?'

She looked quickly round her. Apart from a lorry that had just drawn up by Swan Wharf the area was deserted.

'Yes, it's me. It's an emergency, can you come and get me? I'm soaking wet and hurt.'

'I don't understand. What's happened?'

'There isn't time to explain,' she gabbled. 'I'll hide in the little alley by the side of Harry's club. Can you bring an old blanket or something? I'm covered in stinking mud.'

'But . . .!'

'I've got to go before someone sees me.' She cut him off before he could finish his question. 'Please don't let me down, I'm desperate.'

'OK.' He sounded awake now. 'The alley by the side of the club. Should take around ten minutes unless the traffic's bad.'

'Thank you.' The word came out with a sob and she put the receiver down.

Back in the alley, crouched down behind a dustbin, she took stock of the damage. Her jeans, shoes and jumper were caked in the stinking muck, already drying in the wind. The sharp pain in her leg was subsiding to an ache but, now that help was at hand, shock was taking over, making her tremble from head to foot.

The oblong of sky above the alley was an ominous dark grey and in that moment she felt as if there was nothing left on earth to live for.

'Why?' she asked herself. 'Why can't I have a life like other people, where good things happen? I've lost my brother, my gran and now Harry. Is there any point in going on?'

But the pain inside was all for Harry. When she closed her eyes she could see his brilliant blue eyes, and feel the silkiness of his skin. How could she have even considered loving another man? He was in her heart, and she would give everything she had just to see him one last time.

Josh's car stopped at the end of the alley, the roof down. He didn't open the door but leaped over the top and ran to where she crouched, with a blanket tucked under his arm.

'Oh, Tara!' He recoiled in shock as he got close enough to smell her. 'What on earth is it?'

He was unshaven, his curly hair tangled as if he'd just jumped into his jeans and sweater. But no-one could have looked better to her.

'Seagull shit, stagnant water, the filth of centuries.' She tried to smile but it didn't happen.

'Take everything off,' Josh suggested. 'I won't look.' He stood with his back to her as she hastily stripped off to her underwear.

'That's better.' She breathed a sigh of relief as she wrapped the blanket round her like a cloak. 'It's just my hair, hands and face now.'

'Are you going to dump those clothes?' Josh turned back to her and looked at the fetid pile on the ground.

'I can't, they're my best jeans!' she said in horror. 'They'll wash!'

'I think there's a plastic bag in the boot.' Josh held his nose and took a step back. 'Won't be a minute.'

'Don't let it rain until we get home!' Josh looked up at the threatening sky as they tore through the deserted City streets with the hood still down. 'I love you dearly, Tara, but that smell is something else!'

'I think Harry's dead,' she blurted out. She couldn't say anything more as emotion overtook her. Great shuddering sobs welled up from inside, banishing all prospect of explanation.

'It's OK, baby,' he said soothingly. 'Let's get you back to my place. Once you've had a bath and got a cup of tea inside you we can talk it out.'

'We've got to call the police,' she said over and over again. 'They've killed Harry, that man Duke is an impostor.'

'You can tell me everything properly once you've calmed down,' Josh said evenly. 'Then I'll go down the nick and do what I can while you have a sleep.'

She had only been to his place a couple of times. It was a tall, thin townhouse in Jubilee Place, just off the King's Road. His garage was under the house, and Josh drove straight in through the open door.

'There now.' He turned and smiled at her. 'I'll just shut the doors and you can hop in.' He pointed out the door that led to his kitchen.

Tara lay right down under the bath water. Every bone in her body ached now and she could feel bruises in a dozen different places.

Josh's house was just like him, ostentatious, bold and colourful. The bathroom was like something from the Arabian Nights, with a huge sunken bath in the centre, fake marble pillars, and murals of wonderful gardens.

'Are you nearly ready?' Josh called out. 'I've put some clothes outside the door.'

He smiled as Tara joined him in the kitchen. She looked like a waif, with her wet, straight hair, an oversized shirt and baggy jeans dangling over her feet.

'Whose knickers are they?' she asked, eyes brimming with tears.

'A sample!' he retorted. 'We sold them at Christmas if you remember. Do you really think I'd give you another girl's underwear?'

Tara dropped her eyes, feeling foolish. Now he'd reminded her, they had sold red satin knickers, in heart-shaped boxes designed to hang on a tree.

The kitchen was bright and sunny, made brighter still by its yellow and white theme.

'You should eat,' Josh reproved her as she pushed the scrambled eggs away, barely touched.

'I can't,' she said. 'I just keep thinking about Harry.'

'Come on, tell me about what happened.' Josh took away her plate and started eating it himself. 'Pour yourself another cup of tea, then start from the beginning.'

She went through getting into the club and hiding, the long wait, then the search after everyone had gone.

'Then I found his wallet and passport with a gun.' She caught hold of his arm, her face contorted with grief. 'I just know he's dead, Josh. I had to get out of there and the only way was out of the top window. It was awful.'

Josh came round the table and knelt in front of her, wiping her eyes.

'Why did you go there? It was so silly,' he said gently. 'You could have been killed yourself climbing down from that roof, and suppose you'd set off the burglar alarm?'

'You don't believe he's dead, do you?' Tara turned big, sorrowful eyes on him.

Josh shook his head. 'You'll hate me if I tell you what I really think,' he said.

'No I won't! Tell me.'

He looked reluctant, but Tara insisted.

'I think he's into something big.' Josh shrugged his shoulders. 'It's probably drugs. I reckon he's just gambled on one big job that will set him up for life.'

'He wouldn't do that,' she cried. 'He promised me he was over all that. Someone has kidnapped him and now they've killed him!'

'Oh, Tara.' Josh took her hands and gently rubbed them in his. 'He's rung people, he's been in and out of his flat. I know it's painful for you to think he's less than perfect but he's just like all of us, lured by easy money.'

'But his wallet and passport!'

'He's been back to the club and left them there,' said Josh. 'Maybe he's even got a forged passport! You need a body before you can say someone's murdered, and as I see it we haven't got one piece of evidence to suggest anything's happened to him.'

'But I can't just sit and wait,' she cried out angrily. 'I have to know what's happened.'

'OK.' Josh got up, spread his hands wide in a gesture of giving in. 'I go down the nick and say Harry Collins has gone missing. They ask me how I know. I say his girl says he hasn't phoned her.'

'You're taking the mickey!' she said angrily. 'I heard Duke talking yesterday afternoon and he said something about a signal on Friday, about training and men being cooped up. Don't you think that's suspicious?'

'I'm not taking the mickey.' He put his hand on her head and ruffled her damp hair. 'I'm only trying to show you how they'll see this. What you heard could be something quite innocent. The police will go steaming into the club, just because they hope something has happened to him. But what will they find? The staff will tell them he's phoned several times, been back to his flat. What are they going to think, darling?' He looked quizzically at her.

'That Harry's avoiding me.' Her eyes dropped from his in utter dejection. 'And what you're trying to say is that, if I go making waves, I might blow the whole thing up.'

'I think that's it in a nutshell.' Josh rubbed his chin thoughtfully. 'Well, I've got to get ready for work, darling. Have a shave and stuff. Why don't you get into my bed and have a snooze?'

Tara nodded, too exhausted for more argument. 'I'll just get my things out of your car and put them in a bucket of water to soak.' She got up and walked towards the garage door.

'The utility room's the other door,' Josh called as he went into the bathroom. 'You'll find a bucket there. I'll put them all in the washing machine later if you just rinse out the worst.'

The smell made her gag as she lifted her clothes out of the car. She dropped them to the floor hastily and went off to get a bucket of water. Sweater first, then her plimsolls and the canvas bag. Finally her jeans, but just as she was about to put them in, too, she remembered the list of telephone numbers in the pocket. She tossed the damp folded paper on to the front seat of the car then shoved the stinking jeans into the soapy water.

Tara came back out of the utility room a few minutes later. She'd sluiced the clothes through and left them to soak in clean water. As she leaned over the front seat to retrieve the list of numbers, she noticed a small piece of paper tucked down the back of the seat.

It was just a parking ticket, the sort you got in any car-park. It must have blown off the dashboard and lodged there. But it jolted her because it was like the one she'd found in Harry's office. She bent down to examine it, fully expecting it to be from Chelsea municipal car-park, but it wasn't.

A shudder ran down her spine. She closed her eyes and then looked again, sure she'd made a mistake. But it was no mistake. The ticket said Lympne airport. Fear rushed through her veins like a shot of poison. Her mouth went dry and her legs started shaking uncontrollably.

'You're taking your time,' Josh called out. 'Or have you dropped off out there?'

Anger pushed back the fear, and she opened her mouth to roar out some abuse, but stifled it in the nick of time. There might be a good explanation, but she needed time to think this thing through. With trembling hands she picked up the ticket, grabbed the folded list from the boot and shoved them both into her pocket.

'Is there something the matter?' Josh asked as she came back in. He was standing at the sink, washing the breakfast things, singularly unconcerned.

She was aware she was still shaking; she was clammy with sweat, suspicion ate at her innards.

'No, nothing.' She shook her head. 'Just exhausted.'

'Off you go to bed then.' He patted her bottom towards his room. 'We'll talk when I get home later. Maybe you should go home for a bit, have a holiday. Ring your mum if you want to.'

Tara lay in Josh's big bed listening to him getting ready in the bathroom next door. He was in a hurry to get out, or was that her imagination?

His bedroom was done up like a high-class brothel, with dark red wallpaper, a mirror on the ceiling and huge erotic Indian paintings. She hadn't been a bit surprised the first time she saw it, it was as characteristic of him as his gold medallion. But now, as daylight came in the windows, it took on a decadent, kinky note that made her unease even worse.

Could he be involved? What were the odds on finding two tickets for the same obscure place within hours of one another? But what motive could Josh have? Nothing sprang to mind other than simple jealousy, but surely a man like Josh, with the world at his feet, couldn't feel jealous of Harry?

'I wish I could stay with you.' Josh came into the bedroom and smiled down at her. 'But it's an important meeting, I'm afraid. Help yourself to anything. I'll be home around five-thirty.'

'Thank you for everything.' She deliberately let her eyelids droop so she couldn't be expected to talk more.

'Sleep tight,' he said and left, shutting the door behind him.

Sleep was the last thing on her mind. She wanted to believe there was a simple explanation to that ticket, yet in her heart she knew there wasn't. What a fool she'd been, blurting everything out to him. Maybe it was even things she'd said to Josh in the past that had helped this plot along?

Tara waited till his car left the garage, then she sat up and pulled out the parking tickets. They were identical, only the dates were different. Tara counted back on her fingers.

'Last Friday,' she said thoughtfully. 'He said he was going to Birmingham for the day. So where is this place?'

Wearing only Josh's shirt she padded into his lounge and looked along the bookshelves. Right at the bottom she found a road map.

'Lympne, Kent,' Tara muttered. '4 D, page 29.'

There it was, a tiny little place which seemed to have no significant feature other than its airport, about four or five miles from Hythe, nine or ten from Folkestone, around a mile from the coast. Yet as Tara stared at the map, the place name and its position seemed strangely familiar. Had someone told her something about this village?

Why would both Duke and Josh use an obscure airport? If they were catching a plane to France or Germany it would take longer to drive there than the actual flight. Could they be picking something up from there?

But if there was an innocent explanation, why had Josh said he was going to Birmingham?

She sat on the settee for a moment, the map on her knees. Then she went over to Josh's desk, hoping it might shed some light on the question. It was a Chinese lacquered one and she'd been with him when he bought it in Chelsea antiques market. It was a year ago and she'd been staggered to think anyone would spend eight hundred pounds on a whim. Lifting down the writing flap, she began to search it.

The first thing she found was a small bag of white powder, tucked in with a lump of cannabis. She had no idea whether it was heroin or cocaine, and right now she didn't care. A whole clump of letters were held together with a bulldog clip. At first she put them to one side, but out of the corner of her eye she saw 'Final Notice' stamped on the top one.

Taking the bundle over to the settee, she flicked through them. Every one was a final demand, some for small amounts from mills and knitwear companies, but there was a demand from the Inland Revenue for eight thousand pounds, another for the rates of another two thousand, and the mortgage on this house was almost a year in arrears, with the threat of repossession.

'So you're up to your ears in debt,' she whispered. 'How on earth were you intending to pay for the alterations to the shop?'

She put the papers back where she found them and continued her search. There was nothing else to interest her, certainly nothing to explain what he was doing in Kent last week.

Opening the doors on to the balcony she leaned her arms on the wrought iron and looked thoughtfully down into the garden below, wondering what to do next.

Josh said he rarely went out there, yet the initial effort he'd put into it by planting so many shrubs had paid off. They climbed the walls and drifted over one another, creating a beautiful jungle effect. A statue of a nude woman stood in one corner, a purple clematis clambering over her; even a little white wooden bench had been taken over by a clump of marguerites.

As she looked at the statue it seemed to be telling her something, but she didn't know what. Why would a statue have any significance? Wasn't she just tired and getting her thoughts jumbled up?

'Phone Mum,' she said wearily. 'Perhaps you'd better go home for a few days.'

Mum! It was as if a door flicked open in her mind. Her mother had told her a story about statues, but what was it?

Tara sat down on the settee, a cup of coffee beside her, and rang Greg's number. There was no reply so she tried the farm. It rang for some time before her mother answered, panting as if she'd been running.

'Is there something the matter?' she said immediately. 'Aren't you at work? This is a funny time to be calling.'

'I've got the day off, I'm feeling a bit poorly.' Tara already felt irritated. Why couldn't Amy just say what a lovely surprise it was instead of wondering how much it cost? 'I was just thinking I could do with a bit of a holiday, but I didn't want to come and get in your way.'

'Don't be ridiculous,' Amy snapped. 'You wouldn't get in the way.'

'Well, don't try to sound too welcoming,' Tara said indignantly. 'Perhaps I'd better ring off and try again another day?'

'I'm sorry.' Amy's voice changed immediately. 'I didn't mean it that way. It's just I seem to be on the go all the time at the moment. You know how the farm is

617

in the summer, so much more work, and what with the wedding plans –.'

'Well, maybe I could take some of the chores off your hands,' Tara said.

Suddenly she really wanted to be there, to put on a pair of shorts and a suntop, to be out weeding the garden or hoeing the vegetable patch.

'Is everything all right with Harry?'

'He's fine. We just aren't seeing much of each other nowadays,' Tara said airily. 'Josh is expanding in a different direction and he wants me to design for it. But I'll tell you all about that when I come down.'

'That sounds very exciting, darling.' Amy's voice rose in pleasure. 'But I'm sorry about Harry!'

'Just one of those things.' Tara forced herself to laugh lightly. 'By the way, Mum, did you ever tell me something about a statue?'

'A statue?' Amy sounded bewildered. 'What sort?'

'I don't know,' Tara said, feeling a little foolish. 'I just saw one in a garden and I got this feeling of *déjà vu*. It seemed to be connected in some way with you.'

Her mother was silent for a moment. 'There were statues in a garden once, a place your father took me to. I expect I told you about that.'

Goose-pimples came up on Tara's arms. 'Where was it?' she asked.

'Oh, in Kent somewhere.' Amy sounded a little impatient. 'Not far from Folkestone.'

'Was this place special or anything?' she asked, shreds of memory coming back thick and fast.

'It's the place you were conceived.' Amy's voice sounded slightly embarrassed. 'My seventeenth birthday. Bill took me there for the day out. We spent the day in the garden of a lovely old house. No-one lived there, you see, it was just lying empty.'

'What was it called, the house?' Tara asked. A sick feeling was growing inside her.

'Port Lympne,' Amy said. 'Your dad found it when he was stationed at Shorncliffe barracks near Folkestone. It was tucked away in woods, overlooking the marshes. It was his special place.'

It was all she could do not to bang the phone down right away and run for the door, though somehow she made general conversation, about the farm, the wedding and Greg. Yet all the time she was imagining that house in the woods and Harry lying there, dead.

'Look, Mum, I will come on down to see you if that's OK, but I'm going to stop off in Reading to see a friend first, so I'm not sure when I'll be with you. I'll phone when I'm on my way.'

Wording a note for Josh was difficult. She didn't want him checking up and she needed to reassure him she had come to terms with Harry walking out on her. She sat sucking on a pen for some time before she found the right words.

'Dearest Josh, I felt odd here so I got a taxi back to my place, then I'm going to make tracks for Somerset and home. I need time and space to think about what I'm going to do with the rest of my life and who I'm going to do it with. I can't thank you enough for helping me, for making me see the truth at last. I'll ring you in a few days when I've got my head together again. Love, Tara.'

It was almost two when the train left Charing Cross and it was raining heavily. She had got a taxi back to her flat, changed, then got the Tube to the station.

In jeans, a waterproof jacket, stout flat shoes and carrying a small rucksack, she could have passed for a hiker or student. There were only two other people in her carriage, both engrossed in magazines, and she wished she'd had the presence of mind to buy one too.

If only she knew the area! Now she was actually on

her way, questions kept popping up and she didn't have answers to any of them.

Her plan was weak. She'd take the train to Hythe, then a taxi out to the airport at Lympne. Back in her own flat she'd almost rung George or Needles and confided in them, but she knew they'd pour cold water on the idea. They might even pity her because she kept on pursuing Harry. So here she was, dressed up like a hiker with a Stanley knife, the only weapon she could find, tucked among her packet of sandwiches, apples and a drink.

'I'll just take a look,' she told herself as the blocks of flats and Victorian terraces turned to semi-detached houses with big gardens. 'If I see anything suspicious, if there's any sign of any of them, I'll go and call the police straight away.'

Hythe station looked so small and pretty in the rain, with polished brass on the waiting-room doors, and white painted tubs filled with geraniums and petunias.

'Can I get a taxi anywhere?' she asked the ticket collector. He was entirely in character with the station, in full uniform and highly polished boots.

'They don't come out much until the six o'clock,' he said as he clipped her ticket. 'You could try phoning the rank in the town but I don't expect there'll be anyone there just now. It's not that far to walk though, love. Just keep going down the road.'

He had already lost interest in her and was reaching out to grab the tickets from other passengers, touching his cap for certain regulars.

'I didn't want the town,' she said weakly. 'I wanted to get out to Lympne airport. Is that too far to walk?'

'Lympne airport?' A tall, thin man in a dark business suit who was just flashing his season ticket stopped short.

'Yes, do you know it?' Tara asked.

'I'm going that way myself. I can drop you off in Lympne village, if that's any help. It's only a bit further on from there.'

Tara thanked him profusely and followed him out to the car-park.

'Do you go by train to London every day?' she asked as he unlocked a green Morris Minor.

'Oh, yes.' He flung his briefcase into the back seat and got in. 'I'm a barrister, you see. I don't normally arrive home till sevenish but I was lucky today, my case was postponed.' He turned away from the town and up a winding road overhung with trees.

'Meeting someone at the airport?' he asked.

'Yes, an old friend.' She was frightened to elaborate as she had no way of knowing where the planes flew to and from there. 'Do you know Lympne well?'

'Not really. Mind you, there isn't much to know about.' He laughed heartily. 'Blink and you miss it! I don't live there, you see. I live in Hythe. But I'm picking my wife up from a friend's house.'

'My mother went there once when she was a girl. She said there was a lovely old house called Port Lympne. Is it still there?'

'Indeed it is. Though I've never seen the place myself, it's kind of buried in the woods. There's been talk of someone turning it into a wild-life park, that fellow Aspinall who owns a gambling club in London.'

'When's this going to happen? Does anyone live there now?'

'Oh, it's all in the planning stage, nothing definite yet.' He looked at her curiously. 'Don't think anyone's lived there for donkey's years, place must be in ruins. Why, thinking of dropping in?'

Tara laughed nervously. 'No, of course not. But like I say, my mother went there once and she's got romantic memories of it. If it was possible I'd take a photo for her. I expect it's all boarded up, though.'

They had turned on to a wider road which was signposted back to London, but after a couple of miles he turned off to the left.

'This is as far as I go,' he said, pulling over just before a T-junction. 'Just walk on up there and turn right. You'll see the airport straight away, there's a windsock outside. That old house is just about opposite it, though you can't see it from the road. There's an old gate, I believe, but mind how you go, it is private property.'

'Thank you so much for the lift.' She held out her hand to shake his. 'It was very kind of you.'

A pub overlooked the junction, but once Tara was past that, she paused. Ahead there was just one lone cottage to her left, the airport with its windsock to her right. It was small; one Dan Air plane and around five or six small ones were out on the runway.

Butterflies started to flutter again in her stomach. It was very open and very isolated. Since she had turned into this road only two cars had passed and it wasn't even five o'clock yet.

If only it wasn't raining. In London you hardly noticed rain, you just wore your usual clothes and stuck up an umbrella. Here it seemed to soak so quickly. The bottoms of her jeans were wet already and the hood of her coat obscured her vision on either side.

The cottage had a narrow lane beside it. Tara turned into it, hoping it might give her a glimpse of the house. Some springer spaniels were in the yard by the side and they opened up a barrage of barking. Tara walked on. To her right were impenetrable-looking woods. There was a barbed wire fence but in places it was broken down entirely.

The road turned slightly and Tara stood for a moment or two looking at the view. She had a strange feeling of *déjà vu* again. The rain looked like a grey mist over the greeny-grey fields, the few trees growing down on the marsh looked twisted and stunted by the wind. It was a wild, lonely place but for some inexplicable reason she felt at one with it.

The woods were thinner now and through them she could see what must be the grounds of Port Lympne – a high privet hedge, a tennis court overgrown with weeds and wild flowers. There were so many different trees, a rose garden and a wisteria-covered pergola. But she couldn't see the house. It had to be further back, against the woods. The gardens were built in a series of terraces and she was sure all she was seeing here were the lower ones.

Looking all around to check no-one was watching, she slipped through a hole in the fence and into the woods. Rain dripped down her face, finding its way under her anorak into her jumper. Leaves slapped at her, spraying her with more water, but she carried on, stepping gingerly through the undergrowth.

The woods gave way to a rhododendron walk; one moment she was knee-deep in ferns and weeds, the next on a shingle pathway with bushes towering over her head. But at last she could see the old house. All the way down on the train she'd had a mental picture of an ancient house tumbling into decay, but Port Lympne was neither so old nor so neglected. Its creamy stone was clean, windows intact and the sweeping gravel drive leading to the pillared porch and front door looked almost weed-free.

Tara understood exactly why her father liked this place, she could feel herself being bewitched by it. Her eyes swept over the grounds, taking it all in. A swimming pool, empty of course, with weeds growing out the sides, a rose garden, and graceful urns and statues ornamenting the steps down on to the lower terraces. Once it must have required a whole team of gardeners to keep it in shape, and obviously one at least had been kept on to cut the hedges and trim the grass.

There was no sign of people staying here, at least there were no cars left on that gravel drive. Until now Tara hadn't thought about being cautious. She had a vague plan in her head that if anyone stopped her she would pretend to be a hiker who'd strayed in by mistake. Reason told her that if this was indeed where Duke and his men had brought Harry, the headquarters from where they were organising crime, they could kill her, too, just for being there.

'I need to get closer,' she whispered to herself. In front of her a four-foot hedge stretched down to the drive. She ducked down behind it, following it to the end.

The hedge ended close to a semi-circular lawn flanked by privet and statues. Hidden between the hedge and the surrounding wall of the terrace, Tara peered at the house again.

There was no sign of anyone, and no sound apart from the drip of rain and the occasional rustle of leaves. It was dry where she crouched. Tara took a sandwich out of her bag and ate it while she thought about what to do next.

Maybe openness was the best idea! Just breeze up there, peer into windows and, if anyone came, front it out. Even if Josh was in on it and had told Duke about her, this place hadn't been mentioned. As she slipped out of her hiding place and back on to the proper path her heart was pounding, her mouth dry. The gravel drive was the worst part, the crunching noise would surely wake even the dead. She crossed it swiftly and walked closer to the house where the path was smoother.

There was nothing in the downstairs rooms she peered into, beautiful, graceful rooms still in good decorative order. The front door looked as if it hadn't been opened in years. She went right round to the back until her way was blocked by bushes but, though there was a door there, it was locked. Despondently she walked back around the front and down the far side, feeling she'd made a mistake and it was time she found her way back to the station.

But as she reached the bushes growing right up to the back of the house she saw broken branches, a few dog-ends on the ground and a smooth path beaten by feet. Her heart began to pound again. She looked at her watch. It was half-past six. As she moved further round it was clear that many people had come and gone this way, and the feet marks ended at the fire escape.

'Go on,' she urged herself. 'You can't walk away now!'

She took off her rucksack and stood for a moment staring around her, the light drizzle dripping from the hood of her coat. The air was heavy with the scent of wet soil, privet and decaying vegetation, a lone bird chirruped somewhere in the distance.

Taking a deep breath she rummaged in her bag for the Stanley knife and slipped it into her jeans pocket. It made her feel tougher, and she folded the bag over and pushed it out of sight under a bush.

She put her first foot on the rusting stairs, then the second, but she was so frightened she felt faint. 'Harry might be in there,' she said to herself. 'Go on, just have a quick look. If there was anyone around they'd have spotted you by now.'

Steeling herself she walked on up the stairs. She could see a sash window open just a crack and she tried to think of nothing more. The window glided up as if it had been oiled. The room was empty and the door shut. She climbed in and closed the window behind her.

Opening the door of the room was a moment of pure terror. But no hand came down on her, no crow-bar on her neck or cobweb on her face as she walked out into the landing. It was light and airy here, some of the light coming from a long window over the staircase to her left, more from the room opposite.

This room was being camped in. Three brown sleeping bags lay on the floor, next to a box full of magazines, a primus stove and a plastic washing-up bowl with some clean plates in it.

Tara moved quickly. She was certain they were out, they had to be, and she must get away before they returned. A bathroom had shaving stuff on the sink, the lavatory was filthy and a bottle of aspirin sat on the windowsill. She felt more confident going downstairs as she knew they weren't in any of the front rooms. The kitchen was the only room in use here, and even that was tidy.

'Very military,' Tara murmured, seeing a box of food carefully packed, presumably ready to be lifted up at a moment's notice.

She smelled the cellar before she even saw the steps leading down to it, an earthy, musty smell, and as she moved nearer she felt the chill.

Her courage left her as she looked down into the darkness. Her mouth was so dry she could barely swallow. Her heartbeat seemed to be in her ears, and her legs were so tense she wasn't sure she could even make it down there. The steps were almost slimy, the rail under her hand rusting and cold to the touch. She longed to turn back and run, but slowly she took one step after another. But at the bottom she could see a chink of light, the clear line of a door and a small grille in the middle.

As she crept closer she heard a groan. Not the loud sound of someone trying to make themself heard, just an involuntary gasp of pain. Instinct told her it was Harry. She ran forward, exultation banishing her fear. Her hands scrabbled to find a handle on the door, but it was locked.

'Harry!' she called out, not caring if anyone heard now. 'Harry, is it you?'

Straining her ears she put her face right up to the small grille, and called again. There was just enough light to make out a second door, with an identical grille. The lamp was in this inner room and presumably Harry, too.

'Tara!' His voice was faint, but it was him. 'Tara, are you really here?'

'I'm here at this door, but it's locked,' she called. 'I'll have to go out and get the police.'

Suddenly she saw his head illuminated in the grille.

'Get out now!' he called out, his voice intensely fierce. 'If they catch you they'll kill you, that's what they intend to do with me. Run for it! NOW!'

Chapter 35

'How are you feeling, darling?' Josh called as he approached the bedroom door, kicking it open with his foot because his hands were full of roses, chocolates, and a Josh carrier bag with a selection of trousers and tops. His smile faded when he saw the carefully made bed.

'Shit!' he exploded. 'Where the hell's she gone now?' Dumping the parcels on the bed he went quickly into the lounge. A note was propped up on the coffee table; he read it quickly, then threw it down in anger.

It was half-past one. He'd spent the morning in frantic haste just so he could get back quickly. He'd even picked up some travel brochures he was so confident she would soon be his. Tonight he'd planned to cook her a good meal, then tempt her into selecting a holiday with him for after her mother's wedding. But now she'd run off, leaving that irritating fawning note.

A phone call to her flat confirmed she'd already left there, too. Odd that someone so distraught and exhausted should so suddenly pull herself together. Unless, of course, she'd tumbled he was involved?

The thought of it made him tremble. Retracing his steps mentally he tried to recall everything that had happened from the moment he picked her up this morning at the club.

'She wouldn't have told me all that if she knew I was

in on it,' he said aloud. Of course she couldn't know. She would have phoned someone else to pick her up, or even the police. 'Was it because I didn't want to go to the police?' He frowned.

But she was all right about everything then, she seemed resigned. The only time she seemed a bit odd was when she came out of the garage. What was out there? Josh jumped up and ran down to the stairs to look. A stringent search revealed nothing. He couldn't think of one item he had ever had that would lead her to suspect him. Besides, why would she leave him such a warm letter?

Half appeased Josh went back upstairs and read the letter again, then picked up the phone.

'Hullo, Mrs Manning,' he said as Amy answered. 'It's me, Josh. How are you?' He made small talk for some time, asking her if she needed anything for the wedding and what she and Greg would like for a present.

'Oh, I don't know.' Amy giggled as if embarrassed. 'People said we should have a list, but that seems awful to me.'

He agreed he would give her a surprise, then brought the subject round to Tara.

'She's been a bit fraught lately,' he said. 'That's part of the reason I suggested she came home to you for a short break. Did she tell you about the new shop?'

'In passing, she said she'd tell me everything when she got here. I'm not sure when that will be, she's stopping off at a friend's in Reading,' Amy replied.

'Do you know this friend's name or address?' Josh asked. 'It's just there's something urgent I need to ask Tara about.'

'No, I don't.' Amy sounded thoughtful. 'I don't remember her speaking of anyone in Reading before. I was going to ask her who it was but she was a bit touchy with me and I didn't like to. Is that how you found her?'

'It's this Harry business, I think.' Josh lowered his voice in a confidential manner. 'I think she suspects everything and everyone of intrigue.'

'I don't understand.' Amy bristled a little and Josh smiled to himself.

'Oh, dear, I wish I hadn't said anything now.' Josh made himself sound reticent at revealing anything more, but he gave her the bare bones of Harry's disappearance and the fact he hadn't contacted Tara. 'I shouldn't really be telling you this, she wouldn't like it. I expect she'll tell you anyway when she gets there.'

'It doesn't sound like Harry's way, though,' Amy said. 'I tend to agree with Tara that it's a bit odd.'

'Talking of odd things,' Josh was getting bored with this conversation and needed to bring it to a close, 'did Tara speak of anything else? I mean, if I'm to track down this friend in Reading I need the old brain cells jogged.'

'Not really, she wasn't on the line long,' Amy replied. 'She asked me about a place her dad and I went to once, that was all.'

'What place was that?' Josh said casually. 'Somewhere en route to home?'

'Oh, no, it's in Kent,' Amy said. 'A little place called Lympne.'

Josh sat staring into space for some minutes after he'd put the phone down. Sheer panic was tearing at his insides and he didn't know what to do. How had Tara discovered the name of the village? In fact, how on earth did Amy, who'd hardly been out of Somerset in umpteen years, know that particular village in Kent? A pound to a penny that was where Tara was heading. But why? What sparked her off?

It had been bad enough telling Duke this morning about her getting in the club and searching round, but to admit she was hot on Harry's trail – that was something else!

'Never let sentiment cloud your judgment,' Josh muttered. That was his father's motto and it covered hiring and firing, lending and borrowing money.

Well, he'd misjudged Tara in this. He thought she was well on the way to forgetting Harry bloody Collins for good. He'd always seen her as a materialistic girl who would plump in the end for the guy who could give her the most. It seemed he was wrong!

'Duke, there's a fly in the ointment,' Josh said softly into the receiver.

He bitterly regretted the day he hired Joe Spikes to mind Ginger. Without him he would never have met Duke, never been tempted to take this path. The man was more reptile than human, he sucked people into his plans, and once in there was no escape.

'The girl's found out about Lympne and I suspect she's on her way there now. What can we do?'

The momentary silence frightened Josh more than anything. He knew Duke was capable of killing anyone who got in his way.

'You're an arsehole, Josh.' Duke let out his breath in one fierce stream. 'You said you could distract her from Collins.'

'I underestimated her.'

'Well, I hope you don't underestimate me, Josh. When I tell you I don't allow people to get in my way, you do understand what I mean?'

Josh's bowels turned to water.

'You can't have it both ways.' Duke's voice had a steely edge. 'You brought this on yourself and I'm not kissing goodbye to two million for some little tart.'

Josh sat in his lounge, head in hands. However he looked at it, he was in deep trouble.

Tara wasn't the only person to tell him he needed to look more closely at his business; his accountant had been telling him the same thing for over a year. Now he had to choose between the girl who was the linchpin

631

of his company, or enough money to re-float himself. But whichever one he chose, he would lose.

If he let Duke go ahead and deal with Tara in his way, he'd have the money he needed. He could pay off his debts, keep his house, his car, his warehouse. Maybe he could find another designer as good as her.

But at what price?

'Run now,' Harry urged Tara through the grille. 'I overheard them a while ago, they were talking about doing a recce to look for someone. They must know you're here. Go up through the woods at the back of the house, but watch out when you come to the road.'

'Just tell me, Harry, were you in on this?' Tara asked.

'Of course I wasn't,' he called back. 'Need you ask? All I wanted was to sell the club and leave London with you. But go now, before they catch you!'

'I'll call the police,' she reassured him. 'You won't be here long.'

'Tell them the drug pick-up is at first light tomorrow,' Harry said faintly. 'And tell them I'll need an ambulance. I've been shot in the leg.'

'Does it hurt?'

'Tara, go!' he exploded. 'I love you, babe, but you don't understand how mean they are. Run for it!'

His voice impressed upon her the seriousness of her situation. Without another word she turned and fled, up the cellar stairs, up to the first floor and out of the window to the fire escape. There was no time to listen for car engines, for voices or even feet on the gravel. Instead she jumped down the stairs two at a time and at the bottom threw herself into the bushes, then fought her way through the brambles and undergrowth.

It was hard going. Branches snapped back in her face, brambles snatched at her clothes and she tripped a dozen times, but finally she saw snippets of sky between the trees and knew she was close to the road.

Such a relief! The worst was over now. Soon the police would arrive, Harry would be taken to hospital and she could sleep at last. As she came up to the wire fence she almost shouted with glee. She had been right all along, Harry wasn't a villain and he did love her.

No-one was coming as she climbed over the fence. Running along to the airport on her right was the obvious choice; it meant people, phones and safety.

The dark green Morris Oxford was parked just a few yards before the airport entrance. Two men sat inside, heads close together as if consulting a map.

'Excuse me, can you tell me if this road leads to Ashford?' one of the men called out just as she'd passed them.

Tara stopped and turned. The man was out of his car, just one step behind her.

'I'm sorry, I don't – ' She didn't even get the last word out. She saw him lift his arm, and as she tried to run she felt a blow on the back of her neck.

The sensation was a bit like coming round from gas at the dentist's. A tunnel of darkness was all around her, but a chink of light shone in the centre and she was moving towards it. There was a roaring sound in her ears, a terrible pain which prevented her from opening her eyes, and she felt sick.

'There isn't anywhere else to put her,' a man was saying. 'Besides, they might as well spend the last few hours together.'

It was enough to jolt her memory. She could tell by the distinctive smell of wood that she was back in Port Lympne, but she had no recollection of how she got there.

'How did she find out about this place?' The man's voice was very deep and strangely familiar. It sounded as if he might be leaning over her, studying her. She could smell tobacco and engine oil.

'Dunno. Duke didn't say, just said she was a looker with golden hair and to nab her. We was only just in time. If she'd gone the other way . . . !'

Her wrists were bound, so were her feet, but the pain in her neck dominated everything.

'I don't like this, not women.' This was a younger, anxious voice.

'Neither do I, Micky. But just remind yourself what prison's like and all the dough we've got coming. You'll find you can live with it.'

Hands grabbed her shoulders and ankles and Tara bucked and screamed, her eyes flying open. The man holding her ankles had shoulder-length curly brown hair and a smooth, almost pretty face. He smiled apologetically and caught hold of her legs more firmly.

'Calm down,' he said. 'We're only taking you down to Harry.'

She bucked again, this time to see the other man holding her shoulders. He was older, with a hideous scar on his right cheek which puckered his lips into a sneer, and he was completely bald.

'Don't do this,' she gabbled. 'I left messages all round town about where I've gone. It's only a matter of time before the police get here.'

The bald man laughed, and she felt again that strange *déjà vu*.

'Think we came in on the last banana boat?' he jeered. 'You never got to the phone, remember?'

The two men moved quickly then, out of the hall where she'd been lying, along a passage and down the stone stairs to the cellar. She wriggled and screamed abuse at them, but they ignored her.

'You bastards,' she shouted. 'You won't get away with this. I've told people what's going on. You'll be sorry.' Yet as crazy as it was, she was glad she was going in with Harry. If they both had to die, at least they'd have the comfort of one another.

'You can scream all you like down here, Goldilocks, no-one will hear you,' the bald man sneered.

The young man dropped her feet as he opened the first door, but the bald man held her back tight to his chest, then shuffled her forward while the man he called Micky locked it behind them. Then the second door opened, light flooded out into the dark chamber and she saw Harry hobbling towards her.

'There you go, a playmate for you.' The bald man pushed her forward into Harry's arms. 'See you later!'

The door clanked shut behind them, the key turned in the lock, but Tara was only aware of Harry's face.

He was thinner, his skin looked sallow, his eyes burned too brightly. One leg of his jeans had been slashed to the knee; she could see a blood-stained bandage beneath.

'Your leg!' she gasped. 'How bad is it?'

'A whole lot better now you're here.' He smiled, but his eyes told her he would give his life for her to be safe a hundred miles away.

'I let you down,' she cried. 'I couldn't get to the phone quick enough. They were waiting for me in a car.'

'You were so brave.' He held her face, kissing her eyes, her nose, her cheeks and finally her mouth.

'Foolish.' She moved her head from his. 'I should have followed my instincts and got the police in the first place. I don't understand how they knew I'd be here. What are we going to do?'

'I'm going to untie you.' Harry's voice was gentle, his fingers running down her face and neck in a soothing gesture. 'We can't fight anything in here, Tara, but if we can stay calm, and compare the information we have, we may be able to figure out something.' His composure was comforting, and she found herself smiling down at him as he bent to untie her.

'There's a Stanley knife in my pocket,' she said when

she saw he was finding it hard to untie the rope. 'Will that help?'

The look of joy that flashed across his face made her forget the seriousness of their situation for a moment. 'You've got a Stanley knife?'

She wriggled her hips. 'In the side pocket. That is, unless they found it.'

Harry's hands felt her side and he looked up at her, his bright blue eyes almost worshipping her.

'I can fight them with this,' he whispered. 'It gives us a chance, even if only a slim one.'

He thought he'd died and gone to heaven when Tara called through that grille. He counted every second after she left, imagining her fighting her way through the bushes and finally coming to the road. His faith in her was so strong he almost heard police sirens and the pain in his leg vanished. But then he heard the screaming out on the stairs and once again he was plunged back into despair. Now it was far worse, not just his own life at risk, but hers too.

The rope came off and she watched while he cut a short length from it.

'Another weapon.' He grinned, flexing it between his fists. 'We're getting an arsenal together!'

'Could you strangle someone?'

'Once I'd have said no.' Harry smiled. 'But it's dog eat dog now.'

He put the knife and rope down and took her wrists, rubbing them between his fingers.

'Poor Tara.' His eyes were full of sorrow. 'You must have been through hell.'

Her face was covered in tiny scratches, still more on her hands, her jeans were wet right up to her knees and her coat was torn. She winced as he put his hand on her shoulder; he gently lifted her hair and saw the angry red mark on the nape of her neck.

'Not as bad as you. How serious is that wound?'

'Fairly.' He grinned but she could see pain in his eyes. 'The bullet's still in there. But I reckon I could still thrash that Joe Spikes if I got the opportunity.'

He helped her off with the coat. 'You'd better take off those wet jeans, too.' He ran his hand down her cheek tenderly. 'We don't want you catching pneumonia on top of everything else.'

Tara took off her shoes and jeans, and Harry hung them on the back of the chair. Her checked shirt barely covered her white knickers and she sat down on the bed, tucking her legs up under her. There was so much she wanted to know that she hardly knew where to start.

'Tell me – '

Harry cut her short with a finger on her lips, then sat down next to her.

'I'll tell you anything and everything, but a kiss first,' he said, sliding his arm round her and pulling her closer. 'Thoughts of you are all that have kept me going these past few weeks. Now I want to feel you in my arms.'

It was tenderness rather than passion, a need to hold and be held, yet it was the most memorable kiss Harry had ever given her. She could feel his inner strength, silent reassurance that he would fight to the end to save her, but that he intended to live because there was so much more to do together.

'I love you, Tara,' he said softly. 'I don't know where this is going to end. I can't even promise we'll make it. But if we do, I want your promise that we'll spend the rest of our lives together.'

She could only nod. She knew now that their love would survive anything.

'Just tell me one thing, was it you who phoned the club and Uncle George?'

Harry looked at her, head slightly on one side, as if surprised by the question.

637

'I got captured the night you came back from Paris.'
He reached out and cupped her face in his hands,
turning it towards him. 'I've been in this cell ever since.
Except if you count two days ago when I escaped
briefly, only to get this wound.' He patted his leg
gingerly.

Tara explained to Harry exactly where he was, how
she'd discovered the place and everything else she
knew.

'So Josh is in on it?' Harry shook his head in astonishment. 'He's the missing link! Of course!'

'I can't believe he'd want to hurt you.' Tara felt her
eyes filling up with tears but she brushed them away
angrily. 'You were friends once.'

'Men like Josh Bergman don't know the meaning of
real friendship.' Harry smiled ruefully. 'Looking up to
me as a kid turned to jealousy the moment he met you.
This is about destroying me, gaining a fortune and
having you, too.'

'I don't understand.'

'It's a kind of frame-up.' Harry explained. 'Everything has been arranged as if I'm the instigator. Duke
and all the leading players back in London will have
perfect alibis. You can bet when my body's found
there'll be a nice bit of incriminating evidence with it.
I'll be labelled another Al Capone or Ronnie Kray.'

'How did Josh get to know Duke?'

'I've got a feeling Joe Spikes has the answer to that.
I got word of him when I was in prison. Seems he had
some grudge against me. Josh has plenty of contacts in
the East End still. Maybe they just scratched each
other's backs? They kept their eyes on me, through
you.'

Tara's eyes misted over. Over the years she must
have innocently dropped hundreds of pieces of information about Harry. Was she to blame for all of this?

'So getting someone to impersonate you on the

phone wasn't just to stop people like Needles and your Dad getting anxious about you. It was a smoke screen!' Tara shook her head in wonder.

'Wainwright!' Harry closed his eyes and put his hand on his forehead. 'Of course! Josh must have recruited him when he was in hospital. I couldn't see how he got in on it before, but now it's all becoming clearer.'

'But I still can't really see why Josh would take the risk of doing something criminal. He's got a good business already.'

'Is it that good?' Harry smiled grimly. 'You told me yourself sales were falling. It might have been a golden opportunity to build up the business again, and lose his rival into the bargain.'

Tara remembered the pile of bills and sighed.

'But how could Josh get all these blokes together?' She still couldn't quite believe it. 'That bald man, there's something familiar about him.'

'I don't know if Josh planned it.' Harry tickled her chin. 'I suspect he was picked out by Duke. Maybe word had got around he hated me, and he had some bread to put up. Josh knew enough about me to smooth things along. Funny you should say Joe Spikes seemed familiar, his voice does to me. Every time I hear him speak I do a double take.'

'Maybe it'll come to us.' Tara snuggled closer to Harry. 'So what do you think they're doing now?'

'My guess is that a boat comes up the English Channel, maybe bound for Sweden, Norway or wherever. He drops a parcel overboard tied to a float. Micky let it slip that he was into water skiing. I couldn't understand afterwards why he was so worried that he'd told me, after all it's a pretty harmless hobby. Until I got to think about it.'

'He water skis out to pick it up?'

'Right!' Harry smirked. 'No coastguard is going to

be suspicious about a couple of blokes fooling around in a little motor boat!'

'But why have they gone out now? Surely they aren't going to do it in the dark?'

Harry shrugged. 'Maybe they have to watch where the ship drops it. Send messages, who knows. It's better if they don't get home till the morning – they'll be tired, we might be able to steal a march on them.'

'How, if we're in here?' she asked.

The sound of the outer door opening made them jump. Tara looked at her watch, it was almost nine. She rushed for her jeans and pulled them on. Harry had gone white as a sheet. He stood up defiantly as the key turned in the second door.

It was Micky, with two mugs of tea and a couple of bars of chocolate.

'I thought you might be thirsty,' he said. 'And need the bog.'

Harry hobbled across the room, picked up his bucket and, averting his eyes from Tara, went out.

'What are they going to do with us?' Tara saw no harm in resorting to feminine wiles and trying to prick his conscience. She took the two mugs from him and put them down on the floor by the bed.

'I don't rightly know,' he said, avoiding her penetrating stare. He knew exactly what was planned for both Harry and her and it made him sick to his stomach to think about it. 'I'd like to help you both, but I don't know if they'll give me the chance,' he added in a whisper, inclining his head towards the door.

Harry came back in, limping badly, the bandage wet with fresh blood.

'Do you want to go?' he asked Tara. 'Last chance unless Micky's going to leave the door unlocked.'

'I daren't,' Micky shook his head, mouthing a message that someone was outside. Tara went out to the toilet.

640

'Don't let her cop it, too,' Harry whispered. 'Not just because she's beautiful, or my girl, but her grandmother was murdered just last Christmas, and her brother died in an accident. Her mum couldn't take any more.'

Micky closed the door and drew Harry over to the corner. 'Joe doesn't want to kill her.'

Harry's mouth fell open in shock.

'He's been arguing with Frank and Carl. She wasn't part of the plan.' Micky shook his head. 'Trouble is, I can't see how he can avoid it!'

'You know Josh Bergman's your man in London, do you?'

Micky frowned, obviously surprised at this piece of information.

'We grew up together. He wants Tara for himself,' Harry explained. 'This has all got out of control, Micky. Don't let another man put blood on your hands.'

Micky faltered. He was in this so deep he could see no way out. 'I'll do what I can.' He dropped his eyes from Harry's cool stare. 'You don't know how difficult it is!'

'Oh, I do,' Harry assured him. 'I've been in your shoes, remember? Took the rap for killing a nightwatchman. Everything I've got now I earned after I came out the nick, and it didn't come easy. But I can sleep nights, Micky. I ain't got nothing on my conscience. Carry on the way you are and in a couple of years you won't get no more choices about how you live.'

Tara came back, stopping in the doorway as she heard the last bit of what Harry was saying. Micky turned to look at her.

'Drink your tea while it's still hot. I gotta go now.'

'Do you think that all fell on stony ground?' Tara said as the second of the doors banged shut.

'None of it did.' The shadow of a smile twitched Harry's lips. 'Micky's a good sort, he ain't no killer, but he's scared of the others. The question is whether he'll be strong enough to side with us if it comes down to it.'

'It's bugging me about that Joe.' Tara frowned. 'It's like he's tucked away behind a net curtain in my head. I've almost got it, but not quite.'

'Like an itch you can't scratch?' Harry smiled. 'Well let's forget them for the moment, drink our tea and have a cuddle. Maybe it will come to us.'

He whispered as he held her. The pain in his leg prevented real lovemaking, but his hands reached out for the comfort of her breasts like a small child. He wove dreams about living in the country when all this was over, about the beautiful clothes she would design for her own company. He spoke of their children, of George, Queenie, Amy and Greg, painting a fairytale happy ending.

She couldn't spoil his vision of the future by discussing the possibility of them being led out, shot and buried somewhere. Instead she held him tightly, told him maybe her mother would phone George and pass on her question about Lympne. That even now help might be on the way.

It was when Harry fell asleep that Tara finally remembered who Joe was. Lying tucked against Harry's shoulder, unable to sleep herself, concentrating on that voice was like counting sheep. She went over her life year by year, trying to recall every man she'd ever met, every voice she'd heard. But it was when she analysed the words she'd heard Joe utter that a shutter flew up in her mind.

'Goldilocks.' Suddenly, she vividly recalled a voice calling to her across a school playground. 'Oi, Goldilocks!' The same gravelly Cockney voice, and she could see the face it belonged to so clearly, peering over a fence.

Reason told her it couldn't be the same man, yet she knew it was. He hadn't been bald then, nor did he have an ugly scar twisting his mouth. But it was him.

Her father!

Her immediate reaction was to wake Harry and tell him the news, but one look at his peaceful face stopped her. Instead she turned over on her side to give him more room and considered what this meant.

Bill MacDonald had staged his death so convincingly that the police had closed the file on the murder of Father Glynn. He had re-emerged in the East End as Joe Spikes. The bald head, the fit, muscular body and the hideous scar hid everything that was Bill MacDonald. Had he sought out this job because he wanted to destroy Harry and ultimately wound George? Did he know who she was?

Tara stared hard at the wall in front of her. The musty smell in here reminded her of the flat above Sid's fish and chip shop, and the nervy, miserable feeling inside her was identical to how she'd felt so much of the time back then. But it was a long time ago. No-one else in Whitechapel had ever recognised her as Anne MacDonald, so why should he?

There was no question of sleep now as other images came into her mind. She remembered the mystery of Gran's murder. Could her father have been responsible?

'Are you awake, sweetheart?' Harry's whisper broke through Tara's reverie.

She had thought things through, she even had a plan of sorts, but she knew she couldn't tell Harry. A sigh, a yawn and she turned round to snuggle into his arms, to let him think she'd been sleeping.

'How's your leg?' she asked.

'Pretty bad,' he admitted reluctantly. 'That's what woke me, I think. Could you stand to re-dress it?'

The bandage was soaked in blood and as Tara gently eased it from the wound she winced.

643

'Oh, Harry!' Tears sprang into her eyes when she saw the purple hole and the inflamed area all around. 'Should I wash it?'

'Better not.' Harry screwed up his face in pain and gripped his knee tightly. 'That water's been sitting around uncovered. Just bind it up with a strip of that old sheeting.' He pointed to some material folded up on the table.

'I've got an idea.' Tara held up the material and tore off a four-inch strip. 'When they come back I'll ask if I can talk to Joe because I've got a deal to offer him. Once I'm upstairs I might be able to escape or even talk him round.'

She deftly bandaged the leg, noting the perspiration on Harry's upper lip and the clammy feel of his hands. His leg was infected, he needed treatment fast, but worst of all she doubted he had the strength to fight anyone off.

'What sort of deal?' Harry's voice sounded weak, he slumped back on the bed almost as soon as she'd finished the dressing.

'Well, I'd just bluff,' Tara said vaguely. 'Go on about how important I am to Josh, offer him a bribe. Make out I'm a hard bitch and I value my own life more than you.'

Harry caught hold of her hand fiercely. His eyes were bright with fever.

'Micky said Joe didn't want to kill you. Convince him it's right to let you go,' he said. 'Don't risk anything for me, sweetheart. I'll do what I can when they come for me. I've got the rope, I'll wait behind the door with it.'

Harry knew it was unlikely she'd get away with it, at best all he could hope for was that they'd shoot her cleanly and unexpectedly before she got a chance to panic. His leg hurt so much the fear of death was loosening its grip, but if there was a chance for her, he wanted her to take it.

Tara didn't want to pursue the subject any further. Joe did know who she was! That's why he felt bad about killing her. Well, if he knew who she was then it was almost certain he'd killed Gran! She hated him with every fibre of her body. She would get the better of him somehow!

Four o'clock came, five and six, but still no-one came. Harry was drifting in and out of consciousness now and it crossed Tara's mind that maybe the men might never come back, but leave them there to die of hunger and thirst.

She sat on the side of the narrow bed, dressed and ready, and tried to control the rising panic within her. When she finally heard footsteps in the passage Tara almost shrieked with joy. She jumped up, slid the Stanley knife into her pocket and handed the rope to Harry.

'Just stay where you are,' she whispered. 'If one of them bends over you, use this. You aren't strong enough to stand.'

She had only the briefest look at him as the outer door was unlocked. His eyes were almost closed with pain, his breathing laboured, his mouth boyish and vulnerable.

She kissed him, stroking his face gently. 'I love you, Harry.'

The key was turning in the lock. Tara stood close by it, poised for action.

'Take me up to speak to Joe?' she said the moment the door opened. It wasn't Micky as she'd expected but an older man with short mousy hair, possibly the one called Carl Harry had spoken of. 'It's really important. I must speak to him.'

'Now hold on.' The man was surprised by her calm. 'My brief was just to let you use the bog, nothing else.'

'You must be Carl?' Tara widened her eyes and moved closer to him, reaching out and putting one

645

hand on his arm almost seductively. 'I'm sure a real man like yourself wouldn't want to hurt a lady, particularly if she's got some information which will help you all.'

'I'll have to ask.' Carl's eyes were constantly on the move, flitting nervously round the room. 'Get back in there while I lock the door again.'

The door slammed shut and was locked. After a second the other door slammed behind him.

Tara used Harry's comb to tidy her hair, wishing she had some make-up or could even clean her teeth before she had to face Joe. What if he refused to see her? What if he wouldn't speak to her alone?

Harry was right out now and the bandage was soaked in blood again. He still held the length of rope in his hands but he would never be capable of defending himself.

Footsteps came back down the stairs. Once again the doors were opened and Carl looked in.

'All right, come on,' he said, looking over to Harry. 'But don't even think of any funny business!'

It confirmed everything. Joe knew who she was!

Carl held her arm the whole way, fingers digging into her as if he was prepared for her to make a dash. She had expected to be taken to the kitchen, but instead he marched her right up the stairs to the first floor.

They were all in the room at the front where she'd seen the sleeping bags. Micky was lying down, another young man with dirty straw hair and pale blue eyes was crouching over a radio and Joe sat by the window on a fishing stool. There was a great deal of equipment in the room – wet suits, flippers, fishing rods and the kind of large plastic boxes fishermen use to keep their bait. Tara's eyes scanned it quickly, and she took deep breaths to combat the feeling of panic.

'What's so important?' Joe looked up at her. It was difficult to assess whether he was smiling or scowling, but as Tara looked into his deep brown eyes she knew she was right about his identity.

'It's something only for your ears,' she said in a small voice. She could see something in one of the open fishing boxes that looked remarkably like a gun. 'Could we talk alone?'

Joe looked round at his men and back to her. 'Go and take a walk,' he said.

Carl's fingers still dug into her arm and as Tara took a step nearer Joe his grip tightened. Micky and Frank got up, shot curious glances at her and sauntered out.

'Could he wait outside, too?' Tara asked. 'What I've got to say is very personal.' She didn't dare look directly at the fishing box in case he followed her eyes, but she was ninety-eight per cent certain it was a gun.

Joe got up from the stool, rubbing his back with his hands in a gesture she remembered clearly from her childhood. He was fit now, not a trace of belly hanging over his trousers. The flabby jaw she remembered was tighter, the undamaged skin on his face glowing with health even though he needed a shave. If he had his dark hair back and kept his left side towards her, he would look almost the same as he did in his old Army snaps.

'OK, Carl,' he snapped. 'Wait outside. I'll give her five minutes.'

The moment Carl walked out of the door, Tara moved closer towards both Joe and the box.

'Well, come on,' he said impatiently, sitting down again on the stool. 'What's all this about?'

'Take a good look at me,' she said softly. 'The hair colouring, the eyes.'

She looked straight at him, opening her eyes wide. He knew who she was, she saw it in his eyes, but to her surprise she saw consternation. 'You didn't mind killing me while I didn't know you, I suppose,' she said

647

softly. 'You made the mistake of giving me too much time to think.'

'How did you know?' His voice had lost its harshness.

'The baldness and the scar distracted me,' she said slowly, inching closer towards the box. It was a gun, a small pistol like ones she'd seen in films. Was it loaded? Could she actually fire it if necessary? 'But you couldn't change your voice.'

He was knocked off balance. She could see an almost tender expression, and knew she had to act now before he snapped back to his customary hardness. She opened her arms just a little, as if intending to embrace him, and moved forward.

'Did I turn out as you imagined?' She kept her voice sweet and warm, her eyes on him while she gauged the point at which she must bend and snatch up the gun. 'I changed my name because Anne MacDonald didn't sound like a designer.'

'I never imagined you so pretty.' His voice was hoarse with emotion. 'You were real ginger when you were little.'

The bob down to grab the gun looked like nothing more than a bend to scratch a knee, or even to sit on the sleeping bag lying on the floor. Her hand going to the box could be interpreted as merely steadying herself. But in that split-second her fingers closed round the stock and she drew it out, pointing it at him.

'Back to the same point we left one another all those years ago!' Her voice was strong, even though her hand was shaking. 'I wasn't wrong about you, Dad, not that time, not ever. I should have blinded you with that poker.' She had to bring her other hand up to steady the gun. Sweat was trickling down over her forehead and the sunshine through the window was almost blinding after the cellar's murky light.

'Give me that gun.' His voice roared out with all the power she remembered as a kid.

648

She smiled then. Had it not been loaded his eyes wouldn't be popping out of his head.

'Well, Joe Spikes,' she drawled the name sarcastically. 'The boot's on the other foot now, isn't it? I've got the gun and I intend to shoot you if you even attempt to take it off me. So you'll just obey my orders for now.'

'Come on, darlin'.' He tried to smile but he just looked even more evil. 'I'm yer dad, for God's sake!'

'You'd have killed me regardless.' She raised one eyebrow. 'You killed my gran, didn't you, and that old priest. Paul panicked when he thought you were coming after him, and he died too. So tell me, Dad, what do I owe you?'

'You don't know the half.' His eyes looked wild. 'Paul wasn't my kid, he was George Collins', she deceived me, lied to me. She got George to grass me up. I loved her.'

'You never loved anyone but yourself,' Tara spat at him. 'Paul was your son, he was the very image of you. Mum loved you even after all those beatings, even when she was humiliated and broken. She even cried when the police told her you died in that car crash.'

She could see this shook him by the trembling of his twisted lips, a blurring of his eyes.

'She turned on me,' he said. 'When I came out of prison the first time.'

'Well, you poor bloody thing,' Tara sneered. 'Never occurred to you that she almost starved while you were inside. She adored you, but you just had to ruin everything with your thieving, gambling, drinking and brutality, didn't you?'

'You don't know how things were!' His tone was almost petulant.

'Don't I?' Tara taunted him. 'I've heard Mum's stories about what a prince you were, how you stood up to Gran, even what happened in the garden here.'

He looked up quickly, surprised.

'Yes, she told me,' Tara snapped. 'Don't you feel any shame that you'd plan to kill me in the same place I was conceived in love?'

He couldn't answer that. For a moment his head drooped and she knew she'd touched the part of him that had once been a war hero and a tender lover.

'I didn't expect you to turn up here. You should never have found out about this.'

'Why kill Gran?' she asked. 'What could an old lady do to hurt you?'

'I only wanted to find out where you and Amy were.' His head shot up in defiance. 'I didn't know you all lived there then. I just crept in intending to look through her things and find an address.'

'Gran heard you?' Tara relaxed the gun just enough to be comfortable.

'She caught me in the kitchen.' His eyes flashed dangerously, just the way she remembered. 'She knew who I was immediately.'

Tara lifted the gun a little, just in case.

'But why kill her, a defenceless old woman?'

'She weren't never defenceless, not that one.' He shook his head. 'She'd have shopped me. Both you and Amy would have been shamed.'

'You mean you'd be doing a life sentence as a priest killer.' Tara's lip curled back in disgust. 'Don't make out it was for our benefit! But I've heard all I want to. Now you're coming with me.'

The gun was a bonus she hadn't expected, her plan had consisted of little more than an emotional appeal. But six inches of potential destruction in her hand changed everything. She could force Joe and his men to change places with Harry, call the police and get them to round up the whole gang.

But Joe was looking up at her in astonishment, not taking her seriously.

'I said you're coming with me,' she said more firmly. 'If you don't, I'll shoot you. It's all the same to me.'

He stood up reluctantly. 'Don't do this, Anne!' It sounded like a threat. 'The others, they'll jump you. Let me talk to them and find a way round it.'

'I'm not Anne, I'm Tara.' She tossed her hair back from her face. 'And you mean nothing to me. If anyone tries to jump me I'll kill them, or you. Now move it, to the door, and call Carl.'

Did they have more guns? The question jumped into her head and stayed there. What if the threat to blow Joe's head off didn't work? Could she really squeeze the trigger?

He opened the door. 'Carl!' he yelled. He opened his mouth to add something else, but Tara dug the gun in the small of his back.

'Don't! I explain things.'

Carl came running up the stairs. He paused as he turned on to the landing, instantly suspecting something.

'I've got a gun at his back.' Tara spoke in a strong, clear voice. 'If you do as I say I'll let him go later. If not I'll shoot him, then you. Understand?'

'Eh, yes!' He was clearly startled by this turn of events.

'Have you still got the keys of the cellar?' she asked.

He nodded, his eyes flitting between her and Joe.

'Right then, we'll go down.' She prodded Joe forward. 'Where are the other men?'

'In the kitchen.' Carl turned back to the stairs.

'Well, we'll walk slowly down there. When we get to the kitchen you call them to come out and they join us. Any trouble, any smart moves, Joe gets it and I'll go on shooting till the bullets run out.'

Her mouth was dry, her heart pounding with fear as Carl began to move down the stairs. She prodded Joe and the pair of them followed Carl.

'Call them out, Joe,' Tara ordered as they reached the

kitchen. She could hear Frank talking to Micky and she wondered whether Harry was right in believing that Micky would help them if the chips were down.

'Frank, Micky!' Joe's voice boomed out. 'Here.' It was ridiculous for her to even think they'd be loyal to Joe, she saw that immediately in Frank's foxy, mean face. He stood in the doorway of the kitchen and looked contemptuously at her.

'Down the stairs to the cellar,' Tara ordered. 'Go on, or I shoot.'

'I don't give a fuck who you shoot, lady,' he sneered. 'It won't be me, that's for certain.'

'Don't push me,' she said. 'I want Harry out of that cellar and I'll do whatever it takes. Tell them to do it, Joe!' She prodded his back, but she was feeling dwarfed now by the four men all packed into the narrow passage.

'You heard the lady,' Joe said, but she couldn't see his face and she sensed he was giving them some silent directive. In panic Tara stepped back on to the stairs so she could see above their heads. Joe was now just a couple of feet from her, Carl perhaps a yard in front. Frank stood scowling in the kitchen doorway, Micky was just behind him. It was another five feet or so from the kitchen to the cellar stairs and she knew they could easily overpower her there. She had to scare them now.

'Get moving.' She forced herself to keep her voice steady and she lifted the gun, moving it from side to side to imply she hadn't decided who she would shoot. 'Frank, you first. Down to the cellar.'

He leaned back on the doorpost and crossed his arms defiantly; she saw he had 'love' and 'hate' tattooed on his knuckles and a spider's web round each elbow.

'I said move.' She shouted this time, lifting the gun and aiming it at Frank's legs. 'Or you won't move under your own steam again.'

He just shrugged his shoulders and stared insolently

at her. Anger rose like bile in her stomach. She waved the gun between them, brought it to rest pointing it at Frank's knees and squeezed the trigger. The bang and the impact made her stagger back. A trail of smoke hid Frank for a moment but she could hear a howl of pain.

'Does that show you I'm serious?' she screamed, going up another step and looking down at all four of them. Frank was clutching at his crotch, bent over double and blood spurted out on to the floor. 'I'm not a good shot. I aimed at his knees, but I suppose that has the same crippling effect.'

'You fucking bitch.' Frank looked up at her, eyes streaming, lips quivering.

Tara waved the gun again, looking to each of the men in turn. Joe turned towards her and she saw a glint of admiration.

'OK, time to make a deal,' he said. 'We give you the keys of the cellar. We scarper now. Can't say fairer than that!'

'No deals! Get down those steps now,' Tara commanded. 'Micky, take the keys from Carl, go first and help Harry out. Any funny business and I'll blast one of you.'

The gun was warm in her hand, it had become an extension of her body. She understood why some men revered guns, they gave instant power. Now she had conquered her fear of it, she knew she could pull that trigger again, even if that meant killing someone.

Chapter 36

'What a nice surprise! How are you, love?' Queenie purred down the phone. 'No, Tara's not here. What's up, you sound a bit agitated?'

'Oh, Queenie,' Amy blurted out. 'I'm probably totally off my trolley imagining things, but I'm worried about Tara.' She hastily explained the telephone conversations with her daughter and Josh. 'Josh almost seemed to be checking up on her, whatever he said, and he told me Harry was missing!'

'Well, he ain't officially,' Queenie said. 'I mean he's phoned here. But there is something funny going on, 'Arry don't sound like hisself.'

The two women talked their way round everything they knew for certain.

' 'E's never asked once 'ow George's back is,' Queenie said. 'And like 'e always used to ask what I was baking, and pound to a penny if 'e was away 'e'd say, "Save me a bit, Queenie". But we didn't get none of that, just what 'e was doin' and stuff. I might not be so clever, Amy, but I don't think our 'Arry would change just 'cos he was in Germany.'

'So you don't think it's him phoning?'

'I dunno, Amy. Needles is getting worried, too. He tried to complain to 'Arry about something what Duke was doing at the club and 'Arry told him to mind his own business. A couple of days later Duke comes down on 'im like a ton of bricks, threatening 'im wiv the sack.'

'Well, Queenie, I honestly think Tara's got some idea where he is and she's gone off to find him. But the more I think about the place she mentioned, the more scared I get.'

Queenie reassured her she would pass all this on to George and get him to phone back the minute he came in.

'What is it you fear about Lympne?' Greg asked Amy as she sat staring into space after her call to Queenie.

It was a warm evening, the windows in Greg's sitting room were wide open, but Amy was shivering, her face drawn and pale.

'Bill,' she said simply, tossing back her blonde hair. 'Don't you think it's too much of a coincidence that Tara should ask me about her father's secret place?'

'Bill's dead,' Greg said gently.

'But what if he isn't?' She raised her face to look at him, eyes dark with anxiety. 'His brother identified the body, not me. He hated George and Harry, he burned down their warehouse. Maybe he's been planning this for years. Suppose it was him who killed Mother?'

'You're being silly now,' Greg sat down beside her and drew her close, ruffling her hair. Deep down he shared her anxiety. 'Would you feel better if we went and talked to the police about it?'

'Let's just wait for George to phone back.' She smiled weakly. 'Who knows! Tara might walk in through the door any minute.'

It was after seven when the phone finally rang. Amy leaped across the room to answer it.

'Oh, George.' She sighed with relief. 'Tell me I'm imagining things?'

'I can't, darlin',' he said in his strong voice. 'Unless

655

I'm going loopy, too. I've just had a word with Needles and Tony and they aren't any happier than us.
Apparently Duke's sacked some of 'Arry's old staff
and replaced them with new people. They don't know
whether they can trust Dennis and Alec, either. It's
very 'ard for them to be totally blunt with me, because
for all they know my boy might be right in up to his
ears with Duke, planning some big scam. But all three
of us have this feeling it ain't 'Arry that's been phoning. Oh, 'e gets the voice right, but 'e ain't got the soul
of 'Arry. None of the little jokes, know what I mean?'

'What should we do then? Do you think it's relevant
that she asked me about a place called Lympne?' She
told him all she remembered about the place and how
Bill felt about it.

'I can't see 'im coming back to the East End even if
he didn't die in that accident,' George said firmly. 'If
he put so much as one foot in the manor, someone
would talk. But one thing Needles told me was interesting. Someone broke into the club last night. Well,
not broke in. Stayed in after it closed. Nothing was
taken, it seems, but 'e 'eard Duke talking about a
drawer being forced up in one of the games rooms and
a window left open up in the attics. Needles reckons it
was Tara.'

'And she found something about Lympne?'

'Could be! You say Bill found this place while he was
in the Army, 'e could've told one of his mates. Or it
could be they's using the airport. But I think I'll go
down the nick now and get them to check it out. Let's
just hope I don't make things worse.'

'George, if Harry's being held at Lympne and that
Duke's a phoney, it stands to reason something big is
going on. If Tara has gone there alone to try and rescue
Harry –' She stopped, fear twisting her stomach as she
imagined her daughter walking straight into a gang's
hideout.

'I'll go down the nick now,' George said gently. 'Now don't get yer knickers in a twist. We could 'ave it all wrong.'

George knew they hadn't got it wrong. He'd lived among villains for too long to misread foul play. He'd been certain it wasn't Harry on the line during the third telephone call when Harry failed to wish him a happy birthday. But knowing something and proving it were two different matters, especially when your son was involved with heavy-duty rascals. To speak out too loudly was to court disaster. Harry could be in concrete boots at the bottom of the Thames by now and if Tara got too close it would be curtains for her too.

'Whatcha goin' to do then, love?' Queenie asked as he sat staring into space.

'I'll have to go down the nick.' He looked up at Queenie and saw the distress in her eyes. 'If 'Arry's got himself in over 'is 'ead and Tara gets hurt by it, I'll never forgive 'im. Where did I go wrong with 'im, Queenie? I thought by just lovin' 'im, keepin' 'im close to me, it would be enough, but it ain't.'

Queenie didn't reply for a moment, but put her arms round George and enveloped him in her large bosom.

'Don't ever think you failed 'im,' she said softly. 'You're a good man, George, and so is that son of yours. Now you get down that nick with your head held high. Believe in your boy, stand by 'im. That's what Tara's doing.'

'Best day's work I ever did was marry you.' He lifted his head. 'You was given the right name sure enough, you're a real queen!'

'I just want you to get on to the local police down there, get them to check out that 'ouse,' George repeated. 'There's something going on, something nasty, and a young girl's gone down there and walked right into it.'

It was well after midnight and George had been

657

given the runaround ever since he arrived at the police station three hours earlier. They behaved as if it were a joke, especially when he brought up the subject of Bill MacDonald being alive.

'You what?' Inspector Ronald Harrison gave a loud guffaw, his sallow face suddenly brighter. 'Leave it out, George! We got enough trouble on our patch without Bill MacDonald rising from his coffin.'

George had known Ron since they were boys. Ron was a good copper, but his opinion of George's story was coloured by Harry's record, the clientele who drank and gambled at his club and a conviction that the whole place was kept alive by dirty money.

'You know as well as I do that MacDonald burned down my ware'ouse,' George insisted. 'You know 'e killed Father Glynn. Well, what starting price would you put on 'im staging his own death to avoid capture, then planning the ruin of my boy and me? He could 'ave strangled Mabel Randall down in Somerset, Amy says this 'ouse in Kent was his favourite place and we all know that stretch of coast is a smugglers' haunt.'

'Bill MacDonald weren't bright enough for all that. He was drunk all the time!'

'You've forgotten his Army service, ain't you?' George raised an eyebrow quizzically. 'War hero, survived in the jungle for God knows 'ow long. I'd say something like this was right up 'is street.'

Ron Harrison saw the conviction in George's eyes. In recent weeks he'd heard several stories about Harry. He was in Germany, he'd been buried in a tunnel doing a robbery and was dead before he could be dug out, he was supposed to have run off to South America after a death threat. Putting all the rumours and facts together one thing was clear; Harry Collins had disappeared and the Top Cat Club was almost certainly the base for some criminal activity.

'OK, leave it with me,' he sighed. 'I'll contact the

local police and get them to have a sniff round. When did you say Tara phoned her mother?'

'About ten this morning. Josh Bergman phoned Amy around one-thirty, 'e said she'd already left 'er flat. So if she went to Hythe she could have been there by three or four in the afternoon.'

'Leave me your number and Amy's,' Ron said. 'Now for God's sake, clear off, George. I'll ring as soon as I've got something to tell you.'

As George was leaving the police station, Josh was struggling to get his key in the door. He was drunk, falling down, unable to form words. Yet he still hadn't managed to silence the raging fear inside him.

He and Duke had met at eight, in the Markham in King's Road. He was sober then, but when he heard that Tara had been captured at Lympne, he started to drink in earnest.

'She's locked up with Harry. They'll deal with them both in the morning after they've made the pick-up.' Duke reported it as coldly as if he were talking about two stray dogs.

'I didn't plan on murder,' Josh whispered. The pub was crowded with stoned students and hippies listening intently to Santana. 'There's got to be another way.'

'You wanted Harry out of the picture, as I remember,' Duke reminded him, casting his cold blue eyes derisively around the bar. 'If you play for big stakes there's always the chance the game can go against you. It's no good blaming us about the girl, that poncy actor friend of yours could have phoned her, too. It was your bright idea to let her think Harry was sick of her.'

'But she's so talented. I don't know what I'll do,' Josh pleaded. 'My business will fail without her.'

Duke looked at Josh contemptuously. 'I've always been a bastard,' he hissed through thin, cruel lips. 'I've made a living out of being one. But I've never resorted

659

to foul play to get a woman. Even with Harry out the way you wouldn't get her. She's too fuckin' bright, for starters. You'd better pray they put her down, because if they don't she'll come gunning for you.'

'I could cool her down.' Josh's brown eyes welled up with tears.

Duke snorted with laughter. 'Cool her down! You must be joking! That girl's got guts. She'd eat you for breakfast! Stop snivelling, man. You'll have enough money to do anything you want by tomorrow. Even a pathetic little Yid can pull a bird if he's got money.'

'How dare you speak to me like that?' Josh's eyes flashed with anger. 'I put up the money for this. I don't expect to be attacked by someone who works for me.'

'Let's just get one thing straight,' Duke snarled, his thin lip curling back like a savage dog. 'You just bought into this job. Until you got careless and left something in your house for that girl to find, there wasn't even a connection between you and the rest of it. You've put everything in jeopardy and, if you end up in the firing line when they find her body, too bloody bad!'

Duke left the pub after that, but that last line of his nagged all night. It didn't matter how much drink he downed, it was still there like a toothache. Tara had to go, there was no alternative, but the thought of someone firing a bullet into that lovely body was a nightmare vision.

It wasn't meant to be like this. Duke was supposed to disappear from the club once this deal was all settled. Then Harry's body would turn up after several weeks, along with enough evidence to put him firmly in the frame. Josh was actually planning to be the one who made the police look for Harry, so Tara would feel indebted to him. But now everything had gone wrong.

He fell on to his lounge floor and just lay there. The

room was spinning round and he knew he was going
to vomit, but he couldn't get up. He could see Tara
standing in the doorway as she had earlier in the
day, in that big shirt and the too big jeans, her hair
hanging wet around her beautiful face. Why couldn't
he be satisfied with having her as a friend and his
designer? What kind of evil was there in him that he had
to possess everything?

He knew as he vomited across his carpet that things
would never be good again for him. His father was
very fond of the expression, 'As ye sow, so shall ye
reap', and now it was harvest time.

George beckoned to Needles through the club doorway. Any other time it would be heartening to hear the
raucous laughter from the packed bar and observe the
group of six in evening dress going upstairs to the
gaming rooms, but tonight George would rather see
the place torched.

'What is it, George?' Needles came out, glancing
back to make sure he wasn't being observed.

Briefly George related his conversation with Ron
Harrison down at the nick. 'I'm not happy to wait until
the plod stir themselves,' George explained. 'Do you
fancy coming down there tonight?'

Needles' big face lit up with boyish delight. 'Not 'alf.
The only trouble is we ain't going to finish early tonight, there's a big game on.'

'Can't you make out you're ill?' George suggested.
'Or your wife is?'

'I'll do me best, but it would be better to wait and
take Tony too.' A cloud came back to the big man's
face. 'Don't wanna be funny, George, but you ain't so
young and sprightly no more!'

'I'd walk through fire to protect my boy,' George
said fiercely. 'But I suppose you're right, one push and
I'd go down. Look, I'll go home. Phone me when you

get out and I'll pick you up.'

George sat down heavily on the settee. It was after two and he was very tired.

'Come and lie down till they phone,' Queenie suggested as she came in with a cup of tea.

It was cosy in his lounge, imitation coals flickering even though there was no heat and the soft Dralon settee soothing under his old body.

'When this is over we should retire and sell up,' he said, taking the tea.

Queenie perched on the arm of his chair and slid her arm across his shoulders.

'Where would we go? The seaside?'

George looked up at her and smiled. She was still a remarkably handsome woman, her skin was unlined, pink and white like a girl's, her eyes full of youthful vitality. He knew her hair had long since turned grey, but seen in the soft light of a table lamp it looked natural blonde, curling on her plump shoulders.

'Wherever you like, darlin',' he said. 'Some nice little cottage where we can stay in bed all day if we want, and a nice garden to potter in.'

'That sounds lovely.' She bent to kiss him and she smelled of rose soap and handcream. 'Now stop worrying and come with me.'

The telephone rang, making them both jump. George picked it up, his eyes wide and frightened.

'It's me, Ron Harrison.'

'Any news?' George asked.

'Afraid not,' Harrison said. 'The Hythe police station is only manned part time, but a couple of men from Folkestone drove out to the house to take a look. It was all in darkness, doors and windows secured, didn't look as if anyone had been there in years, so I guess you were mistaken. They're going back tomorrow in daylight just to be certain.'

'Didn't they go in the house?'

'Even the police can't break and enter,' Harrison said. 'Had the door been broken in or a window left open they would have, but they shone their torches through and there was nothing doing. Even the drive gate was padlocked. There wasn't even any sign of tyre marks. It sounds to me like you're barking up the wrong tree, George.'

'OK,' George's voice was flat with disappointment. 'Could you check it out tomorrow again, though, and ask them to see if the girl was spotted around there?'

'Will do. I'm sorry, George. I can imagine how you feel, but we'll be keeping a close watch on the club, too. Something just might pop up when we least expect it.'

George buried his head in Queenie's shoulder.

'I was so sure they'd find something. I don't know if it's worth going down there now with Needles and Tony.'

'There certainly isn't any point till daylight,' Queenie said sensibly. 'If the police can't see anything, neither will you. Go around six or seven, that's soon enough, and meanwhile come to bed.'

'I'll just phone Needles.' George sighed deeply. 'No point in him making up a cock and bull story for nothing.'

Duke picked up the receiver a second after it had been answered downstairs at the reception desk. He had got into the habit of doing this since the time he listened in by accident and heard one of the barmaids slagging him off to another. Tonight he had another reason for snooping; he'd seen Tony and Needles whispering together in the passage down by the bogs. He smirked when he recognised George's voice.

'I won't keep you. Just rang to say we won't bother tonight, but go around six when it's light. Plod's been out there and they can't see nuffin'. Maybe there ain't nuffin' to see anyway. Is that OK?'

'Yeah!' Needles' thick voice showed no curiosity or emotion. 'The club opens at nine till around half two. We take bookings for private parties.'

'Someone ear-wigging?' George asked.

'Certainly, sir,' Needles answered briskly. 'We look forward to meeting you.'

Duke had to be quick with the phone so Needles didn't notice a click. So they were going down there and the police had already been and checked it out?

If George and Needles left at six, on a clear road they could be there around half seven, eight at the latest. He doubted the police would go any earlier than that, especially after one wild goose chase.

Anxiety gnawed at his innards and made him feel nauseous. Bergman had sickened him earlier with his whining and blubbering, now it was George and Needles getting up his nose. The lads would be back from the pick-up before seven. He could nip down there now, collect the stuff and shoot off again, leaving orders for Joe to dispose of the girl and Harry immediately.

Duke got up, smiling to himself as a brilliant idea came into his mind. No doubt George, Needles and probably Tony would go down there tooled up. His men had only Joe's small handgun and the shotgun between them. There was a fair chance some of his men would be killed, with luck all of them. After all, George would be savage when he found they were too late to save Harry and his girl.

But he'd be fine. He had the money and he'd be long gone from the house with the drugs. All he had to do was slip back into his real identity, and Duke Denning would be just another name in East End mythology.

He poured himself a small measure of brandy, just enough to calm those butterflies, and flicked back his sleeve to look at his watch.

'You'll be looking at a gold one soon,' he told himself. 'Lying on the beach in Florida without a care in the world!'

He opened the roll-top desk, removed his personal address book and diary and slid them into his briefcase. Then, taking the safe key from his pocket, he opened that too. Ironically it had been the best night since Harry went, over five thousand put into the safe already during the evening. He took the previous day's takings out of their green bank bag and shoved them loose in his case, then did the same with tonight's. A pile of envelopes from the stationery cupboard made a good substitute back in the bags. When Needles or Tony put the final takings away they wouldn't notice anything different.

There was only his suit jacket to put on now and as he adjusted his tie in front of the mirror he took one last look at Harry's photographs of old boxers and film stars. For a moment he felt strangely sad. He liked this club, the customers and even the staff. But they had always belonged to Harry. Even if he had been a real buyer for the place it would never be as successful as it was for Harry.

He wasn't going to waste his energies on regrets, after all he'd planned to make himself a fortune and now it looked as if he wouldn't even need to give the men their final pay-off. But all the same, you didn't meet many men of Harry's calibre in a lifetime!

'I'm watching every move!' Tara shouted down the stairs as the men started the trek down into the darkness. 'Open the door, Micky. You other three, stand back where I can see you!'

It felt as if every pore in her body was pouring out sweat. Her stomach ached with a combination of terror, hunger and nausea, and she knew with utter certainty these men weren't going to stand by and let

665

her herd them into a cell, however much she waved that gun.

Frank was moaning loudly, still bent over double. Natural concern for his injury conflicted with a suspicion he was laying it on thick, just to distract her attention long enough for Joe or Carl to whack her on the head.

Micky had reached the outer door now. Even in the gloom Tara could see him hesitating, trying to gauge the feelings around him.

'Open it, Micky!' she yelled. 'The rest of you wait there, don't move!'

She heard the clunk of a key turning in the lock.

'Good, Micky,' she called out. 'Now you go forward and open the other door.'

Unless she had read him entirely wrong, she was sure he'd look after Harry. But as Micky stepped into the area between the two doors she felt a surge of hatred for her from the other men. Frank turned his face towards her, lips curled back. Carl's face was cold. He was watching every move she made, and she knew he was waiting to spring.

Her father, meanwhile, was standing at the bottom of the stairs as calmly as if he was queuing to go into a public toilet, and it was this attitude which unnerved her more than anything.

The lock clicked through to Harry's cell and a shaft of dim light spilled out.

'Harry!' she bellowed. 'Come on out!' A shadow knocked out the beam of light and suddenly there was Harry, supported by Micky. She knew he'd lost an enormous amount of blood because she could no longer distinguish a bandage round his leg.

'Are you OK?' she called out.

'Better for seeing you,' he mumbled in a slurred voice.

'Move over here with him.' She waved the gun

666

towards the part of the passageway furthest away from the cell. 'Joe, Carl, Frank, inside!'

They didn't move an inch.

'You heard me, move!' She yelled louder this time, but still they just stood there.

She knew they were testing her, sure she'd never fire, that Frank's injury frightened her. Her hands were so sticky with sweat she could hardly hold the gun; she had to brace herself, legs apart, to stop them shaking.

'If I pull this trigger it will be aimed at one of you,' she assured them. 'I'm not scared to kill any of you. I don't intend to waste bullets. So move, or one of you gets it!'

She saw them exchange looks of pure defiance. She had no choice! Aiming at Carl's legs she squeezed the trigger, holding the stock in both hands. Once again she recoiled with the report, her view obscured for a moment by blue smoke.

She heard him collapse. It sounded like a sack of potatoes hitting the ground and as the smoke cleared she saw the appalled look on both Joe's and Frank's faces. He looked dead. The bullet had hit him in the side and blood was rapidly staining his light shirt, his mouth gaping.

'Drag him in the cell, Joe!' she ordered. 'And you, Frank, unless you want to see my next trick.'

They moved then – Joe hoisted Carl up and Frank took his other side, shuffling forward to the cell.

She had to go down now. She couldn't trust Micky to lock the door on them, and anyway Harry needed help. Walking briskly to the inner cell door, the gun still in her hand, she removed the keys.

'I'm not as inhuman as you were,' she said sharply. They had laid Carl on the bed, Frank sat by his side and Joe was looking down at them both. 'You can get water and use the toilet. The police won't be long, or medical attention!'

667

She slammed the outer door after her and locked it; only then did she get a good look at Harry. He was slumped against Micky as if his life was ebbing away.

'Oh, Harry.' She rushed over to him, tucking the gun into her jeans, and took his face in both hands. 'It's almost over now, hang on a little bit longer, we'll get you up the stairs.'

She tucked the keys in her back pocket and put her shoulder under Harry's arm. Micky took up the other side and slowly they made their way up the stairs.

Harry's breath was laboured, his legs like India rubber, and blood was trickling out through the bandage, running down an already dry furrow of blood on his shin.

'I thought they'd killed you,' he rasped.

At the top of the stairs they laid him down on the wooden floor. Micky looked haunted, dark curls falling into his eyes, biting on his lip as he considered his position. Tara thought hard.

'Micky, I'm going to let you go, I'll even forget what you look like. All I ask is that you go into the airport and telephone for an ambulance. Can I trust you to do that?'

The troubled expression vanished from his face.

'Promise me?' she begged, clutching at his arm. 'I love Harry and he'll die without help. Don't let me down.'

A groan from Harry made them both lean over him.

'Come to me when all this is over,' Harry wheezed out. 'Thanks, mate!'

'I'll go now. Don't worry, I won't let you down.' Micky ran upstairs briefly, coming down seconds later with a leather jacket and a small holdall. He was out of the back window and off through the bushes like a jack rabbit and Tara turned back to Harry, sitting down on the floor beside him.

His eyes opened at her touch on his brow and his lips moved to speak.

'Don't try.' She kissed her finger and laid it across his lips. 'I reckon it will take ten minutes before he gets to the phone, another ten for the ambulance to get here. Within twenty minutes you'll be safe. Can you hold on?'

It wasn't a nod exactly, more a movement of the eyes, then he closed them as if trying to blank out the pain. She had never seen anyone look so ill. His cheeks were sunken, the bones standing out gaunt and sharp, skin like parchment, each breath laboured.

Tara found an old tea towel in the kitchen. She soaked it in cold water and wrung it out, then went back to sit beside him and sponge his face and hair.

It was so strange sitting there on the cool floor in the gloom. The early morning sun was filtering through the front windows, but not reaching the passage where she was. She could hear the birds singing, wind rustling leaves and the occasional faint noise from the cellar.

She felt so dirty and tired. After two nights without sleep she'd reached the stage where if she just leaned back against the wall she would drop off.

The gun was digging in her waist. She took it out and gazed at it reflectively, stunned that she'd actually pulled the trigger. It was too big for her back pocket, so she tucked it into her bra and buttoned her shirt up round it.

Harry groaned softly and she leaned nearer him. His breath was sour and rasping and there was an evil smell coming from his wound. But one thing had come out of all this. She knew the full measure of her man. He had pride, courage and integrity and she loved him so much it hurt.

'Won't be long, sweetheart,' she murmured into his ear. 'He must have reached the phone by now.'

She didn't hear a sound. It was just a faint shadow that made her turn her head.

Duke stood in the kitchen doorway, wearing an army combat jacket and trousers, white blond hair immaculately combed, pointing a gun at her. Her scream was involuntary.

'Move away from him,' he ordered. 'Stay sitting, just shuffle back.'

Tara did as he ordered. She didn't know if he was alone or whether he had caught Micky running away, all she could do was play for time and try to stay calm.

The gun tucked into her bra made her feel more confident. If he got distracted she could reach for it.

'Where are my men?' he asked. His thin lips were set in a straight line, eyes colder than ice, she could see he was like a coiled spring and she guessed he'd have no hesitation in shooting her.

'They ran off,' she replied. He couldn't have got Micky or he wouldn't need to ask this. 'I think they took the stuff too.'

'How did you get out?' The question came out like a bullet and she saw suspicion in every line of his taut body.

'I charmed them,' she said defiantly. 'I promised I wouldn't remember what any of them looked like when the police got here. I only got as far as this with Harry. I was just going to get help for him.'

'He looks beyond help.' Duke came closer and kicked Harry's arm. Harry didn't even open his eyes, only a low gurgling moan proved he still held on grimly to life.

'Don't!' Tara blurted out. 'Please don't hurt him any more!'

His lip curled derisively, then a banging sound made his head spin round.

Tara's heart sank.

670

'What's that?' He listened, his head cocked to one side, as Frank roared out abuse from the cellar.

'They're bloody well down there!' Duke dragged her to her feet by her hair. 'How did you get them in there?'

'I, I . . . ' she stuttered. 'I had a knife.'

She knew it was futile. Any moment he would find out the truth from the men, or kill her anyway. All she could do was play for time and hope the police got here first.

'Don't talk stupid!' He cracked the gun barrel on the side of her head so hard it made her see stars, and jerked her back with her hair.

'I have got a knife. It's in my pocket,' she insisted. 'Shall I show you?'

Holding the gun to her head, he pushed her back against the passage wall and let go of her hair. He ran his left hand down her hips, then changed the gun into his other hand to try the other side. His fingers caught on the knife. He drew it out, looked at it with a sneer and put it in his pocket. His hand went round on to her bottom next and he pulled out the bunch of keys.

'Right, let's go down there and ask them what happened,' he said, grabbing her hair again.

It was only a matter of time, she told herself. Do everything as slowly as possible, string it out, even the answers to his questions. If Micky told the emergency services it was a gun shot wound they'd be bound to send police as well. Any moment now she would hear sirens.

'Joe!' Duke called out as they went down into the gloom. 'How did she get you all in there?'

'She shot Carl and Frank,' Joe called back.

'Whose gun?'

'Mine.' Joe's voice was subdued.

'Where is it now?'

They were down in the cellar now.

'She's still got it.' This time it was Frank who called out. 'Fuckin' get us out of here, Duke. Carl's dying and

671

I'm bleedin like a fuckin' pig. You gotta get help for us.'

'Where's Micky?' Duke turned to Tara, pushing her up against the wall and sticking the gun almost up her nose.

'He ran off,' she said. 'I used him to help me get Harry upstairs and he got out the window while I was distracted.'

'Where's the gun?' Duke stuck his right into her temple.

'Upstairs. I put it down once Micky had gone.' She made herself whimper, wishing she could turn tears on at the drop of a hat.

Duke gave her a long, hard look which turned her insides to jelly, yanked her forward by the hair and opened the cell door. Frank hobbled out first, clutching at his crotch.

'Give me the gun and I'll finish her right off,' he snarled. His jeans were soaked in blood and his face was chalky in the gloom.

'Carl's in a bad way,' Joe called from over by the bed. 'If we move him again I don't reckon he'll make it. He needs hospital.'

'Leave him there for now,' Duke called out, still holding Tara tightly. 'I just came to pick up the stuff and I've gotta run. You clear up here first, then get out. Make sure you don't leave anything behind.'

'So whatcha going to do about her?' Frank asked.

'Joe and you can sort that out, and Harry too,' Duke snapped. Pushing her ahead of him with his gun, he led the way back up the stairs.

Two things struck Tara as odd as Duke pushed her down to the ground with Harry. One was that he seemed to be in a tearing hurry, the other that he showed no concern for either of his wounded men. He tossed his own gun over to Joe.

'Watch them,' he said. 'Frank, find Joe's gun!'

Frank lurched off into the kitchen, the hand holding

his wound covered in blood. Duke went upstairs, leaving Tara with Harry, her father standing guard over them.

'Duke's going to scarper with the drugs,' Tara said softly. 'Forget about us and watch him.'

She read the emotions in his face as clearly as she did as a child. For a moment she forgot the scar, the bald head and even the evil inside him. He was her father, and somewhere deep within her bubbled a little vestige of affection.

He didn't want to kill her, but he knew he must. He didn't want the other men to know she was his daughter, yet he was looking at her with pride. He too had sensed what Duke was up to, and he suspected she'd sent Micky for help. But most of all she read despair. He knew that, whatever way he jumped now, he was trapped.

'It ain't in here,' Frank yelled. 'Bet she's still got it stuffed down her drawers.'

Duke came down the stairs, a holdall in his hand. Frank came out into the passage and Joe just stood there with the gun pointing at her.

'He wants you blamed for everything, Joe.' Tara spoke fast as Duke came nearer. 'He's going to run away with that bag and leave you to take the blame for everything. Shoot him, not me!'

Duke leaped towards her. She saw in his eyes that he'd suddenly realised where the gun was hidden, perhaps even noticed the lump under her shirt. As he reached forward to grab her Joe's voice rang out.

'Hands off her and drop that bag!'

But Duke ignored him, ripping at her shirt, exposing her chest with the gun stuck into her bra.

The report of the gun and Duke's exclamation of 'Bitch' came simultaneously, but it wasn't until Duke fell forward on to her that she realised Joe had shot him in the back.

673

She moved sideways, but not quickly enough to prevent Duke crashing down on top of her, knocking her to the floor under him.

'Fuckin' well get her and Harry now,' she heard Frank say.

The gun was in her hand as she pushed Duke's body off her and sat up. Frank's face blanched, he backed towards the open window just inside the kitchen. Joe had the holdall in one hand, Duke's gun in the other, but he stood still, looking at her.

'Fuckin' blast 'er,' Frank yelled. 'Come on, don't go soft now, she's only some scrubber.'

Her mother, Gran and Paul all seemed to be with her in that split-second. She looked into her father's eyes and saw not the scarred thug, not the brute who'd beaten her mother and terrorised her brother, but the man who carried her on his shoulders in Petticoat Lane on Sundays. His eyes begged her to kill him.

'You didn't turn out so bad,' he said softly. 'Do it. Don't let them take me!'

Her shot and the sound of sirens came together.

She was aware of Frank jumping out of the back window; saw blue smoke rise in the air, smelled cordite mingling with the putrid smell of Harry's wound. But her eyes were pinned on her father's body slumped on the floor by her feet.

There was no need to touch him to confirm he was dead. His face was at peace, almost smiling, even the scar was hidden because he'd landed on his side.

'Tara!' Harry's croaking voice drew her attention away from the body. 'Did I hear sirens?'

'You did.' She bent down and kissed his face. 'They'll have you in hospital in minutes.'

'Are you hurt?' He seemed unable to open his eyes, his words were slurred and hardly audible.

'No, sweetheart, I'm fine. Just fine!'

Chapter 37

'Miss Manning!'

Tara forced her eyes open. It was the staff-nurse, a bumptious strawberry blonde of over forty who glared down at Tara over her glasses and pursed her lips in disapproval.

It was dark outside, and still raining as it had been all day, but it was hot and stuffy in the waiting room.

'Why don't you go home? Mr Collins won't be up to visitors for some time. You're on the point of collapse!'

'I can't bear to go away.' Tara's eyes filled with tears. 'Don't make me go!'

The nurse shook her head, implying she considered Tara's behaviour to be melodramatic.

'No-one's throwing you out, my dear. I understand you've been through a harrowing time, but you won't be much good to your boyfriend when he comes round the way you are now.'

Tara stuck out her lower lip petulantly. The nurse shook her head once more and walked away.

It was close to midnight and the day had passed in a strange blur, with only isolated incidents making any kind of impact – the shock on the faces of the police as they came crashing in to find her sitting on the floor with two dead men and one seriously injured; George passing out when he saw two covered bodies on the floor.

675

George, Needles and Tony had arrived just as the police were carrying Carl up from the cellar on a stretcher. Harry was already in the ambulance, but poor George saw only those two lifeless mounds, thought they were Tara and Harry, and keeled over.

Once they reached Folkestone hospital, she had vague recollections of someone saying she needed a stitch in the cut above her eye and the lump on the back of her neck must be painful, yet until then she hadn't been aware of any injuries. Her whole being was centred on Harry, as she waited on the edge of her seat while they removed the bullet and took him into intensive care, praying he would survive.

Police kept coming into the waiting room and asking more questions. Were any of the men in the gang known to her prior to this incident? What was the name of the fourth man who got away? Why did Joe Spikes kill Duke? And the most difficult one of all, why didn't she contact the police before blundering into a house miles from anywhere?

Their questions about Josh washed over her head – she didn't understand how they expected her to know about dates he'd been out of the country, or how he became involved.

She wanted to sleep, but she was afraid to close her eyes. The police were delighted to recover such a large haul of drugs and even more pleased to have the perpetrators in their custody. They praised her incessantly for her courage and marvelled that a girl who knew nothing about guns could bring herself to aim and fire, not just once, but three times.

Well, maybe she was brave then, but now she was scared! How long would it be before they discovered Joe Spikes was in fact Bill MacDonald and all the old skeletons were taken out and given a good rattle?

Would people see her as a heroine when they knew the man she'd killed was her father? And what about

676

Simon Wainwright? He was out there somewhere, watching and waiting. Should she tell the police about him, or let it go?

'Come on, girl, you're coming with me!'

Tara looked round, surprised to hear George's voice through the open waiting-room door. He had gone back to London around midday with Needles and Tony.

'Where did you spring from?' She rubbed her eyes wearily.

'I've booked you, me and Queenie into a little boarding house just across the road,' he said, pulling her to her feet and hugging her as if she was a small child. 'You didn't think I'd stay in London while my boy is poorly, did you?'

'That's better now.' Queenie clucked like a mother hen as Tara came back from the bathroom into the small room at the top of the house, wearing the nightdress Queenie had brought with her from London. She pulled back the covers and waited for Tara to get in. 'A good night's sleep is what you need. Drink that hot milk, we put a drop of brandy in it to send you off to the land of nod extra quick. If you want anything, we're right next door.'

'Thanks, Queenie.' Tara drank the milk and cuddled down under the covers. 'I'm so glad you came, everything feels less scary now.'

'Well, my goodness, you look better!' George exclaimed as Tara came into the dining room the next morning. Aside from the stitch above her right eye, a little swelling and a bruise on her cheek, she looked like her old self, the sparkle back in her eyes.

'I feel better. I just rang the hospital. Harry came round just after we left last night and they've moved him out of intensive care into a surgical ward.' Tara beamed at them both. 'And thanks for these clothes, Queenie. It's good to be in something clean.'

She sat down at the table with them and ordered a cooked breakfast from the landlady. Queenie poured her a cup of tea.

'I suppose I'll have to face a barrage of questions again today?' Tara said in resigned tone. There were three other couples in the room and they all had their ears pinned back.

George and Queenie exchanged glances over their bacon and eggs.

'They can't help it, love.' Queenie smiled comfortingly and dropped her voice to a whisper. 'I mean, they gotta find the whole truth, ain't they? At least yer mum was wrong about yer dad being alive. What a can of worms that would have opened!'

Tara stared at Queenie, teaspoon still stirring her tea.

'Course, I don't suppose you know about that?' Queenie took Tara's silence to be incomprehension. 'See, yer mum got the idea it had to be Bill involved, that house being an old haunt of 'is. The police asked George to look at the bloke down in the morgue.'

'Daft, weren't it?' George chimed in, his voice like a fog-horn in the small room. 'He was about as much like Bill as our 'Arry is to Prince Charles. Bill might have been a bit spoiled with booze, but 'e was a handsome brute. That Joe Spikes looked like summat out a horror film.' George grinned broadly, but at last lowered his voice and continued in a whisper. 'But they already knew it weren't 'im. Bill 'ad a little bluebird tattoo on 'is shoulder, didn't he?'

'Yes,' Tara replied nervously. 'What about Joe?'

' 'E 'ad just about every kind of tattoo you can think of, all over his bleedin' chest, back and arms. But there was no bluebird.'

'I never could stand a man with tattoos.' Queenie pursed her lips in distaste. 'Shows a man's weird, having needles poked into him for fun.'

'He wasn't so bad.' Defending Joe seemed essential,

678

though Tara didn't quite understand why. 'If he hadn't been half reasonable I wouldn't have managed to get his gun. And at the end he chose to shoot Duke rather than me.'

'They found thousands of pounds in Duke's car,' Queenie said, her blue eyes alight with laughter. 'It was a good job he didn't leave his car around 'ome. He'd have got back and found the wheels gone, never mind the money. It come from the club, of course! He was about to run out on the rest of them, they reckon! 'E left the club soon after George rang Needles, seems like he could've listened on the phone.'

'Did they find Frank, the one who ran away?' Tara asked.

'Yeah, they pulled him walking along a country lane, only about half a mile from the house,' George said. 'He's bin squealing like a pig outside the slaughter house. 'E told 'em there'd been six small runs before. Mostly Duke came down to fetch it. Then up at the club they'd arrange a private poker game, the dealers from all over the country would come and buy the stuff. Last night the police watched the club, 'oping to get leads on these dealers.'

Tara clamped her hand over her mouth. 'I'd forgotten. I got a list of telephone numbers from the club. I left it in my rucksack out in the grounds of the house.'

'You can tell 'em later,' George assured her, clearing a space on the table as the landlady brought Tara's breakfast. 'Now eat that all up, you look scrawny!'

'Have the police pulled Josh?' she asked in a low voice, aware now that the other guests were spinning out their breakfasts purposely.

'He's gone to ground.' George shook his head. 'At least, that's what they said last night. It was on the news yesterday, the papers are probably full of it this morning, so it won't be long before someone spots him.'

Tara ate her breakfast with relish. All day yesterday

679

people had offered her food, but she hadn't been able to eat it. But now, after eight hours of sleep and hearing Harry was better, she felt like a new person.

The surgical ward was full of sunshine. It danced on the shiny floor, illuminating the many vases of flowers.

A nurse had shaved Harry. He grinned broadly as Tara came into the ward, and tried to sit up.

'Down,' she said, slapping his wrist. 'You've made a remarkable recovery! Or were you only playing dead?'

'I kept my eyes shut so no-one would shoot me, then I got to like it that way,' he said teasingly. 'Now kiss me so I can find out if all parts of me are working.'

Tara was aware of the other men in the ward watching, but she bent down to kiss him regardless.

'It's working,' Harry whispered. 'It twitched in recognition of your touch. One more and it might stand to attention.'

'There's not a great deal wrong with you.' Tara laughed, pulling up a chair. She took his hands in hers and looked at him. He was so handsome her stomach churned. Even the pale green hospital pyjamas with 'Folkestone General' stamped on the breast pocket gave him an air of a wounded hero.

'Seriously, though, how's your leg?' she asked.

'It hurts, but not as bad as you would expect.' He smirked. 'I dreamed they were amputating it because I'd got gangrene, so when I woke to find it still there, I was over the moon. I don't even care if they've left a bloomin' great hole.'

'I thought you were going to die,' she admitted softly. 'All the time while Joe shot Duke, then I shot Joe, you never moved, moaned or anything.'

'You were something else,' he said, a look of wonder in his eyes. 'You kept your head, you took command. I just wish I'd been fully conscious all the time, what a story to tell our children!'

Tara blushed and giggled. 'Just you watch how you treat me from now on,' she said. 'I might crash you over the head with a frying pan, or run you down with a lawn mower.'

Harry's grin faded, a thoughtful look taking its place. 'It's like a new start.' He took her hand in both of his, wanting to tell her what was in his heart. 'When they shot me and threw me back in the cellar I knew they were going to kill me eventually. That kind of cleared my brain, made me see what was important. I made a deal with Him.' Harry rolled his eyes heavenwards. 'I promised if He'd find a way of saving me I'd reform. A clean life, one where I did some good, not just making money. When you turned up I thought to myself that the message was "Sorry, no deals, but here's a last minute consolation." Then you vanished with Carl and I thought they'd killed you. I wanted to die then, Tara. I wasn't even scared any more, because I knew life without you wasn't worth anything.'

'Oh, Harry.' She reached forward and stroked his long hair away from his face. 'None of it matters now. We're safe. We can start all over again.'

'It was all fuzzy somehow, but I can still see you in that dark passageway, commanding them to get into the cellar.' He gave a tremulous smile. 'I wanted to help, but I couldn't. I thought they would grab you, but then you shot Carl. You were incredible!'

'Put it aside, Harry?' She pleaded with him, seeing his distress.

'No, you don't understand.' He held her hands tightly. 'I took it as a sign, Tara, the deal was struck. I told myself I would never go back to the club. Not ever.'

'You'll have to, until you can sell it.'

He shook his head. 'Tony and Needles can run it for now,' he said. 'I'll keep the building, offer someone the club on a lease for a few years. All that land on the river is going to be worth a fortune in a year or two. If I just hang on and wait our fortune will be made.'

'Our?'

'You haven't forgotten our promise, have you?' he said, reaching out and caressing her face. 'We must get married the moment I get out of here. Let's go and live on the farm?'

Tara heard his words and she knew it was what she wanted. But he'd been through a terrible trauma and maybe in a couple of weeks things would look different.

'We'll talk about that when you're well again. George and Queenie want to come in now, shall I get them?'

'Just as long as you don't use it as an excuse to slide off somewhere.' He grinned. 'One more kiss before you get them?'

Tara bounded along Pembridge Road, a huge bunch of flowers in one hand, a carrier bag of food in the other.

Tomorrow Needles was going to collect Harry and bring him home to her flat. Amy and Greg wanted him brought down to Somerset, Queenie and George wanted him with them. But they'd both had too much of people asking questions and fussing round them. They wanted to be alone.

George and Queenie had come back to London three days ago with the intention of selling the business and going into retirement. Tara had come back a day early just to give the flat a good clean and stock up the cupboards.

Once she knew Harry was getting better, being in Folkestone was like a holiday. She had taken walks down along the front, sunbathed on the beach between hospital visits and read magazines.

Frank had been transferred from Folkestone to a prison hospital, but in fact his wound was only superficial. For Carl it had been touch and go, and it would be some time before he was well enough to stand trial.

But Micky was still free. Although the police knew there had been a fourth man at the house, so far they had been unable to find him. Josh hadn't been found either, but rumour had it he'd skipped the country.

Each day in Folkestone she expected to hear the police had discovered Joe Spikes was in fact Bill MacDonald. Time and again she was tempted to blurt it out to Harry or George, yet somehow she had managed to keep quiet. Yet at night it plagued her, she would lie awake imagining scenarios in which the police came to her with her father's fingerprints. What would she do? Make out she hadn't known? Cry and tell them what a brute her father had been?

Tara stopped short by her flat and frowned. The curtains were closed and she was sure she'd left them open that day she ran in and got changed before going down to Hythe.

'Maybe I pulled them over?' She frowned, trying hard to remember. 'You must have done.' She shrugged her shoulders and dug her key out of her bag. 'You didn't remember telling the police where you'd left the rucksack, either, but you had.'

A pile of letters was waiting for her on the hall table. She picked them up, opened her own front door and walked in, kicking the door shut behind her as she leafed through her mail.

She sensed someone was there a second before she actually saw him. A faint smell of sweat and cigarettes hung in the air.

'Who is it?' A cold chill ran down her spine and her heart began to race.

'It's only me!'

Wheeling round at Josh's voice she saw him curled up on the floor trying to conceal himself in the space between a large chest of drawers and the window. She felt hatred rather than fear.

'What are you doing here?' She sprang forward,

dragging him out by the shoulders.

'Don't hit me!' He covered his head with his hands and in that second hate turned to mere revulsion.

His face was ghostly white, his hair stood on end and his expression was one of pure terror.

'I hadn't got anywhere else to go,' he said in a low voice. 'I needed time to think things out and you'd left a spare key at work.'

Tara looked at him and slowly shook her head. All these years she'd admired him, thought he was courageous, clever and so very special. But now he was just a frightened kid who knew he deserved punishment but hadn't got enough guts to step forward and take it.

'I'm amazed at your cheek,' she snapped. 'You plotted against Harry, you would gladly have seen me killed. You betrayed me in a thousand different ways, then you come here! I'm phoning the police now!'

'Don't, please don't,' he begged her. 'Later maybe, when we've talked, but not yet.'

'Give me one good reason why I should even share the same air as you?'

'I never wanted you hurt,' he said, and his big dark eyes turned to liquid. 'Please believe that, Tara. I just put up the initial stake for a plan that looked like it would make me a quarter of a million. I needed it to pull the business back together.'

'Don't lie to me on top of everything else,' Tara said scornfully. Josh was shaking from head to foot, his clothes were crumpled and he had thick stubble on his chin. 'You wanted to get Harry out the way, that was as important as the money. You watched me breaking my heart because he'd gone, you took me out for the day and tried to make love to me, all the time knowing he was going to be killed!'

His guilt showed clearly in his eyes. 'I'm so ashamed of myself.' He clutched his arms tighter round his knees. 'But I love you, Tara. I wanted to keep you beside me.'

'Don't you know anything, you stupid jerk?' she exploded. 'I always cared about you. There have been times when I thought you were the one for me. Even if I'd married Harry I expect I'd have carried on working for you.' She went over to her phone and picked it up.

'Please, Tara,' he whispered. 'Just let me explain to you first?'

She hesitated, looking back at him. She could see he wasn't dangerous, and perhaps she needed to hear his side of the story.

'OK, get on with it. I'll give you ten minutes.'

'You didn't know.' Josh wrung his hands together. 'I've been sliding into trouble for some time. The only way I could save my business was by investing in this gang so I could get enough cash to revamp the shops. I was desperate. It wasn't me who suggested taking over Harry's club, or kidnapping him, that was all dreamed up by Duke and Joe Spikes.'

Just the mention of that name made Tara uneasy. Did Josh know Joe's true identity?

'Look, Josh.' She put her shopping down on the table. 'I'll make us a cup of tea but don't take that as a sign of weakness. I'm not going to harbour a wanted man.'

'Fair enough.' His face relaxed a little.

'For God's sake, go and have a bath,' she said. 'This room stinks, and most of it's coming from you.'

'I didn't dare run the water.' He looked boyishly apologetic, but he picked up a small holdall and slunk into the bathroom.

Tara winced when she saw her small kitchen. Flies buzzed around dirty plates, all the mugs had been used and just left. The bin was overflowing with empty tins and the cooker top was filthy. She filled the sink with hot, soapy water, pushed the dirty dishes into it, then went to open the curtains and windows. She made a pot of tea, and was putting it on the table when Josh came back in, smelling of Camay soap and clean-shaven, tidy again in grey needlecord trousers and a pale blue shirt.

'That's better,' she said approvingly. 'I always find you can handle anything after a bath and a change.'

'So you say it wasn't your idea to kidnap Harry?'

'No. Well, partly. I mean they had it all worked out, but I told them bits and pieces to help. See I financed it, but I wasn't part of the gang.'

'Was it Wainwright who made the calls?'

He nodded.

'So you struck a deal with him right back when the other business happened?'

'Not exactly. I just kept a contact number in case. He didn't know what was going on. I just fed him the information about Harry and what to say. It was just an acting job and a chance for revenge as far as he was concerned.'

'How could you?' Tara shook her head in total bewilderment.

'Can I have a bit of time before you grass me up?' he asked, his eyes like a spaniel's.

'I'm not grassing you up.' She beckoned for him to sit on the settee opposite her. 'You can give yourself up, or continue to run, whichever you like. Just as long as you don't come near me.'

'I can't bear the thought of prison,' he said, sipping his tea.

'You might not get prison.'

'Pigs might fly,' he said gloomily.

'Don't be such a weed!' she snapped at him. 'Give yourself up! Talk to a lawyer and he'll get you bail. Then you can sort something out about the business. Has it occurred to you the girls at the shops are waiting to be told what's happening? You owe it to them to make an effort.'

'What for? I haven't got the money to pull things together, it won't be long before I go bust. So what's the point?'

'I don't believe things are that bad.' Tara wanted to slap his face he was being so pathetic. 'There are assets out there, your house, cars and the leases on the shops, not to mention stock which could be sold off.'

He closed his eyes and lay back on the settee. 'I'm going to come clean with you,' he said in a small voice. 'I'm burnt out, Tara. What little talent I had I've used up. I've been doing drugs for so long my life revolves round them. These days it's as much as I can do to shave myself, let alone organise a business.'

Tara opened her mouth to protest, but all at once she saw it. The dead eyes, the pallor of his skin. It was obvious. She leaned forward and undid his cuff, rolling up the sleeve. Red and purple track marks from a hypodermic dotted his veins.

'Oh, Josh.' Tears welled up in her eyes. 'Why? You knew the dangers!'

'It was just speed at first,' he explained. 'I needed a boost, there just weren't enough hours in the day. Then it was cocaine and sometimes both. I only started the heroin this year. It seemed the answer at first, I was looking forward, planning and being creative again. But then the heroin took over, I couldn't think of anything but the next fix.'

'I wish you'd told me.' She took his hands in hers and squeezed them. 'I'd have made you stop some-how. It's such a wicked, wicked waste.'

'You're right, of course.' He grimaced. 'Sometimes I loathe myself so much I can't bear it.'

'Go to the police!' Tara knelt down in front of him. 'It's a huge step, I know, but once you've made it it will get easier. I'll do what I can to hold things together until we can find a long-term solution.'

He didn't answer her immediately, just looked into her eyes with his big, sad brown ones.

'I thought you'd reject me,' he said. 'But you've given me the courage I needed.' He leaned forward and held her face in both his hands, kissing her gently on the nose. 'I'll get out of your life now and let you find the kind of peace and happiness you deserve.'

She watched him walking down the road to flag down a taxi, tears pouring down her cheeks. The bold, arm-swinging march she remembered was gone. His hands were in his pockets, face hidden behind sunglasses, and he kept close to the wall, shoulders hunched.

'What a waste,' she sobbed. 'What a terrible waste!'

'Welcome home!' Tara shrieked as Harry climbed out of the car, running down the steps with her arms outstretched.

'Go easy on him, Tara,' Needles reproved her as she smothered his face with kisses. 'The man's an invalid!'

'Invalid my arse!' Harry grinned wickedly. 'My recovery will be complete once Tara gives me a dose of her special medicine.'

'I won't hang around, then.' Needles handed Tara a carrier bag. 'There's a change of clothing there. Just ring me if he needs anything else.'

'Come on in for a drink, or a coffee?' Tara said quickly, hoping she sounded sincere. 'I want to hear about the club and stuff.'

'You don't want me here.' Needles gave one of his big belly laughs. 'You two's got a lotta lost time to make up for.'

'Thanks, Needles.' Harry clapped his friend across the back. 'You've been a diamond. I'll be in touch in a day or two.'

Tara put her arm around Harry to help him up the stairs. He was still limping, but in every other way he looked like his old self.

He stood for a moment just inside the door, looking around the room. It was clear Tara had cleaned and polished for his homecoming; every surface, ornament and picture glass gleamed. There were flowers on the table and the bookcase, and he noted she'd put a little padded stool next to his favourite armchair for him to put his leg up.

'I feel different here,' he said, not really understanding his feelings. 'Like I've left Harry the wide-boy down the road somewhere.'

'That's good.' She had laughter in her voice, but understanding, too. She shut the door behind them. 'Are you hungry?'

'Starving.'

'What would you like, then?' She slid her arms round him and buried her face in his neck.

'I'd like around a hundred kisses. I'd like to peel your clothes off slowly while I nibble every last inch of skin, then see how I feel.' He tilted her face up to his.

His lips were hungry, they devoured hers, holding her so close she felt her ribs might cave in with the pressure.

'I was so afraid I would never do this again,' he gasped eventually, loosening his hold on her long enough to look down at her face in wonder. He moved her then, sweeping her over to the bed, his fingers reaching for her zip, lips on her neck, her shoulders and her breasts.

Harry had been a superb lover from the very first time but now there was extra tenderness in each caress. His lips seemed to savour the softness and perfume of her skin, his fingers were intent on giving her the ultimate pleasure. Slowly he peeled off her clothes and his own and lay back on the bed.

His skin had regained its customary golden sheen through sitting in the hospital garden in a wheelchair. Aside from the thick crêpe bandage round his thigh there was no evidence of how close he had come to

689

death. He reached out for Tara and pulled her on top of him.

'You'll have to do all the work,' he whispered, running his fingers through her hair. 'Kneeling is beyond me.'

It was heaven just to hold him, to tease him by first allowing him to slip inside her, then moving away. She bent to kiss his neck, his ears and chest, listening to his breathing growing hard and fierce. He rolled with her, playing with her, stroking her, but each time pulling her back on top of him.

'Let me in,' he pleaded with her, holding on to her hips and pulling her down hard on to him.

The expression on his face was one of adoration as his hands reached up to cup her breasts. Watching his pleasure heightened her own, and as she leaned forward to kiss him, passion flared up like sugar tossed on to fire.

'I love you so much.' Harry's voice was hoarse with emotion and Tara moved faster on him, her lips clinging to his.

'I can't hold back any longer,' she heard him gasp, his fingers gripping her buttocks as if afraid she might move away. But even as he spoke she felt her own orgasm erupt within her, making her scream out his name and clutch his shoulders as a wild and thrilling sensation overtook her.

'Oh, Tara,' she heard him whisper against her neck. 'That was so beautiful.'

She leaned back a little to look at him and her heart swelled up with love. 'I can't believe that I can feel such love, so much tenderness. It's like being reborn, all clean and shiny.'

As they lay cuddled together voices drifted through the open windows to them from the street.

'I hope they didn't hear us,' Tara murmured. 'It's so decadent making love at midday, we should be ashamed of ourselves.'

690

'This is the best feeling ever.' Harry turned his face into her breasts and closed his eyes. 'I haven't got to go to work and neither have you. We've got the rest of our lives to be happy together.'

'We can't stay in here forever.' She laughed. 'Someone has to do mundane things like earn money to pay the rent, do the shopping and go to the launderette.'

'Don't be practical today,' he urged her, nuzzling again at her breasts. 'We can feast on each other, we don't have to wear clothes, we can even telephone for a carry-out.'

'That sounds pretty good,' she whispered. 'Oh, Harry, I love you.'

The doorbell woke them.

'Who on earth's that?' Tara asked, looking at her watch. It was almost five. They had eaten sandwiches and drunk some wine, made love again and then slept. She pulled on a T-shirt and crawled over to the window to peep out.

'Oh, shit, Harry, it's the police,' she whispered. 'What can they want with us now? Shall we pretend we're not here?'

Harry was propped up on the pillows, long hair tousled, his face soft with sleep.

'They'll only come back.' He smiled. 'Besides, we haven't got anything to hide.'

'Speak for yourself!' She hastily pulled her knickers on and jumped into her jeans. 'Are you going to just lie there?'

Harry pulled over the bedspread, tossed a few cushions on it, then limped off to the bathroom to put his clothes on. The bell rang again just as Tara was going out into the hall, tucking her T-shirt into her jeans.

'Miss Manning?' the older of the two men asked.

'Yes.' Tara felt a pang of fear. 'What is it?'

'Could we come in to speak to you?' he said in a

691

gentle tone she knew meant something unpleasant. 'It's about Joshua Bergman.'

She stared wide-eyed as they described how a neighbour had rung Chelsea police to report that Josh was back in his house late last night.

'We called soon after but we could get no reply and in fact we believed the neighbour was mistaken,' the younger of the two officers said. He was very fair, with almost white eyelashes and pale blue eyes. The older man had gingery thinning hair, with a freckly complexion and a missing front tooth.

'Spare her the blow-by-blow account,' Harry said, putting his arm around her and holding her tightly. 'Is something wrong?'

'We gained entry at ten this morning.' The gingery one looked faintly irritated by Harry's attempt to speed their report up. 'We found Bergman dead on his bed. He had taken a fatal overdose.'

Tara could hear what they were saying, but she couldn't believe it. Josh's last words to her had been that she had given him the courage he needed.

'But why? We talked yesterday. He was going to come to you and give himself up. I don't understand.'

She hadn't told Harry about him being here. Not because she wanted to hide it, but because his presence had put it right out of her mind. Now she felt him bristle.

'I'm sorry, Harry. I should have told you he was here when I got back from Folkestone. It's just we had other things on our minds.'

'It's OK.' Harry hugged her. 'Let the officers explain.'

'From the letter he left I'd say he just couldn't cope with anything any longer,' the older man said.

'He left a letter? What did he say?' Tara wanted to cry, but she forced herself not to give in to it.

'You'll be able to see it later.' The blond officer looked faintly embarrassed now. 'Much of it concerns his feelings about you and the business. I suggest you come with us to the station; we do need your help with some of our enquiries.'

They were ushered into a small room on the first floor of Chelsea police station. It smelled of stale cigarettes and the windows were frosted so interviewees couldn't even be distracted by the view. But Sergeant Baldwin was kind. He went over how Josh was found, showed no surprise at all that Josh had been hiding in her flat prior to her return to London and even less that Josh had failed to give himself up.

'He was probably more frightened of being without his heroin than the actual process of law,' he said gently.

'I should have rung you last night to check he had come to you,' she said brokenly. 'It never occurred to me he would take his life.'

'Tara.' Sergeant Baldwin's voice was firm. 'I can tell you now that it wouldn't have made a scrap of difference. If someone intends to take their life, they find a way. It would perhaps have been worse for you if he'd flung himself under a bus when we arrived to arrest him, or hung himself in a cell. At least this way you know he died peacefully, the way he'd chosen for himself.'

'But it's such a waste, he had so much talent.'

Baldwin shot her a look that suggested he saw no real loss in one more drug addict dying by his own hand, but he reached across the table and patted her hand.

'Don't fret about this,' he insisted. 'You and Mr Collins have both suffered enough, and from what Bergman says in his letter I suspect he'd been trading on your talent for too long. Would you like to see it now?'

Tara looked at Harry. He had been silently supportive, his hand in hers, but she was a little afraid that Josh's last words to her might hurt him.

'Go on,' Harry urged. 'Maybe it'll reassure you he

693

did know what he was doing.'

Sergeant Baldwin handed her the letter.

Just looking at Josh's beautiful copperplate script made her eyes prick with tears. She remembered him telling her he was taught it by a Rabbi after school because his father said you could tell an educated man by his handwriting. But as Tara began to read the letter she could no longer hold back her tears. Here was the real Josh, a man who had never really belonged anywhere.

It was simply marked 'To whoever finds me'.

'I have decided to end my life because I see no further purpose to it. My business is close to failure, I have disappointed my parents. I am a criminal and a heroin addict. I have lied, exaggerated and hyped my way through life, spread my little talent very thinly, and used people rather than befriending them.

I regret most of the shabby stunts I've pulled on people, all the deals which left others with a sour taste in their mouth, and all those women I treated so badly. As I sit here, so terribly in need of a friend, I can't think of one person who I haven't used and discarded, and I know I deserve what's come to me.

But of all the people I used and hurt, Tara Manning is the one who concerns me most. I want it known now that she was always the creative force behind Josh shops. It was her talent as a designer that made my fortune, and yet I stifled her, gagged and blindfolded her so she would never realise just how bright a star she was.

Why? Simple jealousy, that's all. I had been to art school, I had the right background, but I didn't have that spark of brilliance she has.

There isn't much time to make restitution, but I did call on my solicitor Mr William Bennett of Bennett and Legett of Chancery Lane this

694

afternoon, and made a will.

I wish to apologise now to everyone I hurt. To my parents, who will perhaps never understand. To Harry Collins, who I think might. But most of all to Tara, who not only gave me her best but in the end pointed me in the right direction.

Sing no sad songs for me.

Joshua Bergman'

Harry just held Tara while she cried, waiting patiently for the sobs to subside, offering her a handkerchief and smoothing back her hair.

Sergeant Baldwin cleared his throat and shuffled one or two papers round on his desk in faint embarrassment.

'Of course the solicitors Bergman spoke of will get in touch with you in due course, but I'm sure you'd like a rough idea now of what's in the will?'

Harry looked up quickly, eyes bright with interest. 'You know?'

'The gist of it,' the policeman said. 'We were only checking them out to make sure he hadn't deposited any large sums or even drugs in the solicitors' safe-keeping, and of course to discover how Bergman seemed at the time. Anyway, he didn't deposit anything. He was absolutely normal in every way. He told Mr Bennett he was on his way to us, asked him to recommend a brief, and wanted a simple will drawn up before he did so.'

'How sad,' Tara whispered. 'Imagine thinking all that out, trying to put everything right.'

'And they told you what he put in his will?' Harry asked in some surprise.

'Yes, in case it helped our enquiries. Apparently Bergman wanted his solicitors to have this letter and the contents of his will publicised so there would be no quibbling or doubts as to his intentions.'

'Well?' Harry leaned forward impatiently.

'He left his entire estate to you, Miss Manning.'

It was only when they got back home that the full impact hit her. Grief at losing a man who had been so important in her adult life. Guilt because maybe she'd failed him, and anger because he'd laid a burden at her feet she didn't feel strong enough to lift.

'Why leave me his business?' she sobbed. 'How did he expect me to handle it if he couldn't?'

'I expect he assumed you'd be sensible enough to get professional advice,' said Harry, sitting up in bed and hauling her up till she nestled in his arms. 'But you aren't alone in this, babe, you've got me to help. We'll get a report on the shops, find out which ones are draining away profit, which ones make it. Maybe you'll have to shut up a couple of them, sell the leases and use the money to update the remaining ones.'

Tara was silent for some time. She lay curled up against Harry, deep in thought. He made no attempt to break through the silence, aware she was working her way through the events of the day.

'You know how back home in Somerset they have this idea all the women in our family are jinxed?' she blurted out suddenly. 'That's what all this is. Another bloody jinx.'

Harry shook his head. 'Not so. You've underestimated Josh, sweetheart. I reckon he knew you could turn it around. He was another gambler, but he left the tables this time while he still had a good hand. We're picking up that hand, babe, and we're going to win, not just for us, but for Josh, too.'

Chapter 38

August 1970

'Doesn't she look beautiful?' Tara turned to Harry and Queenie, her eyes glistening as Amy walked up the aisle on George's arm.

The church was bright with flowers. The end of each pew had a posy of trailing ivy, marigolds and gypsophila, there were baskets of roses around the pulpit and huge arrangements of delphiniums and carnations on every available surface. But Amy outshone the flowers, radiant in palest pink silk, with a headdress of pink rosebuds. The long dress was simple, her hair hung loose on her shoulders as she wore it most days, but it was the joy in her face that turned her into an object of wonder.

As Amy reached the front pew she looked sideways at Tara and smiled. Greg looked round from his position at the altar rail, his face beatific.

Harry's hand stole into Tara's and squeezed, reminding her that soon it would be them at the altar.

Tara could hear the choir singing the special wedding anthem after Greg and Amy had made their vows, yet her mind was wandering back over the events of the past weeks.

It was hard to believe that since that painfully sad service for Josh at Golders Green crematorium she had found the strength to be totally ruthless with his empire.

She had expected animosity from his parents, but they were too shattered by their son's death to care about his business. His father kissed her on both cheeks, wished her well and told her to do whatever was necessary.

Under Josh's accountant's direction she analysed each of the four shops' profitability and came up with the answer that she could keep only Church Street Kensington. The leases of the other three were sold, and staff given final wage packets. The warehouse in Fulham was sold at auction, bringing in enough to pay off Josh's debts. Finally she gave up her own flat and moved back into the rooms above Church Street.

In all this she couldn't have managed without Harry. Not only did he listen patiently to her worries, but he was quick at grasping figures, astute at assessing people's characters, and he could handle estate agents and prospective buyers better than anyone she'd ever met. But where he really came into his own was with the renovation of Church Street, not only saving a fortune by taking on men to work under his direction, but leaking an artist's impression of the new shop to a Sunday paper and persuading them to do a profile of Tara.

Josh would have loved the way the media swarmed around them. Tragic irony, perhaps, that he had to die to achieve this kind of coverage, but then he was the one who preached capitalising on each and every opportunity.

She and Harry were hot news, a story that had it all – kidnapping, drug-smuggling, murder. It had a handsome gambler of a hero, a beautiful, talented and brave heroine. They felt themselves duty-bound to give it a truly happy ending, by surpassing everything Josh had done.

Everything was just about perfect, except for the guilt!

It didn't make any difference how often she told herself she was withholding the information about her father to protect her mother. She knew the truth. She couldn't face the fact she had shot her father.

The congregation rose for the hymn 'Love Divine, All Love Excelling'. It was time to follow Amy and Greg to the vestry to witness the signing of the register, along with Reg Beamish, the best man, Harry, George and Queenie.

A shaft of sunshine danced on Amy's blonde hair as she sat at the desk.

'Allow me to be the first to congratulate you both.' Reverend Williamson held out a hand first to Amy and then to Greg.

He and Greg had many shared interests – fishing, dogs and cricket. But while Greg was round-faced, tubby and jovial, the vicar was tall and painfully thin, with gold-rimmed spectacles and a lugubrious manner.

'I wish you love and happiness,' he went on, a warm smile lighting up his long face. 'This is a whole new chapter in your lives.'

Harry watched as Tara embraced her mother. As always he marvelled at their beauty. Tara was taller, her red-gold hair and peachy skin so much more dramatic than Amy's English rose complexion. Tara's long pale green dress complemented Amy's pale pink, like two flowers in a garden.

Queenie moved forward to kiss Amy. She too looked beautiful, but like a dalia next to primroses. From the hot pink picture hat to her pink and white polka dot dress and jacket, she was as glamorous as a film star. Harry smiled at his stepmother, loving her for the happiness she'd given his father. George had dressed with restraint today, in a pale grey suit and a sober tie, but even quietly dressed his red, beaming face gave away his true nature.

'Be happy,' Harry said as he kissed Amy. He moved to grasp Greg's hand, but it turned into a hug. Harry felt great admiration for Greg. His quiet strength, his patience, kindness and sense of humour set him apart from other men.

'Hurry up and do it.' Greg grinned, his pale eyes glistening with unshed tears as he returned the embrace. 'I can recommend it!'

It was as Amy put her bouquet on Paul's and Mabel's joint grave that Harry realised Tara was brooding again.

At six in the evening it was still warm, the huge yew tree casting a long shadow across the churchyard. The four of them had walked up to the church after the reception in the Crown and, despite the emotional nature of the trip, both Amy and Tara were in high spirits.

Harry had never been to a wedding reception with such a good atmosphere. The food was good, the wine flowed freely along with conversation and laughter, yet on several occasions Harry noticed Tara withdrawing into herself.

It had happened many times since his discharge from hospital and each time she laughed away his concern, insisting she was only thinking about the shop. But he knew on this occasion she'd left business back in London, so it seemed safe to assume the thing that was troubling her was here, connected with her mother.

He and Greg sat down on the old decapitated market cross steps in a patch of sunshine, while Tara and Amy crouched down by the grave.

'Something's bugging Tara,' Harry blurted out without really thinking.

Greg looked round at him, his jolly face serious for a moment. 'I know.' He nodded. 'Amy's noticed it.'

'Has she got any ideas?' Harry leaned forward,

resting his elbows on his knees. 'I mean, Tara claims she's only thinking about business, but I know it's not that.'

Greg shrugged. 'She thought it was Mabel's death until yesterday evening. They went into the farm to see Stan, and Amy asked her if she was frightened to go back in there. Apparently Tara just laughed and said "He won't come back".'

'He won't come back!' Harry repeated. 'Paul? Or the murderer?'

'I don't know.' Greg shook his head. 'Amy tried to keep her talking but she just clammed up.'

Harry and Greg broke away from one another then as the women came back to join them.

'Time we were going.' Amy smiled at Greg, blonde hair gleaming in the sunshine. 'Otherwise we won't get there before dark.'

'Fancy a walk?' Harry asked Tara.

Greg and Amy had left for their honeymoon in Porlock over an hour earlier, and Queenie and George were nodding off in their armchairs. Greg had invited them all to stay for a holiday. Harry and Tara couldn't manage more than a weekend, but it was apparent George and Queenie felt quite at home. Winston was taking advantage, stretched out on the settee with one eye open, as if daring them to chase him off.

'Where to?' Tara asked as they went out into the hall. 'Down to the lake?'

'I thought we'd go to the farm,' Harry tossed over his shoulder casually. 'Just look around and see how we both feel about it now.'

Tara shrugged her shoulders. Moving back to the farm hadn't been mentioned by either of them since Harry was in hospital. They had both been too busy winding up Josh's affairs, and thinking no further ahead than the wedding.

'We can't get rid of it even if we want to!'

'All the more reason to go and look, then.' Harry followed her out and pulled the door shut behind him. 'We should make some long-term plans, it's not fair to Greg and your mother to leave them all the responsibility without putting them in the picture.'

Tara didn't reply for a moment, just tucked her hand into his arm as they walked across the gravel drive into the High Street. She had changed her clothes since the wedding reception to a long Indian skirt, a cheesecloth top and sandals.

'Gran shouldn't have left it to me,' she said suddenly as they turned towards the farm. 'Mum deserved better treatment.'

'I think your gran was a clever old bird,' Harry replied. 'By keeping it till your thirtieth birthday she made sure you and your mum had time to consider everything. The way land prices are going it will have increased in value by then, and meanwhile it still provides a living and a home for Amy if she needs it.'

Tara stopped on the bridge just before the farm and rested her arms on the parapet.

'You don't get views like that in London,' Harry said, stopping beside her.

The river wound its way through the meadow, going round the back of the farm. As far as they could see fields and trees stretched on to infinity.

'They say it cures warts,' she said.

'What?' Harry asked.

'The water down there.' Tara pointed out a hollowed-out place down on the stone balustrade. 'I don't know if it works, I haven't ever had one to try.'

'What about secret troubles?' Harry leaned over, dipping one finger in the water collected there and dabbing it on her forehead. 'Would it cure those?'

A guarded look came into her eyes. She wanted to tell Harry everything, it was too big a secret to keep to herself, but something always stopped her.

'I wouldn't know. I haven't any of those either,' she said too glibly.

'Don't tell porkies,' Harry said sternly. 'Tell me what's bothering you.'

She leaned further over the bridge, looking intently at the water.

'I know there's something,' he insisted. 'And don't say it's worrying about the business, because I won't believe you.'

He stood behind her, resting one hand on each of her shoulders, and gently massaged with his fingers.

'Well?'

She sighed and stood up, turning to look at him.

'If you had a secret that could make things bad not only for yourself, but for everyone you loved, would you tell it?'

'That depends.' Harry hedged his bets. 'If it was something like having an incurable disease, I'd probably want to keep it to myself. But would that be fair? George, Queenie and you might all be angry when I popped off because I hadn't given you all time to say and do the things you wanted to.'

'Let's walk on.' She turned back to him and took his hand. 'I want to go in the farmhouse.'

She stopped as they passed the wall where Paul met his death. A few years earlier Amy had coaxed some hardy plants to grow on it by pushing compost into the cracks. A shower of little purple flowers mixed with some red and pink ones, and in some strange way it looked like a memorial to Paul.

'It looks pretty.' Harry realised he would get nothing out of her by direct questioning. 'Amazing how mother nature can disguise so effortlessly.'

'At the time I thought I'd never be free of that image,' Tara said softly. 'Every time I closed my eyes I'd see his little body on that machine. But I never think of him like that any more. I only seem to recall the happy times.'

'Mother nature again.' Harry stroked her cheek. 'I expect I'll look at the scar on my leg one day and find I can't remember how much it hurt, or how scared I was.'

The yard looked just as it always did. The barn door stood open, a few chickens wandering in and out. Wind coming across the meadow brought the smell of freshly cut hay, and Amy's geraniums cascaded over the edge of an old sink. Harry opened the top of the stable door and Betsy whinnied a greeting.

'I still remember clearly how evil my dad was to Mum and Paul,' Tara blurted out from behind him. 'The years didn't dim that for me. I was glad when the police came here and told us he was dead, really glad.'

Harry turned from the old mare. Tara's eyes were flashing with fire, her hair turning red in the sunset.

'That's understandable,' he said soothingly, worried by her intense expression. 'Let's go in and make some tea.'

She broke away from him, marching quickly to the back door, lifting out the loose brick where the key was kept and pulling it out.

'Mum didn't share my delight,' she said in a low voice. 'I could never understand it, Harry. She cried when the police said he was dead. She knew he'd killed a priest, he'd hurt her and Paul countless times, made all of us suffer, but she still cried for him.'

'Well, she loved him once. Maybe love doesn't die entirely, not even after all that he did.'

'She made me feel bad about being pleased.' Tara turned the key in the lock and the door opened.

'Pleased isn't the right word to use.' Harry followed her in. 'Relieved, maybe.'

'Same thing,' Tara retorted, lifting the lid of the Aga through force of habit and shutting it again once she remembered it hadn't been alight for months.

Harry shook his head, picking up the electric kettle and filling it from the sink. Tara didn't speak again for some time. She busied herself looking into cupboards and drawers, taking out cups and putting them on the table, running her fingers over ledges, checking for dirt.

Harry sat down at the table. It was almost dark outside now, the sun as red as a blood orange behind the church tower. He could feel Mabel's presence in the room so clearly he could swear she was sitting opposite him.

'I didn't think Mum would like to come in here.' Tara's voice had a slight edge to it. 'Don't you find it odd that she keeps it so nice?'

'Not odd. Nice!' Harry looked round from the table, concerned more with Tara being odd than with Amy. 'It means she doesn't feel threatened, she isn't scared. That's good, isn't it?'

Tara didn't answer, just reached up to the shelf above the Aga and took down the tea caddy.

He knew it was the familiar movement, the memory of all those times he'd seen Mabel go through the same routine, but for a split-second the girl in front of him was wearing a dark Victorian dress, and her hair was braided in fat, shiny coils on each side of her head.

'Harry!' Tara's voice cut through the vision. Once again the girl was Tara, looking at him strangely.

'What's up? You went all weird!'

Harry smiled. 'Thinking about your gran,' he said. 'It feels as if she's still here.'

'She told me once that she often felt her own mother's presence here.' Tara put the teapot on the table. 'She said it was comforting, but she never felt it again after Mum, Paul and I moved in.'

They drank their tea in companionable silence, the room becoming darker as the sun slipped out of sight.

When Tara stood up Harry expected her to switch on the light, but instead she lifted an old candleholder down from the dresser, took a new candle out of the drawer, pushed it in, then lit it.

'Hold me, Harry,' she whispered, putting the candle down on the table.

Harry held out his arms and pulled her on to his lap.

'What is it?' he asked gently, his lips moving down to her throat.

'I don't know,' she whispered back. 'I've got the feeling this house has some answers, something has to happen here. I can't explain.'

Harry knew, though he couldn't have put it into words.

Tara looked ethereal in the candlelight, her hair gleaming, eyes sparkling, lips plump and moist.

'I want you,' Harry said, sliding her blouse off one shoulder and leaning forward to kiss her gleaming skin. She smelled of lilac and he could hear her heart beating faster as he began to open the buttons on the front of her blouse. She bent down to him, drawing his head up between her hands, her lips reaching out for his, tasting faintly of lemon.

'I love you,' she panted, turning round on his lap till her legs straddled his, pushing herself hard up against him.

Her blouse fell to the floor. Harry pulled the skirt apart, her knickers to one side and pushed his fingers hard into her.

'That's so nice.' She sighed, arching her back and leaning back, undulating on his fingers. 'More!'

His lips were on her nipples, one hand caressing her and the other holding her on to his lap. His cock was so hard it hurt and for a moment he considered laying her down on the kitchen floor and screwing her there.

But the lilac smell of her skin, her silky hair on his face and her lemon-tasting lips reminded him of all the

706

other beautiful women who'd lived, loved and lost in this house. Instead he stood up, holding her tightly, her legs round his waist.

'Upstairs,' he said hoarsely, his lips still on her breast. 'Hold the candle!'

It was Mabel's old room he went to, without knowing why, and as he opened the latch the scent of the orange and clove pomanders she hung in her cupboards filled his nostrils.

'Why this room?' Tara murmured, her lips on his neck, thighs gripping him tighter still.

'To lay ghosts!' Harry whispered back and pushed the door open wide.

The old carved bed, covered in a colourful patchwork quilt, seemed to beckon them. Harry put Tara down and by the time she'd placed the candle on the bedside table, he'd shed his clothes.

She looked like a goddess as she stood to untie her skirt at the waist – full, firm breasts partially covered by her hair, her skin glowing in the candlelight. She smiled as her skirt fell to the floor. Harry lay back against the pillow and watched as she put her thumbs into the elastic of her white knickers and slowly pushed them down.

'Come here!' he whispered. 'I'm going to love you till you cry for mercy!'

They had experienced so much memorable lovemaking, but this eclipsed everything. Harry held back his desire to enter her, using his tongue and fingers to bring her to the brink of orgasm again and again. He kissed and stroked every inch of skin, breathed deeply the smell and taste of her, knowing that no other woman would ever make him feel this way.

'Fuck me now,' Tara called out as his tongue probed deep inside her. Her fingers dug into his hair, dragging him up over her stomach, breath coming in hard, hot bursts.

'Say it again.' Harry knelt between her legs. She was tossing from side to side, her tongue flickering across her swollen lips, her hands reaching out desperately for him.

'Fuck me now,' she repeated, her lovely amber eyes glowing in the dim light.

She was so hot and wet inside. Her legs folded round his back, pulling him closer, nails digging into his back, and he felt her come almost immediately.

'I love you,' he said as he drove himself harder and deeper into her. 'I'll love you forever.'

It was very late when a cold chill crept into the room and made them shiver as they lay in each other's arms.

'We should go home,' Harry whispered.

'This is our home,' Tara whispered back. 'I can feel it welcoming me, wanting me here.'

Harry pulled the patchwork quilt over them and drew Tara back into his arms.

'All the answers lie here,' he said softly. He didn't know what prompted him to say that, or even what exactly it meant.

'I know.' Tara burrowed into his shoulder. 'I even understand why Dad put Gran into bed.'

Harry felt as if he had to suspend even breathing until she'd explained that strange statement.

'She reminded him of me once he'd strangled her, and he couldn't leave her tied to that chair. He carried her up here just as tenderly as you carried me, and tucked her into this bed.'

The candle was spluttering as it reached its end, leaving just enough light for Harry to see Tara's face glowing with a mysterious knowledge.

'He didn't come here to hurt anyone, he thought he could creep in, find out how we were, where we were, then go. But Gran heard him, recognised his voice just as I did.'

'I don't understand,' Harry said, just as the candle finally died.

'Joe Spikes was my father, Harry. That's why we got free and why he shot Duke.'

The sun was coming up, weak pink light catching the top right-hand corner of the window as if it was trying to peep in.

Tara had spilled out the true story and then fallen into a deep, peaceful sleep. Harry had dozed intermittently, but his mind was whirring with such conflicting emotions he was unable to let go entirely.

He was astounded that she'd kept such a secret to herself, he felt a little foolish that the truth hadn't dawned on him before, and hurt she hadn't trusted him enough to share it. But honesty was the only way to heal Tara completely. Later today he would take her to the police and let them decide how to handle it.

MacDonald was cunning, twisted and ruthless, and there was no doubt in Harry's mind that if Tara hadn't turned up when she did, he would be dead now. Yet there was this one thread of decency that redeemed him. He'd died in preference to hurting his daughter.

A slight breeze made Harry turn towards the door and he felt a presence. It was coming closer, a warmth, a sweetness. Even though he could see nothing he felt a hand on his brow, as light as a dandelion clock, as tender as the remembered touch of his mother's hand when he was a small child.

A warmth ran through him, strength and joy. He knew all the women of this house were at peace now. He could marry Tara, live here happily with their children, nothing bad would ever happen again. Tara knew this too, that's why she slept so deeply.

He smiled, then he slept, as soundly as Tara.

*

Tara paused before crossing Church Street and smiled. The dark green paintwork, the sparkling windows and the gold letters reading 'Tara Manning' made her want to whoop with joy.

It was the first of November, and already the shops had Christmas displays. They had reopened in a blaze of publicity just two weeks ago and now it was clear they had the formula for success. As she had so often insisted to Josh, people didn't mind paying for quality; her own special evening-wear designs were selling brilliantly.

But she and Harry weren't going to stay in London and play shops. In three weeks they would be married and living on the farm. Harry, for all his flair at organisation, didn't want to spend his life in ladies' fashions. Solly Bergman had put them in touch with a small factory ideally suited to making up her designs, and the staff she'd inherited from Josh were all good people. She could design at home and perhaps twice a month make lightning trips to London to check things out.

Their children would be brought up with grass under their feet, with trees to climb, animals to love and space to grow, along with the child Amy and Greg were so joyfully expecting.

She had done what she set out to do, proved herself, stamped her name on a portion of London. But her life and heart belonged to Harry, and the farm.

She held the box of cream cakes carefully as she dodged across the street through the traffic. The girls had worked so hard since they opened and buying a few cakes on a Friday afternoon seemed little enough to show her appreciation.

'There's a gentleman to see you,' Annabel, a leggy Knightsbridge debutante whom Tara had taken on as manageress, came bustling forward as Tara came in. 'I showed him into the office. I hope that's OK?'

Tara had offered this job to Angie, but she'd giggled and insisted she found someone classy. Miranda had at last broken into modelling; now they were all new faces.

'A rep?' Tara enquired.

'I don't think so.' Annabel's smooth, rather large forehead furrowed in a frown. 'I think he's a police-man.'

Tara glanced round the shop. It was beautiful with its smooth pine fittings and dark green carpet, mirrors and subdued lighting. Sometimes she got a wave of nostalgia for those early days with Josh, the soul music blasting out, girls in mini skirts clamouring to get in the communal changing room. But those days were gone, wiped out like the smell of joss-sticks and patchouli oil from the old shop. It was glam rock now, sequins and satin.

Josh would've liked that. He'd have paraded around in his platforms and a sequinned jacket, playing his air guitar and singing his favourite line from The Who, 'Hope I die before I get old'.

'Well, he got his wish,' she said to herself as she walked towards the stairs. 'Age wouldn't have suited him.'

'I hope this isn't bad news?' Tara was slightly out of breath from running up the stairs. It was some weeks now since she and Harry made a clean breast of everything to Inspector Morris at Bow Street police station, but she had guessed from Annabel's words that it had to be him.

He looked like a policeman, even though his rank had removed him from the beat many years ago. He was tall and thick-set, with a determined jaw, eyes like gimlets and a shock of white hair.

'Sorry to call in working hours,' he said pleasantly. 'But I though it might be less intimidating than ringing you and making an appointment.'

711

'You haven't come to arrest me, then?' Tara tried to smile, but she was nervous.

'Of course not.' He smiled encouragingly. 'Any chance of a cuppa? We can talk easier then.'

It took ten minutes to make tea for the girls downstairs, deliver the tray with the cakes and then sit down with him.

'Well, what have you decided?' she asked, having a sip of tea for courage.

'To leave well alone.' In all his years of service Ron Morris had seen and heard so much that virtually nothing surprised him. But Tara Manning had knocked him for six.

He'd known MacDonald, as just about every other officer on the force did, and to be told by this beautiful, softly spoken girl that she was his daughter was incredible. It got wilder as she unfolded the hidden story about Joe Spikes. But as she blurted it all out with such emotion, he could see the burden slowly lifting from those slender shoulders, and he knew then he wasn't going to give her any more trauma.

'Well, Tara, look at this from the police's angle. It was us who claimed the crash victim was MacDonald. We've poked around again and we think we've discovered the real identity of that body and, believe you me, there isn't anyone out there grieving for him.'

'You mean you aren't going to do anything?'

'What is there to do?' He shrugged his shoulders. 'Dig up a piece of police bungling, for what? It won't bring Father Glynn back, or your grandmother. MacDonald, or Joe Spikes, he's as dead as a joint of mutton and he admitted the crimes to you. If we announce all this the only people to be punished are you and your mother.'

Intense relief, happiness and gratitude surged through her.

'Are you sure? It doesn't seem right,' she whispered, hanging her head a little.

'It would seem a great deal worse to me if you got hurt after your bravery in coming forward.' Morris shook his head.

'But the tattoo thing keeps bugging at me,' she said softly. 'It's the one thing I still don't understand.'

'Well, that's quite a pretty story.' Morris smiled. 'I discovered all the men your father led through that jungle in Malaya had one. They had been through hell together and, when they finally made it to safety, all six of them had the same tattoo, the bluebird of happiness, I suppose. The man who died in the car was one of them. Like your father, he'd turned to crime when he couldn't find the right niche in civilian life. You'll be glad to know the other four kept to the straight and narrow, all family men.'

'So Joe got all those other tattoos done to conceal it?'

Morris nodded. 'I guess so. But I prefer to think he felt bad about his friend dying in that car. You see, he must have been in it too and jumped clear. His hands had been burned, and his right leg and side. That's probably how he got that fearsome scar, too, because he fell on rocks, and why we couldn't get a complete finger print. We'll never know what he went through after that accident, he must have holed up somewhere, gone through hell having such terrible injuries. I suppose that's why he lost his hair, too.'

'So you aren't going to do anything?' Tara could feel a smile starting in her toes and creeping up her body.

'The matter's closed.' He smiled back at her, then lifted his tea to his lips and took a sip. 'The man Wainwright knew no-one but Bergman, his motive for getting involved in the job was purely spite against Harry and we've marked his card. Joe and Duke are both dead, the other men awaiting trial. In my opinion, matters are pretty well settled.'

'I almost wish I'd never admitted the truth to Mum,' Tara said with a sigh.

'I think you'd have found the knowledge becoming like a wedge between you,' Morris said understandingly. 'As it is you've laid the ghosts once and for all.' He drank the rest of his tea and put his cup on the table. 'I'll be off now, Tara. I wish you luck and happiness.'

Tara took his outstretched hand and gripped it with both of hers.

'Thank you so much.'

'I'll tell you one thing,' the policeman smiled a little uncertainly. 'MacDonald's biggest punishment was not seeing you as you are now. I'd be so proud if you were my daughter!'

'So that's it? It's over?' Harry's bright blue eyes danced with delight.

'Buried for good.' Tara smiled. 'Case closed.'

Harry reached out to hug her, closing his eyes and rocking her in his arms.

'I'll just have to tell you my good news now then,' he said, dropping little kisses on to her nose and cheeks.

'What good news?'

'I've sold the club, or at least granted a five-year lease on it.' He grinned. 'Most of the staff, including Needles and Tony, are staying on with the new owner. I've got a fat little nest egg to modernise the farm. In a few years' time we'll sell the freehold of the club for a packet and meanwhile I've got a nice little regular sum coming in from the rent. What could be sweeter?'

'Being carried off to bed by you, with a bottle of chilled Champagne to celebrate?' Tara raised one eyebrow.

One moment she was standing, the next he had her up in his arms and was walking with her towards the door.

'I haven't got any Champagne right now.' He laughed as he made towards the stairs with her. 'But I don't need asking twice to carry you off to bed!'